Samuel Johnson vs the Darkness Trilogy

John Connolly

HODDER

First published as three separates volumes:
The Gates © John Connolly 2009

The Infernals © John Connolly 2011
First published as Hell's Bells in Great Britain in 2011 by Hodder & Stoughton

The Creeps © Bad Dog Books Limited 2013
First published in Great Britain in 2013 by Hodder & Stoughton

This paperback trilogy edition published in 2020 by Hodder and Stoughton
An Hachette UK company

4

Copyright © Bad Dog Book Limited 2020

A CIP catalogue record for this title is available from the British Library

Paperback ISBN 978 1 529 31207 2
eBook ISBN 978 1 529 31208 9

Typeset in Garamond MT

Printed and bound in Great Britain by Clays Ltd, Elcograf S.p.A.

Hodder & Stoughton policy is to use papers that are natural,
renewable and recyclable products and made from wood grown in sustainable
forests. The logging and manufacturing processes are expected to conform
to the environmental regulations of the country of origin.

Hodder & Stoughton Ltd
Carmelite House
50 Victoria Embankment
London EC4Y 0DZ

www.hodder.co.uk

THE GATES

JOHN CONNOLLY

For Cameron and Alistair

'Scientists are not after the truth; it is the truth that is after scientists.'

Dr Karl Schlecta (1904–1985)

CHAPTER I

In Which the Universe Forms,
Which Seems Like a Very Good Place to Start

In the beginning, about 13.7 billion years ago, to be reasonably precise, there was a very, very small dot.[1] The dot, which was hot and incredibly heavy, contained everything that was, and everything that ever would be, all crammed into the tiniest area possible. The dot, which was under enormous pressure due to all that it contained, exploded, and it duly scattered everything that was, or would be, across what was now about to become the Universe. Scientists call this the 'Big Bang', although it wasn't really a big bang at all because it happened everywhere, and all at once.

Oh, and just one thing about that 'age of the Universe' stuff. There are people who will try to tell you that the Earth is only about 10,000 years old; that humans and

---

[1] Scientists call the dot the 'singularity'. People who are religious might call it the mote in God's eye. Some scientists will say that you can't believe in the singularity and the idea of a god, or gods. Some religious people will try to tell you the same thing. Still, you can believe in the singularity *and* a god, if you like. It's entirely up to you. One requires evidence, the other faith. They're not the same thing, but as long as you don't get the two mixed up, then everything should be fine.

dinosaurs were around at more or less the same time, a bit like in the movies *Jurassic Park* and *One Million Years B.C.*; and that evolution, the change in the inherited traits of organisms passed from one generation to the next, does not, and never did, happen. Given the evidence, it's hard not to feel that they're probably wrong. Many of them also believe that the Universe was created in seven days by an old chap with a beard, perhaps with breaks for tea and sandwiches. This may be true but, if it was created in this way, they were very long days: about two billion years long, give or take a few million years, which is a lot of sandwiches.

Anyway, to return to the dot, let's be clear on something, because it's very important. The building blocks of all that you can see around you, and a great deal more that you can't see at all, were blasted from that little dot at a speed so fast that, within a minute, the Universe was a million billion miles in size and still expanding, as the dot was responsible for bringing into being planets and asteroids; whales and budgerigars; you, and Julius Caesar, and Elvis Presley.[2]

Oh, and Evil.

Because somewhere in there was all the bad stuff as well, the stuff that makes otherwise sensible people hurt

---

[2] In fact, about one per cent of the static that sometimes appears on your television set is a relic of the Big Bang and, if your eyes were sensitive to microwave light instead of just visible light, then the sky at night would appear white instead of black, as it continues to glow from the heat of the Big Bang. And because atoms are so small, and are constantly recycled, every breath you take contains atoms that were once breathed by Julius Caesar and Elvis Presley. So a little bit of you once ruled Rome, and sang 'Blue Suede Shoes'.

one another. There's a little of it in all of us, and the best that we can do is to try not to let it govern our actions too often.

But just as the planets began to take on a certain shape, and the asteroids, and the whales and the budgerigars and you, so too, in the darkest of dark places, Evil took on a form. It did so while the Earth was cooling, while tectonic plates shifted, until, at last, life appeared, and Evil found a target for its rage.

Yet it could not reach us, for the Universe was not ordered in its favour, or so it seemed. But the thing in the darkness was very patient. It stoked the fires of its fury, and it waited for a chance to strike . . .

CHAPTER II

*In Which We Encounter a Small Boy, His Dog,
and Some People Who Are Up to No Good*

On the night in question, Mr Abernathy answered
the door to find a small figure dressed in a white sheet
standing on his porch. The sheet had two holes cut into
it at eye level so that the small figure could walk around
without bumping into things, a precaution that seemed
wise given that the small figure was also wearing rather
thick glasses. The glasses were balanced on its nose,
outside the sheet, giving it the appearance of a short-
sighted, and not terribly frightening, ghost. A mismatched
pair of trainers, the left blue, the right red, poked out
from the bottom of the sheet.

In its left hand, the figure held an empty bucket.
From its right stretched a dog lead, ending at a red collar
that encircled the neck of a little dachshund. The dachshund stared up at Mr Abernathy with what Mr
Abernathy felt was a troubling degree of self-awareness.
If he hadn't known better, Mr Abernathy might have
taken the view that this was a dog that knew it was a
dog, and wasn't very happy about it, all things considered. Equally, the dog appeared to know that Mr
Abernathy was not a dog for, in general, dogs view

humans just as large dogs that have learned the neat trick of walking on two legs, which only impresses dogs for a short period of time. This suggested to Mr Abernathy that here was a very smart dog indeed – freakishly so. There was something disapproving in the way the dog was staring at Mr Abernathy. Mr Abernathy sensed that the dog was not terribly keen on him, and he found himself feeling both annoyed and slightly depressed that he had somehow disappointed the animal.

Mr Abernathy looked from the dog to the small figure, then back again, as though unsure as to which one of them was going to speak.

'Trick or treat,' said the small figure eventually, from beneath the sheet.

Mr Abernathy's face betrayed utter bafflement.

'What?' said Mr Abernathy.

'Trick or treat,' the small figure repeated.

Mr Abernathy's mouth opened once, then closed again. He looked like a fish having an afterthought. He appeared to grow even more confused. He glanced at his watch and checked the date, wondering if he had somehow lost a few days between hearing the doorbell ring and opening the door.

'It's only October the twenty-eighth,' he said.

'I know,' said the small figure. 'I thought I'd get a head start on everyone else.'

'What?' said Mr Abernathy.

'What?' said the small figure.

'Why are you saying "what"?' said Mr Abernathy. 'I just said "what".'

'I know. Why?'

'Why what?'

'My question exactly,' said the small figure.

'Who *are* you?' asked Mr Abernathy. His head was starting to hurt.

'I'm a ghost,' said the small figure, then added, a little uncertainly: 'Boo?'

'No, not "What are you?" *Who* are you?'

'Oh.' The small figure removed the glasses and lifted up its sheet, revealing a pale boy of perhaps eleven, with wispy blond hair and very blue eyes. 'I'm Samuel Johnson. I live in number five hundred and one. And this is Boswell,' he added, indicating the dachshund by raising his lead.

Mr Abernathy, who was new to the town, nodded as though this piece of information had suddenly confirmed all of his suspicions. Upon hearing its name spoken, the dog shuffled its bottom on Mr Abernathy's porch and gave a bow. Mr Abernathy regarded it suspiciously.

'Your shoes don't match,' said Mr Abernathy to Samuel.

'I know. I couldn't decide which pair to wear, so I wore one of each.'

Mr Abernathy raised an eyebrow. He didn't trust people, especially children, who displayed signs of individuality.

'So,' said Samuel. 'Trick or treat?'

'Neither,' said Mr Abernathy.

'Why not?'

'Because it's not Halloween yet, that's why not.'

'But I was showing initiative.' Samuel's teacher, Mr Hume, often spoke about the importance of showing initiative, although any time Samuel showed initiative Mr Hume seemed to disapprove of it, which Samuel found very puzzling.

'No, you weren't,' said Mr Abernathy. 'You're just too early. It's not the same thing.'

'Oh, please. A chocolate bar?'

'No.'

'Not even an apple?'

'No.'

'I can come back tomorrow, if that helps.'

'No! Go away.'

With that, Mr Abernathy slammed the front door, leaving Samuel and Boswell to stare at the flaking paintwork. Samuel let the sheet drop down once more, restoring himself to ghostliness, and replaced his glasses. He looked down at Boswell. Boswell looked up at him. Samuel shook the empty bucket sadly.

'I thought people might like an early fright,' he said to Boswell.

Boswell sighed in response, as if to say, 'I told you so.'

Samuel gave one final, hopeful glance at Mr Abernathy's front door, willing him to change his mind and appear with something for the bucket, even if it was just a single, solitary nut, but the door remained firmly closed. The Abernathys hadn't lived in the street for very long, and their house was the biggest and oldest in town. Samuel had rather hoped that the Abernathys would decorate it for Halloween, or perhaps turn it into a haunted house, but after his recent encounter with Mr Abernathy he didn't think this was very likely. Mr

Abernathy's wife, meanwhile, sometimes looked like she had just been fed a very bitter slice of lemon, and was searching for somewhere to spit it out discreetly. No, thought Samuel, the Abernathy house would not be playing a very big part in this year's Halloween festivities.

As things turned out, he was very, very wrong.

Mr Abernathy stood, silent and unmoving, at the door. He peered through the peephole until he was certain that the boy and his dog were leaving, then locked the door and turned away. Hanging from the end of the banister behind him was a black, hooded robe, not unlike something a bad monk might wear to scare people into behaving themselves. Mr Abernathy put the robe back on as he walked down the stairs to his basement. Had Samuel seen Mr Abernathy in his robe, he might have reconsidered his position on Mr Abernathy's willingness to enter into the spirit of Halloween.

Mr Abernathy was not a happy man. He had married the woman who became Mrs Abernathy because he wanted someone to look after him, someone who would advise him on the right clothes to wear, and the proper food to eat, thus allowing Mr Abernathy more time to spend thinking about things. Mr Abernathy wrote books that told people how to make their lives happier. He was quite successful at this, mainly because he spent every day dreaming about what might have made him happier, including not being married to Mrs Abernathy. He also made sure that nobody who read his work ever met his wife. If they did, they would immediately guess how unhappy Mr Abernathy really was, and stop buying his books.

Now, his robe heavy on his shoulders, he made his way down the stairs into the darkened room below. Waiting for him were three other people, all dressed in similar robes. Painted on the floor was a pentagram, a five-pointed star, at the centre of which stood an iron burner filled with glowing charcoal. Incense grains had been sprinkled across the coals, so that the basement was filled with a thick, perfumed smoke.

'Who was it, dear?' asked one of the hooded figures. She said the word 'dear' the way an executioner's axe might say the word 'thud' if it could speak as it was lopping off someone's head.

'That weird kid from number five hundred and one,' said Mr Abernathy to his wife, for it was she who had spoken. 'And his dog.'

'What did he want?'

'He was trick or treating.'

'But it's not even Halloween yet.'

'I know. I told him that. I think there's something wrong with him. And his dog,' Mr Abernathy added.

'Well, he's gone now. Silly child.'

'Can we get on with it?' said a male voice from beneath another hood. 'I want to go home and watch the football.' The man in question was quite fat, and his robe was stretched taut across his belly. His name was Reginald Renfield, and he wasn't quite sure what he was doing standing around in a smoke-filled base-ment dressed in a robe that was at least two sizes too small for him. His wife had made him come along, and nobody argued with Doris Renfield. She was even bigger and fatter than her husband, but not half as nice, and since Mr Renfield wasn't very nice at all, that made Mrs Renfield very unpleasant indeed.

'Oh, Reginald, do keep quiet,' said Mrs Renfield. 'All you do is complain. We're having fun.'

'Are we?' said Reginald.

He didn't see anything particularly amusing about standing in a cold basement wearing a scratchy robe, trying to summon up demons from the beyond. Mr Renfield didn't believe in demons, although he sometimes wondered if his friend Mr Abernathy might have married one by accident. Mrs Abernathy frightened him, the way strong women will often frighten weak men. Still, Doris had insisted that they come along and join their new friends, who had recently moved to the town of Biddlecombe, for an evening of 'fun'. Mrs Abernathy and Mrs Renfield had met in a bookshop, where they were both buying books about ghosts and angels. From then on their friendship had grown, eventually drawing in their husbands as well. Mr Renfield didn't exactly like the Abernathys but a funny thing about adults is that they will spend time with people they don't like very much if they think it might benefit them. In this case, Mr Renfield was hoping that Mr Abernathy might buy an expensive new television from Mr Renfield's electrical shop.

'Well, some of us are having fun,' said Mrs Renfield. 'You wouldn't know fun if it ran up and tickled you under the arm.' She laughed loudly. It sounded to her husband like someone pushing a witch in a barrel over a waterfall. He pictured his wife in a barrel falling into very deep water, and this cheered him up a bit.

'Enough!' said Mrs Abernathy.

Everyone went quiet. Mrs Abernathy, stern and beautiful, peered from beneath her hood.

'Join hands,' she said, and they did so, forming a circle around the pentagram. 'Now, let us begin.'

And, as one, they started to chant.

Most people are not bad. Oh, they do bad things sometimes, and everyone has a little badness in them, but very few people are unspeakably evil, and most of the bad things they do seem perfectly reasonable to them at the time. Perhaps they're bored, or selfish, or greedy, but, for the most part, they don't actually want to hurt anyone when they do bad things. They just want to make their own lives a little easier.

The four people in the basement fell into the category of 'bored'. They had boring jobs. They drove boring cars. They ate boring food. Their friends were boring. For them, everything was just, well, *dull*.

So when Mrs Abernathy produced an old book that she had bought in a second-hand bookshop, and suggested, first to her husband, and then to their slightly-less-boring-than-the-rest friends the Renfields, that the book's contents might make for an interesting evening, everyone had pronounced it a splendid idea.

The book didn't have a name. Its cover was made of worn black leather, emblazoned with a star not unlike the one painted on the basement floor, and its pages had turned yellow with age. It was written in a language none of them had ever seen, and which they were unable to understand.

And yet, and yet . . .

Somehow Mrs Abernathy had looked at the book and known exactly what they were meant to do. It was almost as if the book had been speaking to her in her head, translating its odd scratches and symbols into words that she could comprehend. The book had told her to bring her friends and her husband to the basement on this particular night, to paint the star and light the charcoal, and to chant the series of strange sounds that were now coming from each of their mouths. It was all very odd.

The Abernathys and the Renfields weren't looking for trouble. Neither were they trying to do anything bad. They weren't evil, or vicious, or cruel. They were just bored people with too much time on their hands, and such people will, in the end, get up to mischief

But just as someone who wears a sign saying 'Kick Me!' will, in the normal course of events, eventually be kicked, so too there was enough mischief being done in that basement to attract something unusually bad, something with more than mischief on its mind. It had been waiting for a long time. Now that wait was about to come to an end.

CHAPTER III

*In Which We Learn About Particle Accelerators,
and the Playing of 'Battleships'*

Deep beneath a mountain in the heart of Europe, nothing was happening.

Well, that wasn't entirely true. Lots of things were happening, some of them quite spectacular, but because they were happening at an infinitesimally small level, it was quite hard for most people to get excited about them.

The Large Hadron Collider was, as its name suggested, very big. It was, in fact, some 17 miles long, and stretched inside a ring-shaped tunnel burrowed through rock near Geneva in Switzerland. The LHC was a particle accelerator, the largest ever constructed: a device for smashing protons together in a vacuum, consisting of 1,600 electromagnets chilled to -271 degrees Celcius (or, to you and me, 'Crumbs, that's *really* cold. Wonder what would happen if I licked it?'), producing a powerful electromagnetic field. Basically, two beams of hydrogen ions, atoms that have been stripped of their electrons, would whiz around the ring in opposite directions at about 186,000 miles per second, or close to the speed of light, and then collide. When they met, each beam would have the energy of a big car travelling at 1000 miles per hour.

You don't want to be in a car travelling at 1000 miles per hour that crashes into another car travelling at the same speed. That would not be good.

When the beams collided, enormous amounts of energy would be released from all of the protons they contained, and that was where things got really interesting. The reason scientists had built the LHC was in order to study the aftermath of that collision, which would produce very small particles: smaller than atoms, and atoms are already so small that it would take ten million of them laid end to end to cover the full stop at the end of this sentence. Ultimately, they hoped to discover the Higgs boson, sometimes called the 'God Particle', the most basic component of everything in the material world.

Take our two cars travelling at 1000 miles per hour before pounding into each other. After the crash, there isn't likely to be much of the cars left. In fact, there will probably only be very small pieces of car (and possibly very small pieces of anyone who was unfortunate enough to be inside the cars at the time) scattered all over the place. What the scientists at CERN, the European Organization for Nuclear Research, hoped was that the colliding beams would leave behind little patches of energy resembling those that existed seconds after the Big Bang, when the dot of which we spoke at the start exploded, and among them might be the Higgs boson. The Higgs boson would stick out because it would actually be much bigger than the two colliding protons that created it, but it wouldn't hang about for very long as it would vanish almost instantly. It would be as though our two colliding cars had come together and formed a truck, which then immediately collapsed.

In other words, the scientists hoped to understand just how the Universe came into being, which is a big question that is a lot easier to ask than to answer. You see, scientists – even the clever ones – only understand about four per cent of the matter and energy in the universe, which accounts for all the stuff we can see around us: mountains, lakes, bears, artichokes, that kind of thing.[3] That leaves them scratching their heads over the remaining 96 per cent, which is a lot of scratching. To save time, and prevent unnecessary head injuries, the scientists decided that about 23 per cent of what remained should be called 'dark matter'. Although they couldn't see it, they knew that it existed because it bent starlight.

But if dark matter was interesting to them, whatever accounted for the remaining 73 per cent of everything in the universe was more interesting still. It was known as 'dark energy', and it was invisible; entirely hidden. Nobody knew where it came from, but they had a pretty good idea of what it was doing. It was driving galaxies farther and farther apart, causing the universe to expand. This would lead to two things: the first was that human beings, if they didn't start inventing fast ways to move

☠ [3] And even all that stuff added together still amounts to much less than one per cent of not very much at all, since more than 99 per cent of the volume of ordinary matter is empty space. If we could get rid of all the empty space in the atoms of our bodies, the whole of humanity could be squeezed into a matchbox, with room left over for most of the animal kingdom too. Mind you, there would be nobody left to look after the matchbox.

somewhere else, would eventually find themselves alone, as all the neighbouring galaxies would have disappeared beyond the edge of the visible universe. After that, the universe would start to cool, and everything in it would freeze to death. Thankfully, that's likely to happen hundreds of billions of years in the future, so there's no need to buy a thick coat just yet, but it's worth remembering the next time you feel the need to complain about the cold.

The LHC would probably be able to help scientists better understand all of this, as well as providing evidence of other really fascinating stuff like extra dimensions, which as everyone knows are filled with monsters and aliens and big spaceships with laser cannons and . . .

Well, you get the picture.

At this point, it's a good idea to mention the whole Might-Cause-The-Destruction-Of-The-Earth-and-The-End-Of-Life-As-We-Know-It issue. It's a minor thing, but you can't be too careful.

Basically, while the LHC was being built, and lots of men in white coats were chatting about dark matter and high-speed collisions, someone suggested the collider might create a black hole that would swallow the earth. Or instead it could cause particles of matter so strange they're called 'strangelets' to appear and turn the earth into a lump of dead grey stuff. It's safe to say that this chap wasn't invited to the scientists' Christmas party.

Now you or I, if told we were about to do something that might, just might, bring about the end of the world, would probably pause for a moment and wonder if it was a good idea after all. Scientists, though, are not like you or me. Instead the scientists pointed out that there was only a tiny chance the collider might bring about the end of all life on Earth. Hardly worth bothering about, really, they said. Not to worry. Take a look at this big spinning thing. Isn't it pretty?[4]

All of which brings us back to the important things happening in the Large Hadron Collider. The experiments were being monitored by a machine called VELO. VELO detected all of the little particles given off when the beams crashed. It could tell their position to within one two-hundredth of a millimetre, or one-tenth of the thickness of a human hair. It was all terribly exciting, although not exciting enough for two of the men who were responsible for watching the screens monitoring what was happening, so they were doing what men often do in such situations.

They were playing Battleships.

'B Four', said Victor, who was German and blessed with lots of hair that he wore in a ponytail, with some left over for his chin and upper lip.

☠ 4 Anyway, the scientists figured, if the end of the world did happen, there wouldn't be anybody left to blame them. There would probably be just enough time for someone to say, 'Hey, you said it wouldn't cause the end of—' before there was a bit of a bang, and then silence. Scientists, while very intelligent, don't always think things through. Take, for example, the first caveman who found a nice rock, tied it to a stick with a piece of vine, and thought, 'Hmm, I've just invented a Thing For Banging Other Things Into Things With. I feel certain that nobody will use this to hit someone over the head with instead.' Which someone promptly did. In fact, they probably hit *him* with it so that they could steal it. This is how we end up with nuclear weapons, and scientists claiming that they'd only set out to invent something that steamed radishes.

'Miss,' said Ed, who was British and blessed with hardly any hair at all, and certainly none that could be spared for his face. Nevertheless, Ed quite liked Victor, even if he felt Victor had been given some of the hair that should, by rights, have come his way.

Victor's face creased in concentration. Somewhere in the not very vast vastness of Ed's board lay a submarine, a destroyer, and an aircraft carrier, yet, for the life of him, Victor couldn't seem to hit them. He wondered if Ed was lying about all those misses, then decided that Ed wasn't the kind of person who lied. Ed wasn't very imaginative and, in Victor's experience, it was imaginative people who tended to lie. Lying required making stuff up, and only imaginative people were good at that. Victor had a little more imagination than Ed, and therefore lied more. Not much, but certainly a bit.

Ed heard Victor sniff loudly.

'Ugh!' said Victor. 'Was that you?'

Now Ed smelt it too. There was a distinct whiff of rotten eggs in the room.

'No, it wasn't me,' said Ed, somewhat offended.

For the second time in as many minutes, Victor wondered if Ed might be lying.

'Anyway,' said Ed, 'it's my turn. E Three.'

'Miss.'

Beep.

'What was that?'

Victor didn't look up. 'I said it was a miss. That's what it was: a miss.'

'No,' said Ed. 'I meant, what was *that*?'

His right index finger was pointing at the computer

screen, which was occupied by a visual representation of all of the exciting things happening in the particle accelerator, and which had just beeped. The image on the screen looked like a tornado, albeit one that was the same width throughout instead of resembling a funnel.

'I don't see anything wrong,' said Victor.

'A bit just whizzed off,' said Ed. 'And it went *beep*.'

'A *bit*?' said Victor. 'It's not a bicycle. Bits don't just whizz off.'

'Right then,' said Ed, looking miffed. 'A particle of some kind appears to have disengaged itself from the whole and exited the accelerator. Is that better?'

'You mean that a bit just whizzed off?' said Victor, thinking: who said we Germans don't have a sense of humour?

Ed just looked at him. Victor stared back, then sighed.

'It's not possible,' he said. 'It's a contained environment. Particles don't simply leave it to go off, well, somewhere else. It must have been a glitch.'[5]

'It wasn't a glitch,' said Ed. He abandoned the game and began furiously tapping buttons on a keyboard. On a second screen he pulled up another version of the visual representation, checked the time, then began running it backward. Twenty seconds into the rewind a small glowing particle came into view from the left of the screen and appeared to rejoin the whole. Ed paused

---

[5] Whenever someone uses the word 'glitch', which means a fault of some kind in a system, you should immediately be suspicious, because it means that they don't know what it is. A technician who uses the term 'glitch' is like a doctor who tells you you're suffering from a 'thingy', except the doctor won't tell you to go home and try turning yourself on and off again.

the image, then allowed it to run forward again at half-speed. Together, he and Victor watched as the bit whizzed off.

'That's not good,' said Victor.

'No,' said Ed. 'It shouldn't even be possible.'

'What do you think it is?'

Ed examined the data. 'I don't know.'

Both men were now working on keyboards. Simultaneously, they pulled up the same string of data on the screen as they tried to pinpoint a reason for the anomaly.

'I'm not seeing anything,' said Ed. 'It must be buried deep.'

'Wait,' said Victor. 'I'm seeing— No! What's this? What's happening?'

As he and Ed watched, the data seemed to rewrite itself. Strings of code changed; zeros became ones, and ones became zeros. Frantically, both men tried to arrest the progress of the changes, but to no avail.

'It must be a bug,' said Victor. 'It's covering its own tracks.'

'Someone must have hacked into the system,' said Ed.

'I helped to build this system,' said Victor, 'and even I couldn't hack into it, not like this.'

And then, less than a minute after it began, the changes to the code were completed. Ed tried rerunning the image of the particle separating itself from the accelerator, but this time only the great tunnel of energy appeared on the screen, filled with protons behaving exactly as they should.

'We'll have to report it,' said Ed.

'I know,' said Victor. 'But there's no evidence. There's just our word.'

'Won't that be enough?'

Victor nodded. 'Probably, but –' He stared at the screen. 'What did it mean? And, more to the point, where did it go?'

'And what is that *smell . . . ?*'

Scientists were not the only ones who had been monitoring the collider.

Down in the dark places where the worst things hid, an ancient Evil had been watching the construction of the collider with great interest. The entity that existed in the darkness had many names: Satan, Beelzebub, the Devil. To the creatures that dwelt with it, he was known as the Great Malevolence.[6]

The Great Malevolence had been squatting in the blackness for a very long time. He was there billions of

---

⊙ [6] 'Malevolence' for those of you who were off "sick" from school that day means 'hatred', but hatred of a very vicious, evil kind. Incidentally, when you put inverted commas round a word in this way, as I just did round the work "sick", it means that you don't believe that the word in question is true. In this case, I know that you weren't really sick that day: you just felt like having a morning off to watch children's television in your pyjamas. Hence "sick", instead of, well, sick. If you really want to annoy someone, you can make little inverted commas by holding up two fingers of each hand and twitching them gently, as though you're tickling an invisible elf under the armpits. For example, when your mother calls you for dinner, and dinner turns out to be boiled fish and broccoli, you can say to her 'Well, I'll just eat my "dinner", then', and do the little inverted commas sign. She'll love it. Seriously. I can hear her laughing already.

years before people, or dinosaurs, or small, single-celled organisms that decided one day to become larger, multi-celled organisms so they could, at some point in the future, invent literature, painting, and annoying ring-tones for mobile phones. He had watched from the depths of space and time – for rock and fire and earth, vacuums and stars and planets were no obstacle to him – as life appeared on earth, as trees sprouted and the oceans teemed, and hated all that he saw. He wanted to bring it to an end, but could not. He was trapped in a place of flame and stone, surrounded by those like him, some of whom he had created from his own flesh, and others who had been banished there because they were foul and evil, although none quite as foul or as evil as the Great Malevolence himself. Few of the legions of demons who dwelt with him in that distant, fiery realm had even laid eyes upon the Great Malevolence, for he existed in the deepest, darkest corner of Hell, brooding and plotting, waiting for his chance to escape.

Now, after so long, he had just made his first move.

CHAPTER IV

In Which We Learn About the Inadvisability of Attempting to Summon Up Demons, and of Generally Messing About With the Afterlife

Samuel and Boswell sat on the wall outside the Abernathy house and watched the world go by. As it was a quiet evening, and most people were indoors having their tea, there wasn't a whole lot of the world to watch, and what there was wasn't doing very much. Samuel shook his bucket and heard the sound of emptiness which, as anyone knows, is not the same thing as no sound, since it includes all the noise that someone was expecting to hear, but doesn't.[7]

[7] This is similar to the old problem about whether or not a tree falling in a forest makes any noise if there is nobody there to hear it. This, of course, assumes that the only creatures worth being concerned about when it comes to falling trees are human beings, and ignores the plight of small birds, assorted rodents, and rabbits who happen to be in the wrong place at the wrong time and find a tree landing on their heads.

In the eighteenth century, a man named Bishop Berkeley claimed that objects only exist because people are there to see them. This led a lot of scientists to laugh at Bishop Berkeley and his ideas, because they found them silly. But according to quantum theory, which is a very advanced branch of physics involving atoms, parallel universes, and other such matters, Bishop Berkeley may have had a point. Quantum theory suggests that the tree exists in all possible states at the same time: burnt, sawdust, fallen, or in the shape of a small wooden duck

Samuel didn't want to go home. His mother had been preparing to go out for the evening when Samuel left the house. It was the first time that she had dressed up to go out since Samuel's dad had left, and something about the sight of it had made Samuel sad. He didn't know who she was going to meet, but she was putting on lipstick and making herself look nice, and she didn't go to that kind of trouble when she was heading out to play bingo with her friends. She hadn't questioned why her son was dressed as a ghost and carrying a Halloween bucket when it was not yet Halloween, for she was well used to her son doing things that might be regarded as somewhat unusual.

The previous week Samuel's teacher, Mr Hume, had rung her at home to have what he described as a 'serious conversation' about Samuel. Samuel, it emerged, had arrived for show-and-tell that day carrying only a straight pin. When Mr Hume had called him to the front of the class, Samuel had proudly held up the pin.

'What's that?' Mr Hume had asked.

'It's a pin,' said Samuel.

'I can see that, Samuel, but it's hardly the most exciting of show and tells, now is it? I mean, it's not exactly a rocket ship, like the one that Bobby made, or Helen's volcano.'

Samuel hadn't thought much of Bobby Goddard's rocket ship, which looked to him like a series of toilet-rolls

---

that quacks as it's pulled along. You don't know what state it's in until you observe it. In other words, you can't separate the observer from the thing being observed.

covered in foil, or for that matter Helen's volcano, even if it did produce white smoke when water was poured into its crater. Helen's father was a chemist, and Samuel was pretty sure he'd had a hand in creating that volcano. Helen, Samuel knew, couldn't even put together a bowl made of lollipop sticks without detailed instructions and a large supply of solvent remover to get the glue and assorted lollipop sticks off her fingers afterwards.

Samuel had stepped forward and held the pin under Mr Hume's nose.

'It's not just a pin,' he said solemnly. Mr Hume looked unconvinced, and also a little nervous at having a pin somewhat closer to his face than he might have liked. There was no telling what some of these kids might do, given half a chance.

'Er, what is it, then?' said Mr Hume.

'Well, if you look closely . . .'

Despite his better judgement, Mr Hume found himself leaning forward to examine the pin.

'Really closely . . .'

Mr Hume squinted. Someone had once given him a grain of rice with his name written upon it, which Mr Hume had considered interesting but pointless, and he wondered if Samuel had somehow managed a similar trick.

'You might just be able to see an infinite number of angels dancing on the head of this pin,' finished Samuel.[8]

☠ [8] It was St Thomas Aquinas, a most learned man who died in 1274, who was supposed to have suggested that an infinite number of angels could dance on the head of a pin. In fact he didn't, although he spent a lot of time thinking

Mr Hume looked at Samuel. Samuel looked back at him. 'Are you trying to be funny?' asked Mr Hume.

This was a question Samuel heard quite often, usually when he wasn't trying to be funny at all.

'No,' said Samuel. 'I read it somewhere. Theoretically, you can fit an infinite number of angels on the head of a pin.'

'That doesn't mean that they're actually there,' said Mr Hume.

'No, but they might be,' said Samuel reasonably.

'Equally, they might not.'

'You can't prove that they're not there, though,' said Samuel.

'But you can't prove that they *are*.'

Samuel thought about this for a couple of seconds, then said: 'You can't prove a negative proposition.'

'What?' asked Mr Hume.

'You can't prove that something doesn't exist. You can only prove that something *does* exist.'

'Did you read that somewhere too?' Mr Hume was having trouble keeping the sarcasm from his voice.

'I think so,' said Samuel, who, like most honest,

---

about whether or not angels had bodies (he seemed to think not), and how many of them there might be up in heaven (rather a lot, he concluded). The problem with St Thomas Aquinas was that he liked arguing with himself, and it's very hard to nail down exactly what he thought about anything at all. Still, the question of how many angels can dance on the head of a pin is probably of interest mainly to philosophers and, one presumes, dancing angels, since the last thing an angel doing the foxtrot wants to worry about is how crowded the pin is getting, and the possibility of falling off the edge and doing himself an injury.

straightforward people, had trouble recognising sarcasm. 'But it's true, isn't it?'

'I suppose so,' said Mr Hume. He realised that he sounded distinctly sulky, so he coughed, then said with more force: 'Yes, I suppose you're right.'[9]

Samuel continued: 'Which means that I have as much chance of proving that there are angels on the head of this pin as you have of proving that there aren't.'

Mr Hume rubbed his forehead in frustration. 'Are you sure you're only eleven?' he asked.

'Positive,' said Samuel.

Mr Hume shook his head wearily.

'Thank you for that, Samuel. You can take your pin – and your angels – back to your desk now.'

'Are you certain you don't want to keep it?' asked Samuel.

'Yes, I'm certain.'

'I have lots more.'

'*Sit down*, Samuel,' said Mr Hume, who had a way

☠ [9] Actually, this is not entirely true. It may well be the case that one cannot prove the existence of a nine-eyed, multi-tentacled pink monster named Herbert, but that does not mean that, somewhere in the universe, there is not a nine-eyed, multi-tentacled pink monster named Herbert wondering why nobody writes to him. Just because he hasn't been seen doesn't mean he isn't out there. This is known as an *inductive argument*. But the argument is probable, not definite. If there's actually a pretty good chance he exists, there's at least as good a chance that he doesn't exist. So you can prove a negative, at least as much as you can prove anything at all.

In addition, again according to quantum theory, there is a probability that all possible events, no matter how strange, may occur, so there is a probability, however small, that Herbert may exist after all.

Still, it's a good argument with which to confuse schoolteachers and parents, and on that basis alone Samuel is to be applauded.

of making a hiss sound like a shout, a sign of barely controlled rage that even Samuel was able to recognise. He went back to his chair and carefully impaled his desk with the pin, so that the angels, if they were actually there, wouldn't fall off.

'Anyone else got anything they'd like to share with us?' asked Mr Hume. 'An imaginary bunny, perhaps? An invisible duck named Percy?'

Everyone laughed. Bobby Goddard kicked the back of Samuel's seat.

Samuel sighed.

So that was why Mr Hume had called Samuel's mother, and afterwards she had given Samuel a talking to about taking school seriously, and not teasing Mr Hume, who appeared to be, she said, 'a little sensitive'.

Samuel glanced at his watch. His mother would be gone by now, which meant that Stephanie the babysitter would be waiting for him when he returned. Stephanie had been OK when she had first started looking after Samuel a couple of years before, but recently she had become horrible in the way that only certain teenage girls can. She had a boyfriend named Garth who would sometimes come over to 'keep her company', which meant that Samuel would be rushed off to bed well before his bedtime. Even when Garth wasn't around, Stephanie would spend hours talking on the phone while watching reality TV shows in which people competed to become models, singers, dancers, actors, builders, or anything other than what they really were, and she preferred to do so without the benefit of Samuel's company.

It was now dark. Samuel should have been home

fifteen minutes ago, but the house wasn't the same any more. He missed his dad, but he was also angry at him and his mum.

'We should be getting back,' he told Boswell. Boswell wagged his tail. It was getting chilly, and Boswell didn't like the cold.

At which point there was a bright blue flash from somewhere behind them, accompanied by a smell like a fire in a rotten-egg factory. Boswell nearly fell off the wall in shock, saved only by Samuel's arms.

'Right,' said Samuel, sensing an opportunity to delay returning home, 'let's go and see what *that* was . . .'

In the basement of 666 Crowley Avenue, a number of cloaked figures were covering their faces with their sleeves and spluttering.

'Oh, that's disgusting,' said Mrs Renfield. 'How horrid!'

The smell really was terrible, particularly in such an enclosed space, even though Mr Abernathy had earlier opened the basement window a crack to let in some air. Now he rushed to open it wider and, slowly, the stench began to weaken, or perhaps it was just that there was now something else to distract the attention of the four people in the basement from it.

Hanging in the air at the very centre of the room was a small, rotating circle of pale blue light. It twinkled, then grew in strength and size. Slowly, it became a perfect disc, about two feet in diameter, from which wisps of smoke were emerging.

It was Mrs Abernathy who took the first step forward.

'Careful, dear,' said her husband.

'Oh, do be quiet,' said Mrs Abernathy.

She kept advancing until she was mere inches from the circle. 'I think I can see something,' she said. 'Wait a minute.' She drew closer. 'There's . . . *land* there. It's like a window. I can see mud, and stones, and the bars of some huge gates.

'And now there's something moving—'

Outside, Samuel crouched by the small window looking down on the basement. Boswell, who was a very intelligent dog, was hiding by the hedge. In fact Boswell was *under* the hedge, and had he been a larger dog, one capable of restraining an eleven-year-old boy, for example, Samuel would have been right there beside him; that, or both of them would have been well on their way home, where there were no nasty smells, no flashing blue lights, and no hints that something bad had just happened, and was likely to get considerably worse, Boswell also being a melancholic, even pessimistic dog by nature.

The window was only a foot long, and opened barely two inches on its metal hinge, but the gap was wide enough for Samuel to be able to view and hear all that was going on inside. He was a little surprised to see the Abernathys and two other people wearing what looked like black bathrobes in a cold basement, but he had long ago learned not to be too shocked by anything adults did. He heard Mrs Abernathy describe what she was seeing, but all that was visible to Samuel was the glowing circle itself. It seemed to be filled with a white fog, as if someone had blown a very big, very dense smoke ring in the Abernathys' basement.

Samuel was anxious to discover what else Mrs Abernathy might have been able to glimpse. Unfortunately those details were destined to remain unknown, apart from the fact that whatever it was had grey, scaly skin and three large, clawed fingers, for that was what reached out from the glowing circle, grabbed Mrs Abernathy's head and dragged her through. She didn't even have time to scream.

Mrs Renfield screamed instead. Mr Abernathy ran towards the glowing circle, then seemed to think better of whatever he was planning to do and settled for plaintively calling out his wife's name.

'Evelyn?' he said. 'Are you all right, dear?'

There was no response from the hole, but he could hear an unpleasant sound from within, like someone squishing ripe fruit. His wife had been correct, though: something was visible through the hole. It did indeed look like a pair of enormous gates, ones which had developed a hole that was now bubbling with molten metal. Through it, Mr Abernathy could see a dreadful landscape, all ruined trees and black mud. Shapes moved across it, shadowy figures that had no place except in horror stories and nightmares. Of his wife there was no sign.

'Let's get out of here,' said Mr Renfield. He began bustling his wife towards the stairs, then stopped as a movement in the corner of the basement caught his eye.

'Eric,' he said.

Mr Abernathy was too concerned with the whereabouts of his wife to pay attention.

'Evelyn?' he called again. 'Are you in there, dear?'

'Eric,' said Mr Renfield again, this time with more force. 'I think you may want to see this.'

Mr Abernathy turned and saw what Mr Renfield and his wife were looking at. As soon as he did so he decided that, all things considered, he might rather not have seen it, but by then, of course, it was too late.

There was a shape in the corner of the cellar, rimmed with blue light. It resembled a large, Mrs Abernathy-shaped balloon, although one that was being filled with water and then jiggled by some unseen force so that it bulged in all the wrong places. In addition its skin, visible only at its face and arms where they emerged from the now tattered and bloodied cloak, were grey and scaly, and the fingernails of each hand were yellow and hooked.

As they watched, the transformation was completed. A tentacle, its surface covered in sharp suckers that moved like mouths, coiled around the figure's legs for a moment, and then was absorbed into the main body. The skin became white, the nails went from yellow to painted red, and something that was almost Mrs Abernathy stood before them. Even Samuel, from where he watched, could see that she wasn't the same. Mrs Abernathy had been quite handsome for someone his mum's age, but now she was more attractive than ever. She seemed to radiate beauty, as though someone had turned on a light inside her body and it was glowing through her skin. Her eyes were very bright, and some of that blue energy flickered in their depths, like lightning glimpsed in the blackest night.

She was also, Samuel realised, quite terrifying. *Power*, he thought. She's full of *power*.

'Evelyn?' said Mr Abernathy uncertainly.

The thing that looked like Mrs Abernathy smiled.

'Evelyn is gone,' she said. Her voice was deeper than Samuel remembered, and made him shiver.

'Well, where is she?' demanded Mr Abernathy.

The woman raised her right hand and pointed her finger at the glowing hole.

'In there, on the other side of the portal.'

'And what is "in there"?' said Mr Abernathy. To his credit, he was being jolly brave when faced with something that was clearly beyond his experience and, indeed, beyond this world.

'In there is . . . Hell,' said the woman.

'Hell?' said Mrs Renfield, entering the conversation. 'Are you sure? It doesn't sound very likely.' She peered into the hole. 'It looks a bit like that place on the moors where your mother lives, Reginald.'

Mr Renfield took a careful look. 'You know, you're right, it does a bit.'

'Bring Evelyn back,' said Mr Abernathy, ignoring the Renfields.

'Your wife is gone. I will take her place.'

Mr Abernathy regarded the thing in the corner.

'What do you *want*?' asked Mr Abernathy, who was cleverer than Mr and Mrs Renfield, and all the little Renfields, had they been there, put together.

'To open the gates.'

'The gates?' said Mr Abernathy in puzzlement, then the expression on his face changed. 'The gates . . . of *Hell* ?'

'Yes. We have four days to prepare the way.'

'Right,' said Mr Renfield, 'we're off. Come along, Doris.' He took his wife's arm and together they began ascending the steps from the basement. 'Thanks for an, um, *interesting* night, Eric. We must do it again some time.'

Mr and Mrs Renfield got as far as the third step when what looked like twin strands of spider web flew from the glowing blue hole, wrapped themselves round the waists of the unfortunate pair, then plucked them from the steps and dragged them through the portal. With a puff of foul-smelling smoke they were gone. The portal grew larger for an instant before the blue rim seemed to disappear entirely.

'Where is it?' shouted Mr Abernathy. 'Where has it gone?'

'It's still there,' said the woman. 'But it's better that it should remain hidden for now.'

Mr Abernathy reached towards where the circle had been, and his hand vanished in mid-air. Quickly he pulled it back again, then held it up before his face. It was coated in a clear, sticky fluid.

'I want my wife back,' he said. 'I want the Renfields back.' He reconsidered. 'Actually, you can keep the Renfields. I just want Evelyn back. Please.' Mr Abernathy might not have been fond of his wife, but having her around was easier than being forced to look after himself.

The woman merely shook her head. There were twin flashes of blue behind her, and two large hairy things moved in the shadows of the basement. From where he crouched, Samuel glimpsed black eyes glittering – too many eyes for two people – and some bony, jointed limbs. While Samuel watched, the shapes gradually assumed the form of Mr and Mrs Renfield, although they seemed to have a bit of trouble finding somewhere to store all their legs.

'I won't help you,' said Mr Abernathy. 'You can't make me.'

The woman sighed. 'We don't want your help,' she said. 'We just want your body.'

With that a long pink tongue slithered from the portal, and Mr Abernathy was yanked from his feet and disappeared into thin air. Moments later a fat blob, green and large-eyed, assumed his shape and took its place beside what looked, to the casual observer, like Mrs Abernathy and the Renfields.

By then Samuel had seen enough, and he and Boswell were running as fast as they could for the safety of home. Had he waited, Samuel might have seen the creature that was now Mrs Abernathy staring in the direction of the small window, and at the faint shape of a boy that hung in the still night air where Samuel had been hiding.

CHAPTER V

*In Which We Meet Nurd, Who is Not Quite As
Terrifying As He Would Like to Be, but a
Great Deal Unluckier*

Nurd, the Scourge of Five Deities, sat on his gilded throne, his servant Wormwood at his feet and his kingdom spread before him, and yawned.

'Bored, Your Scourgeness?' enquired Wormwood.

'Actually,' said Nurd. 'I am extremely excited. I cannot remember the last time I felt so enthused about anything.'

'Really?' asked Wormwood hopefully, and received a painful tap on the head from Nurd's Sceptre of Terrible and Awesome Might for his trouble.

'No, you idiot,' said Nurd. 'Of course I'm bored. What else is there to be?'

It was an entirely understandable question, for Nurd was not in a happy place. In fact, the place in which Nurd happened to be was so far from Happy that even if one walked for a very long time – centuries, millennia – one still would not be able to see even Slightly Less Unhappy from wherever one ended up.

Nurd's kingdom, the Wasteland, consisted of mile upon mile of flat, grey stone, unbroken by anything at all, apart from the odd rock that was less grey, and some pools of viscous, bubbling black liquid. At the horizon, the rock met a slate-grey sky across which lightning occasionally flashed without ever bringing the sound of thunder, or the feel of rain.

It wasn't even a kingdom as such. Nurd, the Scourge of Five Deities, had simply been banished to it for being, as his name had it, a Scourge, although the nature of Nurd's offences was open to some doubt.[10]

The title 'Scourge of Five Deities', which Nurd had come up with all by himself, was technically true. Nurd had been something of a bother to five different demonic entities, but they were relatively minor ones: Schwell, the Demon of Uncomfortable Shoes; Ick, the Demon of Unpleasant Things Discovered in Plugholes During Cleaning; Graham, the Demon of Stale Biscuits and Crackers; Mavis, the Demon of Inappropriate Names for Men; and last, and quite possibly least, Erics', the Demon of Bad Punctuation.

Nurd had been less of a scourge to these worthies and more of a minor irritation, like a fly buzzing against a window in summer or, well, like a stale biscuit that one had rather been looking forward to having with a nice cup of tea, but thanks to the demon Graham, turns out to taste soggy and a bit dusty. Eventually, because he wouldn't go away, and kept trying to muscle in on their operations, the five deities appealed to an aide to

---

💀 [10] A deity, pronounced 'day-it-tee', is a kind of god. There are good deities, and bad deities. Nurd was a bad deity, but in general none of them is to be trusted. The playwright William Shakespeare wrote, in *King Lear*, that 'As flies to wanton boys are we to the gods; they kill us for their sport.' Nasty lot, deities. Don't say that you haven't learned something new by reading this page.

the Great Malevolence himself, which was how Nurd came to be occupying a not-very-interesting piece of nowhere-in-particular with not-very-much-to-do, but had decided to make the best of it by calling it his kingdom. To keep him company, his faithful servant Wormwood had been expelled along with him, an expulsion that Wormwood considered more than a bit unfair because he hadn't done anything wrong at all, except to be careless in his choice of employer.

The Great Malevolence was not entirely without mercy (or, indeed, a sense of humour), for he had seen fit to give Nurd a slightly used throne upon which to sit, and a cushion for Wormwood, as well as a box in which Nurd could keep various bits and pieces that had proved of no use whatsoever during his banishment. Thus it was that Nurd and Wormwood had been sitting in the middle of nowhere, if not for eternity, then since a few minutes past. They had never had very much to talk about. Now they had even less.

Wormwood rubbed his head, where a new bump had been added to the already impressive collection that adorned his misshapen skull, and not for the first time thought that Nurd, the Scourge of Five Deities, really was a bit of a sod.

Nurd, heedless of Wormwood's resentment, yawned once more, and promptly disappeared.

There wasn't a name for the bundle of blue energy that had managed to escape from the Large Hadron Collider. It was part of that 96 per cent of matter and energy unknown to science, and it wasn't an intended result of the collider experiment at all. Rather, in attempting to recreate the circumstances of the Big Bang, the multiple explosions in the collider had, very briefly, opened a portal, and on the other side of the portal the Great Malevolence had been waiting for precisely that moment. The little bundle of energy was the equivalent of a piece of wood that has been wedged beneath a door to keep it open. Now the challenge was to start putting pressure on the door in order to open it wider, because the Great Malevolence was an immense being. What Mrs Abernathy had glimpsed, before she met her unfortunate end, were the gates of Hell, which had been put in place to keep the Great Malevolence within the boundaries of that awful place. The shard of blue energy had created a small hole in those gates, large enough for some of the Great Malevolence's agents to pass through. They were scouts, and guardians of the portal. They also represented the first step in the Great Malevolence's plan to leave his own place of banishment, which wasn't much better than that of Nurd, the Scourge of Five Deities, but did at least have a view, and a few more chairs.

Unfortunately, as soon as anyone or anything starts sending random bursts of energy whizzing through portals between dimensions without being sure of the consequences, there's a good chance that some of that energy may end up in places that it shouldn't, like the sparks from a welder's torch as he works on a piece of metal. In an act of grave misfortune, one of those sparks of energy had ended up creating a small fissure between our world and the space occupied by Nurd's throne or, more particularly, Nurd himself.

The Great Malevolence had managed to wedge open a door, just as he had hoped.

He had also, unintentionally, managed to open a window.

Nurd, the Scourge of Five Deities, was free.

Nurd was feeling dizzy, and somewhat sick, as though he had just climbed off a roundabout.[11] He wasn't sure what had happened, except that it had been very painful, but he knew that he was no longer occupying a throne in a dull, grey world accompanied only by a small demon who looked like a weasel with mange, which meant that this could only be a good thing. He felt air on his skin. (Nurd was vaguely human in appearance, although his ears were too long and pointed, and his head, shaped like a quarter-moon, was too large for his body, and bore a distinctly greenish tinge.) Although he was in darkness, his eyes were already beginning to make out the shapes of unfamiliar things.

'I'm . . . somewhere else,' said Nurd. Although he had never been anywhere other than the Wasteland and, briefly, until he'd irritated the Great Malevolence, certain far-flung regions of Hell itself, he understood instinctively where he was. He was in the Place of People, of Humans. He was a demon of great power let loose among those who, next to him, were powerless and

---

⊙ [11] There was a demon for that feeling too: Ulp, the Demon of Things That Go Round for Slightly Too Long, with additional responsibility for the Smell of Candyfloss When You're Not Feeling Yourself, and the Lingering Odour of Small Children Being Unwell.

insignificant. He began to channel all his rage and hurt and loneliness, creating from them an energy that he could use to rule this new world. His skin cracked and glowed red, like streams of lava glimpsed beneath the shifting rock of a volcanic eruption. The glow moved to his eyes, giving them a ferocity they had not had for a very long time. Steam erupted from his ears, and he opened wide his jaws as he prepared to announce his presence on Earth to all those who would soon know his wrath.

'I am Nurd!' he cried. 'You will bow down before me!'

Light appeared. It was disturbingly regular, forming a huge rectangle, the outline of a door larger than Nurd had ever seen, even in the depths of Hell itself. Then the door opened, flooding Nurd's new world with illumination. A giant being towered above him, a colossus in a pink skirt and white blouse. It had something in its hands, a squat, eyeless creature with a long nose and square jaws.

'Oh, bug—' began Nurd, all he got to say before Mrs Johnson's vacuum cleaner dropped on him, and everything went dark again.

Back in the Wasteland, Wormwood was still trying to work out what, precisely, had happened to his unloved master. He poked the space on the throne that Nurd usually occupied, wondering if Nurd had been hiding the art of invisibility for all this time, and had only now decided to use it in order to break the monotony, but there was nothing there.

Nurd, it appeared, was gone.

And if Nurd was gone, then he, Wormwood, was now ruler of all he surveyed.

Wormwood picked up the Sceptre of Terrible and Awesome Might from the foot of the throne. With his other hand, he grasped the Crown of Misdeeds which had fallen from Nurd's head as he slipped out of existence. He stared at them both, then faced the Wasteland and raised the sceptre and the crown above his head.

'I am Wormwood!' he cried. 'I am –'

There was a sound behind him, as though a Nurd-shaped object were being forced through a very small hole, and wasn't feeling terribly pleased about the process.

– 'very happy to see you again, Master,' concluded Wormwood, as he turned and saw Nurd, seated, once more, on his throne, and looking like a very big Thing of Some Kind had fallen on him. He seemed bewildered and somewhat broken in places.

'Wormwood,' said Nurd. 'I feel ill.'

And he sneezed a single, dusty sneeze.

CHAPTER VI

In Which We Encounter Stephanie, Who is Not a Demon But is Still Not Terribly Nice

The front door opened while Samuel was still fumbling for his key. He had only recently been entrusted with his own house key, and he was so terrified of losing it that he kept it round his neck on a piece of string. Unfortunately it was proving rather difficult to find it while dressed as a ghost and holding on to a small, worried dog, so he was still searching beneath various layers of sheet, sweater, and shirt when Stephanie the babysitter appeared in his line of sight.

'Where have you been?' she said. 'You should have been back half an hour ago.' The expression on her face changed. 'And why are you dressed like a ghost?'

Samuel shuffled past her, but didn't answer immediately. First of all, he set Boswell free of his lead and divested himself of his sheet.

'I thought I'd get an early start for Halloween,' he said, gasping, 'but that doesn't matter now. I've seen something—'

'Forget it,' said Stephanie.

'But—'

'Not interested.'

'It's important.'

'Go to bed.'

'What?' Samuel was momentarily distracted from what he had witnessed in the Abernathys' basement by the injustice of this order. 'It's half-term. I don't have to go to school tomorrow. Mum said—'

'"Mum said, Mum said,"' mimicked Stephanie. 'Well, your mum isn't here now. I'm in charge, and I say that you have to go to bed.'

'But the Abernathys. Their basement. Monsters. Gates. You don't understand.'

Stephanie leaned in very close to Samuel's face and Samuel recognised that there were things even more terrifying than what he had seen at the Abernathys' house, if only because they were very close and their anger was directed entirely at him. Stephanie's face was going red, her nostrils were flaring, and her eyes had grown narrow, like the slits in a castle wall before someone begins firing flaming arrows out of them. She spoke very precisely, through gritted teeth.

'Go. To. *Bed.*'

The final word was delivered at such ear-splittingly high volume that Samuel felt certain his glasses were about to crack. Even Boswell, who was used to Stephanie by now, looked disturbed.

With no other option, Samuel stomped up the stairs to bed, closely followed by Boswell. He was about to slam his door behind him when he heard Stephanie shout: 'And don't you dare slam that door!'

Although sorely tempted to disobey, Samuel decided to err on the side of discretion. There was not a great deal that Stephanie could do to him, although he sometimes wondered what she might have done if she thought that she could get away with it, like burying him in the back garden after drowning him in the bathtub.[12] Still, Stephanie was a tattle-tale and when Samuel had crossed her in the past he had found himself dealing with his mother the following morning. Unlike Stephanie, there were a great many things she could do to make his life uncomfortable, such as denying him television, or his allowance, or, as on one particularly grim occasion after he had dropped a plastic snake down Stephanie's back, both of the above. How was he to know that Stephanie was afraid of snakes, he had argued, even though he had been fully aware of how much she disliked them, and that had been half the fun. He still treasured the memory of her leaping from the couch in shock, and the strange noise that had come from deep within her, a sound that was barely human, as if someone were playing a violin inside her very, very badly. In fact, he could trace the serious deterioration of his relationship with Stephanie to that particular occasion. Not only had his mother punished him but the odious Garth had threatened to stick his head down the toilet and flush him to China

☠ [12] It is a curious fact that small boys are more terrified of their babysitters than small girls are. In part, this is because small girls and babysitters, who are usually slightly larger girls, belong to the same species, and thus understand each other. Small boys, on the other hand, do not understand girls, and therefore being looked after by one is a little like a hamster being looked after by a shark. If you are a small boy it may be some consolation to you to know that even large boys do not understand girls, and girls, by and large, do not understand boys. This makes adult life very interesting.

if he ever pulled a stunt like that again. Samuel, having no great desire to be flushed to China, had not pulled a stunt like that again.[13]

Samuel changed into his pyjamas, brushed his teeth, and climbed between his sheets. Boswell curled up in his basket at the foot of the bed. Usually Samuel would read before turning off the light and going to sleep, but not tonight. He was determined to stay up until his mother returned home, and then he would confront her with what he had learned.

Samuel managed to stay awake for two and a half hours before sleep eventually took him. He thought of all that he had seen and heard in the Abernathys' basement. He wondered if he should go to the police, but he was not an unintelligent boy and he knew that the police would take a dim view of an eleven-year-old with a dachshund who claimed that his neighbours had been transformed into demons intent upon opening the gates of Hell. So it was that Samuel did not hear his mother come in, nor did he hear Stephanie leave, after first informing Samuel's mother that Samuel had broken curfew.

Nor did he see, after all the lights were turned off and his mother was, like him, asleep in bed, the figure of a woman standing at the garden gate, staring intently at his bedroom window, her eyes burning with a cold blue fire.

💀 [13] It is not possible to flush someone to China. Or Australia. Well, not unless they're already there. It is not a good idea, though, to point this out to someone who is threatening to flush you to China or Australia, as there is a good chance that they will try it anyway just to prove you wrong.

CHAPTER VII

In Which the Scientists Wonder What the Bit Was, And Where It Might Have Gone

While Samuel slept, a group of scientists huddled over a series of screens and printouts. Behind them, an uncompleted game of Battleships lay forgotten.

'But there's no record of anything unusual occurring,' said one. His name was Professor Hilbert, and he had become a scientist for two reasons. The first was that he had always been fascinated by science, particularly physics, which is science for people who like numbers more than – well, more than people, probably. The other reason why Professor Hilbert had become a scientist was that he had always *looked* like a scientist. Even as a small boy he had worn glasses, been unable to comb his hair properly, and had a fondness for storing pens in his shirt pockets. He was also very interested in taking things apart to find out how they worked, although he had never discovered how to put any of them back together again in quite the same way. Instead he was always trying to find some means to improve them, even if they had worked perfectly well to begin with. Thus it was that, when he 'improved' his parents' toaster, the toaster had incinerated the bread, and then burst into flames so hot they had melted the kitchen counter. The kitchen had always smelled funny after that, and he was required to eat his bread untoasted unless supervised. After he spent an hour with their radio, it had begun picking up signals from passing military aircraft, leading to a visit from a couple of stern men in uniforms who were under the impression that the Hilberts were Russian spies. Finally young Hilbert was sent to a special school for very bright people, where, to his heart's content, he was allowed to take things apart and put them together again in odd combinations. He had started only one or two fires at the special school, but they were small, and easily extinguished.

Now Professor Hilbert was trying to make sense of what Ed and Victor were telling him. The collider had been shut down as a precaution, which annoyed Professor Hilbert greatly. Turning the collider on and off wasn't like flipping a light switch. It was a complicated and expensive business. Furthermore, it generated bad publicity for everyone involved in the experiment, especially as there were still people who were convinced that the collider would be responsible for the end of the world.

'You say that a particle of some kind separated itself from the beams in the collider?'

'That's right,' said Ed.

'Then somehow passed through the walls of the collider itself, and the solid rock around it, before disappearing.'

'Right again,' said Ed.

'Then the system began rewriting itself to eliminate any evidence of this occurrence?'

'Yes.'

'Fascinating,' said Professor Hilbert.

What was strange about this conversation was that at no point did Professor Hilbert doubt the truth of what Ed and Victor were telling him. Nothing about the Large Hadron Collider and what it was revealing about the nature of the universe was surprising to Professor Hilbert. Delightful, yes. Troubling, sometimes. But never surprising. He was not a man who was easily surprised, and he suspected that the universe was a much stranger place than anyone imagined, which made him anxious to prove just how extraordinary it really was.

'What do you think it might be?' asked Ed.

'Evidence,' said Professor Hilbert.

'Of what?'

'I don't know,' said Professor Hilbert, and rambled off sucking his pencil.

Hours later Professor Hilbert was still at his desk, surrounded by pieces of paper on which he had constructed diagrams, created complex equations, and drawn little stick men fighting one another with swords. He had also gone over the system records for the past few hours and had discovered something curious. The system had overwritten itself, as Ed and Victor had suggested, but it had not done so perfectly. Like someone rubbing out a couple of lines written in pencil, the shadow of what had been there before still remained. Slowly, Professor Hilbert had begun reconstructing it. While he was not able to recreate it completely, he found that, at the precise moment that Ed and Victor had witnessed what was now being termed 'the Event', a batch of strange code had found its way into the system. It was this code that Professor Hilbert was now attempting to reconstruct.

The problem was that the code was not in any known computer language. In fact, it didn't appear to be in any recognisable language at all.

Professor Hilbert's particular area of interest was dimensions. Specifically, he was fascinated by the possibility that there might be a great many universes out there, of which ours was only one. He was part of a group of scientists who believed that our universe might exist in an ocean of other universes, some being born, some already in existence, and others about to come to an end. Instead of a universe, he believed in the possibility of a multiverse. His life's work had been devoted to this belief, which he hoped the collider might help him to prove. If a mini black hole, one that did not swallow up the Earth, say one thousand times the mass of an electron and existing for only 10^-23 seconds, were created in the collider, Professor Hilbert believed that it would provide evidence for the existence of parallel universes.

Now, as he sat at his desk, he looked at the strange code, written in symbols that seemed at once modern yet very, very old and wondered: Is this the proof that I have been seeking? Is this a message from another universe, another dimension?

And if it is, then what does it mean?

Some of you may know who Albert Einstein was. For those who don't, here is a picture of him:

Einstein was a very famous scientist, the kind of scientist who even people who know nothing about science can probably name. He is most famous for his General Theory of Relativity, which concluded that mass is a form of energy, and goes e=mc2 (or energy = mass by the speed of light squared) but he also had a sense of humour. He once said that we were all ignorant, but each of us was ignorant in a different way, which is very wise when you think about it.[14]

It was Einstein who predicted the existence of black holes (there is one at the heart of our Milky Way, but it's obscured by dust clouds; otherwise it would be visible every night as a fireball in the constellation of

[14] As you can see from his picture, Einstein didn't take himself too seriously, at least not all of the time. In general, it's a good idea to avoid people who take themselves too seriously. As individuals, we have only so much seriousness to go round, and people who take themselves very seriously don't have enough seriousness left over to take other people seriously. Instead they tend to look down on them, and are secretly pleased when they get stuff wrong, because they just prove to the too-serious types that they were right not to take them seriously to begin with.

Sagittarius), but Einstein's black holes came with their own inbuilt problem. They had, at their centre, a singularity (there's that word again, remember footnote 1?), a point at which time came to an end and all known rules of physics broke down. You can't make a rule that breaks all the rules. Science just doesn't work that way.

Einstein wasn't happy about this at all. He liked things to work according to the rules. In fact, the whole point of his life's work was to prove that there were rules governing the known universe, and he couldn't very well leave things like singularities hanging about making the place look untidy.

So, like any good scientist, Einstein went back over his work and tried to find a way to prove the singularities didn't exist or, if they did, that they played by the rules. So, after a bit of fiddling with his sums he came to the conclusion that the singularities might in fact be bridges between two different universes. This solved the problem of the singularities as far as Einstein was concerned, but nobody really believed that this bridge, known as an Einstein–Rosen bridge, could actually be used to travel between the universes, mainly because, if it existed at all, it would be very unstable, like building a bridge made from chewing gum and bits of chocolate over a very long drop, then suggesting that someone in a big truck might like to give it a try. The bridge would also be very small – 10^{-34} metres, or so small that it would hardly be there at all – and it would exist only for an instant, so driving a truck across it (a space truck, obviously) would be difficult and, frankly, fatal.

Mathematicians have also suggested the possibility of

what are known as 'multiply-connected spaces', or wormholes – literally, tunnels between universes – that exist at the centre of black holes.[15] In 1963 a New Zealand mathematician named Roy Kerr suggested that a spinning black hole would collapse into a stable ring of neutrons because the centrifugal force pushing out would cancel the inward force of gravity. The black hole wouldn't fall in on itself, and you wouldn't be crushed to death, but it would be a one-way trip, as the gravity would be sufficient to prevent you from returning the way you had come.

Nevertheless, the whole debate was another stage in the great discussion about wormholes, and black holes, and parallel universes, places where the rules of physics might not be quite the same as ours but might work perfectly well in that universe.

Now Professor Hilbert was wondering if something in a universe other than our own might have found a way of breaking through, using a hole or a bridge as yet unthought of in our science, and tried to make contact. If that was the case, then, if the bridge still existed, there

---

● [15] In *Alice Through the Looking Glass*, the book by Lewis Carroll, the looking glass is, in effect, a wormhole. Carroll, whose real name was Charles Dodgson, was a mathematician, and was aware of the theory of wormholes. He liked injecting puzzles into his maths classes. One of his most famous goes as follows: A cup contains 50 spoonfuls of brandy, and another contains 50 spoonfuls of water. A spoonful of brandy is taken from the first cup and added to the second cup. Then a spoonful of that mixture is taken from the second cup and mixed into the first. Is there more or less brandy in the second cup than there is water in the first cup? If you'd like to know the answer – and, I warn you, it will make your head ache more than drinking all of the brandy would – it's at the end of this chapter . . .*

would be an opening in its world, and another opening in ours.

The questions that followed from this were: where was that opening, and what exactly was going to emerge from it?

Back in the basement of 666 Crowley Avenue, four figures stood staring at where there had been, until recently, a spinning circle of blue. Mrs Abernathy had returned from her visit to Samuel Johnson's house to find her three companions in a state of some distress.

'The portal has closed,' said Mr Renfield, who no longer looked or sounded quite like the Mr Renfield of old. His voice emerged from his throat in a series of hoarse clicks, and his skin had already taken on the wrinkled, unhealthy appearance of a rotting apple. The change in his appearance had begun almost as soon as the blue light had disappeared, and a similar decay could be seen in Mrs Renfield and Mr Abernathy. Only Mrs Abernathy remained unaffected.

'They have shut down the collider,' said Mrs Abernathy, a strange expression on her face as she spoke, which she hid from the Renfields, 'as the Great One predicted that they would. But now we know that travel between this world and ours is possible. Even as we speak, our master is assembling his army, and when he is ready the portal will open once again, and he will cross over and claim this place as his own.'

'But we grow weak,' said Mrs Renfield. Her breath smelled bad, as if something inside her was festering.

'*You* grow weak,' said Mrs Abernathy. 'You are here

only to serve my needs. Your energy will fuel me, and when the portal opens once more you will be renewed.'

This was not entirely true. Mrs Abernathy was a more extraordinary demon than her three companions, older and wiser and more powerful than ever they could have imagined. The portal had not closed, not entirely. Mrs Abernathy's will and strength were keeping it open just a crack. Nevertheless, she was content to suck energy from the others as required, and to use the portal only when necessary. She would be the one to explore this new world in advance of her master's coming, and it was important that she blended in without attracting attention. After so long in the darkness, she wanted to experience something of the Earth before it was turned to ash and fire.

---

* Okay, back to Lewis Carroll's brandy and water problem. Mathematically speaking, the answer is that there will be just as much brandy in the water as there is water in the brandy, so both mixtures will be the same. But – and this is where your head may start to ache – when equal quantities of water and alcohol are mixed the sum of them is more compact than their parts because the brandy penetrates the spaces between the water molecules, and the water penetrates the spaces between the brandy molecules, a bit like the way two matching pieces of a jigsaw fit together so that they occupy less space than if you just laid the same pieces side by side. In other words, the mixture becomes more concentrated, so if you add 50 spoonfuls of water and 50 spoonfuls of brandy, you actually end up with less than 100 spoonfuls of the mixture in total. Adding a spoonful of brandy to 50 spoonfuls of water will give you less than 51 spoonfuls of the mixture, because, like we said earlier, it's more concentrated. If you take a spoonful from *that* mixture, it will leave less than 50 spoonfuls in the cup. Then, if you add that spoonful from the concentrated mixture to the cup of brandy, it means that there's more brandy in the brandy cup than there is more water in the water cup. I warned you . . .

CHAPTER VIII

*In Which Samuel Learns That Someone
Trying to Open the Gates of Hell is Not of
Particular Concern to His Mum*

Samuel awoke shortly after eight to the sound of plates banging in the kitchen. He dressed quickly, then went downstairs. Boswell was waiting expectantly for scraps from the breakfast table. He glanced at Samuel, wagged his tail in greeting, then went back to gazing intently at Mrs Johnson and the remains of the bacon on her plate.

'Mum—' Samuel began, but he was immediately cut off.

'Stephanie says that you came in late last night,' said his mother.

'I know, and I'm sorry, but—'

'No buts. You know I don't like you being out late by yourself.'

'But—'

'What did I just say? No "buts." Now sit down and eat your cereal.'

Samuel wondered if he would ever be allowed to complete a sentence again. First Stephanie, and now his mother. If this continued, he'd be forced to communicate entirely through sign language, or notes scribbled on pieces of paper, like someone in solitary confinement.

'Mum,' said Samuel, in his most serious and grown-up of tones. 'I have something important to tell you.'

'Uh-huh.' His mother stood and carried her plate to the sink, disappointing Boswell considerably.

'Mother, please.'

Samuel almost never called his mum 'Mother'. It always sounded wrong, but it had the effect, on this occasion, of attracting her attention. She turned round and folded her arms.

'Well?'

Samuel gestured at the kitchen chair opposite him, the way he saw grown-ups on television do when they invited people into their office to tell them they were about to be fired.

'Please, take a seat.'

Mrs Johnson gave a long-suffering sigh, but did as she was asked.

'It's about the Abernathys,' said Samuel.

'The Abernathys? The people at number six hundred and sixty-six?'

'Yes, and their friends.'

'What friends?'

'Well, I don't know their friends' names, but they were a man and a woman, and they were both fat.'

'And?'

'They are no more,' said Samuel, solemnly. He had read that phrase somewhere, and had always fancied using it.

'What does that mean?'

'They've been taken.'

'Taken where?'

'To Hell.'

'Oh, Samuel!' His mother rose and returned to the sink. 'You had me worried there for a minute. I thought you were being serious. Where do you get these ideas from? I really will have to keep a closer eye on what you're watching on television.'

'But it's true, Mum,' said Samuel. 'They were all in the Abernathys' basement dressed in robes, and then there was a blue light and a hole in the air, and a big claw reached out and pulled Mrs Abernathy inside, and then she appeared again except it wasn't her but something that looked like her. Then spiderwebs took their fat friends and, finally, Mr Abernathy was yanked in by a big tongue, and when it was all over there were four of them again, but it wasn't them, not really.

'And,' he finished, playing his trump card, 'they're trying to open the gates of Hell. I heard Mrs Abernathy say so, or the thing that looks like Mrs Abernathy.'

He took a deep breath and waited for a response.

'And that's why you were half an hour late coming back last night?' asked his mother.

'Yes.'

'You know that you're not supposed to be out past eight, especially now that the evenings are getting dark.'

'Mum, they're trying to open the *gates* of *Hell.* You know: Hell. Demons, and stuff. Monsters.' He paused for effect, then added: 'The Devil!'

'And you didn't eat your dinner,' said his mum.

'What?' Samuel was floored. He knew that his mother tended to ignore a lot of what he said, but he had never lied to her. Well, hardly ever. There were some things she didn't need to know, such as where her private stash of chocolate kept disappearing to, or how the rug in the living room had been moved slightly to cover some nasty burn marks after an experiment involving match heads.

'Don't say "what", say "pardon",' his mother corrected. 'I said you didn't eat your dinner.'

'That's because Stephanie sent me to bed early, but that's not the point.'

'Excuse me, Samuel Johnson, but that's precisely the point. You came in so late that you couldn't eat your dinner. There was spinach. I know you don't like it, but it's very healthy. And you annoyed Stephanie, and it's hard to get good babysitters these days.'

Samuel was by now completely bewildered. His mother could be very strange. According to her, this was how the world worked:

THINGS THAT ARE BAD

1. Coming in late.
2. Not eating spinach.
3. Annoying Stephanie.
4. Trying to confuse Mr Hume with talk of angels and pins.
5. Not wearing the hat his grandmother had knitted for him, even if it was purple and made him look like he had a swollen head.
6–99. Lots of other stuff.
100. Trying to open the gates of Hell.

'Mum, haven't you heard anything I've said?' asked Samuel.

'I've heard everything that you've said, Samuel, and it's more than enough. Now eat your breakfast. I have a lot to do today. If you want to, you can help me with the shopping later. Otherwise you can just stay here, but no television and no video games. I want you to read a book, or do something useful with your time. It's all those cartoons and monster-killing games that have given you these ideas. Honestly, dear, you live in a world of your own sometimes.'

And then she did something completely unexpected. Having spent the last five minutes complaining about him, and not believing anything that he'd told her, she came over and hugged him, and kissed his hair.

'You do make me laugh, though,' she said. She looked into his eyes, and her face grew sad. 'Samuel, all this stuff – these stories, the angels on the pin – it's not to do with your dad, is it? I know you miss him, and things have been a bit difficult since he left. You know I love you, don't you? You don't need to go looking for attention from me. I'm here, and you're the most important person in my world. You will remember that, won't you?'

Samuel nodded. His eyes felt hot. They always did when his mum talked about his dad. He'd been gone for two months and three days now. Samuel wished that he'd come back, but at the same time he was angry with him. He wasn't sure what had happened between his mum and dad, but his dad was now living up north, and Samuel had only seen him twice since the break-up. From a whispered but angry phone conversation that he'd overheard between his mum and dad, someone called Elaine was involved. Samuel's mum had called Elaine a very bad name during the conversation, and then had hung up the phone and started crying. Samuel was sometimes angry at his mum too, because he wondered if she might have done something to drive his dad away. And, on occasion, when he was feeling particularly sad, Samuel would try to remember if he himself had done anything to make his dad leave, if he'd been bad, or mean to him, or had let his dad down in some way. For the most part, though, he sensed that his dad was the one who was most to blame, and he hated the fact that his dad made his mum cry.

'Now eat your bacon,' said Samuel's mum. 'I've left it under the grill for you.'

She kissed him on the head again, then went upstairs.

Samuel ate his bacon. Sometimes he just didn't understand adults. He wondered if he ever would, or if there would come a time, after he become a grown-up himself, when it would all suddenly make sense to him.

He finished his food, fed the scraps to Boswell, then washed his plate and sat down at the table again. He looked at Boswell. Boswell looked at him. There was still the not-so-small matter of the opening of the gates of Hell to be dealt with, and his mum had been no help at all with that.

'Now what are we supposed to do?' asked Samuel.

If Boswell could have shrugged, he would have.

The doorbell rang at number 666. It was Mrs Abernathy who answered. Standing before her was the postman, holding a large parcel. He wasn't the usual postman, who was on holiday in Spain, and he had never seen Mrs Abernathy before, but he thought she was extremely good-looking.

'Parcel for Mr Abernathy,' he said.

'That would be my –' Mrs Abernathy, unused to talking to someone who wasn't another demon, had to think for a moment – 'husband,' she finished. 'He's not here at the moment.'

'No problem. You can sign for it.'

He handed Mrs Abernathy a pen, and a form on a clipboard. Mrs Abernathy looked confused.

'Just sign, er, there,' said the postman, pointing to a line at the bottom of the form.

'I don't seem to have my glasses,' said Mrs Abernathy. 'Would you mind stepping inside for a moment while I look for them?'

'It's just a signature,' said the postman. 'On a line. That line.' Once again, he pointed helpfully at the line in question.

'I don't like signing anything that I haven't read,' said Mrs Abernathy.

It takes all sorts, thought the postman. 'Right you are, then, ma'am. I'll wait here while you look for your glasses.'

'Oh, please, come inside. I insist. It's so cold out, and it may take me a moment or two to find them.' She moved further into the house, still holding the clipboard. That clipboard was very important to the postman. It contained details of all of the parcels and registered letters that he had delivered that day, and he wasn't supposed to let it out of his sight. Reluctantly he followed Mrs Abernathy into the house. He noticed that the blinds and curtains were drawn in the rooms adjoining the hall, and there was a funny smell, like rotten eggs and recently struck matches.

'Bit dark in here,' he said.

'Really?' said Mrs Abernathy. 'I like it this way.'

And the postman noticed, for the first time, that there seemed to be a blue glow to Mrs Abernathy's eyes.

The door closed behind him.

But Mrs Abernathy was in front of him, so who could have closed it?

He was turning to find out when a tentacle curled itself round his neck and lifted him off the floor. The postman tried to say something, but the tentacle was very tight. He had a brief glimpse of a huge mouth, and some big teeth, and then everything went dark for ever.

Humans were puny, thought Mrs Abernathy. She had been sent to find out their strengths and weaknesses, but already she could tell that the latter far outweighed the former.

On the other hand, they didn't taste bad at all.

Mrs Abernathy licked her lips and went into the dining room, where the curtains were also drawn. Three figures sat upon chairs, doing nothing in particular apart from smelling funny. Mr Abernathy and the Renfields were starting to turn an ugly shade of purple, like meat that was going bad, and their fingernails had begun to drop off. That was the trouble with destroying the life force of another being, and taking on its shape. It was like opening a banana, throwing away the fruit, and then sewing up the skin in the hope that it would continue to look like a banana. It would for a while, but then it would start turning black.

'I'm concerned about the boy,' said Mrs Abernathy.

Her husband looked at her. His eyes were milky.

'Why?' he asked, his voice little more than a croak as his vocal cords began to decay 'He's just a child.'

'He will talk.'

'Nobody will believe him.'

'Somebody might.'

'And if they do? We are more powerful than they can ever be.'

Mrs Abernathy snorted in disgust. 'Have you looked in a mirror lately?' she said. 'The only powerful thing about you is your smell.'

She shook her head and walked away. That was the problem with lower demons: they had no cunning, and no imagination.

Mrs Abernathy was of the highest order of demons, only a level below the Great Malevolence himself. She had knowledge of humans, for the Great Malevolence had spoken of them to her, and with him she had watched them from afar, as if through a dark window. What he saw fed his hatred and jealousy. He rejoiced when men and women did bad things, and howled with rage when they did good. He wanted to reduce their world to rubble and scarred earth, and destroy every living thing in it that walked, crawled, swam, or flew. It was Mrs Abernathy who would pave the way for him. The Great Malevolence, and the humans' machine with its beams and particles, would do the rest.

But there remained the problem of the boy. Children were dangerous, Mrs Abernathy knew, more so than adults. They believed in things like right and wrong, good and evil. They were persistent. They interfered.

First she would find out what Samuel Johnson knew. If he had been a naughty little boy, one who had been sticking his nose in where he had no business sticking it, he would have to be dealt with.

CHAPTER IX

In Which We Learn a Little About the Gates of Hell, None of Which is Entirely Helpful

After his mother left to do her shopping, Samuel spent some time at the kitchen table, his chin cupped in his hands, considering his options. He knew that Mrs Abernathy, or the entity that now occupied her body, was up to no good, but he was facing a problem encountered by young people the world over: how to convince adults that you were telling the truth about something in which they just did not want to believe.

His mother had told him not to play computer games, but that didn't mean he couldn't use his computer at all. With Boswell at his heels Samuel went up to his bedroom, sat at his desk, and began to search the Internet. He decided to start with what he knew for certain, so he typed 'gates of Hell' into the search engine.

The first reference that came up was to a huge bronze sculpture entitled *La Porte de l'Enfer*, which in English means *The Gates of Hell*, by an artist named Auguste Rodin. Apparently Rodin was asked to create the sculpture in 1880, and promised to deliver it by 1885. Instead Rodin had still been working on it when he died in

1917. Samuel did a small calculation and discovered that Rodin had been 32 years late in delivering the sculpture. He wondered if Rodin might have been related to Mr Armitage, their local painter, who had been supposed to paint their living room and dining room over a single weekend and had in fact taken six months to do it, and even then had left one wall and part of the ceiling unfinished. Samuel's father and Mr Armitage had had a big argument about it when they met in the street. 'It's not the ceiling of the Sistine Chapel,' Mr Armitage had said. 'I'll get round to it when I can. You'll want me flat on my back painting angels next.[16]

Samuel's father had suggested that if Mr Armitage *had* been asked to paint the ceiling of the Sistine Chapel, he would have taken twenty years instead of four, and still would have left God without a beard. At that point, Mr Armitage had said a rude word and walked away, and

---

💀 [16] The artist Michelangelo painted the ceiling of the Sistine Chapel in Rome between 1508 and 1512. He had to use scaffolding to do it, but because the ceiling was so high he couldn't build the scaffolding from the floor up, so instead he made a special flat wooden platform that hung from bolts beside the windows. Painting the ceiling was a very uncomfortable business, as you can probably imagine, but it's a myth that Michelangelo had to lie flat on his back to do it. Instead he stood upright, with his head bent back, for four years. By the end of it, he was so sore that he wrote a poem about it:

My beard turns up to heaven; my nape falls in
Fixed on my spine: my breast-bone visibly
Grows like a harp: a rich embroidery
    Bedews my face from brush-drips, thick and thin.

And so on for a few more verses, which can be summarised basically as 'owww...'

Samuel's father had ended up finishing the ceiling and wall himself.

Badly.

Anyway, while Rodin's gates looked very impressive, they didn't seem to have a blue light around them, and Samuel read that they had been inspired by a writer named Dante, and his book *The Divine Comedy*. Samuel suspected that neither Dante nor Rodin had ever really seen the gates of Hell, and had just taken a guess.[17]

After that, Samuel found some dodgy heavy metal groups who either had songs named after the gates of Hell, or simply liked putting images of demons on their album covers in order to make themselves seem more terrifying than they really were, since most of them were just hairy chaps from nice families who had spent too much time alone in their bedrooms as teenagers. Samuel did discover that the Romans and Greeks believed the gates were guarded by a three-headed dog called Cerberus, who made sure that nobody who

---

💀 [17] *The Divine Comedy* is not funny, but it's not supposed to be, despite its name. In Dante's time, a comedy meant a work that reflected a belief in an ordered universe. Also, serious books were written in Latin, and Dante wrote in a new language: Italian. Some of Shakespeare's comedies *are* funny, though, but not if you're being forced to study them in school. In school, everything Shakespeare wrote starts to seem like a tragedy, even the ones that aren't tragedies, which is a bit unfortunate, but that's just because of the way they're taught. Stick with them. In later life, people will be impressed that you can quote Shakespeare, and you will sound very intelligent. It's harder to quote trigonometry, or quadratic equations, and not half as romantic.

entered could ever leave, but they also believed a boatman took dead people across the River Styx, and Samuel had seen no sign of a river in the Abernathys' basement.

He tried 'doors of Hell', but didn't have any more luck. Finally, he just typed in 'Hell', and came up with lots of stuff. Some religions believed that Hell was hot and fiery, and others thought it was cold and gloomy. Samuel didn't think any of them could know for certain, since by the time someone found out the truth he would be dead and the information would probably be too late to be useful. What he did find interesting was that most of the world's religions believed in Hell, even if they didn't always call it that, and lots of them had names for whatever they believed ruled over it: Satan, Yanluo Wang, Yamaraj. The one thing everyone seemed to agree on was that Hell wasn't a very pleasant place, and was not somewhere that you wanted to end up.

After an hour, Samuel stopped searching. He was frustrated. He wanted answers. He wanted to know what to do next.

He wanted to stop Mrs Abernathy before she opened the gates.

Samuel's mother was trying to work out if two small cans of baked beans were better value than one big can when a figure appeared beside her. It was Mrs Abernathy.

'Hello, Mrs Johnson,' said Mrs Abernathy. 'How lovely to see you.'

Mrs Johnson didn't know why exactly it was lovely for Mrs Abernathy to see her. She and Mrs Abernathy barely knew each other, and had never exchanged more than a polite 'hello' in the past.[18]

'Well, it's lovely to see you too,' Mrs Johnson lied. Something about Mrs Abernathy was making her uneasy. In fact, now that she thought about it, there were lots of things not quite right about the woman standing next to her. She was wearing a lovely black velvet overcoat, which was far too nice to wear for shopping unless you were shopping for an even lovelier black overcoat and wanted to impress the salesperson. Her skin, although very pale, paler than Mrs Johnson remembered from their previous brief meetings, had a bluish tinge to it, and the veins beneath her skin were more obvious than before. Her eyes, too, were very blue. They seemed to burn with a faint flame, like a gas fire. Mrs Abernathy was wearing lots of strong perfume, but she still smelled a little funny, and not in a ho-ho way.

As Mrs Johnson looked at Mrs Abernathy, and inhaled her perfume, she felt herself growing sleepy.

☠ [18] Adults say lots of things that they don't quite mean, usually just to be polite, which is no bad thing. They also say things that are exactly the opposite of what they appear to mean, such as:

1) 'To be perfectly honest . . .', which means 'I am lying through my teeth.'
2) 'I hear what you're saying . . .', which means 'I hear it, but I'm not really listening, and I don't agree with you anyway.' And
3) 'I don't mean to be rude . . .', which means, 'I mean to be rude.'

There are some people who use phrases like this more often than anyone else, and who become very good at using them to avoid answering questions or telling the entire truth. These people are known as 'politicians'.

Those eyes drew her in, and the fire within them grew more intense.

'How is your delightful son?' Mrs Abernathy asked. 'Samuel, isn't it?'

'Yes,' said Mrs Johnson, who couldn't remember anyone calling Samuel 'delightful' before. 'Samuel.'

'I was wondering if he ever mentioned me to you?'

Mrs Johnson heard the words emerge from her mouth before she was even aware that she was thinking them.

'Why, yes,' she said. 'He was only talking about you this morning.'

Mrs Abernathy smiled, but the smile died somewhere around her nostrils.

'And what did he say?'

'He seemed to think . . .'

'Yes?'

'. . . that you were trying . . .'

'Go on.'

'. . . to open . . .'

By now, Mrs Abernathy was leaning in very close to Mrs Johnson. Mrs Abernathy's breath stank, and her teeth were yellow. Her lipstick was bright red, and slightly smeared. In fact, thought Mrs Johnson, it looked a little like blood. Mrs Abernathy's tongue flicked out, and for just a moment, Mrs Johnson could have sworn that it was forked, like a snake's tongue.

'. . . gates . . .'

'What gates?' said Mrs Abernathy. '*What* gates?' Her hand reached for Mrs Johnson, gripping her shoulder. Her nails dug into Mrs Johnson's arm, causing her to wince.

The pain was enough to bring Mrs Johnson out of her daze. She took a step back, and blinked. When she opened her eyes Mrs Abernathy was standing farther away from her, a strange, troubled look on her face.

Try as she might, Mrs Johnson couldn't remember what it was they had been talking about. Something about Samuel, she thought, but what?

'Are you all right, Mrs Johnson?' asked Mrs Abernathy. 'You look a little unwell.'

'No, I'm fine,' said Mrs Johnson, although she didn't feel fine. She could still smell Mrs Abernathy's perfume and, worse, whatever it was the perfume was being used to disguise. She wanted Mrs Abernathy to go away. In fact, she felt that it was very important to stay as far from Mrs Abernathy as possible.

'Well, take care,' said Mrs Abernathy. 'It was nice talking to you. We should do it more often.'

'Yes,' said Mrs Johnson, meaning 'No.'

No, no, no, no, no.

When she arrived home Samuel was sitting at the kitchen table, drawing on a sheet of paper using crayons. He hid it away when she entered, but she glimpsed a blue circle. Samuel looked at her with concern.

'Are you OK, Mum?'

'Yes, dear. Why?'

'You look sick.'

Mrs Johnson glanced in the mirror by the sink.

'Yes,' she said. 'I suppose I do.'

She turned to Samuel. 'I met—' She stopped. She

couldn't remember whom she had met. A woman? Yes, a woman, but the name wouldn't come to her. Then she wasn't certain that it had been a woman at all, and seconds later she wasn't sure she'd met *anyone*. It was as though her brain was a big house, and someone was turning off the lights in every room, one by one.

'Met who, Mum?' asked Samuel.

'I . . . don't know,' said Mrs Johnson. 'I think I'm going to lie down for a while.'

Mrs Johnson was beginning to wonder if she might not be coming down with something. The day before, she could have sworn that she'd heard a voice coming from the cupboard beneath the stairs, just as she was putting away the vacuum cleaner.

She left the kitchen and Samuel heard her go upstairs. When he went to check on her minutes later, his mother was already asleep. Her lips were moving, and Samuel thought she might have been having bad dreams. He wondered if he should call one of her friends, maybe Auntie Betty from up the road, then decided that he would just keep a close eye on his mother. He would let her sleep for now.

Samuel went back downstairs, and finished his drawing. He worked very slowly and carefully, trying to capture exactly what he had seen in the Abernathys' basement. It was the third such drawing he had done. He had thrown the first two away because they weren't quite accurate, but this one was better. It was nearly right, or as close to it as he was going to get. From a distance it looked more like a photograph than a drawing, for if there was one thing that Samuel was good at, it was art.

When he was done, he hid it carefully in his big atlas. He would show it to someone. He just had to decide who that someone should be.

Mrs Johnson didn't get up until later that evening. Samuel stayed downstairs and watched television, reckoning that his mum wouldn't mind, despite what she had said earlier. After a time, he got bored and did something else he wasn't supposed to do.

He went out to the garage at the back of the house to sit in his dad's car.

The 1961 Aston Martin DB4 Coupe was his dad's pride and joy, and Samuel had been for only a handful of trips in it before his dad had left, and even then his dad had seemed to resent Samuel's presence slightly, like a child forced to allow another child to play with his favourite toy. Because his dad was living in a flat with no garage, he had decided to leave it in Biddlecombe for now. In a way Samuel was pleased, because he believed that meant his dad might return home at some point. If he took the car away permanently, though, there would be nothing of him left. It would be a sign, thought Samuel, a sign that the marriage was over and it was now just Samuel and his mum.

When Mrs Johnson rose they ordered takeaway pizza, but his mum couldn't finish hers and went back to bed. Every time she tried to recall what had happened at the supermarket her head began to hurt, and intermingled smells came to her, perfume and something else, something foul that the scent would be able to hide for only so long.

That night Mrs Johnson had bad dreams; but they were only dreams.

Samuel's nightmares, on the other hand, came alive.

CHAPTER X

*In Which We Learn of the Difficulties
Involved in Being a Monster Without a
Clearly Defined Form*

Samuel woke to find there was a monster under his bed. He didn't just *think* there was a monster under there, the way very small boys and girls sometimes do; Samuel was no longer a very small boy and had accustomed himself to believe that, in all probability, monsters did not inhabit the spaces under beds. They particularly did not occupy the space under Samuel's bed because there wasn't any, every spare inch being taken up by games, shoes, sweet wrappers, unfinished model aircraft, and a large box of toy soldiers with which Samuel no longer played but which he was most reluctant to get rid of, just in case.

Now many of those objects were scattered across his bedroom floor, and a sound was coming from beneath his bed that resembled pieces of jelly being tossed from hand to hand by a troupe of tiny jugglers. In addition, Boswell was standing on the bed, trembling and growling.

Samuel felt a sneeze coming on. He tried every trick he knew to stop it. He held his nose. He took deep breaths. He pressed the tip of his tongue against the top row of his teeth, the way that Japanese samurai used to do when they didn't want to reveal their presence to an enemy, all to no avail.

Samuel sneezed. It sounded like a rocket taking off. Instantly, all noise and movement from below his bed ceased.

Samuel held his breath and listened. He had the uncomfortable sense that a very squishy creature was also holding its breath, if it had any to hold. Even if it didn't, it was definitely listening.

Maybe I imagined it, thought Samuel, even though he knew that he hadn't. You didn't imagine something squishing under your bed. Either it squished, or it didn't, and something had definitely squished.

He looked around, and saw one of his socks lying at the end of his bed. As an experiment, he leaned forward to pick up the sock, then dangled it over the edge of the mattress before dropping it on the floor.

A long pink thing that might have been a tongue, or an arm, or even a leg, grabbed the sock, and pulled it under the bed. Samuel heard chewing, and then the sock being spat out and a voice saying, 'Ewwwww!'

'Hello?' said Samuel.

There was no reply.

'I know you're under there.'

Still no reply.

'Look, this is silly,' said Samuel. 'I'm not getting off this bed. You can stay there for as long as you like. It's just not going to happen.'

He counted to five in his head before he heard a sigh from beneath the mattress.

'How did you know?' said a voice.

'I heard you squish.'

'Oh. I'm new at this. Still getting the hang of it. You tricked me with that sock thing. Very clever, that. Tasted horrible. You need to get something done about your feet, by the way. They must stink something awful.'

'It's a gym sock. I think it's been there for a while.'

'Well, I suppose that explains it, but still. You could knock someone dead with a sock like that. Lethal weapon, that sock. It's made me feel quite ill.'

'Serves you right,' said Samuel. 'You shouldn't be hanging around under people's beds.'

'Well, it's a job, innit?'

'Not much of a job.'

'Agreed, but you try being a demon of no set form in this day and age. It's not like I'm going to get work looking after puppies, or singing babies to sleep. Frankly, it's this or nothing.'

'What do you mean, "no set form"?'

The demon cleared its throat. 'Technically, I'm a free-roaming ectoplasmic entity . . .'

'Which is?' asked Samuel, a little impatiently.

'Which is,' said the demon huffily, 'if you'll wait for me to finish, a demon capable of assuming almost any shape or form, based on psychic vibrations given off by its victim.'

'You've lost me,' said Samuel.

'Oh look, it's not that complicated. I'm supposed to become whatever scares you. I just picked the whole tentacled slushy thing because, well, it's a classic, isn't it?'

'Is it?' asked Samuel. 'So you're a bit like an octopus, then?'

'A bit, I suppose,' admitted the demon.

'I quite like octopi.'

'Octopodes,' corrected the demon. 'Don't they teach you anything at school?'

'There's no need to be rude,' said Samuel.

'I'm a *demon*. What do you expect me to be? Pleasant? Tuck you in and read you a story? You're not very clever, are you?'

'No, you're not very clever, turning up here in the dead of night and being caught out by an old sock. *And* you haven't assumed a form that scares me. You're an octopus.'

'I'm *like* an octopus,' said the demon. 'But scarier. I think. It's hard to see under here.'

'Whatever,' said Samuel. 'If it's all about psychic vibrations, then why didn't you take the form of something else?'

The demon muttered something.

'I beg your pardon,' said Samuel. 'I didn't quite catch that.'

'I said, "I can't do psychic vibrations."' The demon sounded embarrassed.

'Why not?'

'They're hard, that's why not. You try it, see how much luck you have with it.'

'So you just take a form and hope that it will be scary? That all sounds a bit casual, to be honest.'

'Look, it's my first time,' said the demon. 'Are you happy now? It's. My. First. Time. And I have to say that you're being very hurtful. You're not making this easy, you know.'

'I'm not supposed to make it easy,' said Samuel. 'What would be the point in that?'

'Just saying, that's all,' said the demon. Samuel heard it sniff dismissively.

'OK,' said Samuel. 'I'm not very keen on spiders.'

'Really?' said the demon.

'Yes.'

'You're not just saying that?'

'No, I really don't like them very much at all. Why don't you start with that and see how you get along?'

'Oh, I will. Thanks very much. Very nice of you. Give me a minute, will you?'

'Take your time.'

'Right you are. Much appreciated. Don't go anywhere, now.'

'Wouldn't dream of it,' said Samuel.

He sat on the bed, humming to himself and patting Boswell. From under the mattress came various squelching sounds, and the occasional grunt of effort. Finally, there was silence.

'Er, a question,' said the demon.

'Yes?'

'Do spiders have ears?'

'Ears?'

'You know, huge big flappy things.'

'No. They feel vibrations with the hairs on their legs.'

'All right, all right, I didn't ask for a lecture. It was just a simple question.'

There was silence again.

'What are the things with big flappy ears, then?' said the demon.

Samuel thought. 'Elephants?' he suggested.

'Elephants! They're the ones. Right, are you scared of them?'

'No,' said Samuel.

'Awwww,' said the demon. 'I give up. Let's forget about the whole shape-shifting thing. Just climb off the bed and we'll get this over with.'

Samuel didn't move. 'What will you do if I climb off the bed?'

'Well, I can eat you, or I can drag you down to the depths of Hell, never to be seen or heard from again. Depends, really.'

'On what?'

'Lots of things: hygiene, for a start. After tasting that sock, I don't fancy eating any part of you, to be honest, so it'll have to be the depths of Hell for you, I'm afraid.'

'But I don't want to go to the depths of Hell.'

'*Nobody* wants to go to the depths of Hell. I'm a demon, and even I don't want to go there. That's the point, isn't it? If I told you that I was going to take you for a nice holiday, or on a trip to the zoo, it wouldn't be much of a threat, would it?'

'But why do you have to drag me off to Hell?'

'Orders.'

'Whose orders?'

'Can't say.'

'Can't say, or won't?'

'Both.'

'Why not?'

'She wouldn't want me to.'

'Mrs Abernathy?'

The demon didn't reply.

'Oh come on, I know it's her,' said Samuel. 'You've already given most of it away.'

'Right then,' said the demon. 'It's her. Happy now?'

'Not really. I still don't want to be dragged off to Hell.'

'Then we have what's known as an impasse,' said the demon.

'How long can you stay down there?'

'First sign of daylight, I have to depart. Them's the rules, just like I can't get you unless you step on the floor.'

'So you can't touch me if I just stay up here?'

'I just said that, didn't I? I don't make the rules. I wish I did. This whole business would run a lot more smoothly, I can tell you.'

'Then I'll simply stay here.'

'Fine. You do that.'

Samuel folded his arms and stared at the far wall. From under the bed, he heard what sounded like tentacles being folded. Lots of tentacles.

'Not much point in you hanging around, though, is there, if I'm not going to set foot on the floor until you're gone?' said Samuel.

The demon thought about this. 'Suppose not,' it said.

'So why don't you just leave? It can't be very comfortable under there.'

'It's not. Smells funny, too. And there's something poking into me.'

Samuel heard scuffling from beneath the bed, and

moments later a stray toy soldier was tossed against the wardrobe. 'You don't even want to know where that was,' said the demon.

'Whatever,' said Samuel. 'Are you going to leave?'

'Not much else I can do, really,' said the demon, 'not if you're going to be difficult about it.'

'Off you go, then,' said Samuel.

'Right. Bye.'

There was a great deal of squelching, then silence.

'You're still under there, aren't you?' said Samuel.

'No,' said a small voice, slightly ashamedly.

'Fibber.'

'Fine, I'll go. Don't know what I'm supposed to tell her, though.'

'Don't tell her anything. Just keep a low profile until dawn, then say that I didn't get up during the night.'

'Might work,' said the demon. 'Might work. You promise not to get up to use the bathroom or anything?'

'Cross my heart,' said Samuel.

'Can't ask for more than that,' said the demon. 'Well, pleasure doing business with you. Nothing personal about all this, you know. Just following orders.'

'You're not going to come back, are you?'

'Oh no, I shouldn't think so. Took a lot of power for her to summon me up. Can't imagine she'll try that one again. She has a lot on her mind, what with keeping the portal open and all. Very unstable, that portal. Someone could do themselves an injury in there if they're not careful. She might look for another way to get at you, though. Then again, she might not. Soon, it won't matter much either way.'

'Why not?' said Samuel.

'End of the world,' said the demon. 'Won't be any beds left to hide under.'

And with a squish and a pop, it was gone.

CHAPTER XI

In Which We Encounter the Scientists Again

No good ever comes of someone sticking his head round his boss's door, a worried expression on his face and a piece of paper in one hand that, if it could talk, would shout, very loudly: 'Bad! This is bad! Run away now!'

Thus it was that when Professor Stefan, CERN's head of particle physics, saw Professor Hilbert hovering on his doorstep with both a) a worried expression; and b) a piece of paper that, despite being white and bearing only a series of numbers and a small diagram, also managed to look worried, he began to feel worried too.

'What is it, Hilbert?' said Professor Stefan in the tones of one who would rather not know what 'it' is at all, thank you very much.

'It's the portal,' said Professor Hilbert. He had always liked the sound of that word, which fitted in with his theories of the Universe. Anyway, since they still didn't know for certain what it was, he could call it anything he liked.

'So you've found out what it is?'

'No, not exactly.'

'Do you know if it's ongoing?'

'We're not sure.'

'Have you even found out if that's actually what opened?'

'Oh, we know it opened,' said Professor Hilbert. 'That part's easy.'

'So you've *proved* that it exists.'

Professor Stefan liked things to be proved before he accepted the fact of their existence. This made him a good scientist, if not a very imaginative one.

'Er, no. But we strongly suspect that it exists. A portal has been opened, and it hasn't closed, not entirely.'

'How do you know, if you can't find it?'

A smile of immense satisfaction appeared on Professor Hilbert's face.

'Because we can hear it speak,' he said.

If you listen hard enough, there's almost no such thing as silence: there's just noise that isn't very loud yet. Oh yes, in space no one can hear you scream, or blow up a big spaceship, because space is a vacuum, and sound can't travel in a vacuum (although think how dull most science fiction films would be if there were no explosions, so pay no attention to grumps who criticise *Star Wars* because you can hear the Death Star explode at the end. Spoilsports.) but otherwise there is noise all around us, even if we can't hear it terribly well. But noises aren't the same as sounds: noises are random and disorganised, but sounds are *made*.

Deep in the LHC's command centre, a group of scientists was clustered round a screen. The screen displayed a visual representation of what had occurred on the night that the collider had apparently malfunctioned. The scientists had painstakingly re-created the circumstances of that evening, restoring lost and rewritten code, and had attempted to trace, without success, the trajectory of the unknown energy particle, which now expressed itself as a slowly revolving spiral.

'So this is what you think happened to our collider,' said Stefan.

'It's still happening,' said Hilbert.

'What? But we've shut down the collider.'

'I know, but I suppose you could say that the damage, if that's what it is, has been done. I think – and I stress "think" – that, somehow, enough energy was harnessed from the collider to blow a hole between our world and, well, somewhere else. When we shut down the collider, we took away that energy source. The portal collapsed, but not entirely. There's a pinhole where there used to be a tunnel, but it's there nonetheless. Listen.'

Beside the screen was a speaker, currently emitting what sounded like static.

'It's static,' said Professor Stefan. 'I don't hear anything.'

The static whooshed slightly, its pattern changing as though in response to the professor's words.

'We wanted you to hear the signal before we cleaned it up,' explained Hilbert.

'Signal?' said Stefan.

'Actually, a voice,' said Hilbert, flipping a switch, and instantly the static was replaced by something that Professor Stefan had to admit sounded a great deal like a low voice whispering. The professor didn't like the sound of that voice at all, even if he had no idea what it was saying. It was like listening to the mutterings of a madman in a foreign tongue, someone who had spent too long locked in a dark place feeling angry with all those responsible for putting him there. It gave the professor, who was, as we have already established, not an imaginative man, a distinct case of the collywobbles. Its effect on the other listeners was less disturbing. Most of them looked excited. In fact, Dr Carruthers appeared to be having trouble keeping his teacup from rattling against its saucer, his excitement was so great.

Professor Stefan leaned in closer to the speaker, frowning. 'Whatever it is, it sounds like the same thing being said over and over. Are you sure it's not someone's idea of a joke? Perhaps there's a bug in the system.'

Hilbert shook his head. 'It's not in the system. We've checked.'

'Well, what's it saying?'

Professor Hilbert looked puzzled. 'That's the thing,' he said. 'It's a known language. We've had it examined. It's early Aramaic, probably from around one thousand BC. It's the same language that we found embedded in our code.'

'So it's coming from somewhere on Earth?'

'No,' said Professor Hilbert. He pointed at the image of the Event. 'It's definitely coming from somewhere on the other side of that. Professor, we may just have proved the existence of the Multiverse.'

Stefan looked doubtful. 'But what's it saying?' he repeated.

Professor Hilbert swallowed. What might have been worry creased his face.

'We think it's saying, "Fear me . . ."'

CHAPTER XII

*In Which We Encounter, Once Again, the
Unfortunate Nurd, Who is About to Take
Another Unexpected Trip*

Nurd, the Scourge of Five Deities, had been devoting a lot of thought to his recent experiences. Given that he didn't have a whole lot else to think about beyond whether or not Wormwood was looking even mangier than usual, or, 'My, isn't it flat around here?' it was quite a welcome distraction.

Among the subjects under consideration was his size. Was he, Nurd wondered, very, very small, small enough to be crushed by what he now believed was a mechanism of some kind? He had never really speculated upon this before, since demons came in all shapes and sizes. Indeed some of them came in more than one shape or size all by themselves, such as O'Dear, the demon of People Who Look in Mirrors and Think They're Overweight, and his twin, O'Really, the demon of People Who Look in Mirrors and Think They're Slim When They're Not.

A great many demons were little more than ethereal beings, wisps of nastiness that floated around like bad thoughts in a dark mind. Some chose physical forms just so that they could hold on to things, which made tea breaks much more satisfying. Others were given form by the Great Malevolence himself, for his own nefarious purposes.[19]

Nurd wasn't privy to the Great Malevolence's plans for the conquest of Earth. Few were, except those closest to him. The Great Malevolence had been stuck in Hell for an extraordinarily long time, marooned in that desolate place with only his fellow demons for company. He had managed to carve out a kingdom for himself, but it was a kingdom of rock and dirt and pain. He could hardly be blamed for wanting to get away from it.

The Great Malevolence was extremely angry, and unfathomably cruel, and what the Great Malevolence hated more than anything else was people. People had trees, and flowers, and dragonflies. They had dogs, and footballs, and summers. Most of all they were free to do pretty much whatever they liked where they liked and, as long as they didn't hurt anybody else along the way, or break the law, life wasn't bad. The Great Malevolence wanted nothing more than to bring that to an end, preferably an end that involved wailing and screaming, and big fires, and demons with pitchforks poking people where they didn't like being poked.

Even though Nurd was a demon, the Great Malevolence frightened him a lot. If Nurd had been the Great Malevolence, he would have been afraid to look

---

[19] 'Nefarious' means very wicked indeed, in a cunning way. If you plan on being nefarious, it pays to look the part: dress in black; wear a hat, preferably one with a wide brim and no flowers; and perhaps grow a moustache that you can twirl. It also helps to have a deep and sinister laugh, to indicate when you're being nefarious. You know the kind: 'BWAH-HA-HA-HA-HA!' That kind.

at himself in a mirror, so frightening was the Great Malevolence. The Great Malevolence probably didn't even *have* a reflection, Nurd thought. Any mirror would be too scared to show it.

Nurd stared out at the Wasteland. Anywhere had to be better than here. If he could make his way to the Place of People, then he could rule it in his own manner, and perhaps be a little nicer about it than the Great Malevolence, once he'd got some of the fireballs and general terrifying of the population out of his system.

But he would need to be ready for his journey, if it were to happen again. He tried to remember the sensations he had experienced as he was dragged from one world to the next, but couldn't. He had been so confused, and so terrified, that the journey was over before he'd realised what was happening, and then someone had dropped a heavy object on him, and that had been the end of that.

He did his best to recall whether he had been given any indication that he was about to pop out of existence in one place and pop up in another not very long afterwards, and remembered that the tips of his fingers had begun to itch something terrible in the seconds before he went off on his unanticipated trip.

Actually, just like they were itching now.

Oh.

Oh dear.

Nurd barely had time to concentrate on making himself very large indeed before there was a loud pop and he vanished from his throne.

* * *

As Professor Hilbert suspected, the Large Hadron Collider had, through only some fault of its own, managed to open a hole between our world and somewhere else entirely. It wasn't quite a black hole, since it obeyed only some of the rules of a black hole while rudely ignoring others, which would have greatly irritated Einstein and many other scientists like him. Neither was it quite a wormhole, although it obeyed some of the characteristics of a wormhole too. Nevertheless, it would do nicely until a black hole or wormhole came along.

Here are some things that are worth remembering about black holes, should it ever seem likely that you're going to encounter one. The first is that if, at some time in the future, a group of nice scientists in white coats suggest that you – yes, you! – have been chosen as the lucky candidate to enter a black hole and find out what's going on at the other side, it would be a good idea for you – yes, you! – to find something else to do, preferably far away and not involving, even peripherally, black holes, space suits, or scientists with an unsettling gleam in their eyes.

Perhaps you've already worked this out for yourself, being a clever person. After all, if sticking a head, or any other part of oneself, into a black hole is such a great idea, then scientists would be queueing up to do it, instead of tapping someone else on the shoulder and inviting him to have a go.

Which brings us to the second thing worth noting about black holes: your life is likely to be very short, but spectacularly eventful, if you go messing about with one. There may well be something fascinating at the other side of a black hole, but you're unlikely to be able to tell anyone what it is. The gravitational force of a black hole is subject to quite dramatic changes, so just as you're thinking to yourself, 'Wow, a black hole. How interesting and swirly it is. Wait until I tell those nice scientists all about it!' your body will be ripped to shreds and then compacted to a point of infinite density.

Which will probably hurt a lot, although not for very long.

Figure 1: You in a black hole

Then again, you might be lucky enough to plummet into a supermassive black hole, where the gravitational changes are a little gentler. In that case you'll still be torn apart, but more slowly, so you might have time to come to terms with what it feels like before, once again, you are crushed to a point of infinite density.

It all depends upon the sacrifices one is willing to make for the sake of science really. It's your choice. Frankly, I'd find a less risky job, if I were you, like being an accountant, or cleaning the teeth of great white sharks with a toothpick and some floss.

As it happened, Nurd, the Scourge of Five Deities, was learning a great deal about the nature of not-quite-black holes since he was, at that moment, plunging through one. He really didn't want to be, either, because he felt that no good was going to come of it. He was pretty certain that he was falling, even though he had no sensation that he was doing so, and he was rapidly approaching a point of light in the distance that didn't seem to be getting any closer, which was very confusing. He did his best to pull himself back in the direction from which he had come, like a swimmer kicking against a strong tide, but here is another interesting thing about black holes: the more you struggle to escape the force of one, the quicker you'll reach that whole part about infinite density, and crushing and stuff, due to time and space being all muddled up.[20]

The sensation that, even though he was trying to move away from whatever he was falling towards, he was still approaching it with increasing rapidity, gave Nurd a headache. Fortunately he was distracted from it by the feeling that every atom of his demonic form

[20] If that sounds confusing, it isn't really. The equivalent effect can be found on Earth, such as when you haven't studied for a test in school and the more you want that test to be put off, the faster the time for the test seems to arrive. The same is true for painful dental appointments, visiting that aunt you don't like at Christmas and waiting for your mum to come home while you try to stick back together her favourite vase that you've just broken. The opposite occurs for events to which you're rather looking forward, like Christmas, your birthday, or the first snows of winter. Someday, a very bright child will create an equation for all this in order to explain it, and other, even brighter, children will look at him in a funny way and wonder why he bothered, since everyone instinctively understood it anyway.

was being stretched on an infinite number of tiny racks, each of which had also helpfully been fitted with a selection of very sharp pins. Then that particular pain came to an end, to be replaced by the way a banana might feel if someone peeled it, briefly balanced it upright on a table, and then dropped a rock on it.

Just as Nurd began to think that this was the end for him, all the pain stopped and he felt firm ground beneath his feet. His eyes were squeezed shut. He opened one of them carefully, then another, and then a third, which he kept for special occasions.

He was standing in the middle of a road, and around him metal objects were whizzing by at what seemed like great speeds. One of them, he noticed, was sleek, and red, and pretty.

I don't know what that is, said Nurd to himself, but I *want* one.

He heard a sound behind him. It was very loud, like the bellowing of some great beast.

Nurd turned just in time to be hit full in the face by a very large version of one of the metal objects.

Samuel was staring out of his bedroom window. He had not yet changed out of his pyjamas, and was reflecting on what had taken place during the night. The area beneath his bed had been a little slimy when he checked it once dawn came, but other than that there was no sign of the demon.

He was wondering if the demon might return, despite its protestations to the contrary, when a figure with greenish skin, a large head and pointed ears, wearing a red cloak and big boots, appeared briefly on the street below in a flash of blue light. The figure looked about, its attention caught by a passing car, and then was promptly hit by a truck. There was another flash of blue light and the figure was gone. The truck driver stopped, climbed out of his cab, tried to find a body and then quickly drove off.

Samuel considered telling his mum, but decided that it was probably better just to add it to the list of Things Nobody Was Likely to Believe.

At least, not until it was too late.

Back in the Wasteland, Wormwood was staring suspiciously at the throne, the crown, and the sceptre. Once again, all three tempted him, but after what had happened the last time he didn't want to be caught waving stuff around if, and when, Nurd returned. Say what you liked about Nurd (and Wormwood had said most things, under his breath), but he wasn't entirely stupid. It had not escaped his attention that he had rematerialised after his earlier disappearance to find a mangy demon holding his sceptre and wearing his crown. Once Nurd had recovered from the shock, Wormwood had earned an extra bump for each offence and one more between the eyes for good luck. Wormwood had now decided to bide his time, but he couldn't hide his disappointment when, not very long after he had vanished, Nurd reappeared, this time looking like an insect that had just been hit by the largest swatter ever created.

'So how did that go, Master?' asked Wormwood.

'Not terribly well, actually,' replied Nurd.

He was about to faint when his fingers and toes began to tingle again. 'Oh, no,' said Nurd, who was hurting in so many places that he was wondering if he'd somehow acquired new body parts just so they could ache. 'I've only just—'

And then he was gone again.

Samuel's bedroom was suddenly lit by a blue flash, which was followed by a loud pop and a smell like eggs burning. Dank mist filled the room. Samuel dived to the floor, closely followed by Boswell, and peered over the edge of his bed.

Slowly the mist began to clear, revealing a green-skinned figure in a red cloak. The figure had one leg raised, and his head covered with his hands, as if he were expecting to receive a nasty blow at any moment. When the blow didn't come, he peered out cautiously from between his fingers, then breathed a sigh of relief.

'Well, that makes a pleasant change,' he said, and started to relax. Unfortunately at that moment, Boswell decided to make his presence known, and gave a bark, causing the new arrival to leap on to a chair and cover his head again.

'What are you doing?' asked Samuel from behind the bed.

'I'm cowering,' said the figure.

'Why?'

'Because every time I shift into this world, I get hurt. Frankly, it's starting to become wearing.'

Samuel stood. Boswell, sensing that the figure on the chair wasn't half as threatening as it had at first seemed, experimented with a growl, and was pleased to see the green-skinned personage tremble.

'Didn't you just get run over by a truck?' asked Samuel.

'Is that what it was?' said Nurd. 'I didn't have time to exchange pleasantries with it before it knocked me into another dimension. The cheek!'

'What *are* you?'

'I'm a demon,' said Nurd. 'Nurd, the Scourge of Five Deities.'

'Really?' said Samuel sceptically. The demon's clothes looked tatty, and Samuel didn't think that demons climbed on chairs to get away from small dogs. 'Are you sure?'

'No, I'm a saucepan,' hissed Nurd testily. 'Of course I'm a demon.' He coughed. 'I'm actually a very important demon.'

He looked at Samuel, who arched an eyebrow at him.

'Oh, I give up,' said Nurd. 'No, I'm not important. I live in a wasteland with an irritating entity called Wormwood. Nobody likes me, and I have no power. Happy now?'

'I suppose,' said Samuel. 'Who sent you here?'

'Nobody sent me. I just got . . . dragged here. Very uncomfortably, I might add.'

Nurd glanced at Boswell. 'What's that?'

'It's my dog. His name is Boswell. And I'm Samuel.'

Boswell wagged his tail at the sound of his name then, remembering that he was supposed to be ferocious, showed some teeth and growled again.

'He doesn't seem very happy to see me,' said Nurd. 'Then again, nobody ever is.'

'Well, you did pop up a little unexpectedly.'

Nurd shrugged. 'Sorry about that. Not my fault. Would you mind if I stopped cowering now? I'm beginning to get a cramp.'

Samuel had a good instinct for people. He could tell a good person from a bad one, often before the person in question had even spoken. Although his experience of demons was rather more limited, something told him that if Nurd wasn't exactly good – and, being a demon, it was hardly part of the job description ('Wanted: demon. Must be good . . .') – he was not entirely bad either. Like most ordinary people, he was just himself.

'All right,' said Samuel, then added, because he'd once heard someone say it in a police movie, 'but no sudden movements.'

'Does shooting off into another dimension count?' asked Nurd.

'No.'

'Fine, then.' Nurd sat on the chair, and looked around the room. 'Nice place.'

'Thank you.'

'You decorate it yourself?'

'My dad did most of it.'

'Oh.'

They were silent for a time.

'If you don't mind me saying so, you don't look very happy,' said Samuel.

'I think I'm in shock,' said Nurd. 'You try being wrenched from one dimension to another, being hit by a truck, sent back home again for long enough to start hurting, and then have the whole thing begin all over. It's not conducive to a healthy outlook on life, let me tell you.'

Nurd put his large chin in his hands, and regarded Samuel.

'Anyway,' he said, 'it's not like you look overjoyed either.'

'I'm not,' said Samuel. 'My dad's left us, my mum cries in the evenings, and I think the woman down the road is trying to kill me. Are you sure she didn't send you?'

'Quite sure,' said Nurd, and for the first time in very many years he felt sorry for someone other than himself. 'That's not very nice of her.'

'No, it isn't.'

'Well, like I said, I live in a wasteland. There's nothing to see, nothing to do, and Wormwood and I have run out of things to talk about. In fact, this interdimensional travel has brightened up my days no end, or it would have if I didn't keep being injured by hard metal objects. This is such an *interesting* place.'

He moved to the window and gazed out. 'Look' he said, and there were aeons of longing and sadness in his voice. 'You have white, fluffy clouds, and sunshine. What I wouldn't give to be able to see sunshine every day.'

Samuel picked up a bag of wine gums from his bedside table.

'Would you like a sweet?'

'A what?'

'A sweet. They're wine gums.'

Tentatively Nurd reached into the bag, and came out with a long red sweetie.

'Oh, those ones are lovely,' said Samuel, popping an

orange one into his mouth and chewing thoughtfully. Nurd followed his example, and seemed pleasantly surprised by the result.

'Ooooh, that's good,' he said. 'That's very good. Fluffy clouds. Wine gums. Big metal things that move fast. What a world you live in!'

Samuel sat down on his bed, and Nurd returned to his chair.

'You're not going to hurt me, are you?' asked Samuel.

Nurd looked shocked. 'Why would I do that?'

'Because you're a demon.'

'Just because I'm a demon doesn't mean that I'm bad,' said Nurd. A piece of wine gum had stuck to his teeth, and he worked at it with a long fingernail. 'I didn't ask to be a demon. It just happened that way. I opened my eyes one day, and there I was. Nurd. Ugly bloke. No friends. Even other demons don't care much for my company.'

'Why? You seem all right to me.'

'I suppose that's it, really. I've never been very demonic. I don't want to torture, or wreak havoc. I don't want to be frightening, or terrible. I just want to potter along, minding my own business. But they told me I had to do something destructive or I'd be in trouble, so I tried to find a role that wouldn't attract too much attention, or cause a lot of bother to people, but all those jobs were taken. You know, there's a demon who looks after the little bit of toothpaste that you can't squeeze out of the end of the tube, even though you know it's there and there's no other toothpaste in the house. There's even a demon of shyness, or there's supposed to be. Nobody's ever seen him, so it's hard to know for sure. I quite fancied a job like that.

'Eventually, some of the other demons just got irritated with me trying to muscle in on their action, and I was banished. It all seemed pretty hopeless, and then suddenly I started popping up here. I just feel like I could make something of myself in this world. There are so many opportunities.'

'This world is hard, too,' said Samuel, and there was something in the boy's voice that made Nurd want to reach out to him. The demon picked up the bag of wine gums, and offered it to Samuel. He picked a green one.

'You can have another too,' he said to Nurd.

'You're sure?'

'Absolutely.'

Nurd beamed. He tried a black one. It tasted a bit funny, but it was still better than anything else he had ever eaten, except for that first wine gum.

'Go on,' said Nurd. 'You were saying?'

'It doesn't matter,' said Samuel.

'No, it does. I want to know. Really.'

So Samuel told him. He spoke of his mother and his father, and of how his dad had left and maybe it was Samuel's fault, and maybe it wasn't. He spoke of how the world doesn't listen to children, even when it should. He spoke of Boswell, and of how he would be lost without the little dog for company.

And Nurd, who had never had a mother and father, and who had never loved or been loved, marvelled at the ways in which feeling so wonderful could also leave one open to so much pain. In a strange way, he envied

Samuel even that. He wanted to care about someone so much that it could hurt.

Thus the boy and the demon passed the hours. The day grew brighter, and they drew closer, talking of places seen and unseen, of hopes and fears. The only shadow cast upon their conversation was Samuel's description of the events in the Abernathys' basement, which made Nurd uneasy, even as he struggled to understand what they might mean. It sounded to him as though there might be other demons in this world, demons with a plan. Well, Nurd had plans of his own, assuming he could find a way to stay in the world of men permanently and not simply spend the rest of his existence whizzing painfully between dimensions.

At last, Nurd's fingers began to tingle again.

'I have to go,' he said, with regret. He smiled, a movement so unfamiliar that at first his muscles struggled with it. 'It really has been very nice talking to you. When I work out how to rule this world, I'll make sure that you're well looked after.'

Just as Nurd was about to vanish, Samuel thrust the bag of wine gums into his hand, so that when Nurd arrived back in the Wasteland he might have something with which to cheer himself and Wormwood up a little.

Nurd reappeared on his throne. He opened his eyes to find Wormwood staring anxiously at him.

'What's wrong with your face?' asked Wormwood.

Nurd tested his mouth with his fingers.

'Wormwood,' he said, 'I appear to be smiling. Here, have a wine gum . . .'

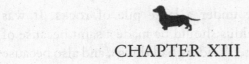

CHAPTER XIII

In Which Samuel Decides to Consult an Expert on Demons and Hell, but Doesn't Get Anywhere

Reverend Ussher, the vicar, and Mr Berkeley, the verger, were standing outside the Church of St Timidus, greeting the congregation as its members filed out on that bright Sunday morning.

The church was named after St Timidus of Biddlecombe, a very holy man who died in 1380 AD at the age of 38. St Timidus became famous when, in 1378 AD, he decided to go and live in a cave outside Biddlecombe so that he would not be tempted to do bad things. It wasn't a very large cave, and when people came to bring him food Timidus would sometimes be able to see them coming, or hear what they were saying. He decided to dig himself another cave next to the one in which he was living, so that there would be absolutely no chance of seeing or hearing someone and being tempted to sin. (It's not entirely clear what sins Timidus was afraid of committing, since he never said, but it probably had something to do with ladies. It often does in such cases.)

Unfortunately, while he was digging the second cave Timidus caused the first cave to fall in on him, and he was buried alive under a large pile of rocks. It was decided that Timidus should be made a saint because of his commitment to avoiding bad things, and also because Biddlecombe didn't have any saints at the time, and there's nothing like a good, old-fashioned saint to bring believers to a place and encourage them to spend money. So it was that plain old Timidus became St Timidus of Biddlecombe.

Now you and I might wonder if Timidus might not have been better off leaving his cave and doing nice things for other people, such as helping old ladies across the road or feeding the poor, instead of hiding himself away and not talking to anyone. After all, not doing bad things is not the same as doing good things, but that is why you and I will never become saints. On the other hand, you and I are unlikely to be buried under a big pile of stones as a result of bad engineering practices, so these things even themselves out in the end.

The bishop of Biddlecombe at the time was named Bernard, but he was known far and wide as Bishop Bernard the Bad. Obviously this wasn't what his parents named him, as that would have been a bit foolish. I mean, if you name someone 'the Bad' then, really, you're just asking for trouble. It would have led to conversations like the following:

Bernard's parents: Hello, this is our son Bernard the Bad. We hope he'll become a bishop some day. A nice one, of course. Not a bad one.

Not Bernard's parents: Er, then why did you
name him 'the Bad'?
Bernard's parents: Oh dear . . .[21]

Bishop Bernard the Bad was given his nickname because
he was very nasty. Bishop Bernard didn't like people who
disagreed with him, especially if they disagreed with his
decisions to steal lots of money, kill people who had
anything that he might want, and have children, even if
he wasn't supposed to have children because he was a
bishop. In fact, he wasn't supposed to do *any* of those
things, but that didn't stop Bishop Bernard. Bishop
Bernard also believed there were few problems in life that
couldn't be solved by sticking a hot poker up somebody's

💀 [21] There are lots of people throughout history with the word 'the' somewhere in their names. Some of these people were rather pleasant, such as Richard
the Lionheart (1157–1199 AD), the English king (even if he didn't speak
much English, oddly enough, although he was very good at French) who
commanded an army by the age of 16, fought in the Crusades, and forgave the
young boy who shot the arrow that fatally wounded him; and Alfred the Great
(849–899 AD), who defended his Saxon kingdom of Wessex against the Danish
invaders and was, well, great.

On the other hand, there were some people with 'the' in their names who
were very unpleasant indeed. Vlad the Impaler (1431–1476 AD) of Wallachia,
who was also known as Dracula and inspired the name of the famous vampire,
liked to stick his enemies on big spikes. Ivan the Terrible of Russia (1530–
1584 AD) was a tyrant and a bully who died while playing chess. It wasn't
the excitement of the game, though: he was probably poisoned with mercury.
Finally, certain historical figures with 'the' in their names were just a bit lame.
Ladies and gentlemen, I give you: Hencage the Dismal (1621–1682 AD), Hugh
the Dull (1294–1342 AD), Charles the Silly (1368–1422 AD), Childeric
the Stupid (died 755 AD), and Wenceslas the Worthless (1361–1419 AD),
who once cooked his chef alive for serving a bad ragout.

bottom. If that didn't work, which was rare, he would put his enemies on a rack and stretch them until they said, 'Ow!' very loudly, or just kill them, often in a slow and painful way. Bishop Bernard knew that people called him Bernard the Bad behind his back, but he didn't care. He rather liked the idea that people were terrified of him.

By the time St Timidus of Biddlecombe, who wasn't bad at all, just a little confused, died in his cave, Bishop Bernard the Bad was getting old. He decided that a church should be built and named after St Timidus, and when he died, Bishop Bernard would be buried in a special vault in that church. That way, Bishop Bernard could pretend that he had something in common with the saint and perhaps, over time, people might forget that he was bad, as he would be the one buried in the church.

People aren't that stupid.

Instead, when he died, Bishop Bernard was buried beneath a little room at the side of the church, the only sign that he was there a stone in the floor with his name on it. Thereafter, he was only ever mentioned when visitors were brought on tours of the old church, and they were only told of the bad things that he had done, mainly because he had never done anything good.

So there you have it: the history of the Church of St Timidus. Why all that is so important we shall discover later. For now, it is enough to know that Reverend Ussher and Mr Berkeley were standing outside its doors, being very polite, when Mr Berkeley saw Samuel approaching and nudged the vicar.

'Look out, Vicar,' he said, 'it's that strange Johnson boy.'

The vicar looked alarmed. Samuel Johnson was only eleven years old, but he sometimes asked the kinds of questions that would challenge elderly philosophers. Most recently, the vicar recalled, there had been a lengthy discussion about angels and pins, which was something to do with a school project, although he couldn't imagine what kind of school, other than a theology college, might require its students to debate the size and nature of the angelic host. To be frank it had made Reverend Ussher's head spin. He thought that Samuel Johnson might possibly be some kind of child prodigy or genius. Then again, he might simply be a rather annoying small boy, of which, in Reverend Ussher's experience, there were already too many in the world.

Now here Samuel was again, his brow furrowed in the kind of concentration that suggested the vicar's knowledge of matters divine and angelic was about to be severely tested.

'Hello, Samuel,' said the vicar, composing his face into some semblance of goodwill. 'And what's on your mind this morning?'

'Do you believe in Hell, Vicar?' asked Samuel.

'Um, well.' Reverend Ussher paused. 'Why are you asking about Hell, Samuel? You're not worried about going there, are you? I can't imagine that a young man like you could have much cause to fear, er, eternal damnation. Or even temporary damnation, come to that.'

Beside him Mr Berkeley stifled a cough, suggesting that he would be quite happy to see Samuel Johnson suffer in a hot, fiery place, if only for long enough to discourage him from asking the vicar awkward questions.

'It's not so much that I'm afraid of ending up there,' said Samuel. 'It's more that I'm afraid of *it* ending up *here*.'

The vicar looked confused. He'd known that he was likely to become confused at some point in the conversation; he just hadn't imagined that it would happen quite so fast.

'I'm not sure that I follow you.'

'I mean, is there a chance that Hell could come here?'

'Come here?' said the verger, intervening. 'It's Hell, not the number forty-seven bus.'

Samuel ignored him. He'd never thought much of Mr Berkeley, who always seemed to be scowling, even on Christmas morning when nobody had any business to be scowling at all.

The vicar quieted Mr Berkeley with a wave of his hand.

'No, Samuel. Even if Hell does exist, and I'm not entirely convinced that it does, it has nothing to do with this earthly realm. It is distinct and of itself. People may end up there, but I can say with some confidence that it will never end up here.'

He beamed beatifically at Samuel. Samuel did not beam back. Instead he seemed about to offer some further argument, but Mr Berkeley had had enough. He gripped the vicar by the elbow and steered him towards less challenging company, namely Mr and Mrs Billingsgate, who ran the local fish-and-chip shop and rarely asked anything more awkward than whether or not one might require vinegar with that.

Samuel stared glumly as the two men walked away.

He'd wanted to say much more to the vicar, but it didn't look like that was going to happen. The vicar seemed very certain about things he couldn't possibly know for sure, but Samuel supposed that was all part of being a vicar. After all, it wouldn't have done for the vicar to stand up before the congregation in church on Sunday and ask if there was any point in their being there. As a vicar, you had to learn to take some things on trust.

As Samuel returned to his mum, who was chatting with friends, he saw Mrs Abernathy by the church wall, watching him. He noticed that she was careful to remain outside the church grounds. She hadn't been at the service either.

She beckoned to Samuel, but Samuel merely shook his head, trying to ignore her.

Samuel.

He heard her voice in his head, as clearly as if she were standing next to him. He glanced at her again. She hadn't moved but a small smile was playing on her face.

Samuel, her voice came again. *We need to talk. If you don't come to me, I'm going to find your little dog, and I'm going to kill him. What do you think of that, clever Samuel Johnson? Would you sacrifice your dog's life because you're too frightened to face me?*

Samuel swallowed. Mrs Abernathy was like the witch in *The Wizard of Oz*, threatening Toto to get back at Dorothy. He left his mother, and approached the woman at the wall.

'How are you, Samuel?' she asked, as though they were friends who had just happened to meet on a pleasant Sunday morning.

'I'm fine,' he answered.

'I'm disapppointed to hear that,' said Mrs Abernathy. 'In fact, I was hoping you wouldn't be here at all.'

Samuel shrugged. Mrs Abernathy's eyes, already blue, seemed to brighten a shade, drawing his gaze towards them.

'You sent the monster who hid under my bed,' said Samuel.

'Yes, and I'm going to have words with him, when I find him. I expended a lot of energy bringing him here. The least he could have done was eat you alive.'

'Well, he didn't,' said Samuel. 'He seemed quite decent, actually.'

Mrs Abernathy's calm expression altered for an instant. She might have been a demon but, in common with most of the human adults who had encountered Samuel Johnson, she wasn't sure if he was being deliberately cheeky, or was just a very unusual child.

'I'm here to seek a truce. I don't know what you saw, or thought you saw, in our basement that night, but you're mistaken. There's nothing for you to be concerned about. We're just . . . *visiting* for a time.'

Samuel shook his head. There was something strangely insistent about Mrs Abernathy's voice. Samuel recalled a play that they had read about in school, one in which a king was murdered by having poison poured into his ear. Listening to Mrs Abernathy, he felt just as he imagined the king must have felt as he started to die.

'I—'

'I don't want to hear it, Samuel. You must learn to keep your mouth shut. If you don't interfere with me then I'll leave you in peace, but if you cross me you won't even live long enough to regret it. Do you understand?'

Samuel nodded, even as he knew that what Mrs Abernathy was saying was a lie. There would be no peace for him, or for anyone, if she succeeded with her plans. But her voice was so sweet and hypnotic, and his eyelids were starting to feel so very heavy.

'Come closer, Samuel,' whispered Mrs Abernathy. 'Come closer, and let me whisper in your ear . . .'

Whisper. Ear. Poison.

At that instant, Samuel sensed the danger he was in. With a great effort of will he pinched himself hard on the hand, using his nails so that the pain was sharp and he drew blood. He took a step back from Mrs Abernathy, his head clearing, and he saw her face cloud with rage. One of her hands reached for him, almost as though it had a will of its own.

'You nasty child!' she said. 'Don't think you can escape me that easily. You'd better be careful, unless—'

'Unless what?' said Samuel, goading her now. 'Unless I want something bad to happen to me, is that it? What could be worse than a monster under my bed waiting to eat me?'

Mrs Abernathy got her anger under control. She smiled almost sweetly.

'Oh, you have no idea,' she said. 'Well then, here it is. Something bad is going to happen to you no matter what you do. The question is: how bad will that something be? When the time comes, I can make it so that you simply fall asleep and never wake up again. But if

I choose, I can ensure instead that you never sleep again, and that every moment of your wretched existence is spent in searing agony, gasping for breath and begging for the pain to stop!'

'It sounds like gym class,' said Samuel, with considerable feeling. He was happy that his voice didn't tremble. It made him appear braver than he was.

Mrs Abernathy looked past Samuel. He risked a glance in the same direction and saw his mother approaching.

'Very funny, Samuel,' said Mrs Abernathy, beginning to move away. 'When my master comes we'll see if he finds you quite so amusing. In the meantime, you keep your mouth shut. Remember when I said I'd kill your dog? Well, if you speak of this to your mother, then I'll kill her instead. I'll smother her in her sleep, and no one will ever know except you and I. I met her in the supermarket yesterday. I know you've been talking about my affairs. Remember this, Samuel: careless talk costs lives . . .'

With that she headed off in the direction of town, trailing strong perfume and a faint whiff of burning.

'What did she want?' asked Mrs Johnson. She was staring at Mrs Abernathy's back with ill-concealed distaste. She couldn't remember why she disliked Mrs Abernathy so much, just that she did.

'Nothing, Mum,' said Samuel resignedly. 'She was simply saying hello . . .'

That evening Samuel decided that there was no point in telling any grown-up in Biddlecombe of what he knew. They simply wouldn't believe him. But perhaps someone his own age might. He could no longer deal with all this alone. Tomorrow, at the risk of being laughed at, he would call upon his friends for help.

CHAPTER XIV

In Which We Learn That it is Sometimes Wise to Be Afraid of the Dark

Samuel's dad called the house that night to speak to his son. Samuel tried to tell his dad about the Abernathys' basement, but his dad only said 'Really?' and 'How interesting', and asked Samuel how he was enjoying his half-term break, and if his mum was OK.

Samuel made one final effort.

'Dad,' he said, 'this is serious. I'm not making it up.'

'You think these people, the Abernathys, are carrying out experiments in their basement?' said Mr Johnson.

'Not experiments,' said Samuel. 'I think they were messing about with something that they shouldn't have been messing about with, and it all went wrong. Now they've opened a kind of doorway.'

'Into Hell?'

'Yes, except it's not working right yet. The door is open, but the gates aren't.'

'Don't you usually have to open the gates before the door?' said Mr Johnson.

'Yes,' said Samuel, 'but—'

He stopped.

'You're making fun of me, aren't you?' he said. 'You don't believe me.'

'Have you been playing those computer games again, those ones where you have to kill demons? Samuel, put your mum on the phone.'

Samuel did, and heard one side of a conversation that seemed to revolve around whether or not Samuel knew the difference between reality and fantasy, and if this was some kind of reaction to the difficulties in their marriage, and if Samuel should see a psychiatrist. The conversation moved on to other matters, and Samuel drifted away.

His mum had a troubled expression on her face when she hung up the phone, as though she realised that she was supposed to remember something important, but couldn't quite recall what it was.

'Samuel, go to bed early tonight,' said Mrs Johnson. 'Read something that doesn't involve demons, or ghosts, or monsters, hmmm? For me. And, darling, be careful what you say to people.'

Then she started crying.

'Your dad's buying a house with that woman, Samuel,' said his mum, through her tears. 'He says he wants a divorce. And he wants to come down and collect that stupid bloody car of his!'

Samuel held his mum, and didn't speak. After a while she told him that it was time for bed. He went up to his room and spent a long time staring out of the window, but he didn't cry. Suddenly, monsters and demons didn't seem so important any more. His dad wasn't coming home again. Meanwhile, he was just a small boy, and nobody – not his mum, not his dad – listened to small boys, not ever. Shortly after nine he changed into his pyjamas and climbed into bed.

Eventually he fell asleep.

It was Boswell who first sensed the coming of the Darkness. He woke at the end of Samuel's bed, where he had now decided to sleep permanently after the nasty slimy thing had briefly taken up residence on the floor beneath. Boswell's nose twitched, and his hair stood on end.

Although he was a very intelligent animal, Boswell, like most dogs, divided the world into things that were Good to eat and things that were Bad to eat, with a small space in the middle for things that might potentially be either, or just Good or Bad generally, but about which he wasn't entirely certain as yet.

Thus Boswell's first impression, upon waking up, was that something was Bad, but he wasn't sure exactly what. He couldn't hear or smell anything out of the ordinary. Neither could he see anything out of the ordinary, although his eyesight wasn't very good at the best of times, so that a whole army of Very Bad Things could have been standing a few feet away and, unless they smelled Bad, or sounded Bad, he would have had no idea that they were there.

He leapt off the bed and sniffed around, then trotted to the window and put his front paws on the sill so that he could peer out. All seemed to be perfectly normal. The road was empty. Nothing was moving.

The streetlight at the nearest corner flickered and

went out, creating a pool of darkness that stretched halfway to the next light. Boswell put his head to one side and whined softly. Then the next streetlight went out and, seconds later, the first light came back on again. Even with his weak eyesight, Boswell caught something slipping from one pool of darkness to the next. The third streetlight, the one directly in front of their house, buzzed and then extinguished itself, and this time it stayed out. Boswell stared at the pool of blackness, and a figure in the shadows seemed to stare back at him.

Boswell growled.

And then the pool of blackness began to change. It extended itself, like oil running down a hill, rivulets of it flowing from the base of the streetlight towards the garden gate of number 501. It slid beneath the gate and oozed along the path until it reached the front door and Boswell could no longer mark its progress.

Boswell dropped down from the window, padded to the half-closed bedroom door and edged his body through the gap. He stood at the top of the stairs and watched as the Darkness slipped under the door, seemed to pause for a second to find its bearings, and then, its speed increasing, flowed to the first step and began to climb, the edge of the Darkness forming fingers that seemed to pull the rest of its mass along. Boswell heard a soft *pop* as the far end of the Darkness slipped beneath the front door, so that now he was staring at a puddle perhaps three feet long making its way inexorably towards him.

Boswell began to bark, but nobody came. Mrs Johnson's bedroom door remained firmly closed, and

Boswell could hear her snoring softly. The Darkness was now halfway up the stairs and, at the sound of Boswell's barks, it began to increase its progress. With no other option, Boswell beat a retreat to Samuel's bedroom door, pushing his way in and then nudging the door closed with his nose. He backed away, still growling. He could see a thin line of illumination between the door and the carpet, and deep in his clever dog mind he sensed that this gap was not a Good Thing.

Slowly the light disappeared, diminishing from left to right until nothing of it remained. For a couple of seconds, all was still. There was only the sound of Samuel's breathing and the distant buzz of Mrs Johnson's snores to disturb the silence.

Boswell jumped onto the bed and barked in Samuel's ear.

'Mwff,' said Samuel. 'Argle.'

Boswell tried licking him, while at the same time keeping an eye on the door. Samuel just pushed him away, not even waking up properly to do so.

''S early,' he mumbled. 'No school.'

Just then, with a speed that caused Boswell to jump backwards in fright, the Darkness poured under the door, moving swiftly towards where Samuel lay. It found the leg of the bed and climbed it like a snake, winding its way round the wood before sliding across the blankets. Boswell could smell it now. It reeked of old clothes, and stagnant water, and dead things. It did not shine like oil, even though it moved with the same relentless viscosity. It was absence made solid, nothingness given form and purpose.

And as it moved to smother Samuel, Boswell knew what he had to do.

Standing near the edge of the bed he gripped one end of the Darkness with his teeth, and pulled. He felt it stretch like rubber in his mouth. His tongue grew cold, and his teeth began to hurt, but he did not release his grip. Instead he dug his paws into the blanket and began working his way back to the end of the bed. The Darkness extended towards Samuel, by now almost within reach of his neck. Boswell's paws tore at the blanket as he tried to maintain his position, his teeth tugging with all his might, even as he felt his back legs begin to slide and he fell off the edge of the bed, his bite still hard upon the Darkness.

The impact of Boswell hitting the floor, combined with the sensation of the blanket slipping away from him, finally woke Samuel up.

'What's happening?' he asked, rubbing his eyes.

From the floor came the sound of a struggle, and he heard Boswell whimper.

'Boswell?'

Samuel sat up and looked over the edge of the bed. He saw what appeared to be a blanket of blackness, and beneath it the shape of a small, struggling dog. The Darkness, or whatever was controlling it, had at last recognised the threat posed by the little dachshund, and was doing its level best to extinguish it.

'Boswell!' shouted Samuel.

He reached down and began to pull at the shadow, but even as he did so it froze his fingers and, as he watched in horror, it began to flow up his arms.

'Ugh!' said Samuel.

Meanwhile, Boswell, now freed from the suffocating force, was catching his breath. Seeing his master in trouble, he recommenced his attack, digging his aching teeth in once again. Simultaneously, Samuel began to move backwards, until, at last, the Darkness was stretched between them.

'Don't let go, Boswell,' said Samuel. He pulled the Darkness and Boswell in the direction of the small bathroom that lay to the right of his bedroom. It contained only a toilet and a basin, but it was enough for what Samuel had in mind.

'Stay, Boswell!' he said, as he reached the toilet and Boswell was almost at the door. Holding on to the Darkness with one hand, so that it remained at full stretch, Samuel lifted the toilet seat and, taking a deep breath, told Boswell to open his mouth.

The Darkness sprang from Boswell's mouth, the force sending its bulk flying in Samuel's direction. As quickly as he could, Samuel released his own grip. The Darkness struck the cistern, then fell into the bowl. Immediately tendrils of it extended upwards as it tried to pull itself out, but Samuel was too quick for it. He hit the flush and watched with satisfaction as the Darkness swirled around the bowl for a time and then was swept into the sewers.

Breathing heavily, Samuel leaned back against the sink.

'I'm never using that toilet again,' he said to Boswell, but Boswell was no longer at the door. Instead he had returned to the bedroom window, where Samuel now joined him. Together they watched as the streetlight across from the house came on once more, and the next one extinguished itself, and so on until at last the corner was plunged into darkness for a moment, and something fled away into Stoker Lane.

Before it disappeared, Samuel and Boswell caught a glimpse of it.

It looked like a woman.

In fact, it looked very much like Mrs Abernathy.

CHAPTER XV

In Which Samuel Johnson Begins to Fight Back

Samuel didn't say much at breakfast the next morning. His mother noticed how subdued her son was.

'Is everything all right, dear?' she asked.

Samuel just nodded, and ate his cornflakes. He wanted to tell his mother what had happened the night before with the pool of Darkness, but he couldn't. She wouldn't believe him, and he had no proof. He had no idea where the Darkness had ended up, and was at first a little worried that it might be stuck in one of the household pipes, waiting for a chance to emerge. Once he had thought about it for a while, though, he realised that it was probably lost in a smelly old sewer which was just fine by Samuel. Still, he had taken the precaution of gluing the toilet seat closed using super-strong adhesive. He was the only one who ever used the little bathroom anyway, and as long as he was careful nobody would discover for a while what he had done.

But Samuel was also very frightened, for his mother and for himself. He remembered Mrs Abernathy's threat to kill his mother if he continued to try to convince her of what he knew. The demon under the bed had been bad enough, but at least that could be reasoned with. The Darkness had been something else entirely. He had been lucky last night; Boswell's bravery had saved him, but Boswell might not be able to save him, or his mum, from whatever came next.

Because Samuel was sure of one thing: Mrs Abernathy wasn't going to give up. The Darkness had simply been her latest attempt to silence Samuel. Others would follow, and eventually she would succeed.

Samuel didn't want to die. He quite liked being alive. But as he tried to come to terms with how scared he was, he began to feel angry. Mrs Abernathy was evil. She wanted to do something awful, so awful that the world would never be the same after it, if there was even any world left once the gates were opened. She had to be stopped, and Samuel was determined to fight her until his last breath.

It was at that moment that fortune began to turn in Samuel's favour.

There was a small portable television in the corner of the kitchen. Samuel's mother sometimes liked to watch it while she was having breakfast. The volume was turned down low, and the news was on. Samuel glanced up and saw a man in a white coat talking. Behind him was what looked like an enormous series of pipelines. Samuel knew what it was: the Large Hadron Collider in Switzerland. He had watched a documentary about it earlier in the year and, although he hadn't understood everything that had been discussed, he thought it all sounded like pretty fascinating stuff. He reached for the remote control and turned up the volume.

The scientist, whose name was Professor Stefan, looked a bit embarrassed. It became clear that he was trying to explain why the collider had been shut down. Samuel knew the collider hadn't worked properly the first time it was turned on, and the scientists had been forced to tinker with it for a while before it began running to their satisfaction. Now, after all the money that had been spent on it, it still didn't appear to be working the way that it should.

'Well,' said Professor Stefan, when the reporter pointed this fact out to him, 'that's not entirely true. It was working perfectly, but then there was an, um, unanticipated release of unknown energy.'

'What does that mean, exactly?' asked the reporter.

'Well, to put it in layman's terms, a bit flew off, and now we're trying to find out what it was.'

'A bit?' said the reporter.

'A particle of energy,' said Professor Stefan, 'but one that has not been encountered before, and appears to show unusual characteristics.'

'What kind of characteristics?' said the reporter.

'Well, the collider is a vacuum, and therefore it's sealed. It simply should not be possible for anything to find its way out of there.'

'But now you think that something has?'

'We believe so. It may just be a leak, so we're checking every inch of the collider for possible breaches. As you can imagine, that's a time-consuming procedure. In the meantime, we're going back over our systems in an effort to determine precisely what we're dealing with.'

The reporter thought over what he had just been told.

'Is there any possibility that this "energy" might be dangerous?'

'Oh, none whatsoever,' said Professor Stefan.

Samuel thought that he seemed very sure of this for someone who didn't know what exactly the energy was.

'And when precisely did you become aware of this energy leak?'

'At precisely seven thirty p.m. on October the twenty-eighth,' said Professor Stefan. 'The collider was shut down shortly afterwards.'

Samuel paused, a spoonful of cornflakes suspended between the bowl and his mouth. Seven thirty p.m. on October 28th. At 7.30 p.m. on October 28th Samuel and Boswell had been sitting on the Abernathys' wall when they'd heard the bang from the Abernathys' basement, and they'd seen the blue light and smelled that nasty smell. It might be a coincidence, of course, but for the first time Samuel sensed that there could be someone out there who might be prepared to listen to him.

Samuel sat at his computer and examined the website for CERN. He couldn't find a telephone number, but there was a section entitled 'Ask an Expert'. Samuel didn't know how long an expert might take to answer his question, or even if what he had to say counted as a question at all. He thought very hard, then composed his message to CERN:

Dear CERN,
My name is Samuel Johnson, and I am 11 years old. I have reason to believe that I may have found

your missing energy particle, or know where it ended up. I think it is in the basement of number 666 Crowley Avenue in the town of Biddlecombe, England. It is owned by a couple named the Abernathys. It is very blue, and smells of rotten eggs. The energy, that is, not Biddlecombe. It materialised there at precisely 7.30 p.m. on October 28th. I enclose a drawing of what I saw in the basement, scanned into the computer for your information.

Yours sincerely,
Samuel Johnson

PS I believe Mr and Mrs Abernathy have become possessed by demons, and may be using the energy to open the gates of Hell.

When he was finished, Samuel checked his spelling and went over the letter once again to make sure that he had included all the important details. He had considered leaving out the bit about Hell, but thought it might add a sense of urgency to his message. After all, he didn't know how many people wrote to 'Ask an Expert' every day, or if there was just one expert answering the questions or a whole team. In any case, he thought it was important to attract CERN's attention and, if nothing else, the mention of demons and Hell was likely to make his message stand out.

He pressed Send, and his missive shot off into cyberspace. He considered staying at his computer and waiting for a reply, but he suspected that, even if someone read his message very soon, a certain amount of discussion would still be required before it was answered.

Samuel was not about to sit around doing nothing. It was Halloween, and he had heard Mrs Abernathy say that she and her fellow demons had four days to prepare the way. Samuel didn't know precisely what 'preparing the way' meant, but by any calculation four days from October 28th led to November 1st. He had a terrible feeling that, at some time the next day, the gates of Hell would begin to open.

So Samuel went to the telephone and began making some calls.

It would not be true to say that Samuel was unpopular at school. There were some boys and girls in his class who looked at him a little oddly, especially when he began talking about angels and pins, but for the most part he got on well with nearly everyone. He was also very happy to spend time by himself, though, and after sharing the same small schoolroom with a bunch of kids his own age for two months, he had rather been enjoying being by himself during half-term. His closest friends were Tom Hobbes and Maria Mayer. Tom's father delivered milk for the local dairy, where his mum also worked, and Maria's dad worked for the telephone company. Samuel, Tom, and Maria had planned to go trick or treating that evening, and Tom and Maria had been a little surprised to hear from Samuel so early in the day.

When Samuel said he had something important to tell them, they were both intrigued. They agreed to meet outside the pie shop in the town centre, and Samuel, with Boswell in tow, was already waiting for Tom and Maria when they arrived together shortly after one p.m. The pie shop was called Pete's Pies, even though Pete had died many years before and his son Nigel now made all the pies, but Nigel's Pies didn't sound right and, anyway, everyone would have just kept calling it Pete's Pies even if Nigel had changed the name. People in small towns are funny that way.

There were always tables and chairs outside Pete's Pies, even in winter, which made it a popular place for people to meet. Pete, and then Nigel, never objected to people taking a seat there. Even if they didn't come along with the intention of buying a pie, the smell from the pie shop would cause their mouths to water and, usually in less than a minute, they would be inside buying a pie 'for later'. About one minute after that they would be eating the pie and considering having another, maybe the apple and raspberry, for dessert.

It was one of these same apple and raspberry pies that Samuel was eating when Tom and Maria strolled up to his table. Tom was taller than Samuel by a couple of inches, and never really seemed to have bad days. He was always in good spirits, except when the school cricket team, of which he was one of the star batsmen, lost. Tom didn't mind losing at most things, but he drew the line at cricket. Tom and Samuel only ever argued on the cricket pitch. Samuel was a good bowler, with a strong right arm, but his eyesight was poor, and he had trouble catching balls when fielding. This meant that he was both an asset and a liability on the cricket pitch, and more than one match had ended with him and Tom shouting at each other at the tops of their voices. Still, they remained friends, and Tom was secretly a little in awe of Samuel, whose mind worked in ways that Tom admired, even if he did not fully understand.

Maria, meanwhile, was smaller than both of them, and had very long hair that she tied in a ponytail each day with one of a selection of bows. She sometimes seemed shy and quiet to those who didn't know her well, but Samuel knew she was very clever and very funny. She just didn't like showing off. Maria wanted to be a scientist when she grew up, and was the only person Samuel and Tom knew who did homework for pleasure.

Boswell wagged his tail in greeting at the two new arrivals, then returned his attention to the pie on the table. He knew that Samuel would share some with him eventually. Samuel shared nearly all of his food with Boswell, except chocolate, because that wasn't good for Boswell and gave him wind, and Boswell could be a smelly dog if he was fed the wrong things.

'All right, then,' said Tom, once he and Maria had bought pies of their own and settled down on their seats. 'What's the big mystery?'

Boswell finished the piece of pie that Samuel had fed to him, licked up the last of the crumbs, and began drooling over Tom's shoe instead. Tom decided to give him some pie to distract him before Boswell's spit started to soak through to his socks.

'Well, it's like this,' said Samuel. 'You're probably going to have trouble believing me, and I'm not sure how I'm going to prove that what I have to say is true.

All I'm asking is that you listen to me, because I really need your help.'

He was so serious that Tom stopped eating for a moment and Tom, like Boswell, didn't like to stop eating for no good reason.

'Wow, that sounds serious,' he said. 'Off you go, then. I'm listening.'

He looked at Maria, who nodded. 'We both are.'

So Samuel told them everything, right up to the point at which he'd sent off his message to CERN. When he was finished nobody spoke for a time, then Tom said:

'You're barmy.'

'Tom!' Maria scolded him.

'No, really. You're trying to tell us that this Mrs Abernathy isn't really Mrs Abernathy but a thing with tentacles, and that in her basement is a blue hole that somehow is a tunnel to Hell, and tomorrow some gates are going to open in that tunnel and – what? Demons are going to come out?'

'Something like that,' said Samuel calmly.

'You *are* barmy,' repeated Tom.

Samuel turned to Maria. 'And you?' he asked her. 'What do you think?'

'It is a little hard to believe,' said Maria gently.

'I'm not lying,' said Samuel. He looked at them both, his face serious. 'On my life, I promise you I'm not lying. And ...'

He paused.

'What?' said Maria.

'I'm scared,' said Samuel. 'I'm really scared.'

And they both believed him when he said it.

'Well,' said Tom. 'There's only one thing for it.'

'What's that?' asked Maria, but she already knew the answer.

Tom grinned.

'We'll just have to take a look at the Abernathys' house.'

Meanwhile, at CERN, the technician who had been monitoring the 'Ask An Expert' section of the website approached Professor Hilbert holding a printed message at the bottom of which was a drawing of a blue spiral.

'Professor,' he said, nervously, 'this may be nothing, but . . .'

CHAPTER XVI

In Which We Visit the Abernathy House, and Decide That We Wouldn't Want to Live There

It was determined that they should leave the visit to the Abernathys' house until the light had begun to fade, so Samuel and Maria spent the early part of the afternoon helping Tom to practise his batting. When it began to grow dark they paid a brief visit to Samuel's house to check his e-mail, but there was no reply to his message from CERN.

'Maybe they're very busy,' said Tom, 'what with their big collider thing being broken.'

'It's not broken,' said Samuel. 'Well, not exactly. They've shut it down while they investigate the energy leak.'

'The one that you say has turned up in the Abernathys' basement,' said Tom. 'That's a long way from Switzerland. They're not Swiss, are they?'

Samuel thought about it. 'No, I don't think so. Mr Abernathy didn't sound Swiss when I spoke to him. Mrs Abernathy just smells funny.'

Then again, Samuel had never, to his knowledge, spoken to a Swiss person. He just suspected that Swiss people didn't sound like Mr Abernathy, who spoke with a gruff northern accent, or Mrs Abernathy, who seemed quite posh.

Maria looked out of Samuel's bedroom window. 'It's getting dark now,' she said. 'Are you sure we should be doing this? It doesn't seem right, creeping around somebody's garden in the dark. I mean, what is it that you hope we'll see?'

Samuel shrugged. 'Just . . . something. Something that will make you believe me.'

'And if we do believe you?' asked Maria. 'What then?'

'Well, you'll know I'm not mad,' said Samuel. 'Or a liar.'

Maria smiled fondly. 'I know you'd never lie to us, Samuel,' she said.

'Although you might still be mad,' added Tom, but he too was smiling. 'Well, come on, then. I have to get home for tea, or I'll catch hell from my mum.' He realised what he had just said. 'Catch hell? Get it? See, I'm funny even when I'm not trying to be.'

Maria and Samuel rolled their eyes.

'Oh, please yourselves,' said Tom. 'Some people have no sense of humour . . .'

The Abernathys' house appeared to be empty when they reached it, Boswell somewhat reluctantly in tow.

'Doesn't seem like there's anybody home,' said Tom.

'It looks creepy,' said Maria 'I know it's just a normal house, but maybe it's because of what you've told us about the people who live there . . .'

'No,' said Tom, his tone subdued. 'You're right. I can

feel it. The hairs on the back of my neck are standing up. There's something wrong here.'

'Boswell feels it too,' said Samuel, and, indeed, Boswell was whimpering. The dog planted his small bottom firmly on the ground outside the garden gate, as if to say, 'Right, this is as far as I go. If you want me to go any farther, you'll have to drag me.'

Samuel tied Boswell's lead to the garden gate. 'We'd best leave him here,' he said.

'Can I stay with him?' asked Tom, only half joking.

'Come on, silly,' said Maria taking Tom by the arm and pulling him into the garden, Samuel close behind them.

'Weren't you scared just a minute ago?' whispered Tom.

'I'm still scared,' said Maria, 'but this is *interesting*.'

The expression on Maria's face had changed. She looked excited. Mr Hume had once said that she had the perfect brain for a scientist. She was both curious and careful, and once she got the scent of something that intrigued her, she would pursue it right to the end.

Samuel led them to the basement window. A bare bulb glowed orange in the ceiling, casting a dim light on the room. They crouched down and peered inside, but apart from the usual junk that accumulated in people's basements, there was nothing out of the ordinary to be seen.

'That's where it happened,' said Samuel. 'The blue circle, the big clawed hand, all of it.'

'Well, it's quiet now,' said Tom. 'Mind you, it smells nasty here.'

He was right. A stink of rotten eggs hung around the basement and the area of the garden nearest to it. A concentrated breeze was blowing, carrying the stench on it, as though a hole had been bored in a great wall behind which a wind was blowing.

'Do you feel that?' said Maria. She raised her hand so that it was very close to the glass. The two boys did likewise.

'It feels like static electricity,' said Tom. He moved his hand farther forward, as though to touch the glass, but Maria reached out to stop him.

'No,' she said. 'I don't think that's a good idea.'

'It's just static,' said Tom.

'No,' said Maria, 'it's not.'

She pointed at the frame of the window. There, barely visible to the naked eye, was the faintest blue glow.

Maria moved on, following the wall of the house.

'Where's she off to?' said Tom.

Samuel didn't know, but he decided to follow Maria nonetheless. Tom, not wanting to be left alone, was soon trotting along behind.

The Abernathys' house stood in the centre of a large garden, so that there was nothing to stop someone circling from the front of the house to the back. Maria was pointing at the windows as she went.

'There!' she said softly. 'And there!'

If they concentrated hard, each time they looked they saw that faint blue glow around every window frame.

'I think it might be a kind of alarm,' said Maria. 'They've secured the place, somehow.'

By this time they had reached the rear of the house.

To the left of the back door was a kitchen, which was empty. To the right was a living room, with a TV, some couches, and a pair of armchairs. A lamp was lit in the room, casting a square of light upon the back lawn.

Together, the three children made their way to the window and peered inside.

Boswell was very unhappy at having his lead tied to a garden gate. Like most dogs, he didn't like being tied to anything. If you were tied to something, it was hard to fight if a bigger dog came along, and impossible to run away if fighting wasn't an option. Boswell was not much of a fighter. To be honest, he wasn't even very good at running away, given his short legs and long body.

But if there was anything worse than having his lead tied to a garden gate it was having it tied to this particular one. The big house smelled wrong to Boswell. It wasn't just the stink that the children had also picked up. Boswell's sense of smell was far more sensitive than that of any human. He had 25 times more smell receptors than a person, and he could sense odours at concentrations 100 million times lower than a human could. As he sniffed the air around the big house, drawing it deep down to where the receptors lay at the back of his snout, he picked up hints of tainted meat, of disease, of dead things that shouldn't be touched, or tasted, or even sniffed for very long for fear of being sick. Lurking behind them all was one smell in particular, one that every animal hated and feared.

It was the smell of burning.

Suddenly Boswell stood up. He had heard something,

the sound of footsteps approaching. One of the bad smells started to grow stronger, although it was mixed up with another that wasn't quite so bad, as though the not-so-bad smell was being used to hide the really bad one. The not-so-bad smell was familiar to Boswell, although that didn't mean he liked it. It was too strong and sweet and sickly. It reminded him of the scent that sometimes came from Mrs Johnson, the scent that emerged from some of the little bottles she kept in her bedroom. It smelled of too many flowers.

Even with his poor eyesight Boswell was able to identify the woman as soon as she turned the corner. He had already built up a picture of her using his nose, and now his worst fears were confirmed.

It was the nasty lady, the one who had brought the Darkness.

Boswell began to whine.

There were three people, two men and a woman, sitting in the living room, the walls of which were covered with a strange orange mould that was spreading from the carpet and extending towards the ceiling. The mould covered the chairs on which the three people were sitting, as though they were rotting and their decay was slowly infecting the room. They were not moving, or speaking, but they all had strange, fixed smiles on their faces, like people who had seen something that only someone with a very strange sense of humour would think was funny. Samuel recognised the men as Mr Abernathy and his friend, Mr Renfield. The woman was Mrs Renfield.

They had changed since last he had seen them. He thought that they appeared fatter; bloated somehow, as if by a great internal swelling. He could see Mr Abernathy the most clearly. Mr Abernathy's skin was a grey-green colour, and there were blisters on it. He looked sick. In fact, he looked so sick that Samuel wondered if Mr Abernathy might actually be worse than sick. Despite the time of year the room was filled with flies, and Samuel knew immediately that the people in the room stank very badly. Samuel thought he saw a fly land on one of Mr Abernathy's eyeballs and crawl across it, a black speck against the milky white of the eye. Mr Abernathy didn't even blink.

It was Tom who voiced what Samuel had been thinking.

'Are they . . . dead?' he asked.

As he spoke, the fly buzzed away from Mr Abernathy's eyeball. At the same instant a long tongue unrolled from Mr Abernathy's mouth, like a party favour. It was pink, and covered with little spines that looked sharp and sticky. It plucked the fly from mid-air, then rolled back in Mr Abernathy's mouth. He chewed on the fly for a moment before swallowing it down.

'Oh, I think I'm going to be sick,' said Maria.

'Was that a tongue?' asked Tom. 'That was a tongue! People don't have tongues that long. *Things* have tongues that long.'

Then they heard the sound of frantic barking from the front of the house, and knew that they were in trouble.

*   *   *

As soon as Boswell saw Mrs Abernathy, he began trying to wriggle out of his collar. It was never kept very tight, mainly because Boswell's neck was so thin that no collar fitted him right. He tugged hard against the lead, and felt the collar begin to rise up against the back of his head. It hurt his ears, but he didn't stop. He knew that if he was still tied to the gate when the bad lady came she would hurt him, and then she would hurt Samuel. Nobody was going to hurt Samuel, not if Boswell had anything to do with it.

The collar was halfway over his ears when the sound of the nasty lady's footsteps started to come faster.

Mrs Abernathy spotted the dog as soon as she rounded the corner. It took her only a moment to identify it as Samuel Johnson's pet.

'Oh, you naughty boy!' she whispered. 'You naughty, *naughty* little boy.'

She began to run.

Boswell risked a glance to his left, and saw the nasty lady drawing nearer. He gave a final hard tug against the collar, and felt it pull free, almost taking his ears with it. He barked, alternating glances between the path leading into the garden of the big house and the bad lady. He kept hoping that Samuel and his friends would come, yet they didn't.

Run! he barked. Nasty lady! Run!

But still there was no sign of them. He looked to his left, and saw the nasty lady's shape begin to change. There were shapes moving beneath her coat. Suddenly, the material began to tear, and long pink feelers burst through the holes, each one ending in sharp pincers that snapped at the cold air. One extended itself towards him, the pincers making a clicking sound and dripping foul-smelling liquid on the ground. Instinctively he snapped back at it, and it withdrew, but only for a moment. It rose up, like a snake about to strike. Boswell sensed the danger.

With no other choice, he put his tail between his legs and ran as fast as his little legs would carry him. He thought he felt something graze his coat; but he didn't look back, not until he had reached the corner. He hid under a car and peered out from behind the wheels. The nasty lady stood for a moment at the garden gate, the long pink tentacles waving against the night sky, then turned away and headed into the garden. Seconds later Boswell heard a terrible sound, one so sharp and piercing that it hurt his ears. It was too high-pitched for a human to detect, but Mrs Abernathy wasn't trying to contact any human.

She was alerting her fellow demons.

CHAPTER XVII

In Which Mrs Abernathy Changes Her Plans

Tom peered round the corner of the house, and saw Mrs Abernathy enter the garden and close the gate carefully behind her. The tentacles moved in the still evening air, the moonlight catching the fluid that dripped from their pincers. Tom counted twelve of them. On the ground at Mrs Abernathy's feet lay Boswell's empty collar. Mrs Abernathy took three steps forward, then stopped. She cocked her head to one side, as though listening for something, but she did not move any closer to the house.

She was waiting, guarding the gate.

Tom ran back to where Samuel and Maria were waiting beneath the window.

'We're in trouble,' he said. 'There's a woman in the garden with tentacles sticking out of her back.'

'Mrs Abernathy,' said Samuel. 'What about Boswell?'

'There's no sign of him. His collar is there, but it's empty.'

Samuel looked worried. 'She couldn't have . . . ?' he began to say, then trailed off. He didn't want to think about what Mrs Abernathy might have done to his dog.

Seconds later, he heard Boswell's bark. It sounded farther away than before, but it was definitely him.

'He's OK!' said Samuel.

'Yeah, but we're not,' said Tom. 'If she recognised Boswell, she'll know that you're here.'

Samuel swallowed hard. 'She doesn't know you and Maria are with me. I could distract her, so you two can get away.'

Tom looked at Samuel with something approaching admiration, then hit him hard on the arm.

'Ow!' said Samuel. 'What was that for?'

'For being stupid,' said Tom. 'We're not going to leave you here alone.'

Suddenly Maria's hand was pushed against his mouth, silencing him. She put a finger to her lips, then withdrew it and pointed at the rectangle of light from the window. The shadow of a man could now be seen against it. They remained very still, hardly daring to breathe. The shadow began to alter. As they watched, eight spiny limbs, like spider legs, emerged from it. Then the shadow turned and began to recede, as whoever, or whatever, it was moved away from the window.

'We have to make a run for it,' said Samuel.

'We can't go out the way we came in,' said Tom. 'That woman's guarding the gate.'

'And we can't go over the garden wall,' said Maria. 'It's too high.'

Now noises were coming from inside the house. They heard a vase break, and then shambling footsteps, as though someone who was having trouble walking was approaching the back door.

To their left, Tom saw two plastic boxes filled with empty wine bottles, ready for recycling.

'Do you think you could hit those wine bottles with a stone?' he asked Samuel.

'If I had a stone,' said Samuel.

Tom gestured to Samuel's right, where there was a small rockery dotted with plants. Samuel immediately reached for a stone roughly the size of a cricket ball, took a breath, and threw it overarm at the boxes of bottles. The stone landed slap bang in the middle of them, breaking the necks of the longest and scattering glass on the ground.

'Now!' said Samuel.

They ran to the right, past the rockery and along the side of the house. From behind them came the sound of the back door opening, but by then they were already at the corner of the house, the front gate before them. Mrs Abernathy was gone, and when Maria risked a look round the corner she saw the shadow of a woman moving quickly away from them and towards the other end of the house.

They took their chance and sprinted for the gate, leaping over the flowerbeds and the bushes that had been carefully tended by Mr Abernathy before he was taken over by a thing with no appreciation for the finer points of gardening. Tom was bringing up the rear when his foot caught on a length of trailing ivy and he stumbled, then fell. Samuel and Maria stopped at the gate, Maria preparing to go back and help Tom when Mrs Abernathy, alerted by the noise, appeared at the side of the house.

'Bad children!' she said. 'You shouldn't trespass on other people's property.'

Two of the tentacles grew longer than the rest, then shot at speed towards Tom as he tried to get to his feet. He could see how sharp their pincers were, and could smell the stuff that dripped like spittle from them as they came. He was raising his hand to protect himself when something slashed through the air before him. It was a garden rake, which caught the tentacles a hard blow and drove them to the ground. They remained pinned there beneath the rake's teeth, writhing feebly and spraying thick black blood on the lawn. Mrs Abernathy screamed in shock and pain as Maria let go of the rake and pulled Tom to his feet.

'Come on,' she said and the three children, accompanied by a happy and very relieved Boswell, disappeared into the dusk.

Mrs Abernathy walked across the lawn, her face contorted with rage and agony. The tentacles had retreated into her body, except for the two that the horrid girl had pierced with the rake. Mrs Abernathy knelt down and pulled the rake free, then tossed it away. Slowly, like wounded animals, the tentacles grew smaller, withdrawing into her flesh where they left a series of small holes that bled black against her ruined coat.

Mr Renfield shuffled towards her, eight spiny legs now receding into his body, and what looked like mandibles disappearing back into his mouth. The same bland, humourless smile was still on his face. Behind him, Mrs Renfield and Mr Abernathy appeared, followed by a cloud of flies.

Mr Abernathy stopped beside his wife. He turned to look blankly at her, and she hit him so hard across the face with the back of her hand that his neck broke and his head hung at a strange angle upon his shoulders. He raised his hands and tried to put his head back into place, but it wouldn't stay. Eventually he gave up and left it hanging. It didn't seem to cause him any great discomfort, and his smile remained unchanged.

'You fool,' said Mrs Abernathy. 'Now *three* of them know about us.'

Mrs Renfield joined her. 'What shall we do?' she asked. 'Kill them?'

'We can't wait any longer,' said Mrs Abernathy. 'We have to begin.'

'But all is not ready.'

'Enough will have gathered,' said Mrs Abernathy. 'The gates will open, and the first will pour through. They will prepare the way for the Great Malevolence, and he will finish what they have begun. Go! I will join you in a moment.'

Mr and Mrs Renfield moved away, followed by Mr Abernathy and his wobbling head. Mrs Abernathy strolled to the garden gate and looked to the direction in which the three children and the dog had run. She saw the ghosts of them still hanging in the air before they drifted away like fog.

Perhaps the others were right, she thought. It was not yet time. The Great Malevolence had wanted to enter this new world in glory, provoking awe and terror as he came, his demonic army arrayed behind him. Instead, their attack upon the world of men would commence more slowly. As the demons began to pour through, the portal would grow larger. They would draw the energy that they needed from the collider. It would only be a matter of hours before the gates would melt away, and the Great Malevolence would be unleashed upon the Earth.

A small figure wearing a devil's horns and mask appeared before her.

'Trick or treat,' said a voice from behind the mask.

Mrs Abernathy regarded him curiously, then began to smile. The smile turned to a fearsome, terrible laughter. She put the back of her hand to her mouth, and said: 'How delightful! Oh, this is just perfect!'

Like small boys the world over, the small boy behind the mask, whose name was Michael, didn't care much for things that were 'delightful', or grown-ups who seemed to find things funny when they weren't funny at all.

'Look, are you going to give me something or aren't you?' he asked impatiently.

'Oh, I'll give you something,' she said. 'I'll give you all something, and it will be the last thing you will ever receive. I'll give you death.'

'No sweets, then,' said the small boy.

Mrs Abernathy's laughter faded, and she knelt down before the little boy. He saw a faint blue glow to her eyes. It grew brighter and brighter, until there was nothing in the woman's eye sockets but cold blue light that made him wince with pain. When she opened her mouth, he smelt the foulness of her insides.

'No sweets,' said Mrs Abernathy. 'No sweets ever again.'

She watched the small boy run away, and thought:

Flee! Flee while you can, but there will be no escape, not from me.

And not from my master.

CHAPTER XVIII

In Which the Portal Opens Wide

Mrs Johnson sat on the couch, smiling awkwardly at her visitor, whose name was Dr Planck. Dr Planck was small and dark, with a pointed beard, and black-rimmed glasses. Mrs Johnson had made him tea, and offered him a biscuit. Now she was trying to understand why he was with her in the first place. All she knew was that it had something to do with Samuel. These things always did.

Dr Planck worked at the local university as part of the experimental particle physics research programme, and had been involved with CERN for a number of years. When the message from Switzerland about Samuel's e-mail had come through to him, he had rushed to Biddlecombe. He wasn't certain that a small boy could be entirely helpful to them, but there was something about his drawing, and the description of the rotten egg smell, that had caught the attention of the scientists at CERN. Now here he was, drinking tea and eating Bourbon cream biscuits, and trying to establish if Mrs Johnson's son might just have given them the help they had been seeking.

'Samuel hasn't done anything wrong, has he?' said Mrs Johnson.

'No, not at all,' said Dr Planck. 'He just sent us a very interesting e-mail, and we'd like to talk to him about it.'

'By "us", you mean the CERN people,' said Mrs Johnson.

'That's right.'

'Has Samuel solved one of the mysteries of the Universe, then?'

Dr Planck smiled politely, and nibbled on his Bourbon cream. 'Not exactly,' he said. 'Tell me, what do you know about the people at number six-six-six . . . ?'

Mrs Abernathy stood in the basement, Mr Abernathy and the Renfields behind her. A pinpoint of blue light hung in the air, pulsing softly. Mrs Renfield growled in disapproval.

'It was there all along,' she said to Mrs Abernathy, 'and yet you hid it from us.'

'You did not need to know,' said Mrs Abernathy.

'Who are you to decide such matters?'

Mrs Abernathy turned on her. For an instant, her mouth grew so large that it threatened to engulf her entire head, revealing row upon row of jagged teeth. The huge jaws snapped at Mrs Renfield, who staggered backwards in alarm. Then, almost as soon as it had revealed itself, the monstrous mouth was gone and Mrs Abernathy was restored to her former beauty.

'You will keep a civil tongue in your head, or you will find yourself deprived of both,' warned Mrs Abernathy. 'Remember to whom you are speaking. I have the ear of our master, and I am his emissary here on Earth. Any disrespect shown to me will be communicated to him, and the punishment will be great.'

Mrs Renfield hung her head, quaking at the thought of what punishments might befall her. She belonged to a lower order of demons than Mrs Abernathy,[22] yet she was envious of Mrs Abernathy's power and her closeness to the Great Malevolence, for that which is evil is always jealous, and seeks constantly to advance itself. Now her display of anger had left open the possibility of retribution from their master, because Mrs Abernathy would surely tell him of Mrs Renfield's impertinence. But if she could overcome Mrs Abernathy and take her place, if she, and not Mrs Abernathy, could pave the way for their master, then she would be rewarded, not punished.

And so she made her move. Her jaws widened, and from between her lips her spider chelicerae emerged, two appendages ending in hollow points, each loaded with poison. She approached Mrs Abernathy from behind, her eyes fixed on the pale skin at the base of Mrs Abernathy's neck.

Suddenly Mrs Renfield froze, unable to advance. She felt her throat tighten, as though a hand had gripped it and was slowly choking her. Mrs Abernathy turned, her eyes ablaze with blue fire.

💀 [22] A book named *Le Dragon Rouge* (*The Red Dragon*), possibly written in the sixteenth century, classified the demons of hell in three orders, from officers to generals. Books like this are known as 'grimoires', and to have power they must be written in red ink and, some say, bound in human skin. Lovely. Just lovely.

'You foolish creature,' she said. 'Now you will suffer.'

Mrs Abernathy waved her fingers in front of Mrs Renfield's face. The chelicerae continued to grow from Mrs Renfield's mouth, but now they began to curl down towards her own neck. Mrs Renfield's eyes widened in panic, but she could do nothing to stop what was about to occur. The twin points pierced her skin and she began to pump poison into her own system. Her eyes bulged and her face blackened, until at last she fell to the floor. Her body jerked once before it turned to dust.

Mrs Abernathy returned her attention to the blue light.

'Master,' said Mrs Abernathy. 'Your servant calls.'

The blue light grew larger, and the basement became colder. Mrs Abernathy's breath plumed whitely. Her fingertips were so chilled that they began to hurt.

And then a voice spoke. It seemed to come at once from everywhere and nowhere, echoing around the basement. It was deep and sibilant, like the hissing of a giant snake in a dank cave.

'*Yessssss,*' it said. '*Speak.*'

'Master,' said Mrs Abernathy again, and her voice trembled. Even now, after she had spent so long in the presence of this great evil, so close to an eternity that the difference hardly mattered, it still had the power to terrify her. 'We must act now. We can wait no longer.'

'*Why?*'

'There has been a . . . difficulty,' said Mrs Abernathy, choosing her words carefully. 'Our presence has become known.'

'*To whom?*'

'A child.'

'*Why was this child not dealt with?*'

'We tried. He was lucky. Now he has shared his knowledge with others.'

There was silence. Mrs Abernathy could almost feel her master's rage building.

'*You disappoint me,*' he said at last. '*There will be a reckoning for this.*'

'Yes, Master.' Mrs Abernathy bowed her head, as though the Great Malevolence were standing before her, ready to visit his wrath upon her.

'*So be it,*' said the voice. '*Let it begin.*'

But before they could proceed any further, the doorbell rang.

Deep in the bowels of CERN, the chief scientists were gathered in Professor Stefan's office.

'Is there any word yet from Doctor Planck?' asked Professor Stefan.

Professor Hilbert glanced at his watch. 'He should be with the boy by now,' he said.

'If it's some kind of joke, I'll have that child's hide,' said Professor Stefan.

He reached for his pen, if only to give him something to do with his hands. The pen lay close to the edge of his desk, but before he could get his fingers to it the pen dropped to the floor.

Professor Stefan looked at it curiously. 'That's odd,' he said, just as he began to feel the vibrations running through his desk. A great humming filled the entire facility, and all the lights dimmed for a moment. Computer screens throughout the facility began displaying huge amounts of data, Aramaic mixed with binary code.

'What's happening?' said Professor Stefan.

But he already knew.

Somehow, the collider had started up again.

Mrs Abernathy answered the door. Standing on the step was a small man with a pointed beard. He was sucking on the frame of a pair of dark-rimmed glasses.

'Mrs Abernathy?' he said.

'Yes?'

'I'm Doctor Planck. I'd like to talk with you for a moment, if it's convenient.'

'Actually,' said Mrs Abernathy, 'I'm rather busy right now.'

Dr Planck sniffed the air. He smelled rotten eggs. Then he noticed a faint blue glow coming from the basement, a light that also seemed to be flickering on the window frames of the house, and around the door. A wind blew in his face, its force increasing. As it did so, the blue glow became brighter.

'What are you doing?' said Dr Planck. 'This isn't right.'

'Run,' said Mrs Abernathy.

'What?'

'I said, "Run".'

Her eyes filled with cold fire. Her mouth opened, and the light shone like a beam from it. It felt like ice on Dr Planck's skin.

He ran.

* * *

The basement of number 666 was filled with a vast swirling mass of light and dark, of blue beams and a blackness that was so thick as to be almost tangible. Little tendrils of electricity flickered deep within it like bolts of lightning against the night sky, then shot out to strike Mr Abernathy and Mr Renfield. They began to change shape, shedding their human skins and assuming once again their true demonic forms. Mr Abernathy looked like a grey toad, with unblinking eyes that protruded from his head on long stalks. Mr Renfield became spiderlike, his body covered with spiny hairs, eight black eyes appearing on his head: two large ones at the front, two smaller ones on either side, then four more behind. Eight long, jointed legs burst from his torso, each ending in a sharp claw, yet he remained standing on his human legs, which were stronger and thicker than the rest. Pointed fangs burst from his jaws, their tips glistening with poison.

Mrs Abernathy joined them, but she remained unchanged, the blue fire in her eyes aside. She did not want to assume her true shape, not yet. Although she was restricted by this human body, it had its uses. If necessary it would allow her to move freely through the world of men during the early stages of the attack. Only when victory was secured did she intend to reveal herself as she really was.

The walls of the house began to shudder. Dust fell from the ceiling of the basement, and old paint cans and boxes of nails dropped from shelves and spilled their contents on the floor. The mortar between the bricks crumbled, and the bricks started to float away. As the house came apart more tendrils of blue light appeared, shooting through the gaps and disappearing into the ground. The wind grew stronger, blowing from one universe into another across the portal that was now opening. Mrs Abernathy watched as the gates, those hated prison bars, began to glow white hot, dripping molten metal as her master harnessed the power of the collider to begin to free himself.

Now the first of the demons appeared. They were simple entities, little more than skulls with black wings. Their mouths appeared to have too many teeth, so that the top and bottom rows were snagged and uneven, yet sharp as needles. There were four of them, and they hovered in the air before Mrs Abernathy, their jaws snapping and their wings flapping.

'I have work for you,' she said. She reached out to touch the nearest one, imparting through her fingers knowledge of the three children, the ones who had hurt her and forced her to appear weak before her master, and the little man with the beard, who she sensed meant her harm.

'Find them,' she said. 'Find them all and tear them apart.'

Samuel, Maria and Tom were in Samuel's bedroom, sitting in front of Samuel's computer and staring at the e-mail message that Samuel had accessed through his Google account. Samuel's mother stood over them. The message from Dr Planck read:

VERY INTERESTED IN YOUR E-MAIL. I WILL COME TO YOUR HOUSE THIS EVENING AT FIVE THIRTY TO

DISCUSS IT. HOPE THIS IS CONVENIENT. IF THERE IS
A PROBLEM, I CAN BE CONTACTED AT THE NUMBER
BELOW.

'He waited here for a while, then said he wanted to
take a look at the Abernathys' house,' said Mrs Johnson.
'What have you been telling people, Samuel?'

'What I've been trying to explain to you all along,'
said Samuel. 'The Abernathys are about to do something
terrible, and they have to be stopped.'

This time his mother didn't contradict him. Listening
to Dr Planck, she had begun to remember her encounter
with Mrs Abernathy at the supermarket and about how
frightened she had been to see Samuel talking to her by
the churchyard, even if she hadn't understood why at
the time. Now she knew that Samuel was telling the
truth. Mrs Abernathy was bad. Mrs Abernathy was, in
fact, quite horrid.

There was a mobile phone number with the message.
Using his home phone, Samuel dialled the number. The
phone was answered on the second ring.

'Hello?' said a man's voice. He sounded out of breath.

'Is that Doctor Planck?' asked Samuel.

'Indeed it is. Is that Samuel?'

'Yes. I got your e-mail.'

'Samuel, I'm rather busy right now.'

'Oh.'

'Yes. It appears that I'm being chased by a flying
skull.'

Before Samuel could say anything more, they were
cut off.

Mrs Johnson looked worried.

'Is everything all right?' she asked.

Samuel tried redialling the number, but there was no tone. He handed the phone to Tom.

'It's gone dead.'

'What did he say?'

'That he was being chased by a flying skull.'

'Oh,' said Tom. 'That's not good.'

But before he could say anything else, they heard the sound of glass breaking from somewhere downstairs.

'What was that?' said Mrs Johnson.

'It sounded like one of your windows breaking,' said Tom. He grabbed Samuel's cricket bat from beside the bedroom door. They listened, but could hear no further noise. Slowly they advanced down the hallway towards the stairs, Tom in the lead.

'Careful,' said Mrs Johnson. 'Oh, Samuel, I wish your dad was here.'

They were halfway to the stairs when a white object flew round the corner and then stopped in mid-air, its wings flapping just hard enough to keep it from falling to the floor. Its jaws never stopped snapping, opening wide enough for a moment to take a man's fist before its twin rows of sharp teeth closed on each other again. Two unblinking black eyes were set like dark jewels in its bony sockets.

'What. Is. *That*?' said Mrs Johnson.

'It looks like a skull. With wings,' said Samuel.

'What's it doing in our house?' said Mrs Johnson.

It was Maria who spoke. 'I think it's looking for us.'

As if in response, the wings of the chattering skull

began to beat faster. It changed its position slightly, then shot forward so fast that it was almost a blur. Samuel, Maria and Mrs Johnson dived to the floor, but Tom remained standing. Instinctively he drew back his bat and struck the flying skull when it was about two feet from his face. There was a loud *crack*! and the skull fell to the floor, its jaws still moving but with most of its teeth now knocked out. One wing had broken off, while the other was beating feebly against the carpet. Tom stood over it and hit it once again with the bat. The skull broke into fragments, the jaws ceased snapping, and its eyes went from black to a milky grey.

'Tom!' shouted Maria. 'Look out!'

A second skull appeared at the end of the hallway, followed by a third. The three children and Mrs Johnson backed away until they came to the wall. Tom took a few steps forward, tapped his bat on the carpet, and then took up a stance that would have been frowned upon on a cricket field, the bat raised to shoulder level, ready to strike.

'Tom,' said Mrs Johnson, pulling Samuel and Maria into the nearest bedroom. 'Please be careful!'

'I know what I'm doing,' said Tom. 'Right, then,' he shouted at the skulls. 'Come and have a go, if you think you're hard enough.'

The two skulls flew towards him at the same moment, one travelling slightly faster and lower than the other. Tom crouched and caught the lead skull with a perfect swing, the bat striking so hard that the skull immediately shattered into three pieces, but Tom wasn't quick enough to hit the second skull as well. He was forced to drop to the floor as it zoomed over his head and hit the wall, leaving a mark on the paintwork and dislodging a chunk of plaster. It seemed a little dazed by the contact, but recovered quickly and was preparing to attack again when Samuel flung a blue towel over it, blinding it.

'Now, Tom!' shouted Samuel.

Tom brought the bat down as hard as he could on the top of the skull. It dropped to the floor, still covered by the towel, and he struck at it until he had virtually flattened it.

Samuel, Maria and Mrs Johnson joined him, and all four of them stared at the remains of the skulls that now littered the hallway.

'Well,' said Samuel. 'I think it's begun.'

CHAPTER XIX

*In Which Assorted Foul Things Begin to Arrive,
and Nurd Discovers the Joys of Motoring*

Nurd felt his fingertips begin to tingle again, but this time he was ready. He was wearing an assortment of rusty armour, some of the few possessions he had been permitted to retain in exile, to protect himself from any unseen eventualities. Given that he was about to be torn out of one world and hurled into another, this meant just about every possible eventuality was unseen. Only his head remained uncovered because the helmet no longer fitted correctly.

'Maybe your head has swollen,' Wormwood had suggested somewhat unhelpfully as he tried for the third and last time to force the helmet over Nurd's ears.

Nurd had responded by hitting Wormwood with his sceptre.

'Now *your* head is swollen,' Nurd had replied. 'Leave the helmet. It must have taken a dent.'

The tingling spread to the rest of his body. It was time. Nurd wondered if he would get to see Samuel again. He hoped so. Samuel was the only creature who had ever been truly kind to Nurd and the memory of the boy's company made the demon smile. He was determined to become friends with Samuel, if he could avoid being crushed by household appliances or hit by trucks.

'Goodbye, Wormwood,' said Nurd. 'I'd like to say that I'll miss you, but I won't.'

With that he blinked out of existence, leaving Wormwood alone once again.

'Good riddance,' said Wormwood. 'I never liked you anyway.'

He looked around at the great Wasteland, which stretched emptily in every direction. He felt very lonely.

At CERN, the collider was generating impacts at a startling rate, creating a constant stream of explosions. As the collisions released their energy, the collider filled with more blue light.

In the main control room, Professor Hilbert and his team were frantically trying to turn the collider off, to no avail.

'We're not in control of it,' he told Professor Stefan, who was pacing anxiously in the manner of someone who sees his job about to go up in smoke. Given the amount of energy being given off by the collider, it wasn't the only thing in danger of doing so.

'If we aren't, then who is?' asked Professor Stefan.

Professor Hilbert reached for the volume button on the nearest computer, and turned it up to full. The control room filled with the sound of whispering: many voices speaking in an assortment of ancient tongues. Despite their panic, all activity ceased as the scientists listened, their faces betraying confusion, yet also curiosity. After all, this was fascinating! Dangerous, and very possibly fatal to all of mankind, but undoubtedly fascinating.

Then a single voice rose above the babble, a deep voice filled with aeons of loneliness and jealousy and rage. It spoke just two words.

'*It begins.*'

'I think,' said Professor Hilbert, his face pale, 'that *he* is.'

Nurd popped into existence again in the world of men just at the point where his body felt as though it were about to be crushed to the size of a pea. He immediately began running, wary of standing still for too long after what had happened to him on his previous visits. He got three steps before the ground disappeared beneath him, and he fell down an open manhole into a sewer.

There was a wail, then a splash, followed by a long, smelly silence.

Finally, Nurd's voice spoke from the darkness. He said, somewhat unhappily, 'I appear to be covered in poo.'

The portal in the Abernathys' basement was growing larger with every minute. The flying skulls had been followed by more demonic forms. Most were still primitive, and not very clever, but some of them were big and strong, and all of them were frightening to look at. Mrs Abernathy watched them stumble forth into the Halloween night to sow terror: a pair of pig demons, their snouts moist with mucus, great boar tusks on either side, their little eyes glinting with menace; three winged creatures with the bodies of lizards and the heads of beautiful women, their fingers tipped with nails of steel; and a quartet of horned devils, their bodies entirely black from shovelling coals into the fires of Hell, their eyes transformed into red orbs from centuries of staring into the flames. There were creatures that looked like fossils come to life, their insides protected by hard exoskeletons, carried along on short, plated legs. Others were warped versions of earthly animals, as though the beings emerging had once caught a brief but imperfect glimpse of life on this planet: goat-headed men with long, curved horns; beasts with the heads of dinosaurs and the torsos of mammals; and winged crocodiles with the tails of lions.

And then there were those that bore no resemblance to any living thing that had ever existed, pale, night-marish visions consisting of little more than legs and claws and teeth, with no urge other than to consume.

'Go,' said Mrs Abernathy. 'Begin our master's work. Kill and destroy until there is no building left standing, and nothing left alive. Turn this world to blood and ash. Make it smell of death.'[23]

They lumbered away, and Mrs Abernathy resumed her vigil at the portal. Through the mists she could see more forms approaching, more demons sent to prepare

---

[23] Mrs Abernathy did not like the smell of Earth. Her demonic senses made her acutely sensitive to all nice scents, so that she was even aware that the Milky Way itself smelled bad to her. Actually, astronomers who were recently sifting through thousands of signals from Sagittarius B2, a big dust cloud at the centre of our galaxy, found a substance there called ethyl formate, which is the chemical responsible for the flavour of raspberries and the smell of rum, the drink popular with pirates. Therefore, our galaxy tastes a bit of raspberries and smells of rum, which is nice.

the way for the Great Malevolence. Soon the gates would disintegrate entirely, and their master would be free at last, free to lead his great army into this world.

Nurd climbed from the sewer, unpleasant substances dripping from his armour. He had also managed to hurt his head and there was a large lump behind his left ear, but at least he was still in one piece.

He looked to his right and instantly forgot his aches and the nasty smells that were troubling his nostrils, and his plans to take over this place and rule it. In front of him was a sign that read BIDDLECOMBE CAR SALES. It stood on the roof of a building filled with a number of the small, fast metal things that ran on wheels. One of them, a blue one with stripes along the sides, was particularly lovely.

Nurd ran towards it with great joy, and smacked his face hard against the glass of the showroom. He stumbled back, his hand pressed to his nose. It was bleeding. The pain made his eyes water.

'Right,' said Nurd. 'That's it. No more Mr Nice Demon.'

Using an iron-booted foot, he smashed the glass. Somewhere a bell began to sound, but Nurd ignored it. He laid his hand on the fast blue stripy thing and stroked it lovingly, concentrating hard, trying to come to an understanding of what he was touching.

Car, he thought. Engine. Fuel. Keys.

Porsche.

He explored its workings in his mind until they became clear to him. There was a locked box in a small office at the back of the dealership. When he touched it, he knew that it held the keys to the cars. He ripped the door from it and instantly found the ones he wanted.

Porsche. Mine.

Minutes later, with a screech of tyres and the smell of burning rubber, Nurd was in car heaven.

CHAPTER XX

*In Which It Becomes Increasingly Clear
That the Demons Are Not Going to Have
Things All Their Own Way*

All across the town, some very strange things were starting to happen.

While Tom used flying skulls for cricket practice, a pair of old ladies were called rude names by a dark-eyed entity that appeared to be living in a drain. One of the old ladies poked at it with her umbrella until it gave up and went away, still calling out rude names, some of which she had never heard before but which, she was certain, were meant to be offensive. In her statement to local police some time later, she claimed that it 'looked and smelled like a big, diseased fish'.

Two men on their way to a Halloween party dressed as schoolboys – only grown-ups think that it's fun to dress up in school uniforms; young people, who have no choice in the matter, don't think it's fun at all – reported that a hunched shape resembling a lump of frog spawn, albeit frog spawn with arms like trumpets, was squatting on the roof of the hardware shop and 'absorbing pigeons'.

A taxi, or something that had taken the form of a taxi, stopped to pick up a young lady on Benson Road and subsequently tried to eat her. She escaped by spraying perfume into its mouth. 'At least,' she told a puzzled streetsweeper, 'I *think* it was its mouth.'

Meanwhile, in a house in Blackwood Grove, Stephanie, the babysitter so unbeloved of Samuel, heard noises coming from the wardrobe in her bedroom She approached it warily, wondering if a mouse might have become trapped inside, but when she opened the door she saw, not a mouse, but a very long, very thick snake. The snake, oddly, had elephant ears.

'Boo!' said the snake. 'Er, I mean, hiss.'

Stephanie promptly fainted. For a moment the snake looked pleased, or as pleased as a demon in the form of a snake can look, until it noticed that the girl had not been alone. There was now a large young man staring angrily into the wardrobe. The demon tried to discover some creature of which the young man was frightened in order to transform itself into the relevant animals, but the young man didn't appear to be afraid of anything. Instead he reached out and grabbed the demon by the neck.

'It's the ears, isn't it?' said the demon. 'I just can't seem to get those right.'

The young man leaned forward and whispered something threateningly into one of the ears in question.

'You know,' said the demon in reply, 'I don't think you can flush something all the way to China from here.'

As it turned out the demon was right: you couldn't flush something all the way from Biddlecombe to China.

Still, he had to give the young man credit.

He certainly tried.

* * *

Over in Lovecraft Grove, Mrs Mayer, Maria's mum, was washing the teatime dishes when she saw movement among the rose bushes in her back garden. The rose bushes were her husband's pride and joy. Mr Mayer was not a man with very green fingers. In fact he was the kind of man who, by and large, couldn't even grow weeds and yet something strange and wonderful had happened as soon as he put his mind to the cultivation of roses. When he and Mrs Mayer had bought the house in Lovecraft Grove, there had been a solitary, sad-looking rose bush at the end of the front garden. Somehow it had survived neglect, bad weather, and the deaths of the other rose bushes that had, judging by the rotting stumps surrounding it, once grown there. Mr Mayer seemed to find a soul mate in that rose bush, and was determined to save it. Mrs Mayer didn't hold out much hope, given her husband's previous forays into horticulture, but she held her tongue and did not suggest that he try a cactus instead.

So Mr Mayer had bought every book on the cultivation of roses that he could find. He consulted experts, and haunted garden centres, and lavished the little rose bush, Mrs Mayer sometimes felt, with more care and attention than he did his wife and children.

And in time the rose bush began to flourish. Mrs Mayer could still recall the morning when they had woken to find the first bud poking tentatively from its branches, soon to be followed by others that burst into bright red bloom. It was the only time she had ever seen her husband cry. His eyes shone and a pair of big, salty tears rolled down his cheeks, and she believed that she had loved him more in that moment than ever before.

Over the years, other bushes had been added to the garden. Mr Mayer had even begun hybridising, creating strange new flowers of his own. Now it was the experts who came to Mr Mayer, and he would make them mugs of strong tea and they would spend hours in the garden, in all weathers, examining the rose bushes. Mr Mayer was generous with both his expertise and the flowers themselves, and rarely did a visitor leave the garden without a cutting from one of the roses in his hand. Mr Mayer would watch them go, happy in the knowledge that the sisters and brothers of his roses would soon flourish in strange new gardens.

Only one bush was not permitted to be touched, the original one that Mr Mayer had found in the garden. Now big and strong, its flowers were the brightest and prettiest in the beds. It was Mr Mayer's pride and joy. If he could have taken it to bed with him each night to keep it warm in winter, then he would have, even if it meant being pricked occasionally by its thorns. That was how much Mr Mayer loved the rose bush.

Now there were shapes moving through the beds. It was foggy out, so Mrs Mayer could not discern precise forms, but they looked big. Teenage trick-or-treaters, she thought, pretending to be monsters. Silly sods. Her husband would have their hides.

'Barry!' she shouted. 'Bar-*eeeeee*!'

Oooh, he'd teach them a lesson, make no mistake about that.

Upstairs the Mayers' son, Christopher, was putting together a model aircraft at the desk by his bedroom window. Actually, he was sort of putting it together. He had been distracted by a message from his sister on his phone. It had been a bit garbled, but a few words had stood out. Those words had been 'monsters', 'Hell', 'demonic horde', and 'warn Mum and Dad'.

Christopher had not, of course, warned his mum and dad. He might have been younger than his sister, but he wasn't stupid. If he started babbling about demons and Hell to his dad he'd be locked up, or at the very least given a sound telling-off. Still, Maria had seemed very serious about it all. If it was a joke, she'd clearly been doing her best to convince her brother otherwise.

He was mulling over all this, and wondering how he was going to separate two parts of a tank that had accidentally stuck to each other, when he caught sight of the figures in the rose garden. Christopher's eyesight was very keen and, aided by a brief break in the fog, he had a different impression from his mum of the beings currently trampling his father's beloved bushes. They weren't trick-or-treaters, not unless trick or treaters had somehow found a way to grow seven feet tall, added spectacular horns to their heads, and contrived to make their eyes glow a deep, disturbing red.

'Crikey,' he said aloud. He *knew* that Maria hadn't been lying. Maria never lied.

It was the demonic horde. There really were demons here.

'Bar-*eeeeeeeeeeeee!*' Mrs Mayer called for the third time, just as her son burst into the kitchen.

'Mum!' he said. 'It's—'

'Not now, Christopher,' said Mrs Mayer. 'There are people trampling around in your dad's rose garden.' She walked to the end of the stairs and shouted: 'Barry! I'm talking to you.'

'What is it?' came an irritated voice from upstairs. 'I'm in the bathroom.'

'There's someone in your rose garden.'

'I said—'

'It's not people, Mum,' Christopher interrupted. 'It's things. It's the demonic horde.'

'The what?'

'The demonic *horde*.'

'Oh.' She walked to the kitchen door. 'Barry! Christopher says the demonic horde are in your rose garden. They must be a band or something.'

'What? In my rose garden?'

They heard scuffling from above and a toilet flushing. Seconds later, Mr Mayer appeared at the top of the stairs, fixing the belt on his trousers.

'I hope you washed your hands,' said Mrs Mayer.

'Washed my hands?' said Mr Mayer. 'I know what I'll do with my hands.'

Christopher's dad was a big man who had boxed at amateur level until he started to be knocked down too often for his liking. He now worked for the telephone company, and Christopher and his mum had once passed in the car while his father and another man who was nearly as big as him were together lifting wooden telephone poles, unaided by machinery. It was one of the most impressive sights Christopher had ever seen.

Unfortunately, while Mr Mayer might have been the equal of most men, and was still pretty good with his fists, Christopher didn't believe that he was fully aware of the threat currently making its way towards the house from the direction of the rose garden.

'Dad,' he said. 'I think you should hang on for a moment.'

'Hang on?' said his father incredulously. 'Hang on? There are roses at stake, son. Nobody, and I mean nobody, messes with my roses.'

'That's just it,' said Christopher, his frustration growing. Didn't anyone in this family listen? 'It's not a "body", it's a—'

But it was too late. His dad had flung open the back door, and was preparing to unleash the full force of his rage upon the unfortunates who had trespassed on the most sacred patch of his little empire. His face was bright red and his mouth was open, but no sound was coming out. Instead he was staring at the enormous demon standing five feet away from him. It looked like a hairy black yak that had managed to stand up on its hind legs and replace its hooves with hooked claws. Along the way it had clearly decided that chewing grass was infinitely less fun than chewing something much meatier, so its blunt vegetarian molars had been replaced with sharp, white, tearing teeth. Its eyes were bright red, and smoke was pouring from its nostrils. It drew back its lips and growled at Mr Mayer.

'Right,' said Mr Mayer. 'Well, we'll say no more about it, then.'

He closed the door and said, in a very small voice: 'Run.'

'Sorry, Barry?' said Mrs Mayer, whose view of what lay on the other side of the door had been blocked by her husband, and who was still under the impression that something needed to be done about the trick-or-treaters in their back garden.

'Run,' said Mr Mayer, in a slightly louder voice, then: 'RUN!'

A heavy body hit the back door very hard, rattling it in its frame. Mr Mayer grabbed his wife with one hand, his son with the other, and dragged them into the hallway just as the door burst from its hinges and landed on the kitchen floor. Mrs Mayer looked over her shoulder and screamed, but her scream was drowned out by a bellowing from behind them.

'It's OK, love,' said Mr Mayer, slamming the kitchen door, although he wasn't entirely sure how much good that would do, given what had just happened to the back door. 'Don't be frightened.' He didn't know why he was telling his wife not to be frightened, as there seemed a perfectly good reason to be very frightened, but that was what one did at times like this.

'Frightened?' said Mrs Mayer, yanking herself free from her husband's grasp and storming into the living room. 'I'm not frightened. That's a new kitchen, that is. I'm not just going to stand by while some bull *thing* destroys it.'

She moved with determination to the fireplace and picked up a poker.

'Mum,' said Christopher. 'It's a demon. I don't think a poker will hurt it.'

'It will where I'm going to put it,' said Mrs Mayer.

Mr Mayer looked at Christopher, and shrugged.

'You have to stop her, Dad,' said Christopher.

'I think I'd rather face the demon,' said Mr Mayer, as his wife pushed past him. 'You know your mum when she has her mind set on something.'

He grabbed a pair of coal tongs and followed his wife. From behind the kitchen door came another bellow, and the sound of dishes smashing on the tiled floor. Mrs Mayer entered the kitchen to find the demon standing amid the wreckage of her second-best crockery.

'Right, you!' said Mrs Mayer. 'That's quite enough of that.'

The demon turned, bared its teeth, and caught a poker straight between the eyes. It staggered slightly, then seemed about to recover itself when the next blow sent it to its knees. Meanwhile a second demon, smaller than the first, had just entered through the back door. Mr Mayer caught it by the snout with the coal tongs and twisted hard. The demon let out a pained howl as Mr Mayer forced it backwards and then, holding on to the tongs with his left hand, began to bang the demon across the head with a dustbin lid.

'That's.' *Crash!* 'For.' *Smash!* 'Messing.' *Thud!* 'Around.' *Whack!* 'With.' *Thump!* 'My.' *Whomp!* 'Roses!'

When he had finished, the demon lay unmoving upon the ground. The red light faded from its eyes before disappearing entirely. In the kitchen, Mrs Mayer was growing tired of hitting the demon with the poker, which was just as well as it had stopped moving some time before and its eyes had also gone dark.

Mr Mayer stood in the yard, the tongs in one hand, the dustbin lid in the other, like a knight of old, albeit one who couldn't afford proper weapons. From the rose garden, two more demons watched him warily as their fallen comrades began to disappear in wisps of foul-smelling purple smoke.

'Now listen here,' said Mr Mayer. 'I'm going to count to five and by then you'd better be off those roses, or you'll get what your friends got. One.'

While the demons had no idea what Mr Mayer was *saying*, they were smart enough to understand what he *meant*.

'Two.'

He began moving in their direction. Mrs Mayer appeared behind him, brandishing the poker. The demons exchanged a look and the universal nod of those who have decided that it would be a smart thing to make themselves very scarce as soon as demonically possible. They squatted down and with a single leap propelled themselves over the six-foot-high garden wall, then, their tails between their legs, promptly scarpered.

Mr Mayer walked to the rose garden where he stared down upon his beloved bushes, now trampled into the dirt. Only one remained standing: the original bush. It had survived everything that man and nature could throw at it, and it wasn't about to be crushed by any horde, demonic or otherwise.

Mr Mayer lay down his tong sword and dustbin-lid shield and patted its bare branches fondly.

'It's all right, little one,' he said. 'We'll start again come spring . . .'

CHAPTER XXI

*In Which The Verger Is Assaulted, and a Very
Unpleasant Person Comes Back to Life*

The vicar and verger were preparing the Church of St
Timidus for the following day's early-morning service
when they heard what sounded like a brick dislodging
from the stonework high above their heads and falling
to the ground outside. Both men looked a little concerned,
as well they might. The church was very old, and in a
poor state of repair. Reverend Ussher was always worried
about the roof falling in, or the brickwork collapsing.
Now it seemed that his worst fears were coming true.

'What was that?' he asked the verger. 'A slate falling?'

'It sounded a bit heavier than a slate,' said Mr
Berkeley, who was a fat little man. Both the vicar and
the verger were fat little men. They had played
Tweedledum and Tweedledee in the local drama society's
version of *Alice in Wonderland* earlier that year, and
very good they were too.

The two men went to the front door of the church
and unlocked it. They were about to step outside when
a small, stunned stone gargoyle staggered from a nearby
holly bush, its heavy wings beating slowly. It was a most
ugly creature, more so even than the average gargoyle.

Bishop Bernard the Bad had supervised its creation, just as he had every other detail of the church's construction. This explained why it was a dark, gloomy building, and why all of the faces and creatures carved on its stonework were hideous and scary.

The vicar and verger watched, open-mouthed, as the gargoyle rubbed its head. Small streaks of blue lightning flashed across its body. It coughed once, and spat out what looked like old pigeon feathers.

The gargoyle was very confused. It had wings, but it didn't seem able to fly. When it had come to life, the first thing it had done was attempt to soar elegantly into the air. Unfortunately, things made out of stone don't tend to soar terribly well, so the gargoyle had simply dropped off its perch. Even though it wasn't very intelligent, it knew the difference between flying and falling. It now also knew the difference between landing and just hitting the ground very hard.

More gargoyles, each one uglier than the last, began to descend upon the church lawns. One of them struck a tree and broke on impact, but most seemed to survive the drop more or less intact. Once they had recovered from their shock, they began to converge on the main door of the church where Reverend Ussher and Mr Berkeley were standing, rooted to the spot in amazement. They might have remained that way too, had the verger not been hit on the side of the head with a sharp piece of masonry.

'Oh, you're in trouble now,' said a voice. Mr Berkeley looked to his left and saw that the faces carved into the stonework of the church had also come to life, and the head of a monk, with a pair of hands supporting his chin, was talking to him. At least the hands should have been supporting his chin, but one of them had clearly just thrown a piece of brickwork at the verger's head.

The verger tapped the vicar's shoulder.

'The monk on the wall is talking to us,' he said.

'Oh,' said the vicar. He tried to sound surprised, but couldn't quite manage it.

'Oi,' said the stone monk. 'Fatties! I said, "You're in trouble now." '

'Why would that be?' asked the vicar, tearing his eyes away from the approaching gargoyles.

'End of the world,' said the stone monk. 'Hell is opening up. The Big Bad is coming. The Great Malevolence. Wouldn't want to be in your shoes. He doesn't like humans.'

The stone monk seemed to consider something for a moment.

'Actually he doesn't like anyone, but especially not humans.'

'I say,' said the vicar, 'you're part of the church's stonework. Aren't you supposed to be on our side?'

'Nah,' said the stone monk. 'Infused with the bishop's evil, we are. Couldn't be nice if we tried.'

'The bishop's evil?' said Reverend Ussher. He thought about that for a moment, until another piece of masonry was picked from the church and thrown hard at the verger, who did a little skip in order to avoid it.

'Oooh,' said the monk. 'Tubby's a dancer.'

'You're a nasty piece of stonework!' said the verger.

The monk stuck its fingers in its ears and blew a raspberry at him.

'Sticks and stones, Tubby,' it said. 'Sticks and stones . . .'

One of the gargoyles reached the vicar's foot, opened its mouth, and bit down hard. Fortunately the vicar had been working in his garden that afternoon and was still wearing his favourite steel-toed work boots. The gargoyle lost its fangs and immediately looked a bit sorry for itself.

'Inside,' said Reverend Ussher. 'Quickly!'

He and the verger retreated into the church and locked the door. Outside they could hear gargoyles beating against the wood and scratching at the hinges, but the door was very old and very thick and it would take more than a bunch of foot-high stone monsters to break it down.

'What do we do now?' asked the verger.

'We'll call the police,' said the vicar.

'And what'll we tell them?'

'That the church is under siege from gargoyles,' said the vicar, as if this was the most obvious thing in the world.

'Right,' said the verger. 'That'll work.'

But before he could say anything else he was distracted by another sound, like one stone rubbing against another, coming from the little room to the right of the main altar, used mainly to store old candlesticks, spare chairs and the verger's broken bicycle. The room was kept unlocked, since there was little in it that anyone would be bothered to steal. The floor was made entirely of stone, but one of the slabs had a name on it and this slab was now moving up and down, as though something was pushing at it from beneath.

After almost 900 years, Bishop Bernard the Bad had woken up.

CHAPTER XXII

*In Which the Forces of Law and Order
Take an Interest in Nurd*

Nurd was alternating between jubilation and absolute terror. He had discovered a crucial detail about fast cars: they can go fast. When he touched a foot to the accelerator the Porsche shot off like a speeding bullet and Nurd's braking technique, like his driving, left a lot to be desired. The first time Nurd braked, he bashed his face against the windscreen, since he had neglected to fasten his seat belt. Now his already injured nose had swollen painfully, and there was blood on his hands where he had tried to wipe it. He had thus confirmed an interesting, if alarming, fact about this world: while he was an immortal being, theoretically incapable of being killed, he could experience pain here. Pain and, if he wasn't careful, something a bit like death, except without the nice long rest afterwards. Still, he was having the time of his very long life, and the Wasteland and Wormwood seemed to belong to another, far-off era.

Not for the first time, a pair of red lights whizzed by on either side of the road. Sometimes those lights were green, or even amber, but Nurd liked the red ones best. They reminded him of the fires of Hell, fires that he might never have to see again if he could terrify this world, or even a little part of it, into submission. But before that there was more driving to be done.

A pair of flashing blue lights appeared in Nurd's rear-view mirror, accompanied by a howling noise. Despite his speed, they appeared to be drawing closer and closer. Hmmm, thought Nurd, I wonder what they are. Then the blue lights came near enough for him to see that they were stuck on the top of another car. Nurd wondered if the lights came in red. If they did, he might try to find some and stick them on the top of his car as well. They would look splendid.

The car with the flashing blue lights pulled alongside Nurd. It was white, with writing on the side, and wasn't even half as pretty as Nurd's car. There were two men in uniform in the car, one of whom was waving at Nurd. Not wishing to seem impolite, even if he was a demon, Nurd waved back. The men in the other car looked quite annoyed at this. Nurd suspected that perhaps he had given them the wrong wave, but he didn't know enough about the habits of this world to be sure of what might be the right variety.

The white car pulled ahead of him and then braked, forcing Nurd to slam his foot down hard on his own brake pedal. If his seat belt hadn't been fastened this time, Nurd would probably have gone through the windscreen. Instead the belt pulled him up short, winding him.

Now Nurd didn't know a lot about driving, but he could tell that the men in the white car had just performed a distinctly dangerous manoeuvre, and he had half a mind to tell them what he thought of them and their little blue lights. Then the two men got out of the car and put hats on, and a warning signal went off in Nurd's brain. He knew Authority when he saw it. His lips moved as he tried to read the word on the back of the car.

Po-lice.

One of the police tapped on Nurd's window while the other walked round the car, holding a notebook and still looking annoyed. Nurd found the button that rolled the window down.

'Evening, sir,' said the man at the window, wrinkling his nose at the unpleasant odour emerging from the vicinity of Nurd. Nurd saw that the man had three stripes on his shoulder. Nurd thought they looked very fetching.

'Hello,' said Nurd. 'Are you a police?'

'I prefer policeman, sir,' came the reply. 'That's quite the costume. Off to a fancy dress party, are we?'

Nurd didn't know what a fancy dress party was, but the policeman's tone of voice suggested that 'yes' might be a good answer.

'Yes,' said Nurd. 'A fancy dress party.'

'Any idea how fast you were going back there, sir?'

Oh, Nurd knew the answer to this one. He could tell from the little red numbers on the dashboard.

'One hundred and twelve miles per hour,' he said proudly. 'Very fast.'

'Oh, yes, very fast, sir. *Too* fast, one might say.'

Nurd thought about this. In his current mood, it didn't seem possible that one could go 'too fast'. There was just 'slow' and 'very fast'.

'No,' said Nurd. 'I don't think so.'

One of the policeman's eyebrows shot up like a startled crow.

'Can I see your licence, please, sir?'

'Licence?'

'Licence. Little piece of paper with a photograph of you on it without your Halloween mask, says you can drive a car, although in your case it might have a picture of a rocket ship on it as well.'

'I don't have a licence,' said Nurd. He frowned. He liked the sound of a piece of paper that said he could drive, although he couldn't imagine to whom he might show it, policemen aside. Wormwood might have been impressed by it, but Wormwood wasn't here.

'Oh dear, sir,' said the policeman, who had just been joined by his colleague. 'That's not good, is it?'

'No,' said Nurd. 'I'd like a licence.' He composed his monstrous features into something resembling a smile. 'You wouldn't have one that you could give me, would you? Even if it doesn't have my picture on, it would still be lovely to have.'

The policeman's face went very still.

'What's your name, sir?'

'Nurd,' said Nurd, then added, 'the Scourge of Five Deities.'

'Scourge of Five Motorways, more like,' said the second policeman.

'Very witty, Constable Peel,' said the first policeman. 'Very witty indeed.'

He returned his attention to Nurd. 'A foreign gentleman, are we, sir?' he said. 'Visiting, perhaps?'

'Yes,' said Nurd. 'Visiting.'

'From where, sir?'

'The Great Wasteland,' said Nurd.

'He's from the Midlands, then, Sarge,' said Constable Peel.

The one called Sarge hid a smile. 'That's enough, Constable. Don't want to offend anyone, do we?'

'Not only does he not have a licence, Sarge, he doesn't appear to have any licence plates,' said Peel.

Sarge frowned. 'Is this a new car, sir?'

'I think so,' said Nurd. 'It smells new.'

'Is it *your* car, sir?'

'It is now,' Nurd said.

Sarge took a step back. 'Right you are, sir. Step out of the car, please.'

Nurd did as he was told. He towered at least a foot above the two policemen.

'He's a big lad, Sarge,' said Peel. 'Don't know how he managed to fit in there in the first place. Mind you, he smells a bit off.'

Nurd had to admit that it had been a bit of a squeeze getting into the Porsche, but he was quite a squishy demon. Some demons were all hard bone, or thick shells. Nurd was softer, mainly because he hadn't taken any exercise in centuries.

'That's quite a costume you have there, sir,' said Sarge. 'What exactly are you supposed to be, then?'

'Nurd,' said Nurd. 'The Scourge of—'

'We got all that the first time,' said Sarge. 'Do you have *any* form of identification?'

Nurd concentrated. On his forehead, a mark began to glow a deep, fiery red. It looked like a capital 'B' that had been drawn by a very drunk person. Its appearance on his skin was accompanied by a faint smell of burning flesh.

'You don't see that very often, Sarge,' said Constable Peel. He looked quite impressed.

'No, you don't,' said Sarge. 'What exactly is that supposed to be, sir?'

'It is the mark of Nurd,' said Nurd.

'He's a nutter, Sarge,' said Constable Peel. 'Nurd the Nutter.'

Sarge sighed. 'We'd like you to come along with us, sir, if you don't mind.'

'Can I bring my car?' said Nurd.

'We'll leave, er, *your* car here for the moment, sir. You can come along with us in ours.'

'It's got pretty lights on the top,' explained Constable Peel helpfully. 'And it makes a noise.'

Nurd looked at the policemen's car. It still wasn't as nice as his, not by a long shot, but it was different, and Nurd felt that he should be open to new experiences, especially having spent so long in the Wasteland with no new experiences at all, some curious noises from Wormwood apart.

'All right,' he said. 'I will travel in your car.'

'There's a good Nurd,' said Constable Peel, opening one of the rear doors. Nurd got the uncomfortable feeling that Constable Peel was making fun of him. Constable Peel also made sure to keep the windows rolled down in order to let the smell out of the car.

'When I assume my throne,' said Nurd, 'and I rule this world, you shall be my slave, and your life will be one of pain and misery until I choose to end it by turning you to a small mass of red jelly that I will crush beneath my heel.'

Constable Peel looked hurt as he closed the door behind Nurd. 'That's not very nice,' he said. 'Sarge, Mr Nurd here is threatening to turn me to jelly.'

'Really?' said Sarge. 'What flavour?'

Then, with Nurd squashed in the back, they began the drive back to the station.

CHAPTER XXIII

In Which We Learn That One Should Be Careful About Accepting Anything That Is Offered For Nothing

The Fig and Parrot pub was well known in the village for its Halloween celebrations. The owners, Meg and Billy, decorated it with cobwebs, skeletons and other ghoulish oddities. The grass square outside the pub's main doors was dotted with polystyrene tombstones, and a noose dangled from the thickest branch of the old oak tree at its centre, the rope tight round the neck of a scarecrow.

Inside the festivities were in full swing, as Meg and Billy had arranged for the local brewery, Spiggit's, to offer free pints to those who arrived in fancy dress, and there was nothing that the regulars at the Fig and Parrot appreciated more than free pints. Hence, everyone had made an effort at dressing up, even if, in the case of Mangy Old Bob (as he was known to most people except Mangy Old Bob himself), it consisted of nothing more than sticking a sprig of holly on his hat and claiming to be the Spirit of Christmas. For the most part, the villagers in attendance favoured the old reliables and had come dressed as vampires, ghosts, mummies wrapped in bandages and toilet paper, and the odd French maid. The

French maids were not, it must be said, terribly frightening, except for Mrs Minsky, who was a very large lady, and who had not been constructed to occupy anything as small and frilly as a French maid's outfit.

The two demons who approached the Fig and Parrot that night were not intellectually gifted. This was true of most of the demons that had so far poured through the interdimensional doorway into the village. They were foot soldiers, nothing more. The real horrors had yet to come. This was not to say that the demons who were already in place were not terrifying. Seen in the right light and at an unexpected moment, they might have proved bed-wettingly frightening. Unfortunately, as Nurd had recently discovered, they had arrived on the one evening of the year when lots of people were doing their utmost to look as frightening as possible, and therefore a great many of the demons were simply blending in.

The two demons in question were called Shan and Gath. Facially they resembled warthogs, although their bodies were those of men, albeit rather overweight ones whose leather clothing was a couple of sizes too small for them. Their eyes, like those of a great number of the other minor hellish entities currently exploring the village and its environs, glowed a deep red from exposure to the fiery pits of Hades. Large tusks jutted over their snouts from their bottom jaws, and their heads and faces were covered in short, rough hair. They had two thick fingers on each hand, but no thumbs. They were clumsy, vicious creatures, intent only on doing harm to whomever happened to come their way.

The girl employed by Spiggit's to hand out the free-beer

vouchers, a young lady named Melody Prossett, was currently dressed as a pink fairy and wearing a very short dress, a disguise that did little to hide the fact that Melody was jolly lovely. Melody was studying the history of art at the local university, which made few demands upon her time or, it must be said, her intelligence, which was probably just as well. Melody was as sweet and beautiful as – oh, all right then – as a melody, but she was by no means the brightest bulb in the box. In fact, even a box of very dark bulbs buried in a windowless coal shed might have given Melody some competition in the brightness stakes.

Thus it was that, when Shan and Gath entered the Fig and Parrot, the first person they encountered was Melody Prossett.

'Guys, what great outfits!' Melody shouted. Shan and Gath looked as confused as only a pair of destruction-bent demons can look when faced by a leggy fairy with a cardboard wand. Admittedly, thought Melody, the new arrivals smelled a bit odd (even worse than Mangy Old Bob, who could kill flies with his breath and had mould in his armpits) but perhaps it had something to do with whatever they had used to make their costumes. Then again, those hog heads were very realistic. Melody wondered if they had somehow managed to hollow out real hog heads and fit them over their own. If so, she admired their efforts, although it wasn't something that she would have been inclined to do, not for all the beer in Spiggit's brewery.

Somewhat awkwardly, she managed to fit six vouchers into the demons' cloven hands.

'I'm only supposed to give you one each,' she whispered conspiratorially, 'but you've gone to such trouble . . .'

Shan raised the vouchers to his snout and sniffed them warily.

'Urk?' he said.

'Oh, I expect you're having trouble seeing through your mask,' said Melody. 'The bar's over here. Let me give you a hand.'

She took each demon by an arm and began to steer them towards the bar. Along the way Shan and Gath passed an assortment of beings – vampires, ghouls and the like – that looked vaguely familiar from the depths of Hell. Somewhere in their tiny minds they began to wonder if they might, possibly, have been better employed elsewhere, given that this place seemed to have plenty of foul creatures to be getting along with. Unfortunately they were now firmly in the grip of Melody Prossett, who was determined to be as helpful as possible, because that was the kind of girl she was. Melody Prossett was so helpful that people, even quite elderly people, often ran fast in the opposite direction when they saw her coming, just to avoid Melody's irritating helpfulness.

'Now, each voucher entitles you to a free pint of Spiggit's Old Peculiar,' Melody explained. 'It's new! I've tasted it and it's wonderful.'

This was not entirely true. Spiggit's Old Peculiar was indeed very new, but Melody had not, in fact, tasted it. She had put it close to her nose and decided that it smelled like something a cat might have done; a cat, furthermore, that wasn't feeling at all well. It had also scorched her nasal hairs and when a drop fell on her hand it had turned her skin a funny colour.[24]

Spiggit's Old Peculiar was an aptly named beer. Even those at the brewery who rather liked it took the view that something needed to be done about its nose (the technical term for its smell) and, while the brewers were about it, perhaps its taste, which veered somewhere between 'not very nice' and 'quite nasty', and the fact that, if left too long on the skin, it tended to burn. It was, though, quite amazingly strong, and after the first sip issues of flavour tended to be forgotten, since Spiggit's Old Peculiar managed temporarily to deaden the drinker's taste buds, leaving only the sensation that he had just accidentally consumed a naked flame. Fortunately that sensation was quickly replaced by one of complete intoxication and a sense of goodwill towards anyone within hugging distance until, after a second pint, he fell over and went to sleep.

Shan and Gath had never tasted alcohol of any kind. Given that they were demons, and therefore not troubled by normal appetites, they had never eaten anything other than the odd chunk of coal or grit, and occasionally

---

[24] Be wary of anything that is offered to you for nothing, especially if it is a new product that the makers are anxious to test. Usually, they will have discovered that the bunny rabbits, dogs, or iron-stomached employees who have already tried it have not died or gone blind as a result, and therefore it's about time to try it on people who might, at some point, be expected to pay for it. Unless you've always wanted to be a human guinea pig, it might be wise to think twice before saying yes to something that a stranger hands to you with a smile, free of charge, especially if there is a doctor or a lawyer hovering nervously nearby.

other, smaller demons, although mostly they preferred to chew them and spit them out. So, when Meg handed them their first free pints, carefully removing two vouchers from their misshapen fists along the way, they just stared at them suspiciously to begin with. Gath was about to shatter the glasses and start being properly demonic when Shan noticed a vampire take a long drink from a similar glass. For a moment the vampire looked as though he had just been hit through the heart with a large stake, as the unusual taste of Spiggit's Old Peculiar seared his mouth and erased a few memories. Then a strange, happy smile appeared on his face and he hugged the nearest mummy.

Shan lifted the glass to his snout and sniffed. Shan was used to the stench of Hell itself, but whatever was in the glass still smelled a bit odd, even to him. He took a tentative sip.

Something exploded in Shan's head, and he looked around to see who had hit him and then poked him in the eyes. As his vision began to return and he found there was nobody nearby, Shan realised that it was the stuff in the glass that had somehow managed to hit him. He was considering throwing it at the wall and laying waste to all around him when he started to feel very mellow. He took another sip, longer this time. Now Gath raised his glass and drank. He staggered a bit when the beer began knocking out brain cells, and almost fell over.

'Hurh, hurh,' said Shan. It was a sound that he had never made before and it took him a while to recognise it as laughter.

'Hurh, hurh,' said Gath, as he too began to recover.

They drank some more. Someone began playing the piano. Meg and Billy began dispensing free chips, and Shan and Gath got their first taste of greasy, deep-fried potato. Gath put an arm round Shan. Shan was his best mate. He loved Shan. No, he *really* loved Shan.

They moved on to their second pints of Spiggit's Old Peculiar, and all thoughts of world domination faded away.

Meanwhile, back at Crowley Avenue, Mrs Abernathy was unhappy. The destruction of the flying skulls she had sent after Samuel Johnson and his friends had not gone unnoticed, for each demon that passed through the portal was linked to Mrs Abernathy's consciousness, so she could see through their eyes and assess the progress of the invasion. She was also aware that two hellbulls had been beaten into non-existence with household implements over what appeared to be some trampled rose bushes, but that was not a primary concern. Increasingly, she found herself infuriated by the Johnson boy. Why couldn't he simply die? After all, he was just a child. His continued refusal to accept his fate was like a splinter under one of her fingernails.

She recalled something she had learned from her interrogation, and subsequent torture, of the demon that had so unsuccessfully occupied the space under Samuel Johnson's bed, and her unhappiness began to ease.

Oh yes, she thought, I know what frightens you, little boy.

She closed her eyes, and her lips moved as she issued her summons.

CHAPTER XXIV

In Which Nurd Puts On an Unexpected Show For the Police

The call came through on the police car's radio while Nurd, Constable Peel, and the Sarge, whose name Nurd had now learned was Rowan, were still some way from the station.

'Base to Tango One, Base to Tango One. Over,' said a male voice. It sounded somewhat panicked.

'This is Tango One,' said Sergeant Rowan. 'Everything all right back there, Constable Wayne? Over.'

'Er, not exactly, Sarge,' said Constable Wayne. 'Over,' he added, with a tremor in his voice.

'Clarify the situation, Constable, there's a good lad,' said Sergeant Rowan. 'Over.'

'Well, Sarge, we're under attack. Over.'

Sergeant Rowan and Constable Peel exchanged a look. 'What do you mean, attack? Over.'

'We're being attacked by flying women, Sarge. With the bodies of lizards . . .'

Biddlecombe's police station was a small building set in a field on the outskirts of the town. It had replaced an older building on the main street that had become infested with rats, and which was now a chip shop that nobody frequented unless they were very drunk, or very hungry, or rats visiting their relatives. The station consisted of a small waiting area and a large desk, behind which was an open-plan office and a single cell that was rarely used for prisoners; currently it was filled with Christmas decorations and an artificial tree.

The village had only six policemen, two of whom would usually be on duty at any one time. On this particular night four were on duty, as it was Halloween and people tended to get up to all sorts of mischief involving fireworks and, occasionally, fires.

PC Wayne and WPC Hay were currently holding the fort at the station. 'Holding the fort' is usually a turn of phrase, a bit like 'manning the barricades' or 'fighting a losing battle'. In other words, people use it to describe perfectly mundane situations, like staying at home on a cold night, or keeping an eye on the local shop while the shopkeeper goes for a wee.

Unfortunately PCs Wayne and Hay were now *literally* holding the fort, *literally* manning the barricades and also *literally* fighting a losing battle. The first of the flying lizard women had appeared in the station car park while PC Wayne was having a crafty smoke outside, almost causing him to swallow his cigarette in shock. The woman had a green saurian body and long sharp nails. Her wings were like those of a bat, with curved talons in the middle and at the ends, and she had a long tail that terminated in a vicious-looking spike. Her hair was dark and flowing, and for a moment Constable Wayne thought that she wasn't bad-looking, the whole lizard body and wings thing excepted. Then she opened her mouth and a forked black tongue flicked at the air between the kind of jagged yellow teeth that crop up in dentists' nightmares, and any thoughts of dating her vanished from Constable Wayne's mind.

At that point Constable Wayne decided that the best course of action would be to head back inside and lock the door, which is precisely what he did. There was a large bolt and he pulled that across as well, just to be sure.

'What are you doing that for?' asked Constable Hay. 'The sarge will spit nails if he comes back and finds that you've locked the front door.'

Constable Hay was small and blonde, and Constable Wayne was a little in love with her. He had always thought she was very pretty, but now, after being confronted with a woman who appeared to be made up of bits of other creatures that really didn't belong together, he decided that Constable Hay was quite possibly the loveliest girl in the world.

'There's a woman outside,' said Constable Wayne. 'With wings. And a tail.'

'It's Halloween,' said Constable Hay slowly, as though she were talking to an idiot. She liked Constable Wayne, but he really could be very thick sometimes. 'On my way here, I saw a man dressed as a toadstool.'

'No, this isn't a woman dressed up to look like she has wings and a tail. She *does* have wings and a tail.'

There was a massive *thud* on the door. Constable Wayne backed away from it.

'That's her,' he said. 'The lizard lady.'

'Lizard lady,' said Constable Hay dismissively. 'You'll be telling me she can fly next.'

A woman's face appeared at the barred window to the right of the door. Constable Hay walked determinedly towards it, her finger wagging.

'Now listen here, miss, it may be Halloween but we'll have no more nonsense or . . .'

She stopped talking when she noticed that the woman was hovering two feet from the ground, her huge wings flapping hard to keep her in place. Then, bracing her feet against the outside wall, the flying woman gripped two of the bars with her claws and tried to pull them from the wall.

'See?' said Constable Wayne. 'I told you so.'

From above their heads came the sound of something landing on the roof. Seconds later the first of the slates began to fall into the car park as whatever it was tried to force its way into the station.

'Call the sarge,' said Constable Hay.

Constable Wayne ran to the radio. 'Where are you going?' he asked, as Constable Hay ran past him.

'To lock the back door!'

Inside the police car there was a long pause followed Constable Wayne's description of the attackers. Constable Peel made a gesture of someone drinking from a bottle, followed by an imitation of that same someone being very drunk. Then they heard the sound of glass breaking.

'Constable, what's that noise? Have you been drinking?' said Sergeant Rowan. 'Over.'

'I wish I had,' said Constable Wayne. 'One of them

has broken the front window and there's another on the roof. Oh, crikey: the back door. Get here, Sarge, quickly. Please! We need help. Er, over. Over and out.'

The woman at the window had injured herself breaking the glass, and black blood now covered the shattered pane, but the bars had held. The woman appeared to give up, and flew upwards. Constable Wayne heard her land on the roof and then followed the sound of her footsteps as she ran across it in the direction of the rear of the station. There, Constable Hay was using the full force of her body to try to force the back door closed when Constable Wayne joined her. The problem quickly became apparent: a claw was clutching at the door as the thing outside tried to push its way in. The gap widened slightly and a gnarled foot appeared, and then Constable Wayne saw one of those terrible female faces pressed against the wood, its teeth bared.

'Help me!' cried Constable Hay. 'I can't hold it much longer.'

Constable Wayne reached for his truncheon and began using it to smack the creature on the knuckles. It screeched in pain and withdrew the claw, but its foot remained in place. Constable Wayne tried stamping on it with his size 11 shoes. Its claw appeared again, slashing at him.

'Hold the door!' said Constable Hay, and suddenly Constable Wayne was alone, with only his weight to keep the creature at bay.

'Where are you going?' he cried.

'Just hold it. I have an idea.'

It had better be a great one, thought Constable Wayne, as he heard more footsteps above his head, followed by the sound of flapping wings as a second creature flew down to aid the first.

'Oh no,' said Constable Wayne to himself. 'That's not good. That's not good at—'

The door was struck with such force that Constable Wayne was flung head first across the room. He scrambled to his feet in time to see two of the lizard women trying to force their way through the narrow door at the same time and getting tangled up in each other's wings along the way. Then the larger of the pair pushed aside her smaller sister and stalked inside, her claws raised and her mouth open wide as she advanced on Constable Wayne.

Constable Hay appeared beside the demon, her arm outstretched and a small bottle in her hand.

'Hey!' she said. 'Over here.'

The winged woman turned, and Constable Hay sprayed perfume straight into her eyes. She screeched and tried to rub at the irritant, but that just made things worse. At the same time Constable Wayne picked up a hat-stand and swung it at the second demon, which was trying to sneak round her sister. The hat-stand caught the demon a vicious blow on the side of the head. She reeled away, stunned but still dangerous. Constable Wayne, now using the hat-stand like a spear, began poking at her, forcing her back outside. Meanwhile Constable Hay continued to spray perfume mercilessly into the first demon's face until she stumbled blindly towards the door. Constable Wayne helped her on her way with a sharp kick to the behind, then slammed the door closed.

A series of loud shrieks came from outside and the two coppers watched through a window as the lizard women ascended into the night sky, off to seek easier prey.

'Great,' said Constable Wayne. 'The sarge will never believe us now . . .'

Sergeant Rowan had just hit the lights and Constable Peel was about to put his foot on the accelerator when Nurd tapped on the sheet of toughened plastic that partially separated him from the men in the front seats. He had heard the exchange over the radio and he had also noticed some things that the policemen had not. The first were the little tendrils of blue energy that were shooting across a field in the direction of what looked like a nearby church.

The second was a small being about two feet in height that appeared to be little more than a yellow ball on legs, although most yellow balls didn't have two mouths and a multitude of eyeballs. The yellow ball was chasing a rabbit, which jumped down a burrow, the ball in hot pursuit. Unfortunately for the ball, the hole was smaller than it was and now it seemed to be stuck, its stumpy legs waving wildly.

This isn't a positive development, thought Nurd. He recalled what Samuel had told him about the woman in the basement and about her friends who no longer seemed to be human. Nurd had been hoping that Samuel was mistaken, or that the four people, or demons, or whatever they were, might just have conveniently vanished, or returned home. Now there were yellow balls with eyes chasing rabbits, which disturbed him greatly. It's all very well if I'm the only demon here, he mused, but if there are lots of demons, then there could be problems. And that blue energy, that wasn't just regular old electricity, or even average transdimensional residue. No, it was energy of a very particular kind . . .

Nurd had once glimpsed the Great Malevolence. It was shortly before Nurd's banishment, and he had been summoned to the Great Malevolence's lair to be dealt with by his most trusted lieutenant, the ferocious demon named Ba'al. In the darkness behind Ba'al a huge shape had lurked, taller than the tallest building, wider than the greatest chasm and for an instant Nurd had seen his face: eyes so red that they were almost black, great fanged jaws and a horned crown upon his head that seemed to have grown out from his skull. The sight had so frightened Nurd that he had almost welcomed his banishment, for there could have been worse punishments. He could have been taken by the Great Malevolence himself deep into his lair, there to be slowly torn apart for eternity, always suffering and never dying. Compared to that prospect, banishment was a doddle.

But there was one other thing that he recalled about the Great Malevolence: the contours of his body had rippled with blue energy. It was his power made visible, and now it was here. On Earth. Where Nurd was and, most certainly, was not supposed to be.

'Hello?' he said, knocking on the glass again. 'I think there's been some mistake.'

'Not now, sir,' said Sergeant Rowan. 'We're a bit busy.'

'You don't understand,' said Nurd. 'I'd really like to go home. You can forget about the car. Actually you can have it. I don't want it.'

'I'm not sure that it's yours to give away, sir. Now you'll have to be quiet. We're a little concerned about our colleagues at the station.'

Nurd sat back in his seat. 'This isn't a disguise,' he said softly.

The two policemen ignored him.

Nurd said it again, louder this time. 'This isn't a disguise!'

'Beg your pardon, sir?' said the sergeant.

'Look, I'm not wearing a costume. This isn't "fancy dress." This is me.'

'Very droll, sir,' said the sergeant.

'If it was a costume,' said Nurd patiently, 'could I do this?'

Nurd's head split evenly in half down the centre, exposing his skull. His eyes popped from their sockets, extended themselves on lengths of pink flesh, and examined Sergeant Rowan very intently. Then Nurd's skull separated, revealing his brain. It was held in place by twelve curved purple muscles, which immediately stood upright and wiggled. Finally Nurd stuck out his tongue, which was three feet long at its fullest extension. The top of the tongue had a hole in it, through which Nurd played a short fanfare before restoring his head to its regular form.

Constable Peel drove off the road. He braked

suddenly, and both he and Sergeant Rowan jumped from the car and backed away from it.

'Sarge,' stammered Constable Peel. 'He's a m –, he's a mo –, he's a mons –'

'Yes, he is, Constable,' said Sergeant Rowan, trying to sound calmer than he felt.

'Demon, actually,' said Nurd, shouting to make himself heard. 'Don't mean to be fussy about it, but there's a big difference.'

'What are you –?'

'– doing here?' Nurd finished for him. 'Well, I was going to try to conquer your world and rule it for eternity, but I don't think that'll happen now.'

'Why not?' asked Sergeant Rowan, carefully drawing a little closer to the car once more.

'Funny you should ask, but someone else has his eye on this place, and I don't think he'll fancy any competition. I'd really prefer not to be around when he gets here, so if you could see your way clear to letting me out, I'll be about my business.'

Sergeant Rowan stared at Nurd. Nurd smiled back politely.

'What exactly is happening?' asked Sergeant Rowan.

'Well, it's just a guess,' said Nurd, 'but I think it's the end of the world as you know it . . .'

CHAPTER XXV

In Which Bishop Bernard the Bad Makes His Presence Felt, and the Dead Rise From Their Graves, But Only the Nasty Ones

Maria, Tom, Samuel, and Samuel's mother watched from the darkened house as all manner of infernal creatures slid, jumped, flew or crawled from the direction of 666 Crowley Avenue, where a blue light hung over the adjoining rooftops. They had already been forced to fend off two further attacks, the first from a pair of foot-long slug demons with mosquito-like probosces for sucking blood, which had oozed through the letter box, the slime trail behind them eating away at the carpet as they approached their intended victims. The judicious use of a container of table salt had caused them to dry up into withered husks before disappearing in a puff of smoke.

The second attack was still ongoing, as the house was being buzzed by a pair of giant flies with jaws in their bellies. They struck the windows occasionally, the hooked teeth in their abdomens leaving marks upon the glass, their pink saliva staining it like watery blood. Mrs Johnson monitored their attempts to gain entry, a can of fly spray in each hand. All things considered, Samuel thought she was coping very well with being confronted by demons, but he also felt angry at something she had said earlier. She had wished his dad was with them and for a moment, when he first saw the flying skulls, Samuel had wished that too, but now he no longer felt the same way. He had suggested using salt on the slugs, he had found the fly spray hidden away in the back of a cupboard. With Tom's help, he had secured all the doors and windows, and set up a system of watches so that, between the three children and Samuel's mother, they were able to keep an eye on all the approaches to the house. For the first time since his dad had left, Samuel was starting to feel that if necessary he could look after both his mother and himself.

What he couldn't do, it seemed, was stop Mrs Abernathy. They were trapped inside the house, and they had heard nothing further from Dr Planck.

Soon, Samuel feared, all would be lost.

Back at the parish church of St Timidus, the thumping sounds continued from what should have been the final resting place of Bishop Bernard the Bad but clearly wasn't, since the last thing Bishop Bernard the Bad appeared to be doing was resting. Clouds of dust rose from the stone bearing his name and the dates of his birth and death. One end lifted from the floor. It hung in the air and the vicar and verger could almost feel the dead man below straining to move it higher, but then the stone fell down again and all was quiet.

'He's very strong,' said the verger, as he and Reverend Ussher peered through the small window in the door. He was quite surprised. After all, Bishop Bernard couldn't have been much more than a collection of old bones, and old bones tended to break easily. They shouldn't have been able to move huge slabs of stone. It just wasn't right.

'Limestone,' said the vicar.

'Beg your pardon?'

'The rock beneath the church is limestone,' said the vicar. 'Limestone preserves bodies. Not just that: it mummifies them. Bishop Bernard has been down there for a long, long time. I suspect that, if you were to touch him, his bones would feel as hard as rock.'

'I don't want to touch him,' said Mr Berkeley. 'I really don't.'

The burial slab began to move again, but this time it rose and didn't fall. A skeletal hand emerged from the crack and tried to get a grip on the edge of the stone.

'You may not want to touch him,' said the vicar, 'but I suspect that he would very much like to get his hands on you.'

Reverend Ussher opened the door of the little room and threw himself on the stone, hoping that his weight would push it back down. His right hand reached out and found the verger's bicycle pump, and with it he began hitting Bishop Bernard on the fingers. It took four or five strikes, but eventually the bishop was forced to release his grip. The stone slammed back down and there was silence once more.

'Quick!' said the vicar. 'Give me some help here.'

Reluctantly Mr Berkeley joined him. In one corner of the room was an old stone statue of St Timidus. It had fallen from its plinth beside the front door of the church the previous winter and its right hand had dropped off. There hadn't been enough money to repair it, or the plinth, so it had joined the old bicycle and the chairs in the storage room. With some difficulty, the vicar and the verger together managed to move the statue onto Bishop Bernard's marker stone.

'There,' said the vicar. 'That should keep him occupied for a while.'

The verger leaned against the wall as he tried to get his breath back.

'But why is all this happening now?' he asked.

'I don't know,' said the vicar. 'I don't even know what all "this" is.'

'Do you really think it's like the monk said: the end of the world?'

'I think the end of the world is some way off yet, Mr Berkeley,' said the vicar. He tried to sound confident, but he didn't feel it. This was all very disturbing: gargoyles running about on the church lawn; Bishop Bernard the Bad attempting to escape from his tomb. If it wasn't quite the end of the world, it might well be the *beginning* of the end.

Bishop Bernard began pounding on the floor once again.

'Oh, I do wish he'd stop that,' said the verger. 'He's giving me a headache.'

He knelt on the floor then put his mouth near the stone.

'Now, Bishop Bernard, Your Excellency, be a nice bishop and go to sleep,' he said. 'There's been a bit of a misunderstanding, but we'll get everything sorted out and you can go back to being dead. That sounds lovely, doesn't it? You don't want to be up here in the land of the living. It's all changed since your time. There's pop music, and computers, and, you know, you won't be able to go around sticking hot pokers up people, because that's not allowed any more, not even for bishops. No, you're much better off where you are, believe you me.'

The verger looked at the vicar, then nodded and smiled.

'See,' said the verger. 'All he needed was for someone to have a quiet word with him.'

There came a muffled roar of rage, and then the thud of stone upon stone as Bishop Bernard flung himself, hard, upwards. The statue of St Timidus shifted slightly.

'Oh, wonderful, Mr Berkeley,' said the vicar. 'That was most helpful!'

Bishop Bernard attacked the stone again, and the statue moved a little more. The verger tried to hold on to it, but it was no use. He gave up and retreated to the window.

'We should make a break for it,' said the vicar. 'Those gargoyles seemed rather clumsy and slow. We can easily outrun them, and my car is parked round the back.'

But the verger didn't appear to be listening. Instead, he was looking out of a small side window.

'I say, Mr Berkeley,' said the vicar. 'Did you hear what I said? I think we should run for it.'

'I don't think that would be a good idea, Vicar,' said the verger.

'And why is that?' asked the vicar, now quite annoyed that his plan had been shot down without even a discussion.

The verger turned to him, his face white.

'Because I think the dead are coming back to life,' he said. 'And not the nice ones . . .'

The Church of St Timidus had been in its present location for centuries. Much of its grounds were taken up with old gravestones because, for many generations, the people of the town had been buried beside the church when they died.

Unfortunately, not *everybody* had been buried under the church lawn. Church grounds were known as 'consecrated', which meant that they had been set aside for holy use. But people who committed serious crimes and were executed for them were not allowed to be buried on consecrated ground. For that reason a second graveyard existed not far from the old church, though beyond its walls. No gravestones were placed there and no markers, but everybody knew of it. The townspeople called it the Dead Field and nobody built houses on it, or walked their dogs there, or had picnics on its grass during the summer. Even birds didn't nest in its bushes and trees. It was, everybody felt, a Bad Place.

Now, as the vicar and verger watched, shambling shapes began to emerge from the Dead Field, their progress lit by the lights of the church grounds. Some still wore the tattered remains of old clothing, although there was precious little of it left. Thankfully, their modesty was preserved by the fact that most of them were just bones. The verger saw one skeleton with part of a rope round its neck and knew that here was someone who had been hanged. The end of the rope dangled at its chest, a bit like a necktie. Another skeleton appeared to have lost both its arms. It tripped on a stone and couldn't get back up, so instead began to wriggle its way along the ground, like a bony worm with legs. Occasionally, flashes of blue light were visible in otherwise empty eye sockets.

'I wonder what that blue light is?' said the vicar.

'Maybe they've stuck candles in there,' said the verger sarcastically. 'After all, it is Halloween.'

'Well, we can't go outside now,' said the vicar, ignoring him.

'No, we can't,' said the verger.

And from beneath their feet came what sounded like laughter.

CHAPTER XXVI

In Which Constable Peel Wishes He
Had Pursued Some Other Profession, and
Dr Planck Reappears

Constable Peel and Sergeant Rowan were debating their options. They could a) let Nurd go, which didn't seem like a very good idea given that he was, quite clearly, not a human being and also, if he was to be believed, a demon; b) take Nurd back to the police station and wait for someone with a little more authority to decide what should be done with him; or c) this was Constable Peel's suggestion, run away, because Constable Peel didn't want to see Nurd do that thing with his head again. It had made him feel quite ill.

'He's a demon, Sarge, and he doesn't half smell bad,' said Constable Peel. 'I'm not sure I want to be driving around with a stinky demon in the back of the car.'

'Hello,' said Nurd through the open car window. 'I can hear you. Less of the stinky, please. I fell down a hole.'

'You *have* been driving around with a stinky demon in the back of the car,' Sergeant Rowan replied, trying to ignore Nurd. 'Nothing happened.'

'"Nothing *happened*?"' said Constable Peel. 'His head split open, Sarge. His tongue played a *tune*. I don't know how you usually spend your evenings, but in my book that counts as "something" happening.'

'Careful now, son, you're getting worked up over . . .'

He almost said 'nothing', then realised this might not be entirely helpful, given Constable Peel's current mood.

'. . . over, um . . .'

Constable Peel folded his arms and waited, then said, 'Over what, exactly, Sarge?'

'. . . over . . .'

'. . . over . . . a, let me see, demon in the back of the car?' finished Constable Peel. 'That about covers it, I think. Oh, and he says the world is coming to an end. That qualifies as "something" too.'

'Well, there you have it, then,' said Sergeant Rowan. 'We can't just sit around doing nothing while the world is coming to an end.'

'So what are we going to do, Sarge?'

'We're going to put a stop to it, Constable,' said Sergeant Rowan, with the kind of assurance that had kept the British Empire running for a lot longer than it probably should have.

The sergeant walked over to the car and leaned in close to the window, where Nurd waited expectantly.

'Now look here, sir,' he began, 'what's all this stuff about the world coming to an end?'

'Well,' said Nurd, 'I thought I was the only one who'd come through.'

'Through from where, sir?'

'From Hell.'

'*The* Hell?'

'That's the one.'

'What's it like, then?' asked Constable Peel, who had reluctantly joined them.

'Not very nice,' said Nurd. 'You wouldn't like it.'

'There's a surprise,' said Sergeant Rowan. 'What did you think he'd say, Constable? That it was pleasant on a sunny day? It's not the beach at Eastbourne, you know.'

'I was just asking,' said Constable Peel.

'Anyway, back to the issue at hand,' said Sergeant Rowan. 'So, you've come from Hell and you thought you were alone, but you're not.'

'No, I'm not.'

'And these, er, "ladies" who may have attacked our police station, friends of yours, are they?'

'No, they came some other way.'

'How, exactly?'

'I don't know how!' said Nurd. 'Someone must have opened a portal, and now they're spilling through.'

'This portal, sir? What would it look like?'

Nurd considered the question. 'I think it would be sort of *bluish*,' he said, finally. 'It probably started off quite small, but now it's getting bigger and bigger. And when it gets big enough, well . . .'

'Well what?'

'Well, *he'll* come through. Our master. The Source of All Evil. The Great Malevolence, along with his army. And that'll be that, really. Hell on Earth.'

'Do you think you could find this portal, sir?'

Nurd nodded. He thought that he could already sense it. He'd felt the presence of the blue energy; it made the hairs on the back of his neck tingle. He knew that the closer he got to its source, the more he'd be aware of it.

He was like a walking Evil Energy Detector. Now his hope was that, if he could get near enough, he might be able to sneak back to the Wasteland unobserved. Better yet, if Hell was empty, because all the demons had moved here, he might find a way to leave the Wasteland altogether. He could go and live somewhere else, perhaps in a cosy cave with a nice view of some burning lakes.

'That's decided then,' said Sergeant Rowan. 'This gentleman will show us where the portal is and we can set about stopping all this nonsense. Get on the radio, Constable. Make sure everything is fine back at the station and then tell WPC Hay to alert the army. We'll need all the help we can get.'

Constable Peel prepared to do as he was told. Before he could make the call, WPC Hay came on the radio herself.

'Base to Tango One, over.'

'This is Tango One,' said Constable Peel. 'Is everything all right, Liz? Over.'

'Those flying women have gone and we've got the doors locked, but now we're getting calls left, right and centre. People's houses are being attacked, there are monsters crawling and flying all over the place. And there's some trouble over at the church. Over.'

'What kind of trouble? Over.'

'According to the verger, the dead have started to rise. Over.'

Constable Peel, who already looked unhappy, now looked very, *very* unhappy. He'd joined the police to stop bank robberies and solve the odd murder, neither of which he had yet managed to do as Biddlecombe was rather quiet, and so far the combined total of bank robberies and murders in the town was precisely nil.[25] Constable Peel had most certainly not joined the police to fight demons, not unless he was going to be paid overtime and danger money, and given a great big gun.

He was about to ask another question, and possibly begin shouting at Sergeant Rowan to call out the air force, the US marines, the Swiss Guard, and perhaps the Pope, vampire hunters and anyone else who might be able to sort out dead people popping up from the ground, when a bolt of blue lightning shot across the radio. Seconds later the radio exploded in a shower of sparks and went dead. He looked up and saw that the telephone lines along the road were also glowing blue and sparking at their connections. He reached for his mobile phone, but it too was dead.

Constable Peel banged his forehead against the steering wheel. A very bad situation had just got much worse.

Mrs Abernathy stood in the garden of 666 Crowley Avenue, her arms outstretched, blue energy flying from the tips of her fingers and out of her eyes. She was smiling as she brought down all communications within a

[25] This is unlike the small towns in television detective shows, where so many people die that it's a wonder there's anyone left in the town to kill by the end of the first series. You'd imagine that some of the residents might wonder about this and think, 'Hmmm, our town appears to be populated entirely by murderers, or people who are about to be murdered and since we're not murderers then we must be potential victims. Marjorie, grab the kids and the dog. We're going to live in New Zealand . . .'

ten-mile radius of Biddlecombe. She felt the power surge through her as she set about creating a barrier around the town, invisible to the naked eye but completely impenetrable. It would remain in place until the Great Malevolence himself emerged and then he would unleash himself upon this miserable planet. Behind her, what was left of the walls of the house expanded as though the whole structure had taken a deep breath, and then most of it fell to pieces, to be replaced by a great tunnel of blue light twenty feet across from which more and more creatures began to pour: imps and small dragons, hooded serpents and hunched gnome-like figures armed with axes and blades. And those were just the ones that could be described in recognisable terms: there were others that bore no resemblance to anything ever seen or imagined on earth, monstrous beings that had lived so long in total darkness they struggled to accommodate themselves to their new environment, creatures that had never had a form because it would have been too dark to see them. Now they were trying to construct shapes for themselves, resembling balls of fleshy dough from which arms and claws and tails and legs occasionally emerged before retreating again, accompanied by the odd eyeball to enable them to see what they were becoming.

Mrs Abernathy turned to face them as they streamed past. She stared into the portal and saw the gates were now almost half gone, a huge hole gaping at the heart of them.

Soon. Soon he would be here, and then she would receive her reward. But first, there was one small matter to attend to. She turned to Mr Abernathy, now a toad, and the spider demon by his side, the one that had, until recently, been crammed into Mr Renfield's skin, and instructed them to find Samuel Johnson.

To find the interfering boy who was frightened of spiders and suck his insides dry.

Tom was keeping watch on the street and Maria and Samuel the back when Dr Planck appeared at the front gate.

'Mrs Johnson,' called Tom, 'there's a man coming up the garden path.'

'Are you sure he's a man?' asked Mrs Johnson.

'Pretty sure,' said Tom.

Dr Planck hadn't seen the huge flies, but the flies had seen him. With a loud buzzing they descended upon the scientist, but so intent were they that they didn't notice the front door opening, and Maria and Tom emerging, each with a can of fly spray. Before the flies could get within chomping distance of Dr Planck they had fallen to the ground, writhing and spitting, then had ceased moving entirely before they, like the other demons who had run afoul of their intended victims, vanished.

Samuel joined Mrs Johnson as she approached the front door, clutching a broom handle. Tom waited at the living-room door, Samuel's cricket bat at the ready.

'Hurry up,' Mrs Johnson told Dr Planck. 'We don't know what else is out here.'

As if to confirm her worst suspicions, a batlike shadow flew over the house. Seconds later a creature the size of an eagle, but with spines instead of feathers and a head that consisted of dozens of wriggling worms with a single eye at the end of each, got tangled up in the telephone lines and fell crashing to the ground. Boswell, who had been watching it suspiciously, barked with delight.

Dr Planck looked upon its demise with relief until the door slammed shut, cutting off his view and almost cutting off his nose as well.

'Thank goodness,' he said. 'That thing has been chasing me ever since I locked the skull in a shed.'

'Right,' said Mrs Johnson, waving the broom handle in a threatening manner. 'What's going on? None of your scientific nonsense, now. Keep it simple.'

Dr Planck kept it very simple indeed. 'I don't know.'

'Well, fat lot of good you are, then,' said Mrs Johnson.

'Actually, I was hoping Samuel might be able to help me in that regard,' said Dr Planck.

Samuel stepped forward. 'I'm Samuel.'

At that moment all the lights went out, as Mrs Abernathy deprived the town of its power. Samuel and Dr Planck sat at the kitchen table while Mrs Johnson lit candles and Samuel told him of almost everything that had happened, from the time that Samuel had gone trick or treating at the Abernathys' house to the battle with the flying skulls. Dr Planck said nothing until Samuel was finished, although he did raise his eyebrow when Samuel described Mrs Abernathy's tentacles, then sat back and tapped an index finger against his lip.

'It's incredible,' he said at last. 'Somehow, the power of the collider has been harnessed to create a rip in the fabric of time and space. I mean, on one level it's wonderful. We've proved the existence of other dimensions, even if it was by accident, and we've discovered a way to travel between them. On the other hand, if this Mrs Abernathy creature is right, and it is a gateway between this world and, for want of a better word, "Hell", then we're in a lot of trouble.'

'A lot of trouble' seemed like an understatement to Samuel, but then he wasn't a scientist. Mrs Johnson didn't look very impressed with this description either.

'So all this is your fault?' she said.

'Not exactly,' said Dr Planck. 'We were trying to discover something of the truth about the nature of the Universe.'

'Well, now something has discovered you instead, and the truth is that it doesn't like any of us. I hope you're happy.'

'What can we do?' asked Samuel.

'If the phones were working, or I had access to a computer, I could contact CERN,' said Dr Planck. 'Unfortunately, the last I heard they were having troubles of their own.'

'What do you mean?' asked Samuel.

'I got a call on my way to the Abernathys' house. It seemed that the collider had started up again, and they couldn't shut it down.'

'Could Mrs Abernathy have done that?'

'Mrs Abernathy, or whatever this thing is whose will she is obeying,' Dr Planck said. 'Assuming the two events are linked, then if they can shut the collider down, it should close the portal as well.'

'So all we can do is wait?' asked Mrs Johnson.

'I'm afraid so.'

'What if they don't manage to shut it down in time?'

'We'll just have to hope that they do.'

By now Maria had joined them and it was she who spoke next.

'It can't be very stable, though, can it?'

'What?' asked Dr Planck.

'The portal,' said Maria.

'It's not,' said Samuel. 'The monster under the bed told me as much. He said that Mrs Abernathy was expending a lot of power keeping it open.'

'Monster under the bed?' said Dr Planck.

'It's a long story,' said Samuel.

'I mean, there are only so many possibilities,' Maria continued. 'It could be an Einstein-Rosen bridge, but that doesn't sound likely given its size and duration, or a wormhole of some kind, or even a combination of both. Either way, its stability is dependent on the energy resulting from the explosions in the collider. And there was that wind we felt when we spied on the Abernathy house . . .'

'Wind,' said Dr Planck thoughtfully. 'Yes, I felt it too. It smelt of . . . elsewhere.'

'So perhaps it was coming from the other side of the portal,' said Maria. 'But its force wasn't very strong. You're the expert, Dr Planck, but isn't it true that, in theory, a portal like that would allow only a one-way trip?'

'Well, according to some theories, yes, and assuming the portal was sufficiently stable. It's to do with the force of gravity,' Dr Planck added, to a confused-looking Mrs Johnson and an even more confused-looking Tom.

'But that kind of force would hurl the travellers out the far side, wouldn't it?' said Maria. 'There should be a howling gale tearing this town apart, but there isn't.'

'You may be right,' said Dr Planck. 'I mean, this is all speculative.'

'So there isn't that force of gravity,' said Maria.

'It appears not. There's some, but not sufficient to suggest a perfect balance between gravity and centrifugal force.'

'Then suppose that we collapse it.'

'But how?' Even as he asked the question, Dr Planck seemed to come up with an answer, for his face cleared for the first time since he had arrived at the house. Nevertheless, it was Maria who was left to make the suggestion.

'By sending something in the opposite direction.'

'Like two cars meeting on a narrow bridge and destroying themselves *and* the bridge,' said Samuel.

'Two cars meeting on a narrow, *unstable* bridge,' said Maria.

'You know,' said Dr Planck, 'that just might work. The questions are, where do we find our car, and who will drive it?'

CHAPTER XXVII

*In Which We Meet Bishop Bernard the Bad
At Last, and Constable Peel Enjoys
Himself Immensely*

Over at the Fig and Parrot, Shan and Gath were having a rare old time. Someone had started playing the piano, and Shan and Gath were doing their best to grunt along to 'My Old Man's a Dustman'. Earlier, someone had sung 'Danny Boy', which, although they had never heard it before, Shan and Gath sensed was a very sad song. It had caused a tear to well up in Gath's eyes, leading Shan to give him a consoling hug.

'One more for the road?' asked someone, waving a handful of beer vouchers in their faces.

Why, Shan and Gath thought, spying the vouchers, we don't mind if we do . . .

Reverend Ussher and Mr Berkeley were in real trouble. In the first place the risen dead were proving to be a great deal cleverer than skeletons whose brains had rotted and turned to mush centuries before had any right to be. The windows of the church were set about eight feet above the ground, which made them hard to reach without the aid of a stepladder. In the absence of said stepladder, some of the dead had formed a skeleton pyramid, with three corpses providing support for two further corpses, while a final corpse on top was using one of the stone gargoyles, which was complaining loudly, to break the glass. Two of the small panes had already broken, and Reverend Ussher could see a mouth grinning at him through the gap, a mouth with only a couple of broken black teeth still visible, which said a lot about dental care in olden days.

At the same time, more of the dead were thumping at the front door of the church and at the back door that led into the vestry, from which the verger had called the police to inform them of all that was occurring. The verger thought that the policeman who answered the phone had sounded a lot less surprised than he might have done, under the circumstances. In fact, he sounded like the dead rising was the least of his worries.

The vicar and verger had taken the precaution of pushing chairs and pews up against the doors in an effort to hold off the attacking corpses if they did manage to break through. There also continued to be worrying sounds from the vicinity of Bishop Bernard the Bad's tomb, the marker stone of which was piled high with just about every available piece of furniture and statuary stored in the little room. Between the pounding and the laughing they could also hear what sounded like 'Free me!' along with the occasional swear word.

'Bishop Bernard seems most irate,' said Reverend Ussher, as Mr Berkeley returned from checking on the storeroom. 'I do hope you haven't been trying to reason with him again. And he does swear a lot for a bishop.'

'He shouldn't be able to talk at all,' said Mr Berkeley. 'Limestone or no limestone, he's a corpse.'

'Mr Berkeley,' said the vicar patiently, 'in case you haven't noticed, the dead have arisen, there are gargoyles bouncing around on the church lawn and we have been insulted by a stone monk. Under those circumstances, Bishop Bernard's conversational skills are unremarkable.'

'I suppose you're right,' said the verger. 'We need to do something about those skeletons, though. They'll be on top of us in a minute if we're not careful.'

The vicar grabbed a brass candlestick and moved to the wall of the church. 'Help me up,' he said. The verger leaned down, cupped his hands and with some effort, boosted Reverend Ussher up close to the windowsill, onto which the vicar managed to haul himself with some effort. There were now four broken panes in the window, and the dead had succeeded in breaking the lead that had surrounded them, leaving a considerable gap. As Reverend Ussher steadied himself, a bony hand reached through and grabbed his trouser leg.

'Oh no you don't,' he said as he brought the candlestick down hard upon the skeletal hand. It smashed into pieces, scattering dismembered bones. The rest of the arm was quickly withdrawn.

Through the stained glass, Reverend Ussher could see the pyramid of skeletons tottering. He waited for it to draw closer once again, and for the lead skeleton to reach for the glass. When it did so the vicar opened the lower half of the window from inside, whacking the skeleton on the head and overbalancing the pyramid entirely. The three top corpses tumbled hard, and broke various limbs when they hit the ground. Reverend Ussher whooped in triumph, but his delight was short-lived. Dozens of bodies in various stages of decay looked from the vicar to the broken skeletons, then back again. It was hard for skulls without much flesh to look any angrier than they already did, but somehow these managed it.

'Oh dear.'

'Oh dear what?' asked Mr Berkeley from below.

'I think I've annoyed them.'

'And they were a bit miffed to begin with. Well done, Vicar!'

Hurriedly, Reverend Ussher began to close the window, but it now appeared to be stuck. He tugged, but it just wouldn't move.

'Oh dear,' he said again.

'Don't tell me,' said the verger.

'I really think that I should,' said the Vicar.

'Go on, then.'

'The window won't close.'

Below him, the dead began to form not one but two more pyramids. They were about to attack on twin fronts. At the same time, there came a great crashing noise from the storeroom, and a single word was roared from within.

That word was: 'Free!'

'Oh dear,' said the vicar and the verger together.

And then, just as the two pyramids of the dead began to approach the wall, a police car shot round the corner and ran straight at them, turning twelve rather innovative dead people into a pile of rotting limbs and broken bones. The car spun and came to rest facing the skeleton host and Sergeant Rowan's voice resounded across the churchyard.

'Right, you dead lot,' it said. 'This is the police. We're giving you five seconds to get back to wherever you came from, or there's going to be trouble.'

The dead did not move. To be fair, their hearing wasn't great. In addition, none of them had ever seen a police car before, or indeed anything with four wheels that wasn't being pulled by a horse or an ox.

'Your choice,' said Sergeant Rowan. 'Don't say we didn't warn you.'

Constable Peel gunned the accelerator and then released the brake. He'd had enough of demons and Hell. He was tired of the car smelling like poo. This was payback.

The car shot towards the ranks of the dead. Now the dead may not have known a lot about mechanised vehicles, but they'd seen what had happened to the last bunch who'd been hit by the big white cart and were pretty certain they didn't want the same thing to happen to them. Unfortunately, being dead, they couldn't move very fast. In fact, it had been all that they could manage to move at all. Thus the vicar was treated to the sight of a police car chasing skeletal figures across the churchyard, none of whom was in a position to avoid being run over. The vicar was rather enjoying the show until Mr Berkeley reminded him that some of their troubles were only beginning.

'Er, Vicar,' said Mr Berkeley, just as the door of the storeroom was hit with such force that it split in half, the two pieces shooting across the church floor and coming to rest against the far wall. A shadow appeared, then became a shape as Bishop Bernard the Bad made his entrance.

Bishop Bernard had never been a handsome man. He had, to be honest, been uglier than a wart on a toad's bum, and the centuries spent buried beneath the church had done nothing to improve his looks. His skin was dirty brown, like old leather. His nose was gone, leaving only a hole, and his eye sockets were empty, although they now glowed with a cold blue light. He had kept a lot of his teeth, which were long and yellow and, Reverend Ussher thought, a bit sharper than they should have been, as though Bishop Bernard had spent some of his time underground working on them with a file. One leathery hand held a long staff: the bishop's crosier with which he had been buried. He was also wearing the remains of his robes of office. On his head was his bishop's mitre. It was a bit tattered and the front half lolled forward like a tongue, but it was undeniably there.

As, regrettably, was Bishop Bernard himself, who was now looking at the verger from out of those empty eye sockets, following his progress as Mr Berkeley tried to hide behind the pews.

'He can see!' said the verger. 'How can he see? He's got no eyes. That's not right.'

Above him, Reverend Ussher leaned against the wall, hiding himself from the bishop's view and pressing a finger to his lips.

'Oh wonderful,' said Mr Berkeley to himself. 'Leave me to face him on my own without even a—'

Bishop Bernard raised his hand which like the rest of him looked like old bones wrapped in brown paper, and extended a finger in the verger's direction.

'Thou!' said Bishop Bernard, in a voice like gravel in a liquidiser. 'Thou art the one!'

He began to advance on the verger, who understood immediately that in this case being 'the one' wasn't a good thing. He hadn't won the lottery or, if he had, he wished that he hadn't bought the ticket, because the prize wasn't going to be very pleasant.

'I'm really not,' said the verger.

'Imprisoned in darkness,' continued Bishop Bernard, still advancing. 'My name, a jest. Thou art to blame!'

Mr Berkeley had to admit he had made the odd joke about Bishop Bernard, but it wasn't as if he thought the bishop was listening. After all, he was supposed to be dead. This just didn't seem entirely fair.

'I'm very sorry about that, Your Excellency,' said the verger. 'I thought you were, um, resting. It won't happen again.'

'No, it will not,' said Bishop Bernard, drawing closer and closer. 'Thou wilt be punished. Thou wilt have hot pokers inserted into thy bottom. Thou wilt—'

The vicar landed squarely on top of the bishop and felt something crack. He rolled across the floor and scrambled to his feet, the candlestick raised to defend himself.

Bishop Bernard the Bad had broken in half at the waist. To his credit, it had barely taken the wind out of him, as the saying goes, not that there was much wind in Bishop Bernard to begin with. He released his grip on his crosier and began to crawl along the floor, his hands clutching at the ends of the pews as he pulled himself along, his attention still fixed upon the verger. Meanwhile, his bottom half climbed to its feet and began bumping into things.

'Vicar!' cried Mr Berkeley. 'He's still coming!'

'Bottoms,' shouted Bishop Bernard. 'Pokers.'

The vicar approached Bishop Bernard from behind.

'I'm very sorry,' said the vicar, 'but this really must stop.'

He brought the candlestick down hard on Bishop Bernard's head. It made a ringing sound and Bishop Bernard's mitre fell off. The bishop ceased crawling, then twisted his head to look back at the vicar.

'Bottoms,' he said again. 'Thy bottom!'

'Oh, do be quiet,' said the vicar and hit Bishop Bernard a second time, then a third. He kept hitting him until there wasn't much left of Bishop Bernard and even his severed legs had stopped moving and had just toppled over like two pillars joined at the top.

The vicar wiped sweat from his brow. He put his hands on his knees and tried to catch his breath.

'I don't think,' he said, 'that a vicar is supposed to beat a bishop to death, or even back to death.'

Mr Berkeley looked down upon the remains of Bishop Bernard.

'If anyone asks, we'll say he fell over,' he said. 'Lots of times.'

There was a knocking at the door.

'All safe inside?' said Sergeant Rowan. 'It's the police.'

The vicar and the verger went to open the door.

Sergeant Rowan and Constable Peel stood on the step, looking quizzically at them.

'We are most happy to see you, Sergeant,' said the vicar. 'Happy, and relieved.'

'Sergeant—' began the verger, but he was interrupted.

'Let me finish, Mr Berkeley,' said the vicar.

'Spoilsports,' said the voice of the stone monk from above their heads.

'Just ignore him,' said the vicar. 'Now, perhaps—'

'Sergeant,' said the verger again.

'I said, "Let me finish",' the vicar insisted. 'Please! Now, Sergeant Rowan, we've had the most extraordinary experience, one that you might have found hard to believe had you not seen with your own eyes—'

'*Sergeant*,' said Mr Berkeley, with such force that even the vicar was forced to concede the floor to him.

'Well, what is it?' asked the vicar.

'Sergeant,' said Mr Berkeley, 'I think your demon is running away . . .'

CHAPTER XXVIII

In Which Nurd Makes a New Friend, and
Meets Some Old Acquaintances

Nurd had been very much enjoying his trip in the police car, with its flashing lights and interesting whooping noise. Furthermore, Constable Peel was a much better driver than Nurd, although, in his own defence, Nurd had just been getting the hang of the Porsche when the police stopped him and confiscated it. Still, he had been learning a lot just from watching Constable Peel control the machine, and he was wondering how he might go about making his excuses and leaving the policemen, in order to apply what he had learned to his own driving, when they had turned into the churchyard and Nurd had seen the risen dead.

That wasn't helpful. It was all very well for demons to start pouring into this world from their own – actually, it wasn't very well at all, come to think of it, but compared to the dead rising from their graves it was a picnic in the park. It took a lot of serious demonic energy to raise corpses, and Nurd could tell that this was a particularly nasty bunch of dead people. If he'd been wearing a watch, Nurd would have hidden it in his pocket before passing this lot on the street: thieves and cut-throats, all of them.

But that wasn't what concerned Nurd. What he was witnessing was not the result of some accidental breach between this world and Hell itself. No, there was *intent* at work here. Evil corpses just didn't rise up of their own accord; they had to be willed back into existence. And only one being was inclined to go around summoning brigands and murderers from the grave, which suggested to Nurd that a personal appearance by the Great Malevolence was imminent.

It has already been established that Nurd was not in the Great Malevolence's good books. In fact, Nurd wasn't sure that the Great Malevolence had any good books, since he was the font of all evil. It would be a bit like someone who hated flowers secretly filling his house with pansies. Nevertheless he had a list of demons who had disappointed him and he wasn't the forgiving type. He also didn't care much for demonic entities that disobeyed his commands. When you were banished by the Great Malevolence, you stayed banished. If you decided that you'd had enough of banishment, and were tempted to sneak back into Hell's inner circles in the hope of finding a comfortable dark spot in which to mind your own business, the Great Malevolence would inevitably find out, because that was the kind of bloke he was. Demons couldn't die, but they could be made to suffer, and one of the problems with being immortal was that you could suffer for a very, very long time.

Nurd didn't like suffering. He was quite sensitive, for a demon. He realised that the Great Malevolence had obviously been planning this attack on the Earth for quite some time, and Nurd hadn't known about it. After all it wasn't as if he'd received a note saying:

Dear Nurd,

Hi. It's me. The Great Malevolence. I hope you are well. I am well. I am considering launching an attack on the world of men, and avenging myself upon them for all the time I've been forced to spend here in Hell. Love you to be part of it. Call me.

Yours,

TGM (aka The Beast, Satan, etc.)

:-)

No, Nurd had received no such communication, which meant that he was very much *not* part of the Great Malevolence's plans. If he were still here when the big guy arrived Nurd would be given an opportunity to discover just how sensitive he really was, as the Great Malevolence would do his best to inflict as much pain on him as possible for disobeying orders, even if Nurd hadn't done so intentionally.

It was, Nurd had decided, time to go home and pretend that nothing had happened. His plan, if you could call it that, was to find the portal and sneak back through it to Hell, where he would return to his nice Wasteland until everything calmed down a bit. Nurd wasn't quite sure how he was going to sneak back, given that he would be moving in the opposite direction to every other demon and foul creature. Perhaps he could tell them that he'd forgotten his keys, or had neglected to pack clean underwear. Anyway, he'd work it out when he got there.

So, once the policemen had finished mowing down corpses, and had gone to see what was happening inside the church, Nurd had simply slipped out of the car window and done a runner.

Constable Peel briefly gave chase, but seemed to give up very quickly, Nurd thought. Nurd suspected that Constable Peel was quite happy to see the back of him, especially given how badly he smelled. By now, Nurd was getting tired of smelling himself, so the first thing he did was to take a dip in a local pond to clean himself off, scaring one of the nearby ducks half to death.

He was just finishing washing off his underarms when a large eyeball on the end of an arm popped out of the murk and blinked at him. A second arm quickly followed, this one sporting a mouth.

'I say,' said a cultured voice, 'do you mind? This is my home, not a public washroom.'

'Very sorry,' said Nurd. 'Didn't know this pond was occupied.'

'Suppose I should put up a sign, really. Not to worry, old boy. Just trying to keep a low profile for the moment, don'tcha know. Lot of pillaging and terrifying going on up there. No place for a gentledemon. Still, can't have every Tom, Dick and Harry demon washing his socks in my water, as it were. No offence meant, of course.'

'None taken,' said Nurd. 'I'll be on my way, then.'

'Righty-ho. If anyone asks, you can tell them that this pond has been claimed.'

A third arm appeared, this one holding a homemade flag depicting an eyeball on a red background. It waved the flag in the air.

'Made it m'self,' said the demon proudly. 'All m'own design.'

'Very nice,' said Nurd. 'Very imaginative. Maybe you should put it where people can see it, though.'

'What a jolly good thought,' said the demon. 'You're a clever one, sir, make no mistake.'

A fourth arm grabbed a passing duck and tied the flag to its neck using a piece of pond weed before depositing the startled duck back in the water. The duck made an attempt to fly away, but the demon held it in place until, eventually, the duck gave up and paddled off with the flag hanging limply from its neck.

Nurd stepped onto the bank, smelling faintly of pond, which was better than what he had reeked of before.

'Good luck with everything,' said Nurd.

'Much appreciated,' said the demon. 'You're always welcome to visit.'

The arms plopped back beneath the surface, leaving the pond still and quiet.

'What a nice chap,' said Nurd. 'If only all demons were like him.'

Unfortunately not all demons *were* like the thing in the pond. As Nurd sneaked through the town, trying to make his way to the portal, it became clear that the Great Malevolence's advance guard consisted mainly of some spectacularly vile entities. There was clear evidence of demonic nastiness to be seen: three elderly male members of the Biddlecombe Shooting Club, who had been taking potshots at clay pigeons when the invasion began, had made the mistake of turning their shotguns on a gorgon, its hair a mass of hissing serpents and its eyes so black that they were less organs of sight than dark vacuums, or jellied orbs of nothingness. The shotgun pellets had bounced off the gorgon's body, and the three old gents had immediately been turned to stone when they caught sight of the creature's face, so that they now formed an unusual piece of public statuary outside the post office.

There was a lot more blood in the butcher's shop than there should have been, as the smell of raw meat had attracted some very unpleasant carnivores, hunched beings with white flesh that hung from their frames like wax from a melting candle, their heads smooth but eyeless, their nostrils stretched back against their skulls as though unseen fingers had inserted themselves into the holes and pulled hard. The butcher, Mr Morrissey, had only a few seconds to register the awfulness of the creatures that were invading his premises before their mouths opened and their fine, sharp teeth were revealed, and they descended upon the hanging carcasses and, in their frenzy, upon Mr Morrissey himself. When they were done, only bare bones, animal and human, remained, along with Mr Morrissey's tattered straw hat.

Two members of the Biddlecombe First XV rugby team had been swallowed up during evening training when, somewhat against the laws of nature and, for that matter, rugby, a pair of fins had erupted from the ground and the unfortunate players were dragged beneath it by what very much resembled sharks armed with webbed claws for digging. The rest of the team had promptly harpooned the monsters with the corner flags.

A platoon of imps, two-foot-high red demons armed with small pitchforks, had attacked a florist's shop, only to discover that they were all allergic to pollen. Now they were staggering and wheezing over the street, their eyes streaming and their noses running. This made them easy prey for what was, presumably, the irate owner, a large woman wearing an apron depicting a smiling sunflower, who was beating the imps into submission with a broom.

That was another thing Nurd noticed: the demonic forces were not having things all their own way. The humans were fighting back. He saw a man on a lawn-mower chase a snake demon and turn it into something mushy beneath his blades. A group of schoolchildren dressed as ghouls had encountered half a dozen real ghouls in a park. The ghouls, who were thin and pale and not very interesting-looking, seemed a lot less terri-fying than the schoolchildren, who had gone heavy on the artificial blood. This impression was confirmed when they began pelting the real ghouls with stones, forcing them to beat a hasty retreat and barricade themselves in a sweet shop. The members of the Biddlecombe Ladies' Choral Society had trapped a raiding party of demon dwarfs in a car park and reduced them to small piles of pulp with their handbags and hymn books. Nurd saw parties of humans armed with pitchforks, bats and brush handles, determined looks on their faces as they marched out to reclaim their town. He wished them luck, knowing that when the Great Malevolence came it would all be over for them.

Nurd stepped over a wheezing imp that had staggered into his alleyway. The imp sneezed once and then expired, turning to wisps of smoke that drifted away on the night air. Nurd wondered if the Great Malevolence had anticipated what would happen to his forces once they crossed over from their world into this one: they could be killed. Oh, not permanently killed, but temporarily disposed of as it were. Mortal rules applied in this world. There was simply not enough demonic energy here to sustain the entities, so that when they died their essence was dispersed, to be reabsorbed into the larger energy surrounding the Great Malevolence, there to be reconstituted and sent back into battle. The humans couldn't win, not in the end. All they could hope for were small victories over an enemy that in time would simply return.

And even that would change once the Great Malevolence crossed over, for he would bring with him all his evil power and this world would be transformed into a new Hell.

In the distance, behind some houses, Nurd could see a haze of blue lightning, and he knew that there lay the portal, the gateway between worlds. It was his way home. He thought almost fondly of Wormwood. Almost. Then he remembered Samuel, and hoped that the boy was safe. He wondered if he should go and look for him, but what could he, Nurd, do if he did find him? Take him back to the Wasteland? No, Samuel would just have to fend for himself, but the thought of the boy in danger, or in pain, made Nurd feel sad and guilty.

Nurd left the alleyway and began moving in the direction of the light. He decided that it would be best to stay off the streets, so he climbed a garden wall and used the hedges and bushes for cover, advancing from garden to garden, sticking to the shadows.

He was in his third garden when his skin began to tingle. There was great power nearby. He could sense it. He peered through a gap in a hedge and spied a pair of creatures, one spiderlike, the other a huge toad, scuttling and hopping down the street. He recognised them both.

Nurd sank to the ground and tried to make himself as small as possible. This was grave news. Those demons were bad enough, but they were merely servants of a greater evil. Where they went something much worse inevitably followed, a being intimately acquainted with Nurd and his wrongdoings. That being was Ba'al. Ba'al, the Great Malevolence's trusted lieutenant, the one who had condemned Nurd to eternal banishment, had already crossed over, and Nurd had a pretty good idea of where the senior demon would be.

Ba'al would be waiting at the portal for its master to arrive.

CHAPTER XXIX

*In Which Nurd Proves to Be Rather
Decent, Actually*

It was Samuel who spotted what appeared to be a demon hiding behind the hedge in the front garden. Crouching behind a hedge didn't seem like very demonic behaviour to Samuel, whose experiences of demons until now had shown him they were variously frightening, puzzling, or, in the case of the one that had briefly occupied the space beneath his bed, simply not very good at their jobs; but so far he had encountered only one that appeared to be cowardly.

'What do you think of that?' Maria asked him, as they stood in the darkened kitchen, watching the demon.

'Maybe it's planning to jump out at someone,' said Tom.

'It's a him, not an "it",' said Samuel. 'His name is Nurd and he's the one who popped up in my bedroom. He's obviously frightened. You can see that from here.'

'Well, I don't really fancy asking this Nurd about his problems,' said Tom. '"Excuse me, Mr Demon, is 'oo frightened? Is 'oo having a bad day?" I mean, he's a demon. He's supposed to be frightening *us*. It would have to be something pretty terrible to make a demon tremble.'

They were silent as they considered the implications of what Tom had just said. What could be so frightening that even a demon would be terrified? Samuel watched Nurd. He now appeared to be biting his nails. Nurd may have been a demon, but Samuel knew that there was some good in him, even if Nurd had wanted to rule the world. Anyway, what was that old saying, something about an enemy's enemy being your friend . . . ?

He moved to the kitchen door. 'I'm going to talk to him.'

'Are you sure about this, Samuel?' asked Mrs Johnson. Dr Planck tried to protest, but the others shushed him.

'It's worth a try,' said Samuel. 'If he looks like he's about to turn nasty, we can just lock the door again, or Tom can wave his bat at him, but I don't think that's going to happen. To be honest, I rather like him.'

Samuel opened the door and put his head to the crack. 'Pssssst!'

Nurd, already somewhat tense, almost wet himself at the sound. He looked round to see the head of a small boy wearing glasses poking through a gap in a doorway.

'What are you doing in my garden?' said Samuel.

'What does it look like?' replied Nurd. 'I'm hiding. Go away, Samuel, it's dangerous.'

'Why are you hiding? Aren't they your friends out there?'

'That lot?' said Nurd, gesturing with a big thumb. 'They're no friends of mine. In fact, if some of them found out I was here, I'd be in terrible trouble.'

'Which brings us back to the whole hiding thing,' said Samuel.

'Exactly,' said Nurd.

'Look,' said Samuel, 'if we let you hide in here, will you help us stop all this?'

Nurd risked another glance through the hedge. He clearly didn't like what he saw, because he nodded briskly.

'I'll do my best,' he said. 'I really would just like to go home.'

'Well, come on then,' said Samuel. He opened the door wider and stepped aside as Nurd shuffled across the lawn and shot through the gap. Once the door had closed behind him, Nurd took a relieved breath and looked around. He saw Samuel, looking thoughtful; Tom, holding a bat as though he were aching for an excuse to use it; Maria, sucking on a pencil and wrinkling her nose at the faint smell of pond coming off Nurd and, um, was that poo?; and Mrs Johnson, who was clutching a frying pan determinedly. In one corner of the kitchen a man with a beard was trying to hide under a blanket. Nurd knew exactly how he felt.

'Hello,' said Nurd. 'I'm Nurd. Nurd, the Scourge of Five Deities. Actually, just plain old Nurd will be fine. I don't think I want to be the scourge of deities any more. If I never see a demonic deity again, it will be too soon. Mind if I get up from the floor?'

Most of the people in the kitchen looked dubious.

'Honestly,' said Samuel, 'we can trust him.' Eventually Tom said, 'OK, but do it slowly.'

Nurd did do it slowly, mainly because he had hurt his knee while diving into the kitchen. He took a seat at the table and rested his chin in his hands. He seemed very miserable and entirely unthreatening. A single big tear trickled down one of his cheeks.

'I'm really sorry,' said Nurd, wiping it away in embarrassment. 'It's been a funny old evening.'

Everyone looked sympathetic, even if he was a demon. Mrs Johnson put down her frying pan and pointed to a kettle that was currently simmering on a camping gas stove.

'Perhaps you'd like a cup of tea?' she said. 'Everything feels better after a cup of tea.'

Nurd didn't know what tea was, but it couldn't taste any worse than the stuff in the sewer.

'That would be very nice,' he said. 'Thank you.'

Mrs Johnson poured him a cup of strong tea and added a digestive biscuit to the saucer. Nurd sipped carefully, if noisily, and nibbled at the biscuit. He was pleasantly surprised by both.

'It's nicer if you dunk it,' said Samuel, demonstrating with his fingers.

Nurd dipped the biscuit into the tea.

'That is good, actually,' he said. He dunked the biscuit a second time, but on this occasion he left it in for too long and half of it fell into his cup. He looked like he was about to cry again.

'Just my luck,' he said.

'Never mind,' said Mrs Johnson, rescuing the soggy biscuit with a spoon. 'Plenty more where that came from.'

'So,' said Samuel. 'Perhaps you could tell us what's happening.'

'Well, it's Hell on Earth isn't it?' said Nurd. 'Gates

have opened, demons are pouring out. End of the world and all that.'

'Can we stop it?'

'Dunno. If you're going to do something, you'd best do it quickly because this lot are just the advance guard. As soon as the Great Malevolence himself comes through, it'll be too late. He'll be too strong for anyone to stop.' Nurd chewed glumly on his second biscuit. 'He really isn't very friendly at all.'

'But you came through the gates with the others, didn't you?' said Samuel.

'No, that's just it,' said Nurd. 'I came on my own. Like I told you before, I keep popping from one dimension into the next. One minute I was sitting on my throne in the Wasteland, hitting Wormwood on the head and minding my own business, and the next moment I was here. Now I appear to have ended up here permanently. I tried to make the best of it. In fact –' Nurd coughed ashamedly into his hand – 'I had hoped to rule the world. Oh, I'd have been very decent about it. None of this terrorising and demonic nonsense. All I really wanted was a bit of adoration, and a nice car. Apart from that, I'd hardly have bothered anybody. Unfortunately I think there's going to be some competition for the position, so I've decided to abandon my hopes and go home.'

'So you just sort of teleported[26] here?' asked Tom,

☠ [26] Actually, teleportation is not quite as far-fetched as you might think. Scientists at the Joint Quantum Institute in Maryland recently managed to teleport the quantum identity of one atom to another a few feet away. However, teleportation of humans is a long way off, as the experiment only works once in every 100 million attempts. Therefore the chances of you being teleported

who was a big fan of *Star Trek* and fancied the idea of being transferred from one place to another instantly.

Nurd shrugged, then looked at Maria who was still sucking her pencil and regarding him with an intense gaze.

'Why's she looking at me like that?' said Nurd. 'What've I done?'

'Apart from being a demon and planning to rule the world, you mean?' said Tom.

'Yep, apart from all that,' said Nurd.

'Maria?' asked Samuel. 'What are you thinking?'

'Nurd here said that he flipped back and forth between worlds. I'm just wondering what that might mean for our plan. It may be that we're wrong about the nature of the portal.'

'What plan?' said Nurd.

Nobody spoke.

'Oh, I see,' said Nurd. 'Don't trust the demon.' He sighed. 'Well, can't say I blame you with that lot outside. And for your information, I didn't just flip back and forth, happy as a demon with two tails. The first time I got crushed and found myself back in the Wasteland, and the second time a big truck thing hit me, and the same thing happened. The third time I was with Samuel, and then I wasn't with him. That was the only time something bad didn't happen.'

---

and arriving as interesting goo at the other end, if you arrive at all, are very high indeed. You don't want to be the subject of the following conversation:

'Is he there yet?'

'Well, bits of him are . . .'

He gave Samuel an embarrassed smile.

Maria looked pleased. 'Oh, so the rest of the time you died. Sort of. That's all right then.'

'Thanks very much,' said Nurd. 'It wasn't all right for me. You should try dying sometime. I guarantee that you won't care much for it.'

But now Maria was really interested. 'What's it like, travelling through a portal?'

'It hurts,' said Nurd, with feeling. 'It's like being stretched for miles, and then squeezed into a tiny little ball.'

'That's because of this,' said Maria, pointing at a drawing she had made of an hourglass shape, her pencil poised where the hourglass was at its narrowest. 'That's the point of compression. You shouldn't have been able to pass through it at all, because you should have been torn apart, or squashed to almost nothing. It sounds like this portal has some of the qualities of a black hole, and some of a wormhole. Theoretically, again, it shouldn't exist but then demons shouldn't exist either and yet one is drinking tea with us at this precise moment.'

'Your point being?' asked Tom, impatient because he couldn't follow most of what Maria was saying.

'My point being,' said Maria, 'that Nurd here may be the solution to our problems.'

'Solution?' said Nurd nervously. 'This solution isn't going to hurt, is it?'

'Might do, a bit,' said Maria. 'Scientifically it has lots of holes in it. It may not work at all.'

'Well, it's better than no plan,' said Samuel. 'Assuming Nurd is willing to try.'

'It can't be any worse than what's happened to me already,' said Nurd gloomily. 'Explain away.'

So they did.

'Right,' said Nurd, when they had finished, 'that sounds so foolhardy, dangerous, and completely impossible that it just might work. Now all we need is a car.'

He looked up from the table and his expression changed.

'There is just one more problem,' he said.

'What's that?' asked Samuel.

Nurd pointed a shaking finger at the window, to where a pair of demons, one a toad, the other a spider, stood at the garden gate.

'Them!'

CHAPTER XXX

In Which Mrs Abernathy Loses the Battle, but Sets Out to Win the War

The children crowded at the window, staring out at the demons.

'Ugh,' said Maria, wrinkling her nose at the sight of the ten-legged spider and the great toad. 'They're horrid.'

'The Servants of Ba'al,' said Nurd. 'They look awful and they *are* awful, but Ba'al is like a thousand of them rolled into one, with added nastiness. I'm in trouble now.'

Samuel stared at the two demons; there was something familiar about them. It took him a second to realise that they still wore the remains of black robes.

'They're not after you,' he said to Nurd. 'I'm not even sure they know you're here.'

'Then who are they after?' asked Tom.

'Me, I think,' said Samuel. 'They're two of the people from the Abernathys' basement, or they used to be. Mrs Abernathy must have sent them.'

'Why?' asked Tom. 'You didn't even manage to stop her. The gates are open. She has what she wanted.'

'I got in her way. I don't think she likes people

crossing her. I'm not sure if anyone has ever crossed her before, not like that. She wants to punish me and you lot as well if you're caught with me.'

He turned to Maria and Tom. 'I'm sorry. I should never have got you involved in all this.'

Tom patted him on the back. 'You're right, you shouldn't have.'

'Tom!' said Maria, appalled.

'Only joking,' said Tom. 'I really was,' he added, as Maria continued to glare at him.

'So what do we do now?' asked Maria. 'Run away?'

'Running away sounds good,' said Dr Planck from somewhere beneath the blanket.

'No,' said Samuel. 'We have to face them.'

'Look,' said Tom, 'hitting flying skulls was all very well, but I don't think those two are going to let any of us get close enough to knock them on the head with a bat.'

'We go ahead with the plan,' said Samuel. 'We send Nurd through the portal.'

'There is just one thing,' said Nurd. 'I'd rather they didn't know it was me. Could create difficulties at the other end, assuming I don't get spread over half the universe when the portal collapses. Perhaps you have a disguise of some kind that I could use?'

Mrs Johnson whipped the blanket from Dr Planck, made two holes in it with a pair of scissors and handed it to Nurd.

'But where do we get a car?' asked Tom.

'Mum,' said Samuel. 'Keep an eye on those things. Tom, stay with her. Nurd, Maria: come with me.'

'Where are you going?' asked Tom.

'To steal my dad's car,' said Samuel, and saw his mum smile.

Samuel, Maria and Nurd stood in the garage at the back of the house, looking at the car that Samuel's father had spent years lovingly restoring.

'"Aston Martin,"' read Nurd. He stroked the car gently. 'It's beautiful. Is it like a Porsche?'

'It's better than a Porsche, because it's British,' said Samuel.

'Right,' said Nurd. He wasn't sure that he agreed. He really had liked the Porsche, but this was still a splendid car.

'Are you sure you can drive one of these?' asked Maria.

'I drove a Porsche,' said Nurd. 'I got the hang of that fairly quickly.'

Samuel was having second thoughts about letting Nurd have the car. Samuel's dad would go crazy when he found out.

'You will look after it?' said Samuel to Nurd. 'It's such a lovely car.'

'Samuel,' said Maria, 'he's going to drive it through an transdimensional portal and if things go right, end up back in Hell, or, if things go wrong, in tiny little pieces scattered throughout a wormhole, or even compressed to almost nothing. It's not entirely fair to ask him if he's going to look after it.'

Samuel nodded. 'Perhaps it's better not to know.'

Samuel handed Nurd his father's spare car keys. Nurd

climbed into the driver's seat and put the key in the ignition as Samuel raised the garage door that opened on to a lane at the rear of the house. Maria stood beside the open passenger-side window and spoke to Nurd for the last time.

'Do you know where you're going?'

'Towards the big blue light,' said Nurd. 'It won't be hard to find.'

'No, I suppose not. You'll need to build up quite a head of speed if this is to work.'

'I don't think that will be a problem,' he said.

'Right. Good luck, then,' said Maria. 'And Nurd?'

'Yes?'

'Please don't let us down.'

'I won't,' he said.

'Your dad is going to have a meltdown when he finds out, isn't he?' said Maria to Samuel as he returned from opening the garage door.

'If Nurd fails, or if you're wrong, my dad will have better things to worry about,' said Samuel.

'You'd think so,' said Maria, 'but he'll still find time to kill you.'

'I don't care,' said Samuel. He was not frightened, but neither was he quite as angry as before. In a terrible way, he was getting his own back on his dad for running away. If they weren't quite even, they were getting there.

'Give us a few minutes, then get going,' said Samuel to Nurd. 'We'll distract those things at the gates, just in case they *have* come for you.'

Nurd gripped the steering wheel expectantly.

'I'll count to one hundred,' he said.

'Great,' said Samuel. 'Well, like Maria said, don't let us down.'

He patted the car once more in farewell.

'Is your dad really going to be annoyed?' asked Nurd.

'He'll get over it. After all, it's for a good cause.'

'I hope he understands,' said Nurd. 'You just seem like the sort of person who should be understood.'

'I wish you could stay around,' said Samuel. 'I'd like to get to know you a little better.'

'You were the first person who was nice to me ever,' said Nurd. 'That counts for something, whatever happens.'

They shook hands, and then Samuel gave Nurd a hug that, after a moment of surprise, the demon returned. For the first time, Nurd began to understand how it was to feel sorrow at parting with a friend, and even as it hurt him he was grateful to Samuel for giving him the chance to experience something of what it was to be human.

'Come on,' said Maria. 'Let's go and help the others. That will keep your mind off things.'

'I expect being eaten by a spider or a toad will do that,' said Samuel.

The demons had not moved. They were simply staring at the house, but it was the huge spider that most concerned Samuel, its mouthparts moving, dripping clear venom that turned the leaves black. Samuel's brain was filled with shrieking voices telling him to run. He had always been frightened of spiders, ever since he was a very small child. He couldn't explain why. Now he was being forced to confront a spider so vile that even in his worst nightmares he couldn't have come up with anything like it, even if it did have a pair of human legs sticking somewhat incongruously out of its bottom.

Samuel opened the front door and stepped into the garden. From the back of the house he heard the sound of the Aston Martin starting up.

A flickering figure like a picture on a cinema screen appeared on the path before him, surrounded by blue light. It was Mrs Abernathy, or a projection of herself.

'Hello, Samuel,' she said. 'I'm sorry I can't be there in person to witness your death, but I'm sure my servants will make it as uncomfortable as possible.' Her head turned, as though she were listening to something; then she clicked her fingers and the toad demon, in response to her command, hopped away.

'Was that the sound of your little friends trying to escape?' sneered Mrs Abernathy, and Samuel knew he had been right: Mrs Abernathy had not been aware of Nurd's presence.

Samuel shrugged.

'Well, they won't get very far. Naroth will find them and kill them. It will be a swift death, pleasant compared to what I have planned for you.'

Her ghostly hand touched the remaining spider demon, causing the hairs on its body to stand on end.

'Chelom,' she said. 'Eat him. Slowly.'

Nurd was approaching the end of Poe Street when a large, dark shape appeared on the road before him, its body tensed to jump. Naroth's face was not capable of showing feeling, but if it had been it would have displayed utter astonishment. Instead of the expected children and the adult woman, there was a single figure behind the wheel, its body draped with a blanket in which two eyeholes had been cut. Naroth's senses detected something familiar about the figure, but it couldn't decide what it was.

Nurd stopped the car and stared at Naroth.

'Horrid thing,' said Nurd.

As though it had heard the words Naroth jumped on to the bonnet, causing Nurd to shriek in fright. Nurd put his foot down on the accelerator and the car jerked forward, but Naroth was holding on tight with its sticky toes. It spat concentrated venom on to the windscreen, which began to smoke and melt.

'Oh no you don't,' said Nurd. 'I'm not having you messing up this nice car.'

He braked hard and Naroth was thrown off with such force that it left one of its legs caught in the wing mirror. It landed on its back and began to twist in an effort to right itself. It heard the sound of the engine growling, and redoubled its efforts, finding its feet just as its head was struck by the front of the Aston Martin and its body was dragged beneath its wheels. It had just enough to time to think, 'Ouch, that—' before it stopped thinking altogether and everything went black.

Nurd looked in the rear-view mirror at the mangled remains of Naroth and the satisfying green smear that the toad demon had left along the lower half of Poe Street.

'Serves you right for messing with my motor,' said Nurd. 'You should have more respect . . .'

Chelom began to climb over the garden wall, the weight of its body causing the hedge to collapse. It landed heavily and lumbered towards Samuel. As it did so an arrow whistled by Samuel's ear and buried itself in the spider demon's body, causing yellow liquid to spurt from the wound. The spider demon reared up, then resumed its progress as a second arrow flew towards it. This time it struck one of the black eyes on the demon's head and the demon arched its body in agony, one leg raised as if in an effort to dislodge the arrow from its flesh.

Maria appeared beside Samuel, Samuel's toy bow raised, and another arrow already nocked, its tip sharpened with a blade.

'Now, Tom!' she shouted.

Tom emerged from the kitchen carrying a container of fluid from which a plastic pipe connected to a nozzle in his hand. He squeezed the nozzle and a jet of fluid landed on the grass at Chelom's feet. The spider demon reacted as though the ground were hot when the sensitive taste buds at the tips of its legs came into contact with the liquid. Tom kept pumping, and more of the fluid squirted onto the demon's body and into its eyes and mouth. It tried to retreat but Tom pursued it relentlessly until at last the demon began to twist and writhe before falling on its back. Its legs curled in upon its body, and it stopped moving.

Samuel wrinkled his nose.

'What is that stuff?'

'Ammonia and water,' said Tom. 'Maria thought of it.'

But Maria was not listening and neither, suddenly, was

Samuel. Their attention was concentrated on the image of Mrs Abernathy, who was gazing upon them in fury.

'Come and get me,' said Samuel. He wanted to distract Mrs Abernathy from the portal. He had to buy Nurd some time.

But Mrs Abernathy simply disappeared.

CHAPTER XXXI

In Which Mrs Abernathy Reveals
Her True Colours

Mrs Abernathy stood outside what remained of the house. It was almost time. She had wanted to kill Samuel, but that would have to wait. She would find him and when she did he would wish that the spider had consumed him. Again and again he had defied her, and Mrs Abernathy was not one to tolerate defiance.

The portal had grown to such an extent that all that was left of the house were two walls and a chimney breast. The doors and windows were entirely gone, replaced by a huge spinning vortex with a dark hole at its centre. There were no longer creatures coming through it. All such activity had ceased for a time, and those demons and monsters not otherwise occupied in sowing chaos throughout the town were waiting expectantly for the arrival of their master, the Great Malevolence himself. Winged, purple forms dangled upside down from lamp-posts, like great bats, their heads simply elongated beaks filled with jagged teeth. Around them flew insects as big as seagulls, their iridescent green bodies ending in long, barbed stingers. A phalanx of vaguely human figures had assembled by the corner of Derleth Crescent, dressed in ornate gold armour that was itself alive as the dragons and snake heads with which it was decorated slithered and snapped at the night air, the armour both a means of defence and a weapon. The armour had no face guard and beneath each jewelled helmet there was blackness broken only by the flickering of red, hostile eyes. Above their heads a banner flew: flames in the shape of a flag, burning in honour of he who was to come.

Mrs Abernathy raised her arms in the air and closed her eyes in ecstasy as a great cheer arose from the demons before her.

Nurd watched all that was happening from a side street nearby, the Aston Martin purring softly beneath him. He shivered as the woman lifted her arms, blue energy crackling around her.

There were ranks of demons in Hell, but the very worst of them had hidden themselves away with the Great Malevolence, and were rarely seen by the rest. They were monstrous beings, their appearance so awful that they shrouded themselves in darkness, unable to tolerate even the reaction of other, lesser demons to their blighted state.

Yet there was one great demon that felt no such shame, that did not seek to hide itself. It had become the Great Malevolence's most trusted lieutenant, the demon that knew his every secret and to whom he revealed all of his thoughts, a demon that had studied the humans with hateful fascination, altering itself as it did so, its mind becoming both male and female, although it always preferred the female side, sensing that the female was smarter and shrewder than the male.

Even dressed in the skin of Mrs Abernathy, Nurd recognised the entity before him. After all, it had been responsible for his banishment.

It was Ba'al.

He sank back against the wall.

'I'll never get past her,' he said bitterly. 'I'm done for. We're all done for.'

Mrs Abernathy began to speak.

'Our time has come,' she said. 'Our long exile in the void is at an end. Tonight we have begun to claim this world as our own, and soon we will reduce it to a charred ruin. See! Our master approaches. Gaze upon his might! Feel his majesty! Behold him, the destroyer of worlds!'

She stepped aside and the centre of the vortex grew larger, the dark hole at its heart simultaneously expanding and becoming lighter. The gates were almost entirely gone, and the melting metal steamed and boiled. Slowly, shapes became visible through the murk. They were blurred at first, and shrouded in mist, but gradually they became clearer.

It was an army, the largest army ever assembled in any world, and in any universe. All the peoples of the Earth were as nothing before it. Its ranks outnumbered every grain of sand on the planet, every leaf on every tree, every molecule of water in every ocean. Demons of every shape and size, things formed and without form, had assembled behind the remains of the gates. Above the great army towered a black mountain so tall its top could never be seen, its base so wide that a man might walk for a lifetime and never circumnavigate it. At the heart of the mountain was a massive cave, unseen fires glowing within.

A dark form appeared at the entrance to the cave; from its head sprouted a crown of bone. It wore black armour carved with the name of every man and woman who had ever been born on Earth, and who ever would be born, in order that it would never forget its hatred for them. In its right hand it held a flaming spear and on its left arm it bore a shield made from the skulls and bones of the damned, for in every evil man and woman there was something of the Great Malevolence, and when they died he claimed their remains for himself. He towered above his army, so that they were like insects before him. He opened his mouth, and roared, and they shook before him, for his glory was terrible to behold.

Another cheer arose from the assembled masses. Mrs Abernathy basked in the sound. So consumed was she by the imminent success of their invasion, and the impending arrival of her master, that she failed to notice the cheers had started to fade, to be replaced by mutterings of confusion, and a voice that appeared to be saying, very politely, 'Excuse me . . .'

Mrs Abernathy opened her eyes. Standing before her was Samuel Johnson.

'I have a question,' said Samuel.

Mrs Abernathy was so taken aback that she couldn't reply. Her brow furrowed. Her mouth opened and tried to form words, but none would come. The gates of Hell were about to be opened at last, Earth destroyed, all of its inhabitants torn to pieces, and here was a small boy who seemed to have, not to put too fine a point on it, a question.

Eventually, Mrs Abernathy responded in the only way she could.

'Well, what is it?'

'I just don't see the point,' said Samuel.

'The point?'

'Yes, the point,' said Samuel. 'I mean, if you've all been stuck in horrible old Hell for ages and now you're about to come here instead, why would you reduce it to a ruin and turn it into somewhere that's just as bad as the place you've left? It doesn't seem to make any sense.'

Beside him, a pink demon with four legs scratched itself in puzzlement. Its form had the consistency of marshmallow, so its fingers got rather lost in the process and jabbed themselves into the demon's brain, but at least it was thinking, or giving the impression of doing so.

'And what would you have us do?' asked Mrs Abernathy. 'Leave it as it is?'

'Well, yes,' said Samuel. 'I mean, it's got trees, and birds, and elephants. Everybody likes elephants. You can't not like an elephant. Or a giraffe. And personally, I'm very fond of penguins.'

The pink demon gave a little shrug of agreement, or as much of a shrug as something without a neck can give, which isn't very much at all.

'If you destroy it,' continued Samuel, 'then you'll just be back where you started, with a big lump of rock that doesn't have a whole lot in it, except demons. It's not exactly going to be beautiful, is it?'

Mrs Abernathy took a step towards him.

'And why do you imagine that we would want beauty?' she said. 'Beauty mocks us, for we have none.

Goodness appals us, because we have no goodness. We are all that this world is not, and we are all that you are not.'

She raised a hand to the stars above her.

'And this world is just the first. We have a universe to conquer. We have suns to extinguish, and planets to crush. In time, each of those lights in the sky will fade to nothing. We will extinguish them like candle flames between our fingers, until there is only blackness.'

The little pink demon, still thinking about penguins, gave a disappointed sigh. Mrs Abernathy flicked a finger and he exploded in a puff of pink and red.

'He goes to the back of the line,' said Mrs Abernathy as Samuel wiped a piece of demon from his sleeve. 'And as for you, I am strangely glad to see you. It means I can kill you now, and enjoy our triumph with the knowledge that you are not alive to spoil it.'

Mrs Abernathy grinned. Her body began to bulge. Her skin stretched under the pressure, opening tears in her face and on her arms, but no blood came. Instead, something terrible moved in the spaces revealed.

'Now, Samuel Johnson,' she said, 'look upon me. Look upon Ba'al, and weep.'

Nurd's finger was poised over the ignition key. He saw Mrs Abernathy step away from the portal, but not far enough.

'Come on, Samuel,' he whispered. The little boy was brave, so very brave. Nurd hoped that Samuel wouldn't die, but the odds in his favour weren't good. The odds in Nurd's favour weren't much better, but he was determined to try. He would be brave, if not for his own sake, then for Samuel's. Mrs Abernathy took another step towards the boy; Samuel retreated in turn. Then Mrs Abernathy started to shudder and swell.

'Oh no,' said Nurd. 'Here we go . . .'

Mrs Abernathy's skin fell away in clumps, withering and turning to dry flakes as it hit the ground. A grey-black form was exposed, wrapped up in tentacles that now began to stretch and move as they were freed from the constraints of skin. Only her face and hair remained in place, like a rubber mask, but it was stretched so tightly over what was beneath that it bore no resemblance to the woman who had once worn it. One of the tentacles reached up, separated itself into claws and wrenched the skin mask away.

And still Ba'al grew: six feet, then eight, then ten, on and on, larger and larger. Two legs appeared, bent backwards at the knees, from which sharp spurs of bone erupted. Four arms emerged from the torso, but only two ended in clawed fingers. The second pair ended in blades of bone, yellowed and scarred. A great mass of tentacles sprouted from the demon's back, all of them twisting and writhing like snakes.

Finally Ba'al reached its full height, towering twenty feet above Samuel. There was a cracking sound, and what had looked like a bump in its chest was revealed as its head, which now untucked itself. It appeared to have no mouth, merely two dark eyes buried deep in its skull, but then the front of the skull split into four parts, like a segmented orange, and Samuel realised that it was *all* mouth, the four parts lined with row upon row of teeth, a gaping red hole at its centre from which a multiplicity of dark tongues emerged.

Samuel was too frightened to move. He wanted to run, but his feet wouldn't respond. In any case, his back was against the garden hedge. He could go right or left, but he couldn't go any farther backwards. He felt something brush his leg and looked down to see Boswell, who had escaped from the house and followed his master. Even now, the little dog wanted to be near Samuel.

'Run, Boswell,' he whispered. 'There's a good boy. Run home.'

But Boswell didn't run. He was frightened, but he wasn't going to desert his beloved Samuel. He barked at the nasty, unknown thing before him, nipping at its heels. One of its bladed limbs shot out in an effort to impale him, but Boswell skipped out of the way just in time and the long bone buried itself in the pavement, lodging firmly. Ba'al tried to free itself, but the bone was stuck.

Something in its struggles snapped Samuel out of his trance. He looked around for a weapon and saw a half brick that had been dislodged from the house as the portal expanded. He picked it up and hefted it in his hand. It wasn't much, but it was better than nothing.

With a great wrench, Ba'al managed to pull the blade free, even as Boswell continued to bark and snap. A tentacle, larger than the rest, lashed out at him, catching the little dog around the chest and tossing him into the air. The pincers at the tentacle's end shot out to cut him in two, but they missed him by inches and Boswell fell to the ground, stunned. He tried to get up, but one of his legs was broken, and he was unable to raise himself.

He yelped in pain and the sound cut through Samuel, filling him with rage.

'You hurt my dog!' he shouted. By now he didn't know if he was more angry than scared, or more scared than angry. It didn't matter. He hated the thing before him: hated it for hurting Boswell; hated it for what it had done to the Abernathys and their friends; hated it for what it wanted to do to the whole world. Behind it the portal was visible and Samuel could see the Great Malevolence approaching, his army parting for him so that he could lead the legions of darkness into this new kingdom.

Ba'al bent down before Samuel, surrounding him with tentacles, those four limbs poised to finish him off. Its skull opened up once more, breathing its stink upon him as it hissed and Samuel saw himself reflected in those dark, pitiless orbs.

He threw the half-brick straight into its mouth.

It was a perfect shot. The lump of stone landed in the demon's throat. It was too far down to be spat out, and too big to be swallowed. Ba'al staggered back, black blood and drool dripping from its jaws as it began to choke. Around it, the assembled creatures watching the unequal battle, waiting for the boy to be destroyed, gave a collective gasp of shock. Ba'al tried to reach into its mouth with its tentacles to free the blockage, but the gap was too narrow for them to gain purchase. It collapsed to its knees as smaller demons ran to its aid, climbing up its body in an effort to reach its mouth. Carefully three of them entered its jaws and began working at the brick, trying to free it. Samuel felt hands grasp his arms. Two of the figures in gold armour were securing him, their red eyes glaring as he was held in place. He struggled against them, but they were too strong.

There was a thud and something landed before him. It was the half-brick. Samuel looked up to see Ba'al rising from its knees, and in its black eyes he saw his doom.

At that moment a vintage Aston Martin, driven by a moon-headed figure in a blanket, sped behind Ba'al and disappeared into the portal, leaving behind it only exhaust fumes and a fading 'Goodbyyyyyyyye . . .'

For a second, nothing happened. Everyone, and everything, simply stared at the portal, unsure of what they had just seen. Flashes of white light appeared at its edges, and the portal, which had been spinning in a clockwise direction, reversed its flow and began to move anticlockwise. There was a sense of suction, as though a vacuum cleaner had just been switched on, but it seemed to affect only the demons, not Samuel. First the smaller ones, then the larger, were lifted from their feet and pulled inexorably into the portal. Some struggled against its force, holding on to lamp-posts, garden gates, even cars, but the portal began to spin faster and faster, and one by one they found themselves wrenched from one world and back to the next until the portal was filled with a mass of legs and tentacles and claws and jaws, demons bouncing off one another as they were drawn towards the centre. Two of them, oddly, were desperately trying to hold on to glasses of beer.

At last only one remained. The thing that had once been Mrs Abernathy was heavier and stronger than anything else that had passed into this world, and it did not want to leave. Every limb and every tentacle was stretched to its limit, each clinging to something, however insubstantial, in an effort to fight against the force of the portal, which was now spinning so fast that it was nothing more than a blue blur. Finally it proved too much even for the great demon, until at last only one tentacle remained clinging to the bottom of the garden gate, the rest of the demon's body suspended in mid-air, its legs pointing to the void.

Samuel stepped forward. He stared into Ba'al's pitiless eyes, and raised his right foot.

'Go to Hell,' he said, and stamped down hard on the tentacle with his heel.

The demon released its hold on the gate, and was sucked back to the place from which it had come. The portal collapsed to a small pinpoint of blue light, then disappeared entirely.

Samuel knelt by Boswell and cradled the little dog's head in his arms. A police car pulled up, and people began to emerge from their homes, but Samuel cared only for Boswell.

'Brave Boswell,' he whispered, and despite his pain, Boswell's tail wagged at the sound of Samuel's voice speaking his name. 'Brave boy.'

Then Samuel looked up at the night sky, and he spoke another name, and his voice was filled with regret, and fondness, and hope.

'Brave Nurd.'

CHAPTER XXXII

*In Which Nearly Everyone Lives
Happily Ever After, Or So It Seems*

It took a long time for Biddlecombe to return to normal. People had died or, like the Abernathys and the Renfields, simply vanished. For months afterwards there were scientists, and television crews, and reporters cluttering up the town and asking all sorts of questions that the townsfolk quickly grew tired of answering. Nutcases, and people with nothing better to do, made journeys to the town to see the place in which, for a time, a gateway between worlds had opened. The problem was that, all damage to people and property aside, and the stories told by those who had encountered the demons, no actual evidence survived of what had occurred, apart from the stone statue of three old gents with shotguns. There were no physical remains of monsters, and those who had taken mobile phone pictures of flying creatures, or who had used video cameras to take shots of demonic entities trampling flower beds in the local park, found that there was nothing but static to be seen. Oh, everyone accepted that *something* had happened in Biddlecombe, but, officially, nobody seemed entirely sure of what that something might have been, not even the scientists responsible for the Large Hadron Collider, who, in the wake of what had occurred, decided that in future they needed to keep a very close eye on their experiments. For now, though, the collider would remain powered off and Ed and Victor were left to play Battleships in peace, while Professor Hilbert dreamed of travelling to other dimensions, but only ones that didn't have demons in them.

The collider did have three very special visitors in the weeks that followed. Samuel, Maria and Tom were treated with a great deal of curiosity and respect as they toured the facility, and they did their best to answer all of the scientists' questions as politely as possible. Samuel and Maria decided that they quite liked the idea of becoming scientists, although they were pretty certain that, after all they'd seen, they'd be more careful about what they got up to than the CERN people had been.

'I still want to be a professional cricketer,' said Tom after their visit. 'At least I can understand cricket. And nobody ever accidentally opened the gates of Hell during a test match . . .'

Eventually Biddlecombe began to fade from the headlines, and that suited everyone in the town just fine. They wanted their dull, pretty old Biddlecombe back, and that was what they got.

More or less.

Over at Miggin's Pond, a boy named Robert Oppenheimer was throwing stones at ducks. It wasn't that he had anything against ducks in particular. Had there been a dog, or a lemur, or a meerkat at which to throw stones instead he would happily have done so, but in the absence of any more exotic creatures, ducks would just have to do.

He had managed to hit a few birds, and was looking for more stones, when he was lifted up into the air by one leg and found himself dangling over the surface of the pond. An eyeball appeared on the end of a stalk and, well, eyeballed him. Then a very polite voice said:

'I say, old chap, I do wish you wouldn't do that. The ducks don't like it and frankly, I don't much care for it either. If you persist, I will have no choice but to disassemble you and put you back together the wrong way. As you can imagine, that will hurt a lot. Do I make myself clear?'

Robert nodded, albeit with some difficulty as he was still upside down. 'Yes,' he said. 'Perfectly.'

'Now say sorry to the ducks, there's a good chap.'

'Sorry, ducks,' said Robert.

'Right, then, off you go. Toodle-pip.'

Robert was put back, surprisingly gently, on the bank. He found that all of the ducks were watching him and quacking. If he hadn't known better, he might have thought that they were laughing.

Over time, other people reported similar odd encounters at Miggin's Pond, but instead of calling in investigators, or selling tickets, the people of Biddlecombe simply kept quiet about it, and gave Miggin's Pond a wide berth whenever they could.

* * *

In the staff room at Montague Rhodes James Secondary School, Mr Hume sat staring intently at the head of a pin. During the Halloween disturbances, Mr Hume had been forced to lock himself in a cupboard while a band of six-inch-high demons dressed as elves shouted at him through the keyhole. The whole experience had shaken him a great deal and when he had learned of Samuel Johnson's involvement in the affair he began to consider that the boy might know something about angels and pins that he didn't.

So he stared hard at the pin, and wondered.

And on the head of the pin, two angels who had been performing a very nice waltz, surrounded by lots of other waltzing angels, suddenly stopped what they were doing as one turned to the other and said:

'Don't look now, but that bloke's back . . .'

One night, almost a month after the events of Halloween, when everyone was getting ready for December, and Christmas, Samuel was in the bathroom, brushing his teeth. Boswell watched him from the doorway, one leg still encased in plaster but otherwise his clever, contented self. Samuel had just taken a bath and the mirror was steamed up. He reached out and wiped some of the steam away. He glimpsed his reflection and, standing behind him, the reflection of another.

It was Mrs Abernathy.

Samuel looked round in fright. The bathroom was empty yet Mrs Abernathy was still visible in the mirror. Her lips moved, speaking words that Samuel could not hear. As he watched, she moved forward. A finger reached out and began to write from behind the glass in the steam of the mirror. When she was finished there were four words visible. They were:

THIS IS NOT OVER

A blue light flickered in her eyes, and then she was gone.

CHAPTER XXXIII

In Which We Bid Farewell to Nurd. For Now . . .

In the great Wasteland, Wormwood stared at the Aston Martin that had accompanied Nurd back to his kingdom.

'What is it?' asked Wormwood.

'It's a car,' said Nurd. 'It's called an Aston Martin.'

Nurd was surprised that the car had made it to the Wasteland in one piece, although not as surprised as that he himself had done so with only minor injuries. After all, it wasn't every day that one went the wrong way through a transdimensional portal wearing a blanket and driving a very fast car. He had already decided that if any curious demons asked him how the car had got here, assuming any of them could be bothered to investigate the Wasteland, Hell being a very big place with more interesting areas to explore, he would tell them that it had dropped out of the sky. After all, who would suspect Nurd, that most inept of demons, of being responsible for thwarting the Great Malevolence and his invading army.

'What does it do?' asked Wormwood.

'It moves. It moves very fast.'

'Oh. And we watch it move fast, do we?'

It sounded like fun to Wormwood, although not much fun. Actually he was quite pleased that Nurd was back. It had been a bit quiet without him, and the throne hadn't been very comfortable to sit on. Funny, that. For so long Wormwood had desired the throne and then, when he'd had it, it hadn't been worth desiring after all.

'No, Wormwood,' said Nurd patiently. His trip to the world of men and his encounter with Samuel, had mellowed him, and he was no longer immediately inclined to hit Wormwood for being a bit dim, although he had a feeling that this wouldn't last. 'We sit in it, and then we go fast too.'

Wormwood looked doubtful, but eventually he was convinced to sit in the passenger seat, his seat belt fastened and a concerned expression on his face. Beside him, Nurd started the engine. It growled pleasantly.

'But where will we go?' asked Wormwood.

'Somewhere else,' said Nurd. 'After all, anywhere is better than here.'

'And how far will we get?'

Nurd pointed at one of the bubbling black pools that broke the monotonous landscape of the Wasteland.

'You see those pools, Wormwood?'

Wormwood nodded. He'd been looking at the pools for so long that they almost qualified as old friends. If he'd known the date of his birthday, he'd have invited the pools to the party.

'Well,' Nurd continued, 'what's in those pools is remarkably similar to what makes this car go. Hell, Wormwood, is our oyster.'

'What's an oyster?'

Nurd, who didn't know either, but had seen the phrase on a poster in the car showroom and rather liked the sound of it, began to reconsider his decision not to hit Wormwood quite so often.

'It doesn't matter,' he said. He took a paper bag from his pocket. The bag contained the last of the wine gums that Samuel had given to him. Nurd had been saving them, but now he offered one to Wormwood and took the final sweetie for himself.

'To Samuel,' he said, and Wormwood, who had heard so much about the boy from Nurd, echoed his master.

'To Samuel.'

The Multiverse was unfathomably huge, thought Nurd, but it was still small enough to allow two strangers like Samuel and himself to find each other and become friends.

Together, Nurd and Wormwood drove off, the car growing smaller and smaller, disappearing into the distance, until all that was left to indicate that anyone had ever been there was a throne, a sceptre and an old, rusty crown . . .

Acknowledgments

I would like to thank Alistair and Cameron Ridyard, who were the first two readers of this book. Graham Glusman, and Nicholas and Barney Rees, also came forward with kind words and encouragement at a very early stage. I'm grateful to you all.

Dr Colm Stephens, Administrator of the School of Physics at Trinity College, Dublin, very generously agreed to read this manuscript and offered advice and clarification. In the interests of fiction I was forced to ignore some of it and for that I apologise deeply. His input, patience and expertise were greatly appreciated and any errors are entirely my own. Thanks also to Sally-Anne Fisher, the Communications Officer at TCD, for her assistance.

I seem to have read a great many books and articles during the writing of this novel, but among the most useful were *Black Holes, Wormholes & Time Machines* by Jim Al-Khalili (Taylor & Francis, 1999); *Quantum Theory Cannot Hurt You* by Marcus Chown (Faber and Faber, 2007); and *Parallel Worlds* by Michio Kaku (Penguin, 2005).

Thanks to Sue Fletcher at Hodder & Stoughton and Emily Bestler at Atria Books, whom I am lucky enough to have as editors; to all of those who work with them, particularly their respective assistants, Swati Gamble and Laura Stern; to Darley Anderson and his staff, without whom I would be lost; and to Steve Fisher, for always thinking visually.

Finally, love and thanks to Jennie, as always, for putting up with me.

THE INFERNALS

JOHN CONNOLLY

WARNING

In opening this book, you enter
more than a story.

The dreadful beings on the other
side are always watching, always
waiting, for any way to break
through to our world.

Do you have the courage to unleash
what may be unleashed?

And, when you are done, do you
have the strength to return it
to whence it came?

For Cameron and Alistair

Whenever science makes a discovery, the devil grabs it while the angels are debating the best way to use it.

Alan Valentine (1901–80)

CHAPTER I

In Which We Find Ourselves in Hell, But
Only Temporarily, So It's Not All Bad News

The place generally referred to as Hell but also known variously as Hades, the Kingdom of Fire, Old Nick's Place[1], and assorted other names designed to indicate that this is not somewhere in which you might want to spend eternity, let alone a short holiday, was in a state of turmoil. Its ruler was unwell.

The source of all Evil, the ancient thing that hid itself in the darkest part of Hell, also had many names, but his followers called him the Great Malevolence. He wished for many things: he wished for every star in every universe to be snuffed out like candle flames between his fingers; he wished for all beauty to cease to be; he wished for cold, and blackness, and a great silence that would last for ever.

Most of all, he wished for the end of mankind. He had grown weary of trying to corrupt every human being, one by one, because it was time-consuming, and frustrating, and a lot of human beings continued to defy

☠ [1] Not to be confused with St Nick's Place, which is the North Pole. You don't want to make that mistake, and end up selling your soul to Santa.

him by being decent and kind. While he hadn't exactly decided to give up on his efforts entirely, it just seemed easier to destroy the Earth and have done with it, and so he came up with a plan.

Now for those of you who may not be entirely familiar with our story so far, here is a chance for you to catch up.[2] When last we met, the Great Malevolence, aided by the demon known as Ba'al, was trying to harness the power of the Large Hadron Collider, the massive particle accelerator in Switzerland that was trying to recreate the moments after the Big Bang, in order to open the gates of Hell and force his way into our world. Ba'al passed through a portal connecting Hell to the town of Biddlecombe in England, and disguised itself as a woman named Mrs Abernathy, having first killed the original Mrs Abernathy. At the last minute, just as the Great Malevolence and his army were about to pass through the portal and take over the Earth, Mrs Abernathy's plans were foiled by a small boy named Samuel Johnson, his dachshund Boswell, and an inept, although well meaning, demon named Nurd, the Scourge of Five Deities. The Great Malevolence blamed Mrs Abernathy for this, and as a result was now refusing to meet with her, causing her much hurt and humiliation.

[2] And by the way, what kind of person are you, reading the second part of a series before the first? Now the rest of the readers have to hang around, whistling and examining their fingernails in a bored manner, while I give you special treatment. I bet you're the sort who arrives halfway through the movie, spilling your popcorn and standing on toes, then taps the bloke next to you on the shoulder and says, 'Have I missed anything?' It's people like you who cause unrest . . .

All clear? Good.

The Great Malevolence still wasn't quite sure how his plan had failed, and he didn't care. For a moment, he had glimpsed a hole between dimensions, a possibility of escape from Hell, and then that portal had been closed just as he was about to leave his dreary kingdom behind. All of his bloodied hopes, his shadowy dreams, had come to nothing, and the closeness of his triumph had driven him insane.

This is not to say that he wasn't mad already: the Great Malevolence had always been madder than a bag of badgers, madder even than a colony of bats trapped in a biscuit tin. Now, though, he had passed into another realm of craziness entirely, and significant portions of Hell had been filled with the sounds of his wailing ever since the portal had blinked out of existence. It was a terrible sound, that cry of rage and sorrow, ceaseless and unvarying. Even by the standards of Hell it was very annoying indeed, echoing from the Great Malevolence's lair deep inside the Mountain of Despair, through tunnels and labyrinths, through dungeons and the bowels of the odd dragon, until at last it reached the doorway that led from its hiding place into the dreadful landscape beyond.

The doorway was most impressive, intricately carved with terrifying faces whose expressions were ever-changing, and horrific forms whose bodies intertwined, so that the very entrance itself seemed to be alive. At this precise moment the doorway was being guarded by two demons. In the classic manner of double acts everywhere, they were exact opposites. One guard was tall and thin, with features that suggested an irritating, and somewhat overweight, child had spent a lot of time hanging from the guard's chin, thereby stretching the guard's face into a very mournful expression. His colleague was shorter and fatter. In fact he looked like he might have eaten the irritating, overweight child as a favour to his fellow guard.

Brompton, the thinner of the two, had been guarding the doorway for so long that he had forgotten what he was supposed to be guarding it against, given that the most awful being it was possible to imagine was already in residence inside the mountain. During the centuries that he had spent leaning on his spear, occasionally dozing or scratching himself where polite demons didn't usually scratch themselves in public, he could not, until recently, recall a great many instances of individuals trying to get in who weren't already entitled to pass freely. Oh, a couple of demons had tried to escape from inside the mountain, largely to avoid being torn apart as a punishment for something or other, or occasionally just for a bet, but otherwise things had been very quiet around there, in a Hellish way, for a long time.

His colleague, Edgefast, was a new arrival. Brompton regarded him suspiciously from beneath his helmet. Edgefast wasn't leaning sufficiently on his spear for Brompton's liking, and he had not yet proposed skiving off for a cup of tea, or a nap. Instead, Edgefast seemed to be standing up very straight, and he had a disconcerting gleam in his eye, the kind of gleam associated with someone who actually likes his job and, even worse, plans to do it as well as possible. Brompton, by contrast, had not yet found a job that he might be inclined to like or do well, and was of the opinion that such an occupation did not exist, which suited him just fine. A job, as far as Brompton was concerned, was something that somebody made you do when you'd rather be doing nothing at all.

Edgefast glanced nervously at Brompton.

'Why do you keep staring at me like that?' he asked.

'You're not slouching,' said Brompton.

'What?'

'I said, "You're not slouching." Making me look bad, you are. Making me look untidy. Making me look like I don't care.'

'But, er, you *don't* care,' said Edgefast, who understood, from the moment he had set eyes on Brompton, that here was a demon with 'waste of space' written all over him.

'That's as maybe,' said Brompton, 'but I don't want everyone to know that I don't care. You'll get me fired, looking all enthusiastic like that. I might not like this job, but there are worse ones out there.'

'Don't I know it,' said Edgefast, in the manner of a demon who has seen the worst that Hell has to offer, and for whom anything else is pure gravy.

'Yeah?' said Brompton, interested now despite himself. 'What were you doing before this, then?'

Edgefast sighed. 'You remember that time Duke Kobal lost his favourite ring?'

Brompton did. As demonic lords went, Kobal[3] wasn't

💀 [3] Duke Kobal was officially the demon of comedians, although only the really unfunny ones, with additional responsibility for the jokes in Christmas crackers. You know, like: What's the longest word in the English language? Smiles, because there's a 'mile' between the first and last letters. A mile. No,

the worst, which meant that, when he was sticking sharp needles into your flesh, or finding out just how many spiders you could hold in your mouth at once, he would always provide tea and biscuits for everyone who was watching, and tell you how sorry he was that it had to come to this, even as he tried to fit one last spider between your lips. Kobal had lost his best skull ring down one of Hell's sewers, and it had never been found. Following this incident a law had been passed requiring that all of Hell's rotten vegetables, old food, unidentified limbs, and assorted demonic bodily waste products should be searched by hand before being swept into the Sea of Unpleasantness, just in case anything valuable might have been mislaid.

'Well,' continued Edgefast. 'You know all that searching business?'

'You mean, going down on your claws and knees and raking through poo 'n' stuff?'

'Yep.'

'With your nose right in it, so you could be certain that nothing slipped by?'

'Yep.'

'And with nowhere to wash, so you had to try and eat your sandwich at break by holding it right at the

---

a *mile*. Yes, as in distance. Yes, I know there's not really a mile, but – OK, stop talking. I'm serious, you're starting to annoy me. No, I don't want to wear a paper hat. I don't care if it's Christmas, those hats make my head itchy. And I don't want to see what you've won. No, I really don't. Fine, then. Oh great, a compass. If I take it away, will you get lost? See, that's funny. Well, I thought it was.

Christmas: Duke Kobal loves it.

edges with your claws while hoping that you didn't drop it?'

'Yep.'

'But your hands smelled bad so your sandwich smelled bad too?'

'Yep.'

''Orrible. Just 'orrible.' Brompton shuddered. 'Doesn't bear thinking about. Worst job in Hell. Anyway, go on.'

'Well, that was me.'

'No!'

'Yes. Years and years of it. I still can't look at a toilet without feeling the urge to stick my hand down it.'

'I thought you smelled a bit funny, even for a demon.'

'It's not my fault. I've tried everything: water, soap, acid. It won't go away.'

'Very unfortunate for you, and anyone who happens to be downwind of you, I must say. Well, this must be quite the promotion for you, then.'

'Oh, it is, it is!' said Edgefast fervently.

'Somebody likes you.'

Brompton nudged him. Edgefast giggled.

'Suppose so.'

'Oh yes, you're quite the special one. Satan's little pet!'

'Don't know I'm born,' said Edgefast. 'Happiest day of my existence, getting away from all that.'

Edgefast beamed. Brompton beamed back. Just then, a large slot opened above their heads, and the hourly emptying of Hell's drains began, dousing the two guards in the foulest waste imaginable before coming to rest in a series of large, stinking pits at the base of the mountain. When the last drop had fallen, and the slot had closed, a small demon dressed in wellington boots and wearing a peg on its nose entered the pits and began searching through the latest delivery.

'That was me once, that was,' said Edgefast, carefully removing a piece of rotting vegetation from his ear.

'You lucky, lucky sod,' said Brompton.

They watched the demon quietly for a time.

'Good of them to give us helmets, though,' said Edgefast.

'One of the perks of the job,' said Brompton. 'Wouldn't be half as nice without the helmets.'

'I meant to ask,' said Edgefast. 'What happened to the bloke who had this job before me?'

Brompton didn't get the chance to answer. A long, dismal road led through the pits and on to the dreary plain beyond. That road had been empty ever since Edgefast had arrived for this, his first day on the job, but it was empty no longer. A figure was approaching and as it drew nearer Edgefast saw that it was a woman, or something that was doing a pretty good impression of one. She was wearing a white dress decorated with a pattern of red flowers, and a straw hat with a white ribbon around its crown. The heels of her white shoes made a steady *click-click-click* sound on the stones of the road, and over her left arm hung a white bag fastened by gold clasps. The woman had a very determined expression on her face, one that might have given pause to a more intelligent demon than Edgefast. But, as

Brompton had correctly surmised, Edgefast was an enthusiast, and there's no talking to enthusiasts.

The woman was now close enough for Edgefast to see that the dress was more tattered than it had first appeared. It looked home-made, with uneven seams, and the shoes were crude black boots that had been painted white and then carved so that the heels ended in points. The bag had a frame of bone over which skin had been draped, complete with freckles and hair, and the clasps were, on closer inspection, gold teeth.

None of these elements, peculiar in themselves, represented the strangest aspect of the woman's appearance. That honour went to the fact that the only thing more poorly stitched together than her dress was the woman herself. Her skin, visible at her face and arms and legs, seemed to have been ripped apart at some point, the various pieces then sewn back together again in a rough approximation of what a woman might look like. One eye socket was smaller than the other, the left side of the mouth was higher than the right, and the skin on the lower part of the left leg sagged like a pair of old tights. The woman's blond hair sat untidily on her head like a mess of straw dropped there by a passing bird. What he was looking at, Edgefast realized, was not so much a woman as a woman costume, which made him wonder what might lie beneath it.

Still, Edgefast had a job to do. He stepped forward before Brompton had a chance to stop him and stuck his spear out in a vaguely threatening manner.

'You know, I wouldn't do—' Brompton began to say, but by then it was too late.

'Halt,' said Edgefast. 'Where do you think you're going?'

Unfortunately Edgefast didn't get an answer to that question, but he did receive an answer to his earlier one, which was what had happened to the chap who had previously held the guard's job before him, for Edgefast was about to become intimately acquainted with his predecessor's fate.

The woman stopped and stared at Edgefast.

'Oh dear.' Brompton pulled his helmet low over his eyes, and tried to make himself as small as possible. 'Oh dear, oh dear, oh . . .'

Fearsome tentacles, dripping viscous fluid, erupted from the woman's back, ripping through the fabric of her dress. Her mouth opened wide, revealing row upon row of sharp, jagged teeth. Long nails shot from the tips of her pale fingers, curling in upon themselves like hooks. The tentacles gripped Edgefast, lifted him from the ground, and then pulled him very, very hard in a number of different directions at once. There was a squeal of pain, and assorted pieces of what was once Edgefast were thrown in the air; one of them landed on Brompton's helmet. He peered down to see Edgefast's head on the dirt before him, a puzzled look in his eyes.

'You might have warned me,' said the head.

Brompton put his foot over Edgefast's mouth to keep him quiet as the woman adjusted her now even more dishevelled appearance, patted her hair, and then proceeded to pass through the doorway to the Mountain of Despair, untroubled by any further enquiries as to where she might be going.

Brompton tipped his helmet to her as she passed. 'Morning . . .'

He paused, trying to find the appropriate word. The woman's dark eyes flicked towards him, and he felt a coldness enter his belly, the kind of coldness that comes just before someone rips *you* into little pieces and tosses *your* head at the nearest wall.

'. . . Miss,' he finished, and the woman smiled at him in a 'Yes-I-am-so-pretty-thank-you-for-noticing' way before disappearing into the mountain.

Brompton breathed a sigh of relief, and lifted his foot from Edgefast's mouth.

'That really hurt,' said Edgefast, as Brompton began picking up his limbs and placing them in a large pile in the hope that Edgefast could be put back together in a way that might vaguely resemble what he had once been.

'It's your own fault,' said Brompton. He began to fold his arms, then realized that he was still holding one of Edgefast's arms in each of his hands and it all threatened to get very confusing, so he contented himself with shaking one of Edgefast's severed fingers at Edgefast's head in a disapproving manner. 'You shouldn't be asking personal questions of a lady.'

'But I'm a guard. And I'm not sure that *was* a lady.'

'Shhhhh!' Brompton looked anxiously over his shoulder, as though expecting the woman to pop up again and tear both of them into pieces so small that only ants could find them. 'You know, I don't think you're cut out to be a guard,' he said. 'You're too keen on the whole *guarding* business.'

'But isn't that what we're supposed to be doing?' said Edgefast. 'Our job is to guard the entrance. I was just trying to be good at it.'

'Were you now?' said Brompton. He looked doubtful. 'You know what I'm good at guarding?'

'No. What?'

'My health.'

He popped Edgefast's helmet back on Edgefast's head, and went back to leaning on his spear as he waited for someone to come and take the bits away.

'Who was . . . um, "she", anyway?' asked Edgefast.

'That,' said Brompton, with some feeling, 'is Mrs Abernathy, and she's in a very bad mood.'

CHAPTER II

In Which We Learn a Little About
How Hard It Is To Be In Love

Time is a funny thing. Take time travel: ask a random assortment of people whether they'd prefer to go backwards or forwards in time, and you'll probably get a pretty even split between those who like the idea of seeing the Great Pyramid being built, or of playing tag with a dinosaur, and those who'd rather see if all of those jet packs and laser guns we were promised in comic books have finally made it into shops.[4]

Unfortunately, there is bad news for those who would like to go back in time. Assuming that I, when not writing books or annoying the neighbours by practising the bassoon at odd hours, build a time machine in my

---

[4] Actually, the decision on whether to go backwards or forwards in time might well tell you something important about the person in question. The English writer Arnold Bennett (1867–1931) was reputed to have said that 'The people who live in the past must yield to the people who live in the future. Otherwise, the world would begin to turn the other way around.' What Bennett was saying is that it's better to look forward than to look back, because that's how progress is made. On the other hand, George Santayana (1863–1952), an American writer, said that 'Those who cannot remember the past are condemned to repeat it.' In other words, it's a question of balance: the past is a nice country to visit, but you wouldn't want to live there.

basement, and offer free trips in it to anyone who fancies a jaunt, those who want to visit Queen Elizabeth I to see if she really had wooden teeth (she didn't: they were just rotten and black, and the lead in her make-up was also slowly poisoning her, so she was probably in a very bad mood most of the time), or to find out if King Ethelred the Unready really was unready (he wasn't: his nickname is a mistranslation of an Old English word meaning 'bad advice') are going to be sorely disappointed.

And why is that? Because you can't go back to a time before there was a time machine. You just can't. The earliest time to which you can return is the moment at which the time machine came into existence. Sorry, those are the rules. I don't make them, I just enforce them in books. So the reason why there are no visitors from the future is that nobody has yet managed to build a time machine *in our own time*. Either that or someone has invented one and is keeping very quiet about it so that people don't keep knocking on his door asking him if they can have a go on his time machine, which would be very annoying.[5]

If Mrs Abernathy had been able to go back in time,

☠ [5] There is also the small matter of what is known as the 'Grandfather Paradox': what would happen if you went back in time and killed your grandfather before your mum or dad was born? Would you then cease to exist? But the argument is that you're already in existence, as you were around to travel back in time, so if you do try to kill your grandfather then you'll obviously fail. Hang on, though: is it possible that you might just 'pop' out of existence if you did manage to kill your grandfather? No, because that would imply two different realities, one in which you exist and the other in which you don't exist, which won't do at all. This has led the eminent physicist,

there are a number of things she might have done differently in the course of the attempted invasion of Earth, but principal among them would have been not to underestimate the boy named Samuel Johnson, or his little dog, Boswell. Then again, how could she have imagined that a small boy and his dachshund would prove her undoing? She might have been a demon, but she was also an adult, and most adults have a hard time imagining that small boys, or dachshunds, could possibly be superior to them in any way.

It might have been of some consolation to Mrs Abernathy to learn that while she was struggling with her feelings of rejection and humiliation, the person responsible for most of her problems was experiencing some rejection and humiliation of his own, for Samuel Johnson had just tried to ask Lucy Highmore on a date.

Samuel had been in love with Lucy from the moment he set eyes on her, which was his first day at Montague Rhodes James secondary school in Biddlecombe. In Samuel's eyes, little bluebirds flew ceaselessly around Lucy's head, serenading her with odes to her beauty and depositing petals in her hair, while angels made her school bag a little lighter by helping her with the

---

Professor Stephen Hawking, to come up with the Chronology Protection Conjecture, a kind of virtual ban on time travel. Professor Hawking believes that there must be a rule of physics to prevent time travel, because otherwise we'd have tourists from the future visiting us, and people popping up willy-nilly trying to shoot grandfathers in order to prove a point. In the end, though, if you're the kind of person who, at the first mention of time travel, brings up the possibility of shooting your grandfather, then you're probably not someone who should be allowed near time machines or, for that matter, grandfathers.

burden of it, and whispered the answers to maths questions into her ear when she was stuck. Come to think of it, that wasn't angels: it was every other boy in the class, for Lucy Highmore was the kind of girl who made boys dream of marriage and baby carriages, and made other girls dream of Lucy Highmore falling down a steep flight of stairs and landing on a pile of porcupine quills and rusty farm equipment.

It had taken Samuel over a year to work up the courage to ask Lucy out: month upon month of finding the right words, of practising them in front of a mirror so that he wouldn't stumble on them when he began to speak, of calling himself an idiot for ever thinking that she might agree to have a pie with him at Pete's Pies, followed by a squaring of his newly teenage shoulders, a stiffening of his upper lip, and a reminder to himself that faint heart never won fair lady, although faint heart never suffered crushing rejection either.

Samuel Johnson was brave: he had faced down the wrath of Hell itself, so there could be no doubting his courage, but the prospect of baring his young heart to Lucy Highmore and risking having it skewered by the blunt sword of indifference made his stomach lurch and his eyes swim. He was not sure what might be worse: to ask Lucy Highmore out and be rejected, or not to ask and thus never to know how she might feel about him; to be turned down, and learn that there was no possibility of finding a place in her affections, or to live in hope without ever having that hope realized. After much thought, he had decided that it was better to know.

Samuel wore glasses: quite thick glasses, as it happened, and without them the world tended to look a little blurry to him. He decided that he looked better without his glasses, even though he couldn't be sure of this as, when he took them off and looked in the mirror, he resembled a drawing of himself that had fallen in a puddle. Still, he was pretty certain that Lucy Highmore would like him more without his glasses, so on the fateful day – the First Fateful Day, as he later came to think of it – he carefully removed his glasses as he approached her, tucking them safely into his pocket, while repeating these words in his head: 'Hi, I was wondering if you'd allow me the pleasure of buying you a pie, and perhaps a glass of orange juice, at Pete's emporium of pies on the main street? Hi, I was wondering if—'

Somebody bumped into Samuel, or he bumped into somebody. He wasn't sure which, but he apologized and continued on his way before tripping over someone's bag and almost losing his footing.

'Oi, watch where you're going,' said the bag's owner.

'Sorry,' said Samuel. Again.

He squinted. Ahead of him he could see Lucy Highmore. She was wearing a red coat. It was a lovely coat. Everything about Lucy Highmore was lovely. She couldn't have been lovelier if her name was Lucy Lovely and she lived on Lovely Road in the town of Loveliness.

Samuel stood before her, cleared his throat, and, without stumbling once, said, 'Hi, I was wondering if you'd allow me the pleasure of buying you a pie, and perhaps a glass of orange juice, at Pete's emporium of pies on the main street?'

He waited for a reply, but none came. He squinted harder, trying to bring Lucy into focus. Was she overcome with emotion? Was she gaping in awe at him? Even now, was a single tear of happiness dropping from her eye like a diamond as the little tweety birds—

'Did you just ask that letter box on a date?' said someone close by. Samuel recognized the voice as that of Thomas Hobbes, his best friend.

'What?' Samuel fumbled for his glasses, put them on and found that he had somehow wandered in the wrong direction. He'd stepped out of the school gates and on to the street where he had, it seemed, just offered to buy a pie for the red letter box and, by extension, the postman who was about to empty it. The postman was now regarding Samuel with the kind of wariness associated with one who suspects that the person standing before him may well be something of a nutter, and could turn dangerous at any time.

'It doesn't eat pies,' said the postman slowly. 'Only letters.'

'Right,' said Samuel. 'I knew that.'

'Good,' said the postman, still speaking very slowly.

'Why are you speaking so slowly?' said Samuel, who found that he had now started speaking slowly as well.

'Because you're mad,' said the postman, even more slowly.

'Oh,' said Samuel.

'And the letter box can't come with you to the pie shop. It has to stay where it is. Because it's a letter box.'

He patted the letter box gently, and smiled at Samuel

as if to say, 'See, it's not a person, it's a box, so go away, mad bloke.'

'I'll look after him,' said Tom. He began to guide Samuel back to the school. 'Let's get you inside, shall we? You can have a nice lie-down.'

The students near the gates were watching Samuel. Some were sniggering.

See, it's that Johnson kid. I told you he was strange.

At least Lucy wasn't among them, thought Samuel. She had apparently moved off to spread her fragrant loveliness elsewhere.

'If it's not a rude question, why were you offering to buy a pie for a letter box?' said Tom, as they made their way into the depths of the playground.

'I thought it was Lucy Highmore,' said Samuel.

'Lucy Highmore doesn't look like a letter box, and I don't think she'd be very happy if she heard that you thought she did.'

'It was the red coat. I got confused.'

'She's a bit out of your league, isn't she?' said Tom.

Samuel sighed sadly. 'She's so far out of my league that we're not even playing the same sport. But she's lovely.'

'You're an idiot,' said Tom.

'Who's an idiot?'

Maria Mayer, Samuel's other closest friend at school, joined them.

'Samuel is,' said Tom. 'He just asked out a letter box, thinking it was Lucy Highmore.'

'Really?' said Maria. 'Lucy Highmore. That's ... nice.'

Her tone was not so much icy as arctic. The word 'nice' took on the aspect of an iceberg towards which the good ship Lucy Highmore was unwittingly steaming, but Tom, too caught up in his mirth, and Samuel, smarting with embarrassment, failed to notice.

Just then, he discovered that Lucy Highmore was not elsewhere. She appeared from behind a crowd of her friends, all still whispering, and Samuel blushed furiously as he realized that she had witnessed what had occurred. He walked on, feeling about the size of a bug, and as he passed Lucy's group he heard her friends begin to giggle, and then he heard Lucy begin to giggle too.

I want to go back in time, he thought. Back to a time before I ever asked Lucy Highmore for a date. I want to change the past, all of it.

I don't want to be that strange Johnson kid any more.

It's odd, but people are capable of forgetting quite extraordinary occurrences very quickly if it makes them happier to do so, even events as incredible as the gates of Hell opening and spewing out demons of the most unpleasant kind, which is what had happened in the little town of Biddlecombe just over fifteen months earlier. You'd think that after such an experience, people would have woken up every morning, yawned, and scratched their heads before opening their eyes wide in terror and shrieking, 'The Gates! Demons! They were here! They'll be back!'

But people are not like that. It's probably a good thing, as otherwise life would be very hard to live. It's not true that time heals all wounds, but it does dull the memory of pain, or people would only go to the dentist once and then never return, or not without some significant guarantees regarding their personal comfort and safety.[6]

So, as the weeks and months had passed, the memory of what had happened in Biddlecombe began to fade until after a while people began to wonder if it had really happened at all, or if it had all been some kind of strange dream. More to the point, they figured that it had happened once, and consequently wasn't ever likely to happen again, so they could just stop worrying about it and get on with more important things, like football, and reality television, and gossiping about their neighbours. At least that was what they told themselves, but sometimes, in the deepest, darkest part of the night, they would wake from strange dreams of creatures with nasty teeth and poisonous claws, and when their children said that they couldn't sleep because there was something under the bed, they didn't just tell them that they were being silly. No, they very, very carefully peered under the bed, and they did so with a cricket bat, or a brush handle, or a kitchen knife in hand.

Because you never knew . . .

💀 [6] 'What do you mean, you're giving me a small anaesthetic? I want a *big* anaesthetic. I want the kind that they give to elephants before they operate on them. I want my chin to feel like it's been carved from rock, like my face is part of a statue on the side of a large building. I don't want to feel ANY pain at all, otherwise there'll be trouble, you hear? Why did you become a dentist anyway? Do you like hurting people? Well, do you? You're a monster, that's what you are, a monster!'

Sorry about that, but you know what I mean . . .

In a peculiar way, though, Samuel Johnson felt that they blamed *him* for what had happened. He wasn't the one who had conjured up demons in his basement because he was bored, and he wasn't the one who had built a big machine that inadvertently opened a portal between this world and Hell. It wasn't his fault that the Devil, the Great Malevolence, hated the Earth and wanted to destroy it. But because he'd been so involved in what had happened, people were reminded of it when they saw him, and they didn't want to be. They wanted to forget it all, and they had convinced themselves that they had forgotten it, even if they hadn't, not really. They just didn't want to think about it, which isn't the same thing at all.

But Samuel couldn't forget it because, occasionally, he would catch a glimpse of a woman in a mirror, or reflected in a shop window, or in the glass of a bus shelter. It was Mrs Abernathy, her eyes luminous with a strange blue glow, and Samuel would feel her hatred of him. No other person ever saw her, though. He had tried to tell the scientists about her, but they hadn't believed him. They thought he was just a small boy – a clever and brave one, but a small boy nonetheless – who was still troubled by the dreadful things that he had seen.

Samuel knew better. Mrs Abernathy wanted revenge: on Samuel, on the Earth, and on every living creature that walked, or swam, or flew, or crawled.

Which brings us to the other reason why Samuel couldn't forget. He hadn't defeated Mrs Abernathy and the Devil and all of the hordes of Hell alone. He'd been helped by an unlucky but generally decent demon named Nurd, and Nurd and Samuel had become friends. But now Nurd was somewhere in Hell, hiding from Mrs Abernathy, and Samuel was here on Earth, and neither could help the other.

Samuel could only hope that, wherever he was, Nurd was safe.[7]

☠ [7] Just one more thing about time travel, while we're on the subject. Quantum theory suggests that there is a probability that all possible events, however strange, might occur, and every possible outcome of every event exists in its own world. In other words, all possible pasts and futures, like the one where you didn't pick up this book but read something else instead, are potentially real, and they all co-exist alongside one another. Now, let's suppose that we invent a time machine that allows us to move on to those alternative time lines. Why, then you could set about killing assorted grandfathers to your heart's content, as they're not part of your world but part of someone else's, someone who is not you but is a slightly different version of you, except possibly not with a murderous, inexplicable grudge against his or her grandfather.

And if you think all of these notions of parallel worlds and other dimensions are nonsense, please note that Jonathon Keats, a San Francisco-based experimental philosopher, has already begun selling land in those extra dimensions of space and time. In fact, he sold 172 lots of extra-dimensional land in the San Francisco Bay Area in one day. I'm not sure what that proves, exactly, other than the fact that there are people in San Francisco who will pay someone for things that may not exist, which perhaps says more about San Franciscans than about scientific theory. Also, I'd like to see those people try to enforce their property rights when faced with a ray-gun wielding monster from another dimension. 'Now look here, I paid good money for this piece of land and—' *Zap!*

CHAPTER III

In Which We Delve Deeper Into the Bowels of Hell, Which Is One of Those Chapter Headings that Make Parents Worry About the Kind of Books Their Children Are Reading

After that brief detour to Earth, and that lesson in love, life, and the importance of good eyesight, let's return to Hell. As we are now aware, the woman striding purposefully through the dim recesses of the Mountain of Despair while wearing a severely tattered floral print dress was Mrs Abernathy, formerly known as Ba'al. Mrs Abernathy had been making a daily pilgrimage to the Great Malevolence's lair ever since the attempt to break into the world of men had come to naught. She wanted to present herself to her master, explain to him what had gone wrong, and find a way to insinuate herself into his favour again. Mrs Abernathy was almost as ancient and evil as the Great Malevolence himself, and they had spent eons together in this desolate place, slowly creating a kingdom out of ash, and filth, and flame.

But now the Great Malevolence, lost in his grief and madness, was apparently refusing to see his lieutenant. Mrs Abernathy was cut off from him, and the demon was troubled by this; troubled, and, yes, frightened. Without the protection and indulgence of the Great

Malevolence, Mrs Abernathy was vulnerable. Something had to be done. The Great Malevolence had to be made to listen, which was why Mrs Abernathy kept returning to this place, where foul creatures watched from the shadows in amusement at the sight of one of the greatest of demons, the commander of Hell's armies, reduced to the status of a beggar; a beggar, what's more, who seemed troublingly keen on wearing women's clothing.

Oddly enough, Mrs Abernathy, having initially been distinctly unhappy at being forced to take on the appearance of a lady in her forties, had grown to like wearing floral print dresses and worrying about her hair. This was partly because Mrs Abernathy had until quite recently been neither male nor female: she had simply been a distinctly horrible 'it'. Now she had an identity, and a form that wasn't mainly teeth, and claws, and tentacles. Ba'al might originally have taken over Mrs Abernathy's body, but something of Mrs Abernathy had subsequently infected Ba'al. For the first time there was a use for a mirror, and nice clothes, and make-up. She worried about her appearance. She was, not to put too fine a point on it, vain.[8] She no longer even thought of herself as Ba'al. Ba'al was the past. Mrs Abernathy was the present, and the future.

💀 [8] Lest anyone starts getting offended on behalf of women everywhere, let me just stress that vanity is not unique to the fairer sex. 'Vanity', according to the poet and essayist Jonathan Swift (1667–1745), 'is the food of fools;/ Yet now and then your men of wit/ Will condescend to take a bit.' Vanity can best be defined as taking too much pride in yourself, and the opposite of pride is humility, which means seeing yourself as you are, and not comparing yourself to other people, even bad ones or, indeed, other demons in dresses, should you happen to be a dress-wearing demon yourself.

As she descended deeper and deeper into the mountain, she was aware of the sniggers and whispers from all around her. The great bridge along which she walked was suspended over a gaping chasm so deep that, if you were to fall into it, you would keep falling for ever and ever, until at last you died of old age without ever nearing the bottom. Metal and chains held the bridge in place, linking it to the inner walls of the mountain. Set into it were countless arched vaults, each hidden in shadow, and each inhabited by a demon. The vaults stretched upwards and downwards, as far as the eye could see and farther still, until the flaming torches set haphazardly into the walls, the sole source of illumination to be found in the chasm, became as small as stars before at last they disappeared entirely, swallowed up by the gloom. Here and there beasts peered from their chambers: small imps, red and grinning; fiends of fire, and fiends of ice; creatures misshapen and creatures without shape, formless entities that were little more than glowing eyes set against smoke. There was a time when they would have cowered from her presence, fearful that even by setting eyes on her they might incur her wrath. Now, though, they had begun to mock her. She had failed her master. In time his cries would cease, and he would remember that she should be punished for her failings.

And then, what fun they would have!

For now, though, the wailing continued. It grew louder as Mrs Abernathy drew closer to its source. She saw that some of the demons had stuffed coal in their ears in an effort to block out the sound of their master's grief, while others appeared to have been driven as mad as he was and were humming to themselves, or banging their heads repeatedly against the walls in frustration.

At last the vaults were left behind, and there were only sheer dark walls of stone. In the murk before her a shape moved, detaching itself from the shadows the way that someone might detach a shoe from sticky tar, tendrils of blackness seeming to stretch from the entity back into the gloom as though it were part of the darkness, and the darkness part of it. It stepped beneath the flickering light of a torch and grinned unpleasantly. In aspect it resembled a vulture, albeit one with somewhat human features. Its head was pink and bare, although the light caught the tiny bristles that pocked its skin. Its nose was long and fleshy, and hooked like that of a bird of prey, joining a single lower lip to form a kind of beak. Its small black eyes shone with inky malevolence. It wore a dark cloak that flowed like oil over its hunched shoulders, and in its left hand it held a staff of bone, topped with a small skull; that staff was now extended before Mrs Abernathy, blocking her progress.

The creature's name was Ozymuth, and he was the Great Malevolence's chancellor.[9] Ozymuth had always

---

💀 [9] The chancellor is the secretary and adviser to a ruler, or a king. It's a risky profession, as rulers with great power often tend to react badly to people who try to tell them what to do, or who suggest that they may be wrong about something. Thomas Becket (1118–70), the chancellor to Henry II of England, was hacked to pieces by knights after he and the king differed over how much power the king should have over the church. Famously, Henry VIII of England had his chancellor, Thomas More (1478–1535), beheaded because More didn't approve of the king's desire to divorce his first wife, Catherine of Aragon, in order to marry the younger and prettier Anne Boleyn. Eventually, Henry VIII

hated Ba'al, even before Ba'al began calling itself Mrs Abernathy and wearing odd clothing. Ozymuth's power lay in the fact that he had the ear of the Great Malevolence. If demons wanted favours done, or sought promotion, then they had to approach the Great Malevolence through Ozymuth, and if their favour was granted or they received the promotion that they sought then they in turn owed Ozymuth a favour. This is the way that the world works, not just Hell. It's not nice, and it shouldn't happen, but it does, and you should be aware of it.

'You may not pass,' said Ozymuth. A long pink tongue poked from his beak and licked at something invisible upon his skin.

'Who are you to tell me what I may or may not do?' said Mrs Abernathy, disdain dripping like acid from her tongue. 'You are our master's dog, and nothing more. If you don't show me some respect, I will have you taken to pieces, cell by cell, atom by atom, and then reassembled just so I can start over again.'

Ozymuth sniggered. 'Each day you come here, and each day your threats sound emptier and emptier. You were our master's favourite once, but that time is gone. You had your chance to please him and you threw it away. If I were you, I would find a hole in which to hide myself, and there I would remain in the hope that

---

ended up having Anne Boleyn beheaded too. The lesson to be learned here is not to work for any kings named Henry who seem to have a fondness for lopping off heads. It's a good idea to watch how they take the tops off their boiled eggs: if they do it with too much ferocity, then it might be a good idea to apply for a job somewhere else.

our master might forget I had ever existed. For when his grief ceases, and he remembers the torment that you have caused him, being taken to pieces will seem like a gentle massage compared to what he will visit upon you. Your days of glory are over, "Mrs Abernathy". Look at you! Look at what you have become!'

Mrs Abernathy's eyes blazed. She snarled and raised her hand as if to strike Ozymuth down. Ozymuth cowered and hid his face beneath his cloak. For a moment they stayed like that, these two old adversaries, until a strange sound emerged from under Ozymuth's cloak. It was laughter, a hissing demonstration of mirth like gas escaping from a hole in a pipe, or bacon sizzling in a pan.

'*Tssssssssss*,' laughed Ozymuth. '*Tssssssssssssss*. You have no power here, and if you strike me then you strike our master, for I am his voice, and I speak for him. Leave now, and give up this senseless pilgrimage. If you come here again, I will have you taken away in chains.'

He raised his staff, and the small skull glowed a sickly yellow. From behind him, two enormous winged beasts appeared. In the dim light they had looked like the images of dragons carved into the walls, so still were they, but now they towered above the two beings on the walkway. One of them leaned down, revealing its reptilian skull, its lips curling back to expose long, sharp teeth of diamond. It growled low and threateningly at Mrs Abernathy, who responded by smacking it on the nose with her bag. The dragon whimpered and looked embarrassed, then turned to its companion as if to say

'Well, you see if you can do any better.' The other dragon just shrugged and found something interesting to stare at on the nearest wall. That bag, it thought, was a lot heavier than it looked.

'You have not heard the last of this, Ozymuth,' said Mrs Abernathy. 'I will rise again, and I will not forget your insolence.'

She spun on her heel and began to walk away. Once again, she was aware of the sound of the Great Malevolence's cries, and the whispers from demons, seen and unseen, and the hissing of Ozymuth's laughter. She endured the long walk through the bowels of the Mountain of Despair, seething with hurt and humiliation. As she passed through the entrance and back into the desolate landscape of Hell, a voice spoke from somewhere around the level of her shoe.

'Have a nice day, now,' said Edgefast's detached head.

Mrs Abernathy ignored him, and moved on.

As Ozymuth watched the retreating figure his laughter slowly ceased. A second form appeared from the shadows, tall and regal. The torches cast light upon his pale features, imperious and cruel. His long black hair was braided with gold, and his clothing was of rich, red velvet, as though blood had been woven into cloth. His cloak, also red, billowed behind him even when he was still, like a living extension of its wearer. He reached out a bejewelled claw and stroked absent-mindedly at one of the dragons, which purred contentedly like a large, scaly cat.

'My Lord Abigor,' said Ozymuth, lowering his head in a gesture of utter subjection, which was a very wise idea when in Duke Abigor's presence, as people who forgot to lower their heads around Duke Abigor often found their heads being lowered for them, usually by having them removed from their shoulders with a large blade.

It is said that Nature abhors a vacuum, but so too does power. When someone falls out of favour with a leader, a queue will quickly form to take that person's place. Thus it was that when Mrs Abernathy failed the Great Malevolence, a number of powerful demons began to wonder how they might take advantage of her misfortune to promote themselves. Of these, the most ambitious and conniving was Duke Abigor.

'What say you, Ozymuth?' said Abigor.

'She is stubborn, my Lord.'

'Stubborn, and dangerous. Her persistence troubles me.'

'Our master will not see her. I have made sure of it. With every chance I get, I whisper words against her into his ear. I remind him of how she failed him. I stoke the fires of his madness, just as you asked of me.'

'You are a loyal and faithful servant,' said Abigor, his voice heavy with sarcasm. Abigor made a note to himself to have Ozymuth banished at the first opportunity once he achieved his goal, for anyone who betrays one master cannot be trusted not to betray another.

'I am loyal to the Great Malevolence, my lord,' replied Ozymuth carefully, as though Duke Abigor had spoken his doubts aloud. 'It is better for our master if his lieutenants do not fail him. Or dress in inappropriate women's clothing,' he added.

Abigor stared at the predatory visage of the chancellor. Abigor was not used to being corrected, however gently. It made him even more intent upon disposing of Ozymuth as soon as he could.

'I will remember you when I come to power,' said Abigor, and he let the double meaning hang in the air. 'Our time draws near. Soon, Ozymuth, soon . . .'

Abigor faded back into the shadows, and then disappeared. Ozymuth released a long, ragged breath. He was playing a dangerous game, and he knew it, but if he distrusted Duke Abigor, then he hated Mrs Abernathy more. He gripped his staff and headed deeper into the Mountain of Despair, wincing as the howls of his master grew louder. At the entrance to the inner chamber, he paused. In the gloom his keen eyes espied the massive shape of the Great Malevolence, curled in upon himself in grief.

'It is I, my master,' he said, poison dripping from every word. 'I bear you sad tidings: your faithless lieutenant, Mrs Abernathy, continues to speak ill of you . . .'

CHAPTER IV

In Which We Reacquaint Ourselves with Nurd, formerly 'Nurd, The Scourge of Five Deities', Which Was All Something of a Misunderstanding, Really

From a Perfectly Modest cave in the base of a Not Terribly Interesting mountain in a Nothing To See Here, Move Along Now part of Hell, there came the sound of tinkering. Tinkering, as you may be aware, is essentially a male pursuit. Women, by and large, do not tinker, which is why it was a man who originally invented the garden shed and the garage, both of which are basically places to which men can retreat in order to perform tasks that serve no particularly useful purpose other than to give them something to do with their hands that does not involve eating, drinking, or fiddling with the remote control for the television. Very occasionally, a useful invention may result from tinkering, but for the most part tinkering involves trying to improve pieces of machinery that work perfectly well already, with the result that they stop doing what they were supposed to do and instead do nothing at all, hence requiring more tinkering to fix them, and even then they never work quite as well as they did before, so they have to be tinkered with some more, and so on and so on, until eventually the man in question dies, often after being severely beaten by his wife with a malfunctioning kettle, or a piece of a fridge.

Inside the cave was a car. At one point, the car had been a pristine Aston Martin, perfectly maintained by Samuel Johnson's father, who had kept it in the garage behind their house and only drove it on sunny days. Unfortunately the car had been one of the casualties of the demonic assault on Biddlecombe. Without it, there might not have been a Biddlecombe at all, or not one that wasn't overrun by hellish entities. Samuel's dad hadn't seen things that way, though, once he found out that his car was missing.

'You mean it was stolen by a demon?' he had asked, staring at the empty space in his garage that had until recently been occupied by his pride and joy. Samuel had watched his dad as he searched behind stacks of old paint and bits of lawnmower, as though expecting the car to jump out from behind a tin of white emulsion and shout 'Surprise!'

'That's right.'

It was Samuel's mum who had answered. She seemed quite pleased that her husband was upset at the loss of his car, mainly because Samuel's dad had left them to go and live with another woman while expecting his abandoned wife and son to look after his car for him, which Mrs Johnson regarded as being more than a little selfish.

It wasn't quite true that the car had been stolen. In fact Samuel had given the keys to the demon Nurd so that he could drive it straight down the mouth of the portal between Hell and Biddlecombe, thus collapsing it and preventing the Great Malevolence from escaping into our world. Samuel had nevertheless been grateful to his mother for clouding the truth, even if he felt that it was unfair on Nurd to describe him as a thief.

That same Nurd was now standing with his arms folded, staring at what had once been Mr Johnson's Aston Martin but was now Nurd's. The car had passed through the portal relatively unscathed, which came as a nice surprise to Nurd who had half expected that he and the car would be ripped into lots of little pieces and then crushed into something the size of a gnat's eyeball. He had also been relieved to find that the pools of viscous, bubbling black liquid dotted throughout Hell were wells of hydrocarbons and other organic compounds: or, to put it another way, every one of those pools was a miniature petrol station waiting to be put to use.

Unfortunately the petroleum mix was somewhat crude, and the landscape of Hell had not been designed with vintage cars in mind. Doubly unfortunately, Nurd knew next to nothing about how internal combustion engines worked, so he was ill-equipped to deal with any problems that might arise. Nurd fancied himself as a good driver, but since driving in Hell required him to do little more than point the car in a given direction, put his foot down, and avoid rocks and pools of crude oil, Nurd was not as expert behind the wheel as he liked to think.

But sometimes fortune can smile unexpectedly on the most unlikely of faces, and Nurd's, being green and shaped like a crescent moon, was unlikelier than most.

For being particularly annoying, Nurd had been banished to one of Hell's many wildernesses by the Great Malevolence. To keep Nurd company, the Great Malevolence had sent with him Nurd's assistant, Wormwood, who looked like a big ferret that had recently been given a haircut by a blind barber with a pair of blunt scissors. Now Wormwood was many things – irritating, funny-smelling, not terribly bright – but, most unexpectedly, he had proved to have an aptitude for all things mechanical. Thus, aided by a manual that he had found in the boot of the Aston Martin, he had taken responsibility for the maintenance and care of the car. It went faster than before, drove more smoothly, and could turn on a penny.

Oh, and it now looked like a big rock.

Nurd knew that Mrs Abernathy and her master, the Great Malevolence, would not exactly be pleased that their plan to create Hell on Earth had been foiled. Neither of them seemed like the forgiving type, which meant that they'd be looking for someone to blame. The Great Malevolence would blame Mrs Abernathy, because that was the kind of demon he was, since she was supposed to have been in charge. Mrs Abernathy, in turn, would be searching for someone else to blame, and that someone had last been seen hiding under a blanket and driving a vintage car into Hell. Nurd wasn't sure what would happen if Mrs Abernathy ever got her claws on him, but he imagined that it might involve every atom in his body being separated from the next, and then each one being prodded with a little pin for eternity, which didn't appeal to him at all.

So he had made two decisions. The first was that it would be a very good idea to stay on the move, because a moving object was harder to target.[10] It might also, he felt, be wise to disguise the car, which is why they had acquired a frame made from bits of wood and gauze and metal, and painted it to resemble a big boulder, albeit a boulder that could go from nought to sixty in under seven seconds.

At the moment, though, Wormwood was peering beneath the bonnet of the car and fiddling with some bit of the engine that only he could name. Nurd could probably have named it too, if he was bothered, which he wasn't, or so he told himself. After all, he was the brains of the operation, and therefore couldn't be going around worrying about carburettors and spark plugs and getting his hands dirty. It never struck him that Wormwood, as the individual who actually understood something of how the car worked, might have had more of a claim to being the brains than Nurd, but that's

☠ [10] Interestingly, this might be viewed as a variation on a principle of physics known as Heisenberg's Uncertainty Principle, which states that there is no way to accurately pinpoint the exact position of a subatomic particle – a very small particle indeed – unless you're willing to be uncertain about its velocity (its speed in a given direction), and there is no way to accurately pinpoint the particle's exact velocity unless you're willing to be uncertain about its position. It makes sense, when you think about it: on a very basic level you can't tell exactly where something very, very small is if it's moving. To do that, you'd have to interfere with its motion, thus making your knowledge of that motion more unclear. Similarly, observing its velocity means that the precise position will become more uncertain, so that even the act of observing a very small particle changes its behaviour. Actually, Heisenberg's Uncertainty Principle is a bit more complex than that, but that's the essence of it. Still, if you're asked if you understand Heisenberg's Uncertainty Principle, just say that you're not sure, which will be considered a very good scientific joke at the right party.

often the way with people who don't like getting their hands dirty. You don't necessarily get to be king by being bright, but it does help to have bright people around you.[11]

'Have you worked out the problem yet?' asked Nurd.

'It's the ignition coil,' said Wormwood.

'Is it really?' said Nurd, who tried not to sound too bored, and failed even at that.

'You don't know what an ignition coil is, do you?' said Wormwood.

'Is it a coil that has something to do with the ignition?'

'Er, yes.'

'Then I do. Do you know what a big stick capable of leaving a lump on your head is?'

'Yes.'

'Good. If you need to be reminded, just continue giving me lip.'

Wormwood emerged from beneath the bonnet and wiped his hands on his overalls. That was another thing: on the front of the car manual there had been a photograph of a man wearing overalls and holding a tool of some kind. On the left breast was written his name: Bob. Wormwood had decided that this was the kind of uniform worn by people who knew stuff about engines, and had managed to make himself a set of patchwork overalls from the contents of his meagre bag of clothes.

☠ [11] And if they get too bright and start wondering if they might not make rather good kings themselves, then you can have them killed. That's pretty much Rule One of being a king. You learn that on the first day.

He had even stitched his name on them, or a version of it: 'Wromwood'.

'It's the copper wire on the windings,' said Wromwood – er, Wormwood. 'It's taken a bit of a battering. It would be good if we could find some replacements.'

Nurd turned and stared out from the mouth of the cave. Before them stretched a huge expanse of black volcanic rock, which made a change from the huge expanse of grey volcanic rock that had until recently been the site of their banishment. The sky was dark with clouds, but tinged permanently with a hint of red, for there were always fires burning in Hell.

'We're a long way from copper wire, Wormwood,' said Nurd.

Wormwood joined his master. 'Where are we, exactly?'

Nurd shook his head. 'I don't know, but –' He pointed to his right, where the fires seemed to be burning brighter, the horizon lost to clouds and mists. – 'I'd guess that somewhere over there is the Mountain of Despair, which means that we want to go –'

'Somewhere else?' suggested Wormwood.

'Anywhere else,' agreed Nurd.

'Are we going to have to keep running for ever?' asked Wormwood, and there was something in his voice that almost caused Nurd to hug him, until he thought better of it and settled for patting Wormwood half-heartedly on the back. He wasn't sure what one might catch from hugging Wormwood, but whatever it was he didn't want it.

'We'll keep on the move for now,' he said. He was about to add something more when a shadow passed over the stones before him. It grew smaller and smaller as whatever was above them commenced a circling descent.

'Douse the light!' said Nurd, and instantly Wormwood quenched the flame of the torch, leaving the cave in darkness.

A red figure dropped to the ground within a stone's throw of the cave, its great bat wings raised above its back. It was eight feet tall and had the body of a man, but a forked tail curled from the base of its spine, and two twisted horns protruded from its bald head. It knelt and ran its claws over the rocks before it, then raised them to its nose and sniffed warily. A long forked tongue unrolled from its mouth and licked the ground.

'Oh no,' said Wormwood. He thought that he could almost see the marks of rubber upon the rocks where Nurd had been forced to give the car a little too much gas in order to get them closer to the cave.

The creature on the rocks grew very still. It had no ears, merely a hole on either side of its head, but it was clearly listening. Then it turned its head, and they glimpsed its face for the first time.

It had eight black eyes, like those of some great spider, and mandibles at its jaws. Its nostrils were ragged perforations set in a snout of sharp bone. Nurd saw them widen and contract, glistening with mucus. For a moment the creature stared straight at the mouth of the cave in which they were hiding, and they saw the muscles in its legs tighten as it prepared to spring. Its mandibles clicked, and its jaws made a sucking noise as though it could already taste prey, but instead of exploring further its wings unfolded to their fullest expanse and it shot into the air. The sound of flapping reached their ears, but slowly began to fade as the creature moved away, heading north in the direction of the bright flames.

'Did it see us?' asked Wormwood.

'I think it found the rubber from the tyres,' said Nurd. 'I don't know if it realized we were nearby. If it did, why didn't it come after us? Anyway, we have to go.'

'Was it –?'

'Yes,' said Nurd. 'It was one of hers.'

He sounded tired, and frightened, even to himself. They had been running and hiding for so long that sometimes he thought it might almost be a relief if they were caught, at least until he began thinking about what might happen to them *after* they were caught, for the prospect of being slowly disassembled at the atomic level and then prodded for a very long time usually dispelled such thoughts of giving up. But eventually they would make a serious mistake, or some misfortune would befall them, and then Mrs Abernathy's wrath would rain down upon them. The only consolation for Nurd was that Samuel Johnson was safe on Earth. He missed his friend terribly, but Nurd would willingly have sacrificed himself to keep Samuel safe. He just hoped that it wouldn't come to that, for Nurd liked all of his atoms just where they were.

CHAPTER V

In Which We Encounter Mr Merryweather's Dwarfs – or Elves – and Rather Wish We Hadn't

There are few things more soul-sapping, Mr Merryweather concluded wearily, than being stuck in a van with a bunch of truculent[12] dwarfs. The van in question bore the legend 'Mr Merryweather's Elves – Big Talent Comes in Small Packages'. Alongside the legend was a picture of a small person wearing pointy shoes and a cap with a bell on the end. The small person was grinning happily, and did not look at all threatening, and hence bore no resemblance to the actual contents of the van. Indeed, were one to look closely at the legend about elves and talent and whatnot, one might have noticed that the word 'Elves' had recently been painted over what appeared to be the word 'Dwarfs'.

We'll come to the reasons for the change in our own good time, but to give you some idea of just how difficult Mr Merryweather's dwarfs were currently

---

💀 [12] 'Truculent' is a lovely word. It essentially means to be very self-assertive and rather destructive. This perfectly described Mr Merryweather's dwarfs, who could have given lessons in aggression to Vikings.

being, a family of four was at that moment passing the van on the motorway, and the two children, a boy and a girl, had pressed their noses against the car window in the hope of catching a glimpse of an elf. Instead, they caught a glimpse of a small chap's bottom, which at that same moment was sticking out of one of the van's windows.

'Dad, is that an elf's bum?' asked the little boy.

'Elves don't exist,' said his father, who hadn't noticed the van or, indeed, the bum. 'And don't say "bum". It's rude.'

'But it says on the van that they're elves.'

'Well, I'm telling you that elves don't exist.'

'But, Dad, there's a bum sticking out of the window of the elf van, so it has to be an elf bum.'

'Look, I told you: don't use the word "b—"'

At which point the boy's dad looked to his right and was treated to the sight of a pale bottom hanging in the wind, alongside which were a number of small people making faces at him.

'Call the police, Ethel,' he said. He shook his fist in the general direction of faces and bottom. 'You little horrors!' he shouted.

'Nyaahhhh!' shouted a dwarf in return, and stuck his tongue out as the van sped away.

'See, I was right,' said the driver's son. 'It was an elf. And a bum.'

Inside the van, Mr Merryweather was trying to keep his eyes on the road while ignoring all that was going on in the back.

'Cold out there,' said Jolly, the leader of the group, as he pulled his bottom from the window and made himself look decent again. The rest of his companions, Dozy, Angry, and Mumbles, took their seats and began opening bottles of Spiggit's Old Peculiar. The air in the van, which hadn't smelled particularly pleasant to begin with, now took on the odour of a factory devoted to producing unwashed socks and fish heads.[13] Curiously, this very strong, and very unpleasant, beer appeared to have little effect on the dwarfs apart from exaggerating their natural character traits. Thus Jolly became jollier, in a drunken, unsettling way; Angry became angrier; Dozy became sleepier; and Mumbles – well, he just became more unintelligible.

'Oi, Merryweather,' called Angry. 'When do we get paid?'

Mr Merryweather's hands tightened on the wheel. He was a fat, bald man in a light brown check suit, and he always wore a red bow tie. He looked like someone who should be managing a bunch of untrustworthy dwarfs, but whether he looked that way because of what he was, or he was what he was because he looked that way, we will never know.

'Paid for what?' said Mr Merryweather.

💀 [13] Spiggit's Old Peculiar had recently been the subject of a number of court cases relating to incidents of temporary blindness, deafness, and undesirable hair growth on the palms of the hands. Due to a loophole in the law, it was allowed to remain on sale but it was required to have a warning label on the bottle, and anyone buying the ale had to sign a one-off agreement promising not to sue in the event of any injury caused by drinking it, up to and including death. Spiggit's had decided to make the best of this and its advertising slogan now read: 'Spiggit's – Ask for the Beer with the Biohazard Symbol!'

'For today's work, that's what for.'

The van swerved on the motorway as Mr Merryweather briefly lost control of the wheel, and of himself.

'Work?' he said. '*Work?* You lot don't know the meaning of work.'

'Careful!' called Dozy. 'You nearly spilled my beer.'

'I. Don't. *Care!*' screamed Mr Merryweather.

'What did he say?' asked Jolly. 'Someone was shouting, so I didn't hear.'

'Says he doesn't care,' said Dozy.

'Oh, well that's just lovely, that is. After all we've done for him—'

The van came to a violent skidding halt by the side of the road. Mr Merryweather stood and shook his fist at the assembled dwarfs.

'All you've done for me? All. You've Done. For Me. I'll tell you what you've done for me. You've made my life a misery, that's what. You've left me a broken man. My nerves are shot. Look at my hand.'

He held up his left hand. It trembled uncontrollably.

'That's bad,' agreed Jolly.

'And that's the good one,' said Mr Merryweather, holding up his right hand, which shook so much he could no longer hold a pint of milk in it, as it would instantly turn to cream.

'Abbledaybit,' said Mumbles.

'What?' said Mr Merryweather.

'He says you're having a bad day, but once you've had time to calm down and rest, you'll get over it,' said Jolly.

Despite his all-consuming rage, Mr Merryweather found time to look puzzled.

'He said that?'

'Yep.'

'But it just sounded like "abbledaybit".'

'Ed,' said Mumbles.

'He says that's what he said,' said Jolly. 'You're having a bad—'

Mr Merryweather pointed his finger at Jolly in a manner that could only be described as life-threatening. Had Mr Merryweather's finger been a gun, Jolly would have had a small column of smoke where his head used to be.

'I'm warning you,' said Mr Merryweather. 'I'm warning you all. Today was the last straw. Today was —'

Today was to have been a good day. After weeks, even months, of begging, Mr Merryweather had got the dwarfs a job that paid good money. It had even been worth repainting the van, and altering the name of the business. At last, everything was coming together.

Mr Merryweather's Elves had previously been known as Mr Merryweather's Dwarfs, as the changes to the van's lettering suggested, but a series of unfortunate incidents, including some civil and criminal court actions, had required that Mr Merryweather's Dwarfs maintain a low profile for a time, and then quietly cease to exist. These incidents had included a brief engagement as four of Snow White's seven dwarfs at a pantomime in Aldershot, an engagement that had come to a sudden end following an assault on Prince

Charming, in the course of which he was fed his own wig; two nights as mice and coachmen in *Cinderella*, during which Buttons lost a finger; and a single performance of *The Wizard of Oz* that ended with a riot among the Munchkins, a flying monkey being shot down with a tranquillizer dart, and a fire in the Emerald City that required three units of the local fire brigade to put out.

And so Mr Merryweather's Dwarfs had been reinvented as Mr Merryweather's Elves, a cunning ploy that, incredibly, had somehow managed to fool otherwise sensible people into believing this was an entirely different troupe of little men, and not the horrible bunch of drunks, arsonists, and monkey shooters who had almost singlehandedly brought an end to pantomime season in England. Elves just didn't seem as threatening as dwarfs, and as long as Mr Merryweather kept the dwarfs hidden until the last possible moment, and ensured that they were, for the most part, clean and sober, he began to believe that he just might get away with the deception.

That day, Mr Merryweather's Elves had begun what was potentially their most lucrative engagement yet: they were to feature in a music video for the beloved boyband BoyStarz to be filmed at Lollymore Castle. If all went well, the dwarfs would appear in future videos as well, and perhaps join BoyStarz on tour. There would be T-shirt sales; there was even talk of their own TV show. It seemed, thought Mr Merryweather, too good to be true.

And like most things that seem too good to be true, it was.

First of all, they didn't want to do it, even before they knew what 'it' was.

'I have a job for you lot,' he told them. 'A good one and all.'

'Eh, it wouldn't involve being a dwarf, would it?' asked Angry.

'Well, yes.'

'What a shocker. You know, it's not as if we wake up every morning and think, "Oh look, we're dwarfs. Didn't expect that. I thought I was taller." No, we're just regular people who happen to be small. It doesn't define us.'

'What's your point?' asked Mr Merryweather wearily.

'Our point is,' said Jolly, 'that we'd like to do something where being a dwarf is just incidental. For example, why can't I play Hamlet?'

'Because you're three foot eight inches tall, that's why. You can't play Hamlet. Piglet, maybe, but not Hamlet.'[14]

'Less of that,' said Jolly. 'That's what I'm talking about, see? That kind of attitude keeps us oppressed.'

That, thought Mr Merryweather, and the fact that you all drink too much, and can't be bothered to learn lines, and would pick your own pockets just to pass the time.

'Look, it's just the way the world works,' said Mr Merryweather. 'It's not me. I'm trying to do my best, but you don't help matters with your behaviour. We can't even do *Snow White and the Seven Dwarfs* in panto this year because you fought with Mrs Doris

☠ [14] See what I did there? Comedy gold.

Stott's Magnificent Midgets, so we're three little people down. Nobody wants to watch Snow White and the Four Dwarfs. It just doesn't sound right.'

'You could tell them it's a budget production,' said Angry.

'We could double up,' said Dozy.

'You can barely single up,' said Mr Merryweather.

'Careful,' said Dozy.

After they'd bickered and argued for another half-hour he had eventually managed to tell them about the job, and they had reluctantly agreed to earn some money. Mr Merryweather had climbed behind the wheel and thought, not for the first time, that he understood why people liked tossing dwarfs around, and wondered if he could convince someone to toss his dwarfs, preferably off a high cliff.

They had arrived at Lollymore Castle, not far from the town of Biddlecombe, early that morning. It was cold and damp, and the dwarfs were already complaining before they even got out of the van. Still, they were given tea to warm them up, and then dressed in the costumes that had been specially made for them: little suits of armour, little coats of chain mail, light-weight helmets.

Then they were handed swords and maces, and Mr Merryweather had sprinted from the van to stop them killing someone.

'For crying out loud, don't give them weapons,' he said, grabbing Jolly's arm just in time to stop him from braining an assistant director with a mace. 'They might, er, hurt themselves.'

He patted Jolly on the head. 'They're only little fellas, you know.' He hugged Jolly in the manner of a friendly uncle embracing a much-loved nephew, and received a kick in the shin for his trouble.

'Gerroff,' said Jolly. 'And give me back my mace.'

'Look, don't hit anyone with it,' hissed Mr Merryweather.

'It's a mace. It's *for* hitting people with.'

'But you're only supposed to be pretending. It's a video.'

'Well, they want it to look real, don't they?'

'Not that real. Not *funeral* real.'

Jolly conceded that Mr Merryweather had a point, and the dwarfs went to inspect the castle as the director pointed out their 'marks', the places on the battlements where they were supposed to stand during filming.

'What's our motivation?' asked Angry. 'Why are we here?'

'What do you mean?' said the director. 'You're defending the castle.'

'This castle?'

'Yes.'

'Is it ours?'

'Of course it's yours.'

'I beg to differ. The steps are too big. I nearly did myself an injury climbing up those steps. Almost ruptured something, I did. If we'd built this castle, we'd have made the steps smaller. Can't be ours. Makes no sense.'

The director pinched the bridge of his nose hard and closed his eyes.

'Right then, you captured it from somebody else.'

'Who?' asked Jolly.

'Capsmodwa?' said Mumbles.

'That's right,' said Angry. 'Did we capture if from smaller dwarfs? We're dwarfs – er, elves. I can't even see over the battlements. How are four of us supposed to have captured this castle? What did we do, raid it in instalments?'

'Perhaps it was just abandoned, and you took it over.'

'You can't do that. You can't wander into places without a by-your-leave just because someone's popped out for a pint of milk or a bit of a battle, and then call it home. It's not right. They'd have you up in court, you know. That's illegal entry, that is. That's six months in jail. And I should know.'

The director opened his eyes, grasped Angry by his chain mail, then lifted him from the ground so that he and Angry were on eye level.

'Listen to me,' said the director. 'This is going to be a very long, very wet day, and, if I have to, I will drop you from these battlements as an example to your friends of what happens when people start questioning the logic of a video in which a boy band with perfect teeth and blond highlights attempts to capture a castle from a bunch of little people wearing plastic armour. Do I make myself clear?'

'Abundantly,' said Angry. 'Just trying to help.'

The director put him down.

'Good. Now, I'm going to go down there, and we're going to start filming. Clear?'

'As crystal,' said Angry, Dozy, and Jolly.

'A1,' said Mumbles.

The dwarfs watched the director descend to the castle gate, then tramp angrily across the mud to the assemblage of tents and vans that constituted the video set.

'He's obviously very artistic,' said Angry. 'They're like that, artistic people. They go off at the slightest thing. Them, and wrestlers.'

'Why did they give us plastic armour and real swords?' asked Dozy.

'Dunno,' said Angry. 'Doesn't say much for his battle strategy.'

'Nice castle, though.'

'Oh, yes. Lovely workmanship. Knew what they were doing, these old builders.' Angry tapped his sword approvingly on a battlement, and watched as a chunk of it sheared off and almost killed a lighting technician below.

'Sorry,' said Angry.

He saw the director glaring at him, and raised his sword.

'A bit fell off,' he shouted in explanation. 'We can fix it later,' then added to his colleagues: 'Very shoddy, that. Bet a French bloke built this castle. Wouldn't have that in an English castle. Built to last, English castles. It's why we had an empire.'

But the others weren't listening. Instead, they were gazing slack-jawed at the sight of BoyStarz, who had just emerged from the caravan that was their dressing room. Even by the standards of the average boy band, Boystarz looked a bit soft: their hair was perfect, their skin unblemished, their teeth white. They seemed to be struggling under the weight of their armour, and one of them was complaining that his sword was too heavy.

The director accompanied them to within a few feet of the castle walls, and introduced them to the dwarfs.

'OK, these are the BoyStarz,' he said, and at the mention of their band name some deep-seated instinct kicked in, aided by many months of training involving beatings, bribes, and threats of starvation, and each of the four young men did a little dance.

'Hi,' said the first, 'I'm Starlight.'

'And I'm Twinkle.'

'I'm Gemini.'

'And I'm Phil.'

The dwarfs looked at the fourth member, who wasn't as pretty as the rest, and seemed a bit lost.

'Why is there always one bloke in these boy bands who looks like he came to fix the boiler and somehow got bullied into joining the group?' asked Jolly.

'Dunno,' said Dozy. 'Can't dance much either, can he?'

Which was true. Phil danced like a man trying to shake a rat from his leg.

'We're supposed to hand our lovely castle over to this lot?' said Angry. 'It'd be like surrendering it to powder puffs.'

'No,' said Jolly softly. 'No, there's such a thing as pride, as dignity. We can't have this. We just can't.'

'What are they saying?' Twinkle asked the director nervously. 'They look frighteningy.'

'I want to go home,' said Starlight. 'I don't like the little men.'

'The ground feels funny, and it smells like poo,' said Gemini.

'And I'm Phil,' said Phil.

The director was already backing away. He didn't care for the look in the elves' eyes. He didn't care for it at all.

Hey, he thought, they're not elves. They're dwarfs. They're not Mr Merryweather's Elves, they're Mr Merryweather's –

Dwarfs!

He was already running, four terrified boy band members at his heels, as the first rocks began to rain down on them, for Mr Merryweather's Elves were intent upon defending Lollymore Castle, even if they had to take it apart brick by brick to do so.

CHAPTER VI

In Which Samuel is Reunited With Boswell, and We Learn Why One Should Not Trust a Mirror

As such tales will do, the story of how Samuel Johnson had managed to ask a letter box on a date had made its way around the entire school by the time the bell rang to send everyone home.

'Oi, Johnson!' Lionel Hashim shouted at him as he made his way to the school gates. 'I hear there's a very good-looking traffic light over on Shelley Road. You could ask it to go to the cinema with you. Don't try to kiss it though. It might go red!'

Funny, thought Samuel. Really funny. His bag, and his heart, felt very heavy.

Outside the gates, Samuel's pet dachshund, Boswell, was waiting. Boswell had the worried air of one who suspects that bad news is imminent, and its arrival has only been delayed by the fact that it's looking for some more bad news to keep it company. A series of frown lines creased Boswell's brow, and at regular intervals he would give a sigh. He was a familiar sight around the town of Biddlecombe, but particularly at the school, for Boswell was Samuel Johnson's faithful companion, and was always present to greet his master when the bell struck four.

Boswell had always been a somewhat sensitive, contemplative dog.[15] Even as a puppy, he would regard his ball warily, as though waiting for it to sprout legs and run off with another dog. He displayed a fondness for the sadder types of classical music, and had been known to howl along to Mozart's Requiem in a plaintive manner.

But recent events had given Boswell good cause to think that the world was an even stranger and more worrying place than he had previously thought. After all, he had witnessed monsters emerging from holes in space, and had even been injured by one as he attempted to save his master from its clutches. One of his legs had been broken, and ever since he had walked with a slight limp. Being a dog, although a very clever one, Boswell wasn't entirely clear about the nature of what had occurred during the invasion. All he knew was that it had been very bad, and he didn't want it to happen again. Most of all, he didn't want anything to happen to Samuel, whom he loved very much, and so each

---

💀 [15] The English writer Horace Walpole (1717–97) suggested that 'this world is a comedy to those that think, a tragedy to those that feel'. Unfortunately, since most of us both think *and* feel, we are destined to spend a lot of our time on Earth not being certain whether to laugh or cry. Laughter is probably better, but you don't want to be one of those people who laugh all of the time ('Look, that chap over there's just fallen off a cliff! Ah-ha-ha-ha-ha-ha!') because you'll appear uncaring, or insane. Similarly, if you cry all of the time then you'll look like a sissy, or a professional mourner, and you'll start to smell damp. Best to settle for a wry smile, then, the kind that suggests you're able to endure the slings and arrows of outrageous fortune with a degree of grace while still being able to shed a discreet tear at sad films, and funerals. Incidentally, Horace Walpole looked a bit like a horse in a wig, and was once accused of driving the poet Chatterton to suicide. He was, therefore, probably a 'world as tragedy' kind of person.

morning, regardless of the weather, Boswell would trot along beside his beloved master as Samuel walked to school, and would be waiting for him when he emerged from school at the end of the day. A flap in the front door of the house meant that he could come and go as he pleased. Boswell's duty was to protect Samuel, and he intended to fulfil it to the best of a small dog's ability.

That day Boswell detected a change in Samuel's usually sunny disposition. While some dogs might have made an effort to cheer up their master under such circumstances, perhaps by chasing their tail or showing them something that smelled funny, Boswell was the kind of dog that shared his master's mood. If Samuel was happy, then Boswell was content. If Samuel was sad, Boswell stayed quiet and kept him company. In this, Boswell was wiser than most people.

And so the boy and his dog, each bearing some of the weight of the world upon his shoulders, made their way home, and had anyone taken the time to give them more than a passing glance they might have noticed that both the boy and the dog kept their heads down as they went. They did not look in shop windows, and they avoided puddles. They did not seem to want to see themselves. It was as if they were frightened of their own reflections, or scared of being noticed.

People still occasionally shot funny looks at Samuel and indeed Boswell, but not as often as they used to, or perhaps it would be more accurate to say that the funny looks they shot were of a general kind – 'He's an odd kid, and his dog makes me feel sad' – rather than the specific kind, such as, 'There's Samuel Johnson and his dog, who were involved with all of that demonic business that I'd rather not remember, thanks very much. Actually, now that I see them again, I feel a bit angry at them because I don't want to be reminded of what happened, but by their presence here they remind me of it anyway, so I think I'll just blame them for everything instead of the demons because it's easier to be angry at a small boy and a smaller dog, and less likely to result in me being eaten, or whisked off to Hell, or some similarly horrible consequence.'

Or words to that effect.

Samuel had almost ceased to notice the reactions of other people to his presence, but that was not why he and Boswell kept their heads down. It was true to say that they did not want to be noticed, but it was not their neighbours in Biddlecombe who worried them. The individual who concerned them was much further away.

Further away, yet strangely close.

Most of us do not think very hard about the nature of mirrors. We see the reflection of a room, or of ourselves, in a glass and we think, 'Oh, look, it's the couch', or 'Oh, look, it's me. I thought I was thinner/ fatter/ better-looking/ uglier/ a girl.'[16] But it's not your couch, and

---

☠ [16] If you're bored some time, and want to puzzle your parents:
1) Fill a small plastic glass with a little water.
2) Lift said glass as if to drink from it.
3) Bypass your mouth and instead touch the glass to your forehead.
4) Spill a little of the water down your face.
5) Tell your parents that you thought you were taller.
6) Take a bow. Ask people to tip their waitress. Tell them you'll be here all week.
7) Leave.

it's not you. It's a version of you, which is why the artist René Magritte could paint a picture of a pipe and write beneath it, in French, '*Ceci n'est pas une pipe*', or 'This is not a pipe'. Because it's not a pipe: it's an *image* of a pipe. As Magritte himself pointed out: 'Could you stuff my pipe? No, it's just a representation. So if I had written on my picture, "This is a pipe", I'd have been lying!'

The painting in question, from 1929, is called *The Treachery of Images*. ('Treachery', meaning to trick or deceive, is another great word, especially if you roll that first 'r' on your tongue and really stretch it out: 'Trrrrrrreachery!' you can shout, in a demented way, while waving a sword and alarming the neighbours.) In other words, you can't trust images, because they're not what they pretend to be.

Samuel had become very familiar with this concept, and not in a good way. He had begun to suspect that mirrors were very strange indeed, and that, far from simply providing a reflection of this world, they might in fact be a world of their own.[17] He felt this because very occasionally he would glance at a mirror, or the window of a shop, or some other reflective surface, and would see a figure that should not have been there. It was the figure of a no-longer-quite-beautiful woman in a floral dress. It was Mrs Abernathy.

For Mrs Abernathy, Samuel had decided, walked in the world of mirrors. She couldn't get back into this world, but somehow she could see into it by moving behind the glass. Samuel had caught glimpses of her in the mirror of his bathroom cabinet, in the glass of his front door, even once, most peculiarly, on a spoon, where she was distorted and upside down. She seemed to prefer to come at night, when the windows were dark and the reflections clearer in the glass, as though the clarity of her own image in turn made the world at which she gazed easier to discern.

And each time her eyes were filled with a blue light, and they burned with her hatred for Samuel.

* * *

[17] Actually, we have a tendency to take our reflection for granted at the best of times, when it's really quite extraordinary. When you see your reflection in a window at night, perhaps with a city visible through the glass beyond, it's because ninety-five per cent of the light striking the window has gone straight through while five per cent has been reflected, hence the ghostly image of your face. This proves the particle nature of light, but what's troubling is that the five per cent of reflected particles of energy, or photons, is reflected for no particularly good reason that we can understand, indicating the possibility of randomness at the heart of the universe. There's a one in twenty chance that a photon will be reflected instead of transmitted, which means that we can't know for certain how a given photon will behave. This is very troubling for scientists. If you want to give your science teacher a nervous breakdown, ask why this happens.

Samuel's mother greeted him from the kitchen as he opened the front door and dumped his bag in the hall.

'Hello, Samuel. Did you have a good day?'

'If, by good, you mean embarrassing and soul-destroying, then, yes, I had a good day,' said Samuel.

'Oh dear,' said his mum. 'Sit down at the table and I'll make you a nice cup of tea.'

What was it about mothers, wondered Samuel, that led them to believe all of the problems of the world could be solved with a nice cup of tea? Samuel could have walked in with his head under his arm, blood spurting from his neck and his back quilled with arrows, and his mother would have suggested a nice cup of tea as a means of salving his wounds. She would probably even have tried to rub some tea on his severed head in an effort to stick it back on his shoulders.

But the funny thing was that, more often than not, a cup of tea and a consoling word from your mum were enough to make things at least a little better, so Samuel sat down and waited until a steaming mug of tea was placed in front of him. It really did smell good. He could almost feel it warming his throat already. Today had been bad, but perhaps tomorrow would be better. Tea: our friend in times of trouble.

'Oh bother,' said Samuel's mother. 'We're out of milk.'

Samuel's forehead thumped hard against the kitchen table.

'I'll go,' he said.

'There's a good lad,' said his mum. 'I'll have a fresh

cup waiting for you when you get back. Will you get some bread while you're at it? I don't know: even with your dad gone, we're still getting through as much food as ever.'

Samuel winced. He wasn't sure which hurt more: to hear his mother grow sad when she talked about his dad's absence, or to hear her remark upon it so casually. His mother seemed to notice his discomfort, for she moved to him and enveloped him in her arms.

'Oh, you,' she said, kissing his hair. 'I don't mind you eating. You're a growing lad. And your dad and I, well, we're talking, which is something. I'm not as angry with him as I was, although I'd still hit him over the head with a frying pan given half the chance. But we're OK, you and I, aren't we?'

Samuel nodded, his eyes closed, taking in the comforting smell of flour and perfume from his mother's dress.

'Yes, we're OK,' he said, although he wasn't sure if it was true.

His mother pushed him gently away, and held him at arm's length. She looked at him seriously.

'There's been no more, um, *strangeness*, has there?' she asked.

'You mean demons?'

Now it was his mother's turn to look uncomfortable.

'Yes, if that's what you want to call them.'

'That's what they were.'

'Now, I don't want to get into an argument about it,' said his mum. 'I'm only asking.'

'No, Mum,' said Samuel. 'There's been no more

strangeness.' Not unless you include glimpses of a woman with her face stitched together, staring out from mirrors and glass doors. 'There's been no more strangeness at all.'

CHAPTER VII

In Which We Pay a Visit to Mrs Abernathy's House. Which Is Nice. Not.

Before we go any further, a quick word about Evil. Evil has been in existence for a very long time, long enough to be part of the birth of everything billions and billions of years ago following the Big Bang that brought this universe into being. Unfortunately, for a while after the Big Bang there wasn't much for Evil to do because there wasn't a great deal of life about, and what life there was consisted of little single-celled organisms which had quite enough to be getting along with just trying to become multi-celled organisms, thank you very much, without having to worry about being unkind to one another for no good reason as well. Even when these multi-celled organisms grew incredibly complex, and became sharks, and spiders, and carnivorous dinosaurs, they still didn't provide much amusement for Evil. These beasts operated on instinct alone, and their instinct was simply to eat, and thus to survive.

But then man came along, and Evil perked up a bit, because here was a creature that could choose, which made it very interesting indeed. Being good or bad are not passive states: you have to decide to be one or the other. Evil did everything it could to encourage people to do bad instead of good, and because it was clever it disguised itself well, so that people who did bad things found ways to convince themselves that they weren't really bad at all. They needed more money to be happy, and hence they stole, or they cheated on their taxes; and then they told lies to hide what they'd done, because they were kind of sorry for it, but not sorry enough to admit what they'd done, or to stop doing it. In the end, most of it came down to selfishness, but Evil didn't mind. You could call it what you wanted, as far as Evil was concerned, just as long as you kept on being bad.

And Evil wasn't just busy in this universe, but in a lot of others too, for ours was but one in a great froth of universes known as the Multiverse, each one its own expanding bubble of planets and stars. You might think that this would require Evil to spread itself a little thinly, because there can only be so much Evil to go round, but you'd be surprised what Evil can do when it puts its mind to it. On the other hand, no matter how hard Evil tries, it can never quite match up to the power of Good, because Evil is ultimately self-destructive. Evil may set out to corrupt others, but in the process it corrupts itself. That's just the way Evil is. All things considered, it's better to be on the side of Good, even if Evil occasionally has nicer uniforms.

Mrs Abernathy, who was very evil indeed, sat in a high chamber in her palace, a terrifying construct of spars and sharp edges carved from a single massive slab of shiny black volcanic rock, and stared intently at the shard of glass before her. She had 'borrowed' it a long,

long time before from the Great Malevolence, for he had many such shards, and she had convinced herself that one more or less would make no difference to him. They were his windows into the world of men, each revealing to him some part of the existence that he hated, yet also, in the pit of his being, secretly craved. He would watch the sun set, and lakes turn to gold. He would see children grow up to have children of their own, and become old among those whom they loved, and who loved them in turn. He would gaze upon husbands and wives, brothers and sisters, upon puppies, and frogs, and elephants. He would even gaze upon goldfish in bowls, and hamsters who ran around inside wheels to distract themselves from their tiny cages, and flies struggling in the webs of spiders, and he would envy each and every living thing its freedom, even if it was only the freedom to die.

For so long, Mrs Abernathy had shared her master's desire to turn the Earth into a version of Hell, but something had changed. What that something was might be guessed from the fact that the windows of her dreadful lair, which in its way had long been nearly as awful as the Great Malevolence's Mountain of Despair, but considerably smaller, and with better views, had been decorated with net curtains. The curtains were black and, upon closer inspection, seemed to have been used at some point to catch horrible mutated fish, as the remains of a few were still caught in its strands, but at least someone was making an effort. A long table constructed entirely of tombstones now had a yellow vase at its centre, a vase, furthermore, that bore a pattern of dozing cats. Admittedly, the vase was filled with ugly blood-red flowers that hid sharp teeth inside their petals, and those teeth would have made short work of any real cats that made the mistake of falling asleep within snapping distance, but it was a start, just like the curtains, and the doormat that read 'Please Wipe Your Cloven Hooves!', and the jar of pot-pourri made from the husks of poisonous beetles and scented with stagnant water.

What Mrs Abernathy had discovered, even if she refused to admit it to herself, was that if you go to a place intent upon changing it, then sometimes that place may end up changing you instead. She had returned to Hell, but she had brought back a little of the human world with her, and now she was being altered in ways she did not fully understand.

Mind you, she still hated Samuel Johnson, and his dog. Just because she wanted to make her lair a bit prettier, and maybe spent a few minutes longer than before on making sure her hair was just right before she went out, didn't mean that she wouldn't tear them both limb from limb at the first opportunity. Thus it was that she watched them through the fragment of glass as they trudged from the house, the boy's head low, the dog intent upon his master. Samuel looked unhappy, she thought. That was good. She liked it when he was unhappy. She willed him to look up, to catch a quick sight of her in one of the windows as he was passing. It always gave her pleasure to see him react with fear when she appeared, even if she couldn't do him any real harm, not yet, but he seemed intent upon not noticing her.

She stretched out a pale hand and stared at her fingers. The nails were red, and slightly chipped. She would have to paint them again, once she managed to get a decent supply of suitable blood.

From above her head came the sound of wings flapping. The chamber narrowed into a steeple-like structure at its centre that protruded high above the surrounding plains. At its peak was an opening that now darkened as a figure entered and began to descend. Her Watcher had returned.

When Mrs Abernathy had fallen out of favour with the Great Malevolence, many of those demons who had previously been loyal to her had sought new masters. After all, if someone had failed the Great Malevolence so dreadfully that he had cut her off entirely, refusing even to stare upon her face, it could only be a matter of time before he decided that ignoring her was insufficient punishment, and something more imaginative might be called for. In that case, he might decide that he wanted to stare upon her face again after all, but only if the face had first been removed and nailed to a wall, with the other parts of her body arranged alongside it in an interesting if unconventional manner. When that happened, as most of the cleverer demons seemed to think was increasingly probable, then any of those who had remained close to her were likely to end up in a similar position, except slightly lower down the wall.

In a sense, demons were the embodiment of the law of conservation of matter, which states that matter cannot be created or destroyed, but only transformed from one state to another.[18] When applied to demons, this meant that they could not die, but could still be transformed into various alternative painful versions of existence, and their torments could be made to last an eternity. Nobody wants to spend eternity with his face pinned to a wall and his severed legs crossed underneath his chin, like some ghastly coat-of-arms, so the general wisdom in Hell was that it was unwise to be involved with Mrs Abernathy, because Mrs Abernathy was doomed and would, in turn, doom all those around her.

But there were creatures that had remained loyal to her: some because they were too stupid to know better, some because they hoped that Mrs Abernathy might discover a way to improve her situation, and some because they were as cruel and vicious and intelligent

---

[18] Albert Einstein, aided by the earlier work of Cockcroft and Walton, proved that matter can be changed to energy, and energy to matter, as in an atomic explosion. Thus, it's really the law of conservation of energy *and* matter. But one of the forgotten pioneers in this area is the Frenchman Antoine-Laurent Lavoisier (1743–94), who, in his spare time, became fascinated by the possibility that all of the bits and pieces of stuff on Earth – lions, tigers, budgerigars, trees, slugs, iron, and the like – were parts of a single interconnected whole. He and his wife Marie Anne began rusting pieces of metal in a sealed apparatus, then weighing them along with the air that was lost. They found that the rusted metal, rather than weighing less than before, or the same, in fact weighed *more*, because the oxygen molecules in the air had adhered to the metal. In other words, matter was changing from one form to another, but not disappearing. Lavoisier met a terrible end: he had offended a frustrated scientist, Jean-Paul Marat, and during the Reign of Terror (1793–4) that followed the French Revolution, Marat, who was prominent in the Reign, got his revenge: Lavoisier was tried, sentenced and then beheaded, all in one day. When a plea for mercy was entered on his behalf, the judge responded: 'The Republic has no need of geniuses.' The next time that you burn a match, spare a thought for Lavoisier.

as she was, and couldn't find a better employer, even in Hell. The Watcher appeared to be one of those. It was strong, and tireless, and seemed unquestioningly faithful to its mistress, even if it was a bit disturbed by the changes that had taken place in her appearance recently. It had grown used to serving a monstrous, tentacled demon many times its own height, not a small, blond woman in a print dress. Still, you had to be open to new experiences, that was its philosophy, as long as those new experiences sufficiently resembled the old ones in terms of hurting other creatures.

The Watcher was pleased with itself, and it knew that Mrs Abernathy would in turn be pleased with it. But before it could begin to speak, its mistress spasmed. Her arms shot out from her sides and her back arched. Her mouth gaped and her eyes opened wide. Beams of blue light shot from her jaws, her ears, and the sockets of her eyes. Smaller splinters of energy erupted from every pore of her skin, and she hung suspended in the air like a blue sun.

And the Watcher regarded her, and knew that it had made the right choice.

Mrs Abernathy had been patient: one could not exist for so long without learning the value of patience. She had endured the rejection of the Great Malevolence, continuing to make her regular pilgrimage to his mountain when others laughed at her, reminding them all that she would not be forgotten. When she was not traipsing back and forth between her palace and her master's home, she had been waiting. She had waited for her

Watcher to find traces of the vehicle that had entered the portal and caused it to collapse, dragging them all back to Hell. She had waited for those moments when Samuel Johnson might inadvertently glance in a mirror and find her staring back at him, relishing his fear. She had waited for her chance to avenge herself upon him. But, most of all, she had waited for the humans to do what she knew they most assuredly would do.

She had waited for them to turn on their great Collider once again.

CHAPTER VIII

In Which We Wonder Just How Smart Really Smart People Sometimes Are

Scientists are a funny lot. Oh, they do many great and wonderful things, and without science we wouldn't have all kinds of useful stuff like cures for diseases, and light bulbs, and nuclear missiles, and deadly germ warfare, and . . .

Well, best not go there, perhaps. Let's just say that science has, in general, been very beneficial to humanity, and many scientists have exhibited considerable bravery in the course of their work, although occasionally the more sensible among us might, if given the opportunity to witness some of their experiments, think to ourselves, 'Ooh, I wouldn't do that if I were you'[19], which is why we're not scientists and will never discover anything very interesting, although neither will we accidentally poison ourselves by ingesting the contents of a thermometer.

[19] Alexander Bogdanov (1873–1928), for example, experimented with blood transfusions, possibly in an effort to discover the secret of eternal youth. Regrettably, some of the blood was infected with malaria and tuberculosis, and he promptly died. Meanwhile Karl Scheele (1742–86), the discoverer of tungsten and chlorine, among other chemical elements, liked to taste his discoveries. He survived tasting hydrogen cyanide but not, alas, mercury.

And so, deep in a tunnel near Geneva in Switzerland, a group of scientists was looking a bit anxiously at a switch, while around them the Large Hadron Collider once again went about its very important business. The Collider, for those of you who don't know, was the largest particle accelerator ever built, designed to smash together beams of subatomic protons at enormous speeds – 99.9999991 per cent of the speed of light – and thereby make all kinds of discoveries about the nature of the universe by recreating the conditions that occurred less than a billionth of a second after the Big Bang that created it about 13.7 billion years ago. Unfortunately, when last turned on, the Collider's energy had been harnessed by Mrs Abernathy in order to open a portal between our world and Hell, which was when all the trouble had started. Since then the Collider had remained resolutely switched off, and the scientists had done a great deal of work to ensure that the whole portal to Hell business would never, ever happen again. Promise. Pinky promise. Pinky promise with sugar on top.[20]

[20] Actually, the Collider experiment had been plagued by many difficulties in addition to the unfortunate scientists/demons interface, including a mishap caused by a bird dropping a piece of baguette into the machinery, so that one prominent scientist even suggested it was being sabotaged from the future in order to prevent it being turned on and sucking the planet into a big black hole, or transforming it to ash. On the other hand, those of us who hadn't spent too long hanging around with scientists, and who got out of the house occasionally, thought that the idea of sabotage from the future seemed to be pushing it a bit. Then, strangely, a man was arrested at the Collider who claimed to have come from a future where there were Kit-Kats for everyone, with the precise purpose of sabotaging the experiment. Mind you, he also claimed that his time machine was powered by a kitchen blender, so he may not have been playing with a full deck of cards, if you catch my drift.

'Is anything happening?' said Professor Stefan, CERN's head of particle physics. He sounded both nervous and impatient. Professor Stefan had been present when all that nasty demonic business had happened, and a lot of people had pointed the finger of blame at him, which he felt was a bit unfair as he hadn't *known* that the gates of Hell were going to open because of his nice, shiny particle accelerator. If he had –

Oh dear, that was the thing of it. If he had known, he probably would still have allowed the Collider to be switched on. They'd gone to all that trouble to build it, and had spent all that money: $7 billion, at the last count. They couldn't very well just lock the door, put the key under the mat, leave a note for the milkman cancelling their order, and go back to doing whatever it was they had been doing before the Collider was suggested. That would just be silly. And there would have been no guarantee that the gates of Hell would open anyway, because nobody was sure if Hell even existed. It would be like saying, 'Don't turn that thing on. The Easter Bunny might pop out!' or, 'A fairy's wings might drop off!', or, 'A unicorn might fall over.' That wouldn't be science. That would be nonsense.

On the other hand, the scientists now knew that a) Hell, or something similar to it, did exist; b) it was full of creatures that didn't like them very much, although it wasn't just scientists they didn't like but everything that existed on Earth; and c) somehow the Collider had provided these creatures with a way of poking their heads into our world and eating people.

The general consensus among those who knew about CERN's involvement in the near-catastrophe, and who didn't particularly want to be eaten by demons – thanks very much, ever thought of trying a salad? – was that it probably wouldn't be a very good idea to go turning the Collider on again. The scientists argued that they'd figured out what the problem was (kind of), and they were certain (sort of) that nothing like what had happened before would ever happen again (or probably would never happen again, within a given margin of error. What margin of error? Oh, tiny. Hardly worth bothering about. What, you want to see the piece of paper on which I've made that calculation? What piece of paper? Oh, this piece of paper. Well you can't because – munch, munch – I've just eaten it. So there.)

Eventually they decided that it might just be OK to turn on the Collider again, but the scientists had to be very careful, and if it looked like something bad involving creatures with claws and fangs and bad attitude was about to occur they were to turn off the Collider immediately and go and inform a responsible adult. The scientists were reasonably confident that this would not be necessary, as they had worked hard on what was thought to have been a source of potential weakness. The joints holding the machine's copper stabilizers were discovered not to be strong enough to withstand the forces being unleashed against them – 500 tons per square metre, or the equivalent of five jumbo jets at full throttle being pushed against each square metre – but now the stabilizers had been reinforced, and all was believed to be well.

But the changes and corrections that the scientists had made to the Collider had also enabled them to increase its energy levels. The energies involved in its collisions were measured in terra electron volts, or TeV, with each TeV being equivalent to a million million electron volts. When the first 'incident' had taken place, the Collider was sending twin beams of 1.18 TeV each around its ring, giving collision energies of 2.36 TeV. The new, improved Collider was set to more than double the collision energy to 7 TeV, the first big step toward its routine capacity of 14 TeV.

Which was how the scientists came to be standing around looking at the switch with fingers crossed and lucky rabbits' feet in hand while Professor Stefan enquired if anything had happened yet, and Professor Hilbert, his assistant, who was very curious about all of the Hell and demons stuff because it proved his theory that there were universes out there other than our own, sucked his pencil and wondered if he should confess that he was rather hoping the portal might open again nearby as he'd missed it last time.

'Nothing unusual,' said Professor Hilbert, trying not to sound disappointed.

Professor Stefan let out a deep breath of relief. 'Thank goodness,' he said. 'Everything's going to be fine from now on.'

The other scientists glared at him, because that's just the kind of thing that people say before the roof collapses, the floor cracks, and everything goes to Hell in a handcart, in this case potentially quite literally, assuming someone had remembered to bring along a handcart, but Professor Stefan didn't notice. Neither did he pay any attention to the fact that Professor Hilbert had sidled away, and had disappeared into a small room marked 'Broom Closet – Janitor's Use Only'.

'See,' said Professor Stefan, who just didn't know when to stop tempting fate, 'I told you there was nothing to worry about.'

The broom closet that Professor Hilbert had entered was no longer really for brooms. Instead, an array of monitoring equipment had been set up, and two technicians were staring intently at a pair of screens. Between the screens was a speaker, currently silent.

'And?' said Professor Hilbert.

'It all seems to be working as it should,' said the first technician, whose name was Ed. He was staring at an image that resembled a spider encased in a wire tube dotted with bits of brick.

'I agree,' said his companion, Victor. Behind them was an unfinished game of Battleships, which Professor Hilbert pretended not to notice. 'There is a marginal energy loss, but that could be a joint again. Anyway, it will be contained within the vacuum.'

'Are you sure?'

'No, but it must be. I mean, where else could it go? We've examined every inch of the Collider. Its integrity is now beyond doubt.'

'Really?' said Professor Hilbert. 'I seem to remember that's what was said last time.'

'Well, we were wrong then,' said Ed, with the

certainty of someone who is convinced he knows where his opponent is hiding a submarine and an aircraft carrier, if only he might be allowed to return to the game. 'But we're right now.'

He smiled amiably. Professor Hilbert did not smile back.

'Keep an eye on it,' said Professor Hilbert, as he made for the door. 'And if I catch you playing Battleships again, you'll wish you really were on a sinking aircraft carrier . . .'

Mrs Abernathy slumped to her knees. The beams of blue light withdrew into her body, but her eyes retained a blue glow. It had been there ever since the collapse of the portal, but now it was more intense. She trembled for a moment, then was still. Slowly, a smile spread across her face.

The Watcher had not moved. At last it understood. Yes, Mrs Abernathy had been changed by her time in the world of men, and she had brought back aspects of it with her to Hell: curtains, and vases, and doormats; print dresses, and blond hair, and painted nails.

But it was also she who had first recognized the importance of the Collider experiment. The primal forces involved in the creation of the universe were also present in the most ancient of demons. The recreation of those forces on Earth had formed a connection between universes that she and the Great Malevolence could exploit. The collapse of the portal, and the consequent failure of their invasion, seemed to have severed that connection for ever, but now that appeared not to be so. The connection between worlds remained, but only through her. She had been the first one through the portal, and had held it open initially through sheer force of will. Some small part of the Collider's energy was still being accessed by her. She had to draw upon it slowly and carefully so as not to alert those responsible for the Collider, for she did not want them to shut it down. It would not be enough to stage another invasion, but in time it might be. It was not even enough to enable her to cross over from her world to theirs, for a powerful old demon like herself would require enormous energy to move between universes. But it would be sufficient to pull a human being from their world into hers, and she knew just the human being she wanted. She would drag Samuel Johnson to Hell and present him to her master as a prize. Then she would reveal the secret of the blue light to him and he would love her again.

As she rose to her feet, the Watcher began to speak. It told her of strange tracks in the dirt, of a black substance on rocks, of the smell of fumes and burning in the air. When it was finished she touched its head with her hand, and it bowed low with gratitude.

'All good things come to those who wait,' said Mrs Abernathy. 'All good things . . .'

She began to laugh, a terrible sound. It echoed around the chamber, carried across the plains, and was heard by the demons who had abandoned her. Some fled, fearing her vengeance for their betrayal, but others prepared to return to her, for if Mrs Abernathy was laughing then circumstances had changed, and they might yet profit from it. Foul beings emerged from holes in the ground and caves in black mountains, from pits of ash and pools of fire. They crawled, wobbled and slimed their way from their hiding places, and slowly began to make their way back to her.

CHAPTER IX

In Which Mr Merryweather's Elves Embark on a New Adventure

Mr Merryweather's elves were making good time on the motorway. There had been some initial problems with driving the van, since the only one of them who had a licence was Jolly, and his legs were even shorter than those of his fellow dwarfs and therefore had no chance at all of reaching the brake or the accelerator. This problem was solved by gluing a bottle of Spiggit's Old Peculiar to each of the van's pedals with extra strong adhesive, so Jolly simply had to step on a bottle cap to speed up or slow down.

The dwarfs had been feeling somewhat glum since Mr Merryweather had stomped off down the road, muttering and waving his fists, and vowing never again to work with anyone who couldn't look him in the eye without standing on a chair. Say what you wanted to about Mr Merryweather – and the dwarfs had said virtually everything about him that they could, including a number of insults that would be unprintable in a guide to swearing for sweary sailors – he had at least found them work, and he had stood by them following various incidents of assault, arson and, on one occasion, conspiracy to overthrow an elected government. Without him they were going to struggle to find jobs, and avoid arrest.

Mumbles and Dozy stared mournfully into their glasses of Spiggit's. Even though the van's suspension was suspect and made drinking from a glass difficult, it was generally considered unwise to drink Spiggit's directly from the bottle.[21] In the first place, it was uncivilized, as ale always tasted better from a glass. In the second place, Spiggit's tended to have an odd, cloudy residue that lurked at the bottom of every bottle, rather like one of those strange creatures that live in deep trenches on the sea bed, waiting to snap at the unwary. Jolly had once drunk some of that residue as an experiment.[22] The immediate effect was to cause him to seek the comfort of a toilet for so long that it was suggested he might like to take out a mortgage on it. Three months later, as he told anyone who would listen, his insides still weren't right, for somewhere in his digestive organs Spiggit's Old Peculiar continued to ferment away merrily, as the beer had the kind of long life more usually associated with lethal radiation. He was still prone to attacks of temporary blindness, an occasional inability to remember his own name, and explosive

---

💀 [21] Actually as we have established, it was generally considered unwise to drink Spiggit's at all.

💀 [22] Well, I say 'experiment', but his fellow dwarfs simply sat on him and poured the sediment down his throat, then quickly stepped back to watch what happened. While this is still technically an experiment, it also qualifies as torture, as does almost anything involving the involuntary ingestion of Spiggit's Old Peculiar.

burping, which had led to one of the incidents of alleged arson after he belched a little too close to a naked flame.

So Mumbles, Angry, and Dozy held on tightly to their glasses of ale (particularly since Spiggit's, if spilled on skin or clothing and allowed to remain there for more than five seconds, tended to burn) and wondered how they were going to be able to afford to eat, or drink, without Mr Merryweather to help them. There was a certain urgency to this, as they had only twelve cases of Spiggit's left in the back of the van, along with two boxes of crisps and a couple of sandwiches that appeared to be on the turn. It had been suggested that they dump the two boxes of crisps in order to make room for more beer, but wiser counsel had prevailed, and they had dumped just one of the boxes of crisps, and kept the sandwiches.

'That's the end of us,' said Angry. 'I'll have to go back to my old job.'

'What was that?' said Dozy.

'Not having a job.'

'Take up much time, did it?'

'All day. I had weekends off, though.'

'Well, you would. You'd exhaust yourself otherwise.'

'What about you?'

Dozy shuddered. 'Doesn't bear thinking about. Children's television.'

'No!'

'Yes. Remember that show, *Beefy and the Noodles*?'

'The one set in the bowl of soup?'

'That's the one. I was Percy Pea.'

'Don't remember you saying much.'

'I was a pea. Peas are among your quieter vegetables on account of there not being much air in those pods. You can't get a carrot to shut up, and don't get me started on broccoli. I hated being a pea. And the suit smelled funny. The previous Percy Pea died in it.'

'Really?'

'Contracted something from the soup. We spent hours in that soup. It was horrible. Anyway, he caught a disease from the soup, and he died, but they didn't find out until after the weekend. They thought the suit was empty, so they just pushed him back into his pod and left him there. That suit never smelled the same after.'

'It wouldn't, would it?' said Angry. 'You can't leave a dead person in a pea suit for a weekend and not expect it to smell a bit. Stands to reason. A day, maybe: you can get rid of a day's dead smell, but not a weekend's. What about you, Mumbles, what did you do?'

'Vovos,' said Mumbles.

'Oh,' said Angry.

'Missed that,' said Dozy.

'He says he did voiceovers,' said Angry, who tried to hide his confusion by looking more confused. 'You know, for commercials, and movie trailers, and the like.'

There was a pause while the dwarfs took this in.

'Nice work if you can get it,' said Dozy eventually.

'Have to have a talent for it,' said Angry, who had developed an extra wrinkle in his forehead as he tried to figure out the precise trajectory of Mumbles's career path.

'Anglebog,' agreed Mumbles.

'Indeed,' replied Angry, neutrally. 'Good pronunciation would be the key.'

'What about you, Jolly?' said Dozy. 'What will you do?'

'Do?' said Jolly. 'Do? Listen to you lot. We're not finished yet. We've been through worse times than this. We've been arrested, deported, and almost sold into slavery. You have to be optimistic. I guarantee that opportunity lies around the next bend.'

He was so convincing that they raised their glasses and cheered.

Opportunity did not, in fact, lie around the next bend. What did was a police car, in which Constable Peel and Sergeant Rowan of the Biddlecombe constabulary were checking the speeds of cars and drinking tea from a flask.

'Lovely tea, this,' said Sergeant Rowan. 'How do you get it to taste like that?'

'Honey,' said Constable Peel.

'Fantastic. Never would have thought of it.'

'Honey,' Constable Peel continued, 'and ... elves. With beer.'

Sergeant Rowan sniffed his tea. 'No, I don't get any hint of elves or beer. Honey, yes, but not little people.'

'That's not what I meant, Sarge. There are elves in that van. And they're drinking beer.'

Sergeant Rowan squinted at the side of the van as it passed, and saw glasses of beer being raised in little hands. 'Mr Merryweather's Elves,' he read aloud. He thought for a moment. No, it couldn't be. Not that bunch. Completely different. Admittedly, it did look like the same van. It even looked like the same—

Dwarfs.

'Constable, stop those dwarfs!'

Dozy shifted on his seat. 'Can we stop somewhere? I need to go to the bathroom.'

'Yeah, and I wouldn't mind some food,' said Angry. 'I'm famished.'

'There's no service station around here, lads,' said Jolly. 'Still, that's the exit for Biddlecombe. We can find somewhere there.'

He pulled off the motorway, not noticing the police car that was in pursuit, and quickly found himself on Shirley Jackson Road, which led to the centre of Biddlecombe. As he drove along he passed an ice-cream truck, and a small boy with a dachshund on the end of a leash. Jolly liked small dogs. Being the height that he was, he had to be careful around big ones.

Now there were blue lights in his rear-view mirror, and in his wing mirror. Funny, there seemed to be blue light everywhere. That was—

'Missed!' shouted Mrs Abernathy. 'I missed him.'

She was staring intently at the shard of glass in which she had been monitoring the progress of Samuel Johnson and his little mutt. She had focused all of her energy upon it, intent upon bringing him to her, and instead a vehicle of some kind had got in her way. She concentrated again, feeling already that some of her power had ebbed.

'Careful,' she whispered to herself. 'Careful . . .'

She raised her hands as if the boy were already before her and she was about to clutch his throat, and twin bursts of blue light streaked from her fingers and through the glass. She was aware of an impact of some kind in the world of men, the force of which made her blink hard. When she opened her eyes Samuel Johnson was still in Biddlecombe, except now he had stopped walking and was looking around in bewilderment.

Samuel was puzzled. He could have sworn that, just moments before, a van carrying boozy little men had been about to pass him, but it now seemed to have disappeared. Then a police car had approached him, and that had vanished too. And hadn't there been an ice-cream van nearby? He'd been considering buying a cone for himself, even if the weather was still a bit cold. Perhaps he was working too hard, or he needed to get his glasses changed.

There was something spinning on the road before him. As he drew closer to it it grew still. It was a bottle of Spiggit's Old Peculiar. A faint blue light danced around the cap, causing it to burst and spray beer all over the road. There was more blue light on the bumper of the car beside him, and on the garden gate to his left, and in a puddle of oil on the ground, a puddle in which he could see himself reflected, and Boswell.

And Mrs Abernathy.

'Oh no,' said Samuel, as Mrs Abernathy extended her hands for the final time. Streams of blue light shot from her fingertips and erupted from the puddle, enveloping Samuel and Boswell. For a second there was only a terrible coldness, then suddenly every atom in Samuel's body felt as though it were being torn from its neighbour, and he was falling, falling into blackness and beyond.

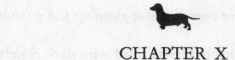

CHAPTER X

In Which Mr Merryweather's Dwarfs
Make an Unpleasant Discovery

It was Dozy who woke first. He was called Dozy because of his ability to take a nap at any time. He could nap on rollercoasters, on a sinking ocean liner, or while his toes were being set on fire – all of which he had actually done. Dozy was the kind of bloke who could take a nap while he was already taking another nap.

He stretched his arms and yawned. He felt as if his body had been stretched on a rack, disassembled, and then reassembled by someone who wasn't particularly worried about whether or not all of the bits were in the right place. Under similar circumstances most people might have wondered why this might be, but Dozy had been drinking Spiggit's Old Peculiar for some time, and was used to waking up feeling that way.

He looked out of the window and saw what appeared to be immense white sand dunes stretching before him. He scratched his head as he tried to remember where it was they were supposed to be going when – well, whenever it was that whatever it was happened. Had they a seaside engagement? Dozy quite liked the sea.

He decided to leave everyone else sleeping and stretch his legs.

The sky above his head was filled with dark clouds tinged with red, so he figured that it was either sunrise or sunset, and it looked like there might be rain on the way. He took a deep breath, but he couldn't smell the sea. He couldn't hear the sea either. Dozy tried to remember if there was a desert anywhere in the vicinity of Biddlecombe, and decided that there wasn't. There was a beach nearby, at Dunstead, but it was mainly stones and old shopping carts, and not like this at all. The sand beneath his feet was very white, and very fine. That sky was odd, though. The clouds kept changing shape and colour, so that at times the sky appeared to be filled with faces tinged fireplace orange and chimney red. If he hadn't known better, he'd have said that it was on fire. There was certainly a smell of burning in the air, and not nice burning either. It smelled as though someone had left a great many steaks on an enormous barbecue for far too long, and then allowed them to rot.

He began to climb the nearest dune in the hope of getting his bearings, whistling as he went. There were more dunes. He climbed another, then another. When he reached the top of the third dune he stopped whistling. He stopped doing anything at all, really, except staring.

Stretched before him, all the way to the flaming horizon, were desks, and at the desks sat small red men with horns on their heads. Each of the desks had a hole on one side, through which other small red men were feeding pieces of something white that emerged from the far side of the desks as fine white sand. A third group of small red men moved back and forth between the desks, loading the sand into buckets and carrying it away, while the little seated men carefully noted the details of the operation in big books.

To his right, at a much larger desk, sat a tall man in a black cloak with scarlet lining. Unlike the little fellows below his skin was very pale, and his horns were larger and seemed to have been polished to a bright sheen. He had a thin moustache on his upper lip, and a beard that came to a pronounced point at the end of his chin. It was the sort of beard worn by someone who is Up To No Good, and doesn't care who knows it. It was a beard that conjured up images of Dastardly Schemes, of women being Tied To Train Tracks and orphans being Deprived Of Their Inheritances. It was a beard that screamed 'I'm A Wrong 'Un, And Make No Mistake About It'.

On the desk, close to where the bearded gentleman's black, pointed boots were currently crossed, there was a sign that read: A. Bodkin, Demon-In-Charge.

Dozy noted that A. Bodkin, Demon-In-Charge, was reading a newspaper called *The Infernal Times*.[23] The headline read:

💀 [23] There usually isn't very much to read in *The Infernal Times*: the weather is always hot with a chance of fireballs; everybody is either miserable, angry, or tormented; and your favourite football team is in the process of losing its most recent match because, in Hell, *both* teams always lose. And keep losing. To a controversial penalty decision. In extra time. And extra time goes on for ever.

GREAT MALEVOLENCE CONSIDERING NEXT MOVE
'Victory Will Be Ours,' says Chancellor Ozymuth.
'Anyone who doubts this will be dismembered.'

A smaller substory announced:

ACTION TO BE TAKEN AGAINST MRS ABERNATHY
'Someone has to take responsibility for the failure of
the invasion,' says Chancellor Ozymuth, 'and I've
decided it should be her.'

This Chancellor Ozymuth seems to be getting around,
thought Dozy. He might not have been the brightest
of dwarfs, but he was developing the uncomfortable
suspicion that all was not quite right here.

'Morning,' he said, then thought about it. 'Afternoon.
Er, Evening?'

A. Bodkin looked to his left to where Dozy was
standing. He puffed his cheeks and blew air from his
mouth in the bored, world-weary manner of middle
managers everywhere whose lot in life is to be disturbed
just when they're about to reach the good bit of something, and therefore never get to experience the good
bit of anything, which makes them even more bored
and world-weary.

'Yes?' said A.Bodkin. 'What is it?'

'Just wondering what all those blokes are doing.'

A.Bodkin lowered his newspaper.

'Blokes? *Blokes?* They're not "blokes": they're highly
trained demonic operatives, not just some imps-come-
lately with lunch boxes and an attitude. Blokes. Tch!'

A. Bodkin returned to his newspaper, muttering about unions, and toilet breaks, and demons being lucky to have a job.

'Yes, but what are they doing?' repeated Dozy.

A.Bodkin rustled his newspaper in an 'I'm very busy and don't want to be disturbed' way then, realizing that the short annoying person by his desk was not about to depart, lowered the paper again resignedly and said:

'Well, it's obvious, isn't it? They're grinding the bones of the dead.'

'Grinding?' said Dozy.

'Yes.'

'Bones?'

'Yes, yes.'

'Dead?'

'Yes. They're hardly going to grind the bones of the living, are they? That would just be messy.'

'Right,' said Dozy. He put his hands in his pockets and kicked idly at the sand, then remembered that it was not sand after all and apologized to it. 'It's nice to have a trade, I suppose.'

He sucked at his lower lip and thought for a moment.

'Where is this, exactly?' he asked.

'Oh, you're not lost, are you?' said A. Bodkin. 'Not another one. I mean, how hard can it be to get this right? You're bad, you die, you come to Hell, you get processed, we find you a job somewhere. You'd think, after all this time, the chaps in Head Office would have this down to a fine art. Tch! I mean, really. Well, you'll just have to make your own way to Central

Processing. I'm far too busy, um, supervising to help you.'

He raised his left arm and examined an hourglass on his wrist to indicate just how busy he was. Sands poured from the upper glass into the lower one, but the level of the sands in the upper glass didn't get any lower, and the level in the lower glass didn't get any higher.

'Just one small thing,' said Dozy. 'Tell you the truth, two small things. Smallish. Actually, not small. Bit big, to be honest.'

He laughed nervously.

'Go on, then,' said A. Bodkin. 'But this had better be the end of it. You're distracting me from my work. Production has already decreased in the time that we've been talking. If I don't keep an eye on this lot, I'll have protests, people asking for tea breaks and time off to visit their aunties or go to the dentist. Look at them: they're already on the verge of revolt!'

Dozy looked at the lot in question. They looked about as likely to revolt as A. Bodkin was to mind a baby without stealing its pram.

'That business about being dead,' said Dozy. 'What did you mean by that, exactly?'

'Oops, sorry,' said A. Bodkin, who didn't look sorry at all. 'You mean you didn't know. Tragic, just tragic.' He stifled a giggle. 'Well, frankly, you're dead. No longer alive. Faithfully departed. If there's a bucket nearby, then you've kicked it. If you were a parrot, you'd have dropped off your perch. And the second thing?'

'Huh?' said Dozy, who was still trying to come to

terms with the first thing, which he hadn't liked the sound of at all. 'Oh, you mentioned something about Hell.'

'Yes?'

'That would be – why?'

'Because that's where you are: Hell.'

'*The* Hell?'

'Are you aware of any other?'

'No, but I didn't think Hell was real.' Mr Merryweather's elves had missed the excitement of the invasion from Hell due to hangovers. Very long, very bad, memory-destroying hangovers.

'Now you know better. Happy?'

'No, can't say that I am. I don't *feel* dead.' He pinched himself. It hurt.

A. Bodkin looked at him in a curious manner.

'You know, you don't *appear* dead either,' said A. Bodkin. 'Most dead people tend to look slightly dead: you know, pale, missing a limb or two, bullet holes, blood, *bleh*.' A. Bodkin let his tongue loll from his mouth and made the whites of his eyes show in a reasonable impression of someone whose best days are behind him and no longer has to worry about brushing his teeth in the mornings. 'But you don't look like that at all.'

Dozy was already backing away. 'Nice talking to you,' he said. 'Good luck with all of the bone stuff. Be seeing you again. Byee-ee!'

He trotted back down the dune. He looked over his shoulder just once, to see A.Bodkin tugging at his beard in a thoughtful way that boded ill for someone.

Dozy started running.

CHAPTER XI

In Which Samuel Arrives, and Nurd Departs

Samuel felt Boswell licking his face. He tried to brush the dog away, but Boswell seemed insistent that he wake up. Samuel didn't want to. His limbs ached, and his head hurt. He wondered if he might not be coming down with something.

Then he remembered: disappearing vans; a blue light; Mrs Abernathy's face in a puddle . . .

Mrs Abernathy.

He opened his eyes.

He was lying on his side by the bank of a dark, muddy river that flowed sluggishly in the direction of a copse of crooked trees. Beneath his cheek was hard ground topped with sparse, blackened grass. He raised himself to his knees, and Boswell yipped with relief. Samuel gathered his dog into his arms and stroked him, all the while looking around and trying to get some sense of where he was. He had a memory of falling, and being aware that he was falling, but when he tried to stop himself he just fell faster. There had been a moment of compression and severe pain, and then nothing.

Above him were black clouds broken by veins of burning red. It was like looking into the heart of a volcano, and he experienced a sensation of dizziness as, briefly, up became down, and down became up, and he had a vision of himself kneeling at the bottom of a great sphere suspended in a furnace. He had to fight the urge to fall back and hold on to the ground. Instead he hugged Boswell tighter and said, 'It's OK, it's all OK,' but he was trying to convince himself as much as the animal.

Mrs Abernathy had done this, he knew, which meant that they could only be in one place: Hell. Somehow she had wrenched them from their world into hers, and that could only be for one purpose: she wanted revenge. Already, she would be looking for them.

Although he was now just thirteen, and no longer considered himself a child, Samuel wanted to cry. He wanted his mother; he wanted his friends. Back in Biddlecombe, when he had faced Mrs Abernathy's wrath, he had done so surrounded by familiar places, and with the support of those whom he loved, and who loved him in return. Here he was alone, except for Boswell, and it says much about the kind of boy Samuel was that, even in the midst of his own fear and sorrow, he wished he had remembered to let go of Boswell's lead before he was transported. His loyal dog had no business being here, yet Samuel was also not a little grateful that Boswell had in fact come with him, for there was at least one other being who was on his side in this terrible place.

No, that wasn't entirely true. Boswell was not the only one who cared about him. There was another. The question was: how could Samuel find him?

Wormwood tapped Nurd on the shoulder.

'Master, why have we stopped?'

The car, still disguised as a rock, had been making good progress across the Vale of Fruitless Journeys, as Nurd put as much distance as possible between themselves and the cave in which they had been hiding. The Vale was formed of massive slabs of brown stone on which the car left no tracks. To the west (or maybe it was to the south, such concepts as direction having little or no meaning in a place where reality struggled to maintain a grip on itself) they ended at the Forest of Broken Forms, where those who had been vain about their looks, and dismissive of those whom they didn't consider as pretty as themselves, were condemned to spend their lives as ugly trees. But that way was too close to the Mountain of Despair for Nurd's liking, and so they had proceeded in another direction, or what they hoped was another direction given that Hell had a habit of confounding such expectations, so that you might head off away from Point A with the best of intentions only to find yourself rapidly back at Point A without ever having veered from a straight line. Ultimately, they wanted to reach the Honeycomb Hills, where they could hide themselves before the Watcher or, worse, its mistress, came hunting for them.

But now Nurd had brought the car to a halt and was

staring into the distance in the troubled manner of someone who thinks he may have left the gas on even though he can't remember ever owning a gas oven.

'Master?' said Wormwood, by now growing concerned.

Nurd's brow furrowed, and a single tear rolled down one of his cheeks as he whispered softly:

'Samuel?'

Mrs Abernathy was not the only denizen of Hell who had been changed by experiencing the world of men at first hand. Nurd too had been altered. To begin with, he was a little kinder to Wormwood than he had been before, and not only because Wormwood knew how to keep the car running. During the long period of his banishment, Nurd had spent a lot of time moping, complaining, and generally bemoaning his lot in life. When he wasn't doing that, he was usually hitting Wormwood on the head for being annoying. But since his return to Hell he had started to view Wormwood as, for want of a better word, a friend. Admittedly he might have preferred a friend who wasn't as prone to waving a finger under Nurd's nose and inviting him to look at what had just been excavated from some orifice of his body, but beggars can't be choosers.

Similarly, Nurd had abandoned any ideas of ruling another world or becoming a serious demon; not that he'd ever been very keen on that to begin with, but he had now dispensed with his self-invented title 'Scourge of Five Deities' and had decided not to go looking for any other demon's job[24] as he was much happier not bothering anyone at all.

But, crucially, Nurd had also brought back with him a deep psychic and emotional connection to Samuel Johnson, the first person who had ever been kind to Nurd, and the first friend that Nurd had ever made. Had they lived in the same world, they would have been inseparable. Instead they were divided by time, and space, and the difficulties of crossing between worlds and dimensions. Despite all of those obstacles, each had held the memory of the other in his heart and there were times as they slept when it seemed to them that they spoke to each other in their dreams. Not a day went by when one did not think of the other, and such feelings have a way of transcending the barriers that life may put in the way of people. An invisible energy linked these two beings, the boy and the demon, just as it connects all those who feel deeply for another, and the nature of that link had suddenly been altered for Nurd. He felt it more intensely than ever before, and he knew at once that Samuel was near. He was in this world, in this foul place where all things were said to reach the end of hope. But that was no longer true, for Nurd now had hope of better times, of a better way of existing, and it was Samuel who had given it to him.

☠ [24] Not even the jobs of the really lame demons like Watchtower, the demon of people who ring the doorbell just as you're about to serve dinner; Eugh, the demon of things found dead in soup, with additional responsibility for flies in ointment; Bob, the demon of things that float when you don't want them to; Glug, the demon of things that sink when you don't want them to; and Gang and Agley, the demons responsible for disrupting the best-laid plans of mice. Mice really hate them. If it wasn't for them, mice would rule the world.

Yet if Samuel was here, then it could not be of his own will. Nothing came to Hell willingly. Even the entities trapped there wished to be elsewhere, or to cease to exist at all, for that would be infinitely preferable to an eternity spent in this realm.

Mrs Abernathy had been hunting, unknowingly, for Nurd, the mysterious driver of the car that had brought an end to her master's hope of escape, but Nurd knew that Samuel was the greater prize she sought. Somehow she had found a way to bring him here. For all Nurd knew, Samuel might already be her prisoner, and he had a terrifying vision of his friend, chained and bound, being brought before the Great Malevolence himself, there to be punished for his part in all that had occurred. But even if Samuel were not yet in Mrs Abernathy's clutches, there were plenty of other foul beings in Hell who would relish the chance to taste a human child. Someone would have to save Samuel, and that someone was Nurd.

Except Nurd didn't have much experience of saving anyone, apart from Nurd himself, and he was having enough difficulty keeping himself from becoming Mrs Abernathy's prisoner without trying to prevent the capture of someone else. He also didn't consider himself particularly bright, or brave, or cunning. But like most people who think that way, Nurd was a lot smarter, and braver, and cleverer than he realized. He simply hadn't been given much opportunity to prove it to himself, or to others.

'Master?' asked Wormwood, for the third time, and on this occasion he received an answer.

'Samuel is here,' said Nurd. 'We have to find him.'

Wormwood didn't look surprised. If his master said that Samuel, whom Wormwood had never met but about whom he'd heard a great deal, was somewhere in Hell, then Wormwood was happy to believe him. On the other hand Wormwood did look a bit startled when Nurd turned the car 180 degrees so that it was facing in the direction from which they had just come.

'Er, Master,' he said. 'You told me that way lay misery, torture, poor food, and certain dismemberment at the hands of Mrs Abernathy.'

'I did indeed, Wormwood, but only Mrs Abernathy could have brought Samuel here, so wherever she is, that's where he will be too.' He put his foot down and gunned the engine. The car lifted slightly, like a horse yearning for the start of a big race. Then Nurd released the brake and they were off.

Wormwood looked at his master in awe. The old Nurd had been cowardly, self-serving, and determined to avoid personal injury at all costs. This new Nurd was courageous, selfless, and apparently keen to have his limbs separated from his body as soon as possible.

On reflection, thought Wormwood, as they sped towards their destiny, I think I preferred the old one.

CHAPTER XII

In Which Dozy is the Bearer of Bad News

Jolly was just waking up when Dozy got back to the van.

'S'matter,' said Jolly, rubbing his forehead in a pained manner. 'What did we hit?'

From the back of the van Dozy heard assorted mutters, yawns, and unpleasant bodily noises as Angry and Mumbles emerged from the land of Nod.

'Listen to me carefully,' said Dozy. 'Precisely which exit did you take from the motorway?'

'Huh? The Biddlecombe exit. I mean, we agreed.'

'And that's what the sign said? Biddlecombe?'

'Yes, Biddlecombe.'

'It didn't say, like, "Hell", by any chance, did it?'

Jolly looked at him suspiciously, and sniffed his breath. 'Have you been drinking already? You know, it's all very well having one or ten to help you sleep, but at least wait until you've had your cornflakes before you start knocking them back in the morning. You'll have a liver like the sole of a shoe, mark my words.'

'I haven't been drinking,' said Dozy. 'Something is very, very wrong.' And he pointed through the front windscreen at the great expanse of pale dunes that stretched before them.

Jolly stared at the vista for a moment before climbing from the van, Dozy, Angry, and Mumbles close behind. Jolly pursed his lips and did a full circuit of the van, looking hopefully for some sign of a church spire, or a chip shop, or a pub.

'Nah, that can't be right,' said Jolly. 'We must have taken a wrong turning somewhere.'

'Where, Purgatory?' said Dozy. 'We're in Hell.'

'It's not that bad,' said Angry. 'It's a trifle toasty, I'll admit, but don't let's get carried away here.' He knelt, picked up a handful of fine sand, and watched it slip through his fingers. Mumbles did the same.

'Look, we must be near the sea,' said Angry. 'It's sand.'

'No, it's not,' said Dozy.

'Course it is. What else would it be?'

'Smesand,' said Mumbles, lifting a handful of grains to his nose and sniffing them warily.

'That's right,' said Dozy. 'It doesn't smell like sand. That's because it's not sand.'

'What is it, then?' asked Jolly.

Dozy crooked a finger at them in a 'follow me' gesture, and they did.

The four dwarfs lay on the side of one of the dunes, their heads peeping over the top, and watched as the imps fed bones into the sides of their workbenches.

'They're bones,' said Angry. 'We're lying on bits of bone. Quite comfortable, actually. Who'd have thought it?'

'Whose bones are they?' said Jolly.

'Dunno,' said Dozy. 'That bloke over there seems to be in charge, but I don't think he knows either.'

They regarded A. Bodkin curiously. He was talking on an old black rotary dial telephone.

'He's a nutjob,' said Jolly. 'That phone doesn't have a wire attached to it.'

'I don't think that matters,' said Dozy. 'I get the feeling that normal rules don't apply here.'

They continued to watch A. Bodkin, who was becoming quite animated. Although they couldn't hear clearly all of what he was saying, it was apparent that he was troubled by Dozy's unexpected appearance beside his desk, and the fact that Dozy did not appear to be dead.

'So he's a demon,' said Angry.

'Yes,' said Dozy.

'And all that lot are demons too.'

'Imps, apparently, but I think it amounts to the same thing.'

'Then this *is* Hell.'

'That's what I've been trying to tell you.'

'How did we end up in Hell? What have we ever done to anyone?'

There was silence as the other three dwarfs gave Angry's brain a chance to catch up with his mouth.

'Ohhhhhh,' said Angry, as all the reasons why they might justifiably be in Hell came flooding back like rubbish at high tide. He shrugged his shoulders. 'Fair enough, I suppose. I don't remember dying, though. I thought that was supposed to be part of the deal.'

'Maybe it's like Jolly said,' offered Dozy. 'We might have hit something and died in the crash.'

'But I don't think we did hit anything,' said Jolly. 'The van seemed fine. More to the point, I feel fine. If I was dead, I'm sure I'd be feeling poorly. And I'd probably smell a bit. Well, a bit more.'

'So we're not dead, then,' said Angry. 'And if we're not dead, this can't be Hell.'

'I don't know,' said Dozy. 'A. Bodkin over there seemed very sure.'

'He was probably just pulling your leg,' said Angry. 'He looks like the kind of bloke who'd think something like that was funny.'

Suddenly a great pillar of pale fire appeared beside A. Bodkin's desk, stretching from the sands right up to the black clouds above. Its appearance was so unexpected that even the imps at their desks briefly stopped converting bones to dust in order to watch what was happening.

A woman's face appeared in the flames, her eyes twin orbs of the brightest blue.

'She looks familiar,' said Jolly. 'I've seen her somewhere before.'

'She was on the front page of his newspaper,' said Dozy. 'Something about being in trouble.'

'But I didn't see his newspaper,' said Jolly.

'Shhh,' said Angry. 'I want to hear.'

As it turned out, hearing what the woman had to say wasn't going to be a problem. Her voice, when it emerged, sounded like thunder. It was so loud that it hurt the dwarfs' ears.

'BODKIN,' said the woman. 'WHAT HAVE YOU FOUND?'

'Here, turn it down, love,' said Jolly. 'The chap's only standing next to you.'

A. Bodkin looked confused. 'Mrs Abernathy,' he said. 'I wasn't expecting to hear from you.'

'I'M SURE THAT YOU WEREN'T,' said Mrs Abernathy. 'NEVERTHELESS, HEARING FROM ME YOU ARE. YOU REPORTED AN INTERLOPER. WAS IT A BOY? TELL ME.'

'To be honest, much as I'd love to help you, I'm not sure that I can answer your question. This really needs to go through official channels.'

Mrs Abernathy's face darkened. Her lips peeled back, exposing teeth that began to grow longer and sharper as they watched. Her face swelled, and she was at once both a woman and a monster, although it was still the woman that appeared the more terrifying of the two.

'Oops, said the wrong thing there, mate,' said Jolly. 'He'll be telling her it's men's business next, and that she shouldn't worry her pretty little head about it.'

'Nah, he couldn't be that stupid,' said Angry.

'Mrs Abernathy,' said A. Bodkin. 'I really must insist: this is a matter for the Senior Council of Demons. Er, that is, the Council of demons that are, um, entirely fixed in their concept of, um, demonality in the non-female sense.'

'I take it back,' said Angry. 'He is that stupid.'

But A. Bodkin, having decided to put his foot in his mouth, was now determined to eat it, possibly with an order of socks on the side. 'You must understand that since your, ahem, transformation and subsequent, ah, fall from favour, senior management has informed us that you are no longer to be included in the decision-making process.' A. Bodkin smiled his most patronizing smile, which was very patronizing indeed. 'I'm sure that you have far more important matters to attend to,' he continued, 'such as –'

'And he's going for broke,' said Angry.

'Oh dear,' said Jolly, shielding his eyes with his hands. 'I can hardly bear to watch.'

'– beautifying yourself, for example,' continued A. Bodkin, 'or making something pretty for—'

The precise purpose of the something pretty in question was lost in a torrent of white-hot fire that shot from Mrs Abernathy's mouth and engulfed the unfortunate A. Bodkin, consuming him entirely and leaving only a pair of smoking black boots in his place.

The pillar of fire moved, turning to face the ranks of seated imps.

'NOW, WOULD ANYBODY ELSE LIKE TO SUGGEST THAT I MIND MY OWN BUSINESS?' said Mrs Abernathy.

Thousands of heads shook simultaneously.

'WOULD SOMEONE PREFER TO TELL ME IF A BOY WAS SEEN HERE, A BOY WITH A DOG?'

Two rows from the front, one of the imps raised a hand.

'YES?'

'Please Miss, it was the size of a boy, Miss, but it wasn't a boy, Miss,' said the demon.

'Ooh, tattle-tale,' said Dozy. 'If he didn't have all his pals behind him, I'd deck him for that.'

'WHAT DO YOU MEAN?'

'It was a little man, Miss. Mr Bodkin didn't think he was dead, Miss, so he reported him, Miss.'

'AND THIS LITTLE MAN WAS ALONE?'

'Yes, Miss. Far as Mr Bodkin could tell, Miss.'

'VERY GOOD. WHAT'S YOUR NAME?'

'I don't have a name, Miss. I'm just a demon imp, third class, Miss.'

'WELL, CONSIDER YOURSELF PROMOTED. FROM NOW ON, YOU MAY CALL YOURSELF B. BODKIN. THE DESK IS YOURS.'

'Oh, thank you very much, Miss. I'll be a very good B. Bodkin, Miss, mark my words.'

The imp rose from its workbench and trotted up to the main desk as the pillar of fire narrowed and then disappeared entirely. It slipped its feet into A. Bodkin's smoking boots. Slowly it began to increase in height, and its appearance started to change. Within seconds it bore a startling resemblance to the original A.Bodkin, right down to the nasty little beard and the superior manner.

'Right, back to work, you lot,' said B. Bodkin. 'The show is over.'

He settled himself into his new seat, put his feet on the desk, and picked up the newspaper. With a collective shrug of resignation, the rest of the imps returned to the grinding, carrying, and recording of bits of bone.

'Did you see that?' said Angry. 'What this place needs is a good workers' revolution.'

'You can organize the masses another time,' said Jolly as the dwarfs slid down the dune and headed for their van. 'We need to find a way to get home. I remember now where I saw that woman. It was back in Biddlecombe. She appeared on my windscreen, and then there was a blue flash, and next thing I knew we were here.' He paused, and scratched his chin. 'And there was a boy with a dachshund.'

He looked back in the direction from which they had come, as though expecting to see that pillar of flame rising high above them and that dreadful woman's voice asking about a boy and his dog. Slowly, Jolly began shuffling pieces of the puzzle around in his brain.

'I wonder,' he said. 'I wonder, I wonder, I wonder . . .'

CHAPTER XIII

In Which We Meet a Ram, and Some Old Friends are Reunited

Samuel had overcome his fear and, Boswell's lead in hand, had decided to seek cover. As the nearest shelter was the forest of crooked, leafless trees, that was where he and Boswell aimed for. Boswell shivered as they drew near to the forest, and plonked his bottom down firmly on the ground. As far as Boswell was concerned nothing in this land smelled good, sounded good, or looked good, but this forest felt particularly unpleasant.

'Come along, Boswell,' said Samuel. 'I don't like this place much either, but it really isn't a good idea for us to be out in the open where anyone can see us. And not just anyone, if you know what I mean.'

Boswell twitched his ears and lowered his head. His life had once been so normal: wake up, go outside for a sniff and a wee, have a bite to eat, play for a while, have a nap, wake up, and repeat. Had he heard the phrase 'a dog's life' used in the sense of one's existence being a bit harsh, he would have been slightly worried. As far as Boswell was concerned, a dog's life was absolutely fine. It was humans who made things complicated; humans, and those nasty creatures with horns, and big teeth, and a stink of burning about them. His senses were flooded with the scent of those creatures now. This was their place, and Boswell loathed it.

Samuel tugged on the lead and, reluctantly, Boswell trotted along beside his master. The branches of the trees met above their heads, as though they were reaching out to one another for consolation, their extremities tangling. Their bark was pitted with hollows that looked like eyes and mouths, faces contorted in expressions of agony. He heard the leaves whispering as though a breeze had briefly blown through them.

But there was no breeze, and there were no leaves.

'Boy,' said a soft voice. 'Boy, help me.'

'Boy,' said another, this time the voice of a woman. 'Free me.'

'Boy . . .'

'Boy . . .'

'. . . help me . . .'

'No, me, help me . . .'

'Boy, I've been here for so long, for so very long . . .'

The mouths in the trees stretched and opened, and the eyes twisted in their wooden sockets. The branches moved, stretching for him. One snagged his jacket. Another tried to pull the lead from his hand.

'Boy, don't leave us . . .'

'Boy, listen to us . . .'

Behind him the forest closed, the trees forming an impenetrable wall through which he could not retreat. Samuel picked Boswell up, shielding him beneath his jacket, and started to run, even as branches cut his face and tore his trousers and tried to trip him as he passed.

They should not have come here. He had made a mistake, but they could not go back. Samuel kept his head down, barely able to see where he was going, and all the time the voices kept calling him: pleading, threatening, promising. Anything at all, he could have anything he desired, if only he would make the pain stop.

A presence appeared in front of him, and a voice said 'Back!'

The trees instantly grew silent and were still. Samuel looked up to see a hunched animal with a distorted mouth, blunt teeth, and ancient, twisted horns protruding from its head, which was bearded with shaggy white fur. It took Samuel a moment or two to see that it was a ram of sorts, but one that had learned to walk on two legs. Its upper hooves had mutated, lengthening to form two pairs of bony fingers, in one of which it held a long staff. Its coat was matted and filthy, and smelled of damp and smoke.

From deep in the forest came another voice, sinister and male.

'What right have you to claim him?' it said.

The branches of the trees parted like courtiers before a king, and Samuel was confronted by an enormous gnarled oak with a complex root system that reminded him uncomfortably of serpents writhing. This was the tree that had spoken. It had two holes in its trunk for eyes, and a twisted gash for a mouth, from which a reeking gas emerged as it talked. It stank of rotting vegetation, and worse: the slow decay of the non-vegetative.

'What right have you?' said the ram in reply. 'He's just a boy.'

'He could help us. He could free us.'

'And how could he do that? You are afflicted things. He cannot help you.'

'Give him an axe, and let him cut us down. Let him reduce us to splinters and sawdust.'

'And then? Do you still believe that mortal rules apply to you? The Great Malevolence would simply start again, reconstituting you into even more grotesque forms for his amusement. That will not bring your pain to an end. It will merely increase it.'

'Then give us the boy, that he might keep us company. We can gaze upon his beauty, and remember what we once were.'

The ram laughed, a low, bleating sound. 'Give him to you so that he can rot slowly in your insides, more like, allowing you to visit some of your anger on him. He is lost, but not forsaken. He does not belong here, and he does not belong to you.'

The great oak seemed to snarl, and Samuel saw deep into the racked, tortured soul of it.

'We will not forget this, Old Ram,' it said. 'Our roots grow longer, our branches sharper. We draw ever nearer to you, and soon you will wake in your hovel to find yourself surrounded by us, and our arms will draw you to us, and your pain will be a source of amusement for us in this miserable place.'

'Yes, yes, yes,' said the ram dismissively. 'Old Ram has heard it all before. You're trees, in case you hadn't noticed. You grow so slowly that even the Great Malevolence himself has ceased to find your misery amusing. Keep staring into your pools of stagnant water, and recalling what you once were. The child has no more business with you.'

He nudged Samuel with his stick.

'Come, my boy,' he said. 'Leave them to their mutterings.'

Samuel did as he was told, but as he went he could not resist looking back at the great oak; for a moment he could have sworn that he saw its roots emerge from the ground. But then the forest closed around it, and he could see it no longer.

Meanwhile, Mr Merryweather's elves, or dwarfs, or however they currently chose to describe themselves, had encountered a serious problem.

Somebody had stolen their van.

'And you're sure this is where you left it?' said Angry. 'You know, a lot of these dunes look alike.'

'Don't take that tone with me,' said Jolly. '*We* left it here. All of us. Not just me. And of course this is where we left it: you can see the tyre marks.'

'Were the keys still in the ignition? Very unwise to walk away and leave the keys in the ignition. Invitation to thieves, that is.'

If a volcano could have assumed the form of a small human being, and had then been photographed on the verge of eruption, it would have looked not unlike Jolly at that moment. When he spoke, though, he was remarkably calm. Dangerously so, one might have thought.

'Yes,' he said. 'I left the keys in it.'

'So that was a bit careless, wasn't it?'

'Well, it might have been – IF SOMEONE HAD DRIVEN IT AWAY!'

The dwarfs looked at the space that had, until recently, been occupied by a bright yellow van decorated with a painting of a happy little person who bore no resemblance at all to themselves, even at the best of times, of which this was definitely not one. There were four marks in the dust where the van's tyres had stood, but there were no tracks indicating the direction in which it might have gone. Simultaneously all four dwarfs raised their heads, shaded their eyes with their hands, and examined the brooding skies above in the hope of catching a glimpse of their vehicle.

'I can't believe someone's nicked the van,' said Dozy. 'I mean, it's not like we left it on a council estate with the doors open. It's a desert. What kind of lowlifes do they have around here, anyway?'

'It's Hell,' Angry pointed out glumly. 'It's probably full of the kind of people who'd nick your feet if your legs weren't attached to them.'

'Suppose so,' said Dozy. 'Still, that's how a place gets a reputation for being unwelcoming to visitors.'

'Leaseraneem,' said Mumbles.

'You're right,' said Jolly. 'There never is a copper around when you need one.'

Which was slightly ironic, given that a) Mr Merryweather's dwarfs were not the sort to court the attention of the police at any time; and b) generally it was not Mr Merryweather's dwarfs who needed the help of the police, but other people who needed it to protect them from Mr Merryweather's dwarfs.

At this point, as if on cue, a police patrol car appeared on top of a nearby dune, its blue lights flashing.

'Blimey,' said Jolly. 'They're efficient around here, I'll give them that.'

Angry squinted at the car as it made its way carefully down the side of the dune.

'You know, I could be wrong, but those coppers don't half look familiar.'

The car drew to a halt. Its doors opened. From one side stepped Sergeant Rowan, and from the other Constable Peel. Both of them scowled at the dwarfs, and on their faces was etched the memory of incidents of assault; drunkenness; unauthorized taking of vehicles, including an ambulance and a bus; arson; breaking and entering, specifically into Biddlecombe's Little World of Animal Wonders, and the removal of a penguin and two ferrets from same; using a penguin and two ferrets as dangerous weapons; and last, but by no means least, stealing a policeman's helmet, namely Constable Peel's, and allowing a penguin and two ferrets to use it as a public convenience. What these incidents had in common was that they had all involved, to some degree or another, one or more of, that's right, Mr Merryweather's dwarfs.

'Oh no,' said Jolly, as his brain registered the two policemen, and all of the unfortunate memories associated with them. 'It's true: this must be Hell.'

CHAPTER XIV

In Which the Forces of Law and Order Assert Themselves

Sergeant Rowan and Constable Peel were deeply, deeply unhappy. To begin with, they had been hauled through an interdimensional portal, which had hurt a lot. Then they had recovered consciousness just in time to see a pink-skinned demon with three heads, too many eyes, and a mouth in its stomach steal the loudspeaker from their roof before running away while wearing it as a hat on its middle head. Then a smaller demon carrying a bucket of white sand had passed them, waved, and disappeared over the top of a dune. He had been followed by another, and another, and another, all of them identical and all of them carrying buckets of white sand. Attempts to engage them in conversation, including such beloved opening gambits as 'Who are you?', 'Where is this?', and 'What are you doing with that bucket?' had met with no reply.

'You know what, Constable?' said Sergeant Rowan, as the never-ending procession of demons passed, each one greeting them with a cheery wave.

'I don't want to know what, Sarge.'

'What?'

'I mean that I don't want to hear what you're about to say, because I know what you're about to say, and I know it's not something I want to hear. So, if it's all the same to you, I think I might just put my fingers in my ears and hum a happy tune.'

And he did just that, until Sergeant Rowan made him stop.

'Now, lad, don't let's be overdramatic,' said Sergeant Rowan. 'We have to face up to the truth here.'

'I don't want to face up to the truth. The truth's nasty. The truth's walking up that dune holding a bucket. The truth has three heads and stole our loud-speaker.'

'Which means?'

Constable Peel looked as if he was about to cry.

'You're going to tell me that the portal's opened again, and all kinds of horrible creatures are pouring out.'

Sergeant Rowan smiled at him. 'I wasn't going to tell you that at all, lad.'

'Really?'

'No, that's not what's happening here.'

'Are you sure?'

'Virtually certain.'

'Oh!' said Constable Peel. He smiled with relief. 'Oh, thank goodness. Phew, don't I feel foolish?'

'I'll bet you do, lad.'

'There was I, worrying that the portal had opened, and monsters were going to pop out of it and try to eat us, and the dead were going to come alive again, and, you know, all that kind of thing. Silly old Peel, eh?'

'Silly old you,' said Sergeant Rowan. 'Monsters aren't going to come pouring through the portal.'

'That's a load off my mind,' said Constable Peel, then thought about what he had just heard. 'But what about the one that stole our loudspeaker, and the little red blokes with the buckets?'

'They didn't come through the portal. None of them did.'

'Why not?'

'Because they're already here. It's we who have come through the portal, Constable, not them. We're in Hell.'

All things considered, thought Sergeant Rowan, Constable Peel had taken the news remarkably well, once he'd stopped raving and calmed down. They had taken the decision to get away from the steady train of bucket-toting, polite, but relatively uncommunicative demons and find someone who might be able to answer a straight question, which is how they had come across four dwarfs standing on a flat patch between dunes, scratching their heads and staring at the sky. Both policemen had recognized them instantly, and their moods had immediately brightened. They might have been in Hell, but they weren't alone, and if there were four individuals that Sergeant Rowan and Constable Peel would like to have seen consigned to Hell more than Mr Merryweather's dwarfs, then they hadn't met those people yet, and probably never would.

'Hello, hello, hello,' said Sergeant Rowan, watching

with pleasure as the four dwarfs looked for a means of escape, and found none. 'What have we here, then?'

'Why, I believe it's the fabled Mr Merryweather's Dwarfs, Sarge,' said Constable Peel.

'Is it really? My, my. Correct me if I'm wrong, Constable, but would they be the same dwarfs who stole your helmet and allowed two ferrets to do their business in it?'

'Two ferrets *and* a penguin, Sarge,' Constable Peel corrected.

'Oh yes, the penguin. I'd almost forgotten about that penguin. Phil, wasn't it?'

'That's right, Sarge. Phil the Penguin. Filled my helmet and all.' He smiled at his own little joke. The thought of getting some revenge on Mr Merryweather's dwarfs was cheering him up no end.

Sergeant Rowan looked around. 'So we have the dwarfs, but where is Mr Merryweather?' He turned his attention back to the dwarfs, and pointed at Jolly. 'You, Mr Jolly Smallpants, you're the leader of this motley crew, but where's the ringmaster?'

'He abandoned us,' said Jolly.

'Hardly blame him,' said Sergeant Rowan.

'He doesn't love us any more,' said Dozy.

'Wonder that he ever did,' said Sergeant Rowan.

'Prifowig,' said Mumbles.

'Whatever,' said Sergeant Rowan.

'We're only little people,' said Angry. He put on his best sad face, made his eyes large, and tried unsuccessfully to force a tear from them. 'We're very small and we're all alone in the world.'

His fellow dwarfs bowed their heads, peered up from beneath their brows, and introduced some trembling to their lips.

'No, you're not alone in the world,' said Sergeant Rowan, his words heavy with consolation. He put his hand on Angry's shoulder. 'You've got us now. And you're under arrest.'

CHAPTER XV

In Which Something of the Nature of this World is Revealed Through Old Ram

Old Ram led Samuel and Boswell through weeds and briars, hacking a path with his staff when the way was blocked. What trees there were appeared smaller here at the edge of the forest. Old Ram had described them as 'new arrivals'. While they still had faces on their trunks, they were confused rather than angry and hateful, and their branches were too small and weak to present a threat.

'Ugly things grow quickly here,' explained Old Ram. 'Each time Old Ram walks, Old Ram has to cut his way through afresh. The forest sets itself against him, but Old Ram will not let it win.'

A stone hovel shaped like a beehive came into view. It had slit windows, and a narrow entrance that was blocked by a door woven from twigs and branches. A thin finger of smoke wound its way upward from a hole in the roof. Above them the dark clouds collided and dispersed, sending flashes of white and red and orange across the sky. As in the forest, Samuel believed that he could discern faces in the clouds, their cheeks billowing, their mouths screaming thunder, forming, swirling, and re-forming in a great tumult of noise and light.

Old Ram followed the boy's gaze.

'They were people once, just as the trees were,' he said. 'The skies are filled with the souls of the angry, turned to storm clouds by the Great Malevolence, so that they can fight and rage for eternity.'

'And the trees?'

'The trees are the souls of the vain. Everything here is given a purpose, a role to play. The Great Malevolence offers each soul a choice: to join his ranks, and become a demon, or to become part of the essence of this world. Most choose to join him, but those in the skies and those in the forest were too wrathful or too self-absorbed to serve even him, and so he found a suitable punishment for them.'

'Those poor people,' said Samuel, and Boswell whined in agreement.

Old Ram shook his head. 'You have to understand that only the very worst end up here: the ones whose anger made them kill, and who felt no sorrow or guilt after the act; those so obsessed with themselves that they turned their backs on the sufferings of others, and left them in pain; those whose greed meant that others starved and died. Such souls belong here, because they would find no peace elsewhere. In this place, they are understood. In this place, their faults have meaning. In this place, they belong.'

Old Ram opened the door, and indicated that Samuel should enter. Samuel paused on the threshold. He was old enough to know that he shouldn't trust strangers, and Old Ram was a very strange stranger indeed. On the other hand Old Ram had saved both Samuel and Boswell from the trees, and they needed help from someone if they were to avoid Mrs Abernathy and find a way home.

Samuel entered the dwelling. It had no furniture, no pictures, no signs of habitation at all except for the lingering odour of Old Ram himself, and the fire that burned in a hollow in the dirt floor. Black wood was piled beside it, ready to the added to the blaze.

'It's . . . very nice,' said Samuel.

'No, it isn't,' said Old Ram, 'but it's polite of you to say so. You may find this odd from one trapped in this kingdom of fire, but Old Ram feels the cold. Old Ram is never hungry, never thirsty, never tired, but Old Ram is always, always cold, so Old Ram keeps the fire burning. Old Ram feeds it with branches from the forest. When there are no fallen branches to be found, Old Ram breaks them from young trees. Old Ram needs his warmth.'

'Is that why the trees hate you so much?' asked Samuel. 'Because you cut their branches?'

'They hate everything,' said Old Ram, 'but most of all they hate themselves. Still, Old Ram has given them much reason to resent him, that's true. If nothing else, tormenting them offers Old Ram something to break the monotony.'

He sat down by the fire, crossing his hind legs beneath him and stretching his forelegs before him to warm his hooves. Samuel and Boswell sat opposite, and watched Old Ram through the flames.

'What did you do to end up here, if it's not rude to ask?' said Samuel.

Old Ram looked away. 'Old Ram was a bad shepherd,' he said. 'Old Ram betrayed his flock.'

And he would say no more.[25]

Samuel was tired and hungry. He searched in his pockets where he found a biscuit and a small apple. It wasn't much. Despite what Old Ram had said about lacking an appetite, Samuel offered him a bite of each, but Old Ram ignored the biscuit entirely, instead sniffing at the apple.

'Old Ram remembers apples,' he said, sadness in his voice, and in his pale eyes. 'Old Ram remembers pears, and plums, and pomegranates. Old Ram remembers . . . everything.'

'You can have a little, if you like,' said Samuel.

Old Ram seemed tempted, but then drew back, as though suspecting Samuel of some plot to poison him.

[25] From this we may surmise that Old Ram was a priest or church minister of some kind. Who knows, he may even have been a pope, for there have been some very dodgy popes over the years. Alexander VI, who was one of the infamous Borgias, and was pope from 1492–1503, sired at least seven children and was described as being similar to a hungry wolf. Benedict IX (who reigned at various points from 1032–48) was pope on three occasions, but surrendered the papacy on two of them in exchange for lots of gold before being hounded out of Rome in 1048. Finally, Stephen VI (896–97) disliked his predecessor, Formosus, so much that he had the corpse dug up and put on trial. Found guilty, Formosus had his garments removed, two fingers cut off, and was then reburied. But Stephen, who was still angry at Formosus, ordered him to be dug up again and Formosus's body was thrown into the Tiber. Stephen probably would have sent divers to find the corpse so he could do something else to it if he hadn't been strangled himself in 897, suggesting that Stephen wasn't much to write home about either when it came to being a pope.

'No, Old Ram doesn't want any. Old Ram isn't hungry. Eat, you and your little dog. Eat.'

Old Ram folded his arms and stared into the fire, lost in his own thoughts. Samuel gave the biscuit to Boswell, then ate the apple himself, Boswell not being much of a fan of fruit.

'How can we get back to our own world?' asked Samuel, when he had finished the apple and grown tired of the silence. Boswell, he noticed, had fallen asleep with his head on his lap. He stroked the dog, who opened his eyes, wagged his tail once, then went back to sleep.

'You can't,' said Old Ram. 'Nothing ever leaves here. Not even the Great Malevolence himself can leave, and he's tried.'

'But they managed to break into my world. If it was done once, it can be done again.'

Old Ram's mouth curled into what might have been a smile.

'Mrs Abernathy,' he said. He bleated his laughter. 'A demon obsessed with being human is a demon no longer. She has fallen from power. Another will take her place, unless she can find a way to make up for her failure.' He glanced slyly at Samuel. 'How did you come here, boy?'

Samuel began to tell him everything, then stopped. 'There was light, a blue light. It flashed as I was walking home with Boswell, and I woke up here.'

'And you saw nothing more, only a light?'

'That's all,' Samuel lied. He chose not to mention his knowledge of Mrs Abernathy to Old Ram. He could not have said why, but he was sure that it would not be a good idea.

Old Ram nodded his head and was silent again. The stone hive was uncomfortably warm, and the smoke was making Samuel drowsy. His eyelids grew heavy. He saw Old Ram watching him, and felt the intensity of the creature's regard, but he was so tired. He lay down and closed his eyes, and was soon fast asleep.

Samuel dreamed. He dreamed that Old Ram was standing over him, and scattering dust upon the flames. There was a sour, acrid smell, and then a face appeared in the fire, black-eyed and insect-jawed. In the dream, Old Ram said: 'Where is your mistress?' and the creature in the fire responded with a series of clicks and hisses that Old Ram seemed to understand.

'When she returns, tell her that Old Ram has a prize for her. Old Ram is tired of this exile. Old Ram wants a place of honour at her table. As she rises again, so shall Old Ram. Tell her this.'

The face in the flames disappeared, and Old Ram sat down again. That was Samuel's dream. But when he opened his eyes the sour smell was still in his nostrils, and Old Ram was not sitting in quite the same place that he had occupied before Samuel fell asleep.

'Rest more,' said Old Ram. 'You'll need your energy. Old Ram will take you to someone who may be able to help you, but first we must wait.'

'Why must we wait?'

'It's too dangerous to travel now. Later, it will be safer.'

Samuel stood, and Boswell stood too.

'I think Boswell and I should leave,' he said. 'We've stayed here long enough.'

'No, no,' said Old Ram. 'Please, sit. Old Ram has things to tell you, important things. You must listen.'

But Samuel was already leading Boswell to the door, although he did not turn his back on Old Ram. Old Ram scrambled upright, and in the light of the fire his eyes took on a red glow.

'You must stay!' he said. 'Old Ram must rise again!'

Thunder roared in the skies above, and lightning flashed, as though the fighting souls had heard Old Ram's cry, but Samuel thought that he discerned another sound hidden beneath the great tumult: a grinding, moaning noise like a mighty engine in motion.

Old Ram moved. He grabbed his staff and swung it at Samuel, barely missing the boy's head.

'Nobody leaves!' shouted Old Ram. 'Nobody leaves until the Dark Lady arrives!'

He made as if to swing the staff again, but instead spun it in his hooves and used it to trip Samuel, who fell heavily to the floor. Boswell snapped and barked, but now Old Ram was standing above them, the staff held high, ready to bring it down on Samuel's skull.

And then the staff was snatched from Old Ram's hooves and disappeared through the hole in the roof, drawn upwards by a snakelike length of wood. The hut began to collapse: stones tumbled down from the ceiling, and fissures appeared in the walls. Black roots and branches thrust their way through, winding themselves around Old Ram's body and neck and legs. The door exploded inwards, and Samuel saw the face of the Great Oak grinning and leering in the gap.

'Old Ram,' said the tree. 'I warned you. We were tormented enough without you adding to our misery. Now we will add to yours instead.'

Old Ram struggled in its grasp, but the ancient tree was too strong for him. More stones dislodged themselves, and an opening appeared close to where Samuel lay. As quickly as he could, he held Boswell under his left arm and pushed himself through the hole. Outside he got to his feet and ran until he came to a boulder which was big enough for him to hide behind. Only then did he risk a look back at the house.

The Great Oak towered above the scattered stones of Old Ram's dwelling, its branches swinging wildly, its roots twisting and curling. Old Ram was held high above the ground, his frightened face close to the Great Oak's features. The Great Oak was laughing at him, and taunting him. Behind it the contorted trees swayed and cried as the Great Oak took its prize and returned to the forest, and the fire in the ruins turned to ash and went out for ever.

CHAPTER XVI

In Which Hell Gets Stranger, and the Scientists Grow More Curious

Not for the first time, Mr Merryweather's dwarfs and the forces of law and order were having a disagreement.

'You can't arrest us,' said Jolly.

'I beg to differ,' said Sergeant Rowan. 'I can, and I have.'

'But someone's nicked our van. It hardly seems fair to arrest us when somewhere out there is a criminal driving a stolen van.'

'But there are four criminals right here,' said Sergeant Rowan. 'A dwarf in the hand is worth two in a van, or words to that effect.'

'Er, Sarge,' said Constable Peel.

'Not now, Constable. I'm enjoying my moment of triumph.'

'It's important, Sarge.'

'So is this.'

'No, really important.'

Sergeant Rowan, still keeping a firm grip on Jolly's collar, turned to Constable Peel and said, 'All right, then, what is—'

He stopped talking. He looked around.

'Constable, where's our car?' he said.

'That's just it, Sarge. It's gone. Someone's nicked it.'

Sergeant Rowan returned his attention to the dwarfs, who all held up their hands in gestures of innocence that, for the first time ever, they actually meant.

'Wasn't us,' said Angry.

'Serves you right,' said Jolly. 'I told you there was a thief about.'

'Nobody saw anything?' said Sergeant Rowan.

'We was too busy being arrested, Sarge,' said Dozy. 'Our rights was being infringed.'

'Nojidell,' said Mumbles.

'Absolutely,' said Angry. 'You have no jurisdiction in Hell. The minute you felt our collars, it was assault. We're going to sue.'

Sergeant Rowan raised a fist in a manner suggesting that, if he was going to be sued for something, he planned to make the most of it and add charges of inflicting serious bodily harm to a dwarf to his list of offences.

'Calm down, calm down,' said Jolly. 'This isn't helping anyone. Look, we all want the same thing here, right? We want to find our vehicles, and get home.'

Dozy's face suddenly assumed an expression of grave loss. 'The booze!' he said.

'What?' said Constable Peel.

'The last of the Spiggit's: it was in the van. It's gone. Oh, the humanity!'

Dozy fell to his knees and started to sob, moving

Constable Peel sufficiently to pat him on the back and offer him a paper tissue.

'There, there,' he said. 'It was probably for the best. Makes you mad, that stuff. And blind.'

Dozy began to pull himself together. Constable Peel helped him to his feet. Together, they listened to 'How Much Is That Doggie in the Window?' being played badly on what sounded like bicycle bells.

'I think all of that beer is making me hear things too, Constable,' said Dozy.

'No, I can hear it as well, and I've never touched a drop of Spiggit's,' said Constable Peel.

'We can all hear it,' said Sergeant Rowan, as an ice-cream van appeared from around the back of a nearby dune and pulled up alongside them. Seated on its roof was a plastic mannequin wearing a peaked cap and holding a plastic ice cream while grinning manically. Red writing on his cap announced him as 'Mr Happy Whip'.

The driver of the van rolled down his window. He wore very thick glasses, which made him look like an owl in a white coat.

'Hello!' he said. 'Which way is the sea?'

'What?' said Angry.

'The sea: where is it?' The driver squinted at Angry. 'Hey, son, fancy an ice cream? Just a quid. Two quid with sprinkles.'

Angry, who was about to punch the driver for mistaking him for a child, found a more immediate outlet for his rage.

'Two quid with sprinkles? You're having a laugh. What are you sprinkling them with, gold dust?'

'Top quality chocolate, son. Only the best.'

'Listen, I expect to bathe in chocolate if I'm paying an extra quid for it. And stop calling me "son". I'm a dwarf.'

'Right you are, son. Anyway, which way is the sea, there's a good lad.'

Angry looked back at his comrade. 'I'll 'ave him,' he said. 'I mean it. He calls me "lad" or "son" again, and I'll sprinkle him, I swear.'

The remaining three dwarfs, and Constable Peel and Sergeant Rowan, gathered round the van.

'I'll have a choc ice, please,' said Constable Peel.

'Now is not the time, Constable,' said Sergeant Rowan. 'Sir, you would be –?'

'I'm Dan,' said the driver. 'Dan, Dan, The Ice-Cream Man, actually. Changed my name when I bought the van. Thought it might be good publicity.'

'Right, Mr Dan. Do you have any idea where you are?'

'On a beach.'

'No, not quite. It's not a beach.'

'Oh, I thought the tide had gone out,' said Dan.

'Where, on the Sahara?' said Jolly.

'It did seem a bit big,' admitted Dan.

'You're in Hell,' said Sergeant Rowan.

'Nah,' said Dan. 'I'm near Biddlecombe.'

'Not any more. Remember a blue flash? A feeling like every atom of your body was being torn apart?'

'Sort of,' said Dan. 'I thought I'd just taken a funny turn.'

'You did take a funny turn: to Hell. Same thing happened to us.'

Dan thought about this for a while. 'Hell is hot, right?'

'Warm, so rumour would have it,' said Dozy.

'Good place to sell ice cream, then,' said Dan brightly.

The dwarfs and the policemen stared at him. It was clear that Dan, Dan The Ice-Cream Man was an incurable optimist. If you told him that his shoes were on fire, he'd have toasted marshmallows on them.

'What did you do before you sold ice cream?' asked Angry.

'I was an undertaker,' said Dan.

'Nice change of pace for you, then.'

'Oh, it's fantastic. I get out. I meet people. I suppose I met people when I was an undertaker as well, but the conversations were a bit one-sided.' He tootled his horn merrily. 'If nobody wants any ice cream, I'll be off, then.'

'Hang on, hang on,' said Sergeant Rowan. 'You don't seem to have grasped the gravity of the situation. You're in Hell. Constable Peel and I have some experience of these matters, and we can say, with a degree of authority, that your time as an ice-cream salesman is going to be very short here, and will probably end with something very large nibbling on you like an ice lolly.'

'You won't like it,' said Constable Peel solemnly. 'It'll hurt.'

'In addition to this, you may have noticed that Constable Peel and I appear to be stranded, and we are therefore forced to commandeer your van in order to unstrand ourselves.'

'Lovely,' said Dan. 'I like a bit of company.'

'What about us?' asked Jolly.

'You can commandeer your own ice-cream van,' said Constable Peel.

'Really? And what do you think are the chances of another ice-cream van coming along any time soon, then?'

'Somewhat slim, I would have said,' said Constable Peel. He did not look unduly troubled by this fact.

'Come on, you can't leave us stuck here. Something might happen to us.'

'That's what I was hoping.'

'That's not very nice of you.'

'You should have thought of that before you encouraged Phil the Penguin to relieve himself in my hat.'

Sergeant Rowan intervened. 'Constable, much as I am tempted to agree with you, I think we have a responsibility as policemen to ensure the safety of civilians, even ones as nasty and criminal-minded as this lot. All right, everybody in the back. I'll take a seat up front with Mr Dan here, and we'll see about getting us home, shall we?'

Everybody did as Sergeant Rowan suggested, because the sergeant just had that way about him. Even though they were trapped in a region that was generally agreed to be the last place in which anyone wanted to end up, with no idea of how they had got there, and no idea of how they were going to get back, they were willing to follow Sergeant Rowan because he had Authority. He had Seriousness.

And he had a big truncheon that he waved meaningfully at the dwarfs in order to encourage them to make the right decision. In these situations, Sergeant Rowan had found, waving a big stick always helps.

Meanwhile, back in that small room supposedly being used for the storage of cleaning products and brooms, Professor Hilbert was engaged in an animated conversation with Victor and Ed. He had just concluded a similar conversation with Professor Stefan, a consequence of a small loss of energy that had occurred shortly after the Collider had been turned on again. Professor Stefan, Hilbert felt, had become slightly hysterical at the possibility that all those demons might start popping up again, although this stemmed as much from his understandable fear of being eaten as from his concern that, if the gateway to Hell did open for a second time, someone would find a way to blame him for it. It had taken all of Professor Hilbert's considerable diplomatic skills to convince Professor Stefan not to close down the Collider again, or not yet. Now, in the broom closet with Victor and Ed, he was using some of his other skills, namely the ones linked to bullying staff in a gentle manner in order to get his way.

Professor Hilbert was a believer in the 'hidden worlds' theory, the idea that there might be universes other than our own somewhere beyond the realm of our senses. He also felt that particle physicists were spending far too much time worrying about the nature of atoms, and refracting light, and other relatively mundane matters related to this world that actually exists, and too little time speculating on the nature of worlds that might exist elsewhere.

Here's the thing: we know that everything we can see around us is made up of some fairly elementary particles, and that various forces, like gravity, help to keep the whole process of existence moving along smoothly without people floating off into the ether or spontaneously collapsing into a muddle of atoms. But suppose that there were other particles, and other forces, operating alongside us, yet which we couldn't perceive because they were beyond the limits of our powers? That would indicate that the cosmos was a great deal more complicated and interesting than it already appeared to be.

In one way, we already know that there are hidden forces at work in our own universe, because only four per cent of the stuff of the cosmos is visible to us. Roughly seventy per cent of what remains is labelled 'dark energy', and is the force causing our universe to expand, sending galaxies racing away from one another. The other twenty-five per cent is called 'dark matter', detectable only by its effect on the mass and gravity of galaxies. Dark matter, then, could be part of the hidden world, and where you have matter you can, in theory, have planets, and life – dark life – assuming that the forces involved are strong enough to hold them all together, as the forces in our own universe are. And what do we know about dark matter? Well, it doesn't cool down, because if it did it would release heat, and we would be able to detect it.

Hmmm. A hidden world. Dark life. Heat. See where Professor Hilbert was going with this? Ed and Victor could, and just in case they were in any doubt he wrote the word in big letters upon a sheet of paper and showed it to them. The word was:

HELL

'Suppose,' said Professor Hilbert, 'that the portal didn't really connect us to Hell at all, because all that stuff about Hell and the Devil is just nonsense. It's a myth. Hell doesn't exist, and neither does this "Great Malevolence". What we could have instead is a dark matter world, filled with dark life, and the only way we can connect to it is through the Collider. If we turn the Collider off, we'll be turning our backs on the greatest scientific discovery of this, or any, age, and endangering the future of the ILC.[26] There's a Nobel Prize in this, mark my words.'

'Will we get the Nobel Prize too?' asked Ed.

'No,' said Professor Hilbert, 'but if I win it I'll give you a day off, and a box of sweeties.'

☠ [26] The ILC, or International Linear Collider, was the proposed next stage in the physicists' attempts to understand the nature of this, and possibly other, universes. It would be a straight-line tunnel 31 km long, and in it electrons and positrons (antimatter electrons) would be fired from opposite ends, reaching accelerations of 99.9999999998 per cent of the speed of light before they collided. The collisions would be more precise than in the Large Hadron Collider, and therefore potentially more likely to provide answers to those big scientific questions: What happened in the Big Bang? How many dimensions are there in space? What is the nature and purpose of the different subatomic particles? And what does the Higgs boson, the theoretical particle that gives matter mass and gravity, look like? Which was all well and good, except that the LHC had already cost $7 billion and the ILC was likely to cost nearly as much again. In scientific terms, this is a little like your parents scrimping and saving to buy you the latest computer games console only for you to tell them that there's a new one coming out in six months time, but this one would just have to do until then. Ungrateful lot, scientists . . .

'But what about the energy loss?' asked Victor, who knew that they had about as much chance of sharing in Professor Hilbert's potential Nobel Prize glory as they had of growing feathers and winning first prize at a 'Lovely Parrot' competition.

Professor Hilbert smiled in that mad way scientists have of smiling just before the lightning strikes and the monster made up of bits of dead people comes to life and starts looking for someone to blame for plugging him into the mains and lighting him up like a Christmas tree.

'But that's the best part!' he said. 'We *should* be losing energy!'

'From a vacuum?' Victor did not sound convinced.

'It's like I told Professor Stefan,' said Hilbert. 'We're searching for the Higgs boson, right?'

'Right,' said Victor, thinking, He's lost it.

'And we realize that the Higgs boson may be the theoretical link between our world and the hidden universe?'

'OK.' Really lost it.

'And we're assuming that the Higgs boson, if it does exist, is present somewhere in the aftermath of the explosions in the Collider?'

'Absolutely.' Look at him: nutty as a bag of hazelnut crackers.

'Well, what if the energy loss is natural? What if the Higgs boson is decaying in the Collider, but is decaying into particles of another world: dark matter. The Collider would register the decay as an energy loss, when in fact it's the nature of the particles that has changed. There is no energy loss, because they're still there. We just can't see them.'

Victor stared at him, jaw agape. Professor Hilbert might have been mad, but Victor was starting to suspect that he was *brilliantly* mad, because this was a really, really interesting theory.

'Did you tell Professor Stefan all this?' asked Ed, who felt the same way that Victor did about Professor Hilbert's ambitions, but was happy enough to be a cog in the wheel of this Nobel Prize-winning operation, in part because he was a modest, unassuming sort of chap, and also because he really liked sweeties.

'Most of it,' said Professor Hilbert[27], and Victor and Ed knew that, in Professor Hilbert's mind, there was only ever going to be one name on the citation from

[27] Translated from lies to truth, this means 'No, I hardly told him anything at all, and what I did tell him was just enough to enable me to continue to pursue my ultimate goal without having him worry about what suit he might wear to the Nobel Prize ceremony, because he's not going. I'm the only one who is going. Just me. Got a problem with that? No, I didn't think so. It's mine, all mine! Ha-ha-ha-ha-ha-ha-ha!' *Laughter fades to madness. Men in white suits arrive with promises of a nice padded cell, three meals a day in pill form, and no nasty sharp edges upon which you might bang your knee and hurt yourself.*

Similar translations from other areas of life of which you should be aware include: 'The cheque is in the post.' (A cheque may be in the post, but it's not your cheque, and it's not going to your letter box.); 'I'll think about it.' (I don't need to think about it, because the answer is 'No'.); 'You don't look a day older.' (You really don't look a day older – you look ten years older, and that's in dim light.); 'You may feel a small sting.' (Only death will hurt more, and that won't take as long.); and the ever-popular 'It's perfectly safe. It isn't even switched on . . .' usually spoken just before moments of electrocution, the loss of a limb due to incorrect use of a hedge-trimmer, and people being blown up by gas ovens.

the Nobel Prize committee, and he wasn't going to endanger that possibility by sharing too much of what he thought with anyone who might have too many letters after his name.

'So we shouldn't worry about the energy loss?' said Victor.

'No.'

'And you don't think the portal to He—, er, this hidden world is in any danger of opening again?'

'The energy loss isn't remotely comparable to last time,' said Professor Hilbert, which wasn't really answering the question at all.

Ed and Victor exchanged a look.

'Two boxes of sweeties,' said Ed. 'Each.'

Professor Hilbert smiled a shark's smile. 'You drive a hard bargain . . .'

CHAPTER XVII

In Which the True Faces of the Conspirators Are Revealed, and An Ugly Bunch They Are Too

Mrs Abernathy was in her element: she sat in her chamber and listened as an array of demons fawned their way into her presence, attempting to find favour with her once again. Even Chelom, the great spider demon, and Naroth, the most bloated of the toad demons, who had fled after the failure of the invasion, now sought a place by her side once again. She wanted to punish them for their disloyalty, but she restrained herself. It was enough that they were coming back to her, and she needed them. She needed them all. Later, she would violently dispense with some of those who had abandoned her, if only to remind the others of the limits of her tolerance.

Mrs Abernathy's original plan had been to target Samuel and Boswell, and bring them straight to her lair. Unfortunately she had reckoned without a number of factors, including:

a. the difficulty of a targeted acquisition between dimensions
b. an ice-cream salesman
c. a police car
d. a van filled with unknown little people.

She had also exhausted herself bringing them all here, and had fallen into unconsciousness for a time. When she woke, she found that she was unable to locate any of them, at least until the insufferable A. Bodkin had tried to send a message to his superiors, a message that she had intercepted. She now knew roughly the area in which at least some of those whom she had accidentally targeted might be, and by extension where she might find Samuel Johnson, but since this was Hell, which, as we have established, tended to play a little fast and loose with concepts such as direction and geography, it was like being told that a needle is almost certainly in a haystack, and then being shown a very large field filled with very large haystacks. Oh, and the field goes up and down as well as across for very long distances. And it's a bit diagonal as well.

Therefore Mrs Abernathy required help if she was to search for the boy, which was why she had decided against immediately torturing those who had earlier turned their backs on her. Instead she listened to their pleas and their excuses before dispatching them to seek out Samuel Johnson. For the most part they had nothing of interest to tell her anyway, but there were certain exceptions. One of those exceptions was standing before her now. Actually 'standing' might be too strong a word for what it was doing, since it had technically oozed beneath her gaze and had now simply ceased oozing, although assorted substances still dripped from its pores in a way that suggested further oozing could only be a matter of time. It resembled a transparent slug with aspirations to be something more interesting, hampered by the fact that it was, and always would be, made of gelatinous material and about three feet tall, and therefore only of interest to other things made of jelly and slightly smaller than itself. Two unblinking eyeballs were set into what was, for now, its front part, beneath which was a toothless mouth. It wore a black top hat, which it raised in greeting using a tentacle that slowly extruded from its body expressly for that purpose, and then was promptly reabsorbed.

'Afternoon, Ma'am,' it said. 'Happy to see you on the up again, as it were.'

'And you are?' said Mrs Abernathy.

'Crudford, Esq., Ma'am. I work in the Pits of Hopelessness. Don't really fit in, though. Not the hopeless type. I've always been a hopeful sort of gelatinous mass, me. The glass is always half full, that's what I say. When you're made of jelly, and only have a hat to your name, it can only get better, can't it?'

'Someone could take your hat,' said Mrs Abernathy.

'Agreed, agreed, but it wasn't my hat to begin with. I just found it, so technically that wouldn't be much of a reversal, would it?'

'It would if I took it, forced you into it, then slowly roasted you, and it, over a large fire.'

Crudford considered this. 'I'd still have my hat, though, wouldn't I?'

Mrs Abernathy decided that Crudford, Esq. might just have to be made an example of at some point in the near future, if only to discourage such a brightness of outlook in others.

'So what can you do for me until then?' said Mrs Abernathy.

'Well, I can ooze. I've worked hard at it. Laboured my way up from just dripping, through sliming, until I hit on a steady ooze. You could say I've perfected it. But I appreciate that it's a skill of limited applicability in most circumstances, if you catch my drift. Still, onwards and upwards.'

'Mr Crudford, if I stood on you, would it hurt?'

'Yes. You'd get ooze on your shoe, though.'

'It's a price I'm willing to pay, unless you give me a good reason why I shouldn't.'

'Suppose I told you about Chancellor Ozymuth, Ma'am, and how he's been plotting against you,' said Crudford, and he was pleased to see Mrs Abernathy's expression of profound distaste change to one of mild distaste, coupled with a side order of interest.

'Continue.'

'As it happens I was there the last time that you came to visit, when you were trying to see our master, the Great Malevolence. It's one of the advantages of oozing, see: you can ooze just about anywhere, fitting into all kinds of small spaces, and nobody ever notices. Anyway, I was there, and I saw what happened after you'd gone.'

'Which was?'

'Someone emerged from the shadows, and it was Duke Abigor, who congratulated Chancellor Ozymuth on how well he was doing in keeping you away from the Great Malevolence, and on telling our master what a bad sort you are. Completely unjustified, I hasten to add. I mean, you are a bad sort, but in the best possible way. Then Duke Abigor slipped away, and having nothing better to do than a bit more oozing I followed him deep underground, until we came to a meeting room, and they were all there waiting for him.'

'Who was waiting?'

'Most of the Grand Dukes of Hell. They were sitting at a big table, and Duke Abigor joined them at the head of it. They started talking about you. Funny thing is, Ma'am, they're back there again now. Just thought you might like to know. I was hopeful about it, you might say . . .'

Duke Abigor looked very unimpressed, a not inconsiderable achievement given that his standard expression veered towards the unimpressed, even when he was impressed, which wasn't very often.

'Tell me again,' he said, as Duke Duscias quivered before him.

'She has found a way to reach out to the world of men,' said Duscias. 'She pulled something from their world into ours, and now she seeks it.'

Duke Abigor was no fool. You didn't end up with sixty legions of demons at your command by being a dolt. Duscias, on the other hand, was a fool, but he was Abigor's fool, and so Duscias's twenty-nine legions were, to all intents and purposes, also under Abigor's command.

'It's the boy,' said Abigor. 'That is the only reason why she would risk opening up a portal without the knowledge of our master. If she has the boy, she can present him to the Great Malevolence for his amusement, and she will be back at his left hand. Our chance to rule will vanish, and she will move against us.'

'But how?' said Duscias. 'She cannot know of our plot. We have kept ourselves well hidden.'

'Because, you idiot, someone will tell her. If she finds a way to worm herself back into our master's trust, then demons will be falling over themselves to betray one another if it increases their chances of a promotion.'

Other figures began to file into the meeting room, their heads hidden by great black hoods that they let fall to reveal their faces: Duke Guares, commander of thirty legions; Duke Docer, commander of thirty-six legions; Duke Borym, commander of twenty-six legions; and Duke Peros, commander of thirty-six legions. These were the ringleaders, the ones who had staked their reputations, and a potential eternity of pain if they failed, on Duke Abigor's ability to convince the Great Malevolence that he should take over from Mrs Abernathy as the Commander of the Infernal Armies. The problem for all concerned was that Mrs Abernathy had not technically been relieved of her post, since the Great Malevolence had simply refused to see her and was still lost in the madness of his grief. Therefore the dukes were engaged in an act of treason against not only their own general, but against the Great Malevolence himself.

'We should have arrested her long before now,' said Duke Docer, once the situation had been explained to him. 'We left her in peace, and the result is that she has outmanoeuvred us.'

'We couldn't have arrested her,' said Duke Abigor with as much patience as he could muster. Duke Docer was a soldier, and without cunning. He had won every battle in which he had fought by charging forwards and overwhelming his foes by sheer might, and now he spent most of his time looking for new foes so that he wouldn't get bored, even if it meant alienating allies to do so.[28] He wouldn't have known a strategy if it bit him. 'There are too many that we have not yet brought over to our side.'

'But the hordes of Hell have no love for her either,' said Duke Peros. 'Most would be glad if she were gone.'

'They may not care for her, but they care as little for me,' said Duke Abigor. 'They may fear her, and hate her, but she is a force that they know and understand. I am an unknown quantity, as are we all.'

'We are more than two hundred legions strong,' said Duke Docer. 'That is all they need to know and understand.'

'It is not enough!' said Duke Abigor. 'We will not go to war unless we are certain of victory, and we do not know which side the Great Malevolence will support once he emerges from his mourning. If we misstep, then we are in danger of being perceived as traitors, and I do not need to remind you what the punishment is for such a betrayal.'

At this the dukes were silent. They had all seen Cocytus, the great lake of ice far to the north in which traitors were kept frozen for eternity. If they were lucky, their heads might be permitted to protrude from the ice, but as traitors not only to the kingdom but also to

---

💀 [28] Evil, unlike good, is constantly at war with those most like itself, and ambition is its spur.

their master, the Great Malevolence, it was more likely that they would be entirely immersed in the cold and darkness, not a fate any of them desired.

'But the Great Malevolence is . . .' Duke Guares searched for the right words, and settled on, 'not well. He may never cease his mourning. What then? Do we let this kingdom that we have hewn from rock and fire fall into decay and strife?'

Duke Abigor eyed Duke Guares warily. Guares was almost as clever as Abigor, and Abigor sometimes wondered if Guares had already guessed Abigor's larger plan. It was true that the Great Malevolence seemed lost to them, but Guares and the others hoped each day that he might recover what passed for his sanity and resume his rule over Hell. Only Abigor wanted the Great Malevolence to remain immersed in his sorrow and his anger. Moreover Abigor wanted that sorrow and anger to grow so much deeper that the Great Malevolence would descend into a fateful madness from which he would never emerge. This was why Abigor had enlisted Chancellor Ozymuth to their cause, for Ozymuth ensured that the Great Malevolence was cut off from all contact with other demons, and Ozymuth whispered in the Great Malevolence's ear that all was lost, lost for ever, and it was Mrs Abernathy's fault that this was so.

'We will track down the boy, Samuel Johnson, before she does,' said Duke Abigor. 'We will find him, and we will lock him away where no one will ever discover him, and deny all knowledge of his whereabouts. Her last hope of earning back her place at our master's left hand will be gone, and we will be able to claim that she is no longer suited to command the Infernal Armies, and a temporary replacement should be appointed as a matter of urgency until our master has found his wits again. You will all put my name forward as the most suitable candidate, and our opponents will have no time to muster a response. If they try to do so, we will wipe them out.'

'And Mrs Abernathy?' said Duke Guares.

Duke Abigor smiled, but such an unpleasant smile that he still looked like an unimpressed demon, albeit one who has just been presented with a head on a plate, and who really likes heads.

'Is she not a traitor? A traitor for failing to achieve the victory we sought in the world of men, a traitor for bringing the boy who caused our defeat to this realm, our realm, and then losing him. She will be tried, and found guilty. We will take her to Cocytus, and we will chain a rock around her neck, and we will throw her through the ice. Let her be frozen for ever as a warning to those who would promise us new worlds, and then disappoint.'

Duke Abigor looked to his co-conspirators, and each of them in turn nodded his agreement. Then one by one they filed from the meeting room, Duke Abigor the last to leave, until all was quiet again.

The silence was disturbed by a soft *glop*.

'Beg pardon,' said Crudford. 'I oozed.'

'Clean yourself up,' said Mrs Abernathy. She had seen and heard everything, crouched behind a crack in the rock wall. The expression on her face was unreadable but Crudford, who was sensitive to emotions, detected fear, and surprise, and disappointment.

And rage: pure, channelled, governed rage.

'Did I do well, Ma'am?' asked Crudford.

'You did very well,' said Mrs Abernathy. 'For this, I'll even find you a new hat.'

Crudford's slimy features parted in a grin. A new hat: it was more than he had dared to hope for.

CHAPTER XVIII

In Which Those Who Will Be of Help to Samuel Begin to Come Together

The Watcher found a quiet cave, where it mulled over what Old Ram had said. Eventually it sought out Mrs Abernathy, but when it tried to speak with her it found her overwhelmed by the attentions of the returning demons as they crowded around her, anxious to make recompense for their lack of faith in her. Their words were a salve to her wounded vanity, and although the Watcher might have fought its way through the mass of stinking bodies in order to reach its mistress, it had not done so. In part this was because it could see the pleasure she derived as they prostrated themselves before her, but there was also a part of the Watcher that still wondered about the boy, and the wisdom of what Mrs Abernathy had done in dragging him to Hell.

In addition, the news that the boy might have been found had almost driven from its mind the discovery of the burnt rubber on the plain; almost, but not quite, for the Watcher had spent the intervening period trying to identify the other smells it had picked up among the rocks, comparing them with the scent memory in its strange, alien brain. The Watcher was an entity apart, even among the many foul and demonic beings that inhabited the various strata of Hell. It had attached itself to what was now its mistress shortly after the formation of Hell itself, and the emergence of the oldest of the demons. No one could recall quite how the Watcher had come into being; its nature was a mystery to all. Not even Mrs Abernathy herself truly understood it: she knew only that it obeyed her will, and when so many others had turned their backs on her, only the Watcher had remained truly faithful.

But the Watcher did not obey her will alone. For as long as it had been in existence, it had reported back to the Great Malevolence himself, for the Great Malevolence trusted no one and nothing, and despite his power he was suspicious of all those around him.[29] But the Watcher had spent so long with Mrs Abernathy that its loyalties had become confused: while it still answered to the Great Malevolence, it did not tell him everything. It could not have said why; it merely understood instinctively that not simply knowledge is power, but *secret* knowledge. So it was that it made its own judgements on what the Great Malevolence needed to be told, and what could safely be hidden from him. In that sense the Watcher was serving two masters, which is never a good idea.

💀 [29] A Scottish proverb says that 'Evil doers are evil dreaders.' In other words, those that do ill, or think ill of others, naturally expect others to do ill to them. Wickedness never rests easily so, in a way, one might almost feel pity for the wicked, for they are destined to live their lives in fear, in a prison of the heart. Or, as the French writer Voltaire put it, 'Fear follows crime, and is its punishment.'

Its situation had been complicated by the Great Malevolence's descent into misery and madness, which meant that, even if the Watcher had wanted to report to him, it could not, for its voice could not be heard above the wailing that filled the Mountain of Despair, and the Chancellor was careful to control all access. Then again, until now there had been little to report: Mrs Abernathy had spent most of her time moving back and forth between her lair and that of the Great Malevolence, seeking an audience that would never be granted, and then brooding over it alone in her chamber until it came time to make the pilgrimage again. When she was not walking, or brooding, she was watching Samuel Johnson in the glass, and hurling curses at him that he could not hear. It was left to the Watcher to try to track down the vehicle that had collapsed the portal, but each time it returned without news Mrs Abernathy's interest in the vehicle seemed to grow less and less, or so the Watcher had thought. Then, when the Watcher had at last returned with evidence of the vehicle's presence, it had been surprised to find that Mrs Abernathy had been plotting quietly all along to open the portal once again, if only to snatch Samuel Johnson from his world and transport him to Hell. She really was a most unusual woman, even leaving aside the fact that she was actually an ancient tentacled demon in disguise, which was one of the reasons why the Watcher's loyalties were split between her and the Great Malevolence.

The Watcher sniffed at the air, recreating the scents it had picked up on the Plain. It had felt presences nearby, watching it, but it was not sure if they were related to the black substance on the rock. Its sunken nostrils twitched.

An old smell, almost forgotten. And another with it: sharper, more pungent. They were familiar, those smells. The Watcher rummaged through its memories, back, back, until it came at last to a pair of cowering figures, its mistress towering above them in her old, monstrous form, banishing them for ever to the Wasteland . . .

Very little surprised the Watcher. It had seen so much that it was almost incapable of surprise. But its realization of who had been responsible for the collapse of the portal nearly caused it to topple over in shock.

Nurd.

Nurd, the Scourge of Five Deities.

Nurd, who barely justified the term 'demon' to begin with, so inept was he at being evil.

Nurd had betrayed them all.

Meanwhile, Nurd and Wormwood were standing on a rise and watching a small van tootling merrily across the Desert of Bones while playing 'How Much Is That Doggie in the Window?' Nurd and Wormwood knew that the piece of music was called 'How Much Is That Doggie in the Window?' because at least four voices were singing along to it, adding 'woof-woof' noises after each mention of the word 'window', and the words 'waggle-waggle' to the bit about 'the one with the waggley tail'.

'What's a doggie?' asked Wormwood. 'And why do they want one?'

'A doggie is a small creature that barks, like Boswell, Samuel Johnson's dachshund,' said Nurd. 'It goes "woof-woof". This one, though, also appears to have a tail that is waggley, which makes it more desirable, I suppose.'

'They do seem to want it very badly,' said Wormwood.

'It doesn't seem like a good idea to go shouting about it, though,' said Nurd. 'The kind of things with waggley tails that live around here tend to have big waggley bodies too, and waggley heads with waggley teeth.'

'If it's from the world of men, then maybe Samuel is in there too.'

Nurd shook his head. 'No, I'd sense him if he were so close.' Nurd strained to read the writing on the side of the van. 'It says something about ice cream on the side. And sweets.'

'Sweets?' said Wormwood.

'Sweets,' said Nurd.

They looked at each other. Their faces brightened, and both said, simultaneously: 'Wine gums!'

Seconds later, they were in hot pursuit of the ice-cream van.

Constable Peel very much wanted to die. More than that, he wanted to die and take four dwarfs with him, and maybe a driver of an ice-cream van for good measure. He'd been listening to 'How Much Is That Doggie in the Window?' for a good four hours now, and was on the verge of insanity.

'Stop singing,' he said to the dwarfs.

'No,' said Angry.

'Stop singing.'

'No.'

'Stop singing.'

'Say "please".'

'Please.'

'No.'

Constable Peel banged on the glass connecting the back of the van to the front compartment, in which Sergeant Rowan and Dan, Dan the Ice-Cream Man were sitting.

'For the last time,' he pleaded, 'there must be some way to turn that music off.'

Dan shrugged. 'I've told you: it comes on automatically with the engine. I haven't been able to work out how to make it stop without messing up the wiring.'

'You're messing up *my* wiring,' said Constable Peel. 'Can't I at least sit up front with you?'

'There isn't really enough room,' said Sergeant Rowan, who didn't like being cramped.

'Then why don't we swap places for a while, and you can sit back here?'

'With that lot singing? I don't think so. It's bad enough up here.'

Jolly made himself another ice-cream cone. He'd already had twelve, but the sometimes bumpy nature of the terrain meant that he had only managed successfully to eat nine, while the remaining three were smeared all over his face and clothes.

'Lovely ice cream, this,' he said, for the thirteenth time.

'Oi, I hope you're paying for all of those,' said Dan.

'I'm putting them on my tab.'

'You don't have a tab.'

'Oh, now you tell me. You should have said before I started eating them all. Bit late now, isn't it?'

'He was right about the chocolate too,' said Dozy, who had taken to eating the sprinkles by the fistful. 'Very high quality.'

Angry and Mumbles began singing about doggies again, at least Angry did. Mumbles could have been singing about dinosaurs and nobody would have been any the wiser. Constable Peel, his patience now at an end, was stretching out his hands to strangle one or both of them when Dan stopped the van, for there was now something to distract them all from the music.

'That's interesting,' said Dozy. He and the other three dwarfs, each munching happily on Dan's livelihood, hopped from the van, closely followed by the two policemen and Dan himself.

Stretched before them were thousands and thousands of little workbenches, each occupied by an imp. Between the desks walked other imps carrying buckets of bone dust. They poured the bone dust into a hole at one end of each desk, the seated imps turned a lever, there was the sound of grinding and then from the other end of the desks emerged clean, intact bones, which the demons with buckets took from them before walking back the way they had come.

'Well, that explains a lot,' said Jolly. 'Sort of.'

There was a larger desk some distance to their right. The dwarfs left the policemen and Dan and made their way over to it. A demon who bore a remarkable resemblance to the recently vaporized A. Bodkin sat at the desk, snoozing. His name plate read 'Mr D. Bodkin, Demon-In-Charge'.

''Scuse me,' said Jolly, tapping D. Bodkin's boot.

D. Bodkin woke slowly, and stared at Jolly.

'Yes, what is it?'

'Do you know where all of this dust comes from?'

'What dust?'

'The dust that makes the bones.'

D. Bodkin looked at Jolly as though Jolly had just asked him why the sky was grey and black with bursts of purple and red flame currently flashing through it. That was just the way things were.

'Is there something wrong with you?' asked D. Bodkin. 'Look around: there's *only* dust. Hardly going to run out, are we?'

The dwarfs started giggling. D. Bodkin, suspecting that he was the butt of a joke he didn't understand, and who didn't care much for humour at the best of times, glowered at them.

'See over that way,' said Angry, 'where all those little demons with buckets are coming from?'

'Yes,' said D. Bodkin.

'You should take a walk over there. There's a bloke who'd love to meet you. Looks a bit like you. Long-lost relative, you might say.'

'Really?'

'Cross my heart. You and him would have a lot to talk about. You're both in the same business, in a way.'

'Well, I will then,' said D. Bodkin. 'I feel like giving the old legs a stretch. Haven't left my desk in, ooooh –'

He glanced at the hourglass on his wrist which, like Mr A. Bodkin's similar model, was designed to funnel sand very efficiently from one glass to another without ever depleting the store in the upper glass, or increasing the store in the lower glass. This watch though, appeared to have stopped, possibly due to a blockage. D. Bodkin looked perturbed. He tapped the glass with a clawed forefinger.

'Funny, my watch doesn't seem to be working.' He gave his wrist a little shake, and said, 'Ah, that's better.'

Angry leaned forward and noticed that the sand from the lower glass was now running upwards into the upper glass, although, as before, neither glass got any emptier, or any fuller.

'You really have been at this desk for too long,' said Angry, glancing back at his fellow dwarfs and twisting one finger slowly by his right temple in the universal indication of someone else's general absence of marbles. 'It'll be good for you to take a break. We'll keep an eye on this lot until you get back.'

'You won't steal anything, will you?' asked D. Bodkin. 'I'll get into terrible trouble if anything goes missing. Budgets, you know. I have to account for every paper clip these days.'

Angry was the picture of wounded innocence. 'I'm hurt,' he said, blinking away an imaginary tear. He fumbled in his pocket for a handkerchief upon which to blow his nose, discovered one, looked at it, decided that the only thing more disease-ridden than this handkerchief was an actual disease, and put it back where he'd found it. 'I'm so hurt that I don't know what to say.'

'That's insulting, that is,' said Dozy.

'We're just trying to brighten up your day,' said Jolly, 'and you go and say something nasty like that about us.'

'We've been the victims of theft ourselves,' said Angry. 'On that subject, you wouldn't have seen a van anywhere – four wheels, picture of a handsome smiling gentleman somewhat like ourselves on the side – would you?'

'No,' said D. Bodkin.

'What about a police car: four wheels, blue lights?'

'No. I'd like to, though. It sounds very interesting.'

'Hmmm,' said Angry. 'Fat lot of good that does us.'

He and the other dwarfs folded their arms and looked expectantly at D. Bodkin. Jolly tapped his foot impatiently.

'Well,' said Jolly, 'we're waiting.'

Eventually, D. Bodkin took the hint.

'I'm very sorry for what I said just now,' he said. He looked embarrassed. The horns on his head glowed bright red. He put his hands behind his back and traced little patterns of shame in the sand. 'I shouldn't have asked if you were going to steal anything. You can't be too careful, you know. After all, this is Hell. All sorts of rotten types end up here.'

'Apology accepted,' said Angry. 'Off you go, then. Tell the other chap we said hello.'

'Righty-ho,' said D. Bodkin, and began following the line of bone-bearing bucket carriers.

The dwarfs waved him off.

'Nice bloke,' said Jolly.

'Lovely,' said Angry, as D. Bodkin disappeared over a dune. 'This world needs more demons like him.'

'Suckers, you mean?' said Jolly.

'Absolutely,' said Angry. 'Complete and utter suckers.'

Back in the van, Jolly counted their loot.

'That's fifteen pencils, one pencil sharpener, a stapler, a rubber, a mug that says "You Don't Have To Be Diabolical To Work Here, But It Helps", and some stamps,' said Jolly.

'You forgot the desk,' said Dozy.

'And the desk,' confirmed Jolly. He stuck his head out of the side of the van and checked on the desk, which they'd tied to the roof of the van with a length of rope they'd found in Dan's boot.

'You're sure he said that you could take them?' said Constable Peel. He was more than a little suspicious, but at least the dwarfs had stopped singing for a while.

'Absolutely. Told us he was quitting. No future in the job. Said we'd be doing him a favour.'

'Well, if you're sure, although I don't know why you think you need a desk anyway.'

'Question not the need,' said Angry. 'If it isn't nailed down, we'll have it. And if it is nailed down, we'll find a way to un-nail it and have that as well.'

Constable Peel's brow furrowed. A cloud of dust seemed to be following them. As it drew closer he saw that it was being preceded by a fast-moving rock.

'Look at that,' he said. He pulled back the glass separating the front of the van from the serving section. 'Sarge, we're being chased by a rock.'

'You don't see a rock rolling uphill very often,' said Angry. 'Very unusual, that.'

'It's gaining on us,' said Dozy.

'Stop the van,' said Sergeant Rowan. Dan did as he was instructed, but kept it neutral and they all listened.

'That's the sound of an engine, Sarge,' said Constable Peel.

'So it is, Constable,' said Sergeant Rowan as the rock pulled up alongside them, its doors opened, and what looked like a ferret with mange jumped out, closely followed by a cloaked demon wearing big boots and an expectant smile on his green face.

'Two bags of wine gums, please,' said Nurd. 'And two cones with sprinkles.'

He waved a small gold coin in the air, just as Constable Peel's head appeared through the service hatch.

'Well, well, well,' said Constable Peel. 'Would you look at who it is?'

Nurd's jaw dropped. Wormwood helpfully picked it up and reattached it.

'Oh, nuts,' said Nurd.

'No,' said Constable Peel, 'but we do have sprinkles . . .'

CHAPTER XIX

In Which We Encounter Some
of the Other Unfortunate
Denizens of Hell

Samuel and Boswell, frightened and tired, traversed the landscape of Hell. There were great causeways of stone that crossed chasms filled with fire, and dark lakes in whose depths swam nightmarish forms, their fins and tails occasionally breaking the surface as they hunted and were hunted. They saw demons large and small, sometimes in the distance, sometimes up close, but even those upon whose path they stumbled paid them little or no attention. They seemed to assume that if Samuel and Boswell were there, then they were meant to be and were therefore some other demon's concern, not theirs.

But for the most part there wasn't a great deal to see, for Hell looked largely unfinished to Samuel and Boswell. True, the skies above their heads continued to rage, and Samuel sometimes felt that the clouds were looking down and mocking him before resuming their never-ending conflict of noise and light, but vast stretches of Hell's landscape had little or nothing to offer at all.[30] There was just dirt beneath their feet, or cracked stone, or low mounds of short black grass unenlivened by even a single weed.

After a time the ground began to slope upwards, and they ascended a small hill. As they reached the crest they saw arrayed before them an enormous banquet. It covered a table that stretched so far into the distance that Samuel lost sight of it in the dreary white mist always lurking on the horizon, but he could see every kind of food imaginable laid out on it, from breads to desserts and everything in between, with dusty bottles of fine wine interspersed among the bowls and dishes. It was a feast beyond compare, yet although Samuel and Boswell were starving they did not feel their appetites piqued by what they saw. Perhaps it was because the food, regardless of its type, was a uniform dull grey, or because, even as they drew closer, they could detect no smell from it

Or it may have been the behaviour of those seated at the banquet, for chairs stood side by side along the length and breadth of the table, so close that there was no room for anyone else to squeeze in, and they were

---

💀 30 Because Hell was huge, and only a fraction of it was occupied, the Great Malevolence had largely given up on trying to decorate every inch of it in a suitable manner. After all, there's only so much time that you can spend putting up big black mountains that loom menacingly, and building great fiery pits in which demons toil, before you start to think, well, why bother? Thus most of Hell is like the spare room in your house, the one your dad keeps promising to turn into his den but instead just fills with boxes of unread books, and old bills, and that exercise bike he bought and now claims doesn't work properly because it's too hard to cycle, although it'll be fine once he gets around to fixing it, and anyway, it cost a fortune, that bike.

Dads: they're just made that way.

all occupied by thin, wasted people who forced food constantly into their mouths, and guzzled wine while their jaws chomped tirelessly, half-chewed meats and grey liquid dripping from their chins and staining their clothes.

Samuel and Boswell were now close enough to the feast to be noticed by the man seated at the head of the table. He wore a dinner jacket with a crooked bow tie. His shirt buttons were open, and a distended belly bulged through the gap, but it was not the belly of a fat person. Samuel had seen poor, hungry people on television, and he knew that chronic malnutrition made the stomach swell. This man was starving, yet he had more than enough food to eat. While Samuel watched, the man tossed aside a half-eaten chicken leg and began chomping on a juicy, if slate-coloured, steak. As one dish was finished a new one appeared, so that there was never an empty plate on the table.

The man spotted Samuel, but he did not stop eating. 'Get away,' he said. 'There isn't enough for anyone else.'

'There's barely enough for us,' said a woman to his left, who was eating caviar with a huge wooden spoon, shovelling the little fish eggs into her mouth. She wore an ornate ball gown, and her head was topped by a white wig dotted with crystals. 'And you haven't been invited.'

'How do you know?' asked Samuel.

'Because if you were invited there would be a chair for you, but there isn't, so you haven't. Now run along. Don't you know that you shouldn't interrupt people when they're eating? You're making me talk with my mouth full. That's rude.'

'And she's spilling some,' said a tall bald man sitting across from her. 'If she doesn't want that caviar, I'll have it.'

He reached for the bowl, but the woman slapped him hard on the hand with the spoon.

'Get your own!' she snapped.

'But the food has no smell,' said Samuel, almost to himself.

'No smell,' said the man in the tuxedo. 'No taste. No texture. No colour. But I'm *so* hungry, always *so* hungry.' He polished off the steak and moved on to a bowl of trifle, using his hand to scoop up mouthfuls of jelly, sponge, and custard. 'I'm so hungry, I could eat you. And your dog.'

And for the first time in a century, for he had been at the table for a very, very long time, the man in the dinner jacket stopped eating, and began thinking. There was a new hunger in his eyes as he examined Samuel the way a chef might examine a pig that has been offered to him by the butcher, sizing it up for the best cuts. Beside him, the woman turned her gaze on Samuel, her mouth open, caviar falling from her tongue. The tall bald man set aside a fish head, and picked up a sharp knife.

'Proper food,' he whispered. 'Fresh meat.'

The words were taken up by the elderly man beside him, and the wizened old lady whose toothless jaws could only suck the meat from bones, and the children dressed like princes and princesses, passed on and on down the table until they, like the distant, starving guests at the feast, were lost in the mist.

'*Fresh meat, fresh meat, fresh meat . . .*'

Samuel picked up Boswell and backed away from the table. The man in the dinner jacket put his hands on the arms of the chair, preparing to rise, but found that he could not stand. He tried to shift his chair, as if hoping to shuffle it towards Samuel, but it would not budge. His hands stretched for Samuel, but Samuel was beyond his reach. The tall bald man with the sharp knife howled in fury, slashing at the air with the blade as though his limbs might somehow extend far enough to cut Samuel's flesh.

The bewigged woman tried to be more cunning. 'Come here, little boy,' she whispered, offering him a grey piece of chocolate. 'I'll protect you from them. I had a little boy of my own once. I wouldn't hurt a child.'

But Samuel was no fool. He stayed out of her reach, clutching Boswell tightly.

'At least leave us your dog,' said the man in the dinner jacket. 'I hear dog is very tasty.'

All along the table voices were raised, shouting threats, promises, bribes, anything that might convince Samuel to approach, or to hand Boswell over, but Samuel just backed away, never taking his eyes from them, fearful that if he did so they might find a way to free themselves from the prison of their chairs. Then, one by one, their appetites got the better of them until the guests resumed their great, tasteless meal, all but the woman with the wig who stared after Samuel, repeating over and over to herself, 'I had a little boy of my own . . .' and only when Samuel was again at the crest of the hill did she turn back to her caviar and lose herself once more in the feast.

Samuel and Boswell moved on. In time they saw a great wooden horse burning; around it sat Greek warriors, lost in melancholy. Samuel approached them warily, but the warriors did not stir and when he tried to speak to them they did not answer.

'What do you want, child?' said a voice, and Samuel turned to see a woman emerge from the sand: first the head, then the body, until she stood before him, grains tumbling from her hair, her hands, her gown. As Samuel looked more closely at her he saw that she had not merely risen from the sand: she was sand, different textures and hues combining to give the impression of clothing, and colour, and life. Only her eyes were not formed from sand: they blazed a deep, fiery red, and Samuel knew that he was staring at a demon.

'This is . . . the Trojan horse, isn't it?' said Samuel.

'It is.'

'And these are the men who used it to gain access to the city.'

'They are. The one who sits apart from the others, the man alone, that is Odysseus.' She spoke his name softly. 'The horse was his idea.'

'But why are they here?'

'Because it was an act of deception. It was not honest, not truthful.'

'But it was clever.'

'A lie may be clever, but it is still a lie.'

'But don't they say that all is fair in love and war? I heard that somewhere.'

'"They"? Who are "they"?'

'I don't know. Just people.'

'That's what the victorious claim, not the defeated; the powerful, not the powerless. "All is fair." "The end justifies the means". Is that what you believe?'

'I don't know.'

'Is there someone you love? A girl, perhaps?'

'There's a girl that I like.'

'Would you lie to gain her affection?'

'No, I don't think so.'

'You don't think so?'

'No, I wouldn't.'

'And if someone lied to her about you in order to turn her against you, would you feel that was fair?'

'No, of course not.'

'Have you heard it said that sport is war by other means?'

'I haven't, but I suppose it could be true.'

'Do you cheat when you play games?'

'No.'

'Why?'

'Because it's not right. It's not –'

'Fair?'

'No, it's not fair.'

'So all is *not* fair in love, and all is *not* fair in war.'

'I suppose not.' Samuel was troubled. He looked at the warriors, but none of them seemed to have paid any attention to his conversation with the demon. 'It still seems like a harsh punishment,' he said.

'It is,' said the demon, with something like regret in her voice.

'Who decided?' asked Samuel. 'Who decided that they should be here?'

'They decided,' said the demon. 'They chose. Now go, child. Their melancholy is infectious.'

The grains of sand at her eyes formed a tear that shed itself upon her cheek. The demon sank back into the ground, and Samuel and Boswell turned away from the burning horse and continued their journey.

CHAPTER XX

In Which We Meet the Blacksmith

The barren landscape began to change, although not for the better. It was now dotted with objects that seemed to come from another world, Samuel's world: a suit of armour, empty and rusted; a German biplane from World War I; a submarine standing perfectly upright, balanced on its propellers; and a rifle, the largest, longest gun that Samuel had ever seen, so long that it would have taken him an hour or more just to walk around it, made up of millions and millions of smaller guns, all fused together to create a kind of giant sculpture. As Samuel examined it he saw that pieces of the rifle appeared to be alive, wriggling like metal snakes, and he realized that the rifle was still forming, weapons popping into existence in the air around it and slowly being absorbed into the whole.

A huge man appeared from behind the discarded turret of a tank. He wore dirty black overalls and a welder's mask upon his face. In his right hand he held a blowtorch that burned with a white-hot flame. He killed the flame and pushed the mask up so that his face was revealed. He was bearded, and his eyes shone with the same white fire as his torch had, as though he had spent too long looking at metal dissolve.

'Who are you?' he asked. His voice was hoarse, but there was no hostility to his tone.

'My name is Samuel Johnson, and this is Boswell.'

Those white eyes looked down upon the little dachshund.

'A dog,' said the man. 'It's a long time since I've seen a dog.'

He reached out a gloved hand. Boswell shied away, but the hand was too quick. It fastened on Boswell's head, then rubbed at it with a surprising gentleness.

'Good dog,' said the man. 'Good little dog.'

He released his grip on Boswell, somewhat to the relief of the good little dog in question.

'I kept dogs,' he said. 'A man should have a dog.'

'Do you have a name?' asked Samuel.

'I had a name once as well, but I've forgotten it. I have no use for it, for nobody has come here for so very long. Now, I am the Blacksmith. I work with metal. It is my punishment.'

'What is this place?' asked Samuel.

'This is the Junkyard. It is the place of broken things that should never have been made. Come and see.'

Samuel and Boswell followed the Blacksmith beneath the ever-changing gun, and past row upon row of fighter planes and armoured cars, and there was revealed to them an enormous crater, and in it were swords and knives; machine guns and pistols; tanks and battleships and aircraft carriers; every conceivable weapon that might be used to inflict harm upon another person. Like the great gun, the contents of the crater were constantly being added to, so that the whole mass of metal creaked and groaned and clattered and clanked.

'Why are they here?' asked Samuel.

'Because they took lives, and this is where they belong.'

'Then why are you here?'

'Because I designed such weapons, and I put them in the hands of those who would use them against innocents, and I did not care. Now, I break them down.'

'What about the great gun, the one that keeps growing in size?'

'A reminder to me,' said the Blacksmith. 'No matter how hard I work, or how many weapons I break down, still that rifle increases in size. I contributed to the existence of such weapons in life, and I am not permitted to forget it.'

'I'm sorry,' said Samuel. 'You don't seem like a bad person.'

'I didn't think that I was,' said the Blacksmith. 'Or perhaps I just didn't think. And you: why are you here?'

Samuel was still wary of telling the truth about his situation, particularly after his encounter with Old Ram, but something about the Blacksmith made Samuel trust him.

'I was dragged here. A woman – a demon – called Mrs Abernathy wants to punish me.'

The Blacksmith grinned. 'So you are the boy. Even I, in this dreadful place, have heard tell of you.' He fumbled beneath his apron and brought out a piece of newspaper which he handed to Samuel. It was a cutting from an old edition of *The Infernal Times*, and it showed a picture of Samuel beneath two words:

THE ENEMY!

The article that followed, written by the editor, Mr P. Bodkin, detailed the attempt to escape from Hell through the portal, and the failure of the invasion because of the intervention of Samuel and an unknown other who had driven a car the wrong way through the portal. Samuel thought that the article was a little unfair, and only told one side of the story, but then he supposed that the editor of *The Infernal Times* might have found himself in a spot of trouble had he suggested that sending hordes of demons to invade the Earth wasn't a very nice thing to do in the first place.

'I expect she'll be looking for you,' said the Blacksmith.

'I expect so,' said Samuel.

'Well, if she comes this way I won't tell her anything. You can rely on me.'

'Thank you,' said Samuel. 'But I want to get home, and I don't know how.'

The last words caught in his throat. His eyes grew warm, but he fought away the tears. The Blacksmith discreetly looked away for a moment and then, once he was sure that Samuel was in control of his emotions, turned his attention back to the boy.

'It seems to me that if Mrs Abernathy brought you here, then she may have the means of returning you as well.'

'But she won't do that,' said Samuel. 'She wants to kill me.'

'Nevertheless, whatever power she used to drag you here can surely be used to get you back.'

'So I have to face her?'

'You have to find her, or be found by her. After that, you'll have to use your own cleverness to help you.'

'But I'm just a kid. And she's a demon.'

'A demon that you've defeated once before and can defeat again.'

'But I had help that time,' said Samuel. 'I had help from—'

He almost said Nurd's name, but he bit his tongue at the last minute. It was one thing to trust the Blacksmith with his secrets, but another thing entirely to trust him with Nurd's.

'You had help from Nurd,' said the Blacksmith, and Samuel could not conceal his shock.

'How did you know that?'

'Because I've helped him too. I've seen his vehicle. It broke down, and I helped him and his servant, Wormwood, to repair it. Then they insisted upon disguising the car, so I aided them with that as well. Mind you, they seemed intent upon disguising it as a rock, for reasons I still don't fully understand, but he's a strange one, that Nurd. I rather liked him.'

'He's my friend,' said Samuel. 'If he knew I was here, he'd help me.'

'Oh, he knows you're here,' said the Blacksmith.

'How?'

'He can feel you.' The Blacksmith patted his chest,

just where his heart once beat when he lived and perhaps still did, in some strange way. 'Can't you feel him too?'

Samuel closed his eyes, and thought hard. He pictured Nurd in his head, and remembered what they had spoken of in Samuel's bedroom when Nurd had first appeared to him. He recalled Nurd's joy at the taste of a wine gum, and his own surprise that Nurd had never before had anyone whom he could call a friend. He opened his heart to Nurd, and suddenly he had an image of him, an odd, ferret-like creature beside him that could only have been Wormwood, Nurd's hands gripping the wheel of the Aston Martin that had, until recently, been the proudest possession of Samuel's dad.

Then the image changed, and he saw Nurd and Wormwood standing beside –

Hang on, was that an ice-cream van?

Samuel called out to Nurd. He called out with his voice, and his heart. He called out with all the hope that he had left, and all his faith in the automobile-loving demon who was his friend.

He called out, and Nurd answered.

CHAPTER XXI

In Which Nurd Considers Changing His Name to 'Nurd, Unlucky in Numerous Dimensions'

Nurd, the former Scourge of Five Deities, now reformed, wondered how much bad luck a demon could have. First of all, he'd been banished to the Wasteland with Wormwood, where they had spent a very, very long time getting to know each other and wishing that they hadn't. It had been eons of utter monotony, broken only by the capacity of Wormwood's body to produce the most extraordinary odours, and Nurd amusing himself by hitting Wormwood hard on the head with a sceptre in return. Then, in the manner of a great many buses arriving together after you've been standing in the rain for hours waiting for just one, Nurd had found himself sent back and forth through a hole in space and time on no fewer than four occasions, causing his body to be stretched and then compressed in a most uncomfortable manner, as well as being crushed by a vaccuum cleaner, hit by a truck, dropped down a sewer, and then forced to face the wrath of the armies of Hell by undoing the Great Malevolence's plan to invade Earth. What was more he had managed to annoy two policemen, the very same policemen who were now staring at him balefully while surrounded by four hostile-looking dwarfs and a short-sighted ice-cream salesman.

It's just not fair, thought Nurd. All I wanted was a quiet life, and maybe some sweeties and an ice cream.

Constable Peel removed his notebook in an officious manner, licked the tip of his pencil, and prepared to write.

'Ready, Sarge,' he said.

'List of charges,' began Sergeant Rowan. 'Evading arrest. Leaving the scene of a crime, namely an attack on a house of worship by assorted dead people. Soiling a police vehicle.'

'I never did,' said Nurd.

'You made it smell,' said Sergeant Rowan.

'I fell down a sewer.'

'Nevertheless, our car has never smelled right since. Causes Constable Peel here to feel nauseous on a regular basis.'

'And it makes my uniform pong,' said Constable Peel. 'It undermines my authority, having a smelly uniform.'

Nurd was tempted to suggest that the main factor undermining Constable Peel's authority was Constable Peel himself, but decided against it. He was in enough trouble already.

'What else do we have, Constable?' asked Sergeant Rowan.

'Immigration offences?' suggested Constable Peel.

'Right you are. Improper entry. Entering Britain

without a proper visa. Entering Britain without a passport. Illegal alien, you are.'

'I'm not an alien,' Nurd corrected. 'I'm a demon.'

'Don't nit-pick. You were an illegal immigrant.'

'I didn't immigrate,' said Nurd. 'I was sent against my will.'

'You can explain it to the judge,' said Sergeant Rowan. 'Now we get on to the really interesting stuff. Damage to private property. Theft of a privately owned vehicle. Driving without a proper licence. Driving without insurance. Speeding. Theft of a police vehicle. They're going to throw away the key for you, Sonny Jim. They'll put you away for so long that by the time you get out we'll all be living on other planets.'

Nurd folded his arms. He whistled, scratched his pointy chin, then tapped his fingers against it, all of which served to communicate the following message: *Hmmm, I'm thinking here, and I seem to have spotted a fatal flaw in all that you've just told me.*

'Forgive me for pointing this out, officers, but I wasn't aware that you had jurisdiction in Hell. Biddlecombe: yes. Hell: I think not.'

'Got you there, Sergeant,' said Jolly, sticking his oar in and splashing it about merrily. 'Old Moonface is a bit of a jailhouse lawyer.'

'You keep quiet,' said Constable Peel. 'You lot are in enough trouble of your own.'

'Oooh,' said Dozy. 'Make sure you add "stealing ice cream" to our list of charges. We'll get life for that.'

'Listen, you,' said Sergeant Rowan, wagging his finger at Nurd and doing his best to ignore the Greek chorus[31] of dwarfs, 'you have a lot to answer for. You need to come down to the station and explain yourself.'

'You know, I'd actually be happy to do that,' said Nurd. 'Unfortunately, I, like you, am stuck here in Hell, and there are more pressing problems to consider.'

'Such as?'

'You're not the only humans in Hell.'

'What do you mean? Who else is here?'

'Samuel Johnson and his dog.'

Sergeant Rowan frowned. Nurd could almost hear the cogs turning in his brain. The sergeant had been one of the first on the scene after the portal closed, but he'd never managed to find out the full story. He only knew that Samuel had effectively saved the Earth, aided by an unknown person in a stolen Aston Martin who –

Who had bravely driven it into the portal, causing it to collapse.

Sergeant Rowan took a few steps forward and examined the moving rock. More particularly, he examined

---

💀 [31] Plays in ancient Greece always included a group of between twelve and twenty-four actors who would comment on the action on stage, and they were known as the 'chorus'. If you're bored, and fancy amusing your parents (and when I say 'amuse', I mean 'annoy greatly') you can form your own one-person Greek chorus by following your Mum and Dad around the house and giving them a little commentary on their comings and goings. You know: 'Mum takes milk from the fridge. Mum pours milk. Mum puts milk back. Mum tells me to stop talking about her in that weird way.' Or: 'Dad goes to the bathroom. Dad drops pants. Dad rustles newspaper. Dad tells me to go away I or I'll never receive pocket money again.' The long winter evenings will just fly by, I guarantee it.

the wheels of the rock, and then peered into the interior of the disguised car.

'Constable Peel, do you still have your notebook open?' he said.

'Yes, Sarge.'

'You know that page you've just filled with all of the charges against Mr Nurd here?'

'Yes, Sarge. I've written them all down very neatly, in case the judge wants to read them for himself.'

'Tear it out and throw it away, there's a good lad.'

'But—'

'No buts. Just do as I say.'

With considerable reluctance, Constable Peel did as he was told. He tore the page into little pieces and dropped them on the ground.

'Littering,' said a small, cheery voice from somewhere around his belly button. 'That's a fifty-quid fine.'

'Shut up,' said Constable Peel.

'It seems I may owe you an apology, sir,' said Sergeant Rowan.

'No, not really,' said Nurd. 'I did all of the things that you said, or most of them anyway.'

'Well, I think you may have made up for them. Now, what's this about Samuel Johnson?'

And Nurd did his best to explain how he had felt Samuel's presence, and how he believed that it was Mrs Abernathy who had been responsible for dragging Samuel and, by extension, the policemen, the dwarfs, and Dan, Dan the Ice-Cream Man to Hell.

'And what do you suggest we do about that?' asked Sergeant Rowan.

'We find Samuel, and then we try to discover the location of the gateway so we can get you all home,' said Nurd.

'You seem very sure that there is a gateway.'

'There has to be. Even here, certain laws apply. Wherever it is, it has to be close to Mrs Abernathy. I do have one question for you, though?'

'And what's that?' said Sergeant Rowan.

'What is that *terrible* music?'

'It's "How Much Is That Doggie in the Window?"' said Constable Peel glumly.

'Woof-woof,' said Angry, mainly out of force of habit. (He was Pavlov's Dwarf.[32])

'I told you,' said Dan. 'I can't turn it off if the engine is on, and I'm a bit worried about turning the engine off and leaving us stuck here.'

As he spoke Wormwood opened the door of the van, peered beneath the dashboard, and fiddled about a bit. Instantly, the music stopped.

'Thank you,' said Constable Peel. 'Thank you, thank you, thank you. If you didn't look like a rodent, smell funny, and have what I suspect may be a number of easily communicable diseases, I might even hug you.'

☠ [32] Ivan Pavlov (1849–1936) was a Russian scientist who signalled the arrival of his dogs' food by ringing a bell or, occasionally, giving them an electric shock, which wasn't very nice of him. He found that the dogs began producing saliva even before they tasted any food, simply because they'd heard the bell, or received a shock. This is known as 'conditioning'. You have to wonder, though, if the dogs eventually got a bit tired of the shocks and the bells and the absence of food, and made their unhappiness known to Pavlov. This is known as 'biting'.

'Nicest thing anyone has ever said to me,' Wormwood replied. He sniffled, and wiped away a little tear.

'That is a relief,' said Sergeant Rowan. 'Now, where's Samuel?'

Nurd pointed to his left. 'I think he's over there somewhere.'

'Then over there somewhere is where we're going. Lead on, sir.'

Nurd and Wormwood returned to their car, while the policemen and the dwarfs climbed back into the ice-cream van with Dan.

'Hey, what was that song again?' said Dozy, followed quickly by the words 'Ow!' and 'Never mind,' as Constable Peel made his disapproval of such questions felt.

Nurd started the ignition on the Aston Martin and pulled ahead of the van, which was soon rumbling along behind them.

Wormwood tapped Nurd on the arm.

'Look what I found in the van,' he said.

In his hand he held a bag of wine gums.

'If you ever tell anyone I said this, I shall deny it,' said Nurd, 'but, Wormwood, you're a marvel ...'

CHAPTER XXII

In Which We Learn That There Is Always Hope, As Long As One Chooses Not To Abandon It

Samuel's face wore a smile for the first time since he had arrived in that desolate place. He turned to the Blacksmith and said: 'You were right! Nurd heard me. I know he did!'

But instead of congratulating him, the Blacksmith grabbed Samuel and Boswell and threw them behind a Russian T-34 tank that was lying on its side nearby, its tracks shredded and its innards exposed by a hole that had been ripped in its armour. For a moment, Samuel thought that he had misjudged the Blacksmith and, like Old Ram, he was about to betray them, until the Blacksmith whispered to him to be quiet and stay still. Samuel saw shapes moving across the sky, their tattered wings beating, their keen eyes scouring the land below. Then the ground began to tremble, and Samuel heard the beating of hooves, and a voice said, 'Greetings, Blacksmith.'

Samuel peered around the side of the tank, his hand holding Boswell's muzzle to prevent him from barking. Above the Blacksmith loomed a black horse, three times taller than the Blacksmith himself, with the wings of a bat and yellow eyes that glowed like molten gold set into its skull. Black blood dripped from its mouth where it was biting on its bridle, and its hooves struck sparks upon the stony ground. In its saddle sat a demon with two pale horns protruding from his skull, the horns, like those of some great bull, so long and heavy it seemed almost impossible that he should be able to hold his head upright upon his shoulders. His hair was dark and long, his skin very pale, and his eyes bright with a wit and intelligence that made the cruelty writ upon his features seem somehow more terrible. He wore armour of red and gold, and a red cloak that was clasped at his neck with a tusk of bone. The cloak billowed behind him even though there was no wind to carry it, so that it seemed to have a life of its own, to be a weapon in its own right, a shroud that could suffocate and consume. The rider's saddle was heavy with weapons: a sabre, a spiked mace, and an array of knives with ornate, twisted blades.

'My Lord Abigor,' said the Blacksmith. 'I was not expecting such illustrious company.'

Abigor pulled back on the horse's reins, causing it to rear up before the Blacksmith, its monstrous hooves barely inches from his head, but the man did not flinch. Abigor, seeing that his effort to frighten the Blacksmith had proved fruitless, turned the horse and let its front hooves once again touch the ground.

'If I did not know better, I might have said that I detected a tone of mockery in your voice,' said Abigor.

'I would not dare, my lord.'

'Oh, but you would, Blacksmith. Your skill in forging

my weapons only buys you a little tolerance. Be careful how you spend it.'

The Blacksmith hung his head in shame. 'You made me forge them, on pain of greater torment. I would not have done so otherwise.'

'I do recall your misguided attempt at defiance. If I remember correctly, it died when I threatened to sever your toes.'

The Blacksmith's jaw tightened, and Samuel felt his anger. Despite Abigor's fearsome aspect, the Blacksmith was barely restraining himself from an attack. Abigor released his hold on the reins and spread his arms wide, as though daring an assault, but the Blacksmith did not take the bait, and Abigor once again resumed his hold upon the horse.

'I find that pain focuses the mind wonderfully,' continued Abigor. 'Do you need help in that department again, Blacksmith? I would be happy to oblige if I decide that you are withholding information from me.'

The Blacksmith raised his head. 'I don't know what you're talking about, my lord.'

'I seek a boy. He is a trespasser. He can't be allowed to wander freely, and I have reason to believe that he is in this area.'

'I have seen no boy. I have had no visitors since last your lordship came to me.'

'I detect no sense of sorrow that so long has passed without contact between us.'

'I will not lie to you, my lord. You come to me only when you need weapons, and it pains me to forge such implements. It is why I ended up here, and I wish now that I had not been so eager to please men of power in my past life.'

'Regrets, Blacksmith, make poor currency. You can't buy back with them what you most desire.'

'Which would be, my lord?' asked the Blacksmith, sensing that Abigor was waiting for the question to be asked.

'The past,' said Abigor. 'You are being punished for what you have done. Were it so easy to make up for one's failings, then Hell would be empty.'

'And would that be such a bad thing, my lord?'

'Only for its demons, Blacksmith. Without beings like you to humiliate, our existences would be significantly duller.'

Abigor stared at the weapons and devices scattered across the sands. 'And yet what invention you creatures display,' he said, 'what skill, all put to one end: the destruction of those most like yourselves. Sometimes, I wonder if the real demons already rule the Earth.'

'We put our skills to other uses too,' said the Blacksmith. 'We cure. We help. We protect.'

'Do you, now? But which skill does your kind value more: the willingness to help another, or the ability to wipe him out of existence?'

The Blacksmith looked down, unable to meet Abigor's eye. As he did so he saw the tracks left by Boswell and Samuel in the sand. He shifted position slightly so that his body hid them, then slowly he began to move away from Abigor, erasing the marks with his feet as he did so.

'You back away, Blacksmith,' said Abigor. 'Do you fear me so much?'

'Yes, my lord.'

Abigor tapped a clawed finger upon the horn of his saddle.

'You know, I am tempted to doubt your word. You hate me, almost as much as you hate yourself, but I don't think that you truly fear me, and I know that you do not respect me. You are a peculiar man, Blacksmith, but perhaps such strangeness comes with your gifts. And you have seen no sign of a boy, you say?'

'No, I have not,' said the Blacksmith. The traces of paws and footprints were now entirely gone from Abigor's sight. Samuel noticed that the Blacksmith's voice had changed, and he no longer referred to the demon Abigor as 'my lord'.

'But would you tell me if you had, Blacksmith? I have always suspected your loyalties. Sometimes I wonder how you ended up here. I fear there may be a spark of goodness in you, a flicker of conscience, that has not yet been extinguished. One might even call it hope.'

'I have no hope. I left it in my past life.'

Abigor leaned forward. He drew back his lips, exposing perfect white fangs.

'But not your talent for weaponry. There is a war coming, Blacksmith. You may have thought yourself forgotten by others, but the promise of conflict will recall you to them once again. My rivals will seek you out for your skills. What will you do then, Blacksmith?'

'I will turn them down.'

'Will you, now? I think not. Their capacity for inflicting hurt is almost as great as mine. Almost, but not quite. Even if you were loyal to me, which you are not, your loyalty would not be great enough to stand against such pain. So I have decided to demonstrate both my wisdom and my mercy by relieving you of the burden of being forced to betray me in order to end your suffering.'

Abigor drew his sabre, and with a single slashing motion he cut off the Blacksmith's head. The sword rose and fell, rose and fell, over and over until the Blacksmith lay in pieces upon the ground. The Blacksmith's eyes still blinked, and his hands still moved, the fingers clawing at the dirt like the legs of insects. No blood flowed from his wounds, but his face was contorted with agony. From the sky, an imp descended. It picked up the Blacksmith's hands and flew away with them while Abigor stared down at the work of his sword.

'Even were someone to reconstitute you, you could do nothing without your hands. Goodbye, Blacksmith. We will not meet again.'

With that, Abigor urged on his steed. It galloped away, and then its wings began to beat and it rose up into the sky and vanished into the clouds.

Samuel emerged from his hiding place and ran to where the Blacksmith's remains lay.

'You could have told him where I was,' said Samuel. 'You could have told him, and he might have spared you. I'm sorry. I'm so sorry.'

'Don't be,' said the Blacksmith, 'for I am not.'

And as he spoke, his expression changed. He looked puzzled, and his face became filled with a soft glow tinged faintly with amber, like the reflected light of a slowly setting sun.

'There is no pain,' he said. 'It is gone.' He smiled at Samuel. 'I did not betray you. I have redeemed myself. Now, there is peace.'

Slowly, the pieces of his poor, butchered body faded away, and Samuel and Boswell were alone once more.

The Aston Martin and the ice-cream van were hidden beneath the heads of giant green toadstools that had sprouted from an area of damp, noisome earth, a forest of them that extended for miles. Nurd and Wormwood, along with the policemen and the dwarfs, watched as flights of demons passed overhead, some circling and descending, then ascending again once they had examined more closely whatever had attracted their attention on the ground. After a time a great black steed broke through the clouds above and passed among their ranks, their rider urging the demons to ever greater effort. His voice even carried to the odd little group watching him from below.

'Find the boy!' he cried. 'Bring him to me!'

'I don't like the look of him,' said Jolly.

'I don't like the look of any of them,' said Dozy.

'Who's the big lad on the horse, then?' Angry asked Nurd.

'Duke Abigor,' said Nurd. He sounded distracted. This wasn't right. He had to assume that Abigor and his minions were looking for Samuel, but Samuel could only have been brought here by Mrs Abernathy and Duke Abigor and Mrs Abernathy hated each other. Duke Abigor would do nothing to aid Mrs Abernathy, yet now here he was, using his minions to search for the human Mrs Abernathy loathed above all others. It could only mean that Abigor wanted Samuel for his own purposes.

'Whose side is he on?' asked Sergeant Rowan.

'His own,' said Nurd. 'He's looking for Samuel.'

'Why?'

'Perhaps because if he has Samuel, then Mrs Abernathy doesn't. Samuel is her way back to power, and Duke Abigor doesn't want that. Duke Abigor wants to rule. I think that if he could find a way to get rid of the Great Malevolence himself then he'd do it, but he can't, so he'll have to settle for being second-in-command. To succeed, he has to ensure that Mrs Abernathy is out of the picture. That means taking away any hope she has of regaining the Great Malevolence's trust, and her only hope of that is to present him with Samuel.'

Sergeant Rowan looked at Nurd with a new respect.

'When did you get so clever?'

'When I realized that I wasn't as clever as I thought,' Nurd replied. 'We have to move. Samuel is nearby. I'm certain of it.'

But even as he spoke his sense of Samuel's presence began to diminish, and he felt the boy's spirit start to weaken. Something was very wrong, and Nurd willed Samuel to keep going and not to give up.

Hold on, Samuel, he thought. Hold on for just a little while longer . . .

Samuel and Boswell had left behind the crater of weapons, and the memory of the Blacksmith's bravery. In the distance Samuel could see hills. He decided to head in that direction. He and Boswell might be able to find a place to hide there, for they were too vulnerable out here upon the open plain. But he was so tired. He could barely drag one foot along after the other, and he was also carrying Boswell, who was exhausted and had begun limping. Samuel's nostrils burned and his lungs hurt from breathing the noxious air, tinged as it was with the stink of sulphur. His head grew lower with his spirits, for it seemed that his only hope of returning to his own world lay with the very woman he most wished to avoid. He understood the Blacksmith's logic, but he did not want to face Mrs Abernathy again. None of this was fair. He wished that he'd never seen the stupid portal, never tried to save the Earth, never met Nurd.

He shook his head. Where had that thought come from? It wasn't true. Nurd was his friend. How could he think such a thing of a friend? But if Nurd was his friend, then where was he? Samuel had called out to him, but still he had not come. Perhaps Nurd didn't care, and was just like all the rest. Even his father had abandoned him, and his mother had done nothing to prevent it, nothing. What was the point in continuing if even your own parents couldn't be bothered to behave as they should?

He stopped walking. Ahead of him was a vast expanse of pure nothingness, a void that appeared to open blackly before him but was not really black at all, because at least 'black' was something.[33] The hole in time and space into which he and Boswell now stared was a relic of non-existence, the last trace of all that had not been before the Multiverse was created. Looking into it made Samuel's head hurt, because it had no length, or width, or depth. It had no gravity, nor could energy be transmitted through it. What Samuel and Boswell were seeing was not just the end of this dimension, and this universe, but the beginning and end of all universes, and as they gazed upon it they felt a great sadness overcome them; their spirits fell, and their will to continue was finally sapped, for clever young boys and smart, loyal dogs were never meant to face the bleakness of absolute nothingness. Slowly Samuel sank down, Boswell beside him, and together they looked into the void, and the void began to enter them.

[33] When we see colours, what we're really seeing is a certain frequency and wavelength of light hitting our eyes. Photons, which are units of light, have to leave an object in order for us to pick up on pink, or blue, or that strange brown colour only found in damp earth and school uniforms. Without atoms, there can be no photons, and thus no colour, not even black. There is a school of philosophy known as Existentialism which takes the view that life is all a lot of nothing, really, and as a consequence we are all in a state of constant despair. Unsurprisingly, existentialists don't get invited to many birthday parties.

CHAPTER XXIII

In Which Mrs Abernathy Loses Her Temper, and
We Meet Up Again with an Unpleasant
Personage from Earlier In Our Tale

Mrs Abernathy's voice rose to a shriek. Even the Watcher was taken aback at its volume and intensity.

'*Nurd*?' screamed Mrs Abernathy. 'Nurd? You're telling me that imbecile, that miserable excuse for a demon, is responsible for all this? But I banished him. I sent him to the Wasteland with his idiot servant where he couldn't be a nuisance any more. How could –? How did – ? I mean –'

Probably for the first time ever, words failed Mrs Abernathy. Nurd? But he was so inconsequential, so inept, or so it had seemed. How could she have misjudged him so badly? She began to feel what might almost have been admiration for him, even if it was the kind that came before you began inflicting serious pain on the object of said admiration. The scale of what he had achieved, the great enterprise that he had managed to undo, was almost inconceivable. For a moment, the revelation of Nurd's perfidy drove the Watcher's second piece of news – the message from Old Ram that he had Samuel Johnson nearby – from her mind, but it quickly returned.

'I'll deal with Nurd later,' she said. 'For now, Samuel Johnson is our priority. You should have come to me before now, Watcher. I am disappointed in you.'

Had the Watcher been an entity of a different stripe, it might have felt obliged to protest at the unfairness of this, if only to obscure its other reason for remaining silent. After all, Mrs Abernathy had been variously unconscious, over-concerned with her own vanity, and too keen on finding out the identities of those who were plotting against her to even allow the Watcher into her presence. It wasn't entirely its fault that it had taken so long to relay Old Ram's news to her. But the Watcher was not the kind of entity to complain, and had it done so Mrs Abernathy would not have listened, so it forced such thoughts from its mind even as it wondered if thinking them was enough to make it a complainer after all.

Mrs Abernathy spun on her heel, and the Watcher followed. Behind her lair was a stone courtyard, and in the courtyard a massive crested basilisk[34] stood, saddled and ready. It hissed a greeting at its mistress as she

☠ [34] In mythology, the basilisk was known as the 'King of Serpents' because of its crown-shaped crest. Ascribed to it were variously the capacity to kill with its gaze, its breath, or the sound of its cry. It was even said that if a soldier pierced its skin with a spear, the poison in the basilisk's blood would flow up the weapon and kill its assailant. It was rumoured to be hatched by a rooster from the egg of a toad or serpent, thus providing an interesting variation on the question of which came first, the chicken or the egg. Actually, scientists believe that they have now proved the chicken came first, given that a particular protein in eggshells can only be produced inside a chicken. Mind you, it was probably a very surprised chicken that pushed out the first egg: '*Cluck!* Mavis, dear – *cluck, cluck* – you won't believe what's just fallen out of my bottom . . .'

climbed into the saddle. Spurs of bone emerged from Mrs Abernathy's heels, and she urged the creature towards the Forest of Broken Forms, the Watcher shadowing her from above.

Samuel was no longer angry at his mother. In fact, Samuel could no longer remember what his mother looked like. He knew that he had a mother, once, but he could not picture her in his mind. Likewise his father was a blur, but it didn't matter. Nothing really mattered. The void coursed through him, emptying him of all feelings and memories, turning him into a husk, a hollow being. Beside Samuel, Boswell whined and tried to lick his master's hand, but his strength was seeping from him. The sound caused Samuel to turn. He stared down at the dog and struggled to recall his name. Bos-something? Was that it?

And then even that was gone as the light in his eyes began to die.

Mrs Abernathy's basilisk stopped at the edge of the Forest of Broken Forms, beside the ruins of Old Ram's home. She searched among the stones, half expecting to see Samuel Johnson buried in the rubble, but there was no sign of the boy, or of Old Ram. When she examined the ground, and saw the tracks left by the Great Oak, she knew what had happened here. With the Watcher at her heels, she entered the forest, the trees recoiling in terror, clearing a path for her until she and the basilisk reached the Great Oak. Unlike its smaller brethren, it showed no fear of her. If anything it was

Mrs Abernathy who seemed wary of the massive tree, with its coiling roots and its twisted branches. Mrs Abernathy might have been evil incarnate, and capable of acts of immense cruelty and harm, but the Great Oak was ancient, and strong, and dangerous. The vestiges of its humanity made it so.

The Great Oak was also insane, the result of millennia of misery and racked growth. Its madness rendered it unpredictable, and Mrs Abernathy knew that it would not be beyond the Great Oak's capabilities to try to hurt her, or trap her with its roots and keep her here for its own amusement, torturing her as it had been tortured for so long, avenging some of its pain by visiting pain on another. She knew she was especially vulnerable now that she was no longer under the protection of the Great Malevolence, and she was glad of the Watcher's presence beside her.

'It has been a long time since last you set foot here,' said the Great Oak. 'You were not welcome then, and you are not welcome now.'

'What have you done with Old Ram?'

'No more than he deserved,' said the Great Oak, and its trunk split open beneath its gaping mouth like a vertical wound, revealing a hollow interior in which Old Ram hung suspended by ivy, moaning softly as branches tugged and tore at him, and roots dug into his flesh.

'There was a boy with him,' said Mrs Abernathy.

'Boy?' said the Great Oak. 'I saw no boy.'

And Mrs Abernathy heard the surrounding trees laugh.

'Don't lie to me. Do you have the boy?'

'There is no boy here,' said the Great Oak, and Mrs Abernathy sensed that it spoke the truth.

'Then let Old Ram go,' she said.

'And why should I do that, when I enjoy toying with him so much?'

'I must talk with him, and I can't do that while you're hurting him.'

The ivy uncurled, the roots and branches retreated, and Old Ram was released from bondage. He climbed through the gap in the tree and knelt before Mrs Abernathy.

'Thank you,' he said, stroking her feet with his clawed upper hooves. 'Thank you, kind mistress, thank you.'

'The boy,' said Mrs Abernathy. 'Tell me about the boy.'

'Old Ram was holding him for you, him and his dog. He was sleeping, and he trusted Old Ram. Then Great Oak came and tore Old Ram's home apart, and the boy escaped. Old Ram saw him crawl away, but Old Ram could do nothing to stop him. It is all the fault of the Great Oak. Punish him! Punish him!'

Mrs Abernathy turned to the Great Oak.

'Is this true?'

The Great Oak creaked and rustled. 'Old Ram had hurt us. It was Old Ram who had to be punished. I did not know that the boy was yours. It was . . . my mistake.'

The Great Oak lowered two of its biggest branches, as though they were arms and he was extending them in supplication. Suddenly, they slashed at Mrs Abernathy, smaller branches as sharp as knives radiating from their ends. Its roots erupted from the ground at her feet, twisting around her legs. The Watcher grabbed Mrs Abernathy and tried to take flight, but now the surrounding trees were closing in and there was not room for the Watcher's wings to unfold. Mrs Abernathy's basilisk spat venom, instantly rotting branches and roots, but the trees were too many, and lengths of ivy coiled around the basilisk's mouth, forcing it shut; mud and filth were forced into its eyes, obscuring its lethal gaze. Meanwhile Old Ram cowered in the dirt, his hooves curled over his head, bleating in misery and alarm.

Six thick tentacles erupted from Mrs Abernathy's back, topped with sharp beaks that snapped at the branches and nipped at the roots, but the Great Oak was too strong, and too intent upon hurting Mrs Abernathy now that she was within reach. Slowly, she and the Watcher were being enveloped. Already the Watcher's arms were pinned to its sides, and Mrs Abernathy was concealed from the waist down by twisted roots.

'Come to the Great Oak,' said the old tree. 'Come, and be part of us.'

Mrs Abernathy's eyes began to glow whitely. She opened her mouth and clicked her tongue, and a small blue flame appeared between her teeth. She drew a deep breath into her lungs, then exhaled. Fire burst from her lips, a torrent of light and heat that struck at the heart of the Great Oak, igniting it both inside and out. It roared in pain, and instantly its branches and roots began to retreat, freeing Mrs Abernathy and the Watcher. The

Watcher spread his wings and carried them both upwards and out of the forest as the other trees bent away from the flames, crying out in fear as the Great Oak's struggles sent blue sparks in their direction. The basilisk freed itself and tore a path through the remaining trees, and Old Ram fled with it, running on all fours until he found himself at last beside what was left of his home, where Mrs Abernathy was waiting for him.

'The boy,' she said. 'Which way did he go?'

Old Ram pointed to his right. 'He was hiding behind those boulders, and that was the last Old Ram saw of him, but he could not have gone far. He is a child in a strange land, with only a dog for company. Let Old Ram come with you. Old Ram can help you find him. Old Ram is tired of this place.'

He looked back at the forest as blue flame rose from its heart, and he shivered.

'And the Great Oak will recover, and will come again for Old Ram,' he whispered.

Mrs Abernathy strode to her basilisk and mounted it. As she did so she saw two pale demons circling high above, drawn by the flames in the forest, and she knew them to be Abigor's.

'Go where you will,' she said. 'But if anyone asks you about the boy, deny all knowledge of him. If you do otherwise, I will hear of it, and I will have you tied and bound, and let the Great Oak have his way with you for ever.'

Old Ram nodded, and thanked her again. Mrs Abernathy and the Watcher waited until Abigor's demons had descended to the forest before they took off themselves, travelling fast and true, until the basilisk found the trail of footsteps and paw prints left by Samuel and Boswell.

And they knew that he was near.

CHAPTER XXIV

In Which We Speculate On What, If Anything, Might Be Worse Than Evil

If there is anything worse than evil, it is nothingness. At least evil has a form, and a voice, and a purpose, however depraved. Perhaps some good can even come out of evil: a terrible deed of violence against someone weaker may lead others to act in order to ensure that such a deed is not perpetrated again, whereas before they might have been unaware of the reasons why an individual might behave in such a way, or they might simply have chosen to ignore them. And evil, as we saw with the Blacksmith, always contains within itself the possibility of its own redemption. It is not evil that is the enemy of hope: it is nothingness.

As Nurd felt Samuel's life force ebb away, so too did he come to realize just where the boy was. Even in the grim, blasted regions of Hell, there was only one place that could cause such a loss of self, eating away at all the substance of an individual, all that he loved and hated, all that he was and ever would be. It was the Void, the Emptiness, the Eternal Absence that even the Great Malevolence himself feared. So Nurd kept his foot pressed hard upon the accelerator and found himself pulling away from the ice-cream van, loaded down as it was with dwarfs, policemen, and rapidly dwindling supplies of ice cream. But as he drew closer to Samuel so too was the light in Samuel's soul fading. Nurd felt as though he were trying to reach a candle flame before it flickered for the last time, that he might wrap his hands around it and feed it the oxygen it needed to survive. Nurd knew that if Samuel continued to stare into the Void he would eventually be lost entirely, and nobody would ever be able to bring him back. Samuel and Boswell would become like statues of flesh and bone, with an empty place where their spirits once were (for animals have spirits too, and let no one tell you otherwise). Having endured so much, and having been separated by space and time only to be offered the chance of a reunion at last by Mrs Abernathy's vengeance, Nurd did not wish to see his friend's essence sacrificed to the emptiness that underlay the chaos of Hell.

Faster and faster he drove, until Wormwood put a hand on his arm in warning, for now there were sharp and treacherous stones beneath their wheels. Were they to suffer a puncture or, worse, rupture the engine or break an axle, then Samuel and Boswell would not be saved. Reluctantly Nurd slowed down, while high above their heads unseen eyes watched their progress, and reported it to others.

Samuel was almost entirely still. His eyes did not blink, his lips did not open, and he barely seemed to be breathing. Yet had anyone been watching him, they would have seen one small sign of movement. For even as all that had made him what he was – every memory, every thought, every spark of brightness and eccentricity – was being consumed, his right hand continued to stroke Boswell's fur, and, in response, his dog's tail contributed the barest thump on the ground, but a thump nonetheless. Had Boswell not been present, Samuel would already have ceased to exist, leaving nothing more than the shell of a boy seated on the edge of a dark sea; and if Samuel had not been present, Boswell would have been little more than a stuffed animal withering away. But if a child loves an animal, and is loved in turn, there will always be a connection between them: they are spirits intertwined. And if the Void had feelings, which it clearly did not, it might well have experienced a sense of frustration at its inability to break down the defences of the boy and the dog. Deep inside each of them was a wall protecting the best of themselves, but it was crumbling at last, like a dam finally giving way to the flood, and soon they would be drowned. The movements of Samuel's hand began to slow, and the thumps of Boswell's tail became less frequent, and their eyes grew dim as never-ending night fell upon their hearts.

A hand touched Samuel's shoulder, and gently turned him from the darkness. And Boswell was carefully gathered up, and words of comfort were whispered into his ear.

'Good dog. Loyal dog. Brave Boswell.'

Samuel heard a name being called, over and over, and understood that it was his own.

He looked up and saw four dwarfs, two policemen, and a man dressed in white offering him an ice cream. He saw Boswell being held by what looked like a bald rodent in overalls, and the little dog was licking the rodent's face.

And he saw Nurd. Samuel buried his head against his friend's breast, and for the first time since his arrival in that terrible place he allowed himself to cry.

Old Ram left the forest behind, sulking and muttering his discontent all the way, his gaze focused inward, fixed upon his own sufferings. Sometimes a good turn is the worst that you can do for a certain type of individual, because he will hate you for putting him in your debt. Mrs Abernathy had spared Old Ram any further misery, and had permitted him to leave the place of his banishment, but Old Ram had wanted more: he had wanted influence, and recognition. He had wanted power. Instead he had been left to wander in the wilderness. He began to think that he was now worse off than he had been before. After all, he used to have a roof over his head, and fuel for his fire, but what did he have now? No roof, no fuel, and the cold was seeping into his bones. For this, he blamed Mrs Abernathy.

'She hates Old Ram,' he whispered to himself. 'She thinks Old Ram is worthless, but Old Ram is not. Old Ram was great once, and Old Ram could be great again, but none will give Old Ram the chance that Old Ram deserves. Poor Old Ram! Poor forsaken Old Ram!'

So caught up was he in bitterness that he failed to notice the winged horse alight before him, and the flight of demons that quietly descended behind him. It was only when the horse blew a bad-tempered blast of air through its nostrils in warning that Old Ram looked up to find Duke Abigor staring down at him.

'You are far from home, Old Ram,' said Abigor. 'Were you not banished, and forbidden to leave the precincts of the forest?'

'I was, my lord, but Mrs Abernathy freed me.'

'Did she, now? And why would she do that?'

Old Ram, mindful of Mrs Abernathy's injunction to remain silent about the circumstances of his freedom, said nothing, but Duke Abigor was as clever as he was ruthless. He knew much about Old Ram, and was aware that, like so many who had found themselves damned to the Infernal Regions, his vanity was his weakness. Were Abigor to threaten him, or torture him, Old Ram might simply endure his sufferings with clenched teeth, if only to prove to Abigor that, humbled though he might be, Old Ram had his pride. No, there were easier ways to deal with Old Ram.

'Well, no matter,' said Abigor airily. 'It strikes me only that you don't sound very pleased, even though your long period of exile has come to an end. Surely such generosity of spirit on the part of Mrs Abernathy merits a greater show of gratitude?'

He watched Old Ram twist and writhe, a pantomime of hurt, and envy, and loathing.

'Gratitude.' Old Ram spat the word. 'For what? It cost her nothing, and left Old Ram with nothing. Old Ram tried to help her. It's not Old Ram's fault that—'

Old Ram stopped talking. Mrs Abernathy had

warned him not to speak of the boy, but she wasn't here. Duke Abigor was here though, and Old Ram wondered why that might be. Abigor's presence, thought Old Ram, might be used to some advantage.

'Go on,' said Abigor. 'I'm listening.'

'Old Ram has been alone for a long time, my lord,' said Old Ram carefully. 'Old Ram seeks a master. Old Ram would be a good servant.'

'I already have more servants than I need. You would have to offer me something that no one else can.'

Old Ram's yellow eyes narrowed with cunning.

'Mrs Abernathy made Old Ram promise not to tell, but it may be that Old Ram was wrong to make that promise.'

'Promises are made to be broken,' said Abigor. 'Particularly promises made in the face of a threat.'

'Old Ram has no duty of loyalty to Mrs Abernathy.'

'No, he does not. After all, what fealty do you owe to the one who banished you? The greater fault is hers, not yours. So, what can you offer to prove your loyalty to me?'

'I can offer you news,' said Old Ram, 'news of a human child.'

Mrs Abernathy's basilisk reached the edge of the Void just behind the Watcher, and she quickly turned her mount's head away from the emptiness so that neither of them looked upon it for too long. Even the Watcher kept its head down as it examined the tracks on the ground. Its words echoed in her head.

It is the boy and his dog. They were here. Others came and took them away.

'Others?' demanded Mrs Abernathy. 'What others?'

The Watcher sniffed the ground.

Nurd. And humans. Seven humans.

'Can you track them?'

The Watcher stared out over the stony ground, finding the places in which the stones had been disturbed, distinguishing the marks of wheeled vehicles.

Yes, but they travel fast.

'Then we will travel faster.'

She moved on, not even checking to make sure that the Watcher was following, and so she did not see it pause, its red brow furrowing. All of this was wrong, thought the Watcher. *It has all spiralled out of control. My master is mad, and my mistress may be madder still. Something must be done. The bells have been silent for too long. Perhaps the time is coming when they must peal again.*

Old Ram's tongue, once loosened, unburdened itself of all its secrets. He told Duke Abigor of the boy, and the attack by the Great Oak, and Mrs Abernathy's appearance in the forest. He told him of how he had seen the boy hide, and the direction in which he must have walked. As he spoke, he saw Abigor's face darken in anger.

'The Blacksmith lied,' said Abigor. 'He must have seen the boy, but he would not speak of it.'

He turned to one of his demons, who had only just alighted, and ordered it to retrieve the remaining pieces of the Blacksmith, that he might punish him further. He asked first for the Blacksmith's severed hands, that he might crush them so the Blacksmith could never use them again, but the sack containing the Blacksmith's hands was empty. A second demon, who had recently been patrolling the skies for signs of the boy, approached them and told Abigor that the Blacksmith had disappeared, for it had passed over the crater of weapons and detected no sign of him. Furthermore, it said that there had been a peculiar smell in the air: the smell of virtue, of decency, of *humanity*. The Blacksmith, in the demon's opinion, was gone for ever. His soul was no longer in Hell.

Abigor stifled his rage. He had always sensed a fault in the Blacksmith, some residue of hope and decency that should have been snuffed out long before, but he could never have imagined that it would be enough to redeem him. The Blacksmith had not merely been a soul filled with regret, he was a soul who had genuinely repented, even with no prospect that it might end his sufferings, for he must surely have believed that he was damned to Hell for eternity. But repentance would not have been enough; a sacrifice would have been required. The boy, Samuel Johnson, had saved the Blacksmith by allowing the maker of weapons to offer himself up on behalf of another, one worthy of the gesture. Samuel Johnson was a Good Soul, for only such a soul could survive in this place; survive, and provide sustenance to the soul of another. The boy was dangerous, more so than even Mrs Abernathy realized. His presence in Hell was a pollutant. He had to be locked away, hidden from sight. He could not be killed: a mortal could not die in Hell. Nothing could. It was a place of endless torment, and endless torment required the absence of death.

A shadow passed over him, and another of his demons alighted by his side. It announced that it had followed two moving carts as they had passed into the stony place that led to the Void, and there it had watched as the boy and his pet were gathered into safety. It had stayed with them for a time until it was sure of the direction that they were taking, before returning to inform its master.

'Quickly!' cried Abigor. 'Rise up, rise up! Apprehend the boy and bring him to me.'

The demons took flight like crows from the noise of a gun. Duke Abigor was about to follow them into the sky when Old Ram tugged at his horse's reins.

'What about Old Ram?' he said. 'Old Ram told you all. What about Old Ram's reward?'

Duke Abigor's horse reared up, and one of its hooves struck Old Ram a blow to the head, sending him sprawling to the ground.

'How can I trust a pitiful creature who would break a promise, and betray one master for another?' said Duke Abigor. 'There is only one reward for a traitor.'

He raised a clawed finger, and Old Ram's world went black for a time. When he awoke he was trapped in ice, with only his horned head above the surface of the great frozen lake of Cocytus that extended as far as the eye could see, the icy whiteness of it broken only by others like himself: traitors all, betrayers of family and friends, of lords and masters.

Old Ram's teeth began to chatter, for Old Ram hated the cold.

CHAPTER XXV

In Which a Familiar Odour Sends the Dwarfs' Spirits Soaring

There were a great many things that Wormwood had never expected to see in the course of his existence – a tree that didn't want to tear him apart, for example, or a demon that just fancied a bit of a chat and a warm hug instead of inflicting misery and hurt and generally making a nuisance of itself – but high on that list, perhaps higher even than Someplace Other Than Hell, was Nurd showing a genuine, positive emotion. But as he watched Nurd and Samuel hug, and heard them begin to chatter at high speed about all that had happened since last they had met, and saw a big, sloppy tear drop from one of Nurd's eyes, slide down his face, and perform a little jump into the air from the end of his chin, Wormwood thought that if such a thing as Nurd weeping for joy was possible, then anything might be.

'Got something in my eye,' said Jolly, as the friends enjoyed their reunion. He gave a little sniff.

'Very moving,' said Angry, dabbing at his nose with a sleeve that had clearly been used for that same purpose a great many times in the past, and consequently resembled a race track for snails.

'Seeing people happy always makes me want an ice cream,' said Dozy. 'Seriously.'

'Arfle,' said Mumbles, in what might have been agreement.

They looked hopefully at Dan, Dan the Ice-Cream Man, who brandished an empty cone at them.

'There isn't any more ice cream,' said Dan. 'You've eaten it all. I didn't think it was possible, but you have. You're monsters, all of you.'

'Oh well,' said Dozy, 'I'll just have to be happy without one, then, but it won't be the same.'

He returned to watching Nurd and Samuel.

'Come along, you lot,' said Sergeant Rowan gently. 'Let's not make it a spectator sport.'

Somewhat reluctantly, because they were sentimental little men despite themselves, the dwarfs turned away.

Samuel and Nurd walked a short distance, Boswell trotting along happily beside them. They sat on a flat stone while each considered what the other had just told him.

'So you've been hiding away all this time?' said Samuel.

'Well, running and hiding,' said Nurd. 'You see, I'm not sure that Mrs Abernathy knows I was the one who collapsed the portal. She knows about the car, of course, but not about me, so Wormwood came up with the idea of disguising it as a rock.'

Samuel looked at the disguised Aston Martin; the rock exterior – actually a sheet of thin metal beaten and painted to resemble stone – was held in place by struts that sat upon the body of the car, with gauze replacing metal in front of the windows so that the driver had a clear view to the front, the sides, and behind him. There was actually a kind of brilliance to the idea, as long as nobody saw it moving. Then again, thought Samuel, this was Hell, and moving rocks might well exist somewhere in its depths, presumably with diamond teeth to help them munch on smaller rocks that couldn't defend themselves.

'But how did you find me?' asked Samuel. 'I mean, Hell is a big place, isn't it?'

'I've heard it said that it's infinite, or if it isn't it's as close to infinite as to make no difference. If it isn't infinite, then nobody has been able to find the end yet.[35] And if you include the Void, well . . .'

Samuel shuddered at the thought of how he had

💀 [35] Tricky business, infinity, and a lot harder to explain than one might think. One of the more interesting theoretical manifestations of infinity, and the problems and paradoxes associated with it, was proposed by David Hilbert, and takes the form of Hilbert's Hotel. Hilbert's Hotel is always full, but whenever a new guest arrives the hotel can always find room for him, because it's an infinite hotel with an infinite number of rooms. So, if a new guest arrives, he gets put in Room 1, the person in Room 1 moves to Room 2, and so on. Then an infinite coach, full of an infinite number of people, arrives, but the hotel can still fit them in. The manager moves all of the current guests into a room with a number twice as large as their current room – so Room 1 moves into Room 2, 2 to 4, 3 to 6, and so on. This means that an infinite number of odd-numbered rooms are now available for the infinite coach filled with an infinite number of guests. Unfortunately, Hilbert's Hotel can't exist in the real world because there are only ten to the power of eighty atoms in the universe, so there isn't enough matter to create an infinite-sized hotel. You wouldn't want to stay in it anyway: if you ordered room service, the food would take a long time to arrive, and it would always be cold; and if you forgot your key you'd have a terribly long walk back to reception.

almost lost himself in that emptiness. He could still feel a coldness deep inside him, and he wasn't sure if that element of himself touched by the Void would ever fully recover.

'Anyway,' continued Nurd, 'I sensed you as soon as you arrived. There's always been a part of me that's stayed connected to you. I don't know how, or why, but I'm grateful for it.'

'You used to turn up in my dreams sometimes,' said Samuel. 'We'd have conversations.'

'And you in mine,' said Nurd. 'I wonder if we were talking about the same things.'

But before they could continue an anxious-looking Wormwood approached, with Constable Peel close behind. Wormwood was about to say something, but Nurd stopped him with a raised hand.

'Samuel, I'd like to introduce you properly to someone. Samuel Johnson, this is my, well, this is my friend and colleague, Wormwood.'

And Wormwood, who had been called a lot of names by Nurd in his time, but never 'friend', stopped short as though he'd walked into an invisible wall. He blushed, then beamed.

'Hello, Wormwood,' said Samuel. 'It's good to meet you at last.'

'And you, Mr Samuel.'

'Just Samuel. I'm sorry if I was a bit quiet in the car. I wasn't quite myself then.'

'No apologies necessary,' said Wormwood.

Samuel extended his hand and Wormwood shook it, noticing that, when Samuel took his hand away, he didn't try to wipe it on his trousers, or on the ground, or on someone else. It really was a day of firsts for Wormwood.

A cough from Constable Peel, followed by a finger pointed at the sky, brought Wormwood back to reality with a vengeance.

'Oh yes. We need to get moving,' said Wormwood. 'Constable Peel has seen things circling below the clouds. We're being watched.'

They all looked up. The clouds had grown darker and heavier in the time that Samuel had been staring into nothingness, the thunder louder, and the lightning brighter.

'There's a storm coming anyway,' said Nurd. 'We have to get under cover.'

As they looked up, a winged figure broke through the clouds and hovered for a moment. To Samuel it looked at first like a bird with an elongated body, but then it dropped lower and he could pick out its forked tail, its bat wings, and the horns on its head. He thought that he could feel its interest in them before it twisted in the air and shot back into the clouds again.

'There,' said Constable Peel. 'Last time there were two of them.'

Nurd frowned. If Constable Peel was correct, it meant that one was keeping an eye on them while the other went off and informed of their presence. The question was: who was being informed?

Within sight of where they stood was a range of red-hued hills, the same hills that Samuel and Boswell had been making for when they encountered the Void. The hills were separated from them by what appeared to be marshland, over which hung a particularly noxious mist. Nurd knew that the hills were pitted with holes and caves. In any other part of Hell, they would probably have been turned into lairs for unspeakable creatures, but even the residents of Hell preferred to keep their distance from the Void, which was still visible from the higher points of the range.

'We can find a place to hide over there,' said Nurd. 'After that, we can try to plan our next move.'

They all piled into their respective vehicles, and Nurd led them in the direction of the hills, carefully steering a path through the stinking marshes. He was forced to roll down the windows so that he could peer out and check their progress, which made the car smell awful. At one point Samuel saw an eyeball protrude from the swamp, held up by a hand.

'What is it, Gertrude?' Samuel heard a voice say.

'Nigel, I do believe that there's an oik driving two other oiks and a small thingy through our garden.'

A second eyeball popped out of the water.

'I say, you chaps, bit of a cheek, what?'

'Sorry,' said Samuel. 'We didn't know it was your garden. We'll try not to make a mess of it.'

'It's a *swamp*,' hissed Nurd. 'If we did make a mess of it, it could only be an improvement.'

'Heard that!' said Nigel. Another hand emerged from the swamp and made itself into a fist, which it shook in the direction of Nurd's car. 'I'll give you what-for, and no mistake. Taking liberties with another chap's property, insulting his gardening skills. I mean, what's

Hell coming to, Gertrude? I'll get me sticks.' Both hands duly disappeared beneath the swamp.

'Quite right, Nigel,' said Gertrude, just as the ice-cream van emerged from the mist. 'Look! There's another one. I say, it's full of little fellows. How sweet!'

The dwarfs crowded to the serving hatch of the van, joined by Constable Peel.

'You don't see one of those every day,' said Jolly.

'No,' said Angry. 'You usually see two of them. Oi, darling, keeping an eye on us, are you? See what I did there, eh: keeping "an eye"?'

'Mind you don't drop it, love,' said Dozy. 'You won't have anything to look for it with.'

Gertrude, wisely, began to reconsider her opinion of the dwarfs. 'What dreadful little men,' she said, just as her husband's eyeball appeared beside her, and various hands brandishing sticks, clubs and, oddly, a stick of rhubarb.

'Come away from them, dear,' said Nigel. 'They're common, vulgar types. You never know what you might catch.'

'Common?' said Angry. 'We may be common, but we've earned the right to be unpleasant.'

'Sweat of our brows,' said Jolly. 'You've just inherited rudeness. We've had to work at it.'

'You're peasants!' shouted Nigel. 'Vandals! Get off my land!'

'Nyah!' shouted Angry, sticking his tongue out and wiggling his hands behind his ears in that timeless gesture of disrespect beloved in schoolyards every-where. 'Get a proper job!'

They emerged on to firmer ground, leaving the swamp behind. The dwarfs looked very pleased with themselves, and even Constable Peel and Sergeant Rowan seemed to have enjoyed the exchange.

'I love a good shout,' said Jolly.

'We should visit them on the way back,' said Dozy. 'I liked them. Eh, Jolly?'

But Jolly wasn't listening. Instead he was sniffing the air.

'Can you smell that?' he said.

'It's the swamp,' said Angry.

'No, it's different.'

'That was me,' said Dozy. 'It's all the ice cream. Sorry.'

'No, not that,' said Jolly. '*That.*'

They all sniffed.

'Nah,' said Angry, 'it can't be.'

'We're dreaming,' said Dozy.

'It's . . .' said Jolly, so overcome with emotion that he could barely speak. 'It's . . .'

'It's a brewery,' said Mumbles.

Everybody in the van looked at him, even Dan, who could barely see at the best of times.

'You spoke clearly,' said Jolly.

'I know,' said Mumbles. 'But this is important.'

And, to be fair, it was.

CHAPTER XXVI

In Which We Learn of the Difficulties
in Recreating the Taste of
Something Truly Horrible

We have already seen how exposure to life on Earth had changed Mrs Abernathy, and not necessarily for the better, depending upon how one might feel about net curtains and pot pourri. It had also changed Nurd, who had discovered that if he was any kind of demon at all, then he was a speed demon.

But the brief expedition to the world of men had also changed other denizens of Hell in a variety of ways. A shiver of burrowing sharks[36] had become quite fascinated by the game of rugby, even if they weren't very good at it because they kept eating the ball; a group

[36] And what a lovely collective noun that is, a *shiver* of sharks, because it's so apt. Similarly, you have to love a *smack* of jellyfish, which is exactly the sound a load of jellyfish make if you drop them; a *lounge* of lizards – hence the name 'lounge lizard' for a chap who hangs around in bars trying to look sophisticated; a *parliament* of owls, although this one is a little troublesome because owls actually look a lot smarter than most politicians, and therefore might find the use of 'parliament' a bit offensive as a description; an *unkindness* of ravens, who are clever but talk about other birds behind their backs; a *scold* of jays, who are always complaining to ravens for being unkind; and a *sleuth* of bears, as bears make very good detectives due to their foraging skills. Except for the Three Bears, obviously, because they took ages to work out who had burgled their house.

of ghouls, having locked themselves in a Biddlecombe sweet shop to escape from some rather aggressive young people, had become very adept at making chocolate, and were now distinctly tubbier than they had been, and therefore a lot less frightening; and a party of imps that had briefly glimpsed a Jane Austen costume drama on some televisions in a shop had taken to wearing bonnets and trying to find one another suitable husbands.

In the great clamour and disturbance that had followed the failure of the invasion, nobody noticed that two warthog demons, Shan and Gath, had disappeared, and there were now two fewer pairs of arms to shovel coals into the deep fires of Hell. Still, since it wasn't as if anyone was being paid a wage, and the fires of Hell showed no sign of going out any time soon, it was decided that Shan and Gath had merely found more suitable employment elsewhere, and they were quickly forgotten.

Prior to the opening of the portal, Shan and Gath had led uninteresting, fruitless lives. They had never really experienced hunger or thirst, so they didn't need to eat or drink. Occasionally they would gnaw on a particularly interesting rock, just to test its consistency, and they had been known to nibble on smaller demons, if only to see how quickly their limbs grew back. You had to make your own fun in Hell.

But their brief visit to Earth had opened their eyes, and their taste buds, to a new world of possibilities, for Shan and Gath's sole contribution to the invasion had been to spend the night in the Fig & Parrot pub in

Biddlecombe sampling free pints of what was then merely the experimental version of Spiggit's Old Peculiar. And while Spiggit's was, as we have established, a bit strong, and somewhat harsh on the palate, even for those who had previously dipped rocks in Hell's lava before sampling them, just to add a little taste, Shan and Gath still agreed that drinking it had been a life-altering experience, as well as briefly altering their sight and the proper working of their digestive systems. They had returned to Hell with only one purpose in mind: to find a way to replicate this wonderful brew and then do nothing else but drink it for eternity. They had therefore retired to a cave and set about their work, having absorbed a certain amount of brewing lore from some of the regulars at the Fig & Parrot, who had drunk so much beer in their time that their bodies were essentially kegs on legs.

Unfortunately, as Shan and Gath soon discovered, replicating the unique taste of Spiggit's Old Peculiar was considerably more difficult than they had hoped: successive tastings of their early efforts had played havoc with their insides, and it usually took a while for their tongues and sinuses to recover from more than three glasses. They had therefore decided to recruit a taster to test their various brews. The taster's name was Brock, a small, spherical, blue being with a good nature and two legs, two arms, one mouth, three eyes, and the useful ability to instantly reconstruct himself in the event of any unfortunate accidents.

As it happened, this latter quality had turned out to be particularly useful.

Inside Shan and Gath's cave were tubes, bottles, vats of water, and stocks of weeds that closely resembled wheat, oats, and barley. In an effort to imitate as closely as possible Spiggit's distinctive taste, Shan and Gath had also been forced to acquire a number of different acids; three types of mud; assorted dyes and corrosives; grit; oil; rancid fats; and various forms of wee.[37] Each variation was duly fed to Brock by Shan and Gath who, having encountered a couple of people dressed as mad scientists while drinking in the Fig & Parrot on that fateful Halloween night, had made themselves some white lab coats, and carried stone clipboards on which they carefully made notes of their experiments, as follows:

BREW 1: Subject hiccup, then vanish in puff of smoke.

BREW 2: Subject fall off chair. Appear to die.

BREW 3: One of subject's eyes fall out.

BREW 4: Two of subject's eyes fall out.

BREW 5: Subject claim that he can fly. Subject try. Subject wrong.

BREW 6: Subject claim that he can fly again. Subject try. Subject succeed. Gath remove subject from ceiling with broom.

☠ [37] And in case you think the idea of adding wee to beer is disgusting, there is actually a verb, *to lant*, which means to add wee to beer in order to flavour ale and improve its taste. And not just any old wee, but *aged* wee, which is known as 'lant'. Oddly, in olden days lant was also used in wool processing, for cleaning floors, as a glaze on pastry ('This bun tastes a bit funny.' 'Too much wee?' 'No, too little! Is there a shortage? If so, I can help . . .') and, oddest of all, as a means of keeping one's breath fresh, which raises the question: how bad must people's breath have smelled already if adding wee to it made it smell better? Frankly, you really don't want to know . . .

BREW 7: Subject beg for mercy. Threaten to sue. Fall
asleep.

BREW 8: Subject turn green. Become violently ill. Appear
to die again.

BREW 9: Subject say worst version yet. Subject say it wish
it really was dead. Subject plead for mercy.

BREW 10: Subject claim tongue on fire. Gath examine.
Subject's tongue actually on fire.

And so on. Beside each unsuccessful attempt to make
a drinkable version of Spiggit's Old Peculiar, Shan and
Gath had glumly added a big 'X'. But they now had
high hopes for Brew 19. This one looked like ale. It
had a nice frothy head, and its colour was a deep, rich
red. It even smelled like something that one might drink
without a gun being held to one's head.

They handed the stone cup to Brock, who examined
it carefully. He was becoming quite the expert. He
sniffed it, and nodded approvingly.

'That doesn't smell bad at all,' he said.

Shan and Gath nodded encouragingly. Brock took a
sip, held it in his mouth for a time, then swallowed.

'Well, I have to tell you, that's really very—'

Brock exploded, scattering pieces of himself over the
walls, the brewing equipment, and Shan and Gath. They
wiped Brock off themselves, and watched as the various
bits slimed and scuttled across the floor to reconstitute
themselves once again. When he was complete, and
apparently recovered, Brock looked warily at the liquid
that was now smoking on the stones by his feet.

'Needs a bit of work, that,' he said.

Shan sank to the floor and put his head in his hands. Gath groaned. All of that effort, and they still had not managed to create a drinkable beer, let alone a satisfactory imitation of the wonder that was Spiggit's Old Peculiar. They would never succeed, never. A second cup of Brew 19 stood beneath the stone tap. Gath was about to pour it down a hole in the floor when a dwarf entered the cave, followed by three more individuals of similarly diminished stature.

'All right, lads?' said Jolly, rubbing his hands together. 'I'll have a pint of your finest, and a packet of crisps.'

'That'll be two,' said Angry.

'Three,' said Dozy.

'Unk,' said Mumbles, who had reverted to type now that the beer had been found.

Shan and Gath looked confused. Not only were there unexpected dwarfs in their cave, but they were unexpected dwarfs with a death wish if they were actually prepared to sample the local brew.

'I wouldn't if I were you,' said Brock. 'It's got a bit of a kick.'

Jolly saw that Gath was poised to throw away the cup of Brew 19.

'Hey, hey! Don't waste that,' he said. 'Give it here.'

He ambled over to Gath and took the cup from his cloven hoof. Gath was too shocked to do anything more than gape. He had wondered if the dwarfs really existed at all, and had speculated that he had possibly been exposed to too many toxic brewing fumes. Nevertheless, this dwarf did seem to be speaking to him, and Gath no longer had a cup in his hand, so either the dwarfs were real or Gath needed to have a long lie-down.

'You'll never make any money that way,' said Jolly. 'You should pour it back in the barrel if it's bad. Nobody will notice.'

He sniffed at the cup.

'I'll tell you what,' he said to his comrades, 'it's Spiggit's, but not as we know it.'

He took a long draught, swirled it round his mouth, and swallowed. Shan and Gath immediately curled up and covered their heads, not terribly anxious to be covered in bits of dwarf, while Brock hid behind a rock.

Nothing happened. Jolly just burped softly, and said: 'Bit weak, and it's lacking a certain . . . unpleasantness.'

He handed the cup to the others, who each took a sip.

'I'm getting a hint of dead fish,' said Angry.

'Oh, definitely your dead fish,' said Jolly. 'No complaints on that front.'

'Is that petrol?' said Dozy.

'Diesel,' said Jolly. 'Subtle, but it's there.'

'Trusap,' said Mumbles.

The other three dwarfs stared at him.

'He's right, you know,' said Angry.

'Brilliant,' said Jolly. 'He has the tongue of a god, that boy.'

'I might be able to help,' said Dozy. He rummaged in his pockets and pulled out the core of an apple that was so old it practically qualified as an antique. He dropped it into the cup and swirled it around with his finger.

'Try it now,' he said, noticing that his finger was starting to burn, always a good sign when it came to Spiggit's.

Jolly did. For a moment he couldn't see anything at all, and his head felt as though a piano had been dropped on it from a great height. He teetered on his heels so that only the shelf of brewing equipment stopped him from falling over. Slowly his vision returned, and he found some stability.

'Wonderful,' he croaked. 'Just wonderful.'

Shan and Gath appeared at his shoulder.

'Just needed some rotten fruit,' explained Jolly. 'Apples are usually best, although I say that you can't beat a hint of strawberry. More rancid the better mind, but it's all a matter of personal taste.'

He handed the cup to Shan, who tried it and then passed it to Gath. They both winced, and reached out to support each other, then recovered.

'Hurh-hurh,' said Gath.

'Hurh-hurh,' said Shan.

And they held each other and laughed while the dwarfs looked on indulgently.

'It's that Spiggit's moment,' said Angry.

'That special moment,' said Dozy.

'That moment when you realize you're going to survive,' said Jolly. 'Probably. Magic, just magic.'

CHAPTER XXVII

In Which We Hear a Surprising Confession

Samuel, Nurd and Wormwood, with Boswell dozing beside them, sat at the mouth of the cave and watched the acid rain fall. It really was acid, too: it had corroded a coin that one of the dwarfs had dropped, and it left a faint smell of burning in the air after it splashed on the ground. They had managed to get the Aston Martin and the ice-cream van into shelter and Nurd had assured them all that they were safe for now. Nothing hunted or flew during the acid storms. Even demons didn't care much for unnecessary pain, or at least not self-inflicted unnecessary pain.

'What do we do when it stops?' asked Samuel. 'We can't hide for ever.'

'We know that there has to be a portal, and somehow Mrs Abernathy is in control of it,' said Nurd. 'If we find it then we can send you all back.'

A look of what might almost have been grief passed across Nurd's face, and was mirrored by Samuel. They were both thinking the same thing: after being separated and now, against all the odds, reunited, it just didn't seem right that they should be forced to part again so soon. Even though Samuel desperately wanted to return home, and Nurd wanted him to be in a place of safety, their fondness for each other meant that the ending for which they both wished was destined to cause them great unhappiness. All of this remained unspoken yet understood between them.

Strangely, Wormwood knew it too, for as his master and Samuel silently considered the fact that the best-case scenario would see them divided again by time and space and various dimensions, he coughed softly and said:

'I don't mean to be rude, but I'll be glad to see the backs of those dwarfs. They have the potential to be quite, um, troublesome.'

Samuel and Nurd recognized what Wormwood was trying to do, and were grateful to him.

'I don't think it's potential, Wormwood,' said Nurd. 'They are *actively* troublesome. They haven't been potential trouble since before they were born.'

At that moment the dwarfs were happily sharing Shan and Gath's new variation on Brew 19, helped by some frozen fruit salvaged from Dan's van. Dan, who was resigned to the fact that his ice-cream business was unlikely to recover in the current circumstances owing to the consumption of all his ice cream and most of his chocolate, had joined in the tasting, and was now a little tipsy. Even Constable Peel had consented to a 'small one', with Sergeant Rowan's permission, and the sergeant had found some unexpected common ground with Jolly, who had explained to him that the dwarfs' criminal behaviour was all society's fault. Sergeant

Rowan also believed this, mainly because society hadn't found a way to lock them up and throw away the key.

Angry, meanwhile, was demonstrating to Constable Peel the intricacies of pickpocketing, although this was less out of a desire to share hidden knowledge with the policeman than because Constable Peel had caught Angry trying to steal his handcuffs.

'I can't help it,' Angry was explaining in what might almost have been a sincere manner. 'I was just born this way. My mum says she brought me home from the hospital and found a stethoscope and two thermometers in my diaper. I can find a way to steal anything, me. It's a gift. Sort of.'

'I stole something once,' said Constable Peel suddenly.

Angry, along with Dozy and Mumbles, who had been listening to the conversation, looked taken aback.

'Really?' said Dozy.

Constable Peel nodded slowly. His cheeks burned with shame, and a little Brew 19 that had splashed on his skin and begun to irritate it.

'I was four,' he said. 'I was sitting next to Briony Andrews in kindergarten. We always got two biscuits at break, and I'd finished mine, but she had one left. So –'

Constable Peel covered his eyes with one hand and choked back a sob. Angry patted him on the back and tried not to laugh.

'Let it out,' he said. 'Confession is good for the soul.'

Somehow, Constable Peel found the strength to go on.

'So –'

'I can see where this is going,' said Dozy.

'Ungbit,' said Mumbles.

'Absolutely,' said Dozy. 'Briony Andrews is about to be one hundred per cent down in the biscuit department.'

'So –'

'Very tense this,' said Angry.

'I stole her biscuit!' concluded Constable Peel.

'No!' said Dozy, almost managing to sound surprised.

'Go on with you,' said Angry, not managing to sound surprised at all.

'Hardened criminal, you were,' said Jolly, joining in the fun. 'Stealing a little girl's biscuit? That's low, that is.'

'Devious,' said Dozy.

'Underhand,' said Angry.

'Sneaky,' said Jolly.

'I know, I know,' said Constable Peel. 'And it gets worse: I pretended she'd lost it. I even helped to organize the search party.'

'Oh, the hypocrisy!' said Angry, who actually thought that this did demonstrate a certain criminal cunning on the part of the juvenile Peel. It was almost admirable. He began to wonder if he might not have misjudged the policeman.

Constable Peel uncovered his face, revealing a fanatical gleam in his eye. 'But when I went home that day I vowed that never again would I engage in illegal activities, biscuit-based or otherwise. From that day on I was a policeman in spirit, and the law was my mistress.

I was Bob Peel, child lawman, and schoolyard wrong-doers trembled at my approach.'

There was silence as the dwarfs considered this before Jolly said sombrely:

'You must have been an absolute pain in the bum.'

Constable Peel stared at him. His chin trembled. His fists clenched. For a second, there was murder in the air.

'You know, I absolutely was,' said Constable Peel, and their laughter was so loud that dust from the cave roof fell in their beer, improving it slightly.

Back at the cave mouth, Wormwood nibbled on a wine gum as he, Nurd, and Samuel, joined by Sergeant Rowan, assessed their situation.

'The car has taken a beating,' said Wormwood. 'And the ice-cream van isn't going to last much longer. We're also nearly out of fuel, and it will take time to synthesize some more.'

'Is there any good news?' asked Nurd.

'We still have wine gums.'

'Will they power our car?'

'No.'

'Well, it's not really very good news then, is it?'

'No,' said Wormwood. 'Not really. Oh look, the rain's easing off.' He frowned. 'That's not good news either, is it?'

Nurd rubbed his eyes wearily. 'No, it's not.'

Soon the skies would once again be filled with eager, hostile eyes. Their enemies knew that they were in the area, and when the rain stopped they would begin to close in on them. They had no weapons, and little hope. There were days that just seemed to get harder and harder as they went on. Finding Samuel should have been a bright spot; after all, Nurd had spent so long wishing that he and his friend could be together again. Now that Samuel was here, Nurd just hoped to see him gone. Be careful what you wish for, he supposed; he hadn't wanted Samuel to be dragged to Hell just so that they could have another conversation. The dwarfs and Constable Peel appeared by his side, and together the little group gazed out as the rainfall grew gentler, and then ceased entirely.

'This is our chance,' Nurd told them all. 'It will stay dark and quiet for a while now that the rain has stopped. It's the way of things here. There'll be no lightning, and we can make some progress without being seen.'

'And the plan is that we find this woman, or demon, or whatever she is, and make her send us home?' said Angry.

'Or you find her, she tears you apart, and you don't have to worry about getting home any more,' said Nurd. 'It depends, really.'

'On what?'

'On how fast you can run once she spots you.'

'That doesn't sound like much of a plan,' said Jolly. 'And we've only got little legs. We're not really built for speed.'

'That's unfortunate,' said Nurd. 'Speed always helps on these occasions.'

'Doesn't look like you're much of a runner either,' said Angry. 'Big boots, bit of a belly. You're going to have trouble outrunning this Mrs Abernathy too, if she's chasing us.'

'But I don't have to outrun her,' said Nurd reasonably. 'I just have to outrun you . . .'

CHAPTER XXVIII

In Which Everything Goes Horribly Wrong

Preparations began for their departure while Samuel watched the clouds swirl. They moved less violently than before, as though worn out by their earlier efforts, the faces less visible now. There was a faint yellow glow to the sky and although the landscape before him was not beautiful, it was at a kind of peace. The rocky hillside descended to more muddy bogs, across which stretched a stone causeway. As before, a stinking, heavy mist hung over the bogs, and Samuel felt sure that it would hide them from any watchful eyes above as they drove.

He thought about his mother. She would be worried about him. He had lost all track of time since he had arrived in this place, but at least a day and a night had gone by, and perhaps more. Then again, time was different here. He wasn't even sure that there was time, not really. He supposed that, if eternity stretched before you, then minutes and hours and days would cease to have any meaning. But they had meaning for him: they represented moments spent separated from those whom he loved: from his mother, his friends, even his dad. Nurd was here, though, which was something.

Beside him, Boswell gave a little yip and got to his feet. He sniffed the air. His ears twitched, and he looked troubled.

'What is it, Boswell?' asked Samuel, as a shadow fell upon him, and the Watcher clasped a hand over Samuel's mouth so that he could not cry out, and pulled him into the air with a great flapping of his wings. By the time Nurd and the others grasped what was happening, Samuel was already disappearing into low clouds, clasped tightly in the Watcher's arms. Boswell ran down the hillside after them, barking and leaping up on his stubby back legs as though he might yet haul the massive red creature down.

But Samuel was gone, and it was left to Nurd to run to the little dog and hold him lest he get lost, or eaten, Boswell struggling all the time, desperate to follow Samuel, desperate to save him.

A craggy peak rose in the distance. Nurd thought that he saw a figure there, perched on the back of a basilisk. It was looking back at him, and he heard Mrs Abernathy's voice as clearly as if she were standing next to him:

'*I will come for you, Nurd. I have not forgotten your meddling. For now, it is enough punishment for you to know that I have your friend, and I will sacrifice him to my Master. And then it will be your turn.*'

But Nurd did not care about her threats, or about himself. He cared only for Samuel, and how he might be rescued.

* * *

The Watcher flew high. It held Samuel, and Samuel held it, for Samuel feared falling more than he feared the creature holding him. Its skin smelled of sulphur and ash, and was pitted with the scars of deep, long-healed wounds. Samuel felt the creature's consciousness probing at his own, trying to learn about him, exploring his strengths and his weaknesses. But as it tested him, so too it exposed something of itself, and Samuel was shocked by the strangeness of it, and he understood that even by the standards of Hell itself this was a peculiar, solitary being, one entirely unlike him but also unlike any other entity in that place.

No, not quite. It was allied to another, to—

For an instant, Samuel glimpsed the Great Malevolence, and had his first real inkling of the depths of the First Demon's evil, and wretchedness, and madness. It was so awful that Samuel's mind immediately put up a series of blockades to protect his sanity, which had the effect of closing out the Watcher. The rhythm of the creature's flight was momentarily interrupted, as though it were shocked at the strength of the boy's will. It gripped him tighter as a consequence, clasping him against its shoulder so that Samuel was looking back in the direction that they had come, back towards the hills still visible through wisps of cloud, and towards Boswell and Nurd, who were lost from sight.

A pale, emaciated figure broke through the clouds from above, its ribs clearly visible beneath its skin, its belly sunken. Its head was bald, its ears were long and pointed, and it had too many teeth for its mouth, so that they jutted forth from between its lips, snaggled and broken. It paused in mid-air, seemingly surprised to have come across them, then altered its position and began its pursuit. It was a wraith, a batlike demon little taller than Samuel himself. Its wings were attached to its arms, ending in sharp, hooked claws, and it had talons for feet. These talons it now stuck out, poised to strike like a falcon descending on its prey.

Samuel beat on the Watcher's back, and managed to cry out a warning. Instinctively the Watcher turned to its right, and the smaller creature's talons missed them by inches, one of its wings slapping against Samuel's face as it flew by. The Watcher shifted Samuel so that he was held only beneath its left arm, and Samuel felt sure that he would fall. He dug his nails into the Watcher's hard skin, and wrapped his legs tightly around its waist.

The wraith came at them again, this time from below, screaming over and over, summoning others like it to the chase. The Watcher struck out at it with a flick of its right arm, and its nails tore a hole in the attacker's belly. No blood came, but the wraith's wings stopped flapping and it spiralled through the clouds to the ground far below like a fighter plane crippled by gunfire, crying in agony as it fell.

Two more appeared, drawn by the shrieks of their brother. They dived together. One aimed blows at the Watcher's head, distracting it while the second tried to pull Samuel from his grasp, but the Watcher held on tightly. His free hand grabbed the wraith that was scratching at his eyes and broke its neck before discarding it. The second it almost decapitated with a swipe of its hand, leaving the head hanging from a fold of skin, and with that the attack was over, and they were alone in the skies once more. Samuel closed his eyes as they flew on, so that neither he nor the Watcher saw a final wraith that shadowed them for a time from above before it slipped away to report to Duke Abigor all that it had seen.

CHAPTER XXIX

In Which Various Dangerous Personages Put Their Plans In Motion

Mrs Abernathy's basilisk pounded across the warm stones, lost in the clouds of steam that had arisen in the aftermath of the recent showers. There was an acrid smell in the air, the stink of flesh and wood and vegetation corroded and burned by the falling acid, yet already what passed for life in that place was recovering. Clumps of brown seared weeds became slightly less brown; stunted bushes, blackened and smoking, reassumed their usual dull hue; and assorted small demons who had not been quick enough to escape the downpour began growing back arms, legs, toes, and heads. Some of them even grew an extra limb or two while they were about it, just in case an additional appendage proved useful in future. From holes in the ground and through gaps in the bushes they watched Mrs Abernathy pass, and they saw that her face was alive with triumph, and her eyes shone a deep, cold blue. Not all of them knew who she was, for there were parts of Hell where the Great Malevolence was little more than a rumoured presence hidden deep in his mountain fastness, and his dukes and generals and legions could have been figures from old fables for all the impact they had on the existence of these primitive entities. Yet they sensed that this curious figure was immensely powerful, and should probably be avoided if at all possible.

And then she was gone and they instantly forgot about her, for they had more immediate concerns such as when it might rain acid again, and what to do with that extra head they'd just grown.

Mrs Abernathy didn't even notice the movement around her. She sensed the conflict in which the Watcher was engaged far above her head, but she had never been less than certain of its capacity to annihilate any enemy that came within its reach. There had been a moment when she feared the Watcher might drop Samuel Johnson, an eventuality that might have put paid to her hopes of returning to the Great Malevolence's favour. After all, there wouldn't have been much to show of the boy if he'd been dropped from thousands of feet on to hard rock. True, his consciousness would have survived, but she wasn't certain that she could reconstitute a human as easily as a demon, and a mulch of messy blood, bits of bone, and fragments of tissue lacked a certain immediate identifiability. She could, she supposed, have scraped him into a jar, stuck a label on it reading 'Samuel Johnson (Most of Him)', and presented it to the Great Malevolence, but it wouldn't have had quite the same impact as delivering the boy, weeping yet intact, to her Master, and sharing in his revenge on the troublesome little human.

But even as Mrs Abernathy pictured in her mind the details of Samuel Johnson's impending humiliation, she remained troubled by the intervention of Duke Abigor. Abigor had always resented her position, but she was surprised by how quickly he had moved against her following the failure of the invasion. Some of those who had allied themselves to him, Dukes Guares and Borym among them, had once been her allies, and their betrayal stung her. For a moment she entertained herself by running through lists of the various agonies she would order to be visited upon them once she stood again at her Master's left hand, then pushed such pleasant images away, clearing her mind entirely so that she could concentrate on more important matters.

Abigor was risking a great deal by working against her: although she had been banished from the Great Malevolence's presence, no sentence had been passed upon her and she was still, theoretically at least, commander of his armies. Thus Abigor was technically guilty of treason, although she might have difficulty proving it should the necessity arise for as yet Abigor had done nothing directly to undermine her position.

Yet if he had laid hands on Samuel Johnson, what would he have done with him? He could have presented him as a gift to the Great Malevolence, just as Mrs Abernathy planned to do, but he would have experienced some difficulty in explaining how he had managed to drag his captive to Hell. No, Abigor was playing a different game here, the dimensions of which Mrs Abernathy was only beginning to grasp. The Chancellor, Ozymuth, was on Abigor's side, and Ozymuth, if the oozing Crudford was to be believed, was intent upon undermining the Great Malevolence by prolonging, and deepening, his grief. It hardly seemed possible, but Abigor was not interested merely in supplanting Mrs Abernathy. No, he wanted to take the place of the Great Malevolence himself, to become the ruler of Hell in place of its maddened king. And having already enlisted many of the dukes in his scheme, even if they were not yet aware of the full extent of it, he had no choice but to see it through to its end. If he were to abandon it now, and the Great Malevolence were to recover his wits and discover even some small element of the plot – as he most assuredly would, for if Mrs Abernathy did not tell him others involved would, if only in the hope of saving themselves from punishment – then Abigor and his co-conspirators could expect to end up frozen for eternity in the lake of Cocytus, if they were lucky and the Great Malevolence proved to be unexpectedly merciful. Abigor had gone too far to turn back now, and so he would have to gamble everything on the Great Malevolence's ongoing madness and the defeat of Mrs Abernathy. Both were linked to Samuel Johnson, for the sight of his enemy presented to him in chains might well bring the Great Malevolence back to his senses, and Abigor's plans would come to naught. But if Samuel Johnson were to be kept from him, then his mourning and lunacy would continue, and Mrs Abernathy would be doomed.

This was a delicate time. The boy was her captive, and she had to keep him safe from Abigor until she could bring him to the Mountain of Despair. The attack on the Watcher by Abigor's wraiths was just the beginning. Worse would follow.

As if to confirm her suspicions, the ground before her cracked and a wretched beast, yellow, eyeless and quivering, emerged from a hole. It was a Burrower, its lower half segmented like a worm's, its upper half that of a man, with a face resembling that of a rat or a vole. It had the legs of a millipede, except at its fore and rear parts where powerful webbed claws emerged from its body. It dwelt in the earth, only venturing entirely above ground when absolutely necessary, and formed a collective consciousness with its fellows, so that knowledge gleaned by one was shared by all. Although blind, Burrowers could identify the presence of other beings above ground by the vibrations of their footfalls, aided by their excellent sense of taste and smell. Such gifts made them useful spies, and they were loyal to Mrs Abernathy, for she would sometimes hand over her enemies to them, and they would drag the unfortunate creatures underground and feast on them.

'Mistress, we bring news,' the Burrower said. 'There are legions gathering. We hear whispers. They speak of a boy. They intend to besiege your lair, and take him from you. You are to be punished for plotting against the Great Malevolence.'

'Punished?' said Mrs Abernathy. She could barely believe the impudence of her enemies.

'Yes, Mistress. You were tried in your absence by a panel of judges appointed by Duke Abigor, and by unanimous decision found guilty of treason. It is said that you opened a portal between this world and the world of men in the hope of securing the Earth for yourself and creating a kingdom there in opposition to this Kingdom of Fire. You are to be apprehended, and taken to the farthest, deepest reaches of Lake Cocytus, where a place has been prepared for you in the ice.'

Mrs Abernathy was shaken. They had moved so fast against her.

'How much time do I have?' she asked.

'Little, Mistress. Although the forces that oppose you have not yet gathered in full at their place of rendezvous upon the Plains of Desolation, four legions have been sent ahead to secure your palace.'

'Whose legions?'

'Two legions each of Dukes Borym and Peros.'

'And what of my allies?'

'They await your command.'

'Instruct them to gather in the shadow of the Forlorn Hills. Send word to those of the dukes who remain uncommitted. Tell them that the boy is in my power, and the time has come for them to choose sides. Loyalty will be rewarded many times over. Betrayal will never be forgiven.'

'Yes, Mistress. And what of the legions that approach your lair?'

Mrs Abernathy thought for a moment.

'Drag them down, and consume them,' she said.

She spurred on her basilisk and it sprang away, leaving the Burrower licking its lips in anticipation of fresh meat.

CHAPTER XXX

In Which the Watcher Is Torn

Duke Abigor's wraith followed the Watcher's progress until it was almost within sight of Mrs Abernathy's palace, then banked away to report back to its master. But the Watcher had known of its presence all along, and as soon as it sensed that the spy had departed it changed course, using the clouds to hide itself as it made its way to a plateau on the Forlorn Hills. There it laid Samuel upon the ground, and placed a foot lightly on his chest so that the boy could not escape. From its perch, it stared down as Mrs Abernathy's army began to assemble itself below. Demons burst forth from the earth and emerged from caves. They descended from clouds and crawled from dank black pools. They formed themselves from ash, and sand, and snow, from molecules of water and the unseen atoms in the air. Horned beings, winged beings, finned beings; beings familiar, and beings shapeless; beings of fire and rock, and beings of water and ice; beings of tooth and claw, and beings of mind and energy: all had flocked to Mrs Abernathy's call.

Some had come out of loyalty, some out of fear, and

some simply because they were bored, and gambling on the outcome of a battle, even at the possible cost of future pain if they were defeated, at least broke the tedium of damnation. Lightning flashed, illuminating spearheads, and serrated knife edges, and thousands of bladed weapons. The Watcher moved its gaze to the right. In the distance, fiery hooves struck sparks from the ground, and booted feet marched in unison, metal clanking as the first legions of those dukes who had chosen to support Mrs Abernathy marched to her aid.

The Watcher allowed its consciousness to rove still further. It saw the four legions of Duscias and Peros moving purposefully across a cracked plain where once before, long ago even in its conception of time, a great lake of poisonous water had stood, fed by vile rivers that flowed from the surrounding peaks. The Great Malevolence had redirected the rivers to form the Lake of Cocytus, and in time the plain had dried up entirely. Now only dust flowed across it before falling into narrow crevasses that led deep into the ground below.

The four legions picked their way carefully across the treacherous landscape. They marched on foot, rank upon rank of demons, each heavily armoured and each carrying in his hand a pike topped by a thin, hard blade around which curled a second length of metal shaped like a corkscrew, the weapon designed to be thrust into the belly of an enemy, twisted, and then pulled out, dragging with it the internal organs and leaving the wretched victim in agony upon the ground, for even a demon will struggle to recover itself quickly after such a terrible injury. Short stabbing swords hung at their sides, and their gloves, their helmets, even the plates of their black armour were embedded with spikes, so that the armour itself was a weapon.

By the sides of the legions, mounted on skinless horses, their flesh raw and glistening, their muscles lean, rode the captains and lieutenants, their armour more ornate, their weapons bejewelled but no less capable of inflicting grave wounds. Banners waved in the cold wind, red and gold and green, the colours of the Houses of Peros and Borym, but above them all flew a single great standard, depicting a hand of fire against a sable background. This was the banner of the House of Abigor. There was no sign of Hell's own banner, the horned head of the Great Malevolence, the symbol of his armies. The dukes had made their loyalties public and were no longer primarily serving the Great Malevolence, but the demon who wished to succeed him.

It was the horses, their eyes and mouths lit red by the fires within, that first sensed the approach of an unknown threat. They whinnied and neighed, then rose up on their hind legs, almost unseating their riders. Confusion rippled through the ranks as Ronwe, a minor demon who had allied his nineteen legions with Borym and was now the second-in-command of all his forces, turned to shout an order, an order that was destined never to be heard as the ground opened up and swallowed both Ronwe and his steed. The crevasse before the front rank widened, forcing it to halt. Stinking green gases emerged from the revealed pit and the ground at the edges began to crumble, taking two dozen legionnaires with it into the depths. Those who had witnessed what had occurred, and who were thus aware of the danger, tried to retreat, but they were hemmed in by the ranks advancing from behind, and more tumbled down. Captains called out orders, attempting to halt the advance and permit the front ranks to fall back, but their horses were trying to throw them, and the troops were starting to panic, and the ground continued to crack and break, marooning whole cohorts of legionnaires on islands of dry earth that themselves began to crumble.

And then the creatures from below commenced their attack. Massive tentacles, ridged along their length with sticky, poisonous barbs, shot from the pits, dragging demon soldiers into the darkness. Giant red insects, their jaws capable of swallowing a man's head whole, poured forth, their palps twitching, their mouthpieces snapping. The arms of the troops were not strong enough to pierce their carapaces, nor was their armour capable of withstanding the force of the insects' bites. Worms long hidden beneath the earth opened their jaws, and what had once seemed solid ground became a trap filled with teeth, and feet were severed from legs, and heads from bodies.

But some of Duke Peros's finest soldiers had found solid ground at the edge of the lake bed, and were working their way carefully around the killing field, keeping their enemies at bay as best they could by discipline and force of will. They were halfway around the circumference, from which the surrounding hills rose precipitously like the sides of a volcano, when earth began to fall on their heads from above, revealing neat, round holes in the dusty soil, and webbed claws started to pull at their feet and arms and necks, and the Burrowers began to bite.

And the lake bed, long dry, ran red and black with the blood of demons.

The Watcher, distant yet aware, saw it all. This conflict threatened to tear Hell itself apart, but the Watcher remained uncertain of how to proceed, for the sound of the Great Malevolence's wailing still carried to it, and it seemed that the cries would never stop. If a king is mad, then what are his subjects to do?[38] Without the fear that the Great Malevolence inspired, it was inevitable that his subordinates would begin to fight among themselves, jockeying for power and position. But the threat posed by Abigor was greater than mere disorder, for Abigor was now in open rebellion against his lord.

The mass of demons below continued to swell as more and more of Hell's denizens flocked to Mrs

---

[38] For the most part, subjects just have to put up with them until someone kills the king in question. For example, the Roman emperor Caligula (12–41A.D.), who is said to have tried to make his horse, Incitatus, a consul of Rome, was stabbed thirty times. Eric XIV of Sweden (1533–77) was poisoned by pea soup laced with arsenic. Madness is something of a perennial problem when it comes to royalty, as a considerable number of kings have been distinctly suspect on the sanity front. Lesser known royal lunatics include Charles VI of France (1368–1422), also known as Charles the Mad – but not to his face – who believed himself to be made of glass and had iron rods placed in his clothing to prevent him from breaking, and once refused to bathe or change his clothes for five months. Meanwhile, Robert of Clermont (1256–1318), younger son of Louis IX of France, went mad after being hit on the head several times with a sledgehammer in the course of a joust, but then being hit on the head with a sledgehammer will do that to a person.

Abernathy's banner. Grand Duke Aym arrived with his twenty-six legions; Ayperos, Prince of Hell, with thirty-six; and Azazel, the standard-bearer of Hell's armies, took up a position on a great rock and unfurled the flag of the Great Malevolence.

Samuel twisted beneath the Watcher's feet, gazing out at the gathering forces with a mix of terror and amazement. The Watcher regarded him closely, its eight black eyes like dark planets set against the red sky of his skin. Even though the winged demon was more awful than any of the creatures assembled below, Samuel still found the courage to stare back at it in defiance.

'What are you waiting for?' said Samuel. 'Do whatever you're planning, and get it over with.'

He heard a voice speak in his head, and although the Watcher's insectlike jaws did not move, Samuel knew that he was hearing the demon's voice.

We wait.

'Wait for whom?' Even in this time of great peril, Samuel Johnson's grammar remained intact.

For Mrs Abernathy.

Samuel felt much of the courage he had mustered leach away. His body deflated, and all his strength threatened to leave him. He had been foolish to think he could escape her wrath, foolish to think Nurd could save him. He had been doomed ever since that first evening when he had watched as Mrs Abernathy and her loathsome companions had emerged from their world into his through a hole in an otherwise ordinary basement.

All of this, for you, said the Watcher, with what seemed like wonder in its voice. *All of this, because of a boy.*

'I didn't start it,' said Samuel. 'I didn't make Mrs Abernathy kill anyone. I didn't ask for her to invade the Earth. I just wanted to go trick-or-treating.'

But now look. Armies are mustering. Old loyalties have fallen apart, and new loyalties have been forged. Old enmities are forgotten, and new enmities are formed. And all the time, my master weeps. The bells must peal. There is no other choice.

'Your master?' said Samuel, picking up on something in the demon's tone that might almost have been love, but love so twisted and misguided that it was almost unrecognizable as itself. 'But don't you work for Mrs Abernathy? And what bells are you talking about?'

The Watcher did not reply, and Samuel, remembering his brief glimpse of the reality of the Great Malevolence, knew that the demon's loyalties were confused.

'So you work for the Devil, *and* for Mrs Abernathy?'

Yes. No. Maybe.

'You should probably make your mind up.'

Probably.

'I wondered what all that wailing was about,' said Samuel. 'You're telling me that it's the Great Malevolence, crying?'

Yes.

'Why?'

Because, after all this time, he came close to escaping his prison. After all this time, he had hope, and then the hope was gone, and he hates himself for giving in to hope. He, who exists only to kill the hopes of others, could not destroy the hope within himself. He is lost to his madness, and so he weeps.

'Can't say I'm sorry,' said Samuel, and thought to himself, the big crybaby. The Watcher's head tilted slightly, and Samuel was afraid the demon might have picked up on what he was thinking, but if it did, it gave no further sign.

'So why did those other demons attack us in the clouds?'

They are loyal to Duke Abigor. He does not want Mrs Abernathy to have you.

'Why not?'

Because she is going to hand you over to the Great Malevolence, and thus restore him to sanity, and herself to his favour, and he will forgive her for the failure of the invasion, and he will revenge himself upon you instead. But if Duke Abigor can prevent that, he will take Mrs Abernathy's place. He will take—

The Watcher broke off, unwilling to express its worst fear.

'Would Duke Abigor send me home, if he had me?' said Samuel hopefully.

No. Duke Abigor would keep you in utter darkness, and there you would stay for ever, for Death has no dominion here.

'Oh,' said Samuel.

Yes, 'Oh.'

'And what about you? What do you want?'

I want my Master to stop weeping. That is why I will let Mrs Abernathy hand you over to him.

And Samuel's hopes began to fade.

CHAPTER XXXI

In Which We Learn a Little of the Responsibilities of Command, and the Perils of Being Commanded

Duke Abigor slammed a mailed fist into the table of bones, which shattered under the impact, causing a number of the skulls to complain loudly about vandalism, and demons these days having no respect for antiques, and bones not growing on trees, and suchlike. Abigor lifted one of the dislodged skulls, which continued to chatter until it seemed to realize that its fortunes had suddenly taken a turn for the worse, something that, until recently, had seemed virtually impossible, given that it was a skull stuck in a table without much hope of advancement.

'My mistake,' said the skull. 'Don't worry about the damage.'

Abigor increased his grip, giving the skull just enough time to say, 'Gently, now –' before it was crushed to dust.

Abigor was dressed in his finest battle armour, its surface decorated with images of serpents that slithered over the metal and were, when required, capable of rising up and striking at an enemy. His blood-red cloak billowed angrily behind him, responding to the changes in its wearer's temperament.

'Four legions!' shouted Duke Abigor. 'We lost four legions!'

Before him, Dukes Peros and Borym blanched. They were soft, fat demons, conniving and ambitious, yet lacking the ruthlessness and drive that might have made them great. Peros looked like a vaguely ducal candle that had been placed too close to heat: his face appeared to have melted, so that his skin hung in hard folds over his skull, and any features that might once have resembled ears, a nose, cheekbones, and suchlike, had all been lost, leaving only a pair of green eyes sunk deep in the putty of his flesh. Borym's face, meanwhile, was almost entirely lost beneath a massive brown beard, bushy eyebrows, and hair so unruly that it fought back against any attempt to cut it, as a number of Hell's barbers had learned to their cost. Somewhere in Borym's mass of curls were four pairs of scissors, any number of combs, and a couple of very small imps who had been sent in to retrieve these items and become hopelessly lost.

The dukes' armour was even more ornate than Abigor's, but far less practical, for Peros and Borym were of the school of military command that believed ordinary soldiers, not dukes, should fight battles. Dukes claimed the victory, and divided the spoils; soldiers could relish the glory of war, and later raise a drink to their exploits on the field, assuming their hands were still sufficiently attached to their arms to enable them to raise anything more than a stump. So, whereas Abigor's armour, although beautiful, bore the marks of conflicts endured, the suits of Peros and Borym were decorated with feathers, ribbons, unearned medals, and carvings that depicted much slimmer versions of Peros and Borym vanquishing assorted enemies in unlikely ways, and therefore were barely on nodding terms with reality.

'My lord,' said Borym, who was smart enough to see trouble brewing, but not smart enough to avoid sipping from the resulting cup, 'we were only following your orders. It was you who advised us to cross the Lake of Dry Tears in an effort to take Mrs Abernathy by surprise.'

Abigor brushed his hands together, removing the last vestiges of the bone from his gloves. On the stones below, the dust and fragments began to move, flowing across the floor and gradually reassuming the shape of a skull.

'Ow,' said the skull.

'Are you suggesting that it was my fault?' asked Abigor softly.

'No, not at—' the skull began to say, before Abigor's metal boot stamped upon it, shattering it to pieces again.

'Of course not, my lord,' said Borym. 'I meant no such impertinence.'

'So whose fault was it, then?'

'Mine, my lord,' said Borym, in a vain attempt to rescue an already doomed situation.

'And mine,' said Peros, who was too stupid to keep his mouth shut.

'It is noble of you both to accept responsibility for your failure,' said Abigor.

He clicked his fingers and eight members of his personal guard, demons of smoke contained in suits of black steel trimmed with gold, their red eyes the only indication of the life within, surrounded the dukes.

'Cast them into the dungeons,' said Abigor. 'Then throw away the keys. With considerable force.'

Borym and Peros did not even try to protest as they were escorted from the room. Abigor clasped his hands behind his back and closed his eyes. Above him rose a vaulted ceiling like that of a cathedral. Waves of flame moved across it, blending with the fires that rose from slits in the floor and covered the walls in sheets of white and yellow, so that the whole room seemed to be afire. This was the heart of Abigor's residence, the innermost chamber of his great palace. Next to it Mrs Abernathy's lair was almost humble, but Abigor had always believed that nothing impresses quite like vulgar displays of wealth and power.

He should not have entrusted Borym and Peros with the task of surprising Mrs Abernathy and trying to secure the boy's capture. They were imbeciles who would have been hard pressed to catch a cold. Abigor's difficulty was that he had surrounded himself with traitorous dukes. Had he despatched one of his cleverer allies, such as Duke Guares, to attack Mrs Abernathy, then it was possible that Guares might either have forged a separate alliance with her, betraying Abigor, or tried to take the boy for himself. At least Abigor had no concerns about the loyalty of Borym and Peros, only their competence. Nevertheless, Abigor had enough self-knowledge to grasp that the loss of the four legions was, in part, his own fault, although he wasn't about to admit that to anyone else. When leaders started admitting their failings, their followers tended to seek alternative leaders with fewer failings, or less honesty.

A panel in the eastern wall of the chamber opened, and Chancellor Ozymuth stepped through the gap. Abigor did not turn around to acknowledge his presence, but merely said, 'Have you come to criticize me as well, Ozymuth?'

'No, my lord,' said Ozymuth. 'I was listening as you dealt with your fellow dukes, and have no desire to keep them company in their new quarters.'

'Your instincts for self-preservation are as finely honed as ever,' said Abigor. 'Still, Mrs Abernathy is cleverer than I thought and not all of her allies have deserted her.'

'She is a worthy adversary.'

'You sound almost as if you respect her.'

'It is as well to respect one's enemies, but I do not respect her as much as I respect you, my lord.'

Abigor laughed, but there was no mirth to it.

'You have a serpent's tongue, Ozymuth. I trust not one word that falls from it. What news of the boy?'

'He is with the Watcher. They await the return of Mrs Abernathy.'

'And where is she?'

'I was hoping that you might know, my lord.'

'She has avoided my spies, or it may be that my spies have been apprehended, for I have heard no word from any of them.'

Ozymuth shifted uneasily. He had to pose the question that was on his lips, but he risked angering Abigor by doing so.

'My lord, forgive me for asking, but you are still in control of the situation, are you not?'

Ozymuth tensed. Behind him the door in the wall remained open, and he was poised to flee through it and lose himself in the labyrinthine passageways connecting Abigor's palace to the Mountain of Despair should the duke turn on him, but instead Abigor gave the question some consideration.

'As long as the boy has not yet been handed over to the Great Malevolence, then victory remains within my grasp. Dukes Aym and Ayperos have remained loyal to Mrs Abernathy, as have some of the counts, but we outnumber their legions two to one. They have no hope against us on the field of battle, should it come to that.'

'An army is gathering at the foot of the Forlorn Hills,' said Ozymuth. 'Demons are heeding Mrs Abernathy's call to her banner.'

'They are of the lower orders,' said Abigor. 'They are untrained, and undisciplined.'

'Yet they are many.'

For a moment, Abigor looked troubled. 'What will she do, Ozymuth?'

'She will assemble her army to protect the boy, then march on the Mountain of Despair with her prize.'

'So we must ensure that she does not reach it. Go, Ozymuth: continue to whisper your poison into the ear of the old lord. Keep him mad. When I rule Hell, I will make sure he is well looked after.'

Ozymuth bowed low and left the room, the chamber door closing silently behind him. When he was gone,

Abigor clicked his fingers once again, and the captain of his guard entered.

'Inform the dukes that they are to gather their forces before the entrance to the Mountain of Despair,' said Abigor. 'Tell them to prepare for battle!'

CHAPTER XXXII

In Which Samuel and Mrs Abernathy
Meet Again, Which Only Delights
Fifty Per Cent of Those Involved

Mrs Abernathy's basilisk was chained to a post, its scaly skin covered in saliva, its eyes glazed with exhaustion. Mrs Abernathy had ridden it hard and they had encountered a number of obstacles along the way, although Mrs Abernathy had dealt with them admirably. Those obstacles had included five of Duke Abigor's spies, whose heads now hung from the basilisk's saddle, the heads still arguing among themselves about which of them was most to blame for their misfortune. Mrs Abernathy paid them no heed. Her attention was focused on the boy who sat at the base of a large gilded cage not far from the door to Mrs Abernathy's small but perfectly formed palace.

Samuel watched her carefully through his glasses, one lens of which had cracked as he struggled vainly to escape the Watcher's grip when it became clear that Mrs Abernathy's arrival was imminent. Now, face to face with the woman who hated him more than any other creature in the Multiverse, he found himself examining her closely in the hope that some weakness might reveal itself. To be honest, Mrs Abernathy didn't look at all well. Some of the stitches keeping her face together had come loose, exposing a little of the reality of the monstrous form beneath, and her skin was discoloured, marked with patches of green like mould on bread. Her clothing was filthy and torn, her hair matted and dishevelled. As she circled Samuel she nibbled at one of her fingernails, and seemed surprised when it fell off.

'How are you, Samuel?' said Mrs Abernathy at last.

'I could be better,' said Samuel. 'After all, I'm in Hell. With you.'

'It's your own fault. I warned you against meddling in my affairs back on Earth.'

'I didn't have any choice but to meddle in them. You sent demons to kill me.'

'And very unsatisfactory they were too, given that they failed. It's so hard to get good staff these days. That's why I took it upon myself to drag you to Hell and, lo and behold, here you are. If I'd taken the time to kill you myself back in Biddlecombe, think of all the trouble I'd have avoided. Your home would be a place of ash and fire by now.'

'Well, sorry it didn't work out for you,' said Samuel.

'Don't be sarcastic, Samuel. It's a very low form of wit.[39] You know, now that I have you, you seem so much less worthy of the pursuit. I've spent all this time raging against you, planning the horrors I would inflict upon you, and it made me forget that you're really only

---

💀 [39] The people who say that sarcasm is low wit are usually the ones who keep getting caught out by other people being sarcastic at their expense. Sarcasm is the lowest form of wit? Oh, you don't say . . .

a little boy, a little boy who got lucky for a while, and whose luck has now run out. Yet such trouble you've caused me, and so much distress and humiliation.'

'Is that why you're falling apart?'

Mrs Abernathy examined the index finger that had just lost its nail.

'Yes, in a way,' she said. 'Cut off from my master, I am like a tree without sunlight, a flower without water, a kitten without milk, a—'

She stopped talking when she sensed that the examples she was using were hardly appropriate for an arch-demon of Hell. Flowers? Kittens? She was sicker than she thought . . .

She stretched out a hand in the direction of the vast army of demons that had assembled, awaiting her command.

'You're the cause of all this,' she said. 'Armies are marching because of you. Demon stands against demon, duke against duke. I have ordered the annihilation of four legions in order to keep you safe. Hell has never seen such conflict, such turmoil. And all because of a little boy who couldn't keep his nose out of the business of others, and a demon who believed that he could escape my wrath in a fast car.'

At this, Samuel could not hide his shock.

'Oh, that's got your attention, hasn't it?' said Mrs Abernathy gloatingly. 'You thought I didn't know about your friend Nurd, the so-called Scourge of Five Deities?'

'He doesn't call himself that any longer,' said Samuel. 'It's just Nurd. Unlike you, he doesn't have any delusions of grandeur.' Samuel had heard his mother use that phrase about Mrs Browburthy, who was the chairperson of practically every committee in Biddlecombe and ruled them all like a dictator. He was rather pleased that he'd found an opportunity to use it now.

'Delusions?' said Mrs Abernathy. 'No, I have no delusions. I was great once, and then I was humbled, but I will be great again, mark me, and you will be the gift that restores me to my rightful place. As for Nurd, I will hunt him down when I have handed you over to my master. He will be tortured, just as you will be, but the greatest torment that I can devise will be to ensure that you and he never set eyes on each other again. You will have eternity to miss him, and he you, assuming you can find time for such fine feelings amid your own sufferings.'

She leaned in close to the bars and whispered to Samuel: 'And you can't even begin to imagine what I'm going to do to your rotten little dog, but I'll make sure that you can hear his howls of misery from wherever you are.'

Mrs Abernathy turned her back on Samuel and walked to the edge of the cliff that overlooked her army. She raised her right hand, and opened her mouth.

'Heed me!' she cried. The demons assembled below grew silent and gave her their attention. 'We are close to the moment of our triumph. The boy, Samuel, who foiled our invasion of Earth, who ensured that we would continue to suffer in this place, is in my grasp. We will take him to our master, the Great Malevolence, and we will offer the boy to him like a juicy fly to a spider. Our Dark Lord will arise from his grief, and all who were loyal to me will be rewarded, and all those who took arms against me and, in doing so, betrayed our master, will be punished for ever.'

A great cheer rose from the demons, and blades and claws and teeth flashed.

'But first our foes must be vanquished,' Mrs Abernathy continued. 'Already they gather before the entrance to the Mountain of Despair, intent upon instituting a new order in Hell, as if their ambitions can ever compare to the purity of our master's evil. They are led by the traitor Abigor, and great will be his suffering when victory is achieved. Now, look upon our prize!'

The Watcher ascended, and its claws grasped the ring at the top of the cage. The gilded prison rose into the air before suddenly Samuel was falling fast as the Watcher descended over the lines of demons, tens of thousands strong, all screaming their hatred at him as the cage flew barely inches above their heads, their spears and knives and sharp claws aimed at him as though hoping that they might save the Great Malevolence the trouble of ripping him apart. Samuel saw demons mounted on dragons and serpents, on toads and spiders and living fossils. He saw battle machines: catapults, and cannon, and great spiked wagons. He saw, amid the chaos of the lesser demons, the massed, ordered ranks of the legions, their loyalties distinguished by the banners of each duke, although those banners always flew lower than the standards depicting a horned figure set against a black background.

At last Samuel was lowered on to a flat wagon, where

Mrs Abernathy was already waiting for him. She ordered a black cloth to be placed over the cage, 'a taste of the greater blackness to come', and Samuel's last sight as the cloth fell was of Mrs Abernathy's triumphant, grinning visage.

The Watcher resumed its perch above the gathering. It saw the legions take the head of a column that began to snake toward the Mountain of Despair, the untrained masses falling loosely into place behind the troops. A fresh mount had been found for Mrs Abernathy, a massive hybrid of horse and serpent, its snake head snapping at its bridle, upon which she sat sidesaddle at the head of her army. She had even donned a new dress for the occasion, a little blue number with a lace collar. The wagon bearing the covered cage was surrounded by a phalanx of legionnaires who had been gifted to Mrs Abernathy by the allied dukes, and now bore a new coat of arms: a lady's handbag, decorated with a yellow daisy.

Curious, thought the Watcher. Appropriate, but ... curious.

CHAPTER XXXIII

In Which a Third Force Intervenes
in the Conflict

The wagon rumbled beneath Samuel, tossing him from side to side as its rough-hewn wheels passed over the uneven ground. The repeated impacts against the cage were bruising his body, so he tried to hold on tight to the bars to prevent himself from being injured further. The cloth that covered the cage was quite thick, although Samuel's silhouette was still visible to those outside when lightning flashed, and he could just make out a tiny sliver of landscape visible through a hole in the material. When the wagon at last found itself on even ground, Samuel crawled over to the hole, knelt down, and peered out.

Elevated as he was above the surrounding horde, Samuel could see some distance across the Plains of Desolation. The Mountain of Despair rose before him, so big that it dominated the entire horizon, the extent of its base impossible to measure, its peak lost amid the battling clouds. There was an opening visible at the foot of the mountain, tiny by comparison with the great mass of black rock, but still huge enough to accommodate a hundred men standing on one another's shoulders, with room to spare so that the topmost man would not bang his head. Samuel had seen that opening before: through it, the Great Malevolence had briefly emerged just as it seemed his invasion of the world of men was destined to succeed. The memory reminded Samuel of what he was about to face: the vengeance of the most fearful being the Multiverse had ever known, an entity of pure evil, a creature without love, or pity, or mercy.

Terrified though he was, Samuel did not weaken. It is one thing to be brave in front of others, perhaps for fear of being branded a coward and becoming diminished in their eyes, but another entirely to be brave when there is nobody to witness your courage. The latter is an elemental bravery, a strength of spirit and character. It is a revelation of the essence of the self, and as Samuel crouched in his cage, slowly approaching the place in which his doom would be fixed, his face was calm and his soul was at peace. He had done nothing wrong. He had stood up for what he believed was right in order to protect his friends, his mother, his town, and the Earth itself. He did not rail at the unfairness of what was to come, for he understood in his heart that it would serve no purpose and would only make his torment harder to endure.

Had there been a soul inside Mrs Abernathy for her to examine, or had her vanity and lust for power and revenge not clouded her insight, she might have come to understand that she did not so much hate Samuel Johnson as fear him. There was an essential goodness to him that she could not touch, a decency that remained untainted by all that he had experienced so far in his short life. Samuel Johnson was human, with all of the flaws and foibles that came with his species. He could be jealous and sad, angry and selfish, but in him a little part of the best of humanity glowed brightly, just as it illuminates so many of us if we choose to let it. What Mrs Abernathy did not grasp was that, despite all that she or her master might visit upon him, she would never, ever defeat Samuel Johnson, and no matter how deep or dark the place in which he was interred, his soul would continue to shine.

The wagon ascended an incline, and as it reached the top Samuel gasped, for arrayed on the plain before him was another mighty army: row upon row of demon legionnaires, their long shields catching the reflection of the bolts of lightning that broke through the clouds above with greater and greater frequency and ferocity, as though the angry spirits in the skies were urging on the opposing forces, seeking on the battlefield below a reflection of their own wrath. Mounted cavalry were moving into position, the eyes of their skinless steeds like hot coals set in ash, their hooves striking sparks from the stony ground.

Behind the main ranks strode the monsters of the underworld: cyclopses, and minotaurs, and snake-headed hydrae; gigantic gorgons, their faces masked with plates of gold until the order came to reveal themselves, but their serpentine locks already writhing in anticipation of the fighting to come; and lurching, predatory creatures with the bodies of men and the heads of vicious animals. Many of the beasts seemed familiar to Samuel, and not merely because they had formed part of the huge force originally destined to conquer the earth. These were the monsters that shadowed all of the Earth's mythologies and religions, the beings that had appeared to the ancients in nightmares and had found their way into legends and fairy tales, books of myths and books of faith.

Allied with them were jumbled entities that had never been imagined before, for only madness could have conjured up such visions: heads on legs, scuttling sideways like crabs, sharp teeth snapping; creatures that were hybrids of shark and spider, of toad and bat, of earwig and dog, as though segments of every animal that ever existed on Earth had been tossed in a great vat and allowed to fuse with one another.

And then there were beings that bore no resemblance to anything from Samuel's world, even in the most passing of ways: shifting masses of matter that reached out with wisps of darkness, probing for prey; fleshy globes with a thousand mouths; and entities that existed only as painful sounds, or poisonous smells. It seemed that no force could stand up to such horrors and triumph, yet similar creatures, and worse, had gathered to serve Mrs Abernathy. Her army might have been more ragged and less disciplined, with fewer of the trained legions to array themselves meticulously for battle, but Samuel believed that Mrs Abernathy's strength was greater overall. The conflict would be a test of strategy against might, of military training against sheer weight of numbers.

But regardless of who won, Samuel would ultimately lose, for all here wished him harm.

The Watcher flew high over the battlefield, higher even than the winged scout demons of Mrs Abernathy and Duke Abigor, so high that the gathering combatants were lost to it and there was only cloud below and the peaks of the Moutain of Despair rising before it. The Watcher had made its decision. It could not stand by and watch Hell torn apart. Its loyalty was to one, and one only: the Great Malevolence.

It was time for the bells to ring.

At the entrance to the Mountain of Despair Brompton and Edgefast were regarding the awesome armies, the greatest ever gathered in conflict in Hell's long history, with the slightly bored air of men who are watching a repeat of a football game to which they already know the score, and which hadn't been very interesting first time around.

'Busy out there today,' said Edgefast. Despite the fact that he could quite easily have had himself reassembled after Mrs Abernathy tore him apart, he was still a severed head resting beside a pile of assorted limbs and bits of torso, although he now had a cushion, thanks to an uncharacteristic moment of weakness on the part of Brompton. Edgefast had elected to remain a talking head because a) he claimed that his experience had altered his view of Hell, and he now saw the world, quite literally, from a different angle; b) he no longer had to worry about laundry, or tying his shoelaces;

and c) he could spot anyone really small who might try to sneak in. This had seemed perfectly acceptable to Brompton, who didn't want to have to bother getting to know another new guard.

'Suppose so,' said Brompton, picking at his teeth. 'If you like that kind of thing.'

'Makes a change, though, doesn't it, all them demons milling around? Very exciting, I'd say.'

'I don't approve of change,' said Brompton. 'Or excitement.' He shifted from one foot to another, and looked uncomfortable. 'Mind you, I shouldn't have had that last cup of tea. Gone right through me, that has. I'm about to have an accident. Look, mind the shop for five minutes while I go and, you know, make myself lighter in a liquid way.'

'Right you are,' said Edgefast. 'I'll look after things.'

Desperate though he was to relieve himself, Brompton took a moment's pause.

'Now, you know this is a big responsibility.'

'Yes, absolutely.'

'You can't let anyone in who isn't supposed to be allowed in, and since nobody is supposed to be allowed in – Chancellor Ozymuth's orders – then you mustn't let anybody in, full stop.'

'Understood.'

'Not anybody.'

'They shall not pass,' said Edgefast sternly.

'No passing. Not a one.'

Brompton moved away, then came back again.

'Nobody, right?'

'No. Body. Nobody.'

'Good.'

Brompton shuffled off. Edgefast whistled a happy tune. It was his first time alone at the entrance, and he liked being in charge. He was a good guard, was Edgefast. He didn't nip off for naps, he took his job seriously, and he was happy to serve. He had the right spirit for a guard.

Unfortunately he had the wrong body, namely none at all.

He heard the beating of wings and two large red feet landed in front of him. Since he couldn't move his head, Edgefast did his best to look up by raising his eyebrows and squinting. The Watcher's eight black eyes stared down at him in bemusement.

'Nobody's allowed in, mate,' said Edgefast. 'You'll have to leave a message.'

The Watcher considered this possibility for a moment, then simply stepped around Edgefast and marched into the heart of the mountain.

'Oi!' shouted Edgefast. 'Come back. You can't do that. I'm the guard. I'm guarding. You can't just step around me. It's not fair. Seriously! You're undermining my authority. Back you come and we'll say no more about it, all right?'

The sound of the Watcher's footsteps grew distant.

'All right?' repeated Edgefast.

There was silence, then more footsteps, this time lighter, and approaching with the reluctant shamble of someone who is returning to work but really would prefer not to be.

'Yeah, all right,' said Brompton. 'Feel much better, thanks. Forgot to wash me hands, but never mind. Anything I should know about?'

Edgefast thought carefully before answering.

'No,' he said. 'Nothing at all.'

CHAPTER XXXIV

In Which We Encounter Some Cunning Disguises

There were many curious and alarming vehicles dotted among the opposing sides on the battlefield: war wagons, their steel-rimmed wheels accessorized with bladed spikes, their beds protected by layers of metal to shield the driver and the archers beneath; primitive tanks with long turrets through which oil could be pumped and then ignited by a standing flame at the mouth of the turret; siege weapons shaped like serpents, and dragons, and sea monsters; and field catapults crewed and ready for action, their cradles filled with rocks.

A word about the rocks, or, indeed, a word *from* the rocks, which might be equally appropriate: as we have already seen, there were numerous entities in Hell – trees, clouds, and so on – that were sentient when, under ordinary circumstances, they should not have been. Among them were certain types of rock that had developed little mouths, some rudimentary eyes, and an overestimation of their own value in what passed for Hell's ecosystem.[40] Thus it was that a number of

---

☠ [40] Like a great many organisms straining for sophistication, they had also created their own basic form of music. Please insert your own joke here.

the rocks residing in the cradles of the catapults were complaining loudly about their situation, pointing out that they would, upon impact, be reduced to the status of pebbles or, even worse, rubble, which is the equivalent of a king or queen being forced to live in a tent and claim unemployment benefit. Nobody was listening, of course, since they were rocks, and there's a limit to the amount of harm a rock can do unless someone gives it a bit of help by flinging it at someone or something with considerable force. As these rocks would very soon be headed in the direction of the enemy, it was felt that they could address their complaints to interested parties on the other side, assuming the individuals in question a) survived having a rock flung at them; and b) were in the mood to consider the rock's complaints about its treatment in the aftermath, which seemed unlikely.

So when a large rock with four eyes began pressing through the ranks of Mrs Abernathy's demons, it barely merited a second glance, even if it did appear to be growling more than most rocks tended to. Neither did the vehicle following in its wake attract much attention, even if its effectiveness as a machine of war was debatable given that its weaponry consisted solely of four wooden posts stuck to its front and rear parts, the remainder of its body being covered by a white dust-proof cloth with slits at eye level. What was beyond question, however, was the ferocity of the four small demons riding upon its back. Horns protruded from their foreheads, and their faces dripped with disgusting green and red fluids of indeterminate origin. Somehow they contrived to be even more terrible than the two warthog demons escorting the larger vehicle, and who discouraged those unwise creatures who tried to peer under the dustcloth from investigating further by hitting them very hard with big clubs.

'Coming through,' shouted Jolly. 'Mind your backs.' He nudged Dozy. 'And stop licking that raspberry and lime from your face. You're ruining the effect.'

'One of my horns is coming loose,' said Angry.

'Then use more chewing gum,' said Jolly. 'Here, take mine.'

He removed a lump of pink material from his mouth and handed it to Angry, who accepted it with some reluctance and used it to stick his ice-cream cone horn more securely to his forehead.

'Grrrrrr!' said Mumbles, waving one of D. Bodkin's staplers in a threatening manner.

'Let us at them!' said Dozy. 'We'll tear their heads off and use them for bowling balls.'

'Sissies, the lot of 'em,' cried Angry, getting into the spirit of the thing and making a variety of rude gestures at Duke Abigor's forces in the hope that at least one of them would be understood as an insult by the opposing side.

'Easy, lads,' said the voice of Constable Peel from somewhere under the dustcloth. 'We don't want to attract the wrong kind of attention.'

'What kind of attention would that be?' asked Angry, and received his answer as a black arrow whistled past his ear and embedded itself in the body of the ice-cream van. 'Oh, right. Fair enough.'

The little convoy made its way slowly alongside the wagon on which rested Samuel's hooded cage. Dozy and Mumbles produced some paper cups and began pouring drinks for the demons surrounding the wagon.

'Drink up, boys,' said Dozy, handing down the cups. 'And girls. And, er, whatever you are. Haven't you ever heard of having a drink before the war?'

And while the demons drank, temporarily sacrificing their eyesight, their balance, and their desire to live to cups of not-quite-right-but-still-not-too-bad-all-things-considered imitation Spiggit's, Angry and Jolly dropped from the roof on to the bed of the wagon. Mumbles threw them a sack, and the two dwarfs, with their burden, slipped silently under the cloth.

Mrs Abernathy raised a hand to halt her troops. Three horses, on which were mounted members of Abigor's personal guard, advanced from the opposing lines. A white banner fluttered from a pike held by the leader of the three, the captain of the guard. They rode to within hailing distance of Mrs Abernathy, and halted.

'By order of Duke Abigor, we demand the surrender of the traitor, Mrs Abernathy,' said the captain.

In the distance Mrs Abernathy could see Abigor mounted on his great steed, his red cloak bleeding into the air behind him. Surrender? Could he be serious? She thought not. He was covering himself in case questions later arose about his conduct. Yes, he could say, I gave her the opportunity to surrender and avoid conflict, but she refused, and so I had no choice but to proceed against her.

'I know of no traitor by such a name,' said Mrs Abernathy. 'I know only of the traitor Abigor, who has taken arms against the commander of Hell's forces. If *he* surrenders to *me*, and orders his demons to lay down their weapons and disperse, then I can promise him . . . nothing at all, actually. Regardless, he is doomed. It is merely a matter of how deep in the great lake of Cocytus I choose to inter him.'

'He also demands that you hand over the boy, Samuel Johnson,' said the captain, as if Mrs Abernathy had not spoken. 'He is an interloper, a pollutant, and an enemy of the state. Duke Abigor will ensure that he is imprisoned securely, that he may do no further harm.'

'That, too, I refuse,' said Mrs Abernathy. 'Is there anything else?'

'Indeed there is,' said the captain. 'Duke Abigor orders you to reveal the whereabouts of the portal between worlds, a portal that was opened without the knowledge or approval of our master, the Great Malevolence, and threatens the stability of this realm.'

Mrs Abernathy said nothing for a time, as though composing a suitable response. Eventually the captain of the guard grew tired of waiting.

'What answer should I bring to Duke Abigor?' he said. 'Speak now, lest he unleash his wrath upon you.'

'Well,' said Mrs Abernathy, 'you can say – oh, never mind, I'll let you work it out yourself.'

From her back emerged her lethal tentacles. Before the three riders could react, they were enveloped, and within seconds they and their horses had been ripped apart. Mrs Abernathy gathered up the remains, crushed them into a ball of flesh and bone, leather and metal, then hurled it in the direction of Abigor's lines. The mess rolled as far as Abigor's mount, where it bounced off the horse's front legs and came to rest.

'I think that was a "no",' said Abigor. 'I was rather hoping it would be. Jolly good. Carnage it is, then.'

The Watcher moved swiftly through the Mountain of Despair. The arches and alcoves that had echoed with laughter and mockery during Mrs Abernathy's last visit were now silent. The creatures that dwelt within them retreated to the shadows, fearful of drawing the attention of the Watcher to themselves, and only when it had passed did they peer out at it. It was a long time since the Watcher had walked through those great halls, but the memory of it had remained. Its presence in the mountain was a reminder of an older order, and as it walked it seemed to grow larger and more powerful, as though feeding upon an energy meant for it alone.

Chancellor Ozymuth waited for it at the end of the causeway. He raised his staff and the Watcher halted.

'Go back, old one,' said Ozymuth. 'There is no place for you here. Your time is over. A new force rises.'

The Watcher's black eyes stared at him implacably. In them, Ozymuth was reflected eight times, a pale figure against the darkness, as though he were already lost.

'The Great Malevolence is mad,' continued Ozymuth.

'Another will rule in his stead until his wits are restored. Mrs Abernathy must bow to the inevitable, and you must find some dusty, forgotten corner of this kingdom where you may fade from remembrance, lest you share the fate of your doomed mistress. Cocytus is wide and deep, and there is a place in it for you, should you continue to resist the inevitable. Your time of service to your mistress has come to an end.'

The voice of the Watcher spoke in Ozymuth's head.

Mrs Abernathy is not my mistress.

Ozymuth's desiccated features formed themselves into the semblance of a grin. 'You see sense, then?'

I serve another.

'You speak of Duke Abigor? It may be that he can find some use for you.'

No. I serve another.

Ozymuth frowned. 'You answer in riddles. Perhaps age has addled your brain after all. Go! I am done with you. We are all done with you. Your fall will be great.'

Ozymuth was about to turn away when one of the Watcher's hands grasped him by the throat and lifted him from the ground. Ozymuth tried to speak but the Watcher's grip was too tight, and Ozymuth could only gurgle as he was held over the edge of the causeway, his eyes widening in understanding. Beneath him opened a swirling vortex of red like the interior of a volcano, but its very centre was dark, the blackness within stretching for ever.

You have poisoned my master. You have brought us to the brink of war.

Ozymuth managed to shake his head, his feet kicking,

his hands clawing at the Watcher's arms as he heard the last words he would ever hear.

It is your fall that will be great.

The Watcher released him, and Ozymuth began his eternal descent.

CHAPTER XXXV

In Which Battle Commences, and a
Rescue Mission is Mounted

Samuel turned at the sound of his cage bars rattling. A match flared, and he experienced a moment of pure terror at the sight of the demonic figures revealed until one of the ice-cream cone horns fell from Angry's forehead once again, and Jolly rubbed some of the 'blood' from his face, licked his fingertips, and said, 'It's just raspberry ripple! Oh, and sweat.'

'All right, son?' said Angry. 'We'll have you out of there in no time, as long as the lightning holds off for a minute or two.'

From somewhere on his person he produced a set of picks, and began working on the lock.

'What's happening?' asked Samuel. 'I can't see much from in here.'

'Well,' said Jolly, striking another match as the first one died, 'that Mrs Abernathy woman was asked to surrender and hand you over, but she didn't think much of that idea so she tore the messengers apart, rolled them in a ball, and sent them back where they came from. Strong female, she is. Model of her kind, assuming anyone could tell what kind she is exactly. My guess is that, any time now, there's going to be a lot of shouting, and stabbing, and general warmongering going on all around us.'

'What about Nurd, and Boswell, and the others?'

'All fine, and all nearby.'

There was a loud *click*, and the cage door opened.

'Barely worth the name "lock", that was,' said Angry. 'I've had cans of beer that were harder to open.'

'So what's the plan?' asked Samuel, as he clambered out of the cage.

'It's Mr Nurd's,' said Jolly. 'And it's genius.'

He opened the sack and revealed what lay within.

'You can't be serious,' said Samuel.

But they were.

Duke Abigor raised a hand, and a horn rang out. From behind him came the sound of a thousand arrows being nocked, and a thousand bowstrings being drawn tight.

'On my command!' cried Abigor, then let his hand fall. Instantly the arrows were released, darkening the sky as they hurtled towards the enemy lines.

'Oh, crumbs,' said Constable Peel, peering through the slit in the cloth that covered Dan's ice-cream van. 'That's a lot of arrows.'

But just as the arrows reached the top of their arc and began to fall, they burst into flames, and a cheer rose up the ranks of Mrs Abernathy's army. The lady in question was visible upon her mount, her arms raised and smoke and flames pouring from her fingers.

'I'm glad she's on our side,' said Constable Peel.

'Only until she finds out that we are on *her* side,'

said Sergeant Rowan. 'Then she'll take a very different view.'

Another flight of arrows was unleashed against them, but this time in greater number, and some of them broke through Mrs Abernathy's fiery defences and embedded themselves in the flesh of demons. The demons didn't seem terribly perturbed about their injuries, though, and for the most part just stared at the arrows in mild annoyance.

'Well, they don't seem to be doing much harm,' said Constable Peel, just as a nearby entity, a hunched being of black fur and bad teeth, tugged at the arrow in its chest and promptly exploded in a shower of flesh and white light.

'On the other hand . . .'

Abigor ordered his first wave of cavalry to attack, and the skinless horses carried their riders towards Mrs Abernathy's army. The cavalry wielded heavy lances with vicious, multi-bladed tips, and although half of them fell beneath the onslaught of spears, arrows, and complaining rocks that ripped through their ranks, the remainder hit the first line with incredible force, tearing a hole in the shield wall and impaling the soldiers behind before casting the long lances aside and swinging maces and swords to brutal effect.

A second wave of cavalry attacked, followed by the demonic rank and file, led by Duke Abigor and his personal guard. Meanwhile two legions had commenced a flanking movement, hoping to encircle Mrs Abernathy's army entirely. In response, Mrs Abernathy's forces unleashed torrents of flame and clouds of arrows, while

Mrs Abernathy herself waded into her opponents, the tentacles on her back whipping and writhing, pulling riders from their horses and ripping them apart like bugs. The gorgons at last revealed their hideous visages, turning to stone those who did not look away in time, while those who did hide their faces found themselves vulnerable to attack. The cyclopean giants swung their clubs, tossing aside ten soldiers at a time. Dragons on both sides set hair and skin and flesh burning, while sirens attacked from above like birds of prey, their outstretched claws impaling themselves in flesh and armour, inflicting awful wounds that turned instantly black as the poison in their talons infected the tissue. The fighting drew closer and closer to where the disguised car and the ice-cream van stood, hemmed in by the thronging mass of demons anxious to join in the fight.

'Guard the cage!' screamed Mrs Abernathy, for the discipline of Abigor's legions was beginning to tell, and she felt the battle turning against her. A second line of demons surrounded the wagon, their blades unsheathed, forming a wall of sharp metal and sharper teeth through which none could penetrate. Only a few noticed that the original guards were more than a little unsteady on their feet, and seemed to be having trouble focusing, but then more arrows began to descend and avoiding impalement took precedence over all else.

There was blood, and screaming, all lit by bolts of lightning from above as Hell tore itself apart.

CHAPTER XXXVI

In Which a Certain Someone Wakes Up
With a Sore Head

It was Dozy, now back in the relative safety of the ice-cream van, who noticed it first, just as he finished helping Jolly and Angry back inside after the successful completion of their rescue mission.

'Did you hear that?' he said.

'All I can hear is the noise of battle,' said Constable Peel.

'No, it was something else. Like an echo, but before a sound has been made to cause it.'

Slowly, bells began to toll deep in the heart of the mountain, growing louder and louder. The sound of them was so loud and so resonant that all who heard them covered their ears in pain. The vibrations caused the ground to tremble. Cracks appeared on the plain. In the Hollow Hills caves collapsed, and from the icy mountains to the north great avalanches flowed down and smothered the faces of those unfortunates who broke the surface of Cocytus. The Sea of Unpleasantness was riven by earthquakes beneath its surface, and tsunamis of black water rose up and broke upon the barren shores. On the battlefield weapons fell from hands, and horses threw their riders. Ears bled, teeth were loosened in their gums. Demons cowered, wailing in agony. Over and over the bells sounded, shaking stones from the Mountain of Despair, until the very notion of Hell itself was reduced to a single essence: the awful pealing of the bells that had been silent for so long, heard only at the times of greatest crisis in that place.

And then suddenly they stopped, and demons of all shapes and forms turned their heads in the direction of the Mountain of Despair. Flames flickered deep in its heart as a shape appeared in the doorway. It was the Watcher, now many times taller and broader than before, its red skin glowing as though the creature had recently been forged in the fires within, a being of metal or stone that would slowly cool to grey and black.

'How did it get in?' hissed Brompton to Edgefast, as the shadow of the Watcher advanced before them.

'It must have sneaked by,' said Edgefast, trying not to catch Brompton's eye.

'It's forty feet tall! What did it do, wear a hat and dark glasses? Some guard you are.'

But all questions about the Watcher, and any amazement that the guards, and the two armies, and Mrs Abernathy and Duke Abigor, might have felt at its altered appearance faded away as it became clear that another presence was emerging from the mountain, a figure that dwarfed the Watcher just as the Watcher towered above most of the demons arrayed on the field. A fierce stench of sulphur swept across the plain and the light from within the mountain was lost, the flames hidden by the mass of the approaching creature. All was utter stillness and silence among the assembled armies. Even the dwarfs were quiet, seemingly frozen into muteness and immobility by what they were seeing. In Nurd's Aston Martin, Boswell buried his muzzle in Samuel's armpit, and closed his eyes in terror, just as his nose twitched at the stink of what was coming, forming a picture of it in his dog brain that he was unable to erase.

So enormous was the Great Malevolence that he had to crouch in order to pass beneath the lintel of the mountain's door. When he stood erect at last there was a grandeur to the sight; a sense of awe infected all who witnessed it, for here was not merely the most ancient and ferocious of evils, but the element of Evil itself given form. From this being flowed all that was wrong, all that was foul, all that blighted hope in world upon world, universe upon universe. His crown was formed from spurs of bone that grew from his own skull, jagged and yellow. His great frame was still sheathed in the armour that he had donned in expectation of his crusade upon Earth, etched with the names of every man and woman born and yet to be born, for he hated them all and wanted to remember his fury at each one, the great litany of names constantly being added to as more humans entered the world. Some of those names burned, for there were those who had damned themselves by their actions, and so were destined to join him.

Most of the flesh on the Great Malevolence's face had long since decayed, leaving a thin layer of brown, leathery skin draped over his bones, broken at his cheeks so that the muscles and bone beneath were clearly visible. His teeth were jagged and double-rowed, set in blackened, diseased gums, and a pale pink serpent's tongue licked at his rotted lips.

But terrible though his face was, it was his eyes that truly chilled, for they were almost human in the depth of their feeling, filled with unbounded rage and a dreadful, poisonous sadness. From where he watched inside Nurd's car, Samuel understood at last why this being hated men and women so much: he hated them because they were so like himself, because the worst of them was mirrored in him. He was the source of all that was bad in men and women, but he had none of the greatness, and none of the grace, of which human beings were capable, so that only by corrupting them was his own pain and regret diminished, and thus his existence made more tolerable.

Now he stared out over the battlefield, the Watcher poised before him, and as he spoke all trembled in fear. 'WHO HAS DARED TO RAISE OPPOSING ARMIES IN MY REALM? WHO SETS DEMON AGAINST DEMON?'

As if by a prearranged signal the armies separated, putting as much space as possible between themselves and their commanders, so that Mrs Abernathy and Duke Abigor stood isolated.

'My lord and master,' said Abigor, bowing his head. 'It is good to see you restored to us. Without your hand to guide us we have been lost, and we have been betrayed by our own. I have been forced to act to protect this great kingdom against the treason of one who was once beloved of you, this –' he gestured at Mrs Abernathy with disgust – 'polluted personage, this patchwork woman.' He seemed about to say more, but the Great Malevolence raised a clawed finger and Duke Abigor was silent as his master turned his attention to Mrs Abernathy.

'DOES ABIGOR LIE?'

'No, my master,' said Mrs Abernathy. 'For we have been lost, and we have been betrayed, but the treason was not mine. Look to the standards: I fight under your banner, but Abigor fights only under his own.'

'Permit me to explain—' began Abigor, but his words turned to fat black flies that buzzed against his cheeks and tongue, and Mrs Abernathy allowed herself a sly grin as her opponent tried to spit out the insects, but with each one that he ejected two more came into being until Abigor's mouth was filled with them.

'I set out to make amends to you for my failings, and I have done so,' continued Mrs Abernathy, now that she had silenced Abigor for a time.

'YOUR FAILINGS WERE GREAT. SO TOO MUST BE THE RECOMPENSE.'

'And it is,' said Mrs Abernathy. 'For I have brought you the child who sabotaged all that we had worked for. I have brought you Samuel Johnson!'

She waved to the wagon driver, who urged on his horses, bringing the covered cage to the clearing on the battlefield. Beside her Abigor had found enough power to disperse the flies, and interrupted her.

'She lies, my master! I fight beneath my own banner only because she uses your standard to hide her treason.

She has compounded betrayal with more betrayal. She stole the child from me. It was I who found a way to open the portal, but she took the boy from my castle that she might claim credit for his capture.'

The wagon drew nearer, its prize waiting to be revealed, lightning flashing to reveal the shape inside the cage.

'And where is the portal that you opened, Duke Abigor?' asked Mrs Abernathy. 'Show it to us, that we may marvel at it. Display it for our master, that we may harness its potential for another invasion.'

'It vanished,' spluttered Abigor. 'I could not keep it open for long. I could only find time to snatch the boy before it closed again.'

Mrs Abernathy raised her arms.

'Let me give you proof of his treason, my master,' she said. 'For I know the location of the portal. I know, for it lies ... within me!'

Her eyes shone a cold blue, and a blue glow filled her mouth. The air around her seemed to swirl, forming a column of dust and ash that caught the light coming from within her, so that she became the centre of her own blue world. As she grew taller and taller she was both Mrs Abernathy and her old, ancient self, the demon Ba'al, its tentacles writhing, its massive head visible beneath Mrs Abernathy's stretched skin, like one transparent image overlaid upon another. Her segmented jaws opened wider and wider – ten, twenty, thirty feet in width – revealing a tunnel of dark light with a blue heart.

'Behold, my master!' she cried. 'Behold the portal! And behold – Samuel Johnson!'

The wagon master whipped away the black cloth, and the crowd gasped at the figure of Mr Happy Whip, grinning his plastic grin at the assembled forces of Hell.

And at that moment a rock with four eyes shot from the ranks, followed closely by a cloth-covered wagon adorned with unimpressive horns. The disguises fell away, revealing Dan, Dan the Ice-Cream Man, hunched over the wheel of his beloved van, urged on by Sergeant Rowan, and Constable Peel, and four determined dwarfs; revealing Samuel Johnson in the Aston Martin once owned by his dad, Boswell held tightly in the crook of one arm, the other hand resting on the shoulder of a goggle-eyed Wormwood.

And revealing Nurd: Nurd, no longer Nurd the inept, Nurd the coward; no longer Nurd, the Scourge of Five Deities. No, this was a Nurd transformed. This was Nurd, the Vanquisher of Demons. This was Nurd, the Triumphant.

This was Nurd, the Frankly Terrified.

Before Mrs Abernathy could react, Nurd had driven the car straight into her mouth, the ice-cream van barely inches behind him. As they disappeared through the portal, the faint strains of 'How Much Is That Doggie in the Window?' floated from Mrs Abernathy's jaws over the great plain.

Even on a battlefield where two massive armies faced each other, and the Devil himself towered over them both seeking an explanation for what was going on, a pair of motorized vehicles driving straight down a demon's throat, a throat recently transformed into a gateway between universes, still counted as something quite out of the ordinary. Nothing happened for a number of seconds, apart from the occupants of the two vehicles falling through a wormhole of sorts, with all that entailed, including being stretched to the point of agony and then compressed in a similarly painful manner, but all this was hidden from the denizens of Hell, who continued to stare at Mrs Abernathy to see how she might respond to this recent turn of events.

Mrs Abernathy might have hidden the seeds of the portal within herself, but she had not intended it to be used in the manner to which Samuel, Nurd and company had just put it. She had planned on manifesting it at a point outside herself and then, with her master's help, drawing all the power that she could from the Collider in one fell swoop and reversing the portal's direction of travel, so that instead of moving objects from Earth to Hell, it would move them from Hell to Earth. It would not be enough to pass an army through, but it would be enough to transport the Great Malevolence and herself to the world of men, and there they would create a new Hell, just the two of them. Unfortunately that plan now looked like it would have to be put on the back burner, for Mrs Abernathy had more pressing concerns.

Her body shuddered. She gagged and choked, like someone who has swallowed a piece of food that has gone down the wrong way, which in a vehicular sense was more or less what had happened. The blue light grew stronger and brighter, so bright that the assembled demons, even the Great Malevolence himself, were forced to look away from it, so bright that it turned from blue to white, and burned so strongly that Mrs Abernathy screamed.

The portal collapsed, and Mrs Abernathy imploded, her being turning in upon itself, the substance of her spiralling inward as every atom in her body was separated from the next. Her disguise of human skin was sucked from her, revealing the old monster within. Her segmented jaws were pulled into her throat, her tentacles folded themselves over the front of her body as though to protect her, and there was a soft popping sound as the portal closed and the fragments of her being were scattered throughout the Multiverse.

CHAPTER XXXVII

In Which We Get to the
'Happy Ever After' Part

There was a blue flash on Ambrose Bierce Drive and two vehicles appeared: an Aston Martin, its windows so cracked that it was impossible to see through them, its four wheels splayed outward like the legs of a collapsing animal so that the car rested on its underside; and a very battered ice-cream van, containing four similarly battered dwarfs covered from head to toe in raspberry ripple; two policemen whose hats had melted; and one bewildered ice-cream salesman with smoking hair.

'Next time we take the train,' said Jolly, staggering from the back of the van. 'I feel like I've been dragged through a washing machine backwards.'

His fellow dwarfs joined him, Dozy utilizing one of his horns to scrape up the last of the ripple. Acrid smoke began to emerge from beneath the van, quickly followed by flickering flames. Dan, Dan the Ice-Cream Man looked on mournfully as the remains of his business went up in smoke.

'Perhaps I wasn't really cut out to be an ice-cream

salesman,' he said. 'At least the insurance will cover it, I suppose.'

Jolly tapped him on the arm. 'Think you'll buy a new van, then?'

'Probably. Don't know what I'll do with it, though.'

'Funny you should mention that,' said Jolly, adopting his most trustworthy of expressions. 'How would you feel about transporting four hard-working, self-motivated individuals to a variety of business engagements?'

'Sounds all right,' said Dan.

'It does, doesn't it?' said Jolly. 'I wish we actually *knew* four hard-working, self-motivated individuals, but in their absence, how about driving the four of us around instead?'

Sergeant Rowan and Constable Peel helped Nurd, Wormwood, Samuel and Boswell to free themselves from the Aston Martin, as the doors had buckled badly when they travelled through the portal.

Nurd patted the roof of the car sadly. 'I think she may have taken her last trip,' he said, as Wormwood wiped a tear from his eye. Wormwood had grown to love the Aston Martin almost as much as he loved Nurd; more so, even, as the car had never hit him with a sceptre, used unpleasant language towards him, or threatened to bury him upside down in sand for eternity.

'At least you have a car, or what's left of one,' said Constable Peel. 'How are we going to explain the loss of our patrol car, Sarge? And where did it go?'

'We'll never know, son,' said Sergeant Rowan.[41]

Suddenly there was movement in the flaming ice-cream van, and seconds later Shan and Gath emerged from the conflagration, patting out small patches of fire on their fur.

'Forgot about them,' said Angry, with the casual air of someone who has left a shoelace undone rather than abandoned two creatures to an inferno of metal, plastic and assorted ripples.

'Where did they come from?' asked Constable Peel.

'We hid them in the fridges while you were up front with the sarge and Dan,' said Jolly. 'Sorry. I mean, it wasn't like we could leave them in Hell, not after that winged bloke found Samuel at their cave. It wouldn't have been fair.'

💀 [41] Somewhere in the depths of Hell, a massive invisible floating demon named Fred had just arrived home to his invisible wife, Felicity, and invisible child, Little Fred. 'Where have you been, then?' asked his invisible wife. 'I don't know what you think you are, sauntering about like you haven't a care in Hell, leaving me all alone to keep Little Fred amused. Most of the time, it's like you're never here at all.' Fred, being invisible, was tempted to point out that, even when he was there, it was like he was never there at all, but he didn't think this was the time, as, although he was invisible, and therefore should have presented a hard target for his beloved missus, she seemed to have an uncanny ability to score direct hits upon him with various household objects. Instead he put a police car and a van beside Little Fred, or where he thought Little Fred might roughly be. In the manner of kids everywhere, Little Fred immediately picked up the vehicles and banged them together, before running their wheels across the dirt while making 'brrrmmmm-brrrmmmm' noises.

'They're supposed to come with little men', said Fred, 'but I know he'd just lose them.'

'What about me?' asked Felicity.

'Just a kiss for you, my love,' said Fred.

He pecked lovingly at the air.

'I'm over here, you idiot . . .'

'We've brought four demons to Earth,' said Sergeant Rowan. He had gone rather pale. 'They'll have my stripes.'

Constable Peel grinned. 'I don't have any stripes.'

'I know. They'll have your guts for garters instead.'

'Oh.'

'Yes, "Oh." Not grinning now, are you?'

'But we'll get into terrible trouble, Sarge, and I've had enough trouble to last a lifetime. The chief constable isn't going to approve of us bringing demons back from Hell. He doesn't even like going abroad for his holidays because it's full of foreigners. If we tell him what we've done, we'll be directing traffic for the rest of our lives.'

Sergeant Rowan looked at Shan and Gath. Having put out the flames on their fur, they were now fortifying themselves with the last of their home brew.

'Then we won't tell him,' said Sergeant Rowan.

'But we can't just leave them and Nurd and Wormwood to wander around. It wouldn't be right.'

'We're not going to leave them to wander around either,' said Sergeant Rowan. 'Constable Peel, I have a plan . . .'

Nurd looked at the blue sky above his head, clouds scudding across it, lit by the amber glow of a beautiful setting sun. He smelled flowers, and grass, and burning ice-cream cones. He saw a cat scratching its back against a pillar, and a bird pecking seeds from a feeder. He felt exhilarated, and free.

And very afraid. He was an alien creature here, a demon. They might hate him, or fear him, and lock him away. What about Wormwood? Wormwood had barely been able to look after himself in Hell. Without Nurd he'd be lost, but even Nurd wasn't sure how they were going to survive in the world of men.

A hand grasped his, squeezing it tightly. Nurd looked down and saw Samuel. Beside him, Boswell wagged his tail.

'It's going to be OK,' said Samuel. 'Look, it's a brave new world.'

The whole trip to Hell, with all of its traumas and triumphs, had lasted a mere three hours on Earth, and his mother, although worried, had not yet begun to actively fret, although she did as soon as Samuel explained to her what had occurred. A cup of tea was definitely in order, but this time Mrs Johnson went out to get the milk herself while Samuel had a bath. When Mrs Johnson returned Wormwood was in the bath, and Nurd was wearing one of Mr Johnson's old bathrobes and blowing bubbles from a small plastic pipe.

'What are we going to do about those two?' asked Mrs Johnson as she arranged tea and cake on a tray. 'They can't stay here for ever. We don't have enough room.'

'There's a plan,' said Samuel.

And there was.

Samuel went to school as usual the following morning. To those who were perceptive enough to spot the changes, like Tom and Maria, he seemed older somehow, but also stronger and more determined, even before he told his two closest friends all that had happened the previous day. Then, his spare glasses fixed firmly upon his nose, he strode up to the canteen, where he found Lucy Highmore and two of her friends finishing some homework at one of the tables.

'Hello,' said Samuel to Lucy. 'Can I talk to you for a moment?'

Lucy nodded, and her friends packed up their books and departed, giggling. Lucy looked hard at Samuel Johnson for the first time. She had never been very unkind to him, but neither had she exchanged more than a couple of words with him before. They were in different classes, and only mixed at assembly. Now, face to face and with no distractions, she thought that he was quite handsome in a funny way, and although they were the same age there was a sadness, and a wisdom, in his eyes that made him appear older than she.

'My name's Samuel.'

'I know.'

'Yesterday I asked out a letter box, thinking it was you.'

'Do I look like a letter box?'

'No, not really. Not at all, actually.'

'So it wasn't an easy mistake to make, then?'

'No.'

'That's good to know.'

'Yes, I would expect so.'

There was a silence between them for a time.

'Well?' said Lucy.

'Well,' said Samuel, 'I was rather hoping that you might like to join me at Pete's for a pie after school on Friday, if you weren't busy.'

Lucy considered the offer, then smiled regretfully.

'I'm sorry. I'm busy on Friday.'

'Oh,' said Samuel. He bit his lip, and turned away. At least I tried, he thought.

'I'm not busy on Saturday, though.'

'How did it go?' asked Maria, when she encountered Samuel in the corridor later that day.

'She said "yes",' said Samuel.

'Oh, good,' said Maria, and walked away, and Samuel thought that she seemed to be troubled by something in her eye.

Life can be difficult. In fact life is often difficult. It's especially difficult when you're young and trying to find your place in the great scheme of things, but, if it's any consolation, most people do find that place in the end.

In a basement deep in the headquarters of Spiggit's Brewery, Chemical Weapons & Industrial Cleaning Products Ltd, Shan and Gath, dressed in pristine white coats, moved intently around a laboratory equipped with the latest in brewing technology. Beside the laboratory were their living quarters, with comfortable beds, seats, a television, and a pinball machine, a game at which Shan in particular was surprisingly adept, when he had the time and inclination to play it, which wasn't very often. After all, Shan and Gath had discovered one of the secrets of happiness: find something that you would have done anyway as a hobby, and convince someone to pay you good money to do it instead.[42] Their days were now spent developing Spiggit's new boutique range of beers: Spiggit's Summer Rain Ale, Spiggit's Gentle Sunbeam Amber, Spiggit's Strawberry Sunrise Lager, that kind of thing, beers of gentle fragrance and delicate taste designed for the gentler, more discerning drinker.

Or big girly men, as Shan and Gath liked to think of them.

They were also responsible for a separate line of beers for those with a more 'robust' constitution. These included Spiggit's Very Peculiar, Spiggit's Distinctly Unpleasant, and the notorious Spiggit's Old Detestable, which now came in extra-thick glass bottles with a lock on the cap after the yeast in one batch tried to make a break for freedom. But there was always a place in their fridge, and in their hearts, for Spiggit's Old Peculiar.

After all, there was no improving on perfect imperfection.

Some days later, in another, much larger, basement area, within sniffing distance of the chimneys of the Spiggit works, a sleek red sports car careened out of control and struck a brick wall with so much force that its rear wheels lifted from the ground as the hood crumpled

---

☠ [42] Most people will spend their lives doing jobs that they don't particularly enjoy, and will eventually save up enough money to stop doing those jobs just in time to start dying instead. Don't be one of those people. There's a difference between living and just surviving. Do something that you love, and find someone to love who loves that you love what you do.

It really is that simple.

And that hard.

and pieces of engine, car body, and possibly passenger body as well flew into the air. The back of the car seemed to hang suspended in its death throes, then fell back to the concrete with a bang.

For a time, there was only silence.

A creaking noise came from somewhere in the mass of twisted metal. The driver's door opened or, more correctly, the driver's door fell off, and a dazed-looking Nurd staggered from the wreckage. Wormwood ran to him and helped him remove his crash helmet and gloves. Nurd gazed up uncertainly at a long window, behind which various engineers, designers, and safety experts sat, their heads craned to catch Nurd's words. Samuel Johnson stood close to the glass, clearly relieved. No matter how often he watched this happen, he was always glad, and surprised, when his friend survived relatively unscathed.

'Well,' said Nurd at last, 'the seat belt works, but you might need to take a look at the brakes . . .'

As I said, most people, and some demons, find their place in life in the end.

CHAPTER XXXVIII

In Which We Discover the Limitations of the Term 'Happily Ever After'

Professor Hilbert, Professor Stefan, Ed, Victor, and the senior Collider scientists were gathered in a meeting room at CERN, as the Collider rumbled about its business around them.

'And the boy says that he was dragged to Hell?' said Professor Stefan.

Professor Hilbert nodded. 'The return of the Aston Martin, or what's left of it, seems to support his story.'

'And he was there along with four dwarfs, two policemen, their patrol car, an ice-cream salesman, and an ice-cream van?'

Professor Hilbert nodded again.

'An ice-cream van? You're sure it was an ice-cream van?'

'A Mr Happy Whip ice-cream van,' confirmed Professor Hilbert.

'Mr Happy Whip,' repeated Professor Stefan solemnly, as if this fact were particularly important.

'They didn't bring any, er . . .'

'Demons?'

'Yes, demons, they didn't bring any *back*, did they?'

'The policemen, Samuel Johnson, and Mr Dan, Dan the Ice-Cream Man, who is now apparently managing the dwarfs, all confirm the general absence of demons from this world.'

'And the dwarfs?'

'The dwarfs are very unpleasant. In fact, for a time we thought that *they* were demons,' said Professor Hilbert. 'One of them threw a beer bottle at Ed.'

Ed pointed to a large bump on his forehead. 'He was nice enough to empty it first, though.'

'Have you examined the boy?' said Professor Stefan.

'His mother wouldn't let us,' said Professor Hilbert. 'She seems to think that we're partly to blame for his disappearance, since we were the ones who turned on the Collider again. She was quite adamant about that, and used some very strong language to that effect.'

'And the policemen?'

'The policemen wouldn't let us examine them. They also presented us with the bill for a patrol car, with thirty days to pay.'

'And the dwarfs?'

'We tried to examine them, but it didn't go well. Suffice it to say that those dwarfs are *very* unhygienic.'

'But despite all that they say, you claim they weren't really in Hell?'

'Wherever they were, it wasn't Hell,' said Professor Hilbert. 'Hell doesn't exist. Where they were was simply another world, another universe. I believe it to be a dark matter universe. We're close, Professor, very close. We can't shut down the Collider, not now. Our understanding of our place in the Multiverse is about to change utterly. The answer to whether or not we are alone in the Multiverse has been answered. Now we are duty bound to explore the nature of the life forms with which we share it.'

'What do you suggest that we do?'

'Nothing. We say nothing. We do nothing. We ignore the boy and his story. We continue with the experiment.'

'What if they go to the newspapers?'

'They won't.'

'You seem very certain of that.'

'I am. The mother is frightened enough for her child as things stand. She won't want the media camped on her doorstep, assuming they believe the boy's story, and we can make sure they do not. The policemen have been warned by their superiors not to say anything to anyone about what they experienced, and the ice-cream salesman just wants his insurance money. As for the dwarfs, they're not the most reliable of witnesses.'

Professor Stefan still looked uneasy.

'What are the risks?'

'Five per cent. At most.'

'And that five per cent contains the threat of invasion, possible consumption by unknown entities, and the potential destruction of the entire planet?'

'Possibly.'

Professor Stefan shrugged. 'I can live with that. Anyone for a biscuit?'

Deep in the heart of the Mountain of Despair, the Great Malevolence brooded. The time of his madness had passed. Now his mind was clear again.

'A BOY. A BOY, AND A DEMON.'

The Lord of all Evil spoke as though he could not quite believe his own words. The Watcher stood silently at his feet, awaiting its master's command. Above it the great bells, the bells that had pulled its master from his madness, were silent once again. The portal was gone. Mrs Abernathy was gone. Duke Abigor and his allies were frozen in the lake of Cocytus, where they would remain for ever. Only the Great Malevolence prevailed.

'DOES THE COLLIDER STILL RUN?'

The Watcher nodded.

'GOOD.'

The Watcher frowned. The link between Hell and the world of men was no more. Whatever power Mrs Abernathy had harnessed to create the gateway had vanished with her. It would take time to find a way to access the Collider's power again, and surely the men and women responsible for it would be more careful this time. As far as the Watcher was concerned, the kingdom was once more isolated.

The Great Malevolence, seeming to read his servant's thoughts, spoke again.

'THERE IS ANOTHER KINGDOM.'

And the Watcher, almost as ancient as the one it served, understood. There was a kingdom that existed alongside the world through which men walked, a kingdom filled with dark entities, a kingdom of beings who hated men almost as much as the Great Malevolence himself.

The Kingdom of Shadows.

'PREPARE THE WAY.'

The Watcher departed, and the Great Malevolence
closed his eyes, allowing his consciousness to roam
across universes, touching those who were most like
himself, evil creatures intent upon doing harm to others,
and in each mind he left a single order.

*SEEK THE ATOMS. SEEK THE ATOMS WITH
THE BLUE GLOW. FIND HER . . .*

Acknowledgements

Thanks to my editors and publishers at Hodder & Stoughton and Simon & Schuster, my agent Darley Anderson and his staff, and to Dr Colm Stephens, administrator of the School of Physics at Trinity College, Dublin, who was kind enough to read the manuscript and correct my errors. Any that remain are entirely my own fault.

THE CREEPS

JOHN CONNOLLY

For Cameron and Alistair

CHAPTER I

In Which a Birthday Party Takes Place, and We Learn That One Ought to Be Careful With Candles (and Dangling Prepositions).

In a small terraced house in the English town of Biddlecombe, a birthday party was under way.

Biddlecombe was a place in which, for most of its history, it seemed as though little of interest had ever happened. Unfortunately, as is often the case in a place in which things have been quiet for a little too long, when something interesting did happen it was very interesting indeed; more interesting, in fact, than anybody might have wished. The gates of Hell had opened in a basement in Biddlecombe, and the town had temporarily been invaded by demons.

Perhaps unsurprisingly, Biddlecombe had never really been the same since. The rugby team no longer played on its old pitch, not since a number of its players had been eaten by burrowing sharks; the voice of the captain of the Biddlecombe Golf Club could still occasionally be heard crying out from somewhere at the bottom of the fifteenth hole; and it was rumoured that a monster had taken up residence in the duck pond, although it was said to be very shy, and the ducks appeared to be rather fond of it.

But the creature in the pond was not the only entity from Hell that had now taken up permanent residence in Biddlecombe, which brings us back to the birthday party. It was not, it must be said, a typical birthday party. The birthday boy in question was named Wormwood. He looked like a large ferret that had suffered a severe attack of mange[1], and was wearing a pair of very fetching blue overalls upon which his name had been embroidered. These overalls replaced a previous pair upon which his name had also been embroidered, although he had managed to spell his own name wrong first time round. This time, all of the letters were present and correct, and in the right order, because Samuel Johnson's mother had done the stitching herself, and if there was one thing Mrs Johnson was a stickler for[2], it was good spelling. Thus it was that the overalls now read 'Wormwood' and not 'Wromwood' as they had previously done.

Wormwood was, not to put too fine a point on it, a demon. He hadn't set out to be a demon. He'd just popped into existence as one, and therefore hadn't been given a great deal of choice in the matter. He'd never been very good at being a demon. He was too nice for it, really. Sometimes folk just end up in the wrong job.[3]

[1] For those of you unfamiliar with mange, it is an ailment that causes a loss of fur. Think of the worst haircut you've ever received, and it's a bit like that, but all over your body.

[2] Technically, that sentence should read 'if there was one thing *for which* Mrs Johnson was a stickler', as nobody likes a dangling preposition, but I said that Mrs Johnson was a stickler for good spelling, not good grammar.

[3] Such as Augustus the Second (1694–1733), King of Poland and Grand

A chorus of voices rang out around the kitchen table.

'Happy Birthday to you, Happy Birthday to you, Happy Birthday dear Woooorrrrrmmmmmwooo ood, Happy Birthday to you! For he's a jolly good, um, *fellow* . . .'

Wormwood smiled the biggest, broadest smile of his life. He looked round the table at those whom he now thought of as his friends. There was Samuel Johnson and his dachshund, Boswell. There were Samuel's schoolmates, Maria Mayer and Tom Hobbes. There was Mrs Johnson, who had started to come to terms with having demons sitting at her kitchen table on a regular basis. There were Shan and Gath, two fellow demons who were employed at the local Spiggit's Brewery as beer tasters and developers, and who were responsible for a fifty per cent increase in the brewery's profits, as well as a 100 per cent increase in the number of

---

Duke of Lithuania, also known as Augustus the Strong. He managed to bankrupt his kingdom by spending all of its money on bits of amber and ivory, lost a couple of battles that he really would have been better off winning, and fathered over 300 children, which suggests that, in between losing battles and collecting trinkets, he had a lot of time on his hands, but his party piece consisted of gripping a horseshoe in his fists and making it straight. He would probably have been very happy just straightening horseshoes and blowing up hot water bottles for a living, but due to an accident of birth he instead found himself ruling a number of kingdoms. Badly. You should bear this in mind if your dad or mum has a name beginning with the words 'His/ Her Royal Highness', and you are known as 'Prince/ Princess Something-Or-Other'. Unless, of course, your name is really 'Something-Or-Other', in which case you don't have anything to worry about (about *which* to worry – darn it) as your parents didn't care enough about you to give you a proper name, and you are therefore unlikely to amount to anything. Sorry.

explosions due to the instability of the still-experimental Spiggit's Brew Number 666, also known as 'The Tank-buster', which was rumoured to be under consideration by the military as a field weapon.

And then there was Nurd, formerly 'Nurd, the Scourge of Five Deities' and now sometimes known as the Nurdster, the Nurdmeister, and the Nurdman, although only to Nurd himself. Nobody else ever called Nurd anything but Nurd. Nurd had once been banished to the remotest, dullest region of Hell for being annoying, and Wormwood, as his servant, had been banished with him. Now that they had found their way to Biddlecombe, Wormwood preferred to think of himself as Nurd's trusty assistant rather than his servant. Occasionally, Nurd liked to hit Wormwood over the head with something hard and memorable, just to remind Wormwood that he could think of himself as anything he liked just as long as he didn't say it aloud.

But in the end Nurd, too, was one of Wormwood's friends. They had been through so much together, and now they worked alongside each other at the Biddlecombe Car Testing Institute, where Nurd tested the safety of new cars, aided by the fact that he was immortal and hence able to walk away from the worst crashes with only the occasional bruise for his trouble.

Wormwood had never had a birthday party before. Until he arrived on Earth, he didn't even know there was such a thing as a birthday. It seemed like a very good idea to him. You got cake, and gifts, and your friends sat around and sang about what a jolly good fellow you were. It was all quite, quite splendid.

The singing ended, and everyone sat waiting expectantly.

'What do I do now?' asked Wormwood.

'You blow out the candles on the cake,' said Samuel.

When they'd asked Wormwood how old he was, he'd thought that he might just be a few billion years younger than the universe itself, which made him, oh, about ten billion years old.

'The cake's only a foot wide!' Mrs Johnson had pointed out. 'He can't have ten billion candles. They won't fit, and if we try the whole town will go up in flames.'

So they'd settled on one candle for every billion years, which seemed like a reasonable compromise.

Nurd was seated directly across the table from Wormwood. He was wearing a red paper party hat, and was trying unsuccessfully to blow up a balloon. Nurd had changed a lot in the time that they'd been in Biddlecombe, thought Wormwood. His skin was still green, of course, but not as green as before. He now looked like someone who had just eaten a bad egg. His head, which had formerly been shaped like a crescent moon, had shrunk slightly. It was still long and odd looking, but he was now able to walk the streets of Biddlecombe without frightening too many children or causing cars to crash, especially if he kept his head covered.

'This balloon appears to be broken,' said Nurd. 'If I blow any harder, my eyes will pop out. Again.'

That had been embarrassing. Samuel had used a spoon to retrieve them from Nurd's glass of lemonade.

Wormwood took a deep breath.

'Make a wish,' said Maria. 'But you have to keep it to yourself, or else it won't come true.'

'Oh, I think I've got the hang of the balloon now,' said Nurd.

Wormwood closed his eyes. He made his wish. He blew. There was a loud *whoosh*, followed by a *pop* and a distinct smell of burning.

Wormwood opened his eyes. Across the table, Nurd's head was on fire. In one of his hands, he held the charred, melted remains of a balloon.

'Oh, thank you,' said Nurd, as he tried to douse the flames. 'Thank you very much.'

'Sorry,' said Wormwood. 'I've never tried to blow anything out before.'

'Wow,' said Samuel. 'You have inflammable breath. I always thought it smelled like petrol.'

'The cake survived,' said Tom. 'The icing has just melted a bit.'

'I'm fine,' said Nurd. 'Don't worry about me. I love being set alight. Keeps out the cold.'

Samuel patted Nurd on the back.

'Seriously, I'm OK,' said Nurd.

'I know. Your back was on fire, though.'

'Oh.'

'There's a hole in your cloak, but I expect Mum will be able to fix it.'

Mrs Johnson cut the cake and gave everybody a slice.

'What did you wish for, Wormwood?' asked Tom.

'And if you tell me that you wished my head was on fire, we'll have words,' said Nurd.

'I thought I wasn't supposed to say,' said Wormwood.

'That's before you blow,' said Tom. 'It's all right to tell us after.'

'Well, I wished that everything would stay the way it is now,' said Wormwood. 'I'm happy here. We all are.'

Shan and Gath nodded.

And in the general hilarity and good cheer that followed, nobody noticed that it was only Nurd who had not agreed.

CHAPTER II

In Which Someone Sees a Ghost. (Yawn.)

As has already been established, the town of Biddlecombe was a lot odder than it once had been, but the curious thing about Biddlecombe was that it had always been ever so slightly strange, even before the attempted invasion from Hell. It was just that people in Biddlecombe had chosen not to remark upon its strangeness, perhaps in the hope that the strangeness might eventually grow tired of being ignored and just go and be strange somewhere else.

For example, it was well known that if you took a right turn on Machen Street, and then a left turn on Poe Place, you ended up back on the same corner of Machen Street from which you had recently started. The residents of Biddlecombe got round this peculiar geographical anomaly by avoiding that particular corner of Machen Street entirely, instead using the shortcut through Mary Shelley Lane. Visitors to Biddlecombe, though, tended not to know about the shortcut, and thus they had been known to spend a great deal of time moving back and forth between Machen Street and Poe Place until somebody local came along and rescued them.

And then there was the small matter of the statue of Hilary Mould, Biddlecombe's leading architect. Nobody could remember who had ordered the statue, or how it had come to be in Biddlecombe, but the statue had turned up sometime in the nineteenth century, shortly after Mould disappeared under circumstances that might have been described as mysterious if anyone had cared enough about Mould to miss him when he was gone, which they didn't because Mould's buildings were all ugly and awful.

The statue of Hilary Mould wasn't much lovelier than the buildings he had designed, Mould not being the most handsome of men, and it had often been suggested that it should quietly be taken away and lost. But the statue of Hilary Mould had a habit of moving around, so there was no way of knowing where it might be from one day to the next. It was usually to be found near one of the six buildings in Biddlecombe that Mould had designed, as if the architect couldn't bear to be separated from his work.

As with so many of the strange things about Biddlecombe, the townsfolk decided that the best thing for it was to ignore the statue and let it go about its business.

Which was, as we shall come to learn, a terrible mistake.

As it happened, the statue of Hilary Mould was, at that moment, lurking in a still and silent way near what appeared to be an old sweet factory but which now housed a secret laboratory. Inside the laboratory, Brian, the new tea boy, had just seen a ghost.

The effect this had on Brian was quite considerable. First of all he turned pale, so that he bore something of a resemblance to a ghost himself. Second, he dropped the tray that he was carrying, sending three cups of tea, two coffees, and a plate of assorted biscuits – including some Jammie Dodgers, of which Professor Stefan, the Head of Particle Physics, was especially fond – crashing to the floor. Finally, after tottering on his heels for a bit, Brian followed the tray downwards.

It was only Brian's second day on the job at the secret Biddlecombe annexe of CERN, the advanced research facility in Switzerland that housed the Large Hadron Collider, the massive particle accelerator which was, at that very moment, trying to uncover the secrets of the universe by recreating the moments after the Big Bang. The Collider had been notably successful in this, and appeared to have confirmed the existence of a particle known as the Higgs Boson, which was believed to be responsible for giving mass to the universe.[4]

The Biddlecombe annexe had been set up to examine the strange goings-on in the town in question, which had so far included the dead coming back to life, an attempted invasion by the Devil and all of his demonic hordes, and the abduction to Hell of a small boy, his dachshund, a number of dwarfs, two policemen, and an ice-cream salesman. It was clear to the scientists that Biddlecombe was the site of a link between our universe and another universe that wasn't half as nice, and they had decided to set up an office there in the hope that something else very bad might happen so they could watch and take notes, and perhaps win a prize.

💀 [4] It was, to put it simply, the stuff that made stuff stuff.

The problem was that the good people of Biddlecombe didn't particularly want scientists lurking around every corner and asking hopefully if anyone had been abducted, possessed, or attacked by something with too many arms. The people of Biddlecombe were hoping that whatever hole had opened between universes might have closed by now, or been filled in by the council. At the very least they wanted to forget about it because, if they did, then it might forget about them, as they had quite enough to be getting along with, what with rescuing tourists from the corner of Machen Street and avoiding walking into old statues.

The result was that the scientists had been forced to sneak into Biddlecombe and cleverly hide themselves in a secure location. Of course, Biddlecombe being a small place, everyone in the town knew that the scientists had come back. Now they could only pray that the scientists might blow themselves up, or conveniently vanish into another dimension.

The location of the secret facility was slightly – well, considerably – less spectacular than CERN's massive operation in Switzerland. The annexe was housed in the building formerly occupied by Mr Pennyfarthinge's Olde Sweete Shoppe & Factorye,[5] unoccupied ever since a tragic accident involving Mr Pennyfarthinge, an

---

💀 [5] There is a certain type of shop that just loves sticking the letter 'e' on the end of words in the hope it will make said shop appear older and more respectable. Businesses selling candles, sweeties, Christmas decorations, and models of fairies are particularly prone to this, although in reality the only thing that the 'e' adds is ten per cent extra on to the price of everything. Mr Pennyfarthinge's fondness for the 'Olde E' was so extreme as to qualifye as a forme of mentale illnesse.

unsteady ladder, and seventeen jars of gobstoppers. To keep up the pretence, the scientists had reopened the sweete shoppe and took it in turns to serve sherbet dabs, liquorice allsorts, and Uncle Dabney's Impossibly Sour Chews[6] to various small persons for an hour or two each day.

Technically, Brian was not, in fact, a tea boy, but a laboratory assistant. Nevertheless, as he was the new kid, his duties had so far extended only to boiling the kettle, making the tea, and keeping a close watch on the Jammie Dodgers, as Professor Stefan was convinced that someone was stealing Jammie Dodgers from the biscuit tin. Professor Stefan was wrong about this. It wasn't 'someone' who was stealing Jammie Dodgers.

It was everyone.

Brian's proper title was 'Assistant Deputy Assistant to the Assistant Assistant to the Assistant Head of Particle Physics', or 'ADAAAHPT' for short.

Which, oddly enough, was the last sound Brian made before he fell to the floor.

'Adaaahpt,' said Brian. *Thump*.

The noise caused Professor Stefan, who was concentrating very hard on a piece of data analysis, to drop his pen, and Professor Stefan hated dropping pens. They

---

💀 6 Uncle Dabney's Impossibly Sour Chews were banned in a number of countries after the sheer sourness of them had turned the faces of several small boys inside out. See also: Uncle Dabney's Dangerously Explosive Spacedust (tooth loss due to explosions), Uncle Dabney's Glow-In-The-Dark Radiation Gums (hair loss due to radiation poisoning), and Uncle Dabney's Frog-Shaped Pastilles (mysterious disappearance of entire populations of certain frogs). The late Uncle Dabney was, of course, quite insane, but he made curiously good sweets.

always managed to roll right against the wall, and then he had to get down on his hands and knees to find them, or send the Assistant Deputy Assistant to the Assistant Assistant to the Assistant Head of Particle Physics to do it for him. Unfortunately, the ADAAAHPT was now flat on his back, moaning softly.

'What is ADAAAHPT doing on the floor?' said Professor Stefan. 'He's your responsibility, Hilbert. You can't just leave assistants lying around. Makes the place look untidy.'

Professor Hilbert, the Assistant Head of Particle Physics, looked at Brian in puzzlement.

'He appears to have fainted.'

'Fainted?' said Professor Stefan. '*Fainted?* Listen here, Hilbert: elderly ladies faint. Young women of a delicate disposition faint. Assistants do not faint. Tell him to stop all of this nonsense immediately. I want my Jammie Dodgers. He'll have to get some fresh ones. I'm not eating those ones after they've been on the floor. We can give them to the numbskulls in Technical Support.'

'We don't have any Technical Support,' said Professor Hilbert. 'There's only Brian.'

He helped Brian to sit up, which meant that Professor Hilbert was now technically supporting Technical Support.

'Guh—,' said Brian.

'No, it's not good,' said Professor Hilbert. 'It's not good at all.'

'Guh—,' said Brian again.

'I think he may have bumped his head,' said Professor Hilbert. 'He keeps saying that it's good.'

'You mean that he's bumped his head so hard he thinks

good is bad?' said Professor Stefan. 'We can't have that. Next he'll be going around killing chaps and asking for a round of applause as he presents us with their heads. He'll make a terrible mess.'

Brian raised his right hand, and extended the index finger.

'It's a guh—, it's a guh—, it's a guh—'

'What's he doing now, Hilbert?'

'I think he's rapping, Professor.'

'Oh, do make him stop. We'll have no hip-hoppity music here. Awful racket. Now opera, there's—'

'IT'S. A. GHOST!' shrieked Brian.

Professor Hilbert noticed that Brian's hair was standing on end, and his skin was covered in goose-bumps. The atmosphere in the lab had also grown considerably colder. Professor Hilbert could see Brian's breath. He could see his own breath. He could even see Professor Stefan's breath. He could not, however, see the breath of the semi-transparent young woman, dressed as a servant, who was standing in a corner and fiddling with something that was obvious only to her. Her image flickered slightly, as though it were being projected imperfectly from nearby.

Professor Hilbert stopped supporting Brian, who duly fell backwards and would have banged his head painfully had not some Jammie Dodgers absorbed most of the impact.

'So it is,' said Professor Hilbert. 'I say, it's another ghost.'

Professor Stefan peered at the young woman over the top of his spectacles.

'A new one, too. Haven't seen her before.'

Professor Hilbert carefully approached the ghost.

'Hello,' he said. He waved his hand in front of the

ghost's face, but she didn't seem to notice. He considered his options, then poked at the woman's ribs. His finger passed right through her.

'Bit rude,' said Professor Stefan disapprovingly. 'You hardly know the girl.'

'Nothing,' said Professor Hilbert. 'No response.'

'Just like the rest.'

'Indeed.'

Slowly, the image of the girl began to fade, until finally there was only a hint of vapour to indicate that she had ever been there at all, if, in fact, she *had* ever been there at all. Oh, she was certainly somewhere, of that Professor Hilbert was sure. He just wasn't convinced that the somewhere in question was a laboratory in twenty-first-century Biddlecombe.

Brian had managed to struggle to his feet, and was now picking pieces of Jammie Dodger from his hair. He stared at the corner where the girl had been.

'I thought I saw a ghost,' he said.

'Yes,' said Professor Hilbert. 'Well done, you. And on only your second day too. You can't go around fainting every time you see one, though. You'll end up on the floor more often than you're upright if you do.'

'But it was a *ghost*.'

'Just make a note of it, there's a good chap. See that big hardbacked notebook on the desk over there?' He pointed to a massive black volume, bound in leather. 'That's our record of "ghost sightings". Write down the time it began, the time it ended, what you saw, then sign it. Professor Stefan and I will add our initials when you're done. To save yourself some time, just turn straight to page two hundred and seventy-six. That's the page we're on now, I think.'

Brian looked like he might faint again.

'Page two hundred and seventy-six? You mean that you've filled two hundred and seventy-five other pages with ghost sightings?'

Professor Hilbert laughed. Even Professor Stefan joined in, although he was still disturbed at the loss of so many perfectly good Jammie Dodgers.

'Two hundred and seventy-five pages!' said Professor Stefan. 'Young people and their ideas, eh?'

'Two hundred and seventy-five pages!' said Professor Hilbert. 'Dear oh dear, where do we get these kids from? No, Brian, that would just be silly.'

He wiped a tear of mirth from his eye with a handkerchief.

'That's volume three,' he explained. 'We've filled *one thousand*, two hundred and seventy-five pages with ghost sightings.'

At which point Brian fell over again. When he eventually recovered himself, he added the sighting to the book, just as he had been told. He noted down everything he had seen, including the hint of black vapour that had hung in the air like smoke after the ghost had disappeared. Had Professors Hilbert and Stefan taken the time to read Brian's note, they might have found that black vapour very odd.

Outside, the statue of Hilary Mould stared, solid and unmoving, at the old factory. A cloud passed over the moon, casting the statue in shadow.

When the moon reappeared, the statue was gone.

CHAPTER III

**In Which We Travel to a Galaxy Far,
Far Away, But Since It's Not a Long Time Ago
the *Star Wars* People Can't Sue Us.**

Some things are better left unsaid. Among them are
'This situation can't really get any worse,' which is
usually spoken before the loss of a limb, a car going
off a cliff, or someone pushing a button marked DO
NOT PUSH THIS BUTTON. EVER. WE'RE NOT JOKING; 'Well,
he seems like a nice person,' which will shortly be
followed by the arrest of the person in question and
the removal of bodies from his basement, possibly
including your own; and finally, and most better-left-
unsaid of all, 'You know, I think everything is going
to be just fine,' because that means everything is most
assuredly not going to be fine, not by a long shot.

So. Everything is going to be fine. Are we clear on
that?

Good.

In another part of the Multiverse, a couple of dimensions
from Biddlecombe, a small green planet orbited a slowly
dying star. The news that the star was dying might have
proved alarming to the inhabitants of the planet had any
of them been sufficiently advanced to be capable of

understanding the problem, but so far the planet had not produced any form of life that was equipped to do anything more sophisticated than eat while trying not to be eaten itself. Much of the planet was covered by thick coniferous forests, hence its colour from space, although it also boasted some very nice oceans, and a mountain that, at some point in the future, representatives of some species might try to climb because it was there, assuming the star didn't die long before then.

The creature that moved through the depths of one of the planet's oceans didn't have a name since, as we have established, there was nobody around with the required intellectual curiosity to give it one. Also, as the creature was very large, very toothy, and very, very hungry, any contact with it would have gone somewhat along the lines of 'Look, a new species! I shall name it – AAARRGHHH! My leg! Help, help! No, AAARRGGHH! My other leg!' etc., which doesn't tend to look good in history books.

There was very little in the oceans that the creature had not encountered before, and nothing that it had so far not tried, successfully, to eat. But on this particular occasion its attention was caught by a small bright glowing mass, a clump of atoms that vaguely resembled a cluster of blue fish eggs. The creature, always hungry and open to trying new foodstuffs, wolfed the blue mass down and proceeded on its none-too-merry way, already on the lookout for even more tasty and interesting things to eat.

It had been swimming for a mile or so when it began to consider what all of this hunting and eating was about, really. I mean, it swam so it could eat, and it ate so it could keep swimming, and that was the sum of its existence, as far as it could tell. It wasn't much of a life when you thought about it, which it hadn't until only moments before, and there had to be more to it all than that. What would happen, it wondered, if it sent other creatures out to hunt on its behalf while it put its fins up and made plans for the future, among which were the enslavement of the planet's population – hey, we're on a planet? – followed by the building of space-ships and the further enslavement of lots of other planets' populations, upon which it could then feed to its belly's content? That sounded great! Oh, and apparently the star – star? – around which its planet was orbiting was dying, so the sooner it got started on this whole business of building spaceships, whatever they were, the better.

Before it could get to work on the fine print of its grand design, a larger, even toothier, and even hungrier monster bit it in half, and the creature's brain had barely time enough to think, Oh, well that's just great, that is, before its divided body was chomped to mincemeat and began the great journey through the digestive tract of another.

Whereupon *that* large, hungry creature began to wonder about the nature of good and evil, and how evil seemed much more fun, all things considered, and so this might have continued for a very long time until there was an unfamiliar popping sound in the ocean's depths, and into existence popped a wobbly being with one eye. It was wearing a very fetching top hat tied with a piece of elastic beneath what passed for its chin, just to ensure that its hat didn't float away, as it was very fond of that hat.

The massive ocean monster, all teeth and gills and eyes and horns and scales, looked at the new arrival, opened its jaws, and prepared to chew, but before it could start chomping the little hat-wearer shot into its mouth and down its gullet. The monster gave a kind of fishy shrug and swam on, distracted from the peculiar appearance of its latest meal by all of this evil stuff, which sounded just fascinating.

Deep inside the monster's gut, the gelatinous mass, whose name was Crudford, Esq. began searching through half-digested flesh and bone. It stank something awful in there, but Crudford, cheerful and contented by nature, didn't mind. In fact, he even whistled a happy tune just to pass the time. Eventually, somewhere in the newly consumed remains of a giant segmented eel, he found what he had been looking for: a small group of atoms that glowed a bright blue. Crudford lifted his hat, the elastic stretching as he did so, and retrieved from the top of his head a glass bottle. The bottle was sealed with a cork, and the blue atoms in the monster's belly found a kind of reflection in a similar, but larger, cluster already contained inside. Crudford removed the cork and carefully added the new atoms to the old before resealing the bottle and placing it safely under his hat. His jellied features split into a deep smile, and he patted his hat happily.

'There you are, Mrs Abernathy,' he said. 'We'll have all those bits of you back together again in no time.'

With that, he popped out of existence again, and the huge sea creature that had recently swallowed him forgot all about being evil and simply went back to eating things, which was probably for the best.

There were many advantages to being an entity composed entirely of transparent jelly. Actually, there weren't, but Crudford, Esq., who was a creature of boundless optimism, tried to find the bright side of any situation, even his own, which was very *un*bright. Looked at from the outside, he appeared to be on the same level as slime[7], and in possession of only a single hat. But in Crudford's own mind he was a sluglike object on the rise, a wobbling thingummy on the way to greater things. Someday, an opportunity would present itself, and there would be only one gelatinous demon for the job: Crudford, Esq.

Amazingly enough, that day had come when Mrs Abernathy, the left-hand demon of the Great Malevolence, the most evil being in the Multiverse, had suddenly found herself with each of the billions and billions of individual atoms that made up her body separated from its neighbours and scattered through the Multiverse, all because she had messed with Samuel Johnson, his dog, two policemen, four elves, and an ice-cream salesman.[8] Oh, and four of her own demons,

---

💀 [7] Which was probably to be expected, given that the slime was usually his own. 'I've produced more slime, sludge, glop, gunk, mucus and mire than you've had hot dinners,' he would boast proudly to anyone who might listen. Which would usually be enough to put someone about to sit down to a hot dinner right off the idea.

💀 [8] As detailed in *The Infernals*. If you haven't read it, what are you doing

including Nurd the Scourge of Five Deities, who everyone had thought so useless at being a demon that even Crudford was more terrifying than him, and Crudford couldn't help but be nice to everyone he met.

Crudford imagined that being blown apart at the atomic level must have hurt a lot. Unfortunately for Mrs Abernathy, as Crudford had come to realise, she hadn't just been blown apart at the atomic level: the protons, neutrons and electrons that made up her atoms had also become separated from one another, and then the particles *within* the protons and neutrons, known as quarks, had been scattered for good measure. There were three quarks within each proton and neutron, bound together by other particles called gluons, and all of those various bits and pieces were now scattered throughout the Multiverse. Being blown apart on the sub-atomic level must have hurt an awful, awful lot, thought Crudford. Still, look on the bright side: at least Mrs Abernathy was seeing new places.

But cometh the hour, cometh the congealed, hat-wearing jelly being. It turned out that Crudford had always been very good at squeezing into small spaces, and oozing through tiny holes. No one in Hell was entirely sure what Crudford was made from, exactly, but it was remarkable stuff, and there was no other creature remotely like him in that awful place.

And Crudford couldn't just squeeze through cracks

---

here? I mean, what kind of person are you, reading the third book before the second? I strongly advise you to turn to the second footnote in Chapter One of *The Infernals*, which will wag a finger disapprovingly at you for picking up a later book in a series without first reading the earlier ones. I mean, really . . .

in rocks and wood and metal: no, Crudford could ooze through the rips and tears in universes, the holes and flaws between dimensions. It made him the perfect candidate to search for, and gather up, Mrs Abernathy's quarks and gluons and occasional reconstituted atoms so that the process of putting her back together again could begin. At last, Crudford had found his purpose. The recreation of Mrs Abernathy was his responsibility, and his alone. He was searching for subatomic needles in the universal haystacks of the Multiverse, and he loved it.

He could even explore those spaces between universes, although Crudford didn't like hanging about there for long. Like everyone else in Hell, he had always felt that the Great Malevolence, the foulest, most vile entity imaginable – but probably a lovely demon once you got to know it, Crudford tried to believe – was the cherry on the cake when it came to beings of which one ought to be frightened.

But Crudford had come to learn that there were things in the gaps between universes that made the Great Malevolence look like a small flowery unicorn that pooed fairy dust. At least you knew where you stood with the Great Malevolence. Admittedly, that was on the edge of an infinite fiery pit or a cold, bottomless lake of ice, into either of which the Great Malevolence might plunge you if the mood took it, but there was no mystery about the old GM: it hated everything that breathed, especially everything that breathed on Earth, and ultimately it wanted to torment the living for eternity and turn the Multiverse into a realm of ash and fire. Fair enough, thought Crudford. Aim high. Everybody needs an ambition.

But between universes there were entities that didn't feel anything at all, not even hatred. They had no form, and barely a consciousness. They existed only to bring about nonexistence. They put the 'thing' in 'nothing'. When Crudford came close to their non-kingdoms, he was aware of their non-attention coming to rest upon him, their complete and utter uncaringness, and even his relentless optimism would start to flag somewhat.

But the worse of the unknowable entities dwelt in the Kingdom of Shadows. They had taken the concept of nothingness – the aching absence of absolute emptiness – and added one simple ingredient to the mix.

Darkness.

And not just any old Darkness either, but a dense, suffocating blackness that coated the body and the mind and the soul, a Darkness like eternal drowning, a Darkness from which all hope of light had fled because it came from a place in which light had never been known. Even calling the place in which they lurked the 'Kingdom of Shadows' was a kind of mistake because real shadows required light to form. The Great Malevolence, who had seen so much and recorded it all, had shown Crudford the fate of universes invaded by the Darkness, and it had always begun with shadows where no shadows should have been.

So Crudford moved carefully through the spaces between universes, and he carefully watched every shadow. He listened too, for Crudford could hear the rips widening in the fabric of universes, just as he could see the light through the new gaps. Now, as he moved through the Multiverse to return to Hell with his shiny blue prizes, he became aware of a rhythmic, pulsing sound coming from somewhere distant. It was familiar to him.

It was a heartbeat.

Crudford's senses were so keen that he could tell the beating of one heart from another, for each heart had its own unique beat. But this was a very special heart. He alone, sensitive beyond any other demon, had heard its secret rhythm in Hell. It was a human heart through which no blood flowed, only malice.

Somewhere in the Multiverse, Mrs Abernathy's heart was beating.

CHAPTER IV

In Which We Go Shopping, and
Rather Wish That We Hadn't

Let's drift back through Biddlecombe on this cold dark night, drift like smoke.

Like Shadows.

Wreckit & Sons had once been the largest shop in Biddlecombe. It sold almost everything that anyone could possibly want: pins and pots, bread baskets and bicycles, televisions and tea trays. It was four storeys tall, took up an entire block of the town's centre, and its shelves stretched for miles and miles. Its basement was so huge and poorly lit that a man named Ernest Tuttle had once got lost there while trying to buy a tennis racket and a socket wrench, and promptly vanished. His ghost – a pale, moaning figure – was said to haunt the store, until it was discovered that it was not, in fact, Ernest Tuttle's ghost but Ernest Tuttle himself. He had spent two years trying to find a way out, and couldn't understand why people kept running away from him. When they pointed out that he was pale and moaning, he replied that they'd be pale too if they'd been trapped in a basement for two years living only on rice cakes, and they'd probably moan a bit as well. His feet hurt, he told reporters, and he believed that the mice had adopted him as their king. He still hadn't managed to find a tennis racket or a socket wrench either.

The store was another of Hilary Mould's buildings, but it wasn't quite as offensively awful as the others. There was something almost grand about Wreckit & Sons. In the right light – somewhat dim, a bit murky – it resembled a cathedral, or a temple. Arthur Bunce, the man who had originally asked Hilary Mould to design the store, took one look at it and promptly went mad. Instead Mould bought the building himself, and he disappeared shortly after. The building remained empty for many years until a gentleman named Wreckit took a fancy to it, and opened his department store there.

But if Wreckit & Sons sold a lot of things that people might want, it also tried to sell a lot of things that nobody could possibly want. As he grew older, Mr Wreckit became more and more eccentric. He began calling it Wreckit & Sons for starters, which annoyed his daughters greatly, as he didn't have any sons. His buying habits changed. For example, he bought two thousand three-dimensional Chinese-made photographs of the man on the next page. (We put him there so that you can prepare yourselves for the shock when you turn over. Ready? Are you sure? Okay then. Don't say we didn't warn you . . .)

The man's name was Max Schreck, and he was famous for playing the vampire in an old film called *Nosferatu*. Max Schreck was so strange-looking that it was whispered he might even be a *real* vampire. The 3D nature of the photos bought by Mr Wreckit meant that Max Schreck's eyes followed you around the room, and NOBODY wanted this man's eyes following them around the room. Mr Wreckit sold precisely one of the pictures, and that was to himself. He kept it hidden under a blanket.

Mr Wreckit also bought 100 unicycles, but it was only when they were shipped to him that he discovered they were not actual unicycles but merely bicycles that were missing one wheel. If it is hard to ride a unicycle, it is significantly harder to ride a bicycle that is fifty per cent down in the wheel department. Mr Wreckit tried. The resulting bang on the head made him even stranger.

He bought teapots with no spouts, sieves with no holes, and steel piggy banks with a slot for the money to go in but no way of getting it out again. He bought televisions that only picked up signals from North Korea, and radios that tuned into frequencies only dogs could hear. He sold gloves for people with six fingers, and gloves for people with three fingers, but no gloves for people with four fingers and a thumb. His fire extinguishers started fires, and his firelighters wouldn't light. His fridges boiled milk, and his ovens were so cold that when a penguin escaped from Biddlecombe's Little World of Animal Wonders, it was later found to be living in one of them, along with its entire family and a single confused chicken.

Nobody seemed able to reason with Mr Wreckit. He had simply gone bonkers. He was nutty as a fruitcake. Still, as he was the sole owner of Wreckit & Sons due to the absence of any real sons, and refused to talk to his daughters because they weren't men, he was free to run the business into the ground and there wasn't anything anyone could do to stop him.

So Mr Wreckit did, in the end, wreck it. The store went out of business. Mr Wreckit, broke and crazy, retired to a cottage on the Devon coast. When asked what had possessed him to destroy his own business, he replied, strangely, 'That's a very good question. What *did* possess me?'

But he had no answer. On his deathbed, he apologised to his daughters. His last words were: 'The Voice in the Wall made me do it.'

Nobody wanted to take over Wreckit & Sons after that, and the building stayed empty. It stood at the end of Biddlecombe's main street, a great block of not-quite-nothing, for it always seemed as though the spirit of the old store was still present, infusing its bricks and mortar, its wood and its windows, waiting for the moment when its doors might be opened again, and people could get lost in its basement.

But nobody came, and the spirit slept.

* * *

So it was that the store had been closed for what seemed like a very long time – and was, actually, a very long time.[9] Two generations of Biddlecombe children had grown up without any memory of Wreckit & Sons being anything other than an empty shell, its ground-floor windows boarded and its doors locked. Eventually people just stopped noticing it, although strangers would sometimes pass through the town and gaze up at it. And when they asked who had designed such a building, the residents of Biddlecombe would shrug their shoulders and point at the statue of Hilary Mould, assuming they could find it.

But if the history of Wreckit & Sons was odd, its oddness didn't stand out quite so much when monsters and demons began invading Biddlecombe, even if they

💀 [9] Well, long in human terms, which is all that concerns most people. That's a little narrow-minded, though, and if you only think in those terms then perhaps you should take a long, critical look at yourself in the mirror. Frankly, you're not the centre of the Multiverse, no matter what your mum and dad might say, or your nan, or your Auntie Betty who never got married – mainly because, according to your dad, nobody could get her to shut up long enough to ask her – but comes around to 'babysit' occasionally and just seems to drink a lot of your parents' sherry before falling asleep.

Sorry, where were we? Oh yes, long lives. *Anyway*, what seems like a long time to you is the blink of an eye to lots of other species. The Llangernyw Yew is the oldest tree in Europe, and is reckoned to be 4,000–5,000 years old, while certain specimens of black coral have been found to be over 4,200 years old. Meanwhile, the giant barrel sponge *Xestospongia muta*, which lives in the Caribbean, is one of the longest-lived animals on earth, with some such sponges now over 2,300 years old. Mind you, they don't do a lot of shopping your black sponges, and so couldn't really have done much to help Wreckit & Sons stay open. Then again, Wreckit & Sons did *sell* sponges, so the black sponges, had they known, would probably have been quite pleased to see it close. Things that live for thousands of years tend to have long memories, and know how to hold a grudge.

didn't leave a lot of proof behind once they went away again, monsters in ponds and spectral voices from golf courses excepted. Psychiatrists spoke of mass hysteria, and comedians made jokes about the townsfolk. Experts arrived and took readings. They dug in the ground, and tested the air, and poked at people who didn't want to be poked, thank you very much, and warned that, if the experts continued to poke them, they'd find their poking sticks stuck somewhere the sun didn't shine.[10] With so much strangeness going on, suddenly Mr Wreckit's old store began to seem not so strange after all. But it was. It was very, very strange, and strange things have a habit of attracting more strangeness to them.

In the basement of Wreckit & Sons, something moved. It was pale and naked, but it eventually managed to find a suit that fitted it, and a shirt that wasn't too yellowed, and a smart grey tie. As thousands of eyes followed it round the room, it wiped the dust from an old mirror and smoothed its hair.

'What is my name?' it asked.

The Voice in the Wall told him.

You shall be called Mr St John-Cholmondeley.

'How do you spell that?'

The Voice in the Wall spelled the name.

💀 10 'In a cave?'
No.
'In a very deep ocean?'
No.
'Hmmm. Up someone's bottom?'
Possibly.

'But you say it's pronounced Sinjin-Chumley?'
Yes.

'Are you sure that's right?'
Yes.

The Voice in the Wall sounded a bit miffed. It was so difficult to find good help these days.

The newly animated Mr St John-Cholmondeley looked doubtful.

'If you say so.'
I do.

The Voice in the Wall directed Mr St John-Cholmondeley to a safe, and told him the combination. Inside the safe was a great deal of gold, along with details of secret bank accounts. The bank accounts were all in the name of St John-Cholmondeley, even though they had been set up more than a century earlier.

'What do you want me to do?' asked Mr St John-Cholmondeley.

The Voice in the Wall told him, and Mr St John-Cholmondeley set to work.

Wreckit & Sons was about to reopen for business.[11]

---

[11] Are you on the edge of your seats now? If we had a soundtrack to this book (of which more later) that kind of ending to a chapter would come with a three-note theme along the lines of 'Dun-dun-*dah*!' About that edge-of-the-seat business: in a sense, we are *always* on the edge of our seats because of electromagnetic repulsion, which means that the atoms that make up matter never actually touch one another. The closer atoms get, the more repulsion there is between the electrical charges of each atom. It's a bit like trying to make the same poles of a pair of magnets touch: it just doesn't work. So you may at this moment think that you're sitting in a chair reading this footnote, but you're actually hovering ever so slightly above it, suspended by a force of electromagnetic repulsion a billion billion billion billion times stronger than the force of gravity. You are officially a hoverperson.

CHAPTER V

In Which We Go on a Date – Well, Not 'We' as in You and I, Because That Would Just Be Awkward, But We Go on a Date with Other People. No, Hang On, That's Still Not Right. Oh, Never Mind. Just Read the Chapter

There may come a time in your life – I hope that it does not come, for your sake, but it might – when you realise that you may be with the wrong person. By this I don't mean being in Russia with Napoleon just as the weather starts to turn chilly, or on a raised platform while a chap with a hood over his face raises a big axe and looks for a way to make you roughly a head shorter, although neither of those things would be good.[12]

No, what I mean is that you may ask someone out on a date, and during the course of the date you may discover that you have made a terrible mistake. You may even get a clear signal that a terrible mistake has been made. The person sitting across the table from you, or next to you in the cinema, may announce that

---

[12] Similarly, a century ago you would not have been happy to find that one of the passengers on your ship was Violet Jessop. Ms Jessop, a stewardess and nurse, was on the *Titanic* when it sunk in 1912. She was also on the *Britannic*, which was hit by a mine in 1916, and she was onboard the *Olympic*, the *Titanic*'s sister ship, when it collided with HMS *Hawke* in 1910. If Violet Jessop was one of your fellow passengers on a voyage, you might as well have jumped overboard at the start just to get the whole business out of the way.

she wasn't sure that she was going to make the date because she was certain the jury was going to find her guilty, even though she hadn't really murdered anyone because her last boyfriend had simply tripped and fallen on the knife she just happened to be holding at the time, ha-ha-ha, what a silly boy he was, and DON'T EVER MAKE ME MAD! Other subtle signs that you may have erred in asking someone out for an evening include: shooting the waiter for spilling the soup; laughing very loudly any time anyone dies in a film, especially if they die horribly, and everyone else in the cinema is weeping; or telling you that they've never gone out with anyone quite like you before, and when you ask them what that means you get the reply, 'You know, a real person. One that I didn't imagine, or build from Lego.'[13]

Samuel Johnson was having one of those moments. In fact, he'd been having them for quite some time, but had hoped that things might get better. After all, he'd had a crush on Lucy Highmore for so long that he couldn't actually remember a time when he *didn't* have a crush on her. Occasionally in life we will wish for something that may not be very good for us simply because we think it will make us feel better about

---

[13] To quote the title of a famous song, 'Breaking Up is Hard to Do', and people find all sorts of ways to do it. If someone is breaking up with you, they may tell you that 'it's not you, it's me'. This will be a lie. If someone says that it's not you in order to stop going out with you, then it is you. It doesn't matter if they tell you that they want to go off and help little orphans in some obscure part of the world, or sign up for an experimental space mission, or become a monk or a nun, and this is why it's not you, it's still you. You, you, you. Believe me, I know. I'm not bitter though. Not really. OK, maybe a bit.

ourselves, or make us seem more important in the eyes of the world. This is why people buy expensive cars that they don't need, or wear gold watches bigger than their heads. It is also why people will often date someone simply because he or she is wealthy, or famous, or beautiful. In case you didn't already know – and if you're clever enough to be reading a book, and have managed to get this far without stumbling over any words longer than five letters, then you probably *do* know – let me explain a truth to you: it doesn't work. You're trying to fix a flaw in yourself by shoving the problem on to someone, or something, else. It's like having a cut on your finger and bandaging your toe instead. It's like feeling hungry, and hoping that you'll feel less hungry by buying yourself a hat.

A wise man once said that you should be careful what you wish for, because you might get it. Samuel wanted to meet that wise man and ask him why he hadn't been there to advise Samuel when he'd started wishing that Lucy Highmore would go out with him. That was the trouble with wise men: they were never around when you needed them, and by the time you became a wise man yourself it was too late to use any of your wisdom on yourself, and nobody else wanted to listen to you.

Lucy Highmore didn't particularly like Samuel's friends. She didn't like where he lived, and she didn't like how he dressed. She didn't like the sunlight because it damaged her skin, and she didn't like the cold because, well, it made her feel cold. She didn't like going out, and she didn't like staying in. (When Samuel suggested that they could just stand at her front door with one foot inside and one foot outside, she had looked at him in a troubled way.) She didn't like Samuel's dog, Boswell, because he smelled funny. Boswell, who understood people better than people understood him, found this very unfair, as he wasn't one of those dogs inclined to roll in stuff that smelled bad. He had yet to find a dead animal or a pile of deer poo that made him think, Wow, now why don't I have a bit of a spin in that because I bet everyone will want to hug me after, and there's no way they'll make me take a bath that I don't want. Furthermore, Lucy Highmore smelled funny to Boswell too, but there wasn't much that he could do about it. She smelled of peculiar perfumes with French names that sounded like *Mwah-mwoh*, or *Zejung*, names that were only impressive when spoken by an invisible man with a deep voice. She also smelled slightly of vegetables because that was all she seemed to eat. She could live for a week on a stick of celery and half a carrot, and there were camels that consumed less liquid.

On their first date, Samuel had taken Lucy to Pete's Pies. Everyone loved Pete's Pies. It was a small pie shop run – and you're ahead of me here – by a man named Pete. Pete's pies were perfect pastry constructions filled with meat and vegetables, or just vegetables if you were that way inclined, and just meat if you really, really liked meat. The pastry was as golden as the most perfect dawn, the filling never too hot and never too cold. Pete also made what he called his 'dessert pies', triangles of apple, or rhubarb, or pear that made grown men weep for their sheer loveliness, and grown women weep with them. There was nobody – I mean, nobody – who didn't like Pete's pies. No one. You'd have to be mad not to like them. You'd have to be impossible to please. You'd have to be –

Lucy Highmore.

On that first date, Lucy had politely declined to share a pie, and had simply sipped delicately at a glass of water – so delicately, in fact, that natural evaporation caused the level in the glass to drop more than Lucy's sips.

Now, months later, she and Samuel were still together, but both of them were starting to think that they shouldn't be, although neither could quite find the words to say it. They were also back in Pete's Pies. Since Lucy never seemed to eat much, it didn't really matter where they went. She could choose not to eat in Pete's Pies just as easily as she could choose not to eat anywhere else. They were the only people in the pie shop apart from old Mr Probble, who now spent his days reading the *Oxford English Dictionary* in order to improve his word power. He'd started at 'A', and was reading a page a day. This meant that conversations with Mr Probble tended to involve exchanges like the following:

'Hello, Mr Probble. Nice day, isn't it?'

To which Mr Probble might reply, 'Aardvarks amble awkwardly.'[14]

Samuel stared into Lucy's eyes, and Lucy stared into his.

☠ [14] Until he moved on to the letter 'B', when the reply became 'Aardvarks amble awkwardly *but briskly* . . .'

'You know,' she said, 'you ought to get new glasses.'

'Really?' said Samuel.

'Yes, those ones make your face look a funny shape. They also make you seem like you have trouble seeing things.'

'But I do have trouble seeing things,' said Samuel.

'But you don't want everyone to know, do you?' said Lucy. 'It's like ugly people and hats.'

'Is it?' said Samuel, not sure where ugly people came into it, exactly, or hats.

'Of course, silly.'

Lucy patted Samuel's arm. To be honest, 'patted' might have been an understatement. There were wrestling champions who would have screamed 'Ouch!' after being patted by Lucy Highmore. She had quite a swing on her for a thin girl.

'Ugly people wear hats so that people can't see how ugly they are,' explained Lucy. 'The hats cast a shadow, and so they hide their ugliness, and pretty people don't have to feel so bad about being pretty.'

'But . . .' said Samuel, rubbing his arm. He tried to find his train of thought, but it had departed the station long before, with a fat lady on the back waving goodbye with a handkerchief and leaving Samuel stranded on the Platform of Confusion. 'But don't pretty people wear hats too?'

'Yes, sillikins,' said Lucy, and Samuel just prayed that she wouldn't pat his arm again. He still couldn't feel his fingers. 'But they wear them for a different reason. Hats on pretty people make them look prettier! Everything looks prettier on pretty people. It's a law.'

'Right,' said Samuel. If you followed that statement to its logical conclusion, then Samuel's glasses should have made him look prettier – er, more handsome – but only if he was pretty – er, handsome – to begin with. But if they didn't make him look more handsome – there, got it right third time – did that mean he wasn't handsome at all? Samuel sort of guessed that he wasn't, but he was hopeful that the situation might change as he got older. The fact that Lucy Highmore had agreed to go out with him had fuelled that hope.

In a way, both Lucy and Samuel had made two versions of the same mistake. Lucy had agreed to go out with Samuel because, despite what some of the folk in Biddlecombe might have thought or said, he was a kind of hero. He had faced down the hordes of Hell. He had fought demons. He might have been visually challenged, and distinctly awkward, and so attached to his dog that it accompanied him on dates, but he still wasn't like most of the other ordinary boys in Biddlecombe, and Lucy Highmore felt less ordinary for being with him. It was the same reason that she always made sure her hair was perfect before leaving the house, and always wore the prettiest and most fashionable clothes, and always surrounded herself with people who were slightly less pretty and perfect than she was. She did it because, deep inside, she suspected that she wasn't as interesting, or clever, or even as pretty as she liked to believe, but if she acted like she was, and shielded herself with boys and girls who were even more insecure, she might just convince everyone that she was better than they were. If she tried really, really hard, she might even convince herself.

But the main reason that Lucy had agreed to go out with Samuel was because Maria Mayer, one of Samuel's closest friends, was more than a little in love with him. Everyone knew this – everyone, that is, except Samuel, who was a bit thick when it came to girls. If Maria wanted Samuel, thought Lucy, then there must be something there worth having, even if Lucy wasn't entirely sure what that was.

And Samuel? Well, Samuel had always been happy with himself. I don't mean that he was smug, or self-satisfied. He knew he was awkward, and didn't see very well without his glasses, and that, in his case, his best friend really was his dog, but he didn't mind. He got on well with his mum, and with his dad, most of the time, even if his dad now lived in Norwich with a lady called Esther who wore so much make-up that, when she smiled or frowned, or even when she spoke, cracks appeared in her face and cosmetics avalanched to the floor. She had kissed Samuel the first time that they met, and the left side of his face had turned brown.

But he had looked at Lucy Highmore, who had never so much as glanced at him before all of that demon business, and wondered if being with her might make him feel just a bit less awkward, and a little less like an outsider. Who knew, she might even help to make his hair do what he wanted it to do. (Samuel's hair never seemed to want to do anything other than slouch lazily on his scalp like a flat, yellow animal; he had tried using gel on it once, and it had ended up looking like a flat, yellow animal that had somehow become frozen in place just as it was about to attack someone from the top of a small boy's head.) She could advise him on how to dress so that his shirt matched his trousers, or his shoes matched his jacket, or even so one sock matched the other. In the end, Samuel had wanted Lucy to make him better than he was, ignoring the fact that he was doing perfectly well just being himself. The result was that, because she was secretly more unhappy than he was, she had just ended up making him feel worse: about his hair, his clothes, his friends, himself, even about Boswell.

Lucy Highmore wasn't a bad person. She was slightly vain, but she wasn't mean. Samuel wasn't a bad person either. He was just insecure, and tired of being the odd kid out. Together, they were a small mistake that was rapidly becoming a bigger, more complicated one.

'If you like,' said Lucy, 'I'll go with you to help you choose your new glasses. It'll be fun.'

Boswell, lying on the floor of Pete's Pies beside his beloved master, put his head between his paws and sighed a long dog sigh.

CHAPTER VI

In Which We Are Reunited with Some Old Friends, and Keep a Close Watch on our Wallets

The citizens of Biddlecombe woke one morning to find the windows of Wreckit & Sons blacked out. From inside the store came sounds of drilling and hammering, but nobody knew what construction company was in charge, and no one was seen either entering or leaving the building. But the work went on, day and night, and from somewhere in the depths of the store orders were placed for dolls, and games, and model trains.

The rumour was that Wreckit & Sons was about to reopen as a toyshop.

Sometimes, Dan wondered if he was right to be so upbeat all of the time. He had always had a sunny disposition. If life gave him bruised fruit, he made jam. The glass was always half full, even when it wasn't, because Dan would get down on his knees and squint at it from a funny angle until it appeared fuller than it was. Even if there was no glass at all, Dan assumed this was only because someone had taken it away to fill it up again. If he had been told that the world was ending tomorrow, Dan would have shrugged his shoulders and waited patiently for something to prevent it from happening. The asteroid that was about to destroy the Earth could have been visible as a flaming ball in the sky and Dan would have had a scone ready on the end of a fork so he could toast it without switching on the toaster.

Lately, though, it had been hard for Dan to keep a smile on his face. He had been a happy undertaker for many years[15] but had grown tired of having nobody to talk to. (Well, he did have people to talk to, but they didn't answer back, and even Dan might have been a bit concerned if they had started to.) He had then bought an ice cream van on the grounds that he had always liked ice cream, and lots of other folk liked ice cream too, and therefore he was likely to spread good cheer by selling it to them while his chimes played 'How Much Is That Doggie in the Window?' over and over. At the very least, it was likely that people would buy his ice cream just so that he would move on and they wouldn't have to listen to 'How Much Is That Doggie in the Window?' any longer.

Unfortunately for Dan, he and his ice cream van had been dragged to Hell and, although both had returned, the van had been a great deal the worse for wear when it got back, and Dan's insurance didn't cover unexpected trips to Hell. But, as always, something had turned up.

☠ [15] This was not necessarily a good thing. There are many professions that might benefit from a smile and a hearty laugh, but undertaking is not one of them. The last thing people want as they arrive, red-eyed and weeping, to send their beloved Auntie Ethel on her way to the next life is to find someone in a black suit grinning like a loon and opining that it's a lovely day for a funeral. That way, frankly, lies a punch in the face.

Actually, four of them had turned up: Jolly, Dozy, Angry and Mumbles, known collectively as Mr Merryweather's Elves, or Mr Merryweather's Dwarfs, or by whatever name the police were NOT looking for them at any particular moment in time. Currently, they were known as Dan's Dwarfs, which had seemed like a good idea, Mr Merryweather having abandoned the dwarfs for a number of reasons, but mostly because he hated them.

So now Dan drove the dwarfs round, and tried to find them work. And keep them sober. And stop them from stealing. All of which was a lot harder than it sounded, and it already sounded quite hard.

Today, Dan's Dwarfs were on their way to the grand opening of Honest Ed's[16] Used Car Showrooms just outside the town of Biddlecombe. Why Honest Ed felt that a quartet of surly dwarfs would help him sell more dodgy cars was unclear, but Dan took the view that his was not to reason why, but just to take the money and run before something bad happened which, when the dwarfs were involved, it usually did.

This was why, as Dan drove the dwarfs around in a

[16] A quick word here about people who put words like 'Honest' or 'Cheerful' before their names: they usually aren't. Anyone who has to advertise the fact that he's cheerful is probably sadder than a bird without a beak in a birdseed factory, while someone who has to boast about how honest he is will steal the eyes from your head while you're cleaning your glasses. Mind you, this doesn't mean that someone who calls himself Dishonest Bob, for example, is automatically honest. He's just honest about being dishonest, if you see what I mean. Vlad the Impaler (1431–76) still went around impaling people, and Henry the Cruel of Germany (1165–97) was still cruel. They just believed that it paid to advertise. Generally speaking, then, if someone adds a good quality to their name, they're probably lying, and if they add something bad, then they're probably telling the truth.

battered old van, he was wondering if one could really continue to be upbeat when you were responsible for four dwarfs who appeared set on proving that good things did not always come in small packages.

'Lot of traffic today,' said Jolly, who often wasn't.

'It's moving fast, though,' said Angry, who often was.

'Anyone in a car that's moving fast mustn't have bought it from Honest Ed,' said Dozy, who often was as well. 'His cars are so old, they come with a bloke to walk in front of them waving a red flag.'[17]

'Nwarglesput,' said Mumbles, which is self-explanatory.

'Listen, lads,' said Dan. 'Let's not have any trouble, right? We go in, we dance around the cars, we look happy, we collect the cheque, and we leave. It doesn't have to be any more complicated than that.'

'What do you mean, "we"?' said Angry. 'You're not going to be dancing around in a funny hat, only us. There's no dignity to it.'

'There's fifty quid each to it,' said Dan.

'I suppose so,' said Angry. 'It's still no job for a grown man.'

'You're not a grown man,' said Dan. 'That's the point. If you were a grown man, they wouldn't be paying you to dance around a car showroom wearing a hat with

---

💀 17 Curiously, the British Locomotive Act of 1865 (also known as the 'Red Flag Act') required that no self-propelled vehicle (which included cars) could travel faster than four miles per hour in the country, and two miles per hour in the city. Each car was also required to have a crew of three, one of whom had to walk 180 feet in front of the car carrying a red flag. In 1878 the whole flag business was made optional as cars became faster, probably because someone in a car got tired of travelling at two miles an hour and ran over the bloke with the flag, making it hard to recruit replacement flag wavers from then on.

bells on it and a shirt that says "Honest Ed's Cars – The Lowest Prices Around!"'

'We're not actually low,' said Jolly. 'We're small. There's no reason why we should be wearing shirts advertising low prices. Small prices maybe, but not low ones.'

'You're small *and* low,' said Dan. 'You're low to the ground. Can you reach things on high shelves without standing on chairs? No. So you're low.'

'Still don't like it,' said Jolly.

'Never mind that,' said Dan. 'We're nearly there. The local newspaper is sending someone along to take pictures, and a disc jockey from Biddlecombe FM radio – "The Big B!" – will be playing tunes and giving away prizes.'

'What kind of prizes?' asked Jolly.

'Mugs. Stickers. Pens,' said Dan.

'Fantastic,' said Angry. 'I can just see someone winning a pen and dying of happiness.'

'Or a mug,' said Jolly. 'There'll probably be some old lady who's dreamed all her life of having a mug to call her own. She's been drinking tea out of holes in the ground for all these years, and suddenly – bang! – she wins a mug. They'll write songs about it, and people will tell their children of it for generations to come: "You know, I was there the day old Mrs Banbury won a mug."'

Dan tightened his grip on the steering wheel. He tried to find something to be upbeat about, and decided that there was a limit to the amount of trouble that the dwarfs could cause at Honest Ed's. There'd be no beer, and they didn't have weapons. What could possibly go wrong?

* * *

'Well, that went all right,' said Jolly some time later, as the van drove away at speed. 'Sort of.'

Behind them came the sound of an explosion, and a Volkswagen Beetle – 20,000 miles on the clock, one lady owner, perfect motoring order – flew up into the air like a big, fat firework, trailing smoke and burning fuel. A second explosion, larger than the first, quickly followed, as the rest of Honest Ed's stock went up in flames.

'I told you I smelled gas,' said Angry. 'Very dangerous stuff, gas.'

'Absolutely,' said Jolly. 'You can't go messing about with gas.'

'Can't take chances with it.'

'Absolutely not.'

They were silent for a moment or two. In the distance, the horizon glowed in the light of the flames from Honest Ed's former car dealership.

'Probably shouldn't have gone looking for it with a box of matches, though,' said Dan. He was driving faster than was safe, but it seemed like a good idea to put as much distance between the dwarfs and Honest Ed as possible. When last they'd seen him, Honest Ed had been searching for a gun.

'Well, the torch was a bit small,' said Angry. 'And it didn't light things very well.'

'I think we solved that problem,' said Jolly. 'It looks like Honest Ed's is lit perfectly well now.'

'Did we get paid in advance?' Angry asked Dan.

'We always get paid in advance,' said Dan. 'If we didn't, we'd never get paid at all.'

They drove on. The dwarfs sang. Dan went back to trying to be optimistic. Things, he thought, could only get better, mainly because they couldn't possibly get any worse.

In the basement of Wreckit & Sons, Mr St John-Cholmondeley sat at a desk and wrote what the Voice in the Wall told him to write.

WANTED

he wrote.

FOUR DWARFS FOR STORE WORK. EXCELLENT PAY AND PROSPECTS.

Mr St John-Cholmondeley stopped writing.
'Do they really have excellent prospects?' he asked the Voice in the Wall.
Yes, replied the Voice in the Wall. *They have the most excellent prospects.*
Of dying.

CHAPTER VII

In Which We Have a Musical Interlude

The following morning, Dan gathered the dwarfs in the yard behind the offices of 'Dan, Dan the Talent Man, & Company', as he had recently renamed himself and the business. The '& Company' referred to the dwarfs, who each had an equal share in the talent management company, and therefore an equal say in its affairs. This made the monthly company meetings noisy, stressful and, in the case of Mumbles, difficult to understand. Behind Dan was a vaguely van-shaped object covered in a white tarpaulin.

'Now,' said Dan, 'you'll remember that, at our August meeting, we decided that we should buy a new van.'

The dwarfs vaguely remembered this. They didn't pay a lot of attention at the company meetings. They just liked shouting and arguing, and sticking their hands up to vote for things that they didn't understand.[18] They might well have voted in favour of buying a new van. Then again, they might have voted

$\bigodot$ [18] This is how parliaments work.

in favour of buying a spaceship, or invading China. For little people, the dwarfs didn't pay much attention to small print.

'Just remind us: why are we buying a new van again?' asked Jolly.

'Because we can't keep repainting the old one,' said Dan. 'And you didn't want to be known as "Dan's Dwarfs" any more, or even "Dan's Elves".'

'That's because elves don't exist,' said Angry. 'It's like being called "Dan's Unicorns", or "Dan's Dragons".'

'Exactly,' said Dan.

'And we're not "your" elves,' said Jolly. 'It makes us sound like slaves. Which we're not.'

You're definitely not, thought Dan. Slaves might do a bit of work occasionally.

'You don't like being called "little people",' said Dan, 'and you're not sure about "dwarfs", so I had to think up a different name, which I did. I now present to you – the new van!'

Dan whipped away the tarpaulin, and the van stood revealed. It was bright yellow, and very shiny.

Dan glowed.

The van glowed.

The dwarfs did not glow.

'What's that?' said Angry.

'It's a van,' said Dan.

'No, not that. *That!* The writing on the side.'

'It's your new name: Dan's Stars Of Diminished Stature.'

Dan was very proud of the new name for the dwarfs. He'd spent ages thinking it up, and he'd visited the painters every day that they were working on the job just to make sure they got the details right. The words flowed diagonally down both sides of the van. They'd even found a way to continue the writing over the windows without obscuring the view. The van was a work of art.

DAN'S
Stars
Of
Diminished
Stature!

The dwarfs looked at the van. Dan looked at the dwarfs. Dan and the dwarfs looked at the van. Dan's eyesight wasn't very good, and things might have gone on like that until night fell had Angry not said, 'So, nothing strikes you as odd about the van?'

'No,' said Dan.

'Nothing at all?'

'Maybe the letters aren't big enough. Is that it?'

'No, no, the letters are more than big enough. Too big, some might say. It's more how they read that bothers me, so to speak.'

Dan looked again. He spelled out the words, moving his lips. He took a step back. He squinted.

He saw it.

'Oh,' he said.

'Yes, oh,' said Angry. 'In fact, not just "Oh", but "Ess, Oh, Dee, Ess". The side of our van reads "Dan's SODS!"'

'That's not good,' said Dan.

Definitely accurate, he thought, but not good.

The dwarfs and Dan sat in Dan's office. They did not present a happy picture. The van was just the latest in a series of disasters. They had caused a major gas explosion, and they now owned a van that described them as sods.

Oh, and they had recently been dragged to Hell for a time. Let's not forget that.

But their main problem at the moment was that, while they owned a talent agency, it didn't have any real talent to promote.

'What about Wesley the Amazing Tightrope Walker?' said Dan. 'We have him. He's a genius! He can walk along a length of spider web without falling off.'

'He's afraid of heights,' said Dozy. 'It's hard to get excited about a man who can only walk a tightrope that's six inches off the ground. Even then he looks a bit nervous.'

'Jimmy the Juggler?' suggested Dan. 'You've got to admit that the man can juggle.'

'He *can* juggle,' said Jolly. 'He has a gift. He'd be better if he had two arms, though. Strictly speaking, he doesn't juggle: he tosses.'

'Bobo the Clown?'

'He gets angry with children. It's one thing throwing a bucket of confetti over them, but he's not supposed to throw the bucket as well.'

'And then there's, well, *them*,' said Dan.

'Them!' said Jolly, shaking his head.

'Them!' said Angry, casting his eyes to heaven.

'Them!' said Dozy, putting his head in his hands.

'Arble!' said Mumbles.

Which said it all, really.

They followed Dan down a steep set of stairs to the basement and walked along a hallway to a large padlocked door. Dan fumbled in his pocket for the key.

'Do you really need to keep them locked up?' asked Jolly.

'It's for their own good,' said Dan. 'They wander off if I don't.'

'They were never very intelligent,' said Angry. 'It's a wonder they lasted as long as they did.'

'It's sad, really,' said Dan. 'You know, they wouldn't survive a day in the wild.'

He placed the key in the lock and turned it.

'Careful now,' Dan warned. 'They react to the light.'

He removed the padlock and pulled the bolt. The door began to open with a creak. The room beyond was big and comfortable, but very dark. As the door opened further, a rectangle of light appeared on the floor and grew wider and wider, like the beam of a spotlight tracing its way across a stage.

A figure jumped into the light, followed by a second, and a third, and a fourth. They all looked a little bleary-eyed. Their spangled shirts had seen better days, and their trousers bore food stains. Their voices also sounded somewhat croaky, but that was nothing new.

'Hi,' said the first. 'I'm Starlight.'

'Oh Lord,' said Jolly.

'And I'm Twinkle,' said the second.

'Good grief,' said Angry.

'I'm Gemini,' said the third.

'They never stop, do they?' said Dozy.

'And I'm Phil,' said the fourth. 'And together we're—'

'BoyStarz!' they all cried in unison, and performed a small twirl before they began doing to a perfectly innocent song what grape-crushers do to grapes.

'Make them stop,' said Jolly, his hands pressed to his ears. 'Please!'

'It's very hard,' said Dan. 'They see a light and they start performing. I've tried electric shocks, but that just seems to make them livelier.'

These were hard times for the boyband BoyStarz. For a start, they were no longer as young as they had been but 'MenStarz' didn't have the same ring to it. Phil in particular looked like a doorman at the kind of nightclub where people got killed on a regular basis, while Sparkle, Twinkle and Gemini had only enough hair between all three of them for two people to share. Their career had never recovered from vicious rumours that the BoyStarz could not sing, and they simply mimed along to songs recorded by more talented vocalists. This led to the BoyStarz signing up for a special tour to prove the doubters wrong. In this it was successful, to a degree. The tour did prove that the BoyStarz could sing.

Horribly.

One critic compared the sound of BoyStarz singing live to the final cry of a ship's horn as it sinks beneath the waves with the loss of everyone on board. Another described it as only marginally less awful than being trapped in a room with a flock of frightened geese that kept honking in panic as they bumped into the walls. A third wrote: 'If Death had a sound, it would sound like BoyStarz.'

The BoyStarz kept trying. They turned up for the opening of shopping malls, but nobody came. Then they started showing up for the opening of individual stores, but still nobody came. Eventually they grew so desperate that if somebody opened a newspaper, or a packet of crisps, BoyStarz would pop up beside them and start warbling about how love was like a flower, or a butterfly, or a sunny day. People started complaining. Where once the BoyStarz had been driven everywhere in limousines, they now rode bicycles, or they did until someone stole the bicycles to stop them from showing up unexpectedly. It was all very sad, unless you actually liked music, and songs being sung in tune, in which case it wasn't very sad at all.

The dwarfs felt partly responsible for the run of bad luck that BoyStarz had endured because it was they who had ruined the filming of the video for BoyStarz's Christmas single 'Love is Like a Castle (Built for Two)'. They had done this by taking bits of the castle in question and flinging them from the battlements until the castle built for two looked like a shed built for one. When the dwarfs had decided to set up a talent agency with Dan, it seemed only right and proper that they should try to find work for the BoyStarz. So far, the only work they'd found for them was in a hamburger restaurant, and even then they'd only lasted a day because they insisted on singing about how love was like a lettuce leaf, or a chicken nugget, or a bun.

'All right, boys,' said Jolly, 'the song's had enough. Time to put it out of its misery.'

The BoyStarz stopped wailing.

'Has you got work for us?' asked Gemini.

'Is we going to be stars again?' asked Twinkle. As he said the word 'stars', he tossed fairy dust in the air.

'Where do they get that fairy dust from?' asked Angry. 'They never seem to run out, do they?'

'I've searched their cell – I mean, their *room* – and I can't find a trace of it,' said Dan. 'I think they just produce it from their pores, like sweat.'

'What are you feeding them?' asked Dozy.

'Mostly cheese.'

'Well, that doesn't explain it. Whatever you get from eating lots of cheese isn't going to look like fairy dust, or smell like it either.'

'When is we going to sing again?' asked Starlight.

'What does he mean, "again"?' asked Jolly. 'And why can't they tell singular from plural?'

'I think they're becoming a single entity,' said Dan. 'Except for Phil, of course.'

'Ah.'

They all looked at Phil, who bore the same relationship to the other three as an emu might to three ducks. Every boy band had to have someone who looked like Phil in it. It was a rule.

'What are we going to do with them?' said Angry. 'We can't keep them down here forever. Eventually somebody is going to come looking for them.'

'Really?' asked Jolly.

Angry thought about it.

'Possibly not,' he said. 'Still, we have to find something for them to do or else we'll just end up with four old people living in our basement who can't sing, smell of cheese, and appear to be made partly of fairy dust.'

There was a soft thud from above them as a copy of the *Biddlecombe Evening Crier* dropped through the letter box.

'Maybe there'll be a job for them in the newspaper,' said Dozy.

'Unky,' said Mumbles.

'You're right,' said Dozy, 'it is highly unlikely, but you never know. Sometimes good things happen to good people.'

'And what about us?' said Angry.

'Sometimes good things happen to us too,' said Dozy, 'although only by mistake. Or through theft.'

They closed the door on the BoyStarz.

'Goodbye, little men,' said a voice. It might have been Starlight's. Nobody knew for certain. They all looked the same.

Except for Phil.

And through the door came the sound of four voices singing loudly, if not terribly well, about how love was like a little man.

The dwarfs sat in Dan's office and thought about their future. It looked bleak.

'This is terrible,' said Jolly. 'We're broke, and we have a talent-free talent agency.'

'Maybe we could sell the BoyStarz into slavery,' said Angry.

'They wouldn't make very good slaves,' said Jolly. 'They're too delicate. Except for Phil.'

He looked at Dan.

'So?' he said. 'Is there by any chance a job for the BoyStarz in the newspaper?'

Dan beamed at him. At last, a bit of good luck.

'No,' he replied, 'but there's a job for all four of you!'

CHAPTER VIII

In Which the Forces of Law and Order Encounter the Forces of Lawlessness and Disorder

Sergeant Rowan and Constable Peel were enjoying a nice pot of tea and a couple of pea and chutney pies at Pete's Pies. The sun was shining, the pies were good, and all was well with the world.

'Hello, Sergeant,' said a passerby, walking his dog. 'Criminals taking a day off today, are they?'

Sergeant Rowan smiled. When he chose to use it, he had a smile like a fatal gunshot.

'Do you have a licence for that dog?' he said, and the man hurried quickly along.

Constable Peel sipped his tea.

'Do you think criminals actually take days off, Sarge?' said Constable Peel. 'I mean, if they're on holiday and someone leaves a car unlocked or a wallet unattended, do criminals think, no, I'm not stealing that, I'm on my holidays?'

Since he'd been dragged to Hell, and then escaped, Constable Peel had begun to take a different view of life. His philosophy was that any day that didn't involve demons, the undead, or being hauled off to Hell was a good day as far as he was concerned.

'I don't know, Constable, but here comes a criminal. Let's ask him.'

Sergeant Rowan stretched out a hand and gripped a passing dwarf by the collar.

'Bless my soul,' he said. 'If it isn't Mr Jolly Smallpants, off to find something that isn't nailed down.'

'All right, Sergeant Rowan. Always nice to see you,' lied Jolly, his toes almost touching the ground.

'My colleague here was wondering if criminals ever take holidays,' said Sergeant Rowan. 'I thought you might be able to help him with an answer.'

Jolly thought about the question.

'I once stole a yacht. Does that count?'

Sergeant Rowan reminded himself never to shake hands with Jolly Smallpants, or, if he did, to count his fingers afterwards just to make sure that they were all still there.

'When I said "taking" a holiday, I did not mean stealing one,' he said. 'I meant spending time not engaged in criminal behaviour, if you could imagine such a thing.'

'Oh no, Sergeant,' said Jolly. 'If you have a gift, you ought to take it seriously. We're like the law: we never rest. Well, except for you and Constable Peel. You like a rest. And *arrests*.' He chuckled. 'See what I did there?'

'I did,' said Sergeant Rowan, 'and if you do it again I shall drop you on your head. So where were you off to in such a hurry before I felt your collar? Somebody leave a bank vault open? Is there a cow standing in a field with bricks where its legs used to be?'

'No, Sergeant,' said Jolly. 'I'm off to get a job.'

Sergeant Rowan was so shocked that he let Jolly

go, and Constable Peel began choking on a piece of pie until Jolly helped him by slapping him a bit too enthusiastically on the back.

'Thank you,' said Constable Peel, once he could feel his spine again.

'Give him back his whistle, Mr Smallpants,' said Sergeant Rowan sternly.

'Sorry,' said Jolly. 'Force of habit.'

He handed Constable Peel his whistle and, as he was feeling generous, also returned his notebook, his pencil, and his hat.

'You mentioned a job,' said Sergeant Rowan, while Constable Peel tried to store away his belongings until he realised that Jolly had stolen one of his pockets.

'Yes,' said Jolly.

'An honest, paying job?'

Jolly looked slightly ashamed. 'It's only temporary. Desperate times, and all that.'

'And what would this job involve?'

'Christmas elf at Wreckit's,' said Jolly. 'A chance to make children happy, and to lighten the hearts of their parents.'

'Lighten their pockets by stealing their wallets, more like,' said Sergeant Rowan.

'Speaking of pockets . . .' said Constable Peel.

Jolly handed over a scrap of dark blue material.

'Sorry again,' said Jolly. 'Sometimes I don't even know what my own hands are doing.'

At that moment he was joined by Angry, Dozy, Mumbles and Dan, who greeted the two policemen with cheery smiles and the theft of the remains of their pies.

'Don't you lot have a new van?' asked Sergeant Rowan. 'I seem to recall seeing it being delivered yesterday.'

He frowned and tapped a finger to his lips.

'Now what did it say on the side? Was it "Dan's Twits", or "Dan's Thieving Little Gits"? No, wait a minute, don't tell me, it'll come. Ah, I've got it now. "Dan's Sods"! At least you can't be accused of false advertising.'

'Very funny,' said Dozy. 'Cost us a fortune, that van did, and we can't afford new paintwork. How are we supposed to get around now? We only have little legs.'

'It'll just make it harder for you to run away when we come looking for you,' said Sergeant Rowan.

'Why would you be looking for us, Sergeant?' asked Angry.

'Because the last time you lot worked as Christmas elves there were some very nasty incidents, and don't think that I've forgotten about them. That reindeer probably hasn't forgotten about them either.'

'We were just feeding it a carrot,' said Dozy.

'Carrots go in the other end, the mouth end.'

'It was dark in that stable,' said Jolly. 'It wasn't our fault.'

'And then there was the poor bloke playing Father Christmas.'

'We were sure that beard wasn't real,' said Angry. 'I mean, ninety-nine per cent sure. I'd have put money on it.'

'But you didn't put money on it, did you?' said Sergeant Rowan. 'You put *glue* on it. You glued it when he wasn't looking and then asked a child to give it a tug. You thought you'd end up with a small boy with a beard stuck to his hand, but instead you got a Father Chrismas with a small boy stuck to him. Father Christmas had to have his beard cut off, and the kid ended up with hands that looked like the paws of an elderly werewolf.'

'It won't happen again, Sergeant,' said Dan. 'They're changed men.'

'The only thing that will change that lot is Death,' said Sergeant Rowan. 'Even then, they'll probably try to steal his scythe.'

Dan began to hustle the dwarfs along.

'Well, we must be off,' he said. 'We're running late as it is. Good to see you again. Maybe we'll all meet up at the Grand Opening!'

'I can hardly wait,' said Sergeant Rowan.

He turned his chair to face Constable Peel.

'We need to watch them, Constable. We need to watch them like hawks. No, not just like hawks, but like hawks . . . *with binoculars*. We—'

He paused.

'Where's the rest of my pie gone?' he said.

'Sergeant,' began Constable Peel, as an engine started up.

'And my tea. And the teapot!'

The engine was followed by a burst of sirens, but they were quickly silenced.

'Sarge—'

'They've even taken the cups!'

'Sarge!' said Constable Peel with some force.

'What is it?'

'I think they've stolen our car.'

CHAPTER IX

In Which Clever Disguises Are Adopted

Nurd trudged back to Mrs Johnson's house, his head low. Wormwood had chosen to stay late at the car testing centre. There had been some spectacular crashes that day, and Wormwood liked nothing better than rebuilding crashed cars.

Nurd was wearing a bulky jacket, and a hood covered his head. His hands were plunged deep into his pockets. It looked like rain, but he had decided not to take the bus because taking the bus meant being near people. Even though Nurd's appearance had changed a great deal in his time on Earth, he was still strange enough to attract startled glances from passers-by and fellow passengers. Small children sometimes cried at the sight of him, and he had lost count of the number of elderly ladies whom he had caused to faint with fright. It was easier just to walk home, even if it did take him an hour.

Home. Nurd grimaced at the word. Mrs Johnson's house wasn't home. Oh, it was comfortable, and Samuel and his mother did all that they could to make Nurd and Wormwood feel like part of the family, but as time went on Nurd just became more and more aware of how different he was. Earth was better than Hell, but Nurd still didn't belong there, and he didn't think that he ever would.

A bird sang from a nearby tree. Nurd stopped to watch, and listen. The bird took one look at him, let out a startled squawk, and suddenly decided to fly south for the winter, even though it wasn't a migratory bird.

Nurd adjusted his hood until only a tiny circle of his face was visible, and walked on.

Once they had retrieved their car – following a long lecture from Sergeant Rowan to Jolly about the difference between 'borrowing' and 'stealing', which Sergeant Rowan suspected went in one ear and out the other, but not before being relieved of any valuables – the two policemen decided to drive over to Mr Pennyfarthinge's to see what the scientists were up to in their Secret Laboratory That Everybody Knew About. It was part of the Biddlecombe constabulary's weekly routine: pop in, say hello, pretend that the scientists were simply sweet manufacturers working night and day to perfect new types of sherbet, and make sure that they hadn't opened any portals between worlds.

'We should have arrested them for stealing our car,' said Constable Peel as they neared Mr Pennyfarthinge's.

'Some things aren't worth the time or the trouble,' said Sergeant Rowan. 'At least we got it back before they sold it.'

'You're very tolerant of them.'

'Spending time in Hell with people will do that to you.'

'Spending time with them is Hell anyway,' said Constable Peel. 'Spending time with them in Hell was just Hell squared.'

'You know, I think they like you,' said Sergeant Rowan.

Constable Peel couldn't help but feel pleased despite himself.

'What makes you say that, Sarge?'

'Have they burgled you yet?'

'Not that I know of.'

'There you have it. Stands to reason, doesn't it, that they must like you if they haven't burgled your house?'

'I don't think they know where I live.'

'Really? Well, be sure not to tell them, then. You wouldn't want to put temptation in their way.'

They pulled into the yard of Mr Pennyfarthinge's. The factorye – sorry, factory[19] – occupied a big gloomy Victorian monstrosity designed by Hilary Mould. All of Hilary Mould's buildings were gloomy, thought Sergeant Rowan. They might not have started out that way on the plans, but that's how they ended up. Hilary Mould could have designed a Wendy house and made it look like a mortuary. His buildings were the kind of places that were probably advertised in newspapers in the Afterlife:

💀 [19] It reallye is catchinge.

> FOR IMMEDIATE OCCUPATION: Building looking
> for ghost to haunt it. All Dark Corners, Weird
> Carvings, Creaking Doors, Sinister Paintings of
> Relatives Of Whom Nobody Speaks, and Secret
> Rooms Not Listed On Original Plans entirely intact.
> Would suit ghoul, spectre, poltergeist or other
> incorporeal entity. Available for eternity, although
> shorter leases will be considered. Enquiries to the
> wailing, demented spirit of Hilary Mould.

Why Mr Pennyfarthinge had originally chosen a 'Mould' for the location of his business was something of a mystery, but it had certainly thrived there. Its success was helped by the fact that Mr Pennyfarthinge and the mysterious Uncle Dabney were one and the same person, a detail that only emerged following Mr Pennyfarthinge's death by gobstopper. The basement of his factory was found to contain thousands of boxes of unsold Uncle Dabney products, including prototypes for some that had not yet been unleashed on the public: Uncle Dabney's Orange Bombs (which turned out to be actual bombs, with a hint of orange essence); Uncle Dabney's Chocolate Bullets (real bullets covered in rich dark chocolate: not less than fifty per cent cocoa and fifty per cent gunpowder); and Uncle Dabney's Nuclear Blast Toffees (of which the less said the better). There were also samples of Uncle Dabney's Cough Drops, which caused coughing instead of curing it, and enough sachets of Uncle Dabney's Flu Powder to count as a potential epidemic. It was said by some that the building had driven Mr Pennyfarthinge mad. All things considered, it was a very good thing that the jars of gobstoppers had landed on Mr Pennyfarthinge's head when they did, for who knows what he might have ended up inventing if he hadn't been killed.

None of this, of course, concerned the scientists. They were just happy to find a place that they could rent cheaply, and the sale of sweeties – including the remaining Uncle Dabney products that had not been destroyed or classified as weapons – helped to fund their operations. To ensure that their cover remained intact, they had taken to wearing large beards to disguise their faces, for both Professors Hilbert and Stefan had visited Biddlecombe in the past, and were worried about being spotted by locals. Their assistant, Dorothy, also enjoyed wearing a beard. The scientists were not sure why, and didn't like to ask.

Thus it was that, when Sergeant Rowan and Constable Peel knocked on the side door of the factory, they were greeted by three people wearing false beards, one of whom was clearly a woman. Behind them was Brian, the new tea boy. He was not wearing a beard, which was unfortunate as it might have helped to cover some of his very pale, very frightened face.

To their credit, the policemen did not even blink at the peculiar appearance of the scientists. Sergeant Rowan had learned long ago that, if you started each day expecting people to behave strangely, then you would not be disappointed, surprised, or shocked in any way.

'Hello, er, sweet-makers,' said Sergeant Rowan.

'Hello!' said the three scientists in the excessively

cheery manner of people who have something to hide and are doing their best to make sure that it stays hidden.

'Everything all right here, then?' said the sergeant.

'It's all fine, absolutely fine,' said Professor Stefan.

'Nothing strange going on? No unexplained portals opening? No demons looking to take over the Earth?'

'Ha, ha, ha!' didn't laugh Professor Hilbert. 'Jelly babies don't cause portals to open.'

'Ho, ho, you don't get demons from clove drops,' said Professor Stefan.

'The only strange things here are the shapes of our caramels,' said Dorothy, in a voice that started out high and finished suddenly low, in the manner of a skier plummeting from a mountain.

'And we haven't seen any ghosts!' said Brian.

There was an awkward silence.

'Ghosts?' said Constable Peel.

'Yes,' said Brian, realising his error just a little too late, like a lion tamer entering a lion cage only to find himself wearing a coat made of meat. 'The ghosts that we haven't seen. We haven't seen them. Those ones. Can I go now? I don't feel well.'

Brian went away.

'Has he been drinking?' said Sergeant Rowan.

'No,' said Professor Stefan.

'Do you think he should start? I'd give him a stiff brandy, if I were you, especially if he's *not* seeing ghosts.'

Sergeant Rowan, who was a tall man, leaned over Professor Stefan, who was not tall, so that the professor appeared to be standing in the shadow of a collapsing building.

'Because,' said Sergeant Rowan, 'if I were to hear that innocent sweet manufacturers, who are not – I say absolutely *not* – scientists, were having strange experiences in my town and didn't see fit to tell me then I might get very, very annoyed. Do I make myself clear?'

'Yes, Sergeant,' said Professor Stefan. 'Very clear.'

'Right. We'll be off then. Do keep me posted if you continue not to see ghosts, won't you? Have a nice day sir, and you sir, and you, er, miss.'

'Sir,' said Dorothy.

'Don't,' said Sergeant Rowan, raising a finger in warning. 'Just – don't.'

He and Constable Peel got back in their car, and drove away.

'Ghosts?' said Constable Peel, as Mr Pennyfarthinge's receded into the distance.

'Ghosts,' said Sergeant Rowan.

'It's lucky they're not seeing any, isn't it?'

'Very lucky, Constable.'

'Because, if they were, we'd have to do something, wouldn't we?'

'Indeed we would, Constable.'

'And what would that be, Sarge?'

'We'd have to be afraid, Constable. We'd have to be very afraid.'

CHAPTER X

In Which We Pay a Brief Visit to Hell

The Mountain of Despair was the tallest peak in Hell. It dominated the landscape of that terrible place in the way that only something really, really terrible can do, given the general terribleness of the place in which it happened to be. Even though no sun shone in Hell, and the skies above were forever darkened by warring thunderclouds, still the Mountain of Despair somehow managed to cast a shadow over everything, if only in the minds of those who were doomed, or damned, to exist there. It was so big that, no matter how far away you might stand, it never appeared any smaller. A lifetime might be spent trying to walk around it without success. A *short* lifetime might be spent trying to climb it, for some very disagreeable creatures lived among its cracks and crevasses, and they were always hungry.

Mind you, there were some inhabitants of Hell who had no objection whatsoever to the looming presence of the Mountain of Despair. It provided employment to those who were content to ensure that the business of running an empire based entirely on evil, misery and general demonic activity proceeded as smoothly as possible. A job, in their view, was a job, and, as with most jobs, you just had to find that perfect balance between doing as little as possible so you didn't get tired, and just enough so that you didn't get fired.

Two such beings were currently guarding the great carved entrance to the mountain. Their names were Brompton and Edgefast. Edgefast was, strictly speaking, simply a disembodied head,[20] and Brompton was about as much use at guarding as a toy dog on wheels, but they had somehow managed to continue to be employed as guards despite their general uselessness. This was because Brompton and Edgefast were members of the Union of Demonic Employees and Tormentors (Guards Branch), which fiercely protected the rights of its members to lean on their spears and nap any time their eyes got a bit heavy; to take tea breaks at unsuitable times, including during battles, invasions, and serious fires; and not to actually guard anything if they thought that it might place their personal safety at risk. All of

---

[20] In the first chapter of *The Infernals*, Edgefast was torn limb from limb for daring to question the right of Mrs Abernathy to enter the Mountain of Despair. Once again, if you'd read that book then you'd know all of this already. Look, why don't we just arrange for me to give you a telephone call and I can read the book down the line to you, or perhaps I can act it out in your back garden for you and your friends? Or maybe, just maybe, you could go and read *The Infernals*, and maybe *The Gates* as well, and then when I mention a name like Edgefast you'll be able to say 'A-ha, that's the bloke who got torn apart by Mrs Abernathy in the last book!', and be very pleased with yourself, instead of forcing me to take time from the important task of telling the new story just so you don't feel left out. You've just kept everyone else waiting, you know. I hope you're happy. And I bet you didn't even buy this book: you probably received it as a gift, or stole it. Frankly, I don't know why I bother.

this made Brompton and Edgefast as hard to fire as a pair of chocolate cannons. The Mountain of Despair could have been stolen from under their noses and broken down to make garden gnomes and, thanks to the union, Brompton and Edgefast would still have been guarding the place where it once stood, in between taking essential naps and tea breaks.

'Quiet today,' said Edgefast.

'Too quiet for my liking,' said Brompton.

'Really?'

Edgefast couldn't help but sound surprised. Brompton was the laziest demon Edgefast had ever met. Brompton could fall over and make hitting the ground look like an effort.

'Nah, only joking,' said Brompton. 'Not quiet enough if you ask me, what with you piping up every few minutes about how quiet it is.'

'Sorry,' said Edgefast.

He'd only said that it was quiet *once*. It wasn't like he kept repeating the word 'quiet' over and over until nobody could remember what silence had been like.

Edgefast's nose was itchy. He'd have scratched it, but he didn't have any arms. It was one of the problems with not having a body. Still, Brompton was very good about making sure that he had a straw through which to suck his tea, and he usually remembered to pick Edgefast up and take him home when they had finished guarding for the day.

'Would you mind scratching my nose for me?' Edgefast said.

'Oh, it's all about you, isn't it?' said Brompton. 'Me,

me, me, that's all I ever hear. Who made you king, that's what I'd like to know. Must have been when I wasn't looking. All right, your Majesty, I'll scratch your nose for you. There! Happy now?'

Edgefast wasn't, really. He couldn't be, not with the business end of Brompton's spear jammed up one nostril.

''Es bine,' he said. 'Mub bedder, dan gew.'

Brompton withdrew the spear and went back to leaning on it and staring glumly over the blasted landscape of Hell.

'Sorry,' he said. 'Trouble at home.'

'Mrs Brompton?' said Edgefast.

Brompton and Mrs Brompton had a difficult marriage. There were fatal diseases that had better relationships with their victims than Brompton had with Mrs Brompton.

'Yeah.'

'She move out again?'

'No, she moved back in.'

'Oh.'

There was silence for a time.

'I thought you were going to leave her,' said Edgefast.

'I did.'

'What happened?'

'She came with me.'

'Oh,' said Edgefast for a second time. There wasn't much else to say. Brompton always seemed to be unhappy with Mrs Brompton. The trouble was, he was even unhappier *without* Mrs Brompton.

'She'd be lost without you, you know,' said Edgefast.

'Nah, I tried that,' said Brompton. 'She found her way back.'

'Oh,' said Edgefast, for the third time, followed by 'Oh?' and then 'Oh-Oh!'

Crudford manifested himself directly in front of the two guards with a sound like a plate of jelly being dropped on a stone floor. He raised his hat with his left hand and said 'Evening, gentlemen.' Under his right arm he carried a jar, and in the jar a mass of blue atoms seethed and roiled, slowly forming something that became, as he drew closer to Edgefast, a single hostile eye surrounded by pale, bruised skin. The eye seemed to glare at Edgefast, who would have taken a step back if it hadn't been for his shortcomings in the leg department. Edgefast had clear memories of that eye. It had looked at him in a similar way just moments before some very sharp bits of the body to which it was then attached had ripped him apart.

Crudford put his hat back on his head, and patted the jar the way one might pat the comfortable carrying case of a beloved pet.

'Here we are, ma'am,' he said. 'It's nice to be back, isn't it?'

The Great Malevolence, the monstrous fount of all evil, sat in its lair of fire and stone at the heart of the Mountain of Despair, the flames reflected in its eyes so that it seemed almost to be burning from within. It had cast aside its armour for now, and set aside its shield of skulls and its burning spear. The crooked crown of bone that grew from its head glowed red from the heat of the infernos that surrounded it. Its monstrous body, scarred and misshapen, lay slumped on its throne.

The throne was a massive construct of bones that twisted and tangled like pale branches and yellowed vines. There was no comfort to the throne, but that was as the Great Malevolence preferred: it never wanted to grow used to its banishment in Hell, and never wished to find a moment's peace there. It had come into existence milliseconds after the birth of the Multiverse, a force for destruction born out of the creation of worlds. It could, it supposed, have become an agent for good, but it was a jealous being, an angry being, and it had fought against all that was fine and noble in the Multiverse until at last a force greater than itself had grown tired of its evil. The Great Malevolence was cast down to Hell for eternity, and it had conspired to free itself ever since. It had almost succeeded too, but its plans had been spoiled by the boy named Samuel Johnson and his dog, Boswell.

The Great Malevolence had also lost its lieutenant, the demon Ba'al. It was Ba'al who had led the invasion of Earth, occupying the body of a woman named Mrs Abernathy and then, for reasons unclear, deciding that being a woman was altogether nicer than being a demon. When the invasion failed, the Great Malevolence chose to blame Mrs Abernathy, and she was banished from its presence. When she had tried to get back in its good books by opening another portal to Earth, Samuel Johnson had intervened again, and that was when all of the atoms in Mrs Abernathy's body had been separated from their neighbours and scattered throughout the Multiverse.

The Great Malevolence was a being filled with self-pity. It now regretted banishing Mrs Abernathy, not because of any hurt that it might have caused her, but because she had been useful and loyal, and the Great Malevolence's strength was reduced without her.[21] This was why it had ordered the creature named Crudford to find all of the pieces of her and bring them back to Hell so that she might be reassembled. Crudford wasn't much to look at but, like many creatures that appear humble and insignificant, Crudford had turned out to be far more important and gifted than he had first appeared.

Now Crudford oozed into the Great Malevolence's presence and added the eyeball in the jar to the other

---

☠ [21] This is the curse of kings. While you or I might get annoyed with our friends on occasion, we tend not to order their execution simply because they've trodden on our toes or, if we do, people ignore us, which is usually for the best. The trouble with being a king is that, when you lose your temper with someone and order his head to be lopped off, a bloke appears with an axe and promptly does the deed, or someone drops a noose around his neck and — well, you get the picture. Then later, when the king announces that he misses old What's-His-Name and wonders where on earth he's got to because he was always good for a laugh, a courtier has to go through the awkward business of explaining that old What's-His-Name is unlikely to be cracking jokes any time in the near, or distant, future owing to his definite deadness. Henry VIII, for example, who was king of England from 1509 to 1547, ended his days surrounded by a great many young people for the simple reason that he'd had most of his old courtiers exiled or executed. Between the years 1532 and 1540 alone, Henry ordered 330 political executions, probably more than any other ruler in British history. If you worked for Henry VIII then you really didn't need to worry about putting money into your pension fund as you probably wouldn't live long enough to spend it.

body parts that were currently lined up on a stone platform in the throne room. Crudford had been summoned to the Great Malevolence's presence to detail his progress in tracking down the billions of atoms of Mrs Abernathy's being. Crudford was feeling nervous about this. He thought he'd done well in finding as many bits as he had so far. It was no easy business oozing between universes looking for tiny blue atoms. You needed a steady hand, and a good eye, and a lot of luck. On the other hand, the Great Malevolence wasn't very keen on listening to excuses, and it had a habit of tossing those who displeased it into bottomless pits, or leaving them to freeze in the great Lake of Cocytus.

'Afternoon, your Virulence,' said Crudford, lifting his hat in greeting. 'Nice day out there. Not too chilly.'

The Great Malevolence's voice boomed through the chamber. It made dust and pebbles and the occasional napping demon fall from the walls. Its voice really had a rumble to it.

'Show me what you have found,' it said.

It towered above Crudford, and the little gelatinous being felt himself grow cold in the Great Malevolence's shadow.

'Well,' said Crudford, 'we've made some progress, your Unpleasantness.'

He began to move down the line of jars, pointing a gloopy finger at each one in turn.

'This here's an eye, as you can see – and, I suppose, as it can see too, ho-ho. This one's half a pancreas. That looks like a bit of an ear. That one—'

Crudford paused and squinted. He tapped the jar, as if hoping that the atoms might rearrange themselves and give him a clue. They didn't.

'To be honest, I'm not sure what that is, so we'll just leave it for now and ooze along,' he said. 'That's a finger. This is three-quarters of a lung. In there we have part of a lip, and most of a lower jaw. This one here – actually, you don't even want to know what that is. Seriously, you don't. Over here we have . . .'

This went on for some time. When Crudford was finished, the Great Malevolence didn't exactly seem pleased, but the fact that Crudford was still in one piece meant that the Great Malevolence wasn't displeased either.

'How much longer before you find the rest of her?' it asked. 'I want my lieutenant restored to me.'

'Hard to say,' said Crudford.

'It will be harder to say if I freeze you, or feed you to the imps,' said the Great Malevolence.

'Good point,' said Crudford. 'I'll work doubly fast.'

Crudford was about to say something more, but decided against it. The Great Malevolence made a few more threats, and warned of the harm that would come to Crudford if he didn't find the rest of Mrs Abernathy soon. Crudford wasn't offended. The Great Malevolence was just letting off steam. Anyway, Crudford was the only one who could find Mrs Abernathy's atoms. The Great Malevolence couldn't do him any harm: if it did, then it would never get its lieutenant back.

But the search was harder than Crudford had anticipated, and each time he found some of Mrs

Abernathy's atoms he detected hatred in them. It was almost as if Mrs Abernathy didn't *want* to be found. That was what he had almost told the Great Malevolence before good sense made him stay silent. The Great Malevolence didn't need to hear that, just as it didn't want to hear about the beating, somewhere in the Multiverse, of what Crudford was certain was Mrs Abernathy's heart.

Because Mrs Abernathy wasn't supposed to *have* a heart.

CHAPTER XI

In Which We Learn Why People Should Just Call Their Children Simple Names like Jane or John – Especially John, Which is a Very Good Name. Manly. Heroic, Even

The interior of Wreckit & Sons was still in the process of being redesigned, but Dan and the dwarfs could see that it was going to be pretty spectacular when it was finished. Already some of the displays had been set up: there was a giant teddy bear at least twenty feet high that dominated the cuddly toy section, and a train set that followed a circular track suspended from the ceiling of the second floor. There were dolls piled in corners, and toy soldiers, and cars and trucks and spaceships. There were board games, and a sports section, and books. What there didn't seem to be, Jolly noticed, were any computer games. Walking into Wreckit & Sons was like stepping back in time.

'It's not going to last a week, never mind until Christmas,' said Angry. 'Where are all the PlayStations and things?'

'Somebody should tell them that electricity has been invented,' said Dozy. 'It might come as a shock, but they'll be glad to know.'

In addition to the missing games consoles, Dan and the dwarfs could see no sign of any workers.

'I have a funny feeling that I'm being watched,' said Jolly. 'I was thinking of nicking something, just to keep my hand in, but I don't think I will after all.'

They all shared his uneasy sense of being under surveillance, although they could see no sign of cameras or security guards. There was no sign of anyone at all. They had arrived at the side entrance, just as a message had instructed them to do after Dan had called the number at the bottom of the advertisement. There they found the door unlocked and a handwritten note instructing them to proceed to the top floor via the main stairs.

It was Mumbles who caught a flash of movement in a corner as they neared the final flight of steps.

'Oberare!' he said.

He walked warily to the corner. There was a small hole at the base of the wall. He knelt and peered into it. He had the uncomfortable sensation that, from the darkness behind the wall, something was peering back at him.

'What is it?' said Angry.

'Umsall,' said Mumbles.

'Small?' said Angry. 'It was probably a rat. These old buildings are full of rats.'

But Mumbles didn't think it was a rat. He had only caught the slightest glimpse of it as it fled, but it had looked like a very small person.

If he hadn't known better, Mumbles might even have said it was an elf.

* * *

The dwarfs were stunned into silence when they reached the top floor. The entire space was in the process of being transformed into the most spectacular of Christmas grottoes. Frost glittered on the trunks and branches of the immense silver trees supporting the ceiling, and a pathway that felt like marble wound over the floor while snow fell from above.

'It melts,' whispered Dozy. 'When it touches your skin, it melts!'

And it did.

Somehow, the entire area had been lit so that it looked bigger than it was. It was like being in some great northern forest in the depths of winter. It even *felt* cold. As they progressed through it, the dwarfs saw the shapes of reindeer passing by. They appeared so real that the dwarfs could almost have reached out and touched them, running their fingers through the deer's fur.

At the heart of the forest was a cabin made not of logs but of old stones. Smoke poured from its chimney and was lost in the darkness above, which glimmered with stars. Looking up, Jolly had the sense of being just one small person on one small planet in a vast, icy universe. It made him vaguely depressed so he went back to looking at the cabin instead.

Angry was testing the stones with his hand.

'This cabin must weigh a ton,' he said. 'What's underneath it?'

Dozy tried to remember the floor plan of the store.

'I think it was more soft toys. I could go and check.'

'Well, I wouldn't hang about down there if I were you,' said Angry. 'If this thing falls through the floor it won't be just the toys that are soft. It'll reduce little kids to jelly.'

A man appeared from a doorway to their right. He wore a black three-piece suit with a grey tie and a slightly soiled white shirt. His face was blankly pleasant, like a greetings card without a personal message inside.

'Gentlemen,' he said. 'Can I help you?'

Jolly looked at the note in his hand.

'We're here to see Mr Cholmondeley,' said Jolly.

'Chumley,' said the gentleman, his expression unchanged.

Jolly examined the note again.

'No, it's definitely Cholmondeley.'

He handed it to Angry to check.

'That's it,' said Angry. 'Cholmondeley. It's here in black and white.'

'It's *Chumley*,' said the man. A small frown line had appeared on his forehead.

'Listen, mate,' said Angry, 'are you saying we can't read?'

'Not at all. The name is simply pronounced "Chumley".'

'Then why is it spelled "Cholmondeley"?' asked Jolly.

'It just is,' said the man.

'Well, that's nonsense,' said Angry. 'That's like spelling a name S-M-I-T-H and calling yourself Jones.'

'No,' said the man, with some force, 'it isn't.'

'Yes,' said Angry, with equal force, 'it is.'

It was left to Dan to intervene.

'It's a posh thing,' he explained to the dwarfs.

'Oooooh,' they said in unison, nodding in under-standing. Posh people did things differently. Everybody knew that. Jolly had heard that posh people were born with silver spoons in their mouths, which probably explained why they all talked funny.

'Right you are then, guv,' said Jolly. 'We're here to see Mr *Chumley*. Mr Saint John Chumley.'

'Sinjin,' said the man.

'Bless you,' said Jolly.

'No, I didn't sneeze,' said the man. 'It's Sinjin.'

'Beg pardon?' said Jolly.

By now the man had started to look decidedly irritated.

'It's my name!' he said. 'It's Sinjin-Chumley. How hard can it be?'

The dwarfs crowded around Jolly, and all four of them examined the name on the note, running their fingers beneath it, pronouncing the syllables and occasionally glancing up at the gentleman standing before them as though trying to equate his name with the peculiar jumble of letters before them.

'Actually, pretty hard,' said Angry at last. 'You might need to have a think about that one. Don't take this the wrong way, mate, but you'll never get anywhere in life if you have a made-up name that doesn't sound the way it's spelled. You'd better hang on to this job. If you lose it, you'll never get another. It's always easier to hire someone whose name you can say without hurting your tongue.'

Mr St John-Cholmondeley gave Angry a hard stare.

'I take it that you're here about the job,' he said, in the tone of a man who is hoping that he might be mistaken.

'We were "invited to attend for an interview",' said Jolly.

'Indeed. Well, do come in. It shouldn't take long.'

Mr St John-Cholmondeley stepped aside to admit the dwarfs into his office. It was small, and contained only a desk and a chair. The shelves were entirely bare, and there was nothing on the desk except for a single sheet of white paper, a pen, and a small, sad-looking artificial Christmas tree with a red button on its base. Angry, who couldn't resist a red button when he saw one, pressed it. Immediately the tree began to bob from side to side and 'Jingle Bells' emerged from a hidden speaker.

'What language is that?' asked Angry.

'I'm not sure,' said Mr St John-Cholmondeley. 'I think it might be Urdu, or possibly Serbo-Croat. It's difficult to tell. We found a box of them in storage when we began fixing up the shop.'

'Do you think they're going to be big sellers?' asked Dozy doubtfully.

'Possibly if the shop was situated in a country that spoke Urdu or Serbo-Croat,' said Mr St John-Cholmondeley. 'Otherwise, probably not. I do wish you hadn't turned it on, though. It takes a while for it to finish the song.'

They all tried to ignore the tree as the interview began.

'Now, which job might you be applying for?' said Mr St John-Cholmondeley.

The dwarfs exchanged looks. They were in a toyshop. It was coming up to Christmas. The shop had a

Christmas grotto. They were hardly there to audition for roles as Easter bunnies.

'Elves,' said Jolly. 'We're here to be elves.'

'Not Father Christmas?' said Mr St John-Cholmondeley.

'No.'

'You're sure?'

'Are you trying to be clever?' asked Jolly.

'Not at all,' said Mr St John-Cholmondeley. 'I can't just assume that because you're gentlemen of, er, reduced stature you're only here to be elves. That would be wrong. It's all equal opportunities now, you know. I could get into terrible trouble for saying to you, "Oh, you must be here about the elf job, then." I could end up in court.'

'But we *are* here about the elf job,' said Angry.

'Wouldn't you at least like to think about being Father Christmas?' said Mr St John-Cholmondeley.

'No.'

'Why not?'

'Because we want to be elves. We're the right size for elves. It's not, if you'll forgive the pun, much of a stretch for us.'

'Well, I have to offer you the chance to apply for the job of Father Christmas. It's the rules.'

'We don't want to be Father Christmas.'

'You're sure?'

'Yes.'

'Wouldn't you like to try one little "Ho-Ho-Ho!", just a teeny one?'

'No!' said Jolly. 'We want to be elves.'

Mr St John-Cholmondeley scowled at him.

687

'What's wrong with being Father Christmas? Don't you like fat people?'

'What?' said Jolly.

He was confused. Beside him, the singing Christmas tree continued to sing. It seemed to know a lot more verses to 'Jingle Bells' than Jolly did.

'Are you saying you don't want to be Father Christmas because he's fat?' Mr St John-Cholmondeley persisted. 'Are you fattist? You know, we can't have people working here who are fattist. We won't put up with that kind of thing, do you hear? We won't put up with it at all. How dare you come into this store and say unpleasant things about fat people!'

'But—' said Jolly.

'Don't you go making excuses for your behaviour! You should be ashamed of yourselves. I've a good mind to call the police.'

Angry stared very intently at Mr St John-Cholmondeley. The singing Christmas tree continued to chirp away merrily. Angry was starting to hate it.

'Excuse me,' he said, 'but are you a mad bloke?'

'Oh, and I suppose you don't like them either!' said Mr St John-Cholmondeley. 'What if I was fat *and* mad, eh? What then? I suppose you'd come after me with pitchforks and flaming torches. You'd want me hidden away from sight, locked up in a cell somewhere with only bread and water!'

'Locked up might be a start,' muttered Angry.

'I heard that!' said Mr St John-Cholmondeley. 'Don't think I didn't!'

He opened a drawer in his desk, removed a hammer,

and brought it down hard on the Christmas tree.
While the dwarfs watched, he continued hammering
at the tree until it was reduced to little shards of
green plastic. From somewhere in its workings, a
final faint tinkle of bells could be heard before the
tree expired. Mr St John-Cholmondeley moved a bin
into place with his left foot and used his right hand
to sweep the remains of the Christmas tree into it.
They fell on the remains of lots of other Christmas
trees. From what Angry could see, the bin contained
nothing else.

Mr St John-Cholmondeley restored the hammer to
its drawer, opened another drawer, and took a
Christmas tree from it. He positioned it in precisely
the same place occupied by the previous tree.

'Right,' said Mr St John-Cholmondeley. He smiled.
'Where were we?'

There was a long, careful silence.

'A job?' said Jolly. 'For us?'

'Of course! Elves, by any chance?'

'Er, if you like.'

'Oh, fine by me. You seem just the sorts. Very festive.
Very *small*. We like our elves small. Doesn't work if
they're big. Doesn't work at all. This week good for
you to start? Nine until six on regular days, an hour
for lunch, two tea breaks of not more than fifteen
minutes each, although for the grand opening on
Thursday you don't have to get here until sixish. Don't
eat too many biscuits: they'll make you fat, and we
don't want that, do we? Fine for Father Christmas, but
bad for elves. Bad, bad, bad! Sign there.'

He pushed the pen and blank sheet of paper towards them.

'There's nothing on it,' said Dan.

'Doesn't matter,' said Mr St John-Cholmondeley. 'All friends here.'

'What about money?' said Jolly.

'Oh, I don't take bribes,' said Mr St John-Cholmondeley. 'That would be wrong.'

He leaned forward, placed a hand against his face, and whispered secretively.

'And you're supposed to offer me the bribe *before* you get the job,' he said. 'Doesn't work otherwise. Bear it in mind for next time, eh?'

'Er, no, I meant that we do get paid, don't we?'

'Oh! I *see*! Ha! Forget about the bribe stuff, then. Only joking. Our secret, eh? Yes, money. How much would you like? A lot? A little? How about something in between? What about ten pounds an hour?'

'That sounds—' Jolly began to say, when Mr St John-Cholmondeley interrupted him.

'OK, eleven.'

'What?'

'Twelve, but you drive a hard bargain.'

'I think—'

Mr St John-Cholmondeley puffed his cheeks and wiped his brow.

'Thirteen, then, but that's my final offer.'

'If you're—'

'Fourteen, but you're robbing me, ho, ho! You're stealing me blind!'

The dwarfs had no problem stealing anybody blind,

but on this occasion they weren't even trying. It bothered them. It didn't seem fair somehow.

'Listen,' said Angry, but Mr St John-Cholmondeley was too quick for him.

'Fifteen,' he said. 'That's it. I can't go any higher than sixteen. Seventeen's my last and final offer. Absolutely. Eighteen it is.'

Angry reached for the pen. Mr St John-Cholmondeley grabbed it before he could get to it.

'Nineteen!' he said. 'We need elves!'

'Give me the pen,' said Angry. 'Please.'

Mr St John-Cholmondeley burst into tears and buried his face in his hands.

'All right then, twenty,' he said, in a muffled voice. 'Twenty-one pounds an hour, but you'll be making more than I am.'

The dwarfs eventually managed to sign for twenty-five, but it was a struggle, and two of them had to hold on to Mr St John Cholmondeley's arms while the others wrestled the pen from him. They left him in his office, and closed the door behind them. From inside came the sound of 'Jingle Bells' in a foreign language, followed almost immediately by an intense burst of hammering.

Nobody came to show Dan and the dwarfs out of the store. They had to find their own way back to the street, and they were so troubled by their encounter with Mr St John-Cholmondeley that only later did they notice that, throughout the course of their meeting with him, he had not blinked once.

* * *

Mr St John-Cholmondeley sat back in his chair. He was very relieved that the dwarfs were gone.

'I think that went well,' he said to the Voice in the Wall. 'I don't believe they suspected a thing. I acted entirely normal.'

Twenty-five pounds an hour, said the Voice in the Wall. *Do you think I'm made of money?*

Mr St John-Cholmondeley shook his head. Whatever the Voice in the Wall was made of, it wasn't money. Money didn't smell that foul.

'They were tough little negotiators,' said Mr St John-Cholmondeley. 'Very tough indeed. They wore me down.'

They won't live long enough to collect a penny of it, said the Voice in the Wall. *Still, it's the principle.*

'I'll be more careful next time,' said Mr St John-Cholmondeley.

That's nice, said the Voice in the Wall, and Mr St John-Cholmondeley, who couldn't remember his past, failed to hear in its tones the sound of his very short future coming to an unhappy end.

CHAPTER XII

In Which Invitations are Received

T he invitations began to arrive in the days before the grand opening of Wreckit & Sons. Samuel received one, with a special note informing him that, as the hero who had saved Biddlecombe and the Earth from a demonic invasion, he would be a guest-of-honour. He was also warmly requested to bring the courageous Boswell along with him. The note was signed by Mr St John-Cholmondeley on behalf of the new owner, a mysterious Mr Grimly.

'That's very nice of him, isn't it?' said Samuel's mother as she examined the note. 'And look at that invitation! It's printed on ever such expensive paper, and the hand-writing is lovely. It's odd that it's written in red ink, though, isn't it? You'd think they'd have used black, or blue. Maybe they thought it was more festive in red.'

The invitation made Samuel uneasy for reasons he couldn't quite pin down. Perhaps it was the fact that Boswell took one sniff and decided he didn't care for it at all, or that the ink didn't look much like ink. It looked, to be honest, a bit like blood, and Samuel told his mother as much.

'Don't be silly,' said Mrs Johnson. 'You always see the worst in things.'

'Fighting demons and being dragged off to Hell will do that to a person, Mum,' said Samuel.

'Oh, hush,' said Mrs Johnson, who didn't like being reminded of the unpleasantnesses that had befallen her son, even if she did have two demons living in her spare room and making funny smells in the bathroom. She had decided to look upon Nurd and Wormwood as a pair of slightly eccentric lodgers, and leave it at that.

'Anyway,' Mrs Johnson continued, 'it's about time you got some recognition for all that you've done for this town. They should have put up a statue of you, if you ask me.'

In addition to the wandering statue of Hilary Mould, Biddlecombe only had one other such monument, and that was of Brigadier General Sir Charles MacCarthy, the hopeless nineteenth-century British commander, who, while on his way to be knighted in 1820, had stopped for tea in Biddlecombe and left a small tip.[22] It was often suggested that the town needed another statue or two, although this suggestion usually came from mayors or local politicians, who seemed to think

---

💀 [22] Somebody should really have given Sir Charles himself a tip, namely, don't go into battle with only 500 men against 10,000 spear-wielding natives, which is what MacCarthy did in 1824 when he was governor of the Gold Coast in Africa. MacCarthy ordered his men to play 'God Save the King' in the hope that it might scare the natives away. It didn't. The natives attacked and MacCarthy's force was almost entirely wiped out, not helped by the fact that they had accidentally brought macaroni with them instead of spare ammunition. MacCarthy's heart was eaten by the victorious natives, and they kept his head as a souvenir, displaying it on special occasions and holidays.

it would be a good idea if the statue looked a bit like them, and maybe had their name carved underneath.

'I don't want a statue in my honour, thanks,' said Samuel. He could think of nothing worse than having a bronze version of himself providing a convenient head on which pigeons could poo. Life was hard enough as it was.

A thumping sound came from above, and moments later Nurd and Wormwood appeared in the kitchen. They were very excited. Samuel could tell because Wormwood had somehow set himself on fire and hadn't noticed, and the fire had spread to Nurd's coat but he hadn't noticed either. Samuel discreetly put out the flames with a damp tea towel and waited to find out what was going on.

'We've received an invitation,' said Nurd.

'To the opening of the new toyshop in the town,' said Wormwood.

He was positively glowing, which was probably how the fire had started. Wormwood had recently developed an unfortunate habit of bursting into flame when he got angry or embarrassed, or even if he coughed for too long. He would turn bright red, and the next minute you could toast bread on him.

Wormwood had never been invited anywhere before, unless you counted being invited outside for a fight, or to make a room smell better by his absence. Even Nurd had rarely received invitations to events, largely because he had spent billions of years going through a phase of conspiring to rule worlds, and nobody wants to invite someone to a party only to find that he's declared himself king of their house and is now trying on their slippers for size.

'That's very peculiar,' said Samuel.

He examined the invitation that the demons had been sent. It was addressed to Mr Cushing and Mr Lee, the names under which Nurd and Wormwood were living in Biddlecombe. Only a handful of people knew that Nurd and Wormwood weren't exactly human: even most of their employers at the Biddlecombe Vehicle Testing Centre just regarded Nurd as unusually fire-proof, and quite bendy.[23]

'Why is it peculiar?' asked Wormwood. 'We're good company!'

He thought for a moment.

'Well, we might be, if there was nobody else in the room.'

'It's peculiar,' said Samuel, 'because, as far as most of Biddlecombe is concerned, you're just two odd-looking men who happen to be living with us. You haven't been drawing attention to yourselves, have you?'

'No,' said Nurd. 'Wormwood's been drawing flies, but that's nothing new.'

💀 [23] Similarly, only old Mr Spiggit, the founder of Spiggit's Brewery, Chemical Weapons & Industrial Cleaning Products Ltd., knew that Shan and Gath, the chief brewers in his Dangerously Experimental Drinks Department (DEDD), were pig demons. Everybody else just thought they were two big chaps who had drunk too many of their own brews, since the list of side effects caused by sampling Spiggit's Old Peculiar on a regular basis included massive weight gain, hairy palms, moulting, and unusual beard growth.

And that was just what it did to women.

To the list could be added speech difficulties, tooth loss, tooth *growth*, and explosive wind. Basically, it was Shan and Gath in a nutshell.

'I like to think of them as pets,' said Wormwood. 'And, sometimes, as snacks.'

Mrs Johnson felt queasy, but said nothing.

'So why would this Mr Grimly invite you two to the opening of his new shop?' asked Samuel.

It was only after he had asked the question that he realised how unkind it sounded. He hadn't meant it that way. He had been thinking aloud. But now he could see the hurt in Nurd's eyes, and even Wormwood, who was harder to offend than a dead person, looked a little pained. Nurd snatched the invitation back from Samuel.

'Why wouldn't he invite us?' said Nurd. 'We're nice.'

'No, you're not,' said Wormwood.

'And we work hard.'

'No, you don't.'

'And we— Whose side are you on, anyway?' he asked Wormwood.

'Sorry,' said Wormwood. 'Force of habit.'

'I didn't mean it that way,' said Samuel. 'It's just that Mr Grimly shouldn't have heard of you. We don't *want* people to hear about you, because if the wrong kind of people know about you then there'll be all sorts of trouble, and they might take you away. Don't you understand?'

Nurd's shoulders sagged. He wanted to argue, but he couldn't. Samuel was right.

'Yes,' he said, 'I understand.'

'I don't,' said Wormwood. 'But then, I never do.'

'I'll explain later,' said Nurd.

He placed a consoling hand on Wormwood's shoulder,

then looked for somewhere to wipe his fingers. Mrs Johnson gave him a cloth.

'It doesn't matter,' said Nurd. 'Honestly, it doesn't. But just for a while, it felt like we were part of something.'

'You are part of something,' said Samuel. 'You're part of our family. Right, Mum?'

Mrs Johnson didn't answer immediately.

'*Mum?*' urged Samuel.

'Yes, yes, of course they are,' said Mrs Johnson, under pressure. 'I just tell people that they're from your dad's side.'

Nurd tried to smile, but couldn't quite manage it. He took one last look at the invitation, then tore it up and threw it in the bin.

'Let's go upstairs, Wormwood,' he said. 'You can entertain me by making unusual smells.'

They left the kitchen. When they were gone, Mrs Johnson turned to Samuel.

'He has a point, you know,' she said. 'We can't keep them cooped up in here forever when they're not working. If they're going to stay in this world, they have to find their place in it. I don't mean a physical place: they'll always have a home here, even if I do sometimes wonder what Wormwood does in the bathroom, because he certainly isn't washing, or if he is, then it isn't working. No, what I mean is that they need to be happy in it, and to be happy they have to discover what makes them happy. Maybe you should let them go with you to Wreckit's. They'll have a lovely time, and it will help them. I'm sure of it.'

Samuel nodded. 'I suppose you're right.'

'Go on,' said Mrs Johnson. 'Bring their invitation up to them, and tell them to think about what they're going to wear. Now, I'm late for bingo.'

She went into the hallway, grabbed her coat, and rushed out of the door. Samuel knelt by the bin and prepared to fish out the pieces of the torn invitation, but they weren't there.

The invitation had vanished.

CHAPTER XIII

In Which We Learn That Hilary Mould May Have Been Even Odder Than First Suspected

Samuel knocked on the door of the bedroom shared by Nurd and Wormwood and waited until Nurd's voice gave him permission to come in. Samuel was very conscious of giving Nurd and Wormwood as much privacy and space as he could. The little bedroom was their home within the home, although they hadn't done much to change it apart from putting up a few posters on the walls. Nurd had opted for pictures of ancient monuments in far-off countries: the pyramids of Egypt, the temple complex of Angkor Wat in Cambodia, and the Inca site of Machu Picchu in Peru. Wormwood, by contrast, preferred pictures of terrible boy bands. He even had a signed poster of BoyStarz, given to him by Dan and the dwarfs. According to Dan, there were plenty more posters where that came from. Hundreds. Thousands.

Nurd was lying on the top bunk, flicking through the travel supplement from one of the weekend newspapers. Wormwood was listening to music on his headphones. It was loud enough for Samuel to be able to hear some of the words: something about how love was like a garden, or a rosebush, or a snail. Whatever it was, it sounded dreadful, but Samuel said nothing. It made Wormwood happy, which was all that mattered. As if to confirm this, Wormwood gave Samuel a smile and a big thumbs-up. Samuel waved back and climbed the ladder on the bunks so that he could speak face to face with Nurd.

'Is everything all right?' asked Samuel.

'Everything's fine,' said Nurd, although his expression suggested the opposite was true.

'It's just that you don't seem to be yourself lately,' said Samuel. 'I'm worried about you.'

Faced with Samuel's obvious concern, Nurd put the travel section away.

'That's just it,' he said. 'I'm not sure what being myself means anymore. When I was in Hell, I was Nurd, the Scourge of Five Deities. I wasn't very important. I wasn't important at all, really, but I had a name, and I knew my place, even if it wasn't a very nice one. But here on Earth I live under a false name, and I have to hide my face. I crash cars for a living. Don't get me wrong, I like crashing cars, or I used to, but there's only so many times that you can crash a car and survive a fireball before it starts to get a bit samey.'[24]

'What can I do to help?' said Samuel.

'Nothing,' said Nurd. 'It's not your fault. It's just me, that's all. I'll figure something out.'

💀 [24] No matter how great your job is, there will be days when you might wish that you were doing something else. Everybody feels the need to have a bit of a moan once in a while. Your job could be knocking balls through the windows of buildings and every so often you'd still feel the urge to complain that your arm was tired.

Samuel wasn't convinced, but he didn't know how to make life better for Nurd. If he'd had money, he'd have given it to Nurd so that he could travel and see a bit more of the world, but Samuel and his mum were barely making ends meet as it was, even with the wages that Nurd and Wormwood earned from testing cars.

'Look,' said Samuel, 'maybe you should come along to the opening of the toy shop after all. It'll do you good.'

Nurd shook his head.

'No, what you said downstairs was right. We shouldn't attract any more attention to ourselves, and we wouldn't want to frighten anyone.'

He picked up his travel section again. On the cover, a young couple smiled in front of the Taj Mahal in India.

'I'm sorry,' said Samuel, as he climbed down from the bunk. 'I thought you'd be happy here.'

'I am happy,' said Nurd. 'I just wish I was . . . happier.'[25]

Maria, accompanied by Tom, came round to Samuel's house later that evening. Samuel showed the invitation to them, and they were both impressed.

'Maybe if we keep hanging around with you, some of your celebrity will rub off on us and we'll get invited to openings too,' said Tom.

'Well, can you keep rubbing, then,' said Samuel, 'because I don't want to be a celebrity at all.'

'Still, it's nice to be asked,' said Tom. 'I mean, if the only reward for being famous was being chased by

☠ [25] Which is, in a nutshell, the story of life.

demons and dragged off to Hell every so often, then it really wouldn't be worth being famous at all, would it? Are you going to bring someone along with you? I'd go, but my mum and dad are keeping me out of school that day so we can visit my gran in Liverpool.'

'I expect Lucy will want to go,' said Samuel.

Maria winced, but said nothing. The nature of her friendship with Samuel had changed a lot since Samuel had started seeing Lucy Highmore. Lucy didn't like Maria, and Maria certainly didn't like Lucy, so when Samuel was with Lucy he couldn't be with Maria, and even when he was with Maria without Lucy there was now a certain chill between them. Samuel wondered if it was always that way when a group of friends had to deal with the fact that one of them now had a girlfriend or boyfriend. He wished there was somebody he could ask about it, but the person he would usually have asked was Maria. There was no point in asking Tom: Tom was as close to being married to the rest of the rugby First Fifteen as it was possible to be without them all exchanging rings and sprinkling confetti on one another.

'Since we're all here,' said Maria, 'we may as well get some work done on our project.'

Tom groaned.

'I *hate* this project. I have to look at old buildings and try to find something to say about them other than that they're a bit gloomy and should probably have been demolished a long time ago. Yesterday I nearly got knocked out by a piece of brick that dropped off one of them. I'm lucky to be alive. Whose idea was it to write about Hilary Mould anyway?'

'It was *mine*,' said Maria icily. 'And you really will be lucky to stay alive if you don't stop complaining. We either studied the Mould buildings or spent our Saturdays wandering around shopping centres counting shoe shops. At least Mould is interesting.'

'Only if you're a depressed pigeon with no friends,' said Tom. 'And then there's that business with his statue.'

They all agreed that the statue was odd. Nobody ever saw it moving around. It would be in one place for an hour, or a day, or a week, and then it would be somewhere else. Some weeks earlier, Maria had suggested that their science class should do a study of the statue, but Mr Lugosi, the science teacher, didn't believe it was a good idea.

'Who knows what might happen if we start paying attention to it?' he said, a statement which led Maria to suspect that Mr Lugosi wasn't really cut out to teach science.

'Perhaps it's a quantum statue,' Tom had suggested, 'so that it's in every possible place in Biddlecombe until someone observes it.'

'Very clever, Hobbes,' said Mr Lugosi, 'except that the statue appears to have only six known preferred locations.'

'Sir?' called Mooch, who always sat at the back of the class and walked with a slight stoop, as though auditioning for the role of bellringer in an old cathedral.

'Yes, Mooch?'

'Seven, sir.'

'Seven what?'

'Seven places the statue seems to prefer.'

'Why do you say that, Mooch?'

'Sir, it's outside the window.'

And it was.

'Don't look at it,' said Mr Lugosi. 'Ignore it and it will go away.'

Everybody ignored Mr Lugosi instead and looked at the statue, but after a while it began to give them the creeps so they looked away again. Seconds later, the statue had gone.

'If anyone asks, that never happened,' said Mr Lugosi.

But Maria in particular continued to be intrigued, and when Mr Franklin, the geography teacher, had told them to form groups of three and come up with a project on buildings and public spaces in Biddlecombe, she had twisted the arms of Samuel and Tom until they'd agreed to look at the work of Hilary Mould. The subject was now quite topical due to the reopening of Wreckit & Sons.

'This bloke Grimly will have to do something pretty spectacular with Wreckit's if he doesn't want to send little kids home crying and wondering what the point of life is,' said Tom.

'It is a strange building to turn into a toyshop,' said Samuel. 'I know it's right in the centre of town, but it still looks like it should be used for something else.'

'Storing dead bodies,' Tom suggested.

'Storing *undead* bodies,' Samuel offered.

'A rest home for retired vampires.'

'Kennels for werewolves.'

'Will you two shut up!' said Maria. 'Look, I've printed off a map of Biddlecombe. I thought we could use it as the centrepiece for the project, and mark the Mould buildings on it. Then we could add a picture of each building, and a little potted history of it. Now that Samuel is going to the grand opening, maybe he can find a way to interview Mr Grimly. He might have more luck than the local paper has had. How does that sound?'

It was certainly better than anything Samuel or Tom had come up with. There were six Mould buildings in total in Biddlecombe, and they had taken two each to study. Samuel and Tom hadn't done much more than walk by their buildings, which in Samuel's case included Wreckit's, and then move along as quickly as possible, but Maria had already completed her histories and taken her photos. Now, as they sat around the table, she placed dots on the map indicating the location of the six Mould buildings.

Maria sat back. She appeared troubled.

'What is it?' asked Samuel. 'Did you make a mistake?'

'She doesn't make mistakes,' said Tom, which was true. What Maria did, she did well.

'Don't you see it?' said Maria.

Samuel and Tom didn't see anything at all, apart from the names of streets and buildings, and six black dots. Maria picked up her pen again, grabbed a ruler, and began drawing lines on the map, connecting the dots.

'*Now* do you see it?' she asked.

They did. It might have been a coincidence, but if it was, then it was a very large one. The dots, when joined by lines, made a very distinct pattern. It looked like this, with Wreckit & Sons at the centre:

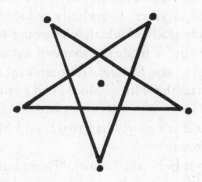

'I could be wrong,' said Maria, 'but that looks very like a pentagram.'[26]

Samuel, Maria and Tom talked for a long time about the pentagram. Maria was the most worried about it, and Tom the least. Samuel was stranded somewhere in the middle. It was unusual, he had to admit, but so what if weird Hilary Mould had set out to position his awful buildings in the shape of a pentagram? It just confirmed what everyone had always thought: he was as odd as two left shoes.

☠ 26 It was only in the nineteenth century that the pentagram – a five-pointed star – came to be regarded as a symbol for evil, and its use in old manuscripts of the supernatural is rare. Just to be clear, if it has one point at the top, then it's a symbol of good, and if there are two points at the top, like the one Maria found, it's a symbol for evil. Then again, like most things in life, it rather depends upon how one looks at it, doesn't it?

'Maybe you shouldn't go to the grand reopening,' said Maria, 'not until we know more. In fact, we should try to have the reopening postponed.'

'Are you mad?' said Tom. 'The reopening is tomorrow, and it's the biggest thing to have happened to Biddlecombe in years. Everybody is looking forward to it. Do you really think they're going to call it off just because you've made the shape of a star on a map?'

'Tom's right,' said Samuel. 'It doesn't mean anything, beyond the fact that Hilary Mould had an unusual sense of humour.'

'But what if it's more than that?' said Maria. 'What if it's dangerous?'

'How can it be?' said Samuel. 'Those buildings have been around for more than a century and they've done nothing worse than make the town look a bit uglier. Why should they start being dangerous now?'

And that was how things ended, because Maria had no answer to Samuel's question. She had only her instincts to go on, and they told her that something was very wrong here. She didn't want anything bad to happen to the people of Biddlecombe, and especially not to Samuel and Boswell. She didn't even want any harm to befall Lucy Highmore.

Or not much harm, anyway.

CHAPTER XIV

In Which the Worst Date in
the History of Dating Begins

Lucy Highmore looked lovely when she arrived at Samuel's house on the evening of the grand reopening. Her dress was lovely, her face was lovely, and her hair was lovely. Her dad had dropped her off at Samuel's house in a car that was so big it qualified as a boat, and he had glowed in the light of his daughter's sheer loveliness. If there had been a town called Lovely and its residents were looking for a statue of Loveliness to represent it, they would have modelled the statue on Lucy Highmore. Samuel felt slightly awkward standing beside her, as though he were somehow dragging her down just by being around.

Lucy Highmore had agreed to go with Samuel to Wreckit & Sons because it was such a big event, even though she knew that, pretty soon, she and Samuel would not be going anywhere together; and Samuel had asked Lucy to go to the special event even though he knew that, pretty soon, he and Lucy would not be going anywhere together; and Boswell had gone with Samuel and Lucy to the special event because Samuel had put a leash on him and said, 'Come on, Boswell,' which was all that Boswell needed to hear.

'You two – um, three – have a lovely time,' said Mrs Johnson as they left the house. 'I just hope that it's a special evening for you.'

Even if the reopening of Wreckit & Sons had been the grandest event that Biddlecombe had ever seen, the evening would not have been destined to go well for these two young people and one small dachshund. As things happened, it was destined to be an opening unlike any other.

Dimensions were fragmenting.

Cracks were appearing in the Multiverse.

The Shadows were gathering.

Eternal Darkness was coming.

Not a good evening for a date then. Not a good evening at all.

CHAPTER XV

In Which Brian the Tea Boy Really Wishes That He Had Found Himself A Safer Job, like Hand-Feeding Great White Sharks, or Juggling Scorpions

Brian the tea boy was still not used to the ghosts. Oh, he understood that they weren't really ghosts as such. Professor Stefan had sat him down shortly after the policemen had paid their visit, and explained to Brian in some detail his theory about why a former sweet factory seemed to be quite the hive of activity for people who had been dead for a long time.

'Think of the Multiverse as a series of bubbles, and each bubble is a universe,' said Professor Stefan. 'But they're not like the bubbles in a glass of fizzy pop. Instead, they're pressed very tightly together, so tightly that the "skin" of one universe almost, but not quite, shares the skin of another. And what is in these universes, you might ask?'

'Ghosts,' said Brian.

'No, Brian,' said Professor Stefan in the tone of a man who has just discovered a large hole in his bucket of patience, and is now considering hitting someone over the head with the bucket, 'not ghosts. Ghosts don't exist. Let's say it together on the count of three. One, two, three. Ghosts don't exist.'

'G – ghosts don't exist,' echoed Brian dully, casting an anxious glance over his shoulder in case one decided to pop up and prove him wrong. Brian felt that he had been reduced to a big jellied spine waiting for a shiver to run down it.

'Very good,' said Professor Stefan. 'If you could say it without stammering, that would be even better.'

'S – sorry,' s-said Brian.

'D – don't – Blast it, you have me at it now. Don't worry, just listen.'

'Right,' said Brian.

'What I think we are seeing in this sweet factory are quantum universes parallel to our own, but we're being given glimpses of different points in their time lines, which is why the people who keep popping up are wearing the clothing of Victorian servants, or Tudor courtiers or, in that slightly disturbing incident involving the elderly gentleman climbing into his bathtub, nothing at all. Similarly, it's entirely possible that somewhere on *their* time lines, people are glimpsing scientists in false beards who are pretending to run a sweet shop.

'Look, people think of time as a single straight line, like this,' said Professor Stefan. He drew a straight line for Brian, just to be helpful.

| **Past** | **Present** | **Future** |

'But suppose,' he continued, 'time isn't like that at all. Suppose time really looks like this.'

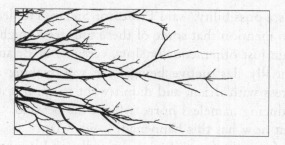

'Handy that you happened to have a picture of twigs with you, wasn't it?' said Brian.

'Yes,' said Professor Stefan. 'I have to explain this often. So, imagine that, every time you made a decision, like whether to come here to work with us—'

'So a bad decision?'

'Yes. No. Maybe. Anyway, suppose that every time you made a decision, the universe branched off, and another universe came into being. So there's this universe, the universe in which you work here, and there's another universe, in which—'

'In which I work somewhere there are no ghosts,' said Brian. 'Sorry, no not-ghosts.'

'Precisely. Now, if you think about all the decisions and actions that you take in a single day, suddenly time begins to seem a lot more complicated, doesn't it, with lots and lots of lines running alongside each other. And perhaps they're not straight lines either. Perhaps they tangle and cross over at points, just like those twigs. And sometimes, if the circumstances are right, we get a glimpse of one of those other universes, those alternative realities.'

'And you believe that's what's happening here?'

'It's a possibility,' said Professor Stefan. He decided not to mention that some of these universes might not contain just other, equally slow, versions of Brian, but potentially destructive beings. He was making some progress with Brian, and didn't want to spoil it all by introducing nameless horrors from the beyond.

'But how has this happened?' said Brian.

Professor Stefan shifted awkwardly on his seat.

'What may have occurred – and I stress "may", because we don't want people blaming us for things that we might not have done, and especially not for things that we might *actually* have done – is that, in the course of the Collider experiments, the skins separating some of the universes within the Multiverse might have been worn a little thin, thus enabling us to peer through them into other realms.'

'Weren't we talking about twigs a moment ago?'

'We were, but forget the twigs. We're back on skins.'

'So why can't the people in these other universes see us when we see them?'

Brian really was asking the most awkward questions, thought Professor Stefan. He began mentally weighing his empty patience bucket and practising his swing.

'Think of them as those windows in police stations that look like plain old mirrors on one side but, if you're sitting on the other side, allow you to watch suspects being questioned.' Professor Stefan had just thought of this explanation, and was quite pleased with it, even if it meant moving from twigs to skins to police stations. 'That would explain why we can see them, but they can't see us.'

'Oh,' said Brian.

It made a kind of sense, in a not very sensible way.

'So we're not going to talk about ghosts any more, OK?' said Professor Stefan.

'OK.'

'Because they're not ghosts, not in the way that you think, and they can't see you or hurt you.'

'Er, yes, right.'

'And we're not going to mention them to policemen, or anyone else, isn't that right?'

'Absolutely.'

'There's a good chap. Now, back to work you go. Milk, two sugars, and a Jammie Dodger, please.'

Brian did as he was told. He made a large pot of tea, put some mugs and a plate of Jammie Dodgers beside it on the tray, added a jug of milk and a bowl of sugar, and looked at his handiwork. It was all very neat and tidy. He picked up the tray, and instantly his hands began shaking so much that the Jammie Dodgers were awash with tea and milk before he even managed to get halfway to the door.

'Oh dear,' said Brian.

He turned round to return to the kitchen counter, and stopped dead.

There was a not-ghost in the room with him.

CHAPTER XVI

In Which a Scientist Tries to be Cleverer than Maria, and Fails

The bell above the sweetshop door jangled. It was Professor Hilbert's turn to sell sweets for a couple of hours, but then it *always* seemed to be Professor Hilbert's turn. Professor Stefan didn't like dealing with children and, on the two occasions Dorothy had been left in charge, she had eaten so many caramel chews that her jaw had swollen on one side, making her look as though she was concealing a golf ball in her mouth. As for Brian, his hands continued to tremble so much that he inevitably poured more sweets on the floor than he managed to put into bags. If Brian and Dorothy had been left in charge, Mr Pennyfarthinge's would have gone out of business in a week.

Professor Hilbert was engaged in mapping reported sightings of strange phenomena in and around Biddlecombe, which was no simple task as *everything* about Biddlecombe seemed strange, even the stuff that people had begun to regard as comparatively normal. For example, it was widely accepted that something unusual was living at the bottom of Miggin's Pond, but attempts to discover precisely what it was had been hampered by the ducks, which were very protective of their new resident and tended to attack anyone who attempted anything more threatening than throwing bread for them. The long-dead, and very unpleasant, Bishop Bernard the Bad, who had popped back to life for a while with the sole intention of sticking hot pokers up people's bottoms, had been reduced to bits of broken bone and mummified flesh, but on quiet evenings his remains could still be heard rattling angrily in the crypt beneath the church. It had been suggested that someone should go down and examine them, but since the person who had made the suggestion was Professor Stefan, and the someone he had in mind was anyone but himself, that suggestion had been put on hold.

Nevertheless, Professor Hilbert had still managed to pinpoint at least five areas of Biddlecombe in which unusual numbers of residents had recently complained of seeing spectral figures. Professor Hilbert shared Professor Stefan's view that these were glimpses of parallel universes, although he also believed that there were other dimensions as yet unknown existing alongside these universes. From his interviews with the boy named Samuel Johnson, Professor Hilbert had come to some understanding of how beings from these other dimensions had entered our own, and had even managed to abduct humans from our world to theirs. Professor Hilbert suspected that Samuel Johnson wasn't telling the scientists everything he knew, but Professor Hilbert didn't mind. Like many adults, he believed that he was cleverer than any child and, quite possibly, most other adults. In this, of course, he was wrong. Being clever is not just about how much you know, but about knowing that you really don't know very much at all.

Professor Hilbert's model of the Multiverse looked something like Professor Stefan's, except that the bubbles[27] weren't all pressed quite so tightly together. There were little gaps between them, and there was life in those gaps. Creatures, intelligent creatures existed in those spaces – and, yes, they were dangerous and evil and wanted to consume humanity, but that didn't make them any less interesting. Somehow, the little town of Biddlecombe had become a focal point for these unpleasant creatures. Professor Hilbert was very curious to find out why.

But now he was about to be distracted from his important thoughts by a small child's need for a bag of bull's-eyes[28] or a quarter-pound of acid drops.[29] Putting in place his false beard, which itched something awful, Professor Hilbert walked from his desk to the sweetshop. A young girl, who looked slightly familiar, was waiting at the counter. Professor Hilbert tried to recall where he had seen her before. He thought that she might be a friend of Samuel Johnson's.

'Can I help you?' he asked.

'My name is Maria Mayer and I'd like to talk to whoever is in charge, please,' said the girl.

💀 [27] Or twigs. Or police stations.

💀 [28] Formerly Uncle Dabney's Special Brand Bull's-Eyes, until it was discovered that the chewy centres were, in fact, actual bulls' eyes.

💀 [29] Again, formerly Uncle Dabney's Unusually Fiery Acid Drops, until, well, you can work it out for yourself . . .

'Of the sweet factory?'

'No, of the scientists.'

Professor Hilbert coughed and straightened his false beard.

'No scientists here, young lady, not unless you count the science of making great sweeties!'

Maria stared hard at him.

'Seriously?' she said.

'Seriously what?'

'Seriously, is that the best you can do? I know you're scientists. The whole town knows you're scientists. I have a pet rabbit named Mr Fluffytail. Even Mr Fluffytail knows that you're scientists, and Mr Fluffytail eats his own poo.'

Professor Hilbert wasn't sure what poo had to do with anything, although he vaguely recalled that Mr Pennyfarthinge's basement had contained a number of boxes of Uncle Dabney's 'Rabbit Droppings'. They appeared to be pieces of chocolate-covered fondant but they'd smelled a bit funny and nobody had been in any hurry to try them out. They'd simply thrown them away, but now Professor Hilbert was wondering if they hadn't missed a trick by not selling them as Christmas treats to the Mr Fluffytails of the world.

'Um, if there were scientists here, which there aren't, what would you want to ask them?' said Professor Hilbert.

'I wouldn't want to "ask" them anything,' said Maria. 'I'd want to *tell* them something.'

'And what would that be?' said Professor Hilbert, only just resisting the urge to add 'little girl' to the end of the question. Even though he managed not to say it aloud, he did speak it in his head, and he got the impression that Maria had somehow heard him say it.

Maria's eyes narrowed. Her scowl deepened.

'Actually, now it's two things. The first thing I'd tell them is that at least one of them needs a lesson in not being a smartypants.'

'Yes, and the second?'

Maria placed a map of Biddlecombe on the desk, a map marked with an inverted pentagram.

'That he's a smartypants in a whole lot of trouble.'

Brian was watching the not-ghost carefully. Its back was to him, but he could tell that it was a woman. She wore a red robe that reminded Brian uncomfortably of a fountain of blood, its sleeves so wide that they concealed her hands, and her long black hair trailed down her back. It was moving slightly, as though buffeted by an unseen breeze, but as Brian continued to stare it began to fan out from her head, and her robes started to billow. Brian realised that, rather than glimpsing someone standing in a breeze, he was looking at a woman somehow suspended under water, an impression strengthened by the fact that the end of her robe was not touching the ground.

Brian's hands, which now tended to tremble at the best of times, began to shake harder. The mugs clinked together. The spoons jangled. The tea slopped. Together, they made what sounded to Brian's ears like the most awful racket.

The not-ghost's head twisted slightly. She seemed to be listening to the sounds coming from the tray, but that couldn't be right. Professor Stefan had said that it was all one-way traffic. We could see them, but they couldn't see us. On the other hand Professor Stefan had said nothing about hearing, but when Brian had seen his first not-ghost he'd dropped his tray in fright, and on that occasion the not-ghost hadn't reacted at all. Perhaps, Brian thought, the not-ghost was listening to something in her own universe. Yes, that was it. She wasn't listening to the noises coming from the tea tray. She couldn't be. Everything was fine. Happy thoughts, Brian, happy thoughts.

Still, just to reassure himself Brian decided to put the tray down on the small table in the kitchen. It was probably for the best. If he didn't he'd end up covered in tea and milk.

Carefully, Brian set the tray on the table to his right. He tried to do it as quietly as possible, but it still made a noticeable sound as it touched the wood.

The not-ghost's head inclined slightly to the right. This time, though, the rest of her body began to follow in the same direction.

Ooops, thought Brian. Oops, oops, oops.

The not-ghost slowly turned 180 degrees in the air until she was facing Brian, except that 'facing' was probably not the word Brian would have used. To face someone, the first thing you need is a face, and the not-ghost had no face at all. There was only darkness, and now Brian saw that what he had believed was hair was not hair at all but tendrils of shadow extending from the blackness where her face should have been.

Brian did what any sensible person would do.

Brian fled.

CHAPTER XVII

In Which BoyStarz Return to the Limelight, Thus Making a Bad Situation Worse

A large crowd had gathered outside Wreckit & Sons to witness the grand reopening of the new store. There were lots of small children doing the things that small children do: talking, crying, complaining they wanted to go to the bathroom and, in the case of one little girl, asking Jolly where he thought he was going with her mother's purse. They were being entertained, if that was the right word, which it probably wasn't under the circumstances, by BoyStarz.

Dan had convinced Mr St John-Cholmondeley to allow BoyStarz to perform some songs at the grand opening. Mr St John-Cholmondeley had never heard of BoyStarz. More importantly, he had never heard them sing, which was why he had agreed to allow them near the store, and had also promised Dan some money, even if Dan was never going to live to collect it. Mr St John-Cholmondley started to regret his decision as soon as he heard the opening lines of 'Love is like a Toyshop', but by then it was too late.

Dan and the dwarfs walked to the rear of the store where Mr St John-Cholmondeley was waiting impatiently at the service entrance. He tapped his watch as the dwarfs approached.

'Is your watch broken?' asked Jolly.

'No, it is not. You're late.'

Jolly looked at his own watch. At least, it was his own watch now, but about five minutes earlier it had belonged to someone else.

'I don't think so. I have us bang on time.'

'I'm telling you —' insisted Mr St John-Cholmondeley, but Angry interrupted him.

'Here, give me a look at that. I'm good with watches.'

Before Mr St John-Cholmondeley could object, the watch was off his wrist and in Angry's hand.

'Ah yes, I see what's wrong here,' said Angry. 'I'll have that fixed in no time.'

The watch vanished into Angry's pocket, never to be seen by Mr St John-Cholmondeley again.

'Now,' said Angry, steering the bewildered Mr St John-Cholmondeley into the store, 'best be getting along. Don't want to keep the little 'uns waiting, do we?'

'Er, no, of course not,' said Mr St John-Cholmondeley. 'By the way, do you think you could make BoyStarz stop singing?'

'What?' said Dan. 'Make them stop? But they've only just started. Listen to them. They're like nightingales, they are.'

'They're more like seagulls,' said Mr St John-Cholmondeley. 'And you can't hear them properly because your ears are stuffed with cotton wool. *All* of your ears are stuffed with cotton wool.'

'Ear infection,' said Dan.

'Very contagious,' confirmed Angry.

Outside the store, BoyStarz finished their first song. There was some applause, but only because people were relieved that they'd stopped.

'Quick, let's get inside before they start up again,' said Jolly, and Mr St John-Cholmondeley didn't try to argue.

He led the dwarfs down the back stairs of the store. They passed no one else along the way, and Wreckit & Sons seemed very quiet.

'Where are all the staff?' asked Dan.

'They're getting a last-minute pep talk from Mr Grimly,' said Mr St John-Cholmondeley.

'Will we get to meet Mr Grimly?' asked Jolly.

'Oh yes,' said Mr St John-Cholmondeley as they reached the dressing room. 'You'll be meeting him very soon, and he's very anxious to meet you too. Dying to meet you, you could say.'

He smiled at the dwarfs the way an anteater might smile at a line of ants, but the dwarfs were too distracted by their elf outfits to notice. In the past they'd worn suits that were either so loose that a bookmark was needed to find the wearer, or so tight around the neck and waist that the wearer resembled a Christmas cracker. Those same suits were often made of the kind of material capable of conducting near fatal levels of static electricity. Angry had stuck to a carpet on one job and had to be removed from it with wooden spoons; on another, Jolly had amused himself by building up a static charge and then poking Mumbles in the arm.

Mumbles had received such a shock that his eyeballs had lit up.

These suits, on the other hand, were made of what felt like velvet. They were red with green trim, and while they might have had too many bells on for Jolly's liking, they were still more than a step above normal.

'I'll leave you to get dressed,' said Mr St John-Cholmondeley. 'Please wait here when you're done, and I'll come and get you in—'

He tried to check his watch, then realised that it was no longer on his wrist.

'Excuse me, about the watch,' he said to Angry.

'What watch?'

'*My* watch.'

'Oh, that watch. I haven't had a chance to look at it yet.'

'Would there be – ? I mean, perhaps I should – ?'

'Out with it, man, out with it,' said Angry. 'We have elf work to do.'

'Well, I was wondering if I might perhaps have a receipt for it?'

When the dwarfs had finished laughing, which took a while, and Angry's sides had stopped hurting, which took even longer, he finally managed to speak.

'Friends don't need receipts,' said Angry.

'Are we friends?' asked Mr St John-Cholmondeley.

He sounded like he didn't believe that this was the case and, if it was, he was wondering if it might be a good idea to put as much distance as possible between himself and his new 'friend'.

'No, but we won't ever be if we start looking for

receipts from each other, will we?' asked Angry reasonably. 'Friendship is about trust. Without trust, what do we have? Nothing.'

Angry put his left hand on his heart. There were tears in his eyes, although they might have been left over from his laughing fit. He put his other hand over Mr St John-Cholmondeley's heart, and discreetly stole his pocket handkerchief.

'Well, since you put it like that,' said Mr St John-Cholmondeley, as he was hustled from the room by the rest of the dwarfs.

'I'd still quite like a receipt though,' he said, as the door closed on him. 'You can even sign it "Your Friend",' he shouted through the keyhole.

Eventually they heard his footsteps move away, but by then they were already changing into their outfits. They fitted almost perfectly, although Dozy's was a little more snug in certain places than he might have liked.

'I think something's being crushed down there,' he said. 'I'll do myself an injury.'

'You'll do someone else an injury if that button pops on your trousers,' said Angry. 'You could take an eye out with it.'

'I must have put on a pound or two since—'

Dozy stopped talking and began thinking.[30] 'Hang

💀 [30] Dozy could do one or the other, but not both at the same time. This is not an uncommon flaw in those who tend to speak before they know what's going to come out of their mouths, and then look a bit surprised at what they hear. Before speaking, it's a very good idea to consider if what you're about to say is better than silence. If it isn't, then perhaps you shouldn't say anything at all.

on a minute, how did they know our sizes? I mean, these suits are very nicely cut. Very good quality, these suits. Not like the usual ones we're given.'

It was a good question. How did the suits fit so well?

'Nipsomash?' suggested Mumbles.

'Yeah, maybe Mr Singing-Chimney has a good eye for fashion,' agreed Jolly.

'If he does, then it's the only good thing about him,' said Angry. 'I wouldn't trust him an inch, and this is me speaking. I don't even trust me, but I trust me more than I'd trust him.'[31]

'It's the moustache,' said Jolly. 'You have to look out for blokes with moustaches. A bad lot, your moustache-growers.'[32]

'I wonder how they'll dress Father Christmas?' said

---

[31] Angry had once stolen one of his own shoes.

[32] The question of why men grow moustaches is one that has troubled philosophers for centuries. At best, a moustache looks like someone has decided to transport caterpillars on his upper lip; at worst, it looks like a bird has flown up his nose. It is also a fact that a great many bad sorts have been wearers of bad moustaches, as can be seen from the line-up below of Stalin of Russia, Hitler of Germany, and our old friend, Vlad the Impaler.

Dan. 'If you've got those threads, his suit must be fit for a king.'

'By the way, where is Father Christmas?' said Jolly. 'We should meet him before all this starts. We don't want any misunderstandings later.'

By 'misunderstandings', Jolly meant that he didn't want Father Christmas complaining when the dwarfs sneaked off for a nap, or took the occasional sip of Spiggit's Old Peculiar to keep their spirits up, or gave the odd annoying kid a clip on the ear.

'We should go and find him,' said Angry. 'Introduce ourselves. Let him know we're on his side, as long as he's on ours.'

'Hang on,' said Dan. 'Mr Snippy-Chinstrap told us to wait here. He seemed very keen that we didn't go wandering off.'

'Well, Mr Saggy-Chapstick isn't around, is he?' said Angry. 'And it's important that we say hello to Father Christmas: we're his elves. Without us he's nothing, and without him we're just small men with no excuse for going round a toyshop where there's lots of stuff that someone could steal if we don't get to it first.'

And so, with Dan in tow, the dwarfs set off to find Father Christmas and set him straight on the difference between 'stealing' and 'borrowing with no real intention of giving back'.

* * *

Now I am not trying to suggest that all those who grow moustaches are secretly demented dictators or bloodthirsty tyrants. That would just be silly. But, as our study shows, having a moustache is a clear sign that you might be one.

The stone house that served as Santa's Grotto sat silent and dark on the top floor of Wreckit & Sons. The trees of the forest seemed to stretch out their branches like arms towards the house. Ivy decorated their trunks, and frost sparkled on the bark. From a distance, it looked almost real. Up close, it became apparent that it *was* real. The trees had rooted themselves in the floor, breaking through the boards and anchoring themselves on the metal supports. A peculiar-smelling sap oozed from the bark, forming sticky yellow clumps that glowed with an inner light. The ivy was growing at a remarkable rate, twisting and coiling as it wound around the trunks of the trees, and extending itself across the floor to form a carpet of green.

And it was cold up there, so very cold. Had there been anyone in the vicinity to exhale, they would have seen their breath form thick white clouds that froze in the air and dropped to the ground with the faintest of tinkles as the crystals shattered. The walls began to disappear as the darkness nibbled away at them, and the little fairy lights in the ceiling blinked out one by one, and were replaced by strange constellations from another universe.

Slowly, a faint humming arose. It came from everywhere and nowhere, as though an unseen hand had set the strings of this universe vibrating. It was a foul, unsettling noise, a melody composed of pain sculpted into notes: if great evil had a theme tune, that is how it would have sounded.[33]

💀 [33] And it wasn't BoyStarz, who at that moment were being bribed to stop singing after the crowd had taken up a collection.

From inside the grotto, a white glow appeared. Tendrils of shadow forced themselves like smoke between the gaps in the stones. In one of the windows the shape of a man became visible and a voice that had, until now, spoken only from the walls found an almost human form.

'Bring them,' it said. 'Bring them to us.'

CHAPTER XVIII

In Which Maria Explains Things
to the Scientists

Professors Stefan and Hilbert eyed Maria's map, then eyed each other. To their right, Dorothy was eyeing them both. She was still wearing her false beard. It struck Professor Stefan that she was growing disturbingly fond of it, and had taken to wearing it even when there was no danger of her being seen by strangers. She also seemed to be wearing a man's suit today, along with a shirt and tie. He made a mental note to have a serious conversation with her, while there was still a 'her' to have a conversation with.

Professor Hilbert, meanwhile, was regretting calling Maria 'little girl', even if he had done so only in his head. She had spotted something that he had missed entirely. It could have been a coincidence, but Professor Hilbert was a scientist and took the view that although coincidences were sometimes just that and nothing more, there were times when coincidences were actually patterns that you had previously failed to spot.

What they were looking at was clearly an inverted pentagram formed by five buildings, all of which had been designed by the mysterious Hilary Mould. It wasn't a perfect pentagram: the crematorium, which occupied the top left point of the star, was slightly too far to the right, but if you included the cemetery next to the Church of St Timidus then it was closer to the mark. Similarly, the Biddlecombe Visitor Centre and Battlefield Experience was slightly too far to the right but, again, if you allowed for the battlefield itself, it was spot on.[34] Throw in the old lunatic asylum, the abandoned prison, and Mr Pennyfarthinge's Sweete Factorye and, hey presto, there was your pentagram.

'Hilary Mould owned all of the land on which the buildings were constructed,' explained Maria. 'He came from a very wealthy family: at one point, the Moulds collected rent from half of Biddlecombe. Mould then offered to design the buildings and contributed half of the cost of construction himself. Biddlecombe didn't really need a prison or a lunatic asylum, or even a visitor centre – it didn't have very many prisoners, only a couple of people who qualified as even slightly odder than usual, and hardly anybody ever came to visit – but getting some new buildings at a bargain price seemed like a good idea to everyone. And then, when the final stone was laid, Hilary Mould simply vanished.'

Professor Stefan shook his head in bemusement.

'But why bother?' he said. 'I mean, what's the point

💀 [34] Biddlecombe had been the site of a famous encounter in 817 AD between Vikings led by Bolverk the Wary, and Saxons led by Oswald the Uncertain. It took quite some time for the battle to get started, and fighting was only believed to have commenced after both sides backed into each other accidentally in the dark.

of creating some kind of notional star in the town of Biddlecombe?'

Behind him, Dorothy coughed. It was a very deep cough. It sounded like a gorilla had just stepped into the room and politely wanted to be noticed.

'I might be wrong,' said Dorothy, 'but it looks like he was building a vast occult generator. You know, a kind of supernatural power station.'

'But powered by what?' asked Professor Hilbert, annoyed that he had been upstaged by a female for the second time that day.

'Death and suffering,' said Dorothy. 'You have a battlefield, a prison, an asylum, a crematorium, and Mr Pennyfarthinge's Sweete Factorye or, more particularly, Uncle Dabney's line in unpleasant eating experiences.'

'It would explain a lot,' said Maria, who was impressed by Dorothy's insights, and regarded them as another blow struck for feminism. 'Like how Biddlecombe became the focus for the invasion from Hell. It couldn't simply have been the Abernathys and their friends messing about in a cellar with things that they didn't understand.[35] They weren't powerful enough, and it made no sense that what was happening at CERN in Switzerland should have found an outlet in Biddlecombe.[36] It was because of Mould and his buildings.'

💀 [35] In *The Gates*, Samuel discovered the Abernathys and their friends trying to summon up demons in the cellar of a house. I really should be charging you extra for these reminders.

💀 [36] Take that, critics. You thought I was just making all this stuff up as I went along, but there was a plan, I tell you, a plan! (Cue maniacal laughter, and a gibbering henchman calling me 'Master!' in an admiring way.)

'But Mould couldn't have known that, more than a century in the future, someone would construct the Large Hadron Collider and turn it on,' said Professor Stefan. 'He couldn't even have imagined people would own watches that didn't need winding, or shoes with wheels in the heels.'

'Perhaps he didn't, but something else did,' said Maria. 'Something much older, something that had been watching humanity for a long, long time, something with a lot of patience and a lot of anger. It guided Mould in the creation of the pentagram, and then added one more building for luck.'

She was about to place her finger at the heart of the pentagram, but Dorothy beat her to it.

'Wreckit & Sons,' said Dorothy.

They all remained silent for a few moments. They might have remained silent for a good deal longer had the quiet not been broken by the sound of a scream and a tea boy's feet running very, very fast.

'What is wrong with that boy now?' said Professor Stefan. 'Honestly, he'll be jumping at the sight of his own shadow next.'

Interestingly for Brian – although 'Terrifyingly for Brian' might have been more apt – he was in the process of doing just that as Professor Stefan spoke. To begin with, he'd been relieved to find that the not-ghost in the red robe wasn't chasing him. He'd taken a couple of glances over his shoulder as he ran, and there was no sign of pursuit. There was just his shadow extending behind him, the way a shadow should.

Unfortunately, his shadow quickly began catching up with him before passing him entirely and finally separating itself from his shoes and assuming a 'this far and no further' position in front of him. It stretched as he watched, growing both wider and taller, until it entirely blocked his way. It also had more substance than a shadow should. Brian thought that, if he poked it with his finger, it would feel like a big, dirty marshmallow, and his finger would be returned to him stained with black, if it was returned at all.

A crack opened in the shadow's head. It might have been mistaken for a smile, but only the kind of smile that a cannibal might wear before tucking into dinner. Teeth appeared in the mouth: they were sharp but wispy, as though the smoke from a series of recently blown-out candles had solidified. A clawed hand reached for Brian, and he ducked just in time to avoid having it close upon his skull. Since he was now heading in the direction of the floor, Brian decided simply to keep going. He dived through the shadow's legs, somersaulted to his feet behind it, surprising himself almost as much as the creature, and recommenced running and screaming. Meanwhile the creature, clearly deciding that two massive arms ending in jagged claws weren't enough for the job, began sprouting a third and a fourth, and grew another head while it was about it, since you never knew when a second head might come in useful. Then, seemingly content with these improvements, it returned to the task of trying to consume Brian.

It was at this point that Professor Stefan opened the door to the main laboratory with every intention of giving Brian a stern talking to about the importance of not mewling and squealing at the slightest sign of Multiversal activity. He got as far as saying 'Now look here—' before he took in the sight of a terrified Brian being pursued by a giant, multi-armed and dual-headed shadow monster.

'Never mind,' said Professor Stefan.

He held the door open for Brian and, as soon as the tea boy was safely inside, slammed it shut.

'Wibble,' said Brian. 'Wibble, wibble wibble.'

He then promptly fainted as wisps of dark matter began seeping through the keyhole.

CHAPTER XIX

**In Which Wreckit & Sons Reopens,
and There Is Much Joy and Good Cheer.
(Part of This Chapter Heading May Be a Lie.)**

At precisely 6.55 p.m., thousands of lights exploded into Christmas cheer on the front of Wreckit & Sons, bathing the crowd gathered below in green and white and gold. There was a collective 'Ooooh!' of appreciation which rose in volume as a grinning Father Christmas formed by red bulbs appeared at the heart of the display, the arrangement of the lights changing as the crowd watched so that Father Christmas's lips seemed to move, although no sound emerged from them, not yet. In truth, he didn't look like a very jolly Father Christmas. His face was a bit too pinched and thin for that, and his eyes were little more than narrow slits. As the lights continued to make his lips move, he looked as though he were threatening a child with something considerably worse than an absence of gifts on Christmas morning. He also, it had to be said, bore more than a passing resemblance to the statue of Hilary Mould.

But any doubts about Father Christmas were overwhelmed by the spectacle unfolding on Biddlecombe High Street. The dark cloths that had so far masked the windows fell away to reveal the most wondrous displays. Polar bears carried gifts on their backs across fields of pure white snow. There were scenes from fairy tales being enacted by mannequins: Snow White accepted a poisoned apple from her wicked stepmother disguised as an unspeakably ugly witch; a huge wolf in a nightdress towered above Red Riding Hood; a troll threatened three billy goats; and another wolf was proving that sixty-six per cent of little pigs were not very good at building houses. They weren't exactly cheerful moments from the history of fairy tales, and there was more blood and gore than was strictly necessary: it was clear that Red Riding Hood's grandmother had already met a nasty end, for the wolf was holding her severed head in one of its paws; the troll wore a necklace of billy goat skulls; and one of the three little pigs was missing most of its lower body, the rest having been reduced to a pile of bacon by a large, steam-powered bacon slicer. But they were very well done, even if it would have been nice had someone taken the time to give proper faces to the human characters. Instead, the dummies appeared to be made from a form of black material, some of which had been used to create the eyes for the other characters, for even the billy goats and the little pigs had eyes like deep, dark pools.

Hang on: weren't there *three* billy goats in the window just a moment ago? And why is that troll licking its lips? It looks very lifelike. Perhaps a bit too lifelike . . .

Meanwhile, what seemed like hundreds of elves danced and sang as they laboured happily in Santa's workshop, although what they appeared to be producing were just more versions of themselves as more elves poured off the production line. Children pressed their noses against the windows, mouths agape. Even their parents were amazed. It was the greatest Christmas display anyone had ever seen. A bit graphic, admittedly, but very impressive.

The main doors of the store opened, and Mr St John-Cholmondeley appeared. Behind him, Wreckit & Sons remained dark. Clearly another surprise was planned, and people remarked aloud that if the windows were that good, imagine what the inside must be like!

'Welcome!' said Mr St John-Cholmondeley. 'Welcome all!'

His voice boomed, even though there was no microphone visible. A hush descended on the crowd.

'On behalf of Mr Grimly, I'd like to say how greatly pleased we are that you could join us on this very special evening. I can assure you it is one that will not easily be forgotten.'

A round of applause came from the crowd, although they weren't entirely sure what they were applauding. Most of them were hoping for some free stuff, just for entering into the spirit of the thing.

'I'm especially pleased to welcome our guest of honour for the evening: Mr Samuel Johnson and, of course, his dog, Boswell.'

There was another smattering of applause, but not much.

'Why him?' someone asked. 'What's he ever done?'

'Well, there was all that invasion from Hell business.'

'Oh, but that was ages ago. What's he done since

then, eh? I mean, yes, he saved the world and all that, but he can't expect us to go around bowing and scraping to him for the rest of our days just because of some demons. Anyway, I heard that they weren't real. It was all made up to promote a film, or a television show, or something.'

Samuel stepped forward, Lucy Highmore on his left arm, and Boswell's leash held tightly in his right hand. A photographer from the local paper popped up and took a couple of pictures, although Samuel noticed that he was pointing his lens at Lucy alone, and the only part of Samuel likely to end up in any photos was his left ear.

Mr St John-Cholmondeley placed a hand on Samuel's shoulder. It felt both hard and strangely light.

'So good of you to come,' said Mr St John-Cholmondeley. 'So very good.'

He looked around, as though expecting someone else to appear.

'And your, um, friends?' he inquired.

'What friends?' asked Samuel.

'Mr Cushing, and Mr Lee. Won't they be joining us?'

'I don't know who you mean,' lied Samuel.

Mr St John-Cholmondeley seemed about to differ, then changed his mind.

'Not to worry,' he said. 'Perhaps they're just a little delayed. They'll join us in time: I'm certain of it.'

He cleared his throat, and raised his hands to silence the crowd, which was getting restless.

'We have two other gentlemen whom we would like to honour this evening. They are the sleepless guardians of the law, the men who keep us all safe at night. May I please ask Sergeant Rowan and Constable Peel to step forward?'

Sergeant Rowan and Constable Peel looked shocked to be singled out in this way. They were simply supposed to be on crowd duty, and nobody had suggested that they would be honoured with anything other than overtime. Now their names were being called out, and the same voice that, moments earlier, had been complaining about Samuel was asking why they were so special, and commenting how, at the rate things were going, everybody in town would be special except him, and what kind of world were we living in, exactly?

The two policemen came and stood awkwardly beside Samuel and Lucy and Boswell. There was a third, generally polite burst of applause, as everybody liked to stay on the right side of the police.

'If all four of you – and, of course, the delightful Boswell – would come into the store for a moment, we have a small presentation we'd like to make,' said Mr St John-Cholmondeley.

'And when we're done,' he continued, addressing the crowd once more, 'the main festivities will begin, and you'll all get what's coming to you.'

Which was an odd way to put it, thought Sergeant Rowan, as he and the others moved towards the darkened interior of the store. He glanced again at the window displays and noted that, close up, the polar bears looked less like bears than some kind of abominable snowmen; and the reindeer had very vicious horns and spiked hooves; and the workshop elves had a mean, spiteful appearance about them; and those machines were producing an awful lot of them, so many, in fact, that pretty soon the window areas wouldn't be big enough to hold them all. They were already piling up, except that they weren't piling up so much as lining up. But the workshop machines were just tossing them on the floor of the store, and there was nobody around to set them on their feet, so how exactly were they ending up in neat rows before the windows?

And why would somebody design Christmas elves with such sharp teeth?

But by then the four humans, along with one small dog, had crossed the threshold of Wreckit & Sons. As soon as they were inside Mr St John-Cholmondeley vanished, and the darkness of the store closed so tightly around them that they could not see their own hands in front of their faces, and they were only vaguely aware of the sounds from outside of glass breaking and people screaming.

'Sarge?' said Constable Peel to the blackness.

'Yes, Constable.'

'Maybe we should have told the man that we didn't want to be special after all.'

'It's a little late for that, Constable, don't you think?'

But Constable Peel didn't get to reply, because the darkness swallowed his words, and then his breath.

And, finally, it swallowed him.

CHAPTER XX

In Which History Comes Alive

Nurd was lying on the top bunk, staring at the ceiling. Mrs Johnson had gone out to bingo again. Nurd suspected that Mrs Johnson was a bingo addict. Whenever anyone mentioned a number in conversation, Mrs Johnson would instinctively try to cross it out.

Nurd was sulking, although it was hard to tell because Nurd's face naturally formed a kind of sulk, even when he was happy.

'I spy with my little eye—' said the voice of Wormwood from the lower bunk.

'I'm not playing any more,' said Nurd.

'Come on. It's fun.'

'No, it's not. "I-Spy" is only ever fun for the person doing the spying. I hate "I-Spy". Anyway, you're on the bottom bunk staring up at the top bunk. So far you've spied a mattress, some wood, and a sheet. You're unlikely to spot a camel, are you, or a spaceship? There's a limit to how interesting it can be.'

'I'll look somewhere else, then.'

'No.'

'Please, just one more? Oooh! Oooh! I've just spotted something. It's great. Seriously. Please? Oh, please?'

Nurd sulked even more. While he really did understand the reason why Sanuel hadn't wanted him to go along to the grand reopening of Wreckit's store, he remained hurt. Once again, Nurd recalled that he had once been a demon with high hopes. He'd even had ambitions to take over the Earth. They hadn't worked out very well because Nurd was useless at being properly demonic, and a squirrel with a nut allergy had a better chance of ruling the world, but at least it had been something to aim for.

Now here he was, sharing a small room with Wormwood, and Wormwood wasn't meant for small rooms. Wormwood could have made a cathedral smell a bit funny. Nurd had grown fond of Wormwood in the way a dog might grow fond of a particularly friendly flea, but he really did wish that they could see a little less of each other.

A lot less of each other.

'Go on, then,' said Nurd. 'But this is absolutely, positively the last time, and I'm only taking three guesses.'

'Understood,' said Wormwood. 'You're the best demonic master I've ever had!'

'I'm the only demonic master you've ever had.'

'You have a point,' admitted Wormwood. 'Now, I spy with my little eye something beginning with "e".'

Nurd thought about it. He was very competitive and he didn't like to lose, not even at I-Spy. He had managed to guess mattress, wood and sheet easily enough. He wasn't about to be beaten on the final try by Wormwood.

'Eiderdown,' he said.

'Wrong!'

Nurd scratched his ear. It helped him to think. He poked at his earhole, and kept poking until the tip of his finger came out of the other ear. Nurd wasn't sure why it sometimes did that. Wormwood had once suggested a possible answer. Nurd had kicked him in the bum for his trouble, but not before putting on his pointiest boots.

'Electric blanket,' said Nurd.

'Wrong again!'

He heard Wormwood sniggering, and wondered where he might have left those pointy boots.

Nurd looked around the room, trying to see it from Wormwood's angle. Electricity? No, that couldn't be it. Samuel's exercise jotter? Possibly, although it was a bit of stretch.

Ah, he had it! On the floor by Samuel's bed was a small, stuffed elephant. It had once been Samuel's favourite stuffed toy, but was now beloved of Boswell, who liked to sleep with it for company.

Nurd made a trumpeting sound, and prepared for his final triumph.

'It is,' he said grandly, 'an elephant.'

'WRONG!' howled Wormwood. 'Wrongedy wrong wrong, Mr Wrongly Wrongington!'

'It has to be an elephant,' said Nurd. 'I've looked. There's nothing else around here beginning with the letter "e".'

'Ring-ring,' said Wormwood. 'Call for you. It has to be for you, because it's a WRONG number.'

'I'm warning you,' said Nurd, who now remembered where he had left those boots.

'You don't have a right hand,' continued Wormwood. 'You just have a left hand and a WRONG hand.'

'I shall inflict grave pain upon you with a pointy boot,' Nurd warned. 'I shall take a very long run-up to do it. It will be such a long run-up that you will have grown old by the time my boot finally reaches you, and I shall kick you so hard that, when you open your mouth, the tip of my boot will be visible at the back of your throat.'

'You lost, you lost . . .'

'Tell me what it was.'

'Don't have to if I don't want to.'

'TELL ŒE!!!!!'

Flames shot out of Nurd's mouth and ears. His cloak billowed like the wings of a bat. His eyes turned red, and his eyebrows caught fire.

'It was an elf,' said Wormwood in a tiny voice.

'Excuse me?' said Nurd, as he regained control of himself.

'An elf,' said Wormwood, a little louder. 'I spied an elf.'

Nurd rubbed his finger along his forehead. He could just about feel where his eyebrows used to be.

'Elves don't exist,' he said. 'Dwarfs exist, not elves. You can't have seen an elf.'

'I did,' said Wormwood. 'And I still spy an elf. It's outside the bedroom window.'

Despite himself, Nurd leaned over the edge of his bed to take a look. Wormwood was right. Standing on the windowsill, wearing a jaunty green hat and a suit of red felt, was an elf. It had unusually sharp teeth, and red dots gave a kind of life to its cheeks. It had very dark eyes. They should have done something about the eyes, thought Nurd. Nobody likes an elf with scary eyes.

'How did that get there?' said Nurd.

'Maybe it climbed up,' said Wormwood.

'It's a Christmas elf,' said Nurd. 'It's made of wood. You might as well expect a clothes peg to climb up.'

Wormwood left his bunk bed and padded to the window. He peered at the elf. The elf peered back.

'It's very lifelike,' he said.

'It's. An. Elf,' said Nurd. 'It can't be lifelike. There's nothing life to be like.'

Wormwood began to open the window.

'What are you doing?' said Nurd.

'I want to take a closer look at it.'

Nurd suddenly had the sense that this might not be a good idea. He couldn't have said why except that they were on the second floor of a house and somehow there was an elf on their windowsill, which meant that either the elf had, as Wormwood suggested, managed to climb up, or, as seemed more likely, someone or something had put it there from above. Whatever the case, opening the window didn't strike Nurd as the wisest of moves.

'I wouldn't do that,' he said, 'not until—', but the rest of the sentence was drowned out by the creak of the window being opened. There was a blast of cold air. In the distance, Nurd could hear sirens and—

Were those screams?

At the Biddlecombe Visitor Centre and Battlefield Museum, the caretaker, Mr Karloff, was closing up for the evening. He wanted to get down to Wreckit's for the grand unveiling of the new store because very little that was exciting ever happened in Biddlecombe, or very little that didn't involve people claiming to have seen demons, or the dead coming to life. Mr Karloff wasn't sure that he believed all of that nonsense. During the supposed invasion of Biddlecombe by the forces of Hell, Mr Karloff had been visiting his sister Elsa in Skegness, and had missed the whole affair. Despite the fact that some very trustworthy people claimed it was all true – honest to goodness, would I lie to you? – Mr Karloff regarded it as evidence of some form of mass hysteria.

It had not been a busy day at the Visitor Centre, but then it was rarely a busy day there. For some reason, tourists didn't want to come to Biddlecombe to stare at a damp field in which, long ago, two small armies led by very cautious men had eventually got around to fighting each other by mistake. The sign above the museum's door read 'We Bring History to Life!', which was not true in any way, shape or form. There were stones with more life than the Biddlecombe Battlefield Museum.

Mr Karloff had tried to make the experience more interesting by constructing a reconstruction of the battle using small plastic soldiers which he had carefully painted with his own hands. There weren't enough Vikings and

Saxons to make it look impressive so he had bulked up the numbers with whatever he had lying around at home. If someone closely examined Mr Karloff's version of the Battle of Biddlecombe, they might have spotted some confused-looking German soldiers painted like Vikings, along with half-a-dozen cowboys and a couple of Indians who had been drafted into the Saxon ranks. The rest of the museum was filled out with some spearheads, broken axes, and the odd bone that had been found poking out of the field after spells of heavy rain.

The centre only opened on Saturdays, Sundays, and every second Thursday. During the summer, coach parties on very cheap tours would occasionally stop there. The money gained from their entry fees, along with what they spent on postcards, chocolate, and pictures of themselves dressed up in the Viking and Saxon costumes that Mr Karloff had put together for the purpose was just about enough to keep the centre open.

But it was now winter, and only seven people had shown up that day. One of them was lost, two of them just wanted to use the bathroom, and the others were visiting Americans who asked some awkward questions about the cowboys and Indians fighting on the Saxon side. Mr Karloff told them that they'd come over to help the Saxons when the Americans heard about their trouble with the Vikings, and they were happy enough with the answer, but it had been a hairy moment. Still, they had bought lots of postcards, and they got a kick out of dressing up as ancient warriors.

In his little office, Mr Karloff counted up the day's takings and put them in an envelope which he folded into his pocket. He would go to the bank with it on Monday once he had added whatever came in on Saturday and Sunday. He was about to turn off the lights when a loud knocking at the front door almost gave him a heart attack.

'We're closed,' he shouted. 'Come back on Saturday.'

He thought that he heard muttered words, and then the knocking came again.

'Oh, really!' said Mr Karloff. 'Some people have no manners.'

He popped his head round the door frame.

'I said we're closed. You'll have to come back at the weekend.'

There was a full moon that night. It shone on the two small glass panels of the door, or would have if most of its light hadn't been blocked by a huge shape holding a large stick. The figure's head was slightly misshapen by what appeared to be a thick feather sticking out of its hair.

The knocking started a third time. It was clear from the movements of the figure that whoever was outside was using the stick to bang on the door. It was probably some young rascal making mischief. No decent, self-respecting person would go round banging on museum doors with a stick.

'He'll have all the paint off, and I only gave it a new coat this summer!' said Mr Karloff aloud. He spent so much time alone at the museum that he had grown used to having conversations with himself.

'Well, I won't have it,' he continued, as he marched to the door. 'I simply won't. Young people these days.

There's nothing wrong with them that a spell in the army wouldn't cure.'

Mr Karloff yanked open the door. His first thought was that perhaps a spell in the army wouldn't solve this chap's problems at all because joining the army was probably what had caused his problems to begin with. Those problems included, but were not limited to, having:

1. No lower jaw in a face that was largely bone and some apologetic grey skin.
2. One completely empty eye socket and one eye socket that was filled by the business end of an arrow, and last but most certainly not least . . .
3. Most of an axe buried in the top of his skull.

In his right hand the new arrival held not a stick, but a spear, a spear that still looked useful in a potentially fatal way despite having spent over a thousand years in the ground alongside its owner.

Mr Karloff had worked long enough at the museum to recognise a Viking when he saw one, especially a dead one. Under other circumstances, such as encountering the dead Viking laid out in a thick glass case, he might even have been pleased. He was slightly less pleased to find a dead Viking standing upright on his doorstep and apparently giving serious thought to abandoning the whole business of being dead and trying out being undead for a while.

The spearhead moved. Instead of pointing straight up in the air, it was now moving in a direction that suggested it fancied making friends with Mr Karloff's insides, although it wasn't planning on staying long because it would very soon pop out of his back, possibly with some of Mr Karloff's insides still attached to it.

'Oh dear,' said Mr Karloff.

Those might have been the last words that he ever said, and they wouldn't have been very memorable, as last words go. He was saved by a whistling sound from the embarrassment of dying without having something witty to say. The whistling sound was followed by a very solid *thunk*, and suddenly the Viking was relieved of the difficulties posed by the axe in his skull and the arrow in his eye by the removal of his head at the neck. His body remained vertical for a second or two, then appeared to think, Actually, why bother?, and collapsed on the doorstep.

Mr Karloff was now staring into the undead face of a Saxon who was holding a sword almost as big as he was. Behind him, Mr Karloff could see more undead Vikings and Saxons digging themselves out of their graves. Those that were above ground were already fighting among themselves.

Mr Karloff gave the undead Saxon his biggest and best smile.

'I'm on your side,' he said. 'Keep up the good work.'

He closed the front door, grabbed his hat, and ran to the back door. That one he didn't bother closing after him. After all, as soon as he heard the front door explode behind him there really didn't seem to be much point.

CHAPTER XXI

In Which the Dwarfs Make
a New Friend. Sort of

Dan and the dwarfs had discovered that getting out of the basement was harder than it looked. To begin with, the basement now seemed much bigger than it had when they arrived, which couldn't be right yet somehow was. They had been walking around for half an hour and still hadn't found the stairs. This development might have worried ordinary people, but the dwarfs were far from ordinary. They were seasoned drinkers of Spiggit's Old Peculiar, and so were well used to walking around small spaces for long periods of time without being able to find the door, often while singing loudly and seeing small multicoloured elephants flying around their heads.

On this occasion, though, the dwarfs were ninety-nine per cent sure that they hadn't been drinking. Dan had been very clear on that point: they needed this job. It was a steady earner until Christmas. Plus, if they made enough money, Dan would be able to have the van repainted, and they would no longer have go around advertising themselves as Dan's Sods.

'Maybe we should split up,' said Dan.

'Why?' said Jolly.

'Because we can cover more ground that way. Two groups: if one group finds the door, it keeps shouting until the other group arrives.'

The dwarfs thought about this.

'That sounds like a great suggestion,' said Jolly after a while. 'Nobody ever got into trouble by separating from his friends in a dark basement and hoping for the best.'

'Absolutely,' said Angry. 'It can't fail.'

So they split into groups, Dan, Jolly and Angry in one, and Mumbles and Dozy in the other.

'Lucky for us that Dan is in charge, eh?' said Dozy to Mumbles as the footsteps of the others faded away. 'We'd be lost without him.'

Which was literally true. Seconds after Dan had left them, Dozy and Mumbles were completely lost.

'Are we there yet?'

'No.'

Pause.

'Are we there yet now?'

'No.'

Pause.

'Are we there—'

'No!' said Dan. 'No, no, no! We're not there. We're here. I don't know where there is. I'm not even sure where *here* is.'

He stomped off to look around the next corner, leaving Jolly and Angry behind.

'I love doing that,' said Jolly. 'Never fails.'

'It's a classic,' admitted Angry. 'Still, I wish we were out of this basement. I'm getting a bit tired of looking at walls and boxes. And I could be wrong, but it does seem to be getting darker down here. I thought your eyes were supposed to get used to the darkness the longer you spent in it, but my eyesight is getting worse.'

He kicked at a scrap of crumpled newspaper. As it rolled away, the dim lightbulb above their heads caught the headline. It announced the defeat of Germany, and the end of the Second World War.

'I think it's been a while since anyone's been down here,' said Angry. 'That, or World War Two took a lot longer to win than I thought.'

There was a door to Jolly's right. They had been routinely opening every door they came to in the hope of finding a stairway, or a lift, or a beer. So far, they'd had no luck on any count. Jolly opened the door and wished silently for a little good luck.

Sometimes, if you squeeze your eyes shut, and you think about good things, happy things – snowflakes, and fairies, and bluebirds singing – and picture your wish coming true, picture it like it's happening in front of you right here and now, then the universe will find a way to make it come true.

This wasn't one of those times.

Reality was fragmenting, and when reality fragments strange things happen.

The tentacled entity inside the closet wasn't sure how it had got there, or how long it had been there, or even what a closet was. All it knew was that one minute it had been minding its own business in a quiet corner of the

Multiverse, idly wondering which tentacle to use to feed a smaller creature into one of its many gaping mouths, and the next it had been squashed into a very small space with spiders crawling across its face. Because the space was so small, the entity was entirely unable to move, and so it had been trying to blow the spiders away with whichever one of its mouths was nearest. It had tried eating one of the spiders by catching it on its tongue and pulling it into its mouth, but the spider's legs had caught in its teeth, which annoyed the entity greatly. The spider hadn't tasted very nice either. Now the entity's tentacles were starting to cramp, and it really needed to go to the toilet very badly, but it didn't want to go to the toilet in the closet because it already smelled bad. In addition, the piece of its bodily equipment that it needed to get to in order to go to the toilet was currently squashed against one of its legs and the entity wasn't sure what would happen if it just took a chance and decided to relieve itself. Frankly, it thought, that stuff could go anywhere.

Suddenly a light shone upon it. One of its heads peered from between a pair of crossed tentacles. Another peered from between its legs. A third popped out of the mouth of the first and squinted at the small figure before it.

Jolly stared at the entity for a couple of seconds, then closed the door. He scratched his chin. He nibbled a fingernail.

He called Angry over.

'What is it?' said Angry.

'Open that door,' said Jolly.

'Why?'

'Just open it.'

'No.'

'Come on, for me.'

'No! I know what's going to happen.'

'I bet you don't.'

'I bet I do.'

'Go on, then. Tell me what's going to happen.'

'I'll open that door, and a broom will fall out and hit me on the head.'

'I promise you that won't happen.'

'A mop, then.'

'No.'

'A bucket.'

'I guarantee,' said Jolly, 'that if you open that door, nothing will fall on your head.'

Angry raised a finger in warning.

'If anything falls on my head . . .'

'It won't.'

'Because if it does, we're going to have a disagreement.'

Jolly took a step back as Angry opened the door.

If the entity was surprised the first time that the door opened, it was better prepared on the second occasion. Jaws snapped. Tongues lolled. Tentacles squirmed ineffectually. It made a horrible sound somewhere between a gibbering howl and an echoing shriek.

Angry gave it a little nod and closed the door softly.

'Did you put that in there?' he asked Jolly.

'Yes,' said Jolly. 'I've been keeping it as a pet, but I didn't want to tell anyone because I thought they might make me hand it over to the zoo.'

'You can't keep that as a pet,' said Angry, on whom

sarcasm was sometimes lost. 'You need a bigger hutch, for a start. It's cruel keeping a – whatever that is – cooped up like that. I ought to report you.'

Jolly punched Angry on the arm.

'Of course I didn't put it in there,' said Jolly. 'I just opened the door and there it was.'

'Well, what's it doing in that closet, then?'

'I don't know!'

'I wonder how long it's been in there?' said Angry.

From behind the door came what sounded like a sigh of relief, and liquid began pouring from inside the closet. Jolly and Angry took some quick steps back.

'Quite a while, I think,' said Jolly.

'We can't just leave it there,' said Angry.

'We can't take it with us,' said Jolly. 'Did you see those teeth? Nasty, those teeth. Not the teeth of a vege-tarian. Never met a bone they didn't like, those teeth.'

On the wall nearby was an ancient blackboard. Fragments of dusty chalk lay on a shelf beside it. Angry picked up one of the pieces of chalk and wrote on the door. The writing was slightly uneven because Angry had to lean at an awkward angle to avoid the liquid that was still spilling from inside the closet.

'What's it been drinking?' said Jolly. 'If he doesn't finish soon, we'll drown.'

'There,' said Angry. He looked admiringly at his handiwork. On the door were now written the words

DO NOT OPEN!

'That should do it,' said Angry.

'Can I have that chalk?' said Jolly.

Angry handed it to him, and Jolly added one more word.

MONSTER!

'Better,' said Angry. 'Much better.'

He slipped the chalk into his pocket.

'Now let's find Dan, just in case we need any more doors opened.'

CHAPTER XXII

In Which All Threats Begin
with the Letter 'E'

Meanwhile, in another part of the basement that should not have been very far away but, because of the strange things happening in the Multiverse, was now much further away than before, Mumbles and Dozy had stumbled upon old Mr Wreckit's selection of unsold Nosferatu photographs. They came in all shapes and sizes, and while most simply lounged against the walls as though recovering from a heavy meal of blood and a long flight home on bat wings, others had been nailed to the walls, creating a gallery of vampiric figures.

Just in case you'd forgotten, or were not having trouble sleeping, some of them looked like this:

Dozy tapped Mumbles on the shoulder and pointed to the nearest picture.

'Your mum's looking well,' he said.

Mumbles kicked him in the shin.

A lightbulb flickered above their heads, casting an unpleasantly sickly light on the faces that surrounded them. It also made them look distinctly alive. The depictions started to seem less like pictures and more like windows through which far too many vampires were peering. It made the dwarfs feel like walking blood banks, and toothy creatures were queueing up to make a withdrawal.

'It's like the eyes follow you round the room,' said Dozy.

It was true. No matter where they stood, the gathered vampires kept a close watch on them.

'Unkebyem?' said Mumbles.

Dozy shrugged.

'I've no idea who'd buy one of those pictures and put it on his wall,' he said. 'Except maybe your dad, to remind him of your mum.'

Mumbles kicked him in the shin again. The bulb above their head flickered one last time, then died.

'This isn't doing us any good,' said Dozy. 'Come on, let's get out of here. I feel like we've been walking in this basement for hours. We must be under the sea by now.'

They trooped on, Dozy limping slightly from the repeated kicks to his shin, and Mumbles sulking in front of him.

'I like your mum,' said Dozy. 'Seriously. You're just lucky you got your looks from your dad.'

Mumbles turned to aim another boot in Dozy's general direction, but he paused mid-kick.

'Erat?'

'Hear what?' said Dozy.

'Er*at*!'

Dozy listened. From the shadows behind came the sound of something landing on the floor. It didn't sound like a big something, which was good. On the other hand, it was definitely *a* something, which was bad. The sound came again, and again, and again. Not a something, then, but lots of somethings.

Which was very bad.

'Rats?' said Dozy. They hadn't seen any rats or mice yet, which he found odd. There were usually rodents in old basements.

Dozy listened harder.

'No,' he said. 'That's not the sound of claws. It's more like soft fruit dropping on a floor. Maybe someone's making jam.'

The two dwarfs faced the darkness. The sounds had stopped, but now there was movement in the gloom

A small object rolled towards them and came to a halt a couple of inches from Dozy's right foot. It looked up at him. It couldn't do much else, since it was a just an eyeball.

'Somebody will be missing that,' said Dozy.

Another eyeball rolled into view, and a third. Very soon, Mumbles and Dozy were looking down on a field of eyeballs. They were all slightly yellowed, and all very familiar, since the last time the dwarfs had seen them they had been lodged in the skulls of the vampiric pictures in the previous room.

I had to say it, thought Dozy. I had to say that the eyes seemed to follow you around the room. Mumbles had just the same reaction.

'Adzaeyfollroo!'

'I didn't mean it literally,' said Dozy. 'It's not like I was hoping it would happen. All right, here's what we're going to do. We're going to ignore them. After all, they're eyeballs. What can they do, stare us to death? We're going to turn around, continue our search, and pretend that they're not there, agreed?'

Mumbles nodded. 'Ooly.'

They each took a deep breath, spun on their heels, and started walking.

It turned out to be a lot harder than they had expected to ignore the eyeballs. Most of us, at some time or another, will have had the sensation that someone is staring at us. Our instinct is to find out who, and why, and make them stop doing it. If lots of people stare at us, we start wondering what might be wrong with us. Has our face turned a funny colour? Do we have a bird on our head? Have we left something unzipped that shouldn't be unzipped in public? Being stared at for any length of time is very unpleasant.

As Dozy was bringing up the rear he was more aware of the eyeballs than Mumbles. He felt hundreds of eyes boring into his back. He could hear them rolling along the dusty floor behind him. It was slowly driving him mad. Occasionally he would cast a glance over his shoulder and the eyeballs would stop moving. They would even stop staring at him for a while and suddenly find something interesting to look at on the ceiling or the walls. If they could, he was sure that they would have started whistling innocently, as if to say, 'Don't mind us, we're not really following you, we just happen to be heading in the same direction.'

'Look—' Dozy began to say, then realised that a) the eyeballs couldn't do anything else and b) what he actually wanted was for them to stop looking, so telling them to look wasn't helpful.

'Listen—' he tried, but that wasn't right either.

'Oh, just go away!' he said. 'We don't want any eyeballs. We have enough of our own. We only need two each. We've nowhere to put any more. We can't keep you in our pockets. It would defeat the purpose.'

The eyeballs looked hurt, or as hurt as it was possible for disembodied eyeballs to look. The eyeballs peered at one another questioningly, then back at Dozy in a vaguely pleading manner.

'No, don't try that with me,' said Dozy. 'I mean it. You've had your fun, now go back to your pictures.'

He began walking again, but had taken only a few steps when he heard the wet rustling of eyeballs rolling, and felt them staring at his back again.

Dozy turned round in a fury.

'That's it!' he said. 'I've had it! For the last time, go back to your pictures!'

Just to be sure that they understood how angry he was, he stamped his foot hard on the floor. Something popped wetly under his heel, and there was the kind of squishing noise that only comes from standing on a round object that is mainly liquid and jelly held together by a thin membrane.

An eyeball, for example.

'Oops,' said Dozy.

He didn't want to look down, but he didn't have much choice. He lifted his foot and winced. He was no expert, but he was pretty certain that this particular eyeball's days of staring at strangers had come to an end.

Mumbles came back to find out why he had stopped walking, and told Dozy not to worry: the bits of eyeball would clean off easily enough.

There was no way that the eyeballs could have heard him, thought Dozy. After all, they were just eyeballs. Even if they had, they probably couldn't have understood him. Nevertheless, Mumbles's words coincided with a burst of activity among the eyeballs. They began to vibrate. The red veins running across them expanded until the eyeballs were no longer big enough to contain them. They burst through the membrane of the eyes to form what to Dozy's mind looked disturbingly like little legs. Each eyeball split beneath its retina to reveal a mouth filled with teeth. The two upper canines were longer than the rest, and needle-sharp.

'Vampire eyeballs!' said Dozy. 'Or eyeball vampires!'

Mumbles said nothing. He was too busy running away.

Meanwhile in the Johnson house, Nurd and Wormwood were about to have problems of their own.

The window was now open, but so far the elf on the

windowsill had not moved. Wormwood poked his head through the gap and peered down.

'Well, look at that,' he said.

'Look at what?' said Nurd.

He was still keeping a close eye on the elf. It was making Nurd very nervous.

'Elves,' said Wormwood. 'Lots of 'em. It's a pyramid of elves.'

Nurd climbed from his bunk and went to the window. He stuck his head out. Wormwood was right: there was a pyramid of elves under the window, each layer supporting the next until the topmost elf would be on the same level as the windowsill. But who would bother to build a pyramid of elves? Nurd twisted his head and tried to see if there was any sign of activity on the roof, but there was none.

'That's quite unusual,' he said.

Wormwood poked the elf on the windowsill.

'You know what else is unusual?' he said.

'What?'

'This elf. It's made of wood, but it feels warm.'

Wormwood leaned back so that Nurd could test it for himself. Nurd reached out a clawed finger and jabbed at the elf's nose.

'Now that you come to mention it—' he said, just as the elf's mouth opened and bit Nurd's finger. Nurd lifted his hand up to examine it more closely. The elf remained dangling from it.

'Er, Wormwood?' said Nurd.

Wormwood had poked his head out of the window again, and was admiring the elves.

'Aren't they pretty?' he said.

'Wormwood, if you have a moment . . .'

Wormwood waved a stubby hand at the elf pyramid. 'Hello, elves!'

All of the elves grinned at Wormwood. One or two even waved back.

Wormwood scratched his chin. He hadn't expected that.

'You know,' he said, quickly pulling his head back in and turning to Nurd, 'I could be wrong, but those elves may be alive.'

Nurd coughed and showed Wormwood his finger, now with added elf. He shook his hand in the hope of dislodging the elf, but the elf wasn't going anywhere. The bell on the end of its hat tinkled.

'Does it hurt?' asked Wormwood.

'A bit.'

'Would you like me to try to get it off?'

'That would be nice.'

Wormwood grabbed the elf by the legs and gave an experimental tug.

'It's holding on very tight.'

'I know that, Wormwood. It is my finger that is involved.'

Wormwood pulled harder.

'Ow!' said Nurd. 'Stop! That's no good.'

'Try knocking it against the wall.'

Nurd did. On the third attempt, the elf released its grip on Nurd's finger and fell to the floor, where it stumbled about holding its head and looking dazed. Nurd examined his finger. There was a ring of small teeth marks around the tip.

'Nasty,' said Wormwood.

Nurd picked up the elf by one leg and stared at it. The elf struggled a bit, and tried to twist its body in order to bite Nurd again.

'Not very Christmassy, is it?' said Wormwood.

'No,' said Nurd. 'I suspect that if you found one of these in your Christmas stocking, you'd write a strongly worded letter to Santa.'

There were noises from outside. The pyramid of elves, seemingly aware that the elf in the bedroom was now a captive, was trying to rearrange itself. One of the two elves who now formed the tip of the pyramid was trying to climb on to the windowsill with the aid of its colleague. The pyramid wobbled uncertainly.

'Wormwood,' said Nurd, 'could you get the football from under your bunk, please?'

Wormwood did as he was asked. He handed the football to Nurd, who exchanged it for the elf. Nurd leaned out of the window.

'Oh elves!' he called.

The elves looked up. Nurd raised his arms, and threw the football with as much force as he could muster.

The pyramid disintegrated, scattering elves and bits of elves over the front garden of the house.

'What about this one?' asked Wormwood, holding up the captive elf.

'Unless you're planning to adopt it, I'd suggest you get rid of it.'

'I can't throw it out the window! It doesn't seem right.'

Wormwood had let the elf get a little too close to his face. It snapped at him, and missed the end of his nose by a finger's width.

'Oh, all right then,' said Wormwood. ''Bye, elf.'

Out of the window it went. They watched it land in a thornbush. It managed to free itself with the help of some of its friends, and shook its little elf fist at Nurd and Wormwood. It then went into a huddle with the other elves. Nurd and Wormwood could hear them giggling. As they watched, more elves were trying the windows and the doors on the ground floor of the house. One of the brighter ones found a stone and threw it at the living-room window, but the elf couldn't send it high enough to hit the glass. Still, it had the right idea. Soon the elves would find a way inside, and then Nurd and Wormwood would be trapped.

'We have to get out before they get in,' said Nurd.

'But what do they want?' asked Wormwood.

'You know,' said Nurd, 'I think they want us.'

CHAPTER XXIII

In Which the Cracks in the Relationship Between Samuel and Lucy Become Greater

All was still and silent on the ground floor of Wreckit & Sons. The darkness had cleared to reveal the store; it was as if they had passed through a tunnel in order to enter. Samuel, Lucy and the two policemen could now see out of the windows perfectly well, and so could take in the unusual sight of the people of Biddlecombe fleeing from elves, abominable snowmen, and various fairy-tale villains that seemed more smoke than substance, but they could hear nothing. When they tried to leave through the door they met only resistance from the air, and ripples like waves on water ran through it from floor to ceiling. Of Mr St John-Cholmondeley there was no sign.

'Well, this isn't much fun,' said Lucy. 'What kind of date is this?'

She glared at Samuel accusingly.

'It's not my fault,' said Samuel.

'Oh, really? And who invited me to this rotten opening in the first place?' said Lucy.

'I didn't invite you,' said Samuel. 'You saw the invitation and sort of invited yourself!'

'So it's all *my* fault, is it? That's typical, just typical!'

There then followed a long speech blaming Samuel for every unfortunate event that had blighted Lucy Highmore's young life so far, most of which Samuel was fairly certain were not his fault, along with a lot of others that he was absolutely certain weren't his fault because he hadn't been born when any of them happened or, if he had been, then they were out of his control, including a number of wars, world hunger, global warming, and the business with the apple in the Garden of Eden. When she had finished, Lucy folded her arms and looked away. Her bottom lip trembled. After a great deal of effort, she managed to force a single small tear from one eye. It hung on her cheek for a second, decided that it wasn't about to have company any time soon, and promptly dried up somewhere around her chin.

Sergeant Rowan and Constable Peel, who had been doing their best not to get involved, or to attract Lucy's attention for fear that they might catch an earful as well, watched her from a distance. When it became apparent that the storm had calmed itself for now, Constable Peel sidled up to Samuel.

'Are you going out with her?'

'I am,' said Samuel. 'Or I was.'

Constable Peel gaped at him.

'Why?' he asked.

'It seemed like a good idea at the time to ask, and she said yes,' said Samuel.

'You live and learn,' said Constable Peel. 'Now you know why some people become monks.'

Sergeant Rowan coughed deliberately.

'None of this is helping,' he said. 'There's some bad

business going on here, and it's up to us to get to the
bottom of it. Come along now, Constable. You too,
Samuel. And you, young lady, suck in your bottom lip.
It looks like someone has built a shelf over your chin.'

Lucy gave Sergeant Rowan her best glare of rage.

'I shall tell my father what you said. He'll have your
job!'

'He can have it if he wants it, miss, although why he
would, I don't know. Constable Peel, are you crying?'

'No, Sarge. Why do you ask?'

'Because I heard crying and simply assumed it was you.'

'Not me, Sarge. I can't say that I'm not tempted, but
I'm holding it in.'

'Very brave of you, Constable.'

'Thank you, Sarge.'

'That said, I can still hear someone crying for mummy.
I think there may be a child in here with us.'

Constable Peel listened.

'More than one, Sarge. I can hear lots of them.'

'Oh, for goodness' sake!' said Lucy. 'They're dolls!
We're in a toyshop. They're probably demonstration
models left out for children to play with.'

To their left was the entrance to the doll section of the
store. It was clear that the sounds were coming from there.

'That's a relief,' said Constable Peel, just as a doll
waddled into view and blinked at them. It was about
eighteen inches tall, with dark hair. It wore a blue dress
and blue shoes. Its eyes were entirely black.

'Mummy,' said the doll, its lips moving to form the word.

'That's very impressive,' said Constable Peel. 'In a
creepy way. And it has quite big teeth for a doll.'

'It has quite big teeth for a *shark*,' said Sergeant Rowan. 'Constable, I'd take a step or two back from it if I were you.'

Constable Peel didn't need to be told twice. More dolls were joining the first. Some walked and some crawled. One doll pushed another doll in a pram. A number of them were armed with knives. The ones that couldn't talk just cried, but the ones that could talk said things like 'Mummy', and 'Bottle', and 'Change me'.

And 'Kill!'

Mr Karloff had managed to stop running for long enough to call the police. PC Wayne and WPC Hay, who were out in a patrol car, were now aware that Biddlecombe was in trouble again. There were rumours of eerie noises from the old prison, and strange lights in the abandoned asylum. They had tried to contact Sergeant Rowan and Constable Peel, with no result, so they had locked up the police station and headed out to investigate.

As it happened, their route back to the centre of town took them by the battlefield. They paused for a moment and took in the sight of dozens of undead Vikings and Saxons merrily attempting to kill one another and, when that didn't work due to the fact that they were already dead, contenting themselves with lopping off limbs and heads.

'Let's just leave them to it, shall we?' said WPC Hay.

'That seems like the best thing,' said PC Wayne.

They drove away, and did not look back.

CHAPTER XXIV

In Which Nurd and Wormwood
Plan a Great Escape

Nurd and Wormwood crouched in the darkness of Samuel's bedroom, watching the activity below. Nurd turned to Wormwood and examined him critically, which wasn't difficult where Wormwood was concerned. He straightened Wormwood's costume, and adjusted his hat.

'This plan will never work,' said Wormwood.

'It might,' said Nurd.

'I look ridiculous.'

'Wormwood, you always look ridiculous. Admittedly, you now look slightly more ridiculous, if such a thing were possible. I did not believe it was, but it seems you have just proved me wrong. How do I look?'

'You look ridiculous too. And it still won't work.'

'Do you have a better plan?' asked Nurd.

'I have never had a plan in my life,' admitted Wormwood, although he was tempted to add that he was currently trying to come up with his first, because whatever he thought of, it couldn't be worse than this one.

They were under a state of siege. The elves had surrounded the house, but so far had failed to enter it.

774

They had found the double-glazing on Mrs Johnson's windows harder to break than expected, mostly because their little arms weren't strong enough to hurl stones at the glass with sufficient force to do any damage, while attempts to squeeze through the spring-loaded letter box had resulted only in severe injury to the elves involved.

In desperation, the elves had resorted to fire.

Nurd and Wormwood had looked on as a gang of elves struggled under the weight of a can of petrol, along with some matches and various rags, all stolen from the shed of Mr Jarvis, who lived next door to the Johnsons and was currently away on business.[37]

'Mr Jarvis won't like that,' said Nurd. 'He doesn't even allow people to borrow his lawnmower.'

This was true. Mr Jarvis was very mean. If Mr Jarvis had been a ghost, he would have charged people for frights.

'What are they going to do with that petrol?' said Wormwood.

'I'm not certain, but I suspect that they're going to try to burn us out.'

'They do know that we're demons, right?' said Wormwood. 'Demons don't burn very well.'

'No,' said Nurd, 'but this house will burn nicely, whether we're in it or not. What do you think Samuel's mum will say if she comes home from bingo and finds her house on fire?'

'She won't be happy,' said Wormwood.

💀 37 You should not play with fire. You are about to discover why.

'She won't be happy at all.'

'Will she blame us?'

'She might, unless we can show her some elves with matches in their hands, but I'd prefer it if the house didn't burn to begin with.'

'I'll start filling buckets with water,' said Wormwood.

'That would be helpful,' said Nurd.

He continued to watch the elves. Even by the standards of not-very-bright creatures, the elves were spectacularly unintelligent. Perhaps it was because they were made from supernaturally-animated wood. Say what you like about wood, but if you're on a quiz team and one of your team members is made from birch, or if you and your fellow prisoners are trying to come up with a cunning plan to escape from prison and one of you is carved out of oak, there's a limit to how much help the wooden representatives are going to be. Animated entities made from wood are usually not clever. So it was that the elves were splashing petrol around, and failing to light matches, and getting themselves wrapped up in bits of rag like small wooden mummies. More and more elves arrived to help, adding a second can of petrol to the first, and more matches, and even more confusion. They began carrying everything to the front door, spilling more petrol as they went.

'Tut-tut,' said Nurd.

'What?' said Wormwood, who had arrived with a bucket of water.

'Very dangerous, mucking about with fire. Someone could do himself an injury, and I think a lot of wooden someones are about to do just that.'

It's a funny thing about fire, but it burns very well when there is wood involved. It burns even better when there is wood and petrol involved, and better still if a little paint is added to the mix for good measure. Basically, Mrs Johnson's garden was now full of small, painted, petrol-soaked pieces of wood.

Suddenly, one of the elves finally managed to get a match lit.

'Weeeee!' it said, with delight, holding the match above its head like a small, and not very impressive, Olympic torch

'Weeeee!' said the other elves.

'Weeeee!' said the first elf again. It watched as the flame neared its fingers.

'Oh-oh!' it said, and dropped the match.

There was a loud *whoosh*, and a burst of flame. Mrs Johnson's garden was immediately turned into an elf bonfire. Somewhere in the middle of it, small figures could be seen running around trying to put themselves out. Bells tinkled hotly before melting.

'Can I make a joke about elf and safety?' said Wormwood.

'No, you can't,' said Nurd.

They waited until the flames began to die down. Some of the elves, now slightly charred, had made it to safety, although they were still stunned by what had happened. In a very short time, though, it was likely that they would overcome their shock and get angry, and then they'd start looking for revenge.

'Now is our chance,' said Nurd. 'If we don't make it, I'd like to say that it's been an honour to have you as a friend, Wormwood. I'd *like* to say that, but I can't, because it wouldn't be true.'

'Thank you,' said Wormwood. He was getting quite tearful. 'That's the nicest thing you've ever said to me.'

'It is, Wormwood. In return, do you have anything you'd like to say to me?'

Wormwood thought for a moment. Nurd picked up a faint smell of burning. He thought it was coming from the elves until he realised that it was the smell of Wormwood thinking.

'I couldn't have asked for a better demonic master,' said Wormwood finally.

'Really?'

'Really. I couldn't have asked, because nobody would have paid any attention.'

'How true, Wormwood, how true.'

Nurd and Wormwood went down the stairs and paused at the front door. They each took a deep breath and crossed their fingers. Wormwood had an extra one on each hand, which made it more complicated for him.

'Ready?' said Nurd.

'Ready,' said Wormwood.

Nurd opened the door, and together they stepped into the garden.

The elves, as we have already established, were not the sharpest tools in the box. They had, until recently, been perfectly anonymous bits of wood before unexpectedly finding themselves infused with supernatural energy. They had only two purposes: to cause as much mayhem as possible in Biddlecombe, and to capture the demons known as Nurd and Wormwood and bring them to Wreckit & Sons. So far they'd been doing reasonably well on the mayhem front, but the attempts to capture Nurd and Wormwood had been less successful. Various elves had lost limbs and heads due to collapsing pyramids and letterbox-related injuries. Half a dozen more had been crushed when stones and rocks thrown optimistically at windows had fallen tragically short of their targets. Finally, fire had taken care of most of the ones that were still standing, leaving only a handful in any condition to resume the mission.

The elves had pictures of Nurd and Wormwood implanted in their minds. They were sure of what the wanted demons looked like. What they did not look like was elves, which was why the remaining elves were slightly puzzled to see two more elves step out of a house previously occupied only by two demons. They were very large elves, and one of them smelled odd, even from a distance, but there was definitely something elfish about them. They had pointy ears, their cheeks were painted a rosy red, and they were wearing hats with bells on the end. They even had white beards, which made them very senior elves, and probably explained why they were so large.

Wormwood tried to keep from scratching at his cotton-wool beard, and from adjusting the Father Christmas hat that Mrs Johnson had bought to be worn on Christmas Day, and which was making his head sweat. He had also borrowed Mrs Johnson's red bathrobe. Nurd, meanwhile, was looking radiant in the green shower curtain from the bathroom, belted at the waist.

The elves stared at them. Anybody would have, really.

'We're going to die,' whispered Wormwood.

'We can't die,' said Nurd. 'We're demons.'

'Then we're going to nearly die, and we're going to continue nearly dying for a very long time.'

'Keep smiling,' said Nurd, while keeping smiling, so that it came out as 'Keek smigink.'

'Keek what?' said Wormwood.

'Keek *smigink*.'

'Oh. Right.'

Wormwood still had no idea what Nurd was saying, so he decided just to keep smiling and hope for the best. Together, he and Nurd walked down the garden path, their gaze fixed on a point somewhere over the heads of the elves, their smiles never wavering. As they passed, the elves fell to their knees in awe.

'It's working!' said Wormwood.

'Keek quige!'

But it *was* working, and it would have kept on working had Nurd's tail not poked out from beneath the folds of the shower curtain. The tail had been growing shorter of late, and Nurd was certain that eventually it would disappear altogether, but it still liked to make an appearance when Nurd was in stressful situations. One of the elves spotted it as it threw itself to the ground.

'Weeee?' it said.

It nudged the elf beside it, and pointed at the tail.

'Weeee!'

The word was passed among the elves. By now, Nurd and Wormwood were at the garden gate. Another step or two and they'd be on the street, and Nurd had Mrs Johnson's car keys in his pocket. He had promised her never, ever to drive again without permission, or unless he was being paid to crash the car in question, but Nurd looked at promises as things you said just to make other people feel better. You never knew what might happen in the future, and you didn't want to go pinning yourself down.

Nurd reached for the keys. The car was in sight. He took one more step towards it and stopped: not because he wanted to, but because his feet wouldn't carry him forward. He looked over his shoulder to find a dozen elves hanging on grimly to his tail. One of them was even gnawing at it. Nurd wished him luck. His tail was tougher than leather, and tasted like it, too.

Nurd sighed. There was a discarded match on the ground beside him. He picked it up and flicked at it with a curved fingernail, causing it to ignite.

'Wormwood?' he said. 'Will you do the honours?'

He held the match out by his side. Wormwood leaned in close, took a deep breath, and blew hard.

The match disappeared in a torrent of flame that continued in the direction of the elves. If they thought the petrol was bad, the effect of Wormwood's lit breath on them was a thousand times worse. Nurd wasn't sure what Wormwood's digestive system was like, but he decided that whatever was happening inside Wormwood must be very horrible, and certainly explained where a lot of those smells were coming from. The elves didn't even burn. They just went straight from wood to black ash without any stops in between.

'Thank you, Wormwood,' said Nurd. 'Well done. Indeed, they're probably very well done now, come to think of it.'

Wormwood stopped blowing. Nurd dislodged the remaining pieces of charred elf from his tail, and lifted the tip to examine it. It, too, was on fire. He gave a little puff of breath, and the fire went out.

'What now?' said Wormwood.

'We go to Wreckit & Sons,' said Nurd.

'Why there?'

Nurd picked up an elf foot that had survived the blaze and pointed to the sole of its little painted boot. On it were written the words *Property of Wreckit & Sons.*

CHAPTER XXV

In Which Battle Commences

Dozy and Mumbles collided with Angry, Jolly and Dan, who had just been reunited. They came together next to a pile of old yellow boxes marked, peculiarly enough, 'Odd Shoes', although nothing could have been odder than what they'd already encountered in that basement.

'You won't believe what happened to us!' said Jolly, then remembered that, not too long before, they'd all been trapped in Hell together. 'Hang on, you probably will believe it.'

'You won't believe what's *still* happening to us,' Dozy managed to gasp, as the first of the running eyeballs rounded the corner and pulled up short. It had been expecting to encounter two dwarfs, but was now facing four, and a human. If it had been gifted with hands, it would have rubbed itself just to be sure that it wasn't seeing things.

'Is that an eyeball on legs?' said Angry.

'One of many,' said Dozy. 'The rest are on their way. Oh look, here they are.'

More eyeballs appeared, and paused to consider Dan and the dwarfs.

'They've got teeth,' said Jolly. 'That can't be right. Why are they chasing you?'

'Because I stood on one of them,' said Dozy. 'I stamped on it hard, to be honest, but it was an accident.'

'Messy,' said Jolly.

'I think I still have some of it stuck to my heel,' said Dozy.

'Nasty,' said Angry. 'Just so we're clear, you stood on one, and then the others got angry, so you ran away from them?'

'That's right.'

'Why didn't you just stamp on the rest of them?'

'Well, they have teeth.'

'Not much they can do with them though, really, is there?' said Angry. 'Bite your feet, maybe, but then you are wearing big boots, which is where the trouble started to begin with, if I'm not mistaken.'

Dozy looked at his boots, and back at the eyeballs.

'Are you suggesting – ?'

'I am.'

'They squish,' said Dozy. 'It made my tummy feel funny.'

'You'll get over it.'

'I suppose you're right. I think I'm almost over it already.'

'There you are, then,' said Angry.

Slowly, deliberately, meaningfully, the dwarfs and Dan advanced on the eyeballs. The eyeballs eyeballed each other. They may not have had ears, but they could see perfectly well, and what they saw was trouble advancing on them in big boots. As one, the eyeballs turned tail and headed back in the direction from which they'd come. Dan and the dwarfs watched them as they scarpered into the shadows.

'See?' said Angry. 'How hard was that?'

'Not very,' said Dozy.

'Bet you feel a bit silly now, don't you?'

'A bit,' Dozy admitted.

'Where did all those eyeballs come from anyway?' asked Jolly.

'Well,' said Dozy, 'there were all these pictures of a bloke with big ears and teeth – a bit vampirish he was – and I said that the eyes seemed to follow you around the room, and next minute the eyes *were* following us around the room. Very unsettling it was, so—'

'Uh,' said Mumbles. He tapped Dozy on the arm.

'Not now,' said Dozy. 'I'm explaining. Anyway—'

Mumbles tapped him on the arm again.

'Really,' said Dozy, turning to give Mumbles a piece of his mind, 'you have to learn some . . .'

What Mumbles had to learn was destined to remain undiscovered. Music was coming from somewhere nearby, the sound of an organ being played in a very dramatic manner, and a shape was emerging from the murk. It was hunched, and wore a long dark coat. The parts of it that were not covered by the coat were very pale. They included its hands, which had long fingers ending in even longer nails. Its head was entirely bald, and its ears were big and pointed like those of a bat. Its two front teeth, to reference the famous song,[38] were not the kind that anyone would want for Christmas. They extended over its lower lip and resembled the fangs of a snake. As for its eyes, when last Dan and the dwarfs had seen them they'd been running along on two little feet and brandishing teeth of their own. They looked more at home in that awful face, and considerably more threatening.

'Oh,' said Dozy.

He had seen many horrible things in this time. He had seen demons. He had seen Hell itself. He had even, due to an unlocked bathroom door, seen Jolly without any pants on. But he believed that he had never seen, and never would see, anything more terrifying than the figure standing before him.

Until he saw the one that appeared next to it, because, unlike its nearly identical twin, it had only one eye. The remains of the other, Dozy guessed, were still stuck in the treads of one of his boots.

'Eh, Dozy,' said Jolly. 'I think there's a gentleman here who'd like a word with you.'

'Should we start running again?' said Dozy.

'I believe,' said Jolly, 'that would be a very good idea.'

* * *

[38] 'All I Want for Christmas is My Two Front Teeth' was written in 1944, although why anyone would want to wake up in the early hours of Christmas Day to find Santa Claus performing some makeshift implant dentistry on them remains to be seen, and would be likely to result in long-term trauma. What next? 'All I Want for Christmas is My Appendix Removed' or '. . . My Nose Broken and Reset'? What's wrong with a train set, or a doll? Some people are very complicated.

Above the dwarfs, in the store itself, Samuel, Lucy and the policemen were fighting a rearguard action against ranks of dolls that had been reinforced by assorted cuddly toys. The humans had retreated to the first floor where Samuel had equipped them with guns capable of firing plastic darts and foam bullets. They were having some effect on the demented dolls and threatening teddy bears and yapping demon dogs with large jaws, most of whom struggled to get back on their feet once they'd been knocked over. Some, though, were made of sterner stuff, so Samuel and Lucy, their relationship problems temporarily set aside in the fight for survival, had begun to collect footballs, basketballs, toy cars, and various heavy objects instead. Now, like soldiers in a castle raining down boulders on the besieging forces, they tossed their ammunition with maximum force at their attackers, and watched with satisfaction as dolls lost heads and teddy bears lost limbs.

'I never liked dolls anyway,' said Lucy, as a particularly well-aimed rugby ball fragmented a Sally Salty Tears. 'They represent the imposition of outdated gender roles on girls too young to know better.'

Samuel looked at Constable Peel, who shrugged. Samuel thought that Constable Peel might have been almost as frightened of Lucy as he was of the attacking dolls.

'Have you noticed anything funny about those dolls?' asked Sergeant Rowan.

Constable Peel goggled at him. He looked like a goose trying to cough up a feather.

'Funny, Sarge? Funny? You mean, apart from the

fact that they've come alive and seem intent upon killing us, or isn't that funny enough for you?'

'Now, now, son,' said Sergeant Rowan, 'panicking won't do us any good. No, what I mean is that they seem to have stopped trying to get up the stairs. It's as if they're happy enough just to have forced us up here.'

The sergeant was right. The initial assault had petered out, helped in part by the fact that so many dolls and soft toys were no longer in a position to do much assaulting because of a lack of legs, arms, and heads. Reinforcements continued to arrive, but instead of attempting to scale the stairs they were retreating to positions of cover, from which they were happy just to bare teeth or wave sharp items of cutlery. There had been a worrying moment when the giant twenty-foot teddy on the ground floor had begun moving and seemed about to join in the conflict, but it turned out to be too big and heavy to get to its feet. It had instead remained slumped in a corner growling, like a fat man who had eaten too many pies.

Samuel took a moment to get his bearings. They were in the games department, and it didn't look like any of the board games, tennis rackets or cricket bats were about to come to murderous life. The walls, he saw, were decorated with lifesize cardboard models of characters from nursery rhymes. He recognised Miss Muffet sitting on her tuffet, Humpty Dumpty on his wall, and Little Bo Peep along with assorted sheep. At the very rear of the floor was another flight of stairs. A thin figure watched them from halfway up it.

'Look!' said Samuel. 'It's that Mr St John-Cholmondeley.'

'He doesn't look very happy,' said Constable Peel. 'Then again, half of his doll department is in pieces on the ground floor.'

Sergeant Rowan stood up. He unbuttoned the top left hand pocket of his jacket and from it removed his notebook.

'Oh, he's in trouble now,' said Constable Peel to Samuel. 'Once that notebook comes out it's not going back in the pocket without someone's name being written down.'

Sergeant Rowan coughed and licked his pencil. It hung poised over the notebook like the Sword of Damocles.[39]

'Right you are, Mr St John-Cholmondley,' said Sergeant Rowan. 'I'd appreciate it if you'd join me here for a moment and explain just what's going on.'

'I'm afraid I can't do that,' said Mr St John-Cholmondeley. 'The answer you seek can only be found by moving higher into the store. The truth lies on the top floor.'

💀 [39] Damocles was reputed to have been a courtier in the court of Dionysius II, a tyrant ruler of Syracuse in the fourth century. Perhaps unwisely, Damocles suggested that Dionysius was quite the lucky fellow to have such a nice throne, and lots of gold, and all of that power, so Dionysius invited Damocles to take a turn on the throne, just to try it out for size. Unfortunately, as with most tyrants, there was a catch, for Dionysius arranged for a big sword to be hung over the throne, held in place by a single hair from the tail of a horse. Not surprisingly, Damocles didn't care much for sitting in a throne under a sharp blade that might, at any moment, drop on his head with unpleasant consequences, and after a while he politely asked Dionysius if he might be allowed to sit somewhere else instead. Dionysius, having had his fun, agreed. The moral is that those in power are always in peril too, especially if they're tyrants whom nobody likes. The Sword of Damocles is thus very famous, much more so than the lesser known Onion of Unhappiness and the Custard Tart of Doom.

'Well, sir, we don't have time to be running around chasing answers and truth. We're policemen, not philosophers. I think you should come down with us to the station and we'll have a chat about it all over a nice cup of tea in one of the cells. Why don't you just open the doors and stop all of this nonsense, there's a good gentleman. In the meantime, I'm going to write your name in my notebook as a "person of interest".'

Sergeant Rowan was just about to do that when he noticed that his pencil was gone.

'Here, who's made off with my pencil?' he asked, as his notebook was yanked from his hand and disappeared into the shadows on the ceiling, leaving only a sticky residue on Sergeant Rowan's fingers. He pulled at it, and saw that it was a spider web. He looked again at the ceiling, and noticed that the shadows on it appeared to be moving.

'Ah,' he said. 'Right.'

Mr St John-Cholmondeley smiled at them from the stairs, then skipped up to the next floor. Samuel barely noticed him go because another figure was moving towards them. It was coming from where the cardboard model of Miss Muffet used to be, except the model was no longer on the wall.

What appeared before them was not Miss Muffet, the beloved figure of nursery rhyme fame.[40] Either this one

---

💀 [40] You know the one:

Little Miss Muffet sat on a tuffet
Eating her curds and whey,
Along came a spider,
Who sat down beside her

loved spiders an awful lot or she hadn't run away fast enough when the first one appeared, and it had brought plenty of friends along with it for company. She was dressed entirely in black, and wore a veil over her face, a veil that, as she drew closer, was revealed to be made, not from fabric, but from spider silk. The little black spiders that crawled across it, and the dead flies trapped in it, gave the game away on that front. More spiders poured from her sleeves and from beneath her skirts: brown ones, black ones, red ones, yellow ones. There were webs between her fingers, and webs under her arms. Beneath her veil of black spider silk her features were almost entirely concealed by sticky white strands, with only the vaguest of holes torn in them for her eyes and her mouth.

A small black spider descended from the ceiling and dropped on to Sergeant Rowan's shoulder. He quickly brushed it away, but another fell, and another. He got rid of them too. One of them scuttled towards Lucy. She stamped on it. When she lifted her foot, it was still there. It looked unhappy but was otherwise unharmed. Lucy tried again, but was still unsuccessful in killing it. This was clearly no ordinary spider.

'Eugh!' said Lucy loudly. 'How horrid!'

And frightened Miss Muffet away.

Or alternatively:

Little Miss Muffet sat on a tuffet
Eating her curds and whey,
Along came a spider,
Who sat down beside her
We lose lots of Miss Muffets that way.

Little Miss Muffet's head turned in her direction. It was one thing trying to crush her pets, but obviously quite another entirely to describe them as horrid.

'*Not horrid,*' said a soft voice from somewhere behind the silk. '*Beautiful.*'

Miss Muffet was having trouble speaking properly. She sounded like she had hairballs caught in her throat. The spider strands around her mouth trembled, and a fat brown spider emerged from between what might have been her lips. It was quickly followed by another, and another, and another.[41]

Sergeant Rowan backed away. Above them, ranks of spiders moved across the ceiling, forcing the humans and Boswell to retreat further to avoid having the spiders drop on them. More of the nasty creatures were spreading across the floor. There was a sense of purpose to their approach. The spiders were herding Samuel and the others, moving them closer and closer to the stairs.

In case they needed any more convincing, a massive shape disengaged itself from the darkest corner of the

---

☠ [41] If swallowing a spider sounds unpleasant, it should be noted that most of us consume bits of spiders and insects every day. In the United States, the Food & Drug Administration has even published a guide to the level of insect fragments permitted in food. Frozen spinach is allowed fifty aphids or mites per one hundred grams, peanut butter can have thirty insect fragments per one hundred grams, and chocolate is allowed to have sixty. Don't worry, though: insects are an excellent source of protein. So eat up, they're good for you.

Incidentally, in 1911 a scientist named C.F. Hodge calculated that if a pair of houseflies started breeding in April and continued until August, their offspring, if they all survived, would cover the earth forty-seven feet deep by August. So by accidentally eating the odd fly here and there, you're saving the earth from being buried by them. Well done, you! Try them with ketchup. They're tasty. (Warning: may not actually be tasty.)

room and moved steadily towards them. A beam of moonlight caught it, causing the eight black eyes in its head to gleam. It was the size of a small car, except small cars didn't have eight legs and long poisonous fangs that dripped venom as the enormous spider detected the presence of prey.

'My pretty,' said Miss Muffet, stroking the dense hairs on the spider's head. 'Pretty is hungry.'

'You know,' said Sergeant Rowan, 'perhaps we should see what's upstairs after all.'

So they ascended to the next floor, and the spiders, thankfully, did not follow.

CHAPTER XXVI

In Which Constable Peel is Reduced to Tears of Unhappiness

Nurd decided that the scenes of Christmas chaos in Biddlecombe were very inventive, even for someone who had previously witnessed an invasion by the forces of Hell itself. It was one thing to encounter people being attacked by, and fighting against, assorted demons, ghouls and chthonic[42] forces, which were, by and large, simply terrifying, and therefore capable of being understood on those terms. It was quite another to witness a running battle in August Derleth Park between the Biddlecombe Ladies' Football Team and a half-dozen very rough-looking fairies that had climbed down from the tops of various Christmas trees with murder on their minds. So far, the Biddlecombe Ladies seemed to have the upper hand, mainly because the Biddlecombe Ladies were bigger than some of the Biddlecombe Gentlemen,

---

💀 [42] *Chthonic* (pronounced *thonic* to rhyme with *sonic*) is a great word of Greek origin, and means of, or relating to, the Underworld. Feel free to drop it into conversations at home, where it has many amusing uses. For example: 'Mum, this broccoli is positively *chthonic*.' Or: 'I'm not sure about that tie, Dad. It looks kind of *chthonic*.' And, of course, the ever popular: 'I'd give that bathroom a minute or two. It smells a bit *chthonic*.'

and had a such a reputation for violence on the pitch that opposing teams had been known to injure themselves at first sight of them, just to save the ladies the effort. The fairies were doing some damage with their wands, though, which had been weaponised by the addition of chains and spiked metal balls.

'Those fairies are walking a bit funny,' said Wormwood.

'You'd walk a bit funny too if someone stuck a Christmas tree up you,' said Nurd.

A large troop of elves crossed their path, struggling beneath the weight of a tree trunk that they were hoping to use to break down the door of the post office. It was quite clear to Nurd and Wormwood that the tree trunk, while heavy enough to use as a battering ram, was too heavy for even a great many elves to carry for any distance.

'Weeeee!' urged one of the lead elves. 'Weeeee!'

Nurd and Wormwood watched as first one set of legs buckled, and then another. By the time the third set went there was only time for a single, worried 'Oh-oh' before the competition between the elves and the tree trunk was won by the trunk with a crushing victory, leaving various elf limbs sticking out from beneath it.

'Ow,' said a small voice.

One lead elf, who had managed to escape being trapped through some nifty footwork, looked pleadingly at Nurd and Wormwood for help.

'Weeeee?' it said. 'Weeeee?'

Nurd trod on it.

Further along the way, they saw a giant ferocious

reindeer with sharp horns and black eyes standing before a herd of local deer as it tried to incite them to rebellion.

'Rise up!' cried the demon reindeer. 'Rise up against the puny humans who know you only as Bambi, the oppressors who think you're cute but occasionally eat you in stews, or with parsnips and a reduction of juniper berries.'

The local deer did what local deer do, which was to glance nervously from the demon reindeer to one another before returning to eating grass in the hope that the demon reindeer would go away and stop bothering them.

'Oh, have it your way, then,' said the demon reindeer. It looked at the grass. It nibbled a bit. Wow, it thought, the grass was rather good. It ate some more. It continued to graze happily until it was joined by a couple of other demon reindeer who'd had no more luck starting the deer revolution than it had.

'What do you think you're doing?' asked the leader of the demon reindeer.

The lone demon reindeer did some quick thinking. 'Trying to win their trust?' it suggested.

'No, you're just eating grass. Stop it and come with us. We must sow fear and chaos. The Shadows are about to fall.'

The demon reindeer nibbled one last piece of grass and joined the rest of the demon reindeer herd. It paused only to look back at the local deer and whisper, 'Don't eat it all, right? Save some for me. Seriously. Please. You're really lovely deer, and very handsome. Sorry I shouted at you.'

The deer ignored it. After all, it wasn't fawning season.[43]

Fires had broken out in houses and gardens. On Wells Street, a large wolf was trying to blow down a house made of bricks while the lady inside threw pots at it from an upstairs window. A troll had hidden under a canal bridge, hoping to spring out and trap unwary travellers, but that was Bill the Tramp's bridge, and he wasn't about to share it with anyone. Bill had tied the unconscious troll to a shopping trolley and left it outside the police station with a note attached that read 'Possibly from abroad'. Meanwhile Mr Thompson the greengrocer, who did not like competition, had found a wicked stepmother going around with a basket of apples for sale and had forced her to hide in a dustbin to escape his wrath, and his well-aimed fruit and vegetables.

A water main had burst and was already starting to freeze. It was growing colder. Nurd hadn't noticed before. He looked at Wormwoood. The tip of Wormwood's nose had turned blue.

'Your nose has turned blue,' Nurd told him.

'Has it? It was feeling a bit funny.'

Wormwood scratched at his nose. It fell off in his hand. He peered at it, then shrugged. These things happened, or they happened to Wormwood. He excavated a disturbingly filthy handkerchief from somewhere on

---

⚫ [43] A very clever joke that plays upon the fact that the word 'fawn', meaning to gain favour through flattery, and 'fawn', meaning a young deer, are spelt the same. See? Oh, please yourself. It's like casting pearls before swine . . .

his person, carefully wrapped his nose in it, then stuck it in his pocket for safekeeping.

'Why did you wrap it in a handkerchief?' asked Nurd.

'In case I sneeze,' said Wormwood. 'I don't want to make a mess.'

'Ah,' said Nurd. 'Very sensible.'

They walked on, offering Nurd time to think about what Wormwood had just said. Nurd stopped walking, gave Wormwood a hard flick on the ear, and they continued on their way.

Snow fell on them. Nurd looked up, but there wasn't a cloud in sight. The night was so clear that the sky was filled with stars, like millions of gemstones scattered across a great swatch of dark cloth. Nurd had never seen so many. They took his breath away, but there was something wrong about this sky. It seemed blacker than he remembered, which made the stars shine brighter. The problem was that they weren't the right stars. The constellations had changed. No, that wasn't quite true. Nurd thought that he could still pick out Gemini, and Draco, and Ursa Major and Ursa Minor, the Great Bear and the Little Bear, but other stars were overlaid upon them. They were dimmer, but growing in intensity. It was as though one solar system was somehow intruding on another.

Nurd found Polaris, the North Star, the centre of the night sky, which had guided travellers on land and sea ever since the earliest days of exploration. Once Polaris was visible it was hard to be lost, for it marked the way due north. There was consolation in its presence.

As Nurd watched, the great star blinked once, and disappeared.

Dan and the dwarfs were still being pursued, although not very quickly. The Nosferati, as Dan had dubbed them, were addicted to sneaking along, their long fingers grasping, their shadows stretching ahead of them, almost touching the heels of Dozy, who was bringing up the rear. But they did so very, very slowly, and had a fondness for stopping occasionally and making scary faces.

And while there was no doubt that they were horrible, and nasty, and smelled of the grave, they might have been more troubling had their every move not been accompanied by music played on an unseen organ. Every footstep, every raised hand, every arch of the eyebrows came with a tune. They were monsters from a silent movie, and in the days of silent movies each cinema would pay an organist to play along with the film. It was part of the deal, and even these Nosferati, liberated from picture frames, had to play by the rules.

'I wish that music would stop,' said Dan. 'It sounds like the ice-cream van from Hell.'

The music was bothering the Nosferati as well. Some of them snatched at the air, as though trying to pull the notes from the ether and grind them into musical dust. It was no good. The unseen organ kept on playing.

It was Jolly who wondered aloud if the Nosferati had ever even heard the organ music before. By now, Dan and the dwarfs had slowed from a run to a stroll, as it was clear that the Nosferati, though a nuisance, weren't likely to catch up with them any time soon.

'I mean, they were in a silent film,' said Jolly, 'which was, you know, silent. It was only in the real world, our world, that the music played. Imagine if, every time you took a step, some bloke was banging away on an organ behind you. It'd drive you mental. They'd have to lock you up before you killed him.'

The Nosferati had stopped making any progress at all. They were now curled up in balls with their coats over their heads, or were trying to jam their fingers in their ears, which didn't work because their fingernails were too long. One of them was banging his forehead repeatedly against a wall.

'See?' said Jolly. 'There's only so much of it you can take before—'

The one-eyed Nosferatu, the one who had had his eye (singular) on Dozy, started to shake. He raised a questioning finger as if to say, 'Hang on a minute, this doesn't feel right,' and then his head exploded. As he had been undead for a very long time, there wasn't much blood or brain to contend with. His head simply disappeared in a puff of grey dust, and his body quickly followed.

This began a chain reaction of exploding heads, and bodies collapsing like old pillars, filling the basement with the dust of the undead. When it finally settled, Dan and the dwarfs were all that remained standing, although they were now covered from head to toe in grey bits of vampire. The few surviving Nosferati who had managed to plug their ears beat a hasty retreat.

Angry coughed up ash.

'I think I swallowed some,' he said. 'That can't be good for me.'

'Look,' said Dozy. 'It's a lift.'

And it was. It was rickety and old and bore an unhappy resemblance to a cage, but it was definitely a lift of sorts. Its floor was made of wood, and its walls were lined with velvet. Instead of a door, it had a metal gate that could be pulled across and secured.

Dozy poked his head inside.

'I don't see any buttons,' he said. 'There's a control lever, though.'

He stepped into the lift and gave the lever an experimental tug, but nothing happened.

'You have to close the gate first, I think,' said Dan.

'Hang on,' said Jolly. 'Don't do anything until we're all inside.'

Dan, Jolly, Angry and Mumbles joined Dozy in the lift.

'All aboard?' said Dozy. 'Right. Up we go!'

He pulled the lever. There came the groaning of ancient machinery. The lift vibrated, and slowly began to rise.

Samuel, Lucy and the policemen had just reached the next floor when they heard a rumbling in the basement.

'What's that?' said Sergeant Rowan.

'Sorry,' said Constable Peel. 'That's me. I haven't been feeling very well.'

'No, not that,' said Sergeant Rowan, although he took a couple of cautious steps back from Constable Peel. '*That!*'

They all heard it now. It was the sound of a lift ascending.

'Over there,' said Samuel.

To their right was a dark, gated shaft, and above it a panel displaying floor numbers had just lit up.

'Something's coming up from the basement!' said Lucy.

'It has to be something nasty,' said Constable Peel. 'There are only nasty things in this shop, present company excepted.'

The number '1' lit up.

'It'll be here in a couple of seconds,' said Constable Peel.

'Be brave, lad,' said Sergeant Rowan.

He gripped his cricket bat tightly. He'd had the foresight to grab a weapon as they ran from the spiders. Samuel and Lucy hefted their pool cues threateningly, for they had been wise enough to do the same.

Constable Peel took his place beside them.

'What are you holding?' said Sergeant Rowan.

'Ping-pong bat,' said Constable Peel. 'It was all I could find.'

'Constable, we need to have a long talk when this is all over.'

'Yes, Sarge.'

The lift came into view. The light on the second floor was poor, and the lift itself remained dark, but as it stopped Samuel and the others could pick out five grey shapes.

'Ghouls!' whispered Lucy.

'Wraiths!' said Constable Peel.

The lift's gate opened. The five figures emerged and stepped into a small pool of moonlight cast through the murky glass of one of the windows. It was Constable Peel who reacted first.

'It's Dan and the dwarfs,' he said. 'Look at them! They're all grey and spooky and sickly. They're dead, but somehow they're still upright. Only the shells of them remain! Oh! Oh!'

He fell to his knees, buried his face in his hands, and began to weep. Jolly raised a hand and opened his mouth.

'Look,' said Sergeant Rowan. 'One of them is trying to speak.'

Constable Peel peered over the tips of his fingers. It was true. He waited to hear the hollow, undead rattle of what had once been Mr Jolly Smallpants.

Jolly didn't speak. He sneezed. The sneeze was so massive that it caused most of the ash to lift from him, and Jolly used the opportunity to step to one side and avoid the dust as it came down again.

'It's all right,' he said. 'It's just bits of dead vampire.'

Constable Peel stared at him for a time, then burst into tears again, crying even harder than before.

'Oh no!' he wailed. 'They're alive. They're *still* alive . . .'

CHAPTER XXVII

In Which The Stars Begin to Go Out

Maria and the scientists, trapped in the sweet factory with a hostile figure apparently made entirely from darkness, had considered their options and done the sensible thing, which was to leave as quickly as possible. They were now in Professor Hilbert's car, heading in the direction of Wreckit & Sons by taking the shortcut through August Derleth Park. Professor Hilbert was driving, Professor Stefan was in the passenger seat, and Maria, Brian, and Dorothy were crammed in the back. Brian was beginning to recover from his encounter with the dark woman, although his entire body continued to tremble involuntarily, and he would occasionally emit a startled squeak.

Dorothy, meanwhile, was still wearing her beard. Maria had tried not to notice, but it was difficult as it was quite a big beard.

Dorothy caught Maria looking at it.

'It's the beard, isn't it?' she said, in her new deep voice.

Maria nodded.

'I was just wondering why you were still wearing it.'

'I like it. It's warm.'

'Right,' said Maria. She would have moved over a little to put some space between herself and Dorothy, but there wasn't room because of the human jelly that was Brian.

'And I don't want to be called Dorothy any more.'

Professor Hilbert, who had been listening, gave Dorothy a worried look in the rear-view mirror. Professor Stefan turned round in his seat. His face wore the confused expression of a builder who has just been handed a glass hammer.

'What do you mean, you don't want to be called Dorothy?' he said. 'It's your name, and it's a perfectly lovely one.'

'I want to be called Reginald,' said Dorothy – er, Reginald. 'Inside, I feel like a Reginald.'

Professor Stefan frowned.

'But why Reginald?' he said. 'Nobody is called "Reginald" these days. It would be like me announcing that I wanted to be called Elsie, or Boadicea.'[44]

'I like the name Reginald,' said Dorothy, or Reginald. 'It was my mother's name.'

Even Brian stopped shaking for long enough to look bewildered, then went back to trembling again.

💀 [44] Boadicea was the queen of the Iceni tribe in Britain who led a rebellion against the Roman Empire in A.D. 60 or 61. Three settlements were destroyed during her war, including the young city of Londinium, or London. She was finally defeated in a battle in the West Midlands, but died without being captured. The Roman historian Dio said of her that she was 'possessed of greater intelligence than often belongs to women'. Mind you, he said that after she was safely dead and gone, otherwise she'd have cut his head off and stuck it on a spike for saying stupid things about women.

'Right,' said Professor Hilbert. 'I'm glad we cleared that one up.'

Any further discussion of the matter was postponed by the appearance of a Viking on the road. He wore a metal helmet, but was otherwise entirely naked. This might have been more disturbing had he not been little more than leathery skin and yellowed bone. In his right hand he held a rusty sword, and a shield hung from his left arm.

'You know, you really don't see that very often,' said Professor Hilbert.

Even though he was a physicist, he had a scientist's general fascination with anything new and unusual in the world, and a naked undead Viking counted as unusual in any world. Issues of personal safety took second place to things that were just plain interesting.

'How splendid!' said Professor Stefan. 'Slow down, Hilbert, so we can take a good look at him.'

Professor Hilbert slowed the car to a crawl, and rolled down his window.

'Hello!' he said to the Viking.

'You look a bit lost,' said Professor Stefan.

The Viking glared at them. Darkness seethed and roiled in its eyes.

'Garrrgghhhh,' it said. 'Urrurh.'

'Ah, yes, of course,' said Professor Hilbert. 'How true, how true.'

He looked at Professor Stefan and shrugged. Professor Stefan rolled his eyes.

'Where. Are. You. From?' said Professor Hilbert. He spoke very slowly and very loudly, which is how

English people who don't speak foreign languages try to communicate with those who do.

'Harruraruh,' said the Viking.

'Where is that?' said Professor Stefan. 'Could he show us on a map?'

'Map?' said Professor Hilbert to the Viking.

He drew squiggles in the air, in the faint hope that the Viking might make the connection. Instead the Viking simply waved his sword and said, 'Rarh!'

'I don't think we're going to get much out of him, I'm afraid,' said Professor Hilbert. 'His English leaves a lot to be desired.'

'What a shame,' said Professor Stefan. 'You'd think the chap might have brought a phrasebook with him so he could communicate a little better. You know, "Hello, I come from Norway." "Where is Buckingham Palace?" That kind of thing. Hardly seems worth making the trip if you can't speak the language. Never mind.'

He waved at the Viking.

"Bye, now!' he said. 'Thanks for visiting.'

'Warrghhh,' said the Viking.

'Ha-ha!' said Professor Stefan. 'Absolutely, yes.'

He puffed out his cheeks as Professor Hilbert prepared to drive off.

'No idea what the chap was saying.'

He gave the Viking a final wave, just in time to witness a Saxon with one leg dragging brokenly behind him hit the Viking repeatedly on the top of the head with an axe.

'And they wonder why tourists don't come here very often,' said Professor Hilbert.

'It's the battlefield,' said Maria.

'What?'

'We're close to the site of the Battle of Biddlecombe. Hilary Mould designed and built the visitor centre there. It's one of the points on the pentagram. I'll bet there's supernatural activity at the old asylum too, and the crematorium, and the prison. Which makes me more certain than ever that the centre of the activity is here.'

She tapped her finger on the map, right on the location of Wreckit & Sons.

A small troop of Christmas elves crossed their path, forcing Professor Hilbert to brake suddenly.

'You don't want to try talking to them as well, do you?' said Maria.

'Don't be silly,' said Professor Stefan. 'They're elves.'

'Of course,' said Maria. 'Duh.'

The elves paid them no notice. They were too busy running from something. Seconds later, one of the groundskeepers appeared. He was carrying a heavy rake, but was still making good progress. He caught up with the elves just as they reached the other side of the road, and began beating them to splinters.

'The sign said,' he screamed, '"KEEP OFF THE GRASS". What part of keeping off the grass did you' – *Bang!* – 'not' – *Smash!* – 'understand?' – *Thud!*'

When the elves were no more, the groundskeeper looked up to see five people watching him. He tipped his hat at them.

'Evening,' he said.

'Evening,' replied Professor Hilbert.

The groundskeeper indicated with a thumb the stack of firewood and splinters that had once been elves.

'Elves,' he said. 'They trampled on the grass.'

'So we gathered.'

'And the flowerbeds,' added the groundskeeper. His tone suggested that, while some might feel reducing elves to kindling for trespassing on the grass was a bit of an overreaction, no sane person could take issue with pummelling them for stepping on the flowerbeds.

He wiped his sweating brow.

'I quite enjoyed that,' he said. 'I think I'll go and look for some more of them.'

And off he went, whistling what sounded like 'Heigh-Ho, Heigh-Ho.'

It struck Professor Hilbert that, if the groundskeeper was anything to go by, the citizens of Biddlecombe were taking the evening's events in their stride. This view was confirmed when they came across the Biddlecombe Ladies' Football Team standing by half a dozen large and very bruised Christmas tree fairies who had been tied to tree trunks with stout rope in order to prevent them from doing any further harm.

Professor Hilbert stopped the car.

'What are you doing?' said Professor Stefan.

'Look!' said Professor Hilbert, pointing to the west.

There was a faint shimmer to the air. Beyond it Maria could see more trees and, some way in the distance, the spire of the church in the nearest village, Rathford, but it was as though a mist had descended upon the landscape, blurring the image. It struck Maria that they shouldn't even have been able to see Rathford. It was night-time, and yet the spire of the Church of St Roger the Inflammable was plainly visible, although there was a touch of shiny grey to it, like an old photographic negative.

Professor Hilbert stepped from the car and walked toward the location of the shimmering. The others followed, even Brian, although he was not so much curious as frightened to be left alone. As they drew closer, they saw that the ground came to a kind of end at the fence surrounding August Derleth Park. Beyond the boundary it was less actual firm ground than the memory of it, and its level didn't quite match the grass on their side of the fence. Worse, the other ground was transparent, and beneath it Maria could see a terrible blackness spotted with the odd lonely star. It felt to her as though Biddlecombe had somehow been set adrift in the Multiverse while still bringing with it the memory of the planet of which it had once been a part. The dividing line was the shimmering, like the heat haze that rises from the earth on sunny summer days, except this one brought with it no warmth.

Reginald/Dorothy reached out to touch it, and only Professor Hilbert's sudden grip on his/her wrist prevented him/her from doing so.[45]

☠ [45] Look, people should be able to call themselves whatever they like, and think of themselves in whatever way makes them happiest, and it really isn't much of anyone else's business at all. So if Dorothy wishes to be known as Reginald, that's perfectly fine, although I do wish I'd known a bit earlier.

It's very troubling when characters take a funny unplanned turn in a book. They really should do what their creators tell them to do, but that brings us to the whole thorny subject of the problem of free will. If I knew what was going to happen at the end of this book — which, at this point, I don't — then characters

'I wouldn't,' he said.

Reginald withdrew their hand. Professor Hilbert's fingers tingled after touching her. It must be the power of the boundary, he thought.

'How can we see Rathford?' asked Maria. 'We shouldn't be able to. It's night, and anyway Rathford

---

like Reginald would have to do whatever I told them to do, because that would be what was needed to make the plot work.

But right now I'm not sure what's going to happen, and I'm discovering the plot of the book as I write it. This makes me a bit like a god, in that I created these characters, but not the type of god who knows everything in advance. The thing is, if I was that kind of god, and characters like Reginald/Dorothy were, in fact, real, would the fact that I knew what was going to happen to them mean that they had no free will of their own?

Some philosophers have argued that, if there is a god, and he knows everything that will happen in the future, then free will doesn't really exist. I'm not sure that's the case because, if it is, then we are all like characters in a book being written by a writer who knows the ending. Maybe it's truer to say that, if there is a god, then he just happens to know how our story ends, and the choices we make are the ones that will lead to that particular ending.

So can we ever really predict what people will do? Perhaps on one level we can: we are biological machines, each of us made up of — remember? — atoms, and those atoms are made up of — yes, that's right — quarks and gluons. If we can predict how each of these particles will behave in a given situation then we can predict how lots of them packed together into a single human body will behave, right?

Yes, theoretically. In practice, it's a bit harder. We like to think that we're something more than just a collection of atoms. We use the term 'I' to describe ourselves. We have a consciousnesss. (Philosophers call this experience of mental states — seeing colours, smelling food, feeling pain — the 'qualia'.) But what if even consciousness is just an illusion, another product of the actions of all those quarks and gluons in our brains? 'I' may not even exist, and if I start having doubts about that, then where does it leave you? You may not exist either. My brain may just have invented you. In that case, you're as real as Reginald, and I can make you do what I want. Right, I want you all to club together to buy me a yacht. You can send it care of my publishers. Thank you. Even an imaginary yacht is better than no yacht at all . . .

is quite far from Biddlecombe. We can't even see the church spire during the day.'

'You can see *a* Rathford,' said Professor Hilbert. 'It's one of an infinite number of Rathfords, or it may be the point at which all of those potential Rathfords are bound together until a decision is made on which one should come into being.'

'We've become unmoored from reality,' said Professor Stefan. 'I believe that a dimensional shift has occurred, and we're just fractionally off-kilter with the rest of the Multiverse.'

'But what's on the other side of that boundary?' said Brian.

'Perhaps a version of Rathford, once you bring it into being by its observation, or nothing at all,' said Professor Hilbert. 'Then again, you might thrust your fingers into another dimension, and who knows what could be waiting on the other side? Or your fingers might end up between dimensions, which could be just as bad. It might be like wearing fingerless gloves in space, which would be very unwise.'[46]

💀 [46] Deepest, darkest space is very cold, so cold that all molecules stop moving. This is called 'absolute zero' and is calculated as −273 degrees Celsius, although the temperature in space is probably closer to −270 degrees Celsius because of three degrees of background microwave radiation.

So how long could you survive in space if you weren't wearing a suit? First of all, you shouldn't try to hold your breath, as that will cause the air in your lungs to expand and burst things that shouldn't burst, so you'd die painfully but quickly. If you didn't hold your breath, you'd probably have about fifteen seconds before you passed out. You wouldn't get frostbite at first, as you would in cold temperatures on Earth, because there's no air in space, and frostbite is a result of heat transfer accelerated by air. But your skin would start to burn because of ultraviolet radiation, and your skin tissue would swell.

'Did we do this?' asked Brian. 'I mean, all that fiddling around with particle accelerations and the nature of reality: could it have caused this?'

Professor Hilbert found something interesting to look at beside his right foot. Professor Stefan whistled and peered at the fathomless depths of space.

Eventually Professor Hilbert said, 'This is not the time to go around blaming people for what may or may not have happened, Brian.'

'When would be a good time, Professor Hilbert?' said Brian.

'When I'm not here,' said Professor Hilbert, 'but preferably when I'm dead and can't get into any trouble. I'd advise you to think very hard about your part in all of this as well, young Brian. You're an important part of our team, which means that you can be blamed too.'

'But I only made the tea!' said Brian.

'Yes, but it was very good tea,' said Professor Hilbert. 'If it had been bad tea then we might not have been so productive, and none of this might have happened or, if it did, then it might have happened much more slowly.'

'Don't forget the biscuits,' Professor Stefan chimed in.

'Oh yes, the biscuits,' said Professor Hilbert. 'Don't

Overall, then, you'd probably have a good thirty seconds before serious, permanent injury occurred, and a minute or two before you'd begin to die. In 1965, a spacesuit leaked in a vacuum chamber at NASA's Manned Spacecraft Center. The gentleman involved, who was rescued and recovered, remained conscious for about fourteen seconds. His last memory was of the saliva on his tongue beginning to boil. I just thought you'd like to know that.

get me started on the biscuits. All I can say is that you're up to your neck in this, Brian, mark my words. If the world comes to an end because of our experiments, you'll be in big trouble. They'll throw the book at you, or they will if there's anyone still around to throw books, or anything else, which there probably won't be. You know, now that I come to think about it, everything is fine at our end. If the world doesn't get destroyed, we're free and clear, and if it does end then there's not much anybody can do to make us feel bad about it.'

Professor Hilbert smiled happily.

'There, glad that's sorted out. Still, all things considered, it would be nice if we could prevent the end of the world from happening. With that in mind, onwards we go.'

He began to lead them back to the car. Brian didn't move. He just stood where he was, looking confused.

'But I only made the tea,' he said.

Professor Stefan steered him towards the car.

'Never mind,' he said. 'Try looking on the bright side.'

'Is there one?'

'Not really.'

'Oh.'

'But if you come up with one, do let us know, won't you?'

And high above their heads the stars were swallowed, one by one.

CHAPTER XXVIII

In Which Crudford Proves to be the Smartest Gelatinous Blob in the Room

The Great Malevolence, the Watcher by his side, had been spending a very long time staring at the bits and pieces of what had once been Ba'al, the most fearsome of its allies, its second-in-command, its left-hand demon, and considering the problem presented by them.

It had seemed like such a good idea to allow Ba'al to travel to Earth, exploiting the gap in space and time created by the experiments with the Large Hadron Collider. Ba'al was an entity of pure awfulness, but Ba'al was also completely loyal to the Great Malevolence, and there weren't many beings in Hell who could be trusted entirely. This was one of the problems with running a business based entirely around evil, destructiveness, and rage. It attracted bad sorts.

Unfortunately, the successful planning of the invasion of Earth had required Ba'al to take on human form, and the particular human form that Ba'al had chosen to inhabit was that of Mrs Abernathy. But Mrs Abernathy had turned out a) to have a strong personality of her own; and b) to be horrible even before she became possessed by a demon. And so the personalities of Ba'al and Mrs Abernathy had become mixed up in one body, and much of Mrs Abernathy had come out on top. This had left the Great Malevolence with a demonic lieutenant who liked to dress up in a lady's skin and clothing. Ba'al didn't even like being called Ba'al any more. It was Mrs Abernathy or nothing. Not that this was a huge problem, but it was unusual.

The Great Malevolence missed Ba'al – sorry, Mrs Abernathy. It wasn't as though they had ever played draughts or tiddlywinks or Twister together, or gone for long walks with a picnic at the end. No, it was simply that, without her, the whole business of trying to take over the Multiverse was a lot harder, and the Great Malevolence, in addition to being great and malevolent, was also more than a little lazy. It came with being in charge: if you can find someone else to do the hard work, then why would you do it yourself?

But now all that was left of Mrs Abernathy were various body parts in jars, and those body parts weren't doing much at all. Quite often, when it came to the residents of Hell, you could disassemble them into all kinds of small pieces, and each bit would do its best to continue being evil. Fingers would crawl across floors and try to poke the nearest eye; jawbones would try to bite; and intestines would slither like snakes and coil themselves around the nearest neck. Really, there was never a dull moment in Hell when it came to tearing things apart.

'Why does she not react more strongly?' asked the Great Malevolence. 'Why does this chamber not vibrate with the force of her evil?'

If Crudford could have shrugged, then he would have. Instead, he lifted his hat and scratched his head in puzzlement. He scratched slightly too hard though, and his fingers appeared inside his head somewhere behind his eyeballs. He pulled them out, thought about wiping them clean, and decided, well, why bother? Slowly, he examined each jar in turn, taking note of its contents on a small notepad that he kept in his hat. When he had finished, he went to work on his notepad. He scribbled and drew. He crossed things out, and did a lot of sucking on his pencil. The Watcher tried to peer over his shoulder to see what was being produced, but Crudford shielded the notepad from view like a small boy worried that his homework was about to be copied by the student next to him.

Eventually, after an hour had gone by, and two pencils had been worn down to almost nothing, Crudford was finished.

'I think I may have the answer,' he said.

'We are waiting,' said the Great Malevolence. It came with the unspoken warning: *This had better be good.*

Crudford turned the notepad to face the Great Malevolence. This is what it contained:

The Great Malevolence looked at the drawing. It then looked at the Watcher. The Watcher shrugged because, unlike Crudford, it could. The Great Malevolence, having nowhere else left to look, looked at Crudford and thought about the many ways in which it could reduce a gelatinous mass to lots of much smaller pieces of jelly.

'It is,' said the Great Malevolence, 'a picture of a lady. It is not even a very good picture of a lady.'

Everyone, thought Crudford, is a critic.

'It's not just a lady,' said Crudford. 'It's Mrs Abernathy. But see here—'

Crudford pointed at the question mark beside the heart shape.

'The heart is missing.'

The Great Malevolence considered this.

'Ba'al does not have a heart,' it said. 'No creature in Hell has a heart. Hearts are not needed.'

'But Ba'al isn't Ba'al any longer, not really,' said Crudford. 'Ba'al is Mrs Abernathy, and Mrs Abernathy is Ba'al, and Mrs Abernathy has a heart because Mrs Abernathy is, or was, human. Those jars contain bits of every organ in the human body except the heart. The heart is missing. All of it.'

'But what is the heart pumping?' said the Great Malevolence. 'Not blood, for Mrs Abernathy's body died the moment that Ba'al took it over.'

'I'm just guessing,' said Crudford, 'but I'd say that it's pumping pure evil. What we're looking for is a big, black, rotten heart-shaped thingy filled with nastiness.'

'Then where is it?' asked the Great Malevolence.

'That,' said Crudford, 'is a very good question.'

Crudford wandered the halls of the Mountain of Despair, alone with his thoughts. 'Wandered' probably wasn't the right word, strictly speaking: 'slimed', 'oozed' or 'smeared' might be closer to the mark, but if Crudford had said that he was just off to slime around the halls for a while then he would probably have been advised to take his gelatinous self elsewhere, or someone would have been following him with a mop and a bucket.

His search of the Multiverse for bits of Mrs Abernathy had not been entirely random. He had been able to narrow it down to specific universes, or corners of them, either because he could smell Mrs Abernathy, or his keen eyesight had been able to pick out the blue atoms in the darkness. There were only two places he had not explored: the Kingdom of Shadows, and Earth.

He had not entered the Kingdom of Shadows because to do so would have been the end of him: the Shadows had no loyalty to the Great Malevolence, and would have snuffed out Hell itself if they could. He had stayed away from Earth simply because he had detected no sign of Mrs Abernathy there, but now he began to wonder if he might not have been mistaken. Just because he could pick up no trace of her did not mean that she was not there, and it was only recently that he had begun to detect the tell-tale beating of her heart. Mrs Abernathy was cunning and wicked. Her dark heart, he realised, must be filled with hatred. And what or, more correctly, who did she hate more than anything else in the Multiverse?

Samuel Johnson.

Crudford snapped his fingers. A small blob of gloop was flicked away by the action and landed on something in the darkness.

'Hey!' said the something.

'Sorry,' said Crudford.

Could it be true? There was only one way to find out.

CHAPTER XXIX

In Which Efforts Are Made to
Console Constable Peel

A question that is sometimes asked by human beings is why bad things happen to good people. It doesn't seem entirely fair that folk who try to make the world a better, nicer place, who don't go around scowling at puppies or frightening kittens, or trying to set someone's shoes on fire when he's asleep, should suddenly find themselves having a run of bad luck including, but not limited to, feeling a bit poorly, running out of money, having heavy objects fall on their heads, or stumbling off cliffs in the dark.

Equally, one might ask why bad things don't happen to bad people, which was just what Constable Peel was asking himself at that precise moment. Somehow, against all the odds, the dwarfs had survived in a basement filled with carnivorous eyeballs, bald vampires, and at least one monster with bladder control issues. If Constable Peel had been stuck in that basement he'd have been dinner for something within seconds, but Jolly, Angry, Dozy and Mumbles had waltzed safely through it all as if it were nothing more dangerous than a field of daisies.

'We appear to have upset him,' said Angry, as Constable Peel continued to weep and curse the gods from his position on the floor.

'He's very sensitive for a policeman,' said Jolly. 'I think he's just relieved that nothing bad happened to us.'

'He's swearing a lot for someone who's relieved,' said Angry. 'He seems to be doing a lot of fist-shaking as well.'

'He's getting rid of tension, that's all,' said Jolly. 'It can be a very emotional experience when you find out that someone you care about has been in danger. Imagine how much worse he must feel knowing that the four of us – and Dan – were almost killed.'

Constable Peel's wailing grew louder.

'I mean, think about it: just one little bit of bad luck and we might not have been here at all.'

Constable Peel began banging his head on the ground.

'Constable Peel,' Jolly concluded solemnly, 'would never have seen us again.'

Jolly shed a tear at the near-tragedy of it all. It fell on Constable Peel's neck. As it trickled down his back Constable Peel reached for his truncheon, and he might have done to Jolly what the eyeballs and vampires and monster had failed to do had not Sergeant Rowan stepped in and ushered Dan and the dwarfs away.

'Give him a little space, lads,' he said. 'Poor old Constable Peel has had a bit of a shock.'

He knelt by his fellow policeman, who was taking deep breaths to try to calm himself.

'Are you going to be OK?' asked Sergeant Rowan.

'It's not right, Sarge,' said Constable Peel. 'Even Hell

couldn't get rid of them fast enough. Every time it looks like we might be about to see the last of them, something terrible happens and they survive.'

'I know, son, I know, but we can't have you beating them to death with your truncheon; we'd have to find somewhere to hide the bodies, and right now we're stuck in a toystore with all kinds of nasties so we don't have the time to go stuffing the bodies of dwarfs into closets or under floorboards.'

He handed Constable Peel a handkerchief. Constable Peel blew his nose loudly and wetly on it and tried to hand it back to the sergeant.

'No, you keep it,' said Sergeant Rowan.

'Very kind of you, Sarge.'

'Not really,' said Sergeant Rowan.

Constable Peel folded the handkerchief, stuffed it in his pocket, and got to his feet.

'When all this is finished . . .' said Constable Peel.

'Yes?'

'And if we survive . . .'

'It's a big "if".'

'But if we do . . .'

'Yes?'

'Can I kill them then?'

Sergeant Rowan handed Constable Peel his hat.

'We'll see, Constable, we'll see . . .'

High above the Earth, within sneezing distance of the moon, a small hole appeared in the fabric of space and time, and Crudford squeezed through it. He gazed down at the small blue planet below. It was, as planets went, nothing to write home about. It didn't have spectacular rings. It wasn't made of diamond. It did not, unlike the planet Cerberus IV in the Dragon Dimensions, have jaws and teeth, and move around the galaxy chewing up smaller worlds. It was just kind of pretty in a blue, watery way.

Crudford floated closer to the Earth. He hovered over England. He narrowed his focus, concentrating on the area around Biddlecombe. He saw that it was there but not there, as if he were seeing the town in a dream. Black smoke swirled around it, great columns of it like tornadoes.

No, not smoke: shadows.

And not shadows, but *Shadows*.

'Oh, the Great Malevolence is not going to like that,' said Crudford. 'It's not going to like that at all.'

CHAPTER XXX

In Which Help Arrives,
Wearing a Very Fetching Hat

The streets of Biddlecombe's town centre were largely deserted as Maria and the scientists drew closer to Wreckit & Sons. Most of Biddlecombe's citizens had barricaded themselves in their homes and businesses, or were off battling elves and reindeer elsewhere. A small crowd had taken refuge inside the Town Hall, where the forces of darkness were being kept at bay by the singing of BoyStarz, as it turned out that even demonic elves and reindeer had a limited tolerance for infinite variations on 'Love is Like . . .' Some of those trapped inside with BoyStarz had tried to make a break for freedom to take their chances with the forces of darkness, but common sense had prevailed, helped by earplugs and the contents of the mayor's drinks cabinet.

Professor Hilbert parked the car outside Mr Tuppenny's Ice Cream Parlour, where a quartet of abominable snowmen had made the mistake of breaking in and eating some of the stock. Mr Tuppenny's ice cream had a reputation for being heavy on the ice and light on the cream. It was said of his Lemon Surprise that the only surprising thing about it was the fact that it eventually melted at all, and lumps of coal had more lemon in them. There were people who swore that they had eaten one of Mr Tuppenny's Special Ice Cream Sundaes in May and still had an icy ball moving slowly and painfully through their lower intestine come September. Mr Tuppenny had only stayed in business because of tourists and mad people. The abominable snowmen had eaten so much Strawberry Swirl that it had made them very unwell, and were now unable to do anything more threatening than wave their claws in frail 'Kill me now and make the icy pain go away' gestures.

It was Professor Stefan who spotted the two figures picking their way through the broken glass and ruined Christmas decorations.

'They're a bit tall for elves, aren't they?' he said. 'Seems to defeat the purpose, having tall elves.'

'They're not elves,' said Maria. 'They're demons! Unlock the car doors, please. I want to get out.'

Professor Hilbert did as he was told, even though it didn't seem like a good idea to go after two large demonic elves. The small ones were bad enough.

Maria leaned over Reginald, opened the door, and clambered out.

'Nurd! Wormwood! It's me!'

Nurd and Wormwood were just as pleased to see Maria as she was to see them. They hugged, and were soon joined by Professors Stefan and Hilbert, and Brian and Reginald, who kept a cautious distance from them.

'When you say "demons", that usually implies a degree of badness,' said Professor Hilbert to Maria.

Maria tried to explain.

'Look, not all demons are demonic,' she said.

'I did try for a while,' said Nurd. 'I just wasn't very good at it.'

'He was useless,' Wormwood added unhelpfully.

'I wasn't useless, I was just . . .'

Nurd tried to find the right word.

'Rotten?' Wormwood suggested. 'Incompetent? Gormless?'

Nurd settled for 'different'.

'Differently useless,' muttered Wormwood.

The scientists were examining Nurd and Wormwood with some curiosity. Professor Stefan poked Wormwood with a pen, which came back with something unpleasant stuck to its tip. As Professor Stefan watched, his pen began to dissolve.

'That does happen if you're not careful,' said Nurd. 'It's best to avoid touching him without gloves, or even with them if you fancy wearing them a second time.'

'You'd better explain how you got here,' said Maria. 'After all that's happened, I don't think it matters much if they know the truth about you now.'

So Nurd did. He covered his banishment in the wilderness, the way he'd been pulled from Hell to Earth, and how he had managed to foil the invasion of Biddlecombe by the forces of Hell using only a borrowed/stolen car. He then explained how Samuel had ended up in Hell, along with two policemen, some dwarfs, and an ice cream salesman,[47] and the manner in which they had all returned to Earth together.[48]

There was a chorus of questions from the scientists when he had finished. They wanted to know about other dimensions, and reverse wormholes, and what the weather was like in Hell. Nurd tried to answer, but each answer seemed to invite ten more questions. Eventually it was left to Maria to call a halt.

'We don't have time for this now,' she said. 'We need to find Samuel. If there are demons, and problems with reality, he has to be involved somehow. And, if I'm right, he's probably trapped somewhere in there.'

They all took in the great mass of Wreckit & Sons. There was a field of energy surrounding the store, but it was different from the one separating Biddlecombe from the rest of the country. When Maria threw a stone at it, the stone simply bounced off, although it was hot to the touch afterwards.

'Do you know what's happening?' she asked Nurd.

'The stars are going out,' he said. 'There's a darkness approaching. Don't you feel it? It's as though the shadows are becoming deeper.'

'Not just that,' said Brian. 'They've developed a life of their own. I should know. I was chased by one.'

'Who is that, and why is he shaking?' said Nurd.

💀 [47] Although unfortunately not Mr Tuppenny the ice cream man.

💀 [48] He did all that in a paragraph. It took me two books. I'm in the wrong business.

'His name is Brian,' said Maria. 'He made the tea, so according to Professor Hilbert this is all his fault.'

'Hello, Brian,' said Nurd. 'Perhaps you should stop making tea. You should probably stop drinking it too. You might not shake so much.'

He returned his attention to Maria.

'Where were we?'

'The darkness, and the shadows. Is it the Great Malevolence?'

'No, I don't think so. It doesn't feel like his work. It's *blacker*.'

'Whatever is causing it, it lives in the shop,' said Maria. 'Wreckit & Sons is at the heart of some kind of supernatural engine designed by the architect Hilary Mould.'

'It's also a trap,' said Nurd. 'It drew in Samuel, and I know that Dan and the dwarfs were given jobs there. It would have taken Wormwood and me as well, but Samuel told us not to go. He didn't think it would be safe for us.'

'So it wanted Samuel, and Dan and the dwarfs,' said Maria. 'It also wanted you and Wormwood, and I wouldn't be surprised if Sergeant Rowan and Constable Peel are in there too. Someone springs to mind.'

'Mrs Abernathy,' said Nurd. 'But I saw her being torn apart. I *felt* it happen. We all did. She's just atoms scattered throughout the Multiverse now. And even if she was involved, she doesn't have this kind of power. She can't darken universes.'

From somewhere at the level of Nurd's knee, something went *glop*.

'Evening, all,' said a small gelatinous being, raising

his hat in greeting. 'My name is Crudford, Esq., and I think I may be able to answer some questions for you.

"And by the way, is it just me, or can everyone else hear what sounds like a big heart beating?"

Crudford had not headed directly to Earth. Upon glimpsing the Shadows above Biddlecombe, his first act had been to take a closer look at them. What he saw confirmed his worst fears: there were faces in the gloom, faces that had never been glimpsed before because the place from which the Shadows came was a kingdom of utter darkness. The Shadows were blind – what good were eyes when there was nothing to see? – but like so many other creatures that lived without light, their hearing was very, very sensitive. They had been listening to the sounds of the Multiverse for almost as long as it had been in existence. They believed that they were the true owners of the Multiverse, for before the Multiverse there was nothing, and they were as close to nothing as one could find. They hated the light, and all that dwelt in it. They even hated the Great Malevolence, and all who resided in Hell, for in Hell too there was light, even if it was the light of red fires. The only thing that had saved the Multiverse from the Shadows was the fact that their realm was sealed off from every other: they were prisoners inside their own Kingdom, for the Multiverse had ways of protecting itself.[49]

☠ [49] So how big is the Multiverse, exactly? According to quantum theory, particles can pop into and out of existence, and there are scientists who believe that our universe was the result of just such a quantum 'pop'. So if one universe

The Great Malevolence had once thought about trying to recruit the Shadows as its allies, but the messengers it sent to their kingdom had never returned. They had been absorbed into the blackness, their eyes taken from them, and eventually they had become Shadows themselves. The Great Malevolence had learned that the Shadows could not be used, and it was better if they were not allowed to pollute the Multiverse or interfere with Hell's efforts to dominate it.

---

can pop into being, why not many universes? This would require extra dimensions, which is where very complicated string theory comes into play. String theory proposes that our universe is made up of very, very small vibrating strings, and when the strings vibrate in different ways they produce different particles. Think of the strings of a guitar producing different notes, and so the universe can be imagined as a great symphony of particles being produced by an unseen orchestra. Pluck one string and you get a proton; pluck another and you get an electron.

One of the difficulties in understanding string theory lies in the fact that it doesn't work in our four-dimensional world (the three space dimensions of up/down, left/right, and forwards/backwards, and the fourth dimension of time). String theory requires eleven dimensions, ten of space – which are buried within our existing three dimensions – and one of time. One of the tasks of the Large Hadron Collider was to find proof of these extra dimensions: if, during the Collider's proton collisions, some of the bits of shattered particles were found to have gone missing from the sealed vacuum, then that would suggest the possibility that they had disappeared into other dimensions.

Anyway, to get back to our original question of how many universes there may be in the Multiverse, some string theorists suggest the number is 10^{500}, or one for every possible model of physics that string theory offers. (See, I told you it was complicated. It's so complicated that this latest version of string theory, the eleven-dimension one, is known as M-theory, and even Edward Whitten, the man who came up with it, isn't sure what the 'M' stands for.) Mind you, there are some scientists who say that the number of universes in the Multiverse could be far more than 10^{500}, and that the only way you can get it down to 10^{500} is by fiddling about with the (coarse) Moduli Space of Kähler and Ricci-Flat (or Calabi-Yau) metrics and then enforcing extra supersymmetry conditions, which is just cheating, obviously. I mean, everybody knows that.

But then the balance of the Multiverse had been disturbed by the actions of men. Humans were endlessly curious, and their curiosity led them to take risks. They had built the Large Hadron Collider to try to recreate the beginnings of their universe, and in the process they had opened a gateway between Earth and Hell that had almost caused the end of their world. They had also begun to investigate the nature of reality, and reality was a delicate business. What was unreal only stayed that way as long as reality and unreality kept to their own sides of the fence. If you opened a gate between the two, then all kinds of confusion reigned. That was how dwarfs ended up being chased by eyeballs, and tentacled entities got trapped in closets, and little girls with a fondness for spiders, and web for skin, climbed down from walls to bother people.

But even all of the messing about with reality might not have come back to bite the humans had they not gone poking their noses into dark matter. It was all very well deciding that, yes, what they saw when they looked through their telescopes was only four per cent of the stuff of the universe, and the other ninety-six per cent had to be made up of something else. They called that something else 'dark matter' and 'dark energy'. Dark matter was the universe's hidden skeleton, giving structure to universes and galaxies, while dark energy was the force changing universes, forcing galaxies farther and farther apart. Humanity decided that the universe was about seventy per cent dark energy and twenty-five to twenty-six per cent dark matter. Heigh-ho, problem solved, who fancies a cup of tea and a biscuit before we clock off early for the afternoon?

But that wasn't right. They should have paid more attention to one important word: 'dark'. The dark was where things hid. The dark was the place where unpleasant creatures that didn't want to be seen waited until the time was right.

The dark was the place in which the Shadows were imprisoned.

By engaging in dark matter detection experiments – including projects such as Multidark, the Dark Matter Time Projection Chamber, and the Cryogenic Dark Matter search – the humans had alerted the Shadows to their existence. Even in their isolated realm, they had been able to hear the humans: voices, music, rockets, wars, the Shadows had listened to them all. When the detection experiments had begun, it was the equivalent of someone tapping on the outside of a prison wall with a pickaxe – *tap-tap-tap* – except that the person doing the tapping didn't know that there were entities imprisoned inside, entities that were very anxious to escape and smother every light in the Multiverse.

Professor Stefan was right: the Large Hadron Collider had worn thin the walls between dimensions, and the pickaxe jabs of the detection experiments had done the rest. A hole had been opened, and now the Shadows were about to pour through.

The Great Malevolence might have wanted to destroy humanity and burn worlds. It might have wanted misery and ruin. But it also wanted the Multiverse to remain in existence. It wanted to transform universes into branch offices of Hell, and to do that required the continued survival of the Multiverse.

The Shadows wanted only nothingness. They were as much a danger to the Great Malevolence as they were to humanity. This was why Crudford, after a quick return visit to Hell, had come down to Earth. He now believed that he knew why Biddlecombe was the place to which the Shadows had come. Mrs Abernathy's heart had hidden itself on Earth, and its blackness had found an echo in the Kingdom of Shadows. She had called out to the Shadows, and an alliance had been formed. She would give the Earth, and then the Multiverse, to the Shadows.

And in return, they would give Samuel Johnson to her.

CHAPTER XXXI

In Which the Funniness of Clowns is Doubted

Things were going from bad to worse inside Wreckit & Sons, which was surprising given how bad things were to begin with. It seemed that, as Samuel and the others drew closer to the highest floor of the store, the nature of reality was becoming more and more distorted. In fact, as far as Samuel was concerned, reality had pretty much given up on Biddlecombe and gone to live somewhere slightly more down to earth.

First off, there were the clowns. Everyone trapped in the store was beginning to realise that Wreckit & Sons had been designed with one purpose in mind: to provide a series of threats that would gradually drive the humans to the top floor. While they had made the best use that they could of whatever weapons they could find – bats, balls, bows and arrows, and foam blasters, for the most part – it wasn't as if the store had been littered with rocket launchers or heavy artillery. The dangers on each floor were simply meant to force them upwards, not kill them, or so Samuel believed, although Dan and the dwarfs were pretty convinced that, had the Nosferati managed to get their fangs into them, they would soon have been singing in some heavenly choir, assuming heaven was willing to let them in.

They saw that the next-to-last floor had been given a circus theme. There was a Ferris wheel in one corner, large enough for very small children to ride, and the wooden façade of a big top. There were signs that read 'Hoop Toss' and, slightly worryingly, 'Ghost Train'. Over them all hovered the head of a ringmaster in a top hat, his black moustache curling almost to his eyebrows, and his smile wide enough to swallow a person.

The ringmaster was Hilary Mould.

Beneath the ringmaster stood three dummies dressed as clowns. One was bald and entirely covered in white-face make up. He wore a suit of broad yellow check, and a little red hat was positioned on the side of his head. Samuel wondered how it stayed in place: glue, perhaps, or a very thin rubber band. It was only as he drew closer to the clown that he saw the hat had been nailed to his skull.

The second clown wore a huge pink wig that looked like the aftermath of an explosion in a candyfloss machine. Only the areas around his eyes and mouth were painted white: the rest of his face was a sickly yellow. He wore a long green coat with tails, and purple trousers decorated with pink polka dots. A huge plastic flower was pinned to the buttonhole of his jacket.

The third clown was female. She was wearing white one-piece overalls decorated with big red fluffy buttons, and her wig was black. So, too, was the make-up around her mouth and her eyes, while the rest of her face was very pale. Strangely, her mouth had been painted into a frown instead of a smile. Her fingernails were long and pointed, and varnished a deep, dark red, as though she had recently been tearing apart raw meat.

Samuel had never seen a female clown before,[50] but then he had only been to the circus once in his life. Samuel didn't care much for the circus, or clowns. He wasn't scared of clowns; he just didn't think they were amusing.[51]

The dwarfs wandered over to join him.

💀 [50] The history of clowning does not record the appearance of female clowns until 1858, which is quite amazing as clowns have been around since at least the time of the Pharoah Dadkeri-Assi in 2500 BC. The first female clown was said to have been Amelia Butler who was part of Nixon's Great American Circus, but the next female clown, Lulu, was not mentioned until 1939. Now, though, lots of clowns are female, and can be found alongside the various trapeze artists, tightrope walkers, and lion tamers of the circus. Interesting fact: no clown has ever been eaten by a circus animal. This is because clowns taste funny.

💀 [51] Coulrophobia is the word for a fear, or phobia, of clowns, which is not uncommon. Some fears are strangely specific, though, and unlikely to be a real problem unless you actively try to scare yourself. For example, Zemmiphobia is a fear of the great mole rat, which is, despite its name, a small, almost hairless, slow-moving rat with protruding teeth that it uses to carve out tunnels for itself. It tends to avoid people and live underground, so it's not like it's knocking on doors and shouting 'Boo!' Similarly, arachibutyrophobia, the fear of peanut butter sticking to the roof of your mouth, can probably be dealt with by not eating peanut butter, or just eating it carefully. Unfortunately, there's not much that can be done about geniophobia, the fear of chins, since you do rather bring that one with you wherever you go. Phobophobia, meanwhile, is the fear of phobias, or the fear of being afraid. Unfortunately, if you have phobophobia then you're already afraid, so the very fact that you're a phobophobe means that you're in trouble from the start.

'They're not going to get many laughs looking like that,' said Dozy.

'Never liked clowns,' said Angry. 'They always seem to be trying too hard.'

'What do you call the gooey red stuff between a circus elephant's toes?' asked Jolly.

'I don't know,' said Samuel.

'A slow clown,' said Jolly. 'Get it? A *slow clown*.'

The female clown turned her head slowly in Jolly's direction. Her fingers tested the air. The bald clown opened his mouth and licked his lips, and the clown with the fuzzy wig put his hand inside his jacket and squeezed the bulb on his plastic flower. A jet of liquid shot from it, which just missed Angry. It sizzled when it hit the floor, and began burning a hole in the carpet. The others immediately stepped out of range, but instead of joining them Angry began shouting at the clowns.

'Losers!' he said. 'I've seen funnier dead people.'

The flower-wearing dwarf tried again, firing a stream of acid in Angry's direction. Again it landed on the carpet and began eating its way through.

'How do you get a clown off your porch?' called Angry. 'You pay him for the pizza.'

By now the bewigged clown was growling and spraying a constant stream of acid at Angry as he circled the trio. The others tried to snatch at him with their fingers, but he was too fast.

'What are you doing?' cried Samuel. 'You're going to get hurt!'

The smell of burning carpet and wood was very

strong now, and a near perfect acid-drenched circle was sizzling at the feet of the clowns. The liquid stopped pumping. The clown's supply of acid was exhausted. He looked at the flower in disgust before deciding to take care of Angry and the others personally. He took one step forward. The other clowns did the same.

The ceiling collapsed, taking the three clowns with it and leaving only a hole where they had previously stood. Carefully, Samuel and the dwarfs peered over the edge at the floor below. The clowns had shattered on impact, like china dolls. The ceiling had also landed on Miss Muffet's giant spider: they could see the tips of eight legs sticking out from under the mass of wood and plaster, and its insides were leaking out. Lucy's boot might not have been strong enough to crush one of the smaller spiders, but three clowns and a heavy ceiling seemed to have done the trick for the big one.

'Like I told you,' said Angry, 'I never liked clowns. Never had much time for spiders either.'

Miss Muffet appeared beside the remains of her spider. She glared up at them.

'*Bad!*' she said, pointing a web-covered finger at them. '*Very bad!*'

'Oh-oh,' said Jolly. 'We've done it now.'

As they watched, Miss Muffet started to make her way to the stairs. She had obviously decided that someone had to pay for the destruction of her spider, but they were distracted from her approach by the ringmaster. His wooden face had contorted into a mask of rage. Thin streams of black smoke poured from his nostrils. Beside him, the Ferris wheel rattled on its foundations. Bolts popped, and its supports collapsed. The Ferris wheel dropped to the floor and headed towards them.

'Incoming!' shouted Jolly.

Samuel and the dwarfs dived out of the way of the rolling wheel. Samuel was relieved to see Lucy and the policemen do the same. They reacted fast, certainly faster than Miss Muffet, who reached the top of the stairs just in time to be hit by the wheel. It rolled halfway down the stairs before striking a wall at speed, tearing through the brickwork and taking Miss Muffet with it. All that was left to show she had ever been there at all was a trail of crushed black spiders.

And that was when the Polite Monster appeared.

To start with, Samuel and the others didn't know that he was polite. When monsters appear, the general approach is to assume that they don't mean anyone any good and set about getting rid of them. If that doesn't work, it's a good idea to make your apologies and leave while you still can. The Polite Monster had a lot of horns, and a great many teeth in its jaws, and four eyes, two on each side of its head. It was about twelve feet tall, and almost as wide, and was covered entirely in coarse red fur. It popped into existence in a puff of purple and yellow smoke, accompanied by the most horrendous smell combining the worst aspects of rotting fish, dog poo, and very old eggs that had been scrambled and fed to someone with bad digestion and worse wind.

The Polite Monster sniffed the air, made a face, and said, 'That wasn't me.'

It had a very cultured voice. It sounded like a monster that liked light opera, and perhaps acted in plays for the local dramatic society, the kind in which chaps called Gussy popped up dressed in tennis whites, and people laughed like this: 'I say, ah-ha-ha-ha!'

By that point, everyone who wasn't a monster had found somewhere to hide. This floor of the shop was devoted entirely to books and some more board games, which had been a relief to everyone until the Polite Monster appeared. There was a limit to how much damage a game of Scrabble could inflict: at worst, it could probably arrange some of its tiles into a rude name.

'Hello?' said the Polite Monster. 'Anybody home?'

Samuel poked his head up from behind a pile of boxes of Risk. The boxes were rattling alarmingly, suggesting to Samuel that some games might be more dangerous than others. This was confirmed when he heard a muffled shot from the topmost box, and a tiny cannon-ball pierced the lid and flew past his ear. A very small voice, muffled by cardboard, shouted, 'Reload!'

'Oh, hello,' said Samuel.

'Ah,' said the Polite Monster. 'I'm terribly sorry for intruding – nine letters, "to force oneself in without invitation" – but I was hoping that you could tell me where I am?'

Samuel was still wary.

'Where do you think you are?'

'I can tell you where I was a moment ago,' said the Polite Monster. 'I was doing a crossword puzzle in my cave. Tricky one. Two down, eight letters: "Insecure now that the horse has bolted".'

'Unstable,' said Constable Peel, who did a lot of crosswords.

'Unstable!' said the Polite Monster. 'Oh that's very good, very good. Let me just—'

It patted its person looking for something with which to write and then it blushed, or blushed as much as a large hairy monster could blush, which wasn't a lot.

'Oh dear,' it said. 'This is most embarrassing – twelve letters, "to be ill at ease". I appear to be completely naked.'

Another cannonball popped from the Risk box. This time it nicked Samuel's left ear, and drew a little blood.

'Hey!' said Samuel. 'That's enough!'

He gave the box a thorough shake.

'Earthquake!' shouted the same small voice.

The Polite Monster was now attempting to cover itself with its arms. Samuel wasn't sure why it was bothering. It really was just one big ball of fur. If it had any bits that it didn't want seen, the fur was already doing a very good job of hiding them.

'Sorry?' said Samuel.

'Naked,' said the Polite Monster. 'Five letters, "to be bare, or without clothes".'

The dwarfs appeared, hauling behind them a large, paint-spattered sheet that had been left behind by the decorators.

'Will this do?' said Angry.

'Oh, yes,' said the Polite Monster. 'Anything would be better than my current situation – nine letters, "a state of affairs".'

It arranged the sheet as best it could over its shoulders

and around its hips. Jolly found a piece of rope, and the Polite Monster used it to secure the sheet. It now looked like a monster that had been cast in the role of Julius Caesar.

'Thank you, that's much better,' said the Polite Monster.

Dan and the policemen joined Sam, Lucy and the dwarfs. It was clear that they were in little danger from the Polite Monster. The Polite Monster looked curiously at the dwarfs.

'I say: little men,' it said. 'Did you have an accident to make you that way – eight letters, "an unforeseen event or mishap"?'

'We're dwarfs,' said Jolly. 'Six letters – "to thump someone who suggests that we're small because something fell on our heads".'

'Oh dear,' said the Polite Monster. 'I seem to have offended you – eight letters – "to cause to feel upset or annoyed". I really am most dreadfully sorry.'

'Apology accepted,' said Jolly.

He hadn't wanted to beat up the Polite Monster anyway. Even if he'd been able to, it wouldn't have been, well, polite.

'And in answer to your question,' Jolly continued, 'you're on Earth, in Biddlecombe, in Wreckit & Sons' toyshop. And it's not a good place to be right now.'

'Oh, isn't it?' said the Polite Monster. 'You all seem very nice, I must say – four letters, "pleasant or agreeable" – and it makes a change from the cave, but I really should be getting back. I was baking scones, you see. Mother is coming to visit.'

'We're all trying to get out of here,' said Samuel, 'but there are vampires in the basement, killer dolls on the ground floor, and spiders just below us. We're being forced higher and higher in the store because I think that whatever is causing this is waiting for us on the topmost floor.'

The Polite Monster adjusted its tarpaulin toga.

'I'm sure there's a perfectly reasonable explanation,' it said. 'We'll just ask politely to be sent on our way, and that will be the end of it. I find that politeness – ten letters, "tact, or consideration for others" – goes a long way. Shall we?'

It extended a hairy, clawed hand, inviting them to take the lead.

'After you,' said Jolly.

'Such manners,' said the Polite Monster, as it stepped past Jolly. 'Wonderful, just wonderful.'

'Four letters to describe that bloke,' whispered Jolly to Angry, once the Polite Monster was out of earshot. 'Here's a clue: hazel-, wal-, or pea- . . .'

CHAPTER XXXII

In Which We Learn That if
One Can't Go Through Something,
and One Can't Go Over It, or Around It,
then There's Only One Way Left to Go

Maria was finding it difficult to keep the minds of the scientists on the problem in hand. As if suddenly finding themselves in the company of two demons from another realm – the scientists seemed reluctant to call it 'Hell', preferring instead to use the term 'climatically challenged dimension' – wasn't enough, they now had the bonus of Crudford, who was a gelatinous demon from the same place with a great fondness for hats. But the answers that Crudford was giving to their questions seemed to be causing them even more problems than the ones they had been receiving from Nurd and Wormwood.

'So,' said Professor Stefan, 'have you always been a gelatinous mass?'

'Indeed I have,' said Crudford proudly. 'I've been a billion years before the ooze. It trails behind me, you see.'

'Yes, I do see,' said Professor Stefan, who had slipped in some of Crudford's ooze and almost landed on his head as a consequence. 'And you say you work for a being called the "Great Malevolence"?'

'That's right,' said Crudford, 'the most evil being that the Multiverse has ever known. It is the fount of all badness, the well from which the darkest thoughts and deeds spring. No single entity has ever contained so much sheer nastiness as the Great Malevolence. On the other hand, I work regular hours, get weekends off, and the canteen's not bad.'

'And what does this Great Malevolence want?' said Professor Hilbert.

'Well, it would really like to see the Earth reduced to a burning plain, with all life on it either wiped out or left screaming in agony. That aside, it would probably settle for Samuel Johnson's head on a plate.'

'Is that what you want?' asked Maria, who was quite shocked to hear Crudford speak of her friend in that way. Once you got over the fact that he was largely transparent, and clearly demonic,[52] Crudford appeared very good-natured.

☠ [52] A small joke playing on the words 'transparent' and 'clear', which mean the same thing, pretty much. It troubles me that I have to explain some of these jokes – not to you, obviously: I know that you're hugely intelligent, and you got that joke straight off, but not everyone is as bright as you. Maybe there should be a test before we allow people to read this book. We could pay people to wait in bookstores and libraries, and when someone picks the book up with the intention of reading it, the tester could then step in with a list of simple questions. You know:

1. If you see a door marked 'Push', should you a) Pull; b) Push?
2. If you see a sign on the street that reads 'Caution: Do Not Cross Here', do you a) cross; b) look for somewhere else to cross?
3. If you are at the zoo, and see a notice on the lions' cage that says 'Dangerous Animals: Do Not Put Hand Through Bars', do you
   a) put your hand through the bars, and waggle your fingers invitingly;
   b) keep a safe distance and, therefore, keep your hand too?

If you have answered a) to any of these questions, then you are not bright enough to read this book, and we also have another question for you, namely: how come you're still alive?

'I don't know Samuel Johnson personally,' said Crudford, 'and he's never done anything to hurt me. I wouldn't like it if my head was lopped off, although I'm pretty sure that it would grow back again. But life is a lot easier when the Great Malevolence is happy, which isn't very often. If you're worried about me trying to cut Samuel Johnson's head off, though, then don't be. I'm not the head-cutting kind. Also, I'm here to help, because right now you have bigger problems than the Great Malevolence. In case you haven't noticed, your town has been dimensionally shifted. It's now stuck in the space between dimensions, and that's somewhere you don't want to be.

'In a way, it's a bit like the Multiverse's equivalent of the back of the sofa: all sorts of stuff gets lost down there, some of it sticky and unpleasant. But it's also a place where things hide, things that aren't supposed to be hanging around between dimensions but should be locked up nice and safe in dimensions of their own. The problem is that there are weak points in the Multiverse, and your experiments with Colliders and dark matter and dark energy have turned those weaknesses into actual holes. That was how the Great Malevolence nearly got through the first time, and it's how the Shadows are trying to get in this time.'

'Shadows?' said Professor Hilbert.

Crudford pointed a stubby finger at the sky.

They looked up. More and more stars were vanishing, and darkness swirled in their place. To Maria it felt like they were trapped inside one of those glass domes that are usually filled with water and imitation snow and a village scene, and beyond the glass the world was filled with smoke. As they watched, the darkness assumed a face. It was a face unlike any they could have imagined, a face constructed by a presence that had only heard stories of faces, but never actually seen one. The mouth was askew, and the chin too long, and one pointed ear set lower than the other. Only the eyes were missing.

'The Shadows,' said Crudford. 'A little of their essence has already managed to get through, otherwise none of this would be happening, but it's the difference between smelling the monster's breath and feeling its teeth ripping into your flesh. They won't be kept out for long, and once they get in here the whole Multiverse will be at risk. Biddlecombe has been turned into a gateway, a bridge between the Kingdom of Shadows and your universe. But all universes are connected, if only by threads, and once the Shadows infect one universe then the Multiverse is doomed. They'll turn it black, and everything in it will suffocate and die, or be turned to Shadows.'

'And the Great Malevolence doesn't want this to happen,' said Maria, 'because it doesn't want the Shadows to have the Earth, or the Multiverse. If anyone is going to destroy all life, it's going to be your master, right?'

'Absolutely,' said Crudford. 'It's the whole point of its existence. Without it, it'd just be bored.'

'But why is this happening now?' said Maria.

'Someone built the engine that allowed Biddlecombe to be shifted,' said Crudford. 'But it had to be powered up, and that power came from elsewhere, from outside.

It came from Hell and, if I'm not mistaken, it took the form of a beating heart. Furthermore, the Shadows are blind. They had to be led to Biddlecombe, and the only way that could happen was with sound. They followed the heartbeats. Can't you hear them? The heart is close, very close.'

But try as they might, they could hear nothing.

'That shop is the core of the engine,' said Crudford. 'We have to get in there and switch it off before it's too late, and move that beating heart out of this universe.'

'But whose heart is it?' asked Maria. 'Whose heart could be capable of powering an occult engine, and leading a legion of Shadows to Biddlecombe?'

'Mrs Abernathy's,' said Crudford, and he sounded almost apologetic. 'The heart of Ba'al.'

In the Mountain of Despair, the Great Malevolence brooded.

Before he had travelled to Biddlecombe, Crudford had popped back to Hell for long enough to let his master know what appeared to be happening on Earth. The Great Malevolence had not been happy to hear about it. In its anger it threw a couple of demons at walls, and tossed a passing imp on the fire. The imp didn't mind too much about the flames as it had fireproof skin, but it had been on its way to do something very important and had now completely forgotten what the important thing was.[53] With nothing else to do, it

---

[53] You will know that you are getting old when you go upstairs to do something and, by the time you get there, you've forgotten what it is that you

found a nice patch of hot ash and settled down for a nap.

'She has betrayed us,' said the Great Malevolence to the Watcher. 'She has betrayed *me*.'

The Watcher, as was its way, said nothing, but there was something like sorrow in its eight black eyes. It had once served Mrs Abernathy, and had even admired her, but its loyalty ultimately lay with the Great Malevolence. Being loyal to the Great Malevolence was better for your health, and ensured that all of your limbs remained attached to your body.

The Great Malevolence felt powerless to act. Had there been a way, it might have sent an army of demons to fight the Shadows, but what good would that have done? They might as well have hacked at smoke with their swords, or tried to run mist through with spears. In the end, the Shadows would simply have swallowed the Great Malevolence's forces, and those whom the Shadows did not destroy would be condemned to an eternity of utter blackness. But the option of battle was not even available to the Great Malevolence: there was no way to move its troops from Hell to Earth, not since the first portal had been closed by the boy named Samuel Johnson and his friends. Only the little demon named Crudford was able to move from realm to realm without difficulty, and now the future of the Multiverse lay in his small, slimy hands.

---

went upstairs to do. You will know that you are *very* old when you get upstairs and can't remember where you are. And you will know that you are very, *very* old when you get upstairs and can't get downstairs again. You may laugh now, but the old age bus has a seat for everyone.

How strange, thought the Great Malevolence, that so much power should reside in such an unthreatening, and curiously contented, little body. Had Crudford been larger, or more vicious, or more cunning, he might even have been a threat to the Great Malevolence itself. Instead, Crudford just seemed happy to help. The Great Malevolence was baffled. It couldn't figure out what Crudford was doing in Hell to begin with. All things considered, he really didn't belong there.

'Go,' said the Great Malevolence to the Watcher. 'Fly to the very edge of our kingdom. Wait there, and when Crudford returns with the heart, bring them both to me.'

The Great Malevolence realised what it had said: *When Crudford returns with the heart.*

'When', not 'if'.

This is very bad, thought the Great Malevolence. I am becoming an optimist. There could only be one reason for it: Crudford, Esq. In some dreadful way, the demon's good nature was starting to infect Hell itself. The Great Malevolence could not allow this situation to continue. It decided that, once the heart had been returned to Hell, Crudford would have to be dealt with. When Mrs Abernathy's heart was cast into the icy Lake of Cocytus, there to remain frozen forever, it would have some company in its misery.

Crudford would be freezing right alongside it.

Back in Biddlecombe, there was silence for a time.

'Who?' said Professor Stefan at last.

'Mrs Abernathy,' said Maria, and set about explaining as best she could. Professor Stefan and Professor Hilbert looked as if they didn't care to believe her, but it was hard to doubt Maria when everything she told them was being backed up by two demons dressed as elves and a third who was polishing his hat.

'She wants revenge,' said Crudford, when Maria had finished speaking. 'She's gone mad. She was always a *bit* mad, but when she travelled to Earth and the Ba'al bits got mixed up with the Abernathy bits, she went completely bonkers. If she's made a deal with the Shadows, then she doesn't care about the Great Malevolence or anything else: all she wants is a last chance to punish Samuel Johnson and everyone who stood alongside him. She will have her vengeance – at any cost.'

'And her heart is somewhere in there?' said Professor Stefan, indicating Wreckit & Sons.

'I think so,' said Crudford. 'I can hear it beating, but it's so loud that I'm not sure where exactly it's coming from any more. All I know is that the heart is close, and the toyshop is the centre of power for all that's happening here, so my guess is that it's in there somewhere.'

'But how do we get in?' said Professor Stefan. 'I mean, there's an immense occult force field protecting the store. We can't go messing about with it. Somebody might get hurt. *I* might get hurt.'

Crudford removed his hat and took out his trusty notebook and pencil. He scribbled away frantically for a few minutes. Finally he shouted 'Eureka!',[54] and showed the results of his efforts to all.

The Great Malevolence would have been familiar with the looks of bafflement that met Crudford's display of his work, for it consisted only of this:

💀 [54] *Eureka*, which comes from Ancient Greek, means 'I have found it', and is reputed to be what the Greek scholar Archimedes (287–212 BC) shouted after he stuck a foot in his bath and noticed that the water level rose. This was because he had realised that the volume of water displaced by his foot was equal to the volume of the foot itself. This meant that, by submerging them in water, the volume of irregularly shaped objects could now be measured, which had been impossible – or very, very difficult – before.

It also enabled Archimedes to solve a problem set for him by King Hiero II, who wanted to know if a gold crown that had been made for him was pure or had been polluted with silver so that the goldsmith could cheat him. Archimedes knew that he could now weigh the crown against a piece of gold of similar weight, and then submerge both in water. If they were of the same density, then they would displace the same amount of water, but if the gold of the crown had been mixed with silver then it would be less dense and would displace less water, and so the king would know that he had been cheated.

Archimedes was supposed to have been so excited by his discovery that he ran naked through the streets of Athens. You can only get away with this sort of thing if you're a genius. If you're not, they'll lock you up or, at the very least, give you a very stern talking to. You may also catch cold, or injure yourself on a gate.

'It's an arrow,' said Brian. 'What are we going to do, attack the shop with Indians?'

Crudford raised his eyes to the darkening skies in frustration.

'No,' he said. 'We're just going to do this.'

He squelched over to the occult barrier, reached down, and lifted up the bottom the way one might raise a curtain on a stage to peek at what lies behind.

'Simple,' said Crudford. 'I'd try not to touch the edge of the barrier as you crawl under. It'll hurt – if you live long enough to feel it.'

CHAPTER XXXIII

In Which Spiggit's Plays an Important Role

The various dolls, teddy bears, and small battery-powered animals that had forced Samuel and the others up to the next level of Wreckit & Sons watched in silence as Crudford led Maria and the others into the store. The aftermath of battle was still visible. There were disembodied limbs lying on the floor, and teddy bears with their stuffing hanging out. A makeshift doll hospital had been set up close to the lift, and dolls wearing the uniforms of doctors and nurses were doing their best to reinsert arms and legs, and the occasional head, into the correct sockets. Some of the larger dolls still clutched knives, and a couple of stuffed toys snarled at the new arrivals, but none of the toys made any attempt to attack.

'What happened here?' asked Maria.

Nurd took in the Nerf bullets and sporting balls scattered across the floor.

'My guess is that this lot tried to attack Samuel and whoever else was trapped, and they got more than they bargained for,' he said.

Wormwood paused by the remains of a small black stuffed bear. Its head had been almost knocked from its body, and was attached to its neck only by a couple of thin threads. Carefully, tenderly, Wormwood picked it up and held it in his arms, cradling its head in his left hand. A large tear dropped from Wormwood's right eye.

'Is this what we have become?' he said. 'We have set human against teddy, doll against man, and this little bear has paid the price! All he wanted to do was give pleasure to some small child, to be his friend in times of joy, and his comfort in times of trouble. Oh, the humanity!'

He lifted the bear and placed it against his shoulder, its small black body stifling his sobs.

'Ow,' said Wormwood, then louder. 'Ow! Ow!'

'What is it?' said Nurd.

'The little swine is biting my ear!' said Wormwood.

He gave the bear a sharp tug, and its body separated entirely from its head. Unfortunately, the head remained attached to Wormwood's ear, its sharp teeth continuing to gnaw at the lobe.

'Get it off!' said Wormwood. 'It really hurts.'

Nurd tried tugging at the bear's head, but its teeth were firmly embedded, and he succeeded only in painfully stretching Wormwood's ear.

'That's not helping,' said Wormwood. 'You're just making it worse.'

'Well, you're the one who picked it up in the first place.'

'I felt sorry for it.'

'And see where it got you,' said Nurd. 'Maybe you can offer to help those dolls sharpen their knives next.'

Maria arrived with a pencil borrowed from Brian. She managed to jam it between the bear's jaws and prise them open just wide enough for Nurd to remove the head from Wormwood's vicinity. He held it in front of Wormwood's face by one of its ears, where it continued to snap at him, just as the elf had earlier tried to get at Nurd. Nurd considered this poetic justice. He didn't want to be the only one being bitten by possessed objects.

'He seems to have a taste for you,' said Nurd. 'Can't imagine why. I bet you taste awful.'

He tossed the head in the direction of the doll hospital, disturbing the final delicate stages of an operation to restore an arm to a Hug-Me-Hattie doll. Hug-Me-Hattie's arm slid under a radiator, and the doll doctors and nurses gave Nurd a look that could only be described as cutting.[55]

'Sorry!' said Nurd. 'As you were.'

The scientists, meanwhile, were watching the toys. With the exception of the clearly lunatic black bear that had nibbled on Wormwood, the toys still showed no desire to approach.

'Why aren't they attacking us?' asked Professor Stefan.

'Maybe it's because we have demons with us,' suggested Professor Hilbert. 'It might have confused them.'

'They don't look confused,' said Professor Stefan. 'They just look hostile.'

☠ 55 Do you need me to explain that joke? No? Good.

'Why don't we see what happens if we try to leave?'

The two scientists, with Brian and Reginald in tow, pretended to depart.

''Bye!' they said. 'Lovely meeting you! Good luck with everything!'

The heads of the toys turned to follow their progress, but no attempt was made to stop them, not even when Brian opened the main door and stepped outside. He might have kept going as well had not Professor Hilbert grabbed him by the collar and pulled him back inside.

'That's quite enough cowardice for today, Brian,' he said.

'It really isn't,' said Brian. 'I have loads left.'

But Professor Hilbert was not to be argued with, and Brian reluctantly trudged back into the store.

'Interesting,' said Professor Stefan. 'Mr Nurd, Mr Wormwood, perhaps you'd like to try, just out of curiosity.'

Nurd and Wormwood did as he asked, but as they approached the door the toys closed in on them, blocking their way with a wall of plastic and fur broken only by the odd knife.

'Ah,' said Professor Stefan. 'That would seem to answer the question, at least partly. Something wants you two to remain here.'

'We should have known,' said Wormwood. 'We were invited to the opening, and we never get invited to anything. Now it looks like the only reason we were asked is because something wants to hurt us.'

He and Nurd looked sad.

'Try not to take it personally,' said Maria.

'I'll try,' said Wormwood, 'but it's difficult.'

Crudford put one hand to the side of his head, even though he didn't have any obvious ears, and listened.

'Can you still hear the heart?' asked Professor Hilbert.

'It's definitely near,' said Crudford. 'I say we go up. It's clear that whatever we're looking for isn't here.'

Brian didn't want go up. He wanted to go out. He could not think of any reason why he should go deeper into this shop of horrors. At that moment, fate intervened – as it often will – to give him a push in the right direction.

'What is that noise?' said Professor Stefan. 'It sounds like music.'

A handful of Nosferati survivors, their ears jammed with dead mice to drown out the sound of the organ, had found the stairs out of the basement. They emerged from the stairwell with their fangs exposed, their clawed hands raised, and their bald heads shining under the emergency lights.

'Me first,' said Brian. He made it to the top of the stairs in record time. Brian might have been a scaredy-cat of the highest order, thought Professor Stefan, but he was very agile when he needed to be. He just hoped that 'me first' wouldn't be Brian's last words.

All of the pieces were on the board – almost. There were two missing, but they were on their way.

The demons called Shan and Gath were probably happier than they had ever been. In Hell, they had been strictly third-level staff: their main task was to shovel coal and tend the Eternal Fiery Pits of Doom, which wasn't very difficult as the Eternal Fiery Pits of Doom were never likely to go out any time soon. That was why they were called the *Eternal* Fiery Pits of Doom, and not the Temporary Fiery Pits of Doom, which doesn't have the same ring about it at all. Every so often they were sent on holiday to the Quarry of Grey Meaninglessness, where they broke rocks for two weeks, and were entertained in the evenings by the swinging sounds of Barry Perry on the kazoo.[56]

Then, during the attempted invasion of Earth, they had discovered the strange joys of a foul beer named Spiggit's Old Peculiar and had never looked back. For a while they had not looked anywhere at all, Spiggit's tending to cause temporary blindness and an overwhelming desire to be dead. Back in Hell, they attempted to brew it themselves, with mixed results, but they had never stopped trying. When they eventually managed to escape from Hell, their ability to consume large quantities of Spiggit's without actually dying, combined with their sensitive taste buds, had brought them the job of a lifetime: as chief tasters and beer experimenters at Spiggit's Brewery, Chemical Weapons, and Cleaning Products Ltd.[57]

💀 [56] Barry Perry had tortured crowds throughout the north of England for much of his life, taking innocent songs that had never done anyone any harm and murdering them with his kazoo. When he died and found himself in Hell, he also discovered that his kazoo had come with him, if only because someone had shoved it up his bottom before he was buried. Retrieving it from his bottom proved too difficult, though, so his shows in Hell tended to be a bit muffled, which was no bad thing.

💀 [57] In case you think this is an odd name for a company, and are wondering how Spiggit's could manage to create so many different products, let me set your mind at ease: it was all the same product, with varying amounts of water

Yes, they were demons. Even Old Mr Spiggit himself, whose eyesight was very poor, and who was generally regarded as a lunatic, could see from the start that Shan and Gath weren't your usual employees. On the other hand, they didn't stand out as much at the Spiggit's Brewery as they might have done elsewhere on Earth. Years of exposure to Spiggit's had caused biological changes to many of the company's employees. Mr Lambert in Accounts had to shave his hands at least twice a week, and had so much facial hair that the only way to be sure that you were talking to his face was to look for the bulge where his nose was; Mr Norris in Sales had a third thumb; and Mrs Elmtree in Quality Control had grown small but noticeable horns. They didn't mind, though, as Spiggit's paid well, and nobody else would employ them anyway because they looked so distinctive.

Shan and Gath had proven particularly good at looking after the more experimental brews, including the lethal Spiggit's Old Notorious, a beer so dangerous that a batch of its yeast had once stolen a car and held up the Bank of Biddlecombe. The yeast had never been caught, and was now believed to be living somewhere in Spain. Shan and Gath had put an end to that kind of nonsense. No yeast was going to cause trouble on their watch.

Very few things could lure Shan and Gath out of

---

added. Supplies rarely got mixed up, not since the Goat & Artichoke pub had received a delivery of weapons-grade Spiggit's by mistake. The pub had since been rebuilt, although some pieces of the landlord had still not been found.

their comfortable home at Spiggit's Brewery, but the invitation that had landed on their doorstep a few days earlier had contained the magic words 'FREE BEER', which was why they were now standing outside Wreckit & Sons wondering where the party was.

Shan approached the occult field. He suspected that it was dangerous, but he wasn't entirely sure. To test his theory he pushed Gath against it. There was a buzzing sound and the back of Gath's coat disappeared, leaving only a smoking hole where the material had once been.

'Hurh-hurh,' laughed Shan, as Gath put out the last of the flames.

'Hurh-hurh,' laughed Gath, before grabbing Shan's right hand and sticking Shan's index finger into the field. The finger promptly vanished, leaving only a smoking stump in its place.

'Hurh-hurh,' laughed Gath again.

'No, hurh-*hurt*,' said Shan.

He would have wagged his finger disapprovingly at Gath, who always took a joke too far, but he was still waiting for it to grow back. When it had done so, he looked again at the invitation.

'Beer,' he said, and pointed at the shop.

'Beer,' said Gath.

But between them and the beer stood the barrier.

Sometimes in life you have to lose a battle to win a war. Shan dug into one of the pockets of his coat and removed from it a black bottle. The bottle was encased in a titanium frame that kept its cork in place, and the following warning was written on the glass.

This bottle contains *Spiggit's Old Resentful*. Do Not Open. Seriously. Even creating this beer was a mistake, but all attempts to destroy it have proved useless. If you <u>do</u> open this bottle, you agree to give up all right to your health, and possibly your existence. Before opening, ask innocent bystanders to stand well back, or suggest that they move to another country. Do not open near naked flame. Do not so much as THINK of a naked flame in your head. Do not even smile warmly. Do not inhale. If inhaled, seek medical assistance within five seconds. If consumed, seek undertaker.
<u>INSTRUCTIONS FOR USE</u>: Open. Run away.

Shan and Gath had often looked longingly at the next-to-last remaining bottle of Spiggit's Old Resentful. It had been developed by Old Mr Spiggit shortly before people spotted that he was clearly as nutty as a nut-brown squirrel in a nut factory. How bad could Spiggit's Old Resentful be, Shan and Gath had wondered. The answer was probably very bad. Spiggit's did not issue such warnings lightly. If your regular beer has a biohazard symbol on it, even one with a smiley face, then the special stuff must be lethal.

And so Shan and Gath had long carried the bottles of Spiggit's Old Resentful around with them, hoping that the day might come when they would have cause to open them. Now, it seemed, that day was upon them.

Shan typed in the seventeen-digit combination on the bottle's lock, and the titanium cage sprang open. As if sensing that its time was upon it, something rumbled in the glass. Shan looked a bit worried. He looked even more worried as the cork began to remove itself from the bottle under pressure from whatever was inside. Like a man who suddenly finds himself in possession of a live hand grenade, he did the only sensible thing: he handed it to the bloke standing next to him, which in this case was Gath, and began backing away. Gath, meanwhile, might not have been very bright, but he wasn't entirely stupid. He tossed the bottle straight back to Shan, who caught it and sent it back to Gath, and so a game of Hot Potato continued until Shan saw that there was barely a finger's width of cork left in the bottle.

He threw the bottle at the occult field. The bottle didn't pass through but exploded on impact, showering the field with a dark brown liquid that looked like mud and smelled like low tide at a herring factory. Shan's eyes watered, and his nasal hairs caught fire. Gath fainted.

The occult field didn't have feelings, exactly. It was just an energy field generated by Hilary Mould's great engine, aided by the entities with which Hilary Mould had allied himself, but it did have a kind of awareness, for it was alive with dark forces. When the bottle of Spiggit's Old Resentful hit it and exploded, that awareness kicked into high gear, and the field made a swift decision to put as much distance between it and whatever was in the bottle as quickly as possible. The occult field vanished, retreating to another dimension where even the foulest of creatures had nothing on Spiggit's Old Resentful.

Shan slapped Gath on the cheeks to bring him back to consciousness. Once the smell had died down to a manageable level, they approached the shattered bottle. All that was left of the Old Resentful was some thick glass, and a large smoking crater in the ground.

Shan and Gath shook their heads sadly, and went to find their free beer.[58]

And so all was now in place.

Maria and the others, joined by Shan and Gath, found Samuel and his group, and a brief, slightly awkward reunion followed. After all, they had other things on their minds.

Like not dying.

☠ [58] To return briefly to the subject of famous last words, which arose in connection with Brian the teaboy, it's a difficult job, coming up with a memorable farewell to life. If death comes unexpectedly, then last words may be something like 'Aaaarrrgggggh!', or 'Ouch!', or 'Of course it isn't loaded,' or 'That bridge will easily support my weight.' It's hard to be clever under pressure. The last words of the writer H.G.Wells were reputed to have been 'Go away, I'm all right,' which was unfortunate as he clearly wasn't. Arguably the worst last words ever spoken came from Dominique Bouhours, an eighteenth-century French essayist, and a big fan of correct grammar, who announced on his deathbed, 'I am about to – or I am going to – die; either expression is correct.' I'll bet they were glad to see him go.

CHAPTER XXXIV

In Which the Great Size of the Multiverse is Revealed

The first thing that struck Samuel as he reached the icy cold top floor was that he had suddenly developed two phobias: acrophobia, a dreadful fear of heights,[59] swiftly followed by astrophobia, the fear of space. Samuel had never been frightened of heights before, and he had always been entranced by the immensity of space. He could spend a happy hour lying on his back in the garden at night, Boswell sleeping beside him, just watching the stars and feeling as though he were adrift among them.

But the top floor of Wreckit & Sons was a different matter entirely, in part because there was no longer really a floor there, or a ceiling. The memory of them remained, the faintest outline of boards beneath his feet and plasterwork above his head, but they resembled little more than chalkmarks that were slowly being

---

[59] The word 'vertigo' is frequently used, incorrectly, to describe the fear of heights, but vertigo is a spinning sensation felt when someone is actually standing still. The correct term for a fear of heights is 'acrophobia'. Good grief, I sound like that grammarian bloke Dominique Bouhours, and he was really annoying. Sorry.

washed away by rain. Even as fear overtook him, Samuel wondered if this was what it was like to be a ghost: perhaps ghosts felt themselves to be real and substantial, and the world around them seemed pale and faded.

Beyond the near-vanished lines of the old store, and the fading shapes of trees, the Multiverse waited. It was a world of light and dark, of stars being born and stars dying, of clusters of swirling galaxies and gaseous columns of nebulae. Samuel could pick out the colours of the stars, shading from the blue of the new to the red of the old. He saw clouds of asteroids, and meteors turning to fire in the atmosphere of unknown worlds, and quasars, the brightest objects in the universe, their light powered by supermassive black holes. He saw universe layered upon universe, like panes of painted glass separated by distances simultaneously great and small. And he himself was both tiny and vast, for all that he saw seemed to revolve around him: he was suspended at the heart of the Multiverse.

The second thing that struck Samuel was a dwarf, as Angry, who had been leading the way, discovered that being a leader is only fun if you're collecting a trophy, or a cash prize. It's not fun if, as leader, you're the first person to put a foot where you expect a floor to be, only to find that a large number of universes have opened up in its place, and it looks like a very long way down. He slammed painfully into Samuel's stomach, knocking the air from Samuel with his elbow.

'Mind your step there,' said Angry. 'There's a bit of a drop.'

The others had paused on the stairs, aware that

there was some problem ahead, but now the steps behind them began to vanish, one by one, as the lower floors of Wreckit & Sons turned to mist and were gone.

'The stairs are disappearing, Samuel,' shouted Maria. 'We have to move up.'

But Samuel couldn't budge. His feet were frozen in place on what little solidity remained. He willed them to move in order to make room for the others to join him, but he couldn't. It was only then that he looked down and saw there was nothing beneath him after all but stars. He waited for himself to begin falling, like a character in a cartoon who manages to run off the edge of a cliff but doesn't start to drop until he realises what he's done, but Samuel did not fall, and he could definitely feel something solid under his shoes. Tentatively, he tapped with his toe. Whatever was beneath him felt like wood, and sounded like wood, which meant that it was, in all likelihood, wood.

Warily, testing the way before he took a step, he made room for the others to join him. Constable Peel was the first up.

'Oh, Lor',' he said, as he took in the view. 'I don't feel at all well.'

For a moment he appeared to want to turn back and take his chances with the vanishing stairs, but Samuel reassured him.

'It's OK,' he told Constable Peel. 'There's still a floor under us. You can see it if you look hard enough.'

Constable Peel didn't want to look. Looking meant seeing infinity, or as good as, waiting right beneath his feet. He stretched out a hand to balance himself, and Angry gripped it.

'It's all right, Constable,' he said. 'I have you.'

'If I fall,' said Constable Peel, 'I'm taking you with me. At least I'll die happy.'

With Angry's help, Constable Peel came to grips with the concept of a floor that both was and wasn't there. They repeated the process as the rest of the group joined them, until at last they were all standing together, alternating between fear and awe at the terror and majesty of the Multiverse, and at the one construction that really didn't seem to be belong in it, for standing before them was Santa's Grotto.

Samuel couldn't understand why they hadn't noticed it before. Maybe they'd been too concerned with not falling, and with taking in the view, but it was hard to ignore a little stone house with smoke pouring from its chimney and snow on its roof – real snow, because it had now begun to descend on them as well, tickling their faces before melting on their skin. The light flickering through its walls turned from white to orange as they watched, as though a great fire were raging inside.

The door opened, and Mr St John-Cholmondeley appeared.

'Look,' said Jolly, 'it's Mr Smokey-Chimney.'

'So it is,' said Dozy. 'Oi, we want a word with you about this job, Slimy-Chopsticks. We're starting to think that we might not want it after all; that, or you need to pay us more.'

Now it was Mr St John-Cholmondeley's turn to glow red.

'It's Sinjin-Chumley!' he screamed. 'How many times do I have to tell you? *Sinjin-Chumley!* It's just two words. How hard can it be?'

Even amid the chaos of the Multiverse, the dwarfs could see that he was annoyed. The dwarfs prided themselves on their sensitivity to the feelings of others.

'Sorry,' said Angry.

'Yes, sorry,' said Jolly and Dozy.

'Applidlespopop,' said Mumbles.

'He says he's sorry too,' said Angry.

'Sorry, Mr . . . ?' said Mr St John-Cholmondeley.

He cocked his head, and waited for a reply.

The dwarfs looked at one another. Somebody had to give it a try. Angry, who had decided that he'd had enough of taking the lead for one day, gave Jolly a nudge.

'Sorry,' said Jolly, 'Mr Slimjim . . .'

He ran out of steam. Dozy gave it a try.

'Sorry, Mr Soapy-Chandling.'

'Mr Slightly-Chafing.'

'Mr Singing-Chutney.'

'Mr Stinky-Cheesecake.'

There is a phrase sometimes used about people who are very angry: 'he was incandescent with rage'. An incandescent light, as I'm sure you know, is one with a filament that glows white-hot when heated. It does not, of course, mean that someone really glows white-hot when annoyed, or it didn't until Mr St John-Cholmondeley came along. As they watched, Mr St John-Cholmondeley's eyes turned bright red, and then changed from red to burning white before bursting into flames. He opened his mouth, and smoke and fire jetted from between his lips. His whole body shook as smoke poured from his sleeves, and the ends of his trousers, and the neck of his shirt.

'It's—' he roared, but he got no further. His suit ignited and his body exploded, but there was no blood or flesh, only bits of plastic. Mr St John-Cholmondeley was simply a showroom dummy in a cheap suit brought to life, and now that existence was at an end. His head, which had soared high into the air with the force of the blast, landed with a thud and rolled across the nearly unseen floor, where Angry stopped it with his foot.

The white light was fading from Mr St John-Cholmondeley's eyes, and his skin was assuming the hardness of plastic. The dark force that had animated him was leaving, but there was a little wretched life left in him yet.

'It's—' he began again, but Mumbles interrupted him.

'Sinjin-Chumley,' Mumbles said, pronouncing it perfectly.

'We knew all along,' said Angry. 'Serves you right for being unpleasant.'

Mr St John-Cholmondeley found the strength to make his eyes glow an angry orange one last time before the light vanished from them and all that remained was a plastic head. Two thin streams of pure darkness poured from his ears and flowed beneath the walls of Santa's Grotto, and that darkness seemed to be mirrored above their heads. More stars were snuffed out, swallowed by swirling clouds like thick black ink. Eyeless faces appeared in the void, but their very blindness made them more threatening. Long grasping fingers stretched out towards the Earth, and black tongues licked at lipless mouths, as though already tasting the planet's light and life before consuming it. But the barrier between the Shadows and the universe held, for now. The Shadows flattened themselves against it, but they could not penetrate. It would not hold for much longer, though. Already cracks were visible, shining red like streams of lava.

Nurd appeared at Samuel's right hand.

'All of this because of us,' said Nurd, and he sounded both amazed and terribly, terribly sad. 'She will sacrifice whole universes to the Shadows in order to avenge herself.'

'What if we just offered ourselves to her?' said Samuel softly, and if Nurd had been astonished by the lengths to which Mrs Abernathy was prepared to go to have her revenge, he was more astonished still at the boy's words, and he felt honoured that he could call such a person his friend. Billions of years in age separated them. One was human, the other demon. Yet in all his long life Nurd had never felt closer to another being than he did to Samuel. The Multiverse had brought them together, and they had both been changed utterly by the meeting. Samuel had crossed dimensions, and now understood something of the true nature of existence. He had confronted the greatest of evils, but he had also been saved by a demon.

And that demon had himself been saved by Samuel: had they not met, then Nurd would still have been living in exile in the bleakest, dullest part of Hell with only Wormwood for company, devising plots that would never come to pass. Nurd would just have been another failed demon, an entity not weak enough to be truly evil, but not strong enough to be good either.

Now this boy was suggesting that they try to lay down their lives not just for their friends but for humanity and for every other life form, known and unknown, that swam or flew or crawled in the Multiverse. As Nurd watched, Boswell, who had been standing just behind Samuel and peering through his master's legs at all that was happening, shifted position, and moved to Samuel's side, where he sat down with his weight leaning against the boy's right leg.

He hears Samuel, thought Nurd, who had long ago learned not to underestimate the little dog. He senses what the boy is thinking of doing, and he will not leave him. This dog will die with its master rather than abandon him. If a small dog is willing to stand beside the boy at the cost of its life, then what choice have I but to do the same?

'We can try,' said Nurd, 'but I fear that Mrs Abernathy is so insane by now that it won't be enough for her to see only us suffer, and she has made her bargain with the Shadows. They will not let her break it easily. Perhaps, though, we can appeal to her vanity. Even the cruellest of beings must sometimes show mercy. If there is a power in taking lives, there is a greater power in sparing them. If we can make her believe that letting humanity survive would better demonstrate her might than allowing the Shadows to consume everything, then we could have a chance.'

Samuel picked up something in Nurd's tone.

'But not a big chance,' said Samuel, and he managed a smile.

'Not really,' said Nurd, 'but that's better than no chance at all.'

Maria joined them.

'What are you two whispering about?' she said, but even as she spoke Lucy bustled forward and plonked herself between Maria and Samuel. Lucy might have been shallow, and very self-obsessed, but she was nobody's fool. She might not have liked Samuel as much as she once thought she did, and she certainly didn't understand him, but there was no way that she was going to let anyone else take him from her.

'He's *my* boyfriend!' she said.

'Er, I've been meaning to talk to you about that,' said Samuel, although it struck him that this probably wasn't the ideal time to bring it up. Then again, if the universe did come to an end, he didn't want to spend his final moments stuck in a doomed relationship with Lucy Highmore.

'*Excuse* me?' said Lucy.

Nurd took a discreet step back. It is said that Hell hath no fury like a woman scorned. Nurd had spent a long time in Hell, and he knew just how furious it was. If scorning Lucy Highmore was going to be worse than Hell, then Nurd didn't want to be stuck in the middle of whatever happened next. He managed to put Constable Peel and two dwarfs between him and the argument.

'Hey, wait a minute,' said Constable Peel, who might

have been dim at times but could see where this was going.

'You're a policeman,' said Nurd. 'You have a duty to protect.'

He kept a tight hold of Constable Peel's shoulders, just in case the policeman got any ideas about seeking cover for himself.

'Look, it's just not working out between us,' said Samuel. 'It's not you, it's me.'[60]

'How dare you!' said Lucy. 'You're saying that it is me!'

'No, I'm not,' said Samuel. 'At least, I don't think that I am. Hang on, I might be.'

'But nobody has ever broken up with me before,' said Lucy. 'I do the breaking up. I even have a speech about how we can still be friends, and how you must be brave, and all that nonsense.'

'Right,' said Samuel, and his mouth began working before his brain could catch up. 'Well, we can still be friends, and I suppose you have to be brave—'

Any further musings he might have had on the future of his dealings with Lucy Highmore were brought to a sudden end by the impact of her right shoe against Samuel's left knee.

'Oooooooh!' said Lucy. 'Well, I'm glad I'm not going out with you any more! You're strange, you're too short, and your shoes sometimes don't match. And by the way, this has been the worst date of my life!'

💀 [60] Please see footnote 13 in Chapter Five and then substitute 'me' for 'you', and 'you' for 'me' in the sentence above.

She turned to face Maria.

'You Jezebel!' she said. 'If you like him that much then you can just have him, and I hope he makes you as happy as he made me.'

She stomped away, then stomped back again.

'Just in case you didn't understand what I meant,' she told Maria, 'I was implying that he didn't make me happy at all, and I hope you're just as unhappy with him as I was.'

'I knew that,' said Maria. 'And I do like him. I think I may love him, actually.'

'Bully for you,' said Lucy. 'I don't want an invitation to the wedding.'

She stomped away for the second time, and stood beside Nurd and Constable Peel with her arms folded, simmering like a pot on a warm stove.

'What are you two looking at?' she said.

'Nothing,' said Nurd.

'Me neither,' said Constable Peel. 'I'm just minding my own business.'

'Just keep it that way,' said Lucy. 'Oh, men!'

Samuel, meanwhile, was staring at Maria with the confused expression of a man who has just learned that day is, in fact, night, and the moon is made of cheese after all.

'What?' he said, as he couldn't think of anything else to say.

'It doesn't matter,' said Maria, then added: 'You're an idiot.'

'What?' said Samuel – again.

'For a smart boy,' said Angry to Jolly, who had been

watching the entertainment and enjoying it immensely, 'he really is surprisingly stupid sometimes.'

'Look, I like you,' said Maria. 'A lot. I've always liked you. A lot. Do you understand?'

'What?' said Samuel, for a third time.

Maria kissed Samuel gently on the lips.

'There,' she said.

'Ah,' said Samuel.

'The light dawns,' said Angry.

'It's like watching a caveman discover fire,' said Jolly.

'Now,' said Maria, 'to return to the original question: what were you and Nurd whispering about?'

Samuel could taste Maria on his lips. His head was swimming. It was such a shame that he was either going to be killed or the Multiverse was about to come to an end, because he realised he had always loved Maria. He definitely didn't want to die now, and he rather hoped that the Multiverse might be saved without his death being part of the bargain, but then he also understood that there really is no sacrifice, and no bravery, unless there is something to be lost.

He put his hand against Maria's cheek.

'Nurd and I are going to offer ourselves to Mrs Abernathy in order to save the Multiverse,' he said.

'Over my dead body,' said Maria.

'That,' said a voice lubricated by poisons, 'can probably be arranged. Oh, and ho-ho-ho.'

CHAPTER XXXV

In Which We End on a Cliffhanger

Samuel and Maria had seen photographs of Hilary Mould, but had obviously never imagined meeting him in the flesh, not that they had lost a lot of sleep over it. Even in life Hilary Mould had not been a very handsome man. He had fish eyes, a misshapen nose, and a chin so weak that a small child could have taken it in a fight. What little hair he had stuck up at odd angles from his head like clumps of bristles on an old, worn paintbrush, and his ears stood out at right angles from his head like car doors that had been jammed open. He was also so pale and sickly that he resembled a corpse that had recently been dug up and then forgotten about.

In a way, this should have meant that *actual* death was unlikely to make him any less appealing than he already was, but anyone hoping that might be the case would have been sorely disappointed. Hilary Mould now looked worse than ever, and his name seemed to suit him even more than it had in life since he was literally mouldy: something unpleasant and green was growing on what was left of his face, and he appeared to be at least thirty per cent down in the finger department. His skin had retreated from his fingernails, making them appear disturbingly long, and it was possible to see the tendons working through the holes in his cheeks as his jaws moved. His big eyes had turned entirely black, and wisps of darkness hung like smoke around his lips as he spoke. The fact that he was dressed as Father Christmas did not help matters.

'Mr Grimly, I presume?' said Sergeant Rowan. 'Or do you prefer Mould?'

'You may call me *Mister* Mould,' said Hilary Mould. 'I've been waiting a long time for this day. Now—'

'Excuse me,' said Jolly.

Hilary Mould tried to ignore him. He'd been walled up in the basement of Wreckit & Sons for a long time, even if his spirit had been able to wander in the form of a possessed statue infused with some of his blood, but that wasn't the same thing as being out and about. He had a big speech prepared. He wasn't about to let himself be interrupted by a dwarf.

'Now, my great—'

'Mister, excuse me,' said Jolly again. 'Still here.'

Jolly waved his hand helpfully, but Hilary Mould was absolutely determined not to be distracted.

'NOW,' he shouted, 'my GREAT MACHINE has revealed itself to—'

'Really need to talk to you,' Jolly persisted.

'Mister, mister,' said Dozy, waving his left arm to attract attention, 'my friend has something to say.'

Hilary Mould gave up. Honestly, it was most frustrating. He'd created an enormous occult engine, and had sealed himself up at the heart of it, undead and not a little bored, waiting for the moment when dark forces might resurrect him, and just at his time of triumph he found himself dealing with chatty dwarfs.

'Yes, yes, what is it?' said Hilary Mould, as he tried to think of ways that the Shadows could make the dwarfs' sufferings last even longer as a personal favour to himself.

'Mister,' said Jolly, 'your hand has dropped off.'

Hilary Mould stared at his left hand. It was still there, minus most of its fingers, but after spending more than a century walled up in a tomb you had to expect a certain amount of minor damage. Unfortunately, when he switched his attention to his right hand he discovered only a stump. The hand itself – his favourite one, as it still had three fingers and a thumb attached – was now lying by his feet.

'Oh, for crying out loud,' he said.

He bent down and picked up the hand.

'You could try sticking it back on,' suggested Angry helpfully. 'I don't think glue will do it, but maybe if you wrapped it up with sticky tape . . .'

'It doesn't matter,' said Hilary Mould through gritted teeth, or through whatever teeth he had left to grit, which wasn't many.

'You could try a hook,' offered Jolly.

'If you wore the right kind of hat, people might think you were a pirate,' said Angry.

'Stop!' screamed Hilary Mould. 'I told you: it's fine. I have another hand. Just let it drop.'

Jolly detected the opportunity for a joke, but Hilary Mould saw it coming and cut him off before he could get a word out. He stuck the severed hand in his pocket, and pointed one of his remaining fingers at the dwarf.

'I'm warning you,' he said.

Jolly raised two hands in surrender – well, one hand. He'd hidden the other one up his sleeve.

Hilary Mould grimaced in frustration. This wasn't going at all according to plan.

'Mister,' said Dozy again.

'Look,' said Hilary Mould, 'please let me finish. I have a lot to get through.'

He fumbled in another pocket and extracted a tattered, folded sheet of paper. He started trying to unfold it, but he immediately ran into trouble due to a lack of fingers.

'Need a hand?' said a dwarf voice.

Hilary Mould didn't rise to the bait. He kept his temper, managed to get the paper open, and checked his notes.

'Um,' he muttered to himself. 'Yes, "waiting a long time for this day" – done. Laugh sinisterly. Move on to description of occult engine, tell them about ruling the world, laugh again in an evil way, hand over to . . . Okay, fine. Right.'

He cleared his throat.

'Ah-ha-ha-ha-ha!' he laughed.

'Mister,' said Dozy.

'WHAT? What do you want this time?'

'Do you wear glasses?'

Hilary Mould looked confused.

'Sometimes,' he said.

'Well,' said Dozy, 'I hate to break it to you, but you might have trouble with that in future.'

'Why?'

'Your right ear just fell off.'

Hilary Mould reached up to check. The dwarf was right. His right ear was no more. He saw it resting by his right shoe.

'Oh, blast!' he said.

He didn't want to leave it lying around. Someone might step on it. His hand, though, was barely managing to hang on to his notes.

'I'm sorry,' he said, 'but would somebody mind picking that up for me?'

Jolly obliged.

'I'll get the other one while I'm down here,' he said, for Hilary Mould's left ear, clearly pining for its friend, had detached itself from his head and headed south.

'Do you want me to put them with your hand?' asked Jolly.

'If you wouldn't mind,' said Hilary Mould.

'Not at all.'

Jolly squeezed the ears into Hilary Mould's pocket. Unfortunately, the pocket was already taken up with the hand, so Jolly had to use a little force to get the ears in there as well. He distinctly felt something snap and crumble as he did so: more than one something, as it happened.

'Do be careful with them,' said Hilary Mould. 'I'm sure there's a way of fitting them on again.'

'Don't you worry,' said Jolly, discreetly using the end of Hilary Mould's jacket to wipe bits of crushed ear from his fingers, 'you'll look a whole new man when they stick those back on.'

Jolly rejoined the others.

'He'll never wear glasses again,' he whispered to Angry. 'And I don't know how he's going to wind his watch.'

Hilary Mould was worried. He had just discovered one of the dangers of walling oneself up in a basement for a very long time: rot tends to set in. Even with a hint of Shadow essence coursing through his remains, he was in very real danger of falling apart entirely before the real business of the evening was concluded.

'I suppose you're wondering why I created my engine,' he said.

'We were, a bit,' said Samuel.

'I knew,' said Hilary Mould, 'that there was a great force of Darkness somewhere out there in the vast reaches of space.'

He gestured grandly at the stars surrounding them. A finger flew off into the blackness.

'Just pretend that never happened,' said Hilary Mould. He continued: 'I felt this Darkness calling to me. I heard the lost voices. And I knew what I had to build: an engine, a great supernatural machine in the form of a pentagram, and then the Shadows would come.'

'What did they promise you in return?' asked Nurd.

'Eternal life!' said Hilary Mould, and added a 'Bwa-ha-ha-ha-ha!' for effect.

'And how is that working out for you, now that you're falling apart?'

'It'll be fine,' said Hilary Mould,

His nose twitched.

'This decay is only temporary, I'm sure.'

There was definitely a sneeze coming. He could feel it.

'Blast this dust.'

Hilary Mould sneezed. His nose shot past Angry, who made a vain attempt to catch it but succeeded only in breaking it with his fingertips.

'If it's any help,' said Wormwood, 'I know just how you feel.'

'I am not worried,' said the now noseless Hilary Mould. 'The Shadows will restore me to my original form, and they will give me the Earth to rule as my reward.'

Samuel looked doubtfully at the Shadows looming above their heads, still waiting for their way into this universe to be revealed. He didn't think that they were likely to keep their side of the bargain with Hilary Mould. If they got through, there wouldn't be an Earth left for him to rule.

'But the engine didn't work, did it?' said Maria. She stood beside Samuel, seemingly fearless. She made Samuel feel braver too. 'Not like you thought it would.'

'There were, apparently, some problems,' Hilary Mould admitted. 'The Shadows still couldn't enter our world. There wasn't enough chthonic power, not in an engine designed only by a human. That was why I hid myself away in the basement, waiting for circumstances to change. The Shadows told me to be patient. They said that, in time, humanity's own inventions would weaken the barriers between dimensions. And they were right: that was precisely what happened, but still, still it was not sufficient. One final ingredient was required: a force greater than the Shadows, greater even than the most advanced machines of men. It was –'

'A heart,' said Samuel, finishing his sentence for him.

For the first time, Hilary Mould looked surprised, and also disappointed. This was to have been his big revelation, and now a boy had deprived him of it. The dwarfs had been bad enough, but this was just too much. He decided that, once the Shadows had entered the universe, he was going to have a long lie down and not talk to any dwarfs or children for eternity.

'Yes, a heart,' he said, making the best of the situation. 'A heart of purest evil; a heart capable of pumping its poison into my engine, providing it with the fuel that it required to break down the walls, to shatter the divide between universes; the heart of a demon with a hatred for the Earth to match the Shadows' own.'

He added another 'Bwa-ha-ha' for effect, but it came out sounding funny because of the absence of his nose.

'And what did you and the Shadows say that you would give to Mrs Abernathy in return?' asked Samuel.

'We promised,' he said, 'to give to her all those on Earth who had conspired against her. Most of all, we promised to give to her Samuel Johnson.'

'Then let her take me,' said Samuel, 'but spare my friends, and spare the Earth and the Multiverse from the Shadows.'

Maria took Samuel's right hand and held it tightly.

'If he goes, then I go.'

'Look,' said Hilary Mould, 'you're *all* going. Don't you understand? You're doomed, every one of you.

She doesn't want to bargain with you. She doesn't *have* to bargain. She gets what she wants, the Shadows get what they want, and I get what I want. I should say, though, that she has a special fate lined up for you, Samuel. Oh, a very special fate.'

'And what would that be?' asked Samuel. He was glad that his voice didn't tremble, although he was sorely afraid.

'She's going to cut out your heart and replace it with her own,' said Hilary Mould. 'You're going to become her new body, the carrier for her evil. And you'll know it, and feel it, because she'll keep your consciousness trapped in there with her like a prisoner locked away in a prison cell. She'll allow you to watch as she destroys your friends, but she'll leave your dog until last: your dog, and your demon friend Nurd. She's going to spend a very long time hurting them. Suns will die, and galaxies will end, but their pain will go on and on, and you'll be a witness to every moment of it.'

Boswell barked at Hilary Mould. He'd heard his name mentioned, and sensed that this dry, foul-smelling man meant him and Samuel no good. Boswell was on the verge of attacking him and depriving him of some more limbs, but Samuel held him back.

Nurd stepped forward.

'You're a fool,' said Nurd.

'And why is that?' said Hilary Mould.

'Because you trust the Shadows, and you trust Mrs Abernathy. When the Shadows come through, they'll smother you along with everything else in this universe, and Mrs. Abernathy won't protect you. She won't even be able to protect herself. The Shadows are the only entities in the Multiverse that the Great Malevolence could not bend to its will. They are its enemies as much as ours. If the Great Malevolence could not make them do its bidding, why do you think one of its lieutenants – a lieutenant, by the way, who has twice been defeated by a boy and his dog – would be able to succeed where it has failed?'

'She is strong,' insisted Hilary Mould.

'She is weak,' said Nurd. 'The Great Malevolence had turned its back on her even before Samuel and the rest of us tore her apart. She had failed the Great Malevolence, and it had no more use for her.'

An expression of unease flickered on Hilary Mould's rotted features. Nurd picked up on it immediately.

'Ah, she didn't mention that, did she? She didn't tell you that she'd been cast aside by her master. We are stronger than she is, and we always have been. You've been tricked, Mr Mould. When the Shadows come, your alliance with her won't save you. If you do get eternal life out of this, you'll spend it in nothingness with the Shadows pressing down on you, and if I were you, I'd rather have no life at all.'

Hilary Mould's confidence was crumbling, just as his body was. He wanted to convince himself that Nurd was telling lies, but he could not. Nurd's words had the weight of truth to them.

'She was only ever using you,' said Nurd. 'That's what she does. She's clever and ruthless. When she's finished using you – and that should be pretty soon, I think – she'll cast you to the Shadows, and you'll wish you had just toddled off and died years ago instead of hanging about in old shops in the hope of ruling the world someday.'

By now, Hilary Mould had no doubts left. Nurd was right.

'The engine,' said Hilary Mould, as the dreadfulness of his fate became clear to him. 'The engine must be turned off.'

'How?' said Nurd.

But before Hilary Mould could reply, his lower jaw dropped to the floor. He knelt to retrieve it, but his left leg shattered below the knee and he toppled sideways. Samuel ran to him. He was thinking of Crudford. If Crudford could find Mrs Abernathy's heart and steal it away, the force powering the engine would be gone, and the Shadows would not be able to escape from their world into this one.

'Where is the heart, Mr Mould?' said Samuel. 'Tell us, please!'

Hilary Mould had only one finger left. He slowly unbent it from his fist, but before he could point it the grotto behind him began to fall apart. Samuel barely had time to get out of the way before the heavy stones fell on Hilary Mould, turning him to dust.

Samuel's ears rang from the sound of the clashing stones. His eyes and mouth were filled with dry matter, some of it almost certainly bits of Mould. He spat them out.

There was a thumping noise in his head: the beating of a heart that was not his own. It was almost as though Mrs Abernathy had already entered him, just as Hilary

Mould had threatened. He tried to find the source of the sound. It was coming from the group of humans and non-humans nearby.

It was coming from *inside* one of them.

The others seemed to realize it at the same time as Samuel. Slowly they moved away from one another – watching, listening – before grouping together again as they narrowed down the source, until at last a single figure was left standing alone, and the identity of Mrs Abernathy's host was revealed.

CHAPTER XXXVI

In Which Mrs Abernathy's Identity is Revealed

The isolated member of their little band said nothing. It was left to Professor Hilbert to break the silence.

'Reginald!' he cried. 'Can this really be true? I'm shocked, I tell you, shocked!'

'Turncoat!' said the Polite Monster. 'Eight letters,' it added, "one who abandons one party or group to join another".'

'I don't think,' said Samuel, 'that Reginald or Dorothy ever really existed at all.'

Professor Hilbert turned to Professor Stefan.

'I thought you hired Reginald,' he said.

'I thought you did.'

'We need a more careful hiring policy,' said Professor Hilbert.

Dorothy/Reginald removed their false beard. What was revealed was a chin that had begun to blacken and decay. They tugged at their hair, and it came away from the skull in clumps until only a bald, spotted scalp remained. Their body started to swell, bursting through their clothing. Their arms and legs lengthened, and everyone clearly heard grinding of bone against bone, and the snapping of sinews. Tentacles exploded from bubbling skin, beaklike endings gulping at the air, as a great black heart flooded its host body with poison, transforming it utterly. The head expanded, horns sprouting from bone, and the mouth grew larger and larger. Human teeth were forced from gums to be replaced by row upon row of sharp incisors. The creature now reminded Samuel of a huge mantis, but there was a hint of Ba'al to its appearance, and more than a little of Mrs Abernathy too. The skin was now slightly transparent, and the bones and muscles beneath it were visible, as was the foul heart that beat at the core of its being, protected by a thick, hard shell of keratinised cells.

But it was the eyes that drew Samuel's attention. They were large and still somewhat human in appearance, but any traces of real humanity were long gone: in their place was only absolute madness. Samuel thought that it was like staring into the centre of a storm, a thing of pure, relentless destruction.

'Hello, Samuel,' said the beast, and the voice was Mrs Abernathy's, and any lingering doubts were banished.

'Hello,' said Samuel, for want of anything better to say. From somewhere near his ankles came the sound of Boswell barking. Mrs Abernathy had once hurt the little dog badly. He had not forgotten, but he was not afraid. Instead, he seemed anxious to inflict some harm of his own upon her in return.

Above their heads, the Shadows converged, the weight of them pressing down upon the Earth. They sensed their time was near. Soon, this world would be theirs, and all other worlds would follow. They would swallow every star in the universe and leave it cold and black before moving on to the rest of the Multiverse. In time they would make their way to Hell itself and put out its fires, for the Shadows wanted no lights left burning. The Shadows wanted only utter darkness, a nothingness beyond imagining.

'Look at you all,' said Mrs Abernathy. 'Look how easily you were lured to me.'

She took in Dan and the dwarfs, and Sergeant Rowan and Constable Peel, and Shan and Gath, and Maria, even the Polite Monster, until finally her lunatic eyes fell on Samuel and Boswell, and Wormwood and Nurd.

'You!' she said to Nurd. 'Twice you have been my ruin. Twice you sided with humanity against your own kind. There will not be a third time.'

A great forked tongue unfurled itself from behind her jaws and coiled around Nurd like a snake. Holes opened on its surface, and each hole was a tiny, sucking mouth lined with teeth. The tongue came close to Nurd, but it did not touch him, and he did not flinch, until at last it was drawn back into her mouth.

'Not yet,' said Mrs Abernathy. 'That would be too quick, too lacking in agony. Mould was right: there are greater punishments in store for you.'

'He should never have trusted you,' said Samuel. 'If he'd given it even a moment's thought, he would have known that you'd kill him in the end.'

'Kill him?' said Mrs Abernathy. 'I didn't kill him. He was already dead. He just didn't want to admit it. And I could feel him turning on me. He was weak, like all of your kind. The Shadows would not have been kind with him: about that, at least, you were right.'

'They won't be kind with you either,' said Nurd. 'They hate demons as much as humans. They'll destroy you without a thought.'

'Perhaps,' said Mrs Abernathy, 'but they'll have to find me first. You know, in a way you did me a favour when you scattered my atoms throughout the Multiverse. Even I had not understood how powerful I was until then, for as my being imploded, as I felt pain beyond that experienced by any being before me, I was given a glimpse of the Multiverse in its totality. For an instant I saw every universe, every dimension, because I was part of them all, and the memory of that moment was absorbed by every atom of my being. I know the Multiverse: I know where it is weakest and where it is strongest. I know the holes between universes. I can stay ahead of the Shadows for eternity, for there will always be new places to hide.'

'And the Great Malevolence?' said Nurd. 'There will be no forgiveness for releasing the Shadows into the Mulitverse. You will have deprived it of its prize, of claiming the conquest of the Multiverse for itself, and the Great Malevolence will hunt you until the last star disappears from the sky.'

'I can stay ahead of our master too,' said Mrs Abernathy. 'I have knowledge beyond that of the Great Malevolence. The old demon has lived too long in Hell. It has grown weary, and slow. It knows only its own rage, but I have knowledge of every nook and cranny of the Multiverse. Perhaps, in time, other demons will come to me, and leave the Great Malevolence to its plotting and planning, its endless hurt. There are ways to defeat the Shadows. There are universes of pure light. Their greed will eventually lead them to such places, and there I will be waiting. The wait may be long, but I have time.'

She turned once more to Samuel.

'And you will be with me, Samuel: you will keep me company in my exile, and you will live with the knowledge of the hurt that you brought upon your family, your friends, and worlds beyond number because of your meddling.'

'Then take me,' said Samuel. 'I'll go with you willingly. You can do what you want with me, but spare the others. Spare all of these worlds.'

'No,' said Mrs Abernathy.

'You can take me too,' said Nurd. 'I'll suffer beside him.'

'You'll suffer anyway,' said Mrs Abernathy. 'You should have listened to Mould: you're not offering me anything that I don't already have in my grasp.'

'But why make them all suffer because of me?' said Samuel.

'Because I want to,' said Mrs Abernathy. 'Because it gives me pleasure.'

Samuel tried to recall what Crudford had said about playing on Mrs Abernathy's vanity.

'But wouldn't it display your power more forcefully if you were to hold back the Shadows, and allow so many to go on living?' said Samuel. 'Isn't there more greatness in sparing lives than taking them?'

Mrs Abernathy swatted away the possibility as though it were a fly, and a very small fly at that.

'No,' she said. 'No, it wouldn't.'

'Frankly,' said Jolly to Angry, 'even I didn't buy that one.'

'It was a long shot,' agreed Angry. 'It would be like telling us that it's better to pay for stuff than to get it for nothing by stealing it. I mean, it might be true, but you're not going to get anywhere by believing it.'

'You know,' said the Polite Monster to Mrs Abernathy, shaking with the kind of suppressed rage of which only the nicest people are capable, 'you really are a very, very rude – four letters, "ill-mannered or impolite" – demon.'

Mrs Abernathy roared, and foul-smelling spittle shot from her jaws.

'Enough!' she said. 'It begins.'

The stones from the collapsed grotto ascended slowly into the air, revealing the dusty remains of Hilary Mould, but also a very old, very battered wooden door. It hung suspended just a foot off the ground, and at its centre was a single lock.

'This is the last barrier, the doorway between the Kingdom of Shadows and this world,' said Mrs Abernathy. 'It needs only the key to open it.'

Her gaze flicked dangerously from one face to the next, until it came to rest on Maria.

'You,' she said. 'I feel Samuel's fondness for you. You will provide the key.'

As she spoke, two of the tentacles on her back lashed out, wrapping themselves around Maria and lifting her off the ground.

'You are the key,' said Mrs Abernathy, 'and the key is blood.'

The surface of the door rippled. Great splinters protruded from the ancient wood, each capable of spearing a human being like an insect on a pin. The keyhole changed shape, becoming a red-lipped mouth waiting to be fed. The last of the stars disappeared from above their heads as the Shadows merged into a single mass of blackness, a great face composed of many entities in one, and galaxies were swallowed in its jaws.

The dwarfs rushed at Mrs Abernathy, and she struck back with her tentacles and her long spindly arms, each ending in claws of spurred bone. Nurd and Wormwood went for her legs, trying vainly to overbalance her and pull her down. The policemen joined the attack, supported by Dan and the Polite Monster. Even Lucy came out of her sulk and joined the fray. They hit her with truncheons and fists, with cricket bats and tennis rackets, but the demon was too strong for them. All they managed to do was distract Mrs Abernathy, but at least they were preventing her from drawing closer to the door, and impaling Maria on its waiting spikes.

Samuel's voice sounded loudly, even amid the chaos.

'Everybody get back!' he cried.

Without thinking, the attackers did as he commanded, creating space around Mrs Abernathy.

'You put my girlfriend down!' said Samuel.

A single black object soared through the air towards Mrs Abernathy, its cork already popping as its contents struggled to escape. The newly-arrived Shan and Gath watched it go with great sorrow.

The dwarfs saw it too.

'Is that—?' said Angry, diving for cover.

'It can't be,' said Jolly, already trying to hide behind Sergeant Rowan.

'I thought it was just a myth,' said Dozy, who had decided that, if someone had to go, it might as well be the Polite Monster, as he would probably be too polite to object, and so had chosen to use him for cover.

'Spiggit's Old Resentful,' said Mumbles, and there was awe in his voice, as well as fear for his safety, for he seemed to be left with nowhere to hide at all. As a last resort, he curled himself into a small ball and prayed.

The bottle struck Mrs Abernathy in the chest and exploded into shards. The yeasty weapon of war sprayed her skin and immediately went to work on it like acid, burning through the shield that surrounded her heart. Mrs Abernathy screamed in pain and dropped Maria. Her tentacles and arms instinctively went for the growing wound as she tried to wipe the fluid from her skin. Instead it simply spread to her other limbs and began to scald them as well. Her screaming grew in pitch and volume, and then turned to a sound so agonized as to be barely audible, for the first of the Spiggit's had found her heart.

Just then, there was a wet popping sound from inside Mrs Abernathy, and her heart moved. It seemed to be forcing itself out of her damaged body, as though trying to escape its fate. At last it was entirely outside her, and it was only when a small gelatinous mass appeared behind it, black gore running down his sides, that the truth of what was happening was revealed.

Mrs Abernathy gurgled. She reached for her heart, but Crudford was too quick for her. He oozed out of reach as Mrs Abernathy's body, weakened by the trauma of her injury, collapsed. The life left her eyes. Just like Mr St John-Cholmondley, her human form had merely been a vessel for an essence of evil. Her foul heart continued to beat in Crudford's arms, for that was where all of her true power resided.

The wooden door collapsed in upon itself. The face of the Shadows opened its mouth in a soundless cry of frustration and rage, and then was gone. The divisions between the dimensions of the Multiverse were slowly concealed, falling upon one another like clear sheets of plastic dotted with stars until at last there was only one familiar set of constellations in the sky, and then even that was gone as the floors and ceilings and walls of Wreckit & Sons became visible once more. Samuel and the others were left standing beside the ruins of the grotto, and there was silence but for the beating of Mrs Abernathy's heart.

'Don't go anywhere,' said Crudford. 'I won't be a—'

And then he, and the heart, vanished.

CHAPTER XXXVII

In Which Mrs Abernathy Finally
Gets Her Just Deserts

A great host had gathered by the shores of Cocytus, in the chilliest, bleakest region of Hell. Jagged peaks towered above the lake, casting their shadows across its frozen surface. Nothing dwelt among their crevasses and caves: even the hardiest of demons shunned Cocytus. A bitter, howling wind blew ceaselessly across the lake's white plain, the only barriers to its progress being the bodies of those not fully submerged beneath the ice.

Cocytus was both a lake and a river, one of five that encircled Hell, the others being the Styx, the Phlegethon, the Acheron, and the Lethe. But Cocytus was the deepest and, where it entered the Range of Desolation, the widest. It was there that the Great Malevolence liked to imprison those who had betrayed it. The lake had four sections, each deeper than the next: those guilty of only minor betrayals were permitted to keep their upper bodies and arms above the surface; those in the second level were trapped up to their necks; those in the third were surrounded by ice, yet a little light still penetrated to where they lay; but the worst were imprisoned in the darkest depths of the lake, where there was no light, and no hope.

The Great Malevolence itself had once been a prisoner of the lake, placed there by a power much greater than its own, but it had been freed by a demon that had melted the ice with cauldrons of molten lava. Each load of lava would melt only an inch of ice, and before the next cauldron could be brought most of the ice would have returned again, so that every cauldron made only the tiniest fraction of difference. Yet still the demon filled its cauldron and carried it to the lake, working without rest for millennia, until finally the ice was weak and low enough for the Great Malevolence to escape.

That demon was Ba'al, later to mutate into Mrs Abernathy.

The Great Malevolence was not a being familiar with sadness or regret. It was too selfish, too wrapped up in its own pain. But Mrs Abernathy's betrayal had hurt it more than it had ever been hurt before. Now it was forced to condemn to the lake the demon that had once saved it from this same ice. Had there been even one atom of mercy in the Great Malevolence, it might have found some way to forgive Mrs Abernathy, or make her punishment less severe, as a reward for her help in times past.

But the Great Malevolence was entirely without mercy.

It had instructed all the hordes of Hell to gather at the Range of Desolation and witness Mrs Abernathy's fate. It would be a lesson to them all. The Great

Malevolence demanded loyalty without question. Betrayal could lead only to the ice.

Arrayed before him were the jars containing the various parts of Mrs Abernathy. At a signal from the Great Malevolence, the jars were emptied on the ice and Mrs Abernathy – part human, part Ba'al – was reassembled until only the space for her heart remained empty. Finally, Crudford appeared accompanied by the Watcher, and carrying the beating black heart in his arms.

'Well?' said the Great Malevolence.

'The Shadows have withdrawn, Your Awfulness,' said Crudford. 'They will threaten you no more.'

The Great Malevolence did not share Crudford's optimism. The Kingdom of Shadows would always be a threat, although the Great Malevolence did not say this aloud: it would display weakness, even fear, and it could not be weak or fearful in front of the masses of Hell. Beside the Great Malevolence, the Watcher fluttered its bat wings briefly, the only sign it gave that it too understood the danger posed by the Shadows.

'And the boy?' said the Great Malevolence. 'What of Samuel Johnson?'

'He fought her,' said Crudford. 'He fought her with all his heart. Without him, she might well have managed to complete the ritual, and the rule of the Shadows would have begun.'

'Such strength,' said the Great Malevolence. 'Such bravery. Perhaps, in time, he might be corrupted, and we could draw him to our side.'

Crudford very much doubted that, but he knew better than to say so.

'And the traitor Nurd?' said the Great Malevolence.

'He remains on Earth with the boy.'

'He should be here. He should be frozen in the ice like all these others who have betrayed me.'

Again, Crudford said nothing. He felt the Watcher's eight black eyes examining him, waiting for Crudford to make an error, to condemn himself with his own words, but Crudford did not.

The Great Malevolence waved a clawed, bejewelled hand.

'Place the heart in its cavity,' it instructed.

Crudford did as he was ordered, and was glad to be rid of the horrid thing. Instantly the heart began to fuse with the flesh around it, and the disconnected parts of Mrs Abernathy's body started to come together. Atoms bonded, bones stretched, and veins and arteries formed intricate networks.

When all was complete, Mrs Abernathy's eyes opened, and she rose to her feet.

'Master,' she said.

'Traitor,' said the Great Malevolence.

'All that I did, I did for you.'

'No, you did it for yourself. You sided with our enemies. You called the Shadows to your cause. You would have given them the Multiverse, and eventually Hell itself, all to avenge yourself on one human child.'

'It's not true,' said Mrs Abernathy. 'It was all a trick on my part. I had a secret plan . . .'

She was frightened now. The ice was already burning her bare feet. She looked to Crudford for help.

'Tell our master, Crudford. Tell it of my loyalty.'

But there could be no comfort from Crudford. Mrs Abernathy was appealing to the only demon in Hell who was incapable of lying. Before she could speak again, the Great Malevolence's right hand closed around her body, and it lifted her high above the lake.

'I condemn you,' said the Great Malevolence, and its voice echoed from the mountains as every demon in Hell looked on. 'You are a traitor, and there is only one punishment for traitors.'

And with all the force that it could muster, the Great Malevolence flung Mrs Abernathy at the ice. She hit the surface and broke through, and the ice gave way before her as she plummeted deeper and deeper into the lake. At last, when she was lower than any of the others condemned to its cold grip, her descent slowed, then ceased entirely. The ice closed above her head, and she was lost to view.

There was only one task left for the Great Malevolence to complete, for there was one demon that most definitely could not be allowed to roam freely throughout Hell and the Multiverse any longer, spreading his optimism and good cheer. There was space in Cocytus for Crudford as well. Looking on the bright side was also a betrayal of all that the Great Malevolence stood for.

But when the Great Malevolence reached for Crudford, the little demon was already gone, and he was never again seen in Hell.

CHAPTER XXXVIII

In Which There is a Parting of the Ways

In the silence of Wreckit & Sons, Samuel and the others stared at the spot from which Crudford had popped from one dimension into another.

'Well, we won't see him for a—' said Jolly, just as Crudford appeared once again. Jolly was ever so slightly unhappy. He'd been hoping to keep Crudford's hat.

'All done,' said Crudford. 'Can I have my hat back please?'

Jolly obliged with as much good grace as he could summon, which wasn't a lot.

Beside them, the mutated form that had, until recently, housed Mrs Abernathy's black heart was already starting to rot. All traces of Nosferati, and spiders, and sinister clowns had vanished. There were toys scattered across the floor below, but they were no longer intent upon inflicting harm on anyone. They were simply toys, although Samuel had the feeling that he'd never look at a teddy bear in quite the same way again.

'Where's the heart?' asked Nurd.

'Back in Mrs Abernathy's body,' said Crudford.

'And where is that?'

'Frozen somewhere near the bottom of Lake Cocytus.'

'Ah. So the Great Malevolence wasn't very pleased to see her then?'

'Oh no, it was pleased,' said Crudford, 'but only because it meant that the Great Malevolence got to freeze her in an icy lake for eternity. I think it would have liked to have imprisoned you there with her, Nurd. I think it would have stuck me in the ice as well if I hadn't made myself scarce.'

'Tut-tut, and after all that you've done for the old miseryguts,' said Nurd. 'Some demons have no gratitude.'

'It's all for the best,' said Crudford. 'I never really fitted in down in Hell. I didn't want to torment people, or be horrible. I always felt that there might be something better around the next corner. There wasn't, of course: there was just more of Hell, but I never gave up hope. Unfortunately, Hell has no place for optimists. Well, it *does* have a place for them, but it's at the bottom of a lake.'

'So you can't ever go back?' said Samuel.

'I don't want to go back,' said Crudford. 'I know my way around the Multiverse, just like Mrs Abernathy. I know all the little back doors, all the cracks and holes. I think I might just explore it for eternity. After all, there's a lot of it to see. It's a wonderful place, the Multiverse.

'And I'm not the only demon who has escaped: there are thousands of demons scattered all over the Multiverse, and only some are vicious and evil. Lots of them are perfectly lovely, with an admirable work ethic. Mr Comestible, for example, has set himself up as a baker only a couple of universes from here. His cinnamon rolls are worth crossing dimensions to try.'

'With all of your knowledge, I don't suppose you could help me to get home?' asked the Polite Monster. 'Not that it isn't nice here, but I left a pot boiling on the stove – five letters, "an apparatus for cooking and heating" – and Mother will be starting to worry. Oh, and I have a crossword puzzle to finish.'

'It would be my pleasure,' said Crudford, and he meant it.

'I'd like to come too,' said a voice. 'Actually, *we'd* like to come.'

It was Nurd who had spoken. Samuel stared at him in shock.

'What?' he said. 'You're leaving? Why?'

Nurd looked at the boy. Samuel was his friend, the first friend that Nurd had ever had if you didn't count Wormwood, which Nurd didn't, or not aloud. (He didn't want Wormwood to think that Nurd might need him. He did need him, and Wormwood knew that he needed him, but it didn't mean they had to get all soppy about it.) Samuel had made Nurd a worse demon, but a better person. For that Nurd would love him forever.

'I don't belong here,' said Nurd. 'I've tried to belong, but I'm still a demon, and I'll always be one. If I stay here, I'll have to keep my true nature hidden forever: if I don't, they'll lock me up, or try to destroy me. Even if I avoid discovery, I can never be myself. I'll just be that strange-looking bloke who lives with the Johnsons, him and his even stranger-looking friend.'

'That's me,' said Wormwood, unnecessarily.

'And what am I to do as you get older?' Nurd continued, having slapped Wormwood semi-affectionately on the back of the head. 'Do I continue living with your mum? Do I come and live with you? How will you explain me to your wife, or your children?'

'So you're running away?' said Samuel. He fought his tears, but they won, and he hated them for winning. 'You're leaving me because of something that hasn't even happened yet, something that might never happen?'

'No,' said Nurd, 'I'm leaving because I have to make a life for myself. I spent so long in Hell, and then you gave me a place here. You showed me a new world. More than that, you gave me hope. Now I want to see what I might become out there in the Multiverse. And you have to make a life for yourself too, Samuel, one in which there aren't two demons peering over your shoulder, always needing you to protect them.'

'Don't,' said Samuel. 'Please don't go. Don't leave me.'

Now Nurd was crying too, weeping big wet tears that soaked his elf costume. It was hard to be dignified while dressed as a large elf.

'Please understand,' he said. 'Please let me go.'

Samuel's face was contorted by grief.

'Go, then!' he shouted. 'Go on and wander the Multiverse. You were only ever a burden to me anyway. All I did was worry about you, and Wormwood just made things smell when he wasn't setting them on fire. Go! Find your demon friends. I don't need you. I never needed you!'

He turned his back on Nurd. Maria tried to comfort him, but he shook her hand off and stepped away.

Slowly, giving Samuel space in his sadness and anger, the others lined up to shake hands with Nurd and

Wormwood. The dwarfs even managed to hug them without trying to steal anything from them. When their farewells were completed, Crudford drew a circle in the air with his finger, and a hole opened. On the other side lay a red ocean, and anchored upon it was a white boat with a yellow sail.

'Where is that?' asked Wormwood.

Crudford shrugged.

'I don't know. Let's find out.'

Crudford and Wormwood waved goodbye as they stepped though the portal and into the boat. Only Nurd remained. He reached out a hand as though he might somehow bridge the distance between Samuel and himself, the space both emotional and physical that had opened between them, but he could not. His let his hand drop. A new universe beckoned. He touched the sides of the portal. They felt solid. He used them to support himself as he placed his right foot into the waiting world.

A finger tapped him on the back. He turned, and Samuel buried his face in Nurd's chest. The boy wrapped his arms around him, and it seemed that he would never let go. Samuel was sobbing, and could barely speak, but Nurd could still make out the words.

'Goodbye,' said Samuel. 'Goodbye, friend. I hope you find what you're looking for. Come back to me someday. Come back and tell me of your adventures.'

Nurd kissed him gently on the top of the head, and Samuel released him. Nurd stepped through the portal. Before he could look back it had closed behind him, and his friend was gone.

CHAPTER XXXIX

In Which We Step Forward in Time

There is a house on the outskirts of a town far from Biddlecombe, a house old and full of character. Its gardens are neatly tended, but there is space in them too for ancient trees and blackberry bushes, for a little chaos amid the order. On this day the sun is shining, and the house is filled with people. There are children, and grandchildren, and even some great-grandchildren. A man and woman, both still lively and bright despite their years, are celebrating their 50th wedding anniversary. There will be cake, and songs, and laughter.

A small table has been cleared in the living room, and on the table sits their wedding album. It contains all of the usual photographs that one might expect to see from such an occasion: the bride arriving, the ceremony, the couple leaving the church in a cloud of confetti, the hotel, the dinner, the dancing. Here are the parents of the bride and the parents of the groom, basking in the happiness of their children; there, guests cheering and raising glasses. It is a record not only of one day, but of many lives lived until that moment, of friends made and not forgotten.

The final photograph is a group picture: all of those in attendance are gathered together, row upon row: tallest at the back, shortest at the front. Most people who leaf through the album just glance at it and move on. They have seen enough photos by then. There is food to be eaten, and champagne to be drunk. There is even some beer, for Spiggit's has brewed a special ale for the occasion. It is called Spiggit's Old Faithful, and those who have tried it swear that it is very good once their memory has returned. The brewers are here some-where too. They are giving rides on their backs to small children, who don't care that they smell odd and can only say 'Hurh!'

But those who take the time to look more closely at this last photograph in the album might pick out what appears to be a small, gelatinous being in the bottom right-hand corner. He is wearing a top hat, and has borrowed a bow tie for the occasion. To his left, wearing a suit with one sleeve on fire, is a man disguised as a ferret, or a ferret disguised as a man. Whatever he is, he is grinning broadly, mostly because he has not yet noticed the flames.

The bride and groom stand in the middle of the front row. Maria looks beautiful, and Samuel looks like a man who knows that the woman beside him is beautiful, and that she loves him, and he loves her. At their feet sits a small dachshund. He is not Boswell, for Boswell has gone to another place, but the son of Boswell, and the spirit of his father lives on in him.

To Samuel's right is a figure dressed in a very elegant dark suit. His skin has a slightly greenish tinge to it, although that might just be a problem with the camera. His chin is very long, and tilts upwards at the end so that, in profile, he resembles a crescent moon. He has a white flower in his buttonhole, and he is content.

Let us leave the album and move back into the sunlight. The oldest of the trees in the garden is a spreading oak. Beneath it, shaded by leaves and branches, is a bench, and two friends are seated upon it. Nearby, Wormwood tends the garden, aided by Crudford. Wormwood, it has emerged, is a skilled gardener, perhaps the greatest the Multiverse has ever known. A dachshund digs beside him, hoping to unearth a bone. This is the great-great-great grandson of Boswell.

His name, too, is Boswell.

There is much of Samuel the boy in Samuel the older man as he sits on the bench, a glass of champagne by his side. His hair, now grey, still flops across his forehead, and his glasses still refuse to sit quite evenly on his nose. His socks still do not match.

Nurd's appearance has not changed. It will never change, for he will never age. He once used to worry about what might happen when Samuel died, for he could not imagine a Multiverse without his friend, but he worries no longer: he has learned the secrets of the Multiverse, and has seen what lies beyond death. Wherever Samuel goes, Nurd will go too. When the time comes, he will be waiting for his friend on the other side.

Waiting along with a host of Boswells.

'Tell me a tale,' says Samuel. 'Tell me a story of your adventures.'

He has heard all of Nurd's tales many times before, but he never tires of them. It is not just in appearance that he resembles the boy he once was. He has never lost his enthusiasm, or his sense of wonder. They have carried him through difficult times, for it is not only Nurd who has led an exciting existence over the years. Samuel's life, too, has always been enjoyably odd and there are stories about him that may yet have to be told.

And as the sun warms them, Nurd begins to speak. 'Once upon a time,' he says, 'there was a boy named Samuel Johnson . . .'

Acknowledgements

Thanks to my editors and publishers at Hodder & Stoughton and Simon & Schuster, my agent Darley Anderson and his staff, and to Dr Colm Stephens, administrator of the School of Physics at Trinity College, Dublin, who was kind enough to read the manuscript and correct my errors. Any that remain are entirely my own fault.

THE MONKS OF
APPALLING
DREADFULNESS

CHAPTER I

In Which We Are Reunited Some Time After the Appearance of the Last Volume. You Look Lovely, By the Way. Have You Lost Weight? And What Have You Done to Your Hair?

The knight was wearing very shiny armour. It wasn't just the sort of shininess that came from hours of buffing, aided by large dollops of *Mistress Dolly's All-Purpose Miracle Polish and Unguent*[1]. Oh no, this was a deep, ingrained gleam, a 'Look at me!' radiance. The wearer could have fallen down a mine shaft, landed in oil, been set on fire, and still have emerged from the whole affair with the sun bouncing off his helm and breastplate, his cuisses and greaves[2]. It was shiny and clean in a way that demanded to be noticed, just as some people really, really want you to know how good they are, or how good they think they are, and never miss an opportunity to advertise it. The armour made you want to kick the person wearing it really hard, even at

☠ [1] *Also Cures Warts, Ingrown Toenails, Fiddler's Elbow, Housemaid's Knee, Dropsy, and Scrofula. Not To Be Taken Orally. If Swallowed Accidentally, Please Consult An Undertaker.*

☠ [2] See, I know stuff.

the risk of breaking a toe. It was a very, very annoying assemblage of bits of metal, and it suited the wearer because he was very, very annoying, too.

The knight's name was Sir Magnific the Outstanding. He hadn't been born Magnific – his real name was Reg – but a lifetime of being unrelentingly good, and always where this goodness would be spotted by the maximum number of people, had resulted in a knighthood and a change of name. Sir Magnific the Outstanding travelled the land with his squire, Orlic the Resigned, rescuing maidens, righting wrongs, and generally making a nuisance of himself, since not all maidens want to be rescued, and wrongness is often simply a matter of opinion.[3]

Sir Magnific the Outstanding was currently seated on his horse, Button. Sir Magnific was smiling the way only someone who is really proud of what he's just done can smile, all teeth and smugness. Button the horse, meanwhile, was not smiling. It's hard to appear happy while a bloke wearing fifty pounds of metal is plonked on your back – a bloke, what's more, who has never been known to say no to a pie.

Before Sir Magnific stood a man dressed in very raggedy rags and an apron that could only have been

---

💀 [3] You, for example, may like Brussels sprouts. I think you're wrong. I also think they've made you smell a bit funny and other people are just too polite to mention it. But I'm not about to wallop you with a mace until you agree to come around to my way of thinking and concede that the whole Brussels sprout business is a big mistake on your part. That would be grossly unfair. Mind you, don't get me started on cauliflower. Wave a piece of cauliflower in my direction and it'll be the last thing you do.

filthier if it had actually been made of dirt. A cloud of flies buzzed around the man's head. Occasionally one of them would land on his hair or skin, think to itself 'Oh, this is a bit of all right, isn't it? Couldn't ask for a more feculent, unsanitary place to lay a few eggs than here . . .' before promptly dying.

The man's name was Peasant. He came from a long line of peasants, all called Peasant, so he was Peasant Peasant, although he had recently worked himself up from Peasant to Chief Peasant. He was very nice to those around him, and was therefore a Pleasant Chief Peasant Peasant. Sir Magnific the Outstanding, though, was testing his patience. Sir Magnific had turned up earlier that morning at the castle gates, spouting some nonsense about righting wrongs and rescuing maidens. He had then proceeded to hit anyone who disagreed with him very hard until they either started agreeing with him or handed in their dinner pail.[4] As a result, the castle was now in flames, the prince had a fatal dent in his head, and Peasant and his fellow peasants – to only some of whom Peasant was actually related – were stuck out in the cold watching a lunatic on a white horse shining brightly while behind him a castle burned.

💀 [4] Not an actual dinner pail, but a turn of phrase meaning 'died'. See also: cash in one's chips, turn up one's toes, kick the bucket, buy the farm, push up the daisies, pop one's clogs, etc., all of which suggest that death might be avoided by holding on to one's chips, keeping one's toes turned firmly downwards, not booting buckets or other vessels used for the storage of liquids, refusing to purchase arable land, resisting the urge to shove daisies or any other wild flowers, and not wearing clogs. Although one probably shouldn't wear clogs anyway because they look silly.

'You are free,' said Sir Magnific the Outstanding to Peasant and the other assorted peasants. 'You are no longer condemned to a life of servitude. Go, and be happy.'

'Go where?' said Peasant. He liked it here, or had until Sir Magnific arrived and began setting fire to stuff.

'Anywhere,' said Sir Magnific the Outstanding. 'The world is your oyster.'

'What's an oyster?' said Peasant.

'It's sort of a fishy thing,' said Sir Magnific, 'except without eyes or skin. Lives in a shell. Slimy. You have to swallow it in one go because it tastes a bit horrible if you let it hang about in your mouth, and if you eat a bad one, you'll get sick and most likely die.'

Peasant looked doubtful.

'I don't think I want my world to be an oyster,' he said. 'How about a piece of stale bread, with most of the green bits cut off, and maybe some only-slightly-rancid water?'

Now it was Sir Magnific the Outstanding's turn to look dubious.

'But "The world is your piece of stale bread, green bits optional, and stinky water" doesn't sound right.'

'Better than an oyster,' said one of Peasant's fellow peasants.

'How about a bun?' suggested another peasant. '"The world is your bun." Stands to reason. Everyone likes a bun.'

'The world is your *bum*?' said a man at the back,

who couldn't hear terribly well due to the absence of fifty per cent of his ears.[5]

'Not *your* bum,' said his neighbour. '*His* bum.'

'Oh, I was worried for a moment,' said the man with one ear. He stared at Sir Magnific in admiration. 'I bet his bum sparkles.'

Sir Magnific the Outstanding's grin was struggling to stay fixed.

'It doesn't matter!' he shouted. 'It's just a figure of speech.'

'The arsonist on the horse is right,' said a woman with one eye[6]. 'It doesn't matter whose bum it is.'

'Easy for you to say,' said the man with one ear. He held up his arms. At the end of each was a hook. 'I have to dip these in a bucket after cleaning mine.'[7]

'Now look here,' said Sir Magnific the Outstanding, who was getting quite annoyed. 'That's enough talk of bums. What's important is that you are free. You are no longer serfs. I, Sir Magnific, have freed you.'

'But I liked my life,' said Peasant. 'One square meal a day, weevils optional; a roof over my head – or most

---

💀 [5] If someone says, 'Hey, come over here and listen to the sound of this crocodile breathing,' the correct answer is 'No, thank you.'

💀 [6] If someone says, 'Take a look through this hole and tell me if you see a bloke with a bow and arrow,' the correct answer is also 'No, thank you.'

💀 [7] Finally, if someone says, 'Hold on to this crocodile for a minute while I run away from that bloke with the bow and arrow,' the correct answer is . . . Yes, you guessed it. Well done. You get to keep all your limbs and organs.

of a roof, but no point in nit-picking, is there? Except for actual nits.'

He dug a nit out of his hair and showed it to Sir Magnific before deciding not to let the protein go to waste.

'What am I supposed to do now?' said Peasant, once he'd finished nibbling on the nit.

'You can find a proper job,' said Sir Magnific the Outstanding.

'There *are* no proper jobs. The only jobs were in the castle, and you've burnt that down.'

'It's only fire damage,' said Sir Magnific the Outstanding. 'You can probably get some work rebuilding it.'

To his rear, the main tower of the castle groaned, like an old man getting up from a chair, before – also like certain old men – toppling over. The rest of the castle quickly followed, collapsing in a massive cloud of dust and smoke. The pile of rubble slowly settled. Peasant looked not entirely unhappy. After all, this represented a lot of rebuilding.

'I suppose we –' he began, when the ground shook, and the remains of the castle disappeared into the bowels of the earth, leaving behind a massive crater.

'Perhaps we can dig it ou –' said Peasant, whose glass was always half-full, even if it wasn't always half-full of anything a sensible person might want to drink, as a huge fireball erupted from the crater, sending more wreckage soaring into the sky. A helmet landed at Peasant's feet, smoking gently. It had once belonged to a guard named Horace. Peasant knew this because Horace's head was still in the helmet, looking surprised.

This was to be expected, under the circumstances, since nobody wakes up in the morning with the expectation that the day – and, for that matter, life itself – might conclude with his head being separated from his body before being shot into some woods. If you knew that was going to happen, you'd stay in bed.

'Oh, that's just great,' said Peasant, as the fireball dispersed. 'Vandalism, that is. Someone could fall in that hole and do himself a mischief.'

'Listen,' said Sir Magnific, 'I'll do you a mischief –'

Which was when a flash flashed, as flashes will, and a bang banged. At the back of the crowd, someone coughed. Although it was a polite cough, it carried a definite threat. It wasn't a cough to be ignored, not unless you wanted a Very Bad Thing to befall you – possibly lots of Very Bad Things, some of them with spikes on the end. The crowd of peasants and Peasants quickly parted, leaving a channel of communication between Sir Magnific and the source of the cough.

Three figures stood in a clearing: one tall, one slightly less tall, and one very short. Of the trio, he would definitely always be the last to learn it was raining. They wore the long grey robes of monks, the hoods raised ominously. No faces were visible under the hoods, but anyone foolish enough to look hard enough might just have picked up wrinkles, blackness and boundless evil, before being killed.

The tallest of the monks removed his hands from his sleeves – well, removed his talons, really, since they were long, thin, scaly, and sharp. The talons were in the process of unrolling a length of thick parchment.

'𝕾𝔦𝔯 𝕸𝔞𝔤𝔫𝔦𝔣𝔦𝔠 𝔱𝔥𝔢 𝔒𝔲𝔱𝔰𝔱𝔞𝔫𝔡𝔦𝔫𝔤?' said a voice from some-where in the depths of the First Monk's robes. It rumbled unpleasantly, like an avalanche limbering up to roll down a mountain.

Sir Magnific might not have been the brightest bulb in the box, but he had the feeling that the monk wasn't about to tell him he'd won a prize. On the other hand, it didn't seem wise to deny that he was who he was a) just in case he *had* won a prize; b) because monks didn't materialize randomly in the vague hope that whoever they were looking for might happen to be there; and c) because if he tried to lie, the unhappy peasantry before him would probably call him on the fib.

'Er, yes,' said Sir Magnific. 'I am he.'

'𝔑𝔬𝔱 𝔣𝔬𝔯 𝔪𝔲𝔠𝔥 𝔩𝔬𝔫𝔤𝔢𝔯,' said the First Monk.

'Beg your pardon?'

'𝔜𝔬𝔲'𝔯𝔢 𝔞 𝔡𝔬-𝔤𝔬𝔬𝔡𝔢𝔯,' said the Third Monk menacingly. '𝔚𝔢 𝔡𝔬𝔫'𝔱 𝔩𝔦𝔨𝔢 𝔡𝔬-𝔤𝔬𝔬𝔡𝔢𝔯𝔰.'

The First and Second Monks turned to stare at him. The Third Monk stared back.

'𝔚𝔢𝔩𝔩,' said the Third Monk, '𝔴𝔢 𝔡𝔬𝔫'𝔱.'

'𝔚𝔢 𝔡𝔬𝔫'𝔱 𝔩𝔦𝔨𝔢 𝔦𝔫𝔱𝔢𝔯𝔯𝔲𝔭𝔱𝔢𝔯𝔰 𝔢𝔦𝔱𝔥𝔢𝔯,' said the Second Monk.

'Sorry,' said the Third Monk. '𝔍 𝔤𝔬𝔱 𝔠𝔞𝔯𝔯𝔦𝔢𝔡 𝔞𝔴𝔞𝔶 𝔦𝔫 𝔱𝔥𝔢 𝔪𝔬𝔪𝔢𝔫𝔱.'

'𝔥𝔢'𝔰 𝔞𝔫 𝔢𝔫𝔱𝔥𝔲𝔰𝔦𝔞𝔰𝔱,' explained the First Monk. '𝔖𝔬𝔪𝔢 𝔬𝔣 𝔲𝔰 𝔧𝔲𝔰𝔱 𝔞𝔯𝔢. 𝔐𝔶 𝔬𝔩𝔡 𝔤𝔯𝔞𝔫𝔡𝔡𝔞𝔡 𝔴𝔞𝔰 𝔢𝔵𝔞𝔠𝔱𝔩𝔶 𝔱𝔥𝔢 𝔰𝔞𝔪𝔢 𝔴𝔞𝔶. 𝔑𝔢𝔳𝔢𝔯 𝔰𝔞𝔴 𝔞 𝔰𝔨𝔲𝔩𝔩 𝔥𝔢 𝔡𝔦𝔡𝔫'𝔱 𝔴𝔞𝔫𝔱 𝔱𝔬 𝔠𝔯𝔲𝔰𝔥 𝔬𝔯 𝔞 𝔱𝔬𝔯𝔰𝔬 𝔥𝔢 𝔡𝔦𝔡𝔫'𝔱 𝔴𝔞𝔫𝔱 𝔱𝔬 𝔡𝔦𝔰𝔢𝔪𝔟𝔬𝔴𝔢𝔩. 𝔥𝔢 𝔴𝔞𝔰 𝔞 𝔩𝔬𝔳𝔢𝔩𝔶 𝔣𝔢𝔩𝔩𝔞.' The First Monk wiped a tear from somewhere approximating an eye. '𝔐𝔦𝔫𝔡 𝔶𝔬𝔲, 𝔱𝔥𝔞𝔱 𝔴𝔞𝔰 𝔴𝔥𝔶 𝔴𝔢 𝔥𝔞𝔡 𝔱𝔬 𝔨𝔦𝔩𝔩 𝔥𝔦𝔪, 𝔟𝔢𝔠𝔞𝔲𝔰𝔢 𝔥𝔢 𝔥𝔞𝔡 𝔱𝔯𝔬𝔲𝔟𝔩𝔢 𝔱𝔢𝔩𝔩𝔦𝔫𝔤 𝔱𝔥𝔢 𝔡𝔦𝔣𝔣𝔢𝔯𝔢𝔫𝔠𝔢 𝔟𝔢𝔱𝔴𝔢𝔢𝔫 𝔣𝔞𝔪𝔦𝔩𝔶 𝔞𝔫𝔡 𝔢𝔳𝔢𝔯𝔶𝔬𝔫𝔢 else. It might have been his eyesight, but you never knew with him. One minute you're all sitting around the table together, happy as the day is long, enjoying a nice brew and a slice of cake, and the next minute Auntie Olive's head is missing and Cousin Albert is bleeding all over the Victoria sponge. I mean, enthusiasm is all well and good, but you have to draw the line somewhere, don't you?'

The First Monk paused.

'Beg pardon,' he said, 'where were we?'

'We were telling Sir Magnific,' said the Second Monk pointedly, 'how we don't like do-gooders.' His tone of voice suggested that perhaps the time had come for a new First Monk if the old First Monk was finding it difficult to concentrate on matters of importance.

'Right, of course. Sir Magnific.'

'Still here,' said Sir Magnific, and gave the crowd a good-humoured look as if to say, Well, what you going to do, eh, if monkish-looking chaps start popping up and arguing amongst themselves? One can but smile politely . . .

'By the powers vested in us,' said the First Monk, 'in accordance with the Doomsday Prophecies, the Chthonic Concordat, and any and all Infernal Dictats and Transdimensional Laws passed or yet to be passed, you, Sir Magnific the Outstanding, have been sentenced to death. Sign here, please.'

The First Monk flicked the scroll until the end hovered just below Sir Magnific's nose.

'Wait, what?' said Sir Magnific.

'You forgot the quill,' hissed the Second Monk.

'Oh, bother,' said the First Monk. He rummaged in

his left sleeve. A bat flew out, followed by a relieved-looking dodo, half a packet of digestive biscuits, a mug without a handle, a handle, and a small silver cup bearing the engraving *Most Improved, Beginners' Embroidery, Mrs Tompkinson's Class*. Finally, the First Monk found a slightly worse-for-wear black quill, which he sent floating towards Sir Magnific.

'Sorry about that,' said the First Monk, before adding: 'Some people bring their own quill, you know. Saves a lot of trouble.'

Sir Magnific was staring at the scroll. His name was printed in very large letters at the top, but everything else was written in very tiny letters, fading to microscopic. An educated ant would have struggled to make them out.

'Be sure to read through the small print,' said the Third Monk. 'We wouldn't want any misunderstandings.'

'But it's *all* small print!' said Sir Magnific.

'What do you expect?' said the Second Monk. 'It's not like we can just go around killing people without dotting the i's and crossing the t's. We're professionals, you know. We take pride in our work.'

'It's not in English,' said Sir Magnific. 'Or Latin. Or even French. How am I supposed to understand it?'

'We didn't say you had to understand it,' said the Third Monk, 'just read it.'

'And sign it,' added the First Monk. 'And I'll want my quill back after.'

The Second Monk nudged him and hissed what might have been a laugh or laughed what might have been a hiss.

'Not that you'll be needing it, um, after,' said the First Monk. 'Or be in much of a position to stop me from taking it.'

Sir Magnific folded his arms, or tried as best he could, given how encumbered he was by metal.

'Well, I'm not signing it,' he said. 'That's a death warrant, that is. Nobody signs his own death warrant, except in metaphors. What are you going to do about that, then, eh? Not so clever now, are—'

There was a muffled explosion from inside Sir Magnific's armour. His visor fell down, obscuring his face, and puffs of blue smoke began to emerge from various cracks, holes, and grilles, followed by what could only have been liquefied bits of Sir Magnific himself. Finally, the now significantly lighter suit of armour tumbled to the ground, landing with a hollow *clang*. Button the horse looked relieved no longer to be carrying a few hundred pounds of combined man and metal on his back.

Orlic the Resigned just sighed. He'd known something like this was bound to happen some day. Okay, maybe without the monks, and the explosion, and that unsavoury liquefying part, but something very much like it.

'It would be nice,' said the First Monk, 'if some day one person agreed to sign the warrant, just one. Hardly worth going to the trouble of getting it done and carting it halfway across the Multiverse if they're not even going to bother reading it, never mind sign it.'

'It would also save a lot of paperwork later,' said the Third Monk.

'Which is why we always forge their signatures,' said the Second Monk, as the quill scribbled Sir Magnific's name at the bottom of the warrant before returning to its owner. 'We hate paperwork.'

'Oooh, that's naughty,' said the Third Monk. He sounded quite shocked. 'You can't go forging people's signatures. You'll get into trouble.'

'We're assassins,' said the First Monk. 'Naughty - I mean, bad - is what we do, and we are trouble.'

He turned to the Second Monk as assorted confused peasants faded from view.

'Right,' he said, 'who's next on the list?'

The Second Monk consulted a small journal. Embossed on the cover were the words *Your First Assassination Notebook*, and an illustration of a unicorn pooing a rainbow.

'Nurd,' said the Second Monk. 'Scourge of Five Deities, or so it says here.'

'Any deities we know?'

'None worth mentioning.'

'He must have annoyed someone important to end up on our list.'

'He did,' said the Second Monk. 'Old Mr Grumpy himself. The Big Badness.'

'You don't say!' said the First Monk. 'Dear oh dear. Tut-tut. Well, well. What was this Nurd fellow thinking? Some chaps just bring trouble down on themselves, don't they? Do we have the warrant?'

'I gave you all the warrants before we left,' said the Second Monk.

The First Monk had another rummage in his sleeves,

then inside his robes, and lastly *under* his robes, exploring from the knees up. The Second and Third Monks exchanged a glance worth a thousand words.

The First Monk gave a sharp tug. His hand reappeared holding a scroll, which he waved triumphantly at his colleagues, who took an alarmed step back.

'What?' said the First Monk. 'I have to keep them all somewhere, and there's only so much room in these sleeves. I think you could at least carry the quill in future. I've done myself some injuries with that quill. The end is very pointy.'

He examined the scroll.

'"Nurd, Scourge of Five Deities,"' he read. '"To be terminated with extreme prejudice, along with his accomplices Wormwood and Crudford, Esq." I suppose it's official, then. Hang on, there's a footnote.'

The First Monk leaned closer to the warrant. Deep in the hood of his robes, eyes of awful malevolence squinted. The First Monk kept meaning to get glasses, but could never find the time, what with all the murdering that needed to be done. There weren't enough hours in the day . . .

'I do wish they'd make the print bigger,' he said. 'This is how mistakes get made. We don't want to go assassinating the wrong person - er, again.'

The other monks waited patiently while their leader deciphered the instructions.

'Right,' he said at last, 'the gist of it is that we're also supposed to kill a boy named Samuel Johnson, a dog called Boswell, and Dan's Stars of Diminished Stature, who are a bunch of little men, along with their manager, the aforementioned Dan.'

'How little are they?' said the Second Monk.

'Doesn't say.'

'What kind of dog?' said the Third Monk.

'Doesn't matter.'

The First Monk rolled the warrant up. He thought about returning it to where he'd found it before remembering that – thanks to the late Sir Magnific – he now had extra space in one of his sleeves, which was a relief. Some things came out a lot easier than they went back in.

'We have a few other outstanding warrants to take care of along the way,' he said. 'Then we can kill the boy, the dog, Dan and the little men, finish up with Nurd and the other two, and be home in time for tea.' He rubbed his scraggy hands together. They rattled like bones in a sack.

'Really,' he said, 'what could possibly go wrong?'

CHAPTER II

In Which We Meet Some Old Friends

The travellers stood at the edge of a large forest, staring at a rippling portal in the continuum[8]. The first traveller had a head shaped like a quarter moon, albeit a moon made of cheese that was slightly on the turn. The second looked like a squirrel with a skin ailment. The third was a clear, slug-like blob wearing a very fetching top hat. Odder trios might have been dotted around the Multiverse, but if so, they were about to face some stiff competition.

The three were, respectively, Nurd, the Scourge of Five Deities; his faithful companion (in the absence of anyone else willing to take the job) Wormwood; and Crudford, a small gelatinous entity of boundless optimism and

☠ [8] The continuum is the name given to the four-dimensional model that combines the three dimensions of space with the fourth of time. It's also sometimes referred to as Minkowski spacetime, after its originator, Hermann Minkowksi (1864-1909). Hermann's brother, Oskar, was a physician and pioneer in the study of diabetes, and his son, Rudolph, became a noted astrophysicist. Another brother, Max, was the French consul in Königsberg, Prussia. Like me, you're probably looking at your own family right now and shaking your head in disappointment.

wetness, as well as a committed wearer of hats. Since each had, to varying degrees, been responsible for foiling the efforts of the Great Malevolence to escape from the infernal regions and destroy the Multiverse, they were very unpopular with certain entities whose initials were GM. They were, in fact, among the most wanted beings in the Multiverse, if by 'wanted' you meant 'wanted dead', but the most wanted of all was Nurd.

The trees were so tall that their crowns touched the sky, casting the ground below into shadow. The only light came from tiny luminous creatures that floated like parasols through the gloom, singing as they went. Unfortunately, they didn't have a note in their heads, and couldn't have carried a tune in a bucket. It made Nurd think fondly of the (in)famous boy band BoyStarz, but only because BoyStarz weren't anywhere nearby. Things could always be worse.[9]

Nurd, Wormwood and Crudford were aware of their unpopularity with the Great Malevolence, which was

---

💀 [9] Which brings us back, briefly to that spacetime business. Our galaxy – the Milky Way – and everything in it is falling in a swirly manner towards the huge black hole that sits at its heart. That black hole is about four million times the mass of our Sun, which itself is 1.989×10^{30} kilograms, or about 333,000 times the mass of the Earth. But before you think that this sounds like a very good reason not to bother doing your homework, or taking that bath you're always promising your mum you'll get around to before Christmas, a single orbit of the black hole by the Milky Way takes about 250 million years to complete. Since the Sun is so large that it forces the Earth into an orbit that takes a year, you now have a pretty clear idea of just how enormous our local neighbourhood black hole happens to be. In other words, we're probably always going to be falling towards it without ever actually reaching it. So, tough break on the homework/bath avoidance front. Don't forget to learn your French grammar, and remember to wash behind your ears.

why they tried not to linger too long in any one location, although the Multiverse, as they were discovering,
was endlessly fascinating, frequently beautiful, and
often awe-inspiring, and one therefore occasionally felt
the urge to potter about watching nebulae forming and
stars collapsing. Then again, bits of the Multiverse were
also kind of dull, and the bits that weren't dull, fascinating, beautiful, or awe-inspiring were sometimes
dangerous. With this in mind, great precaution had to
be taken before progressing from one realm to the
next.

'Right,' said Nurd to Wormwood, 'stick your head
through that portal and tell us what you see.'

Wormwood looked at the portal dubiously.

'Can't someone else do it this time?' he asked.

'No, it's your job,' said Nurd. 'We took a vote on it.'

'I don't remember a vote.'

'We had it while you were asleep. We didn't want to
wake you.'

'Aw,' said Wormwood, 'that was kind.' He thought
for a moment. 'I think.'

'Now, now,' said Nurd, hustling him none too gently
towards the portal, 'don't get caught up with all that
thinking nonsense. You know how your brain hurts
when you do it.'

'If it makes you happier,' said Crudford, 'you can
wear my top hat.'

Wormwood didn't believe that wearing the hat would
make him feel any better about sticking his head through
a hole between dimensions, but he turned out to be
wrong. The top hat suited him better than expected. He

examined his reflection in the portal, and thought he looked very dapper.

'What do you think?' he asked Nurd.

'You look like you're marketing a Monopoly set for rats.'

Wormwood grinned happily.

'My dream,' he said. 'Right, I'm off to explore.'

And with that he bent down, took a deep breath, and popped his head through the portal.

CHAPTER III

In Which We Learn a Little About Gods

The Grand Oblat of Tern, High Priest of the Great God Murcius[10], stretched his horrid limbs, yawned from one of his several mouths, and prepared for another long day of doing his god's work. This mostly involved accepting gifts on Murcius's behalf, which Murcius, being a deity, didn't have much use for, a god's need for food, treasure, and slaves being limited. To save the worshippers any embarrassment, the Grand Oblat took all the gifts for himself, politely explaining that Murcius had made it very clear to the Grand Oblat that this was what he wanted.

The rest of the Grand Oblat's time was spent dealing with all those who didn't believe in the Great God Murcius[11]. This didn't tend to end well for them, the Grand Oblat's view being that the best way to deal with unbelievers was to kill them as quickly as possible so

---

💀 10 Blessed Be His Many Tentacles, Holy Be His Cavernous Jaws, Adored Be His Fetching Red Cotton Dressing Gown and Matching Carpet Slippers.

💀 11 Venerated Be His Seventy Clawed Toes, Glorious Be His Jagged Horns, Revered Be His Nice Hat That He Keeps for Special Wear.

they could start explaining themselves to the Great God Murcius[12] in person.

Here's the funny thing about gods: they're only ever as good or as bad as the people who believe in them. There's nothing especially awful about gods or religion. It's people who make them that way. The Grand Oblat was a rotten sort, and had made the Great God Murcius in his own rotten image. Even the statues of Murcius that cluttered up every town and village in Tern had begun to look suspiciously like the Grand Oblat, right down to the colour of his dressing gown.

Another thing about gods: they cease to exist if everyone stops believing in them, or at the very least they toddle off to do something more fun than listen to strangers ask for next week's lottery numbers or some help with trying to find that missing screwdriver. But the Grand Oblat's power and wealth depended on everyone believing not only in Murcius but also in the Grand Oblat's direct line to Murcius's thoughts and wishes. For this reason, it was very important to the Grand Oblat that the population of Tern should keep believing in the Grand Oblat – sorry, in Murcius, Idolised Be, etc. (Easy mistake to make, that, what with all the statues that resembled the Grand Oblat. Still, you can't be too careful . . .)

So it was that the Grand Oblat had put on his best, most ornate dressing gown and his newest, plushest carpet slippers, and was now about to reveal the latest

---

💀 [12] Cherished Be His – Oh, never mind. You get the picture.

statue of Murcius/the Grand Oblat[13]. A big white sheet concealed the statue, and large numbers of Ternians had gathered to witness the unveiling on pain of being tortured with hot pokers if they didn't, although tea would be served after.

One more thing about gods: they don't like competition. They have their own territories and their own followers, and have reached an unspoken agreement that it would be best for all concerned if they didn't go about intruding on another god's patch.[14] The Grand Oblat had forgotten this, and had been spreading the Word of Murcius rather too widely for some gods' liking. As a result, those rival gods had taken up a collection, and it wasn't for another statue of Murcius.

A hush descended on the crowd because the guards had begun heating pokers just in case of any latecomers, and nothing quietens a crowd like the prospect of hot pokers exploring their nethers. The Grand Oblat took the end of the cloth in one of his tentacles, cleared a number of his throats, and said, 'I now declare this statue of the Great God Murcius unveiled!'

The cloth fell. The crowd gasped. The Grand Oblat looked confused.

The statue of – okay, let's stop beating around the bush here – the Grand Oblat had been vandalised, because the head had been removed and replaced with

---

💀 [13] Please delete as appropriate.

💀 [14] This message doesn't always get through to their believers, which is how wars start.

an orange. Admittedly, someone had taken the trouble to draw a smiley face on it, but it was definitely still an orange.

'Where's the head?' said the Grand Oblat, as the air behind him burst with a *pop*. 'It looks to me like it doesn't have one.'

'Yes,' said the First Monk, 'about that . . .'

CHAPTER IV

In Which We Learn the Importance of Keeping One's Head, Although a Bit Late for the Grand Oblat

The Monks of Appalling Dreadfulness prepared to be on their way. Thanks to his missing head, the Grand Oblat now bore a much closer resemblance to his statue, even down to the orange. The Third Monk had drawn a frowny face on that one.

'Anyone else here fancy being a god?' the First Monk asked, facing the crowd.

There was an unsurprising absence of candidates.

'I didn't think so,' said the First Monk, as he started to disappear.

'It's more trouble than it's worth, being a god,' said the Second Monk. 'Eventually, you always disappoint.'

He, too, began to fade.

'Don't make us come back with more oranges,' warned the Third Monk.

And then they were gone.

Nurd tapped his foot impatiently.

'So,' he said to Wormwood, once the latter's head had grown back, 'how did that go?'

'Not so good,' said Wormwood. He felt his head, and

was relieved to find that it had been restored to its previous state, even if no one else was. In another corner of the Multiverse, the Grand Oblat might have sympathised, except that the Grand Oblat was dead and so wasn't doing a lot of anything anymore.

'What did you see on the other side of the portal?' said Nurd.

'Well,' said Wormwood, 'I saw a mouth, and a lot of teeth, and then not much at all, really, until I saw you again just now with the new eyes in my new head.'

'I don't suppose you managed to save my hat?' said Crudford.

'I'm afraid not,' said Wormwood.

'Pity. I don't suppose you'd care to go back and have a –'

'No,' said Wormwood, 'I wouldn't.'

'Just wondering. I was fond of it. It was very nice, and fitted me perfectly.'

'That's as may be,' said Wormwood, 'but the same could be said for my old head.'

'Don't exaggerate,' said Nurd. 'Whatever bit your head off was probably trying to do you a favour.'

'Still, perhaps we ought to find a safer portal,' said Crudford. 'I'm sure there's another one around here somewhere.'

'I suppose so,' said Nurd. 'I'm tempted to take my chances with that one, though. I can't stand much more of this racket.'

A parasol floated by, warbling merrily. Nurd couldn't be certain because of the sheer tunelessness, but it sounded like 'My Bonnie Lies Over the Ocean' sung by someone with a large spoon stuck in his mouth.

Nurd stared at Crudford, who was now wearing a black beret.

'Where do you get them from?' said Nurd.

'I don't know. They just seem to appear.' He examined his reflection in the portal. 'I feel a strange urge to take up the accordion.'

'You do, and you'll be travelling alone,' said Nurd. 'There's no situation that can't be disimproved by the addition of an accordion.' He poked Wormwood. 'Come on, we'll go and look for a different portal. If we find one, Crudford, we'll whistle. You'll know it's us because it'll be in tune.'

Nurd and Wormwood trotted off, Wormwood still warily stretching his neck to be sure that his head was on properly. It had once grown back the wrong way around and he'd spent a couple of hours bumping into things before he noticed.

You lived and learned.

CHAPTER V

In Which We Return to Biddlecombe Just in Time to Wish We Hadn't

The Monks of Appalling Dreadfulness materialised at the back of a packed Biddlecombe Palace, Home to the Stars. The Biddlecombe Palace was really a converted Boy Scout hall, but its new owner, Mr Pinchfist, had high hopes for it, and intended to transform it into the town's leading entertainment venue and tourist attraction[15]. The Monks went unnoticed by all upon arrival as most of the audience was facing the stage, but also because the Monks were very accomplished at not being seen when they didn't want to be. This prevented their victims from running away or throwing stuff at them. It also cut down on the screaming.

On the stage, an amateur magician was sawing a girl in half.[16] Worryingly, the amateur magician appeared to

---

💀 15 Better, even, than Rocky's House of Rocks. ('For all your rock needs. Stones and pebbles also available. Boulders by order only.')

💀 16 You don't want to see the words 'amateur,' 'sawing,' and 'girl' in the same sentence. You don't even want to see the words 'professional,' 'sawing,' and 'girl' used too often. It's a tricky business, magic. (Ha, see what I did there?) On March 23rd, 1918, the magician William Ellsworth Robinson was performing

be in his mid-teens, and the saw, which was very rusty, didn't look much younger.

'I am now,' said Samuel Johnson, for it was indeed he beneath a cape and a battered hat, 'sawing my lovely assistant Maria in half.'

Back and forth went the saw. 'Ouch,' went Maria.

'No, there shall be no mercy, no matter how loud you shout!' said Samuel, laying it on fairly thick for the crowd while whispering to Maria, 'Keep it up, they're loving it!'

'Ouch,' said Maria again, this time with more feeling. 'Is it supposed to hurt?'

'What?' said Samuel. 'No, I don't think so.'

'Well, perhaps you ought to stop, then.'

'I wondered what the saw was catching on,' said Samuel. 'I knew I should have paid more attention to the instructions in the book.'

Samuel ceased sawing.

'I shall now,' said Samuel, 'stop sawing. Goodnight, and thank you.'

The curtain came down. The members of the audience exchanged puzzled glances. Applause burst from some-

---

a famous illusion in which he was sentenced to be shot to death by a member of the audience. The gun had a concealed second barrel, so that the audience member loaded the first barrel with a real bullet, but the gun actually fired a blank from the second barrel. Unfortunately, Robinson hadn't cleaned the gun properly, and both barrels fired simultaneously when the trigger was pulled. Robinson's last words were 'Something's happened. Lower the curtain.' It should be noted that Robinson, a New Yorker of Scottish heritage, was dressed as a Chinese person at the time. WARNING: DO NOT TRY THIS AT HOME. The gun part, I mean. And the dressing up as a Chinese person. Unless you're actually Chinese, in which case it's probably okay.

where in the middle of the auditorium. It came from Samuel's mother, who was just glad that her son no longer had a saw in his hand. Maria's parents joined in, thankful that their daughter was still in one piece and not two.

'Is that it?' said the First Monk. 'At least we didn't pay for tickets.'

'Was that Samuel Johnson?' said the Second Monk.

'Without a doubt,' said the First Monk. 'Without a dog, too. Did you see what he was up to with that saw? Lucky we're going to be killing him soon, save him from getting arrested. His loss will be magic's gain.'

Lights flashed over the curtain. Glitter was scattered across the stage from a bucket by a man in overalls at the top of an unsteady ladder. A voice announced:

'And now, ladies and gentlemen, the act you've all been waiting for . . .'

The Monks noticed a couple of people making for the doors, only to be forced back to their seats by security.

'Our very special guests, fresh from their pantomime tour of Latvia . . .'

Over at the far wall, a man tried to climb out of a window before his wife pulled him back inside and told him to suffer like everybody else.

'With a new single on the way . . .'

'Please, no,' someone moaned.

'I give you . . .'

'Bring the magician back,' said someone else. 'He can saw me in half. It'll be a mercy.'

But the announcer was not to be dissuaded

'BoyStarz!'

The curtain rose again to reveal the four members of BoyStarz, Britain's 17th Most Popular Boy Band[17]. The years were not being kind to them, for they were no longer a) boys or b) starz, but continued to scrape a living in places desperate for entertainment, but only if all the paint in town had already dried. A backing track began to play. It was a slow song, because all BoyStarz's songs were slow, even the fast ones. Every song they sang concerned falling in love, falling out of love, looking back on love, searching for love, tripping over love, losing love behind the sofa, or watching love being eaten by lions. A BoyStarz concert was like the worst Valentine's Day of your life compressed into ninety minutes.

Thankfully, that evening's performance was limited to just three songs, but it was still at least three songs too many. Halfway through the first song, tormented wailing was heard, and not just from the stage. By the second song, Row C had already formed an escape committee and begun work on a tunnel, and a man in Row E had retreated to his happy place, never to return. But at the end of the performance – after lead vocalist Starlight had strained to reach the final high note of 'Swept From The Chimney Of Your Love', failed, tried again, grasped it, and strangled it to death – a huge round of relieved applause sent the group from the stage, because people are mostly polite and BoyStarz had promised not to come back for an encore.

💀 [17] Of fifteen.

The Monks of Appalling Dreadfulness, who had withdrawn into the foulest, dankest depths of their robes, peered cautiously from their hoods.

'I think it's over,' said the First Monk.

'I don't feel well,' said the Second Monk. 'And my ears have gone funny.'

'I think I nearly liked it,' said the Third Monk, who was already trying to come up with an alternative name for their own band, The Monks of Appalling Dreadfulness being unlikely to cut it in the hit parade.

'Perhaps we should kill BoyStarz as well,' said the First Monk, 'just to be sure.'

Nobody raised an objection, the Second Monk being of the same opinion as the First, and the Third being happy to get rid of the competition. At that moment, raised voices were heard from the corridor outside, and the Monks gloomed in that general direction to see what the fuss was about. They found four small men, accompanied by a larger man wearing thick glasses and a T-shirt bearing the word 'Manager' on the front. They were arguing with a sixth man in a suit. The small men were, the Monks guessed, Dan's Stars of Diminished Stature, formerly known as Mr Merryweather's Elves, and also sometimes as 'the accused'.

In the background hovered BoyStarz, Samuel Johnson, a dachshund, and Samuel's assistant (and girlfriend) Maria, who was now wearing a sticking plaster on her right side. The argument seemed to be about money.

'I'm not handing over cash for that lot,' said the man in the suit, jabbing a thumb at BoyStarz. 'They were terrible.'

'What did you expect, Pinchfist?' said one of the little men. 'They're BoyStarz. Everyone knows they're terrible.'

'But not *that* terrible. I mean, they sound bad on television, and they're not much better on record, but live and up close –' Pinchfist shuddered. 'I'll never think of a chimney the same way again.'

'We had a contract,' said another of the little men.

'For entertainment. That wasn't entertainment, not unless you like the sound of weeping.'

'But the money is going to charity,' said Maria. 'It'll save donkeys.'

'The donkeys,' said Pinchfist, 'will just have to save themselves.'

Even the Monks, who were among the most pitiless beings in the Multiverse, thought this was very harsh.

'So you're not going to pay?' said the first little man.

Pinchfist lit a cigar and took a long puff.

'No, Mr Jolly Smallpants,' he said, 'I most certainly am not.'

The Monks of Appalling Dreadfulness stood by the side of the road, watching as Dan's Stars of Diminished Stature reduced the Biddlecombe Palace to firewood and broken bricks. For little people, the First Monk reflected, they were remarkably strong, and once they committed to a task, they finished it. Mr Pinchfist could only sit and watch, since he had been tied to a chair with an apple in his mouth. Behind him, BoyStarz hummed a sad song.

'Perhaps,' said the First Monk, 'we could deal with the footnote at a later date.'

'Or even forget about it altogether,' said the Second Monk, because some jobs were more bother than they were worth.

'Yes,' said the First Monk, 'that might be for the best.' They'd still be paid for taking care of Nurd, the Scourge of Five Deities, and someone else could just deal with the boy, the dog, the manager, and the little men.

Especially the little men.

The Monks of Appalling Dreadfulness gradually dematerialised, to the sound of the Third Monk whistling the chorus of 'Swept From The Chimney Of Your Heart'.

'Stop that,' said the First Monk.

So the Third Monk just whistled it quietly in his head instead, and dreamed of stardom.

CHAPTER VI

In Which the Monks of Appalling Dreadfulness . . . Well, You'll See

On an icy fjord in Norway, Valgar the Unpleasant, nastiest and most terrifying of Vikings, possessor of the legendary Hinged Helmet of Hrangar the Hrungry[18], consumed another deer leg. He wondered when his dinner would arrive, because he was tired of snacking and was in need of something more substantial. He also had to be up early in the morning because those villages weren't going to pillage themselves.

Valgar was alone in his throne room. Valgar was often

💀 [18] Hrinterestingly – sorry, interestingly – the image of Vikings wearing horned helmets isn't historically accurate, and dates back only to the late 19th century. We can possibly blame Carl Emil Doepler, who designed the costumes for a performance of Wagner's opera *Der Ring des Nibelungen* in 1876, and gave horned helmets to Wotan, god of battle, and the Valkyrie. Another myth is that the Vikings put their dead chieftains in boats, floated them on a lake or river, and set them on fire with flaming arrows. Duh, wrong! Think about it. It takes a lot of dry wood and heat to keep a big blaze going, especially if you're hoping to burn a body, and you're just not going to have enough of that on a Viking longboat, even if you load it with extra wood. Either the fire will go out or the boat will sink, and what are you going to do then, huh? You think Uncle Olaf, charred and damp, would thank you for that kind of botched send-off? I suspect not.

alone because nobody liked him. Also, Valgar sometimes got bored and killed whoever happened to be standing nearby, so it was best to keep one's distance. For this reason, his food wasn't so much served as thrown at him.

Even by the standards of bad men, Valgar was incredibly bad. He was so bad that he discouraged other people from being bad, like a runner who is so fast that nobody wants to race against him anymore since there's no point in turning up only to be humiliated. Valgar's extreme badness meant that there was actually *less* badness in the Multiverse because of him, as a lot of people who might otherwise have been bad had gone off to do something else instead, like grow lettuce or foster widdle bunny wabbits. For this reason, a contract had been taken out on Valgar the Unpleasant, which was why he was suddenly distracted from matters of the stomach by the sight of three monks standing before him. Valgar hated monks, but then Valgar hated everybody, so it was nothing personal.

'Valgar the Unpleasant?' said the First Monk.

'Only my friends call me that,' said Valgar.

'But you don't have any friends,' said the Second Monk.

'That's right, because I've killed them all,' said Valgar. 'And I *liked* them. I don't even know you.'

He grabbed a huge axe that stood by his throne.

'That's why I'm going to cut you into pieces,' said Valgar, 'and use your pelvises as cake stands.'

'Before you go putting yourself to any effort,' said the First Monk, producing a parchment, 'we are the Monks of Appalling Dreadfulness, and we have good news and bad news for you.'

Valgar frowned.

'I'll take the good news first,' he said.

'It's interesting you should say that,' said the Second Monk, 'because the good news and bad news are both the same. You know that spectacular Viking funeral you were looking forward to when you died, with lots of feasting and dancing and fires and stuff?'

'Yes?' said Valgar.

'Well,' said the First Monk, 'it's just been brought forward.'

Back at the portal, Crudford was still inspecting his reflection while positioning his beret at new and interesting angles to consider the result. He tried to recall some French, but failed. He was wondering how he might go about acquiring a striped jersey when three grey shapes shimmered into being beside him.

'Hello,' said the First Monk.

'Hello,' said Crudford, who liked meeting new people.

'We're looking,' said the Second Monk, 'for Nurd, the Scourge of Five Deities.'

'What do you want him for?' said Crudford.

'Well, funnily enough, we want to kill him.'

'Why is that funny?' said Crudford.

'Because he probably doesn't want to be killed,' said the Second Monk. 'Although if he does, that would be funny, too.'

'Technically,' said the First Monk, 'since he's an arcane entity, we won't so much be killing him as excising him, but it amounts to the same thing.'

'It's official,' said the Third Monk. 'We have a warrant and all.'

On cue, the First Monk produced the warrant. He'd worried about the Third Monk at the start, but he really seemed to be getting the hang of things now.

'Who are you, exactly?' said Crudford.

'We,' said the First Monk, 'are the Monks of Appalling Dreadfulness.'

Crudford appeared puzzled. He lifted his beret and scratched the top of his head. Being gelatinous, his fingers passed straight through and floated somewhere behind his eyes.

'Does that mean you're appalling at being dreadful?' he said. 'Because I wouldn't go boasting about something like that, if I were you.'

'No,' said the Second Monk patiently, 'it means that we're not just dreadful, but really, really dreadful.'

'As in being capable of inspiring dread,' said the Third Monk, 'not being bad at something. Because we're very good at being bad. Grrrrr,' he added.

'If you say so,' said Crudford, 'but I'd still rethink the name. And why are you going around killing people?'

'It's what we do,' said the Second Monk. 'We are the Multiverse's most feared transdimensional assassins.'

'We used to be the second most feared,' said the First Monk, 'until a mountain fell on the Nuns of Eternal Doom. Then everybody moved up a place.'

'Well, we say "fell" on the Nuns of Eternal Doom,' said the Second Monk, 'but it was more "pushed", or even "dropped".'

'Still, congratulations,' said Crudford. 'It's always nice to see talent rewarded.'

'𝔗𝔥𝔞𝔫𝔨 𝔶𝔬𝔲,' said the Monks of Appalling Dreadfulness in unison.

'𝔖𝔬,' said the First Monk, getting back on track, '𝔱𝔥𝔦𝔰 𝔑𝔲𝔯𝔡, 𝔡𝔬 𝔶𝔬𝔲 𝔨𝔫𝔬𝔴 𝔥𝔦𝔪?'

'What does he look like?' said Crudford.

The First Monk tapped the warrant, and an image of Nurd appeared in the air. It wasn't a very flattering picture, so it was Nurd down to a T.

'You know, I think I have seen him,' said Crudford. 'Does he pal around with a scruffy demon called Wormwood?'

'That's the one!' said the Second Monk.

'𝔄𝔫𝔡 𝔱𝔥𝔢𝔯𝔢 𝔦𝔰 𝔞𝔫𝔬𝔱𝔥𝔢𝔯 𝔴𝔥𝔬 𝔱𝔯𝔞𝔳𝔢𝔩𝔰 𝔴𝔦𝔱𝔥 𝔱𝔥𝔢𝔪 –' began the Third Monk, but Crudford cut him off before he could proceed any further.

'They were messing around with this portal,' said Crudford, 'just before you arrived.'

'𝔜𝔬𝔲'𝔯𝔢 𝔰𝔲𝔯𝔢?' said the First Monk.

'I saw that Wormwood stick his head through not ten minutes ago,' said Crudford. 'Cross my heart and hope to dry.'

The First Monk turned to his colleagues.

'𝔕𝔦𝔤𝔥𝔱𝔶-𝔥𝔬, 𝔩𝔞𝔡𝔰,' he said. '𝔏𝔢𝔱'𝔰 𝔤𝔢𝔱 𝔱𝔥𝔦𝔰 𝔡𝔬𝔫𝔢.' He patted Crudford on the shoulder, or the part of Crudford that most resembled a shoulder. '𝔗𝔥𝔞𝔫𝔨𝔰 𝔣𝔬𝔯 𝔱𝔥𝔢 𝔥𝔢𝔩𝔭. 𝔜𝔬𝔲'𝔳𝔢 𝔪𝔞𝔡𝔢 𝔬𝔲𝔯 𝔩𝔦𝔳𝔢𝔰 𝔞 𝔩𝔬𝔱 𝔢𝔞𝔰𝔦𝔢𝔯.'

'Oh, I do hope so,' said Crudford.

The First Monk stepped through the portal, followed

quickly by the Second. The Third Monk paused at the threshold and peered at Crudford.

'This Crudford, Esq. who travels with Nurd and Wormwood wears a hat,' said the Third Monk suspiciously. 'Or so I've heard.'

'This isn't a hat,' said Crudford. 'It's a beret.'

'Ah,' said the Third Monk, 'of course. Sorry, my mistake.'

'Don't mention it,' said Crudford, as the Third Monk entered the portal. 'Au revoir.'

For a moment, Crudford thought he heard the sound of chomping from the other side of the portal, but he might have been mistaken.

'No,' he said '"au revoir" isn't right,' as a whistle from nearby indicated that Nurd and Wormwood had found another portal. 'Never mind, it'll come to me.'

Crudford oozed happily in the direction of the whistling, and wondered where he might find a bicycle and a string of onions.